I0639266

THE SANGUINES
OF ALCHEMY

by Steve Zwolinski

Hope for Healing and A Drop Of Cold Blood

ISBN: 978-0-9864330-0-9

Hope for Healing is dedicated to the lifelong friendship of David M. Milkovich, whose insight, imagination, encouragement, wit, and pursuit of passion in thought and in writing is impeccably effective and decidedly essential to one's furthering of knowledge and personality, uttering not to the scribe, but to the awe and wonder of the world.

I

The Beginning

There are always times when you know if one person could change the world, it would begin with you – and probably end with you. It could have all started that day in the delivery room. The hustle and bustle, the meters beeping, the rushing of clogs across the freshly mopped linoleum floor, the clasping of clipboards closing and the automatic door seemingly opening and closing every few seconds.

In bay #5, Carrie Malott, husband in tow, was in the final stages of labor. Nine months of practicing, discussing her firstborn, stating how wonderful the child would be, how she had to answer about how long she had been pregnant, what the name was, would they need furniture, kids pointing to her protruding belly – the scheme had all been there for her. She thought of it as being part of the family finally. Years of being raised in a somewhat awkward purgatory of a life, having boyfriends that turned either to be total jocks or completely in it for her beautiful brown hair and emerald green eyes but not for her good had taken its toll on her. She felt like her parents were expecting the baby more than her own success, and it added to the sum of the pressure that proceeded to fulfill thoroughly this beautifully nightmarish moment.

By her side, grasping Carrie's hand, was her husband, Alex Malott. Alex was the proud father of the day, a personable humble man that had success in his genome. A man of his word, he had spent many of his years fine-tuning his craft as an environmental inspector. It was quite the unusual work – he would often come home late, sweating like a draft horse who had run 5 miles, all because he had spent the day in a "moon suit", essentially a chemically sealed suit that meant his body isolated itself from the world. Alex knew this day was coming; he had bragged about the work sites he had visited that he had indeed wanted to have a child, preferably a baby boy, so that he could be like the fathers seen on primetime television – although Carrie had thought of it as being more like a daytime soap opera.

"I love you very much, honey," the man said to the woman. "You'll be fine through all this. I'm ready when you are." She looked into his eyes, which had the lens effect of a mist as the moment played before them like a somewhat vivid fairytale, a story which felt too real.

She gave a smile, her minimalist makeup never doubting the true virgin glow that had kept on her face for all these years. "I have to pull through this. You just are sitting and waiting, dear." She may have had the hellish pain of contractions, but her quick wit emanated through the room like a warm rush of air from a fire. Then again, as if to lend verity, she smiled, and Alex grasped her hand, shaking it with a mutual smile. It was the perfect moment, and yes, they had all dreamed of it.

As the lights in the room emitted a cool calm in the hustle and bustle, the severe contractions began to hit Carrie like rounds of gunfire. She screamed her lungs out, and the doctors all began to fulfill their obligations and slowly, yet surely, deliver what surely would be one hell of a child. They were there for the past few weeks; one by one, they gave her a little bit of knowledge of the process. But now, they were real. And strong. And the show was on.

"Come on…." "Just one more breath…..Push…." "Push honey, you're doing good….keep going!" "Push, push, pushpushpushpushpush….." And with one final movement, the last scream from the mother came just as the first small scream from the newly born daughter came.

With tears in her eyes from the struggle, but now ever misting from the fact that she had now produced a child, a small edition of her, someone who would carry on her family and make her father proud....she could not resist holding her emotions back.

The baby's cry resonated through the room, to the sigh of relief of many who had been there since the beginning of the day. She had a very lengthy labor, one that was quite painful, even though she had carried it so well for the term of the pregnancy. "She is perfect, Alex." It had to be stated for it to be true, and it was.

"Yes, but what should we name her? She has your eyes and my hair, I guess. Can't think of a name....I'm so nervous." The new father was panicking, never really giving any thought to this, even with nine months' notice. It was shameful for a college-educated man who prided himself on his decision-making skills, especially when working around stuff that could melt his arms off if need be, but he was in the same boat as every other new father – an outsider to his own offspring.

The mother used a morsel of energy. "Well, I hope you can find out something. We can't pass pictures around to my relatives and say 'She who shall not have nomenclature' when we're over Christmas dinner." She really had her street smarts down, which was a minor miracle in that seemingly pressing moment, considering that she had put so much work into her efforts that afternoon and evening. A quick wit, in spite of the pressures she had been under, always got her somewhere in life. Even if it was absent that night they decided to have a child.

But yet some simple answers are derived from simple questions. Struck in the moment with faith, he said "I hope....hope, Hope! We'll name her Hope, Carrie! Hope Malott. That sounds like a name to be proud of. It will get so many calls, and it has a ring to it." And it did draw a smile to the face of the two new parents.

Carrie looked into the new father's eyes. In it was the sign of happiness, the sign of relief that this penultimate moment of 37 weeks of waiting around, carrying her, night sweats, moodiness, and otherwise seeing what was his Puppy wife become more and more bellied. But yet, there was an inherent sadness in the room. The doctors looked around, and one gentleman, nestled in a suit and holding two vials in his hand, began going over the documents. He stepped next to Alex, and shook his hand. "Congratulations, Mr. Malott. We are glad to see the new addition to your family. But she is a special one, a unique one. And this is no ordinary baby. Your obstetrician has some tests, and you must promise to never, ever, reveal what perhaps will be the prime indicative of this birth.

A brief pause followed, and the now advantageously advanced of knowledge man said with a firm nod and the wrinkle of his mouth, and said "Understood." Carrie stated then "Yes, I knew. It had to happen this way. It's only right." It was words that stung at every syllable, and every time he would have to reiterate them in the coming months.

Sighing, he kissed the baby. "Welcome, dear Hope Malott. Welcome to this sad, sad world."

6 YEARS, 2 MONTHS LATER

The summer sun beat down on the pavement outside, shining into the atrium of the red brick house, a large one in truth sitting in the middle of a block of normalcy and respite in the suburbs of west Philadelphia. The Malotts had done plenty to earn this house; Alex had made his money doing what few would do in inspecting and examining chemical spills. Carrie worked as a teacher in the nearby school district. She had dealt with so many kids that annoyed her and drove her crazy in their adolescent antics. "No child left behind, but no child's behind left!" was her motto. The house had wood floors, a relic of late 19th century design. It was a creaky house, lacking many of the drywall- and LED-bulb newness of the more modern houses. By all means, it was an investment. But it was something Alex, Carrie, and Hope were all proud of.

"I'm awake, Daddy!" the young effervescent Hope yelled from the upstairs. "Come and get me, I'm ready for hug time!" And the dad knocked on the door to the room, saying "May I enter, your highness?" like he always would before he would enter. To Alex, this was his little princess. Her grandparents were not upper-class, but believed that she should be raised on the keys of humility, kindness above all, and unselfishness. "Yes, you may, my liege".

And she opened the door, and she ran up to her dad and gave her a hug. "1, 2, 3, noserubnoserubnoserub!" they both yelled as their foreheads tapped. They both laughed, and he raised her in his arms towards the rays of light spread across the ceiling. Carrie looked on, fists at her hips, smiling and shaking her head in simultaneous disgust and disbelief, petty as the love shown in front of her. "You two are soooooo crazy…you know that?" she would say every time, no matter how ridiculous it would sound to her two top loves in the world.

Little Hope smiled, her eyes twinkling like two mineral springs in the snowy Alps. "Daddy loves me more than anything else in the world." She was raised right, and was cute as could be. "I'm his princess." She smiled and clung to her father's leg.

The father smiled. "Can't beat this on a Saturday morning, can I?" He laughed. This made his day, every time, no matter what. It always made Carrie chuckle to do it; mostly because the two of them both had equal, although uniquely standalone of themselves, admiration of the elder woman of the house.

"Come on, you two. Breakfast is ready. It's 10:30 already. Eggs and country sausage today." Carrie knew how to get things moving. She had worked retail for some time before being demoted to middle school, and knew when she had to pull out the transaction finisher.

They both began to walk to the doorway. The little one said "Poor chickies and poor piggies." She smiled, and blew a kiss to her mom. "But I'm hungry. We'll save 'em for another day. They are cutie as pie, but a girl's gotta eat." She began to run down the stairs, past her Mum and away from the suddenly marooned Dad.

Alex smiled, and looked at Carrie. "She grew up so fast, didn't she, hun?" They both gave a sigh, as if to implicitly condone and affirm their common belief. "Can't believe first grade this year." In a way, they were both breathing a sigh of relief. Ever since birth, they had to go and try to work around the fact that she was quite different from the rest of the kids. Sure, she had her falls, her cuts and bruises, and such. In fact, she was possibly the most playful kid in school, one that wasn't afraid to take risks or climb the jungle gym. But she was also naïve to the fact that inside her was a chassis of a material which was not of playfulness and youth but of power and dignity and an impassable beauty that only God could grant. "Yea, she's really growing up. It was just yesterday Hopie was in her onesie, throwing toys and smiling that innocent smile....now all she does is throw the tantrum and the curveball."

As if in a moment of necessary comic relief, Alex chuckled "But she sure as hell still has that smile, doesn't she?" He placed a peck on Carrie's cheek, and began to walk down the hallway. Perhaps it was the hunger, or the fact that he kind of had a guilt trip that had built up in that time period, like it was a masked plea of guilt. And Carrie recognized it spot on. With the single word of "Hunny?" Alex knew something was up.

Carrie's smile began to turn the sides of her mouth into a look of masked displeasure, a sort of melancholy. "You know, she's really starting to get to the point now where she's going to be doing things out of our supervision. Running around, mixing with kids, playing in the dirt." It was perhaps the mothers' creed of protecting what came from her, but it was more along the lines of fearing for something else.

In a way, Alex kind of agreed. "Yes, I know that. She's….well, she's growing up, dear. I mean, we can't always take her hand, and say 'Hopie, don't do this, don't do that, do this instead.' We have to let her explore herself and her mind." It was perhaps emitting like radiation to Alex that this was indeed a serious matter – but what were they to do? Surely, the Oedipus complex of the 21st century, entitled the helicopter parent, was there. "We just have to go with the flow, and let her be the girl we always wanted." And they both smiled. "You know –"

And if on cue, the daughter ran up the stairs and said "Mom! Dad! There's a huge truck out on the street! And they are taking a pinball machine out of the back! Next door! Go look! – " she immediately grabbed both of their hands in a hastened effort to pull their arm sockets out, or at least pull the rest of their bodies to the door. And indeed, there was a large pinball machine going into the house next door.

"Looks like new neighbors, Hopie. They have a big house over there!" Alex noted in a flavorfully playful way to his daughter.

Carrie gave a slightly sarcastic laugh as she began to spoon the now cooling sausage onto the dishes. "So they are moving in finally. About bloodied time, I say. Place has been up for sale for months now."

She is a tough cookie, Alex thought. *Tough, but genuine.*

God, do I love her.

They both shuffled slowly down the stairs of their stoop, completely ignoring the freshly made meal set upon the cherry oak table in the kitchen, and went to inspect and convene with what were the new neighbors. Alex always wanted to explore new things, new ideas. It was sort of a calling that had been instilled in his genes, one that he had passed onto his offspring. At least hopefully, in his deepest wishes. He could often picture his father saying *Y'know, no one ever built bridges unless they built themselves a boat to get across the sea.* What a kind man he was.

As they ventured out, a man pointing out towards the moving van, where two uniformed guys, one short and rather muscular, and another tall but rather portly, were offloading a couch. The door had been propped wide open to the new home, the "FOR SALE" sign still swinging in the breeze like a banner of aluminum. The man yelled "Yea, I have this truck for two more goddamned hours! We need to get this crap in the house – NOW!" He seemed frustrated, mostly due to the dual process of getting out of the heat into the house and dealing with muscular fools passing his furniture like the collection plate – on his dime, mind you – being his two problems.

The tripod of new neighbors shuffled towards the stranger in an almost too friendly welcome to the neighborhood. "Hi there…just noticed you moved in." It was very 50s television like, but somehow, that always seemed to work. At least it did on the digital subchannel at 2 am.

Remain cheery, Alex thought to himself. *This guy could be a total pain. At least the man who used to live there until a tumor on his ass ate him up.*

Wiping sweat from his brow with the back of his hand and wrist, he smiled. "Hi there. Lou Mendoza. Nice to meet you folks." He reached for the hand of Carrie, not bothering to think that perhaps the benefit of actually trying to not share bodily fluids would be a good way to acknowledge the welcome to the neighborhood. Carrie took it in stride, giving an uneasy smile, and somehow valiantly curtsying in her words "It is…nice to meet you, Lou." Lou then reached for Alex's hand, and before he could pull it away, gave a firm, somewhat moist strangling of the digits that a hard-working man could ever give.

The married couple both gave a look of disgust to each other in a brief moment, as if to say, *What the bloody hell just moved into the neighborhood.* It was well understood that perhaps this was just a moment of time when the man was in a state of flux, perhaps incident to that yes, it was hot. They just put it to the back of their minds.

Immediately, Hope pointed towards the doorway. "Look over there!" She saw a girl on the porch, just about by where it began to curl around towards the driveway. She grasped at an overgrown pot of ivy dangling uncontrollably, the product of having grown for the entire season while the prior owner, an older man, had essentially left to the environment to sustain and produce. The leaves were somewhat blowing, the lines of green extending like a giant jellyfish in the sea of the wind.

The father of foresaid child let out a proud smile. "Yes, my dear. That is the love of my life, Adriana. She's my daughter…at least for now, I guess. We're still filling out paperwork…" He snickered, and began to make the Malotts think that virgin ears were about to be exposed to the hierarchy of a lifestyle gone not so perfect.

Before they could grab it and pull her away, Hopie's curiosity sprung into action. "What's paperwork? Sounds like fun! Where do they keep crayons when you get older –" but then Alex said in pure protection of pedagogy "It's like drawing on Daddy's newspaper. Can't do it too often." They were exposed like the ivy that the girl on the porch was fiddling around with.

Nevertheless unfazed by the politic of the situation, the new neighbor said "Why don't you guys go over and meet each other? Make some friends and such. Go!" Just then, one of the moving men said in his version of a thick New York accent "Hey buddy? See this piece of kindling I have? This piece of shit isn't getting any lighter and if I have to hold it and crack my back, I'm going to launch it into the Delaware!" as he wrestled a very large armoire, presumably one of great heritage and even greater mass, up the walkway.

"I'll be right there, Jimmy. Put it in the hallway – I got some folks to help coming over later. In-laws." Lou laughed in nervousness, obviously kind of pulled between finishing the conversation and keeping on time.

"Hey, as long as we're getting paid, I'll do it. Give me an extra fifty, and I'll paint all the walls in the house and carry your mother in law in my hands." This moving man seemed to supplement his muscles with the attitude that one of the gated community culture could only imagine could arise from years of the street and the smarts that popped from working for a living.

Lou had it on the ball. "In plentiful quantities tonight. Got the checkbook in hand!" He smiled and gave a thumbs up in Jimmy's direction. He then shook his head, looking towards the two now stunned folks who had probably wanted to retract the welcome and let cooler heads prevail. "Stupid asshole greaseball's been giving me hell all the day." He then paused, and the jaws of Carrie and Alex hit the floor. "Eh, you didn't need to know that. Care for some Jello and root beer? Only thing I have cool right now." It didn't even have to be said that they all felt like that was the next step.

While all this happened, the curious 6 year old had wandered up the stairs towards Adriana. A shy young girl of Hispanic descent, she had her long hair braided in one large queue, befitting of ethnic culture. She had a glow about her face that indicated somewhat of a shy introverted, melancholy kind of reactivity. Twirling her hair in one hand and a branch of ivy in the other, she looked down.

Never the one to restrict self, Hopie went on. "Hey, hi. My name is Hope Malott. What's yours?" It was probably the question only a kid of her age group could ask, but nevertheless was friendly. She was indeed putting herself out there – even at the precociousness of age she was at.

The young girl began to look up. "Adriana Laura." She smiled very slowly, as if not to disclose too much. "I can't tell you my last name, 'cos Dad said if someone asks, they can take you and turn you into a ghost."

It was kind of strange for someone to say this for anyone, but still, Hope was uncaring. "Well, you can tell me whatever names you want me to call you." She reached in her pocket. "I carry 'round this....it's a bracelet we make on the weekends. Mommy says that when you make a bracelet and give it to someone, you give 'em a promise that you will keep them as friends." She then handed it to Adriana.

For something so meager, this made her give a shy smile. Adriana had a very simple smile, her lower lip being tucked under a row of the remaining baby teeth. She was afraid to look into the eyes of Hope, but somehow, the two of them could find solace in that a friendship had budded on that porch. "Thank you. Here -" she handed her a leaf – "this is the first leaf I grabbed offa this plant. I want you to have that." And even though it was meager, it was a suitable token of instant apprecia-tion, the first olive branch.

Before they could utter another word, the father of the braided princess yelled "Hey, Pook! Come and get some snacks! Come in the side door!"

And then she went and told Hope "Here, I gotta go in! Come in with me!" And so they ran towards the door.

The sun came out from behind the clouds for a short moment, as if to provide the affirmation from a higher power that a true friendship was breeding in the mix. It was only proper that this was supposed to happen. As they began to run about the porch, the moment was there.

Adriana ran ahead, with the new neighbor friend in tow. It was all perfect. They were one in the same, and that first interaction was leading to the first meal between two girls.

All of a sudden, that changed. A board on the wooden deck of the porch, sticking up like a bastard file of a fine craftsman's tool kit, got in the way of a six year old's foot. And like it should have been, Adriana fell to the ground, and began to cry.

Suddenly, the heroics of a girl who had always been taught to do things right sprang into action. Before the dad of her own, or any adult, or the moving people, or the mailman down the street, could utter another word, there was Hopie, her new friend, in need of the first favor of what would likely be a long friendship.

"My wrist! It hurts! I got cut!" Adriana cried between tears, trying to understand what had just happened. "I don't know what to do, Hope!" She was panicking, and her childhood fears and shyness turned into pure shock.

"Here, Adriana Laura!" Hope grabbed her bracelet and the leaf. "Make this a band-aid! Mommy says this can make you better." She put the leaf over the cut, and slowly but surely slid the bracelet over the injured girl's wrist. In a flash, there was an instant cure....despite the meager and somewhat haphazard first-aid provided, she pressed with the leaf on the wound, as the bracelet forming what was pretty much the kindergarten-er's interpretation of a battle tourniquet. Hope's eyes shined, her black hair blowing in the wind.

Just then, the first responders - or more modestly, the local neighbor-hood instant paramedics known as the parents came. "What happened, Pook? Did you fall?" And immediately, she showed her wrist, with the bracelet tied with the leaf serving as a gauze pad. "Look what Hope did. It feels a little better. Thank you, Hope."

Lou gave her pained daughter a hug. "Here, come on in. We'll make you feel better." And they went in.

As they went into the bathroom of their new pad, Lou did the best fatherly act of taking care of his daughter. "Here, dear. Sit down and scooch." What he saw, he could not believe. He pulled back the leaf and bracelet, and said "Oh, my God." The look of fear in his eyes, he could not explain – and it would not be, for many years.

The three oldsters of the block all gathered around the window. "Guess this is the beginning of a good relationship. Poor girl though, getting cut on the first day.

"Wish we could help her."

II

The Discovery

SEVEN YEARS, 32 DAYS LATER

The sun shone bright in the new Pennsylvania school year, and it was indeed the gathering of the middle schoolers, many of which had begun to form their own friendships and groups. When the hormones release, many of the girls of the age begin having eyes that wander, parts growing for the first time, and a brain hellbent on trying to pay attention to beauty, poetry, and, OH, THAT GUY OVER THERRRRE.

A blue Camry pulled into the school parking lot, which was already littered with balloons, children, and lots and lots of banter, some of it quite loud. The school buses filled the air with the smell of hellish hydrocarbons and silly amounts of soot. And in that car was a 13 year old Hope Malott.

She was already anxious. "Do we really have to pull up in the car? All my friends are going to see me in here. Maaaaa-awm, please. Keep away from the door. I don't want Bella and Tracie and Brittney to see me." Clutching at her backpack and then a small department store handbag, she wanted to be out of the scene.

The mother knew her daughter all too well. But she didn't care for being protective at this point. This was her moment — and no one could stop it from occurring. "Well, I'll drop you off at the corner. None of them will see you." She smiled. "I love you too much, sweetie."

As she stopped the car, Hope looked across the console. "I know I'll make it. Eighth grade, and then I'm off to high school. Rule of the roost to being a freshman. Like, yay me." Hope was not her namesake; she was ready to panic.

"Don't try to do too much on the first day. You still got 184 days after this to do all your stuff, 'k? I'll pick you up and we'll go out to dinner tonight. Duck's Pizza House?" She was a consoler of all types, especially to what she had been to her daughter. It was good to back her kid up – she had seen way too many parents treating school as a government-funded daycare and indoctrination/parenting center. A few lived on their street, and it was motivation enough when they would see the kids unlock the door in the afternoon, and the parents come home at 11 PM, work uniforms still on. And the lights would seldom turn on for the long run.

"Duck's it is." Her mom asked for a kiss, for which she placed one on her right cheek. This was it. As she walked slowly towards the main doors of the freshly painted and manicured foyer of the school, a lot of things preoccupied her growing mind, as they did for many of the days that school started Most of them were pretty typical for a sheltered girl like herself: how her friends were doing, whether or not Adriana was wearing the designer shoes that she had boasted her Dad bought her, how Mr. DeBlau, the English teacher, really was now that he no longer wore his eighties glasses, and whether or not the new school mascot's actor really had a pimple that really pulsed after he sneezed and when he had to say a fricative.

What a shame to be worried about such petty things, of course.

No sooner had she walked up the stairs that she saw Adriana, her thick frame "geek" glasses hiding her real feelings. Her hair had grown over the summer to where it reached straight back in one stream to each shoulder. Surveying her new locker for the year, she carefully sorted through and placed the school supplies Lou had packed like sardines into her backpack. Never be underprepared for the new school year, the dad would say all the time. It made it look like she was a bum from that intersection the bus would always pass through near the river. Eventually, she would probably be busted for hoarding, and be even more outcast than she was, well, now. But a girl's locker is also her space, and even if the school could open it, it had to be wardrobe, powdering mirror, social gathering spot, and school desk all in one. And occasionally, it was a place to hide for someone who needed it, a refuge for her best kept secrets. How that could fit in such a small space fools the best of us. Especially when she would leave notes to friends she never had, little reminders to others that she wanted to be there for a friend, but never could pass the notes to them because she was afraid. Adriana could never muster up giving her friends the notes.

And at the end of 7th grade, she threw them all away. As she did for the years before.

The sea of young blood parted seemingly as the last few rays of the sun of summer freedom blended into the fluorescent light of the modern industrial complex of a school built in the Seventies. Hope had walked these halls so many times before, but yet, the air of mystery seemed to pervade the young girl. As she walked towards her assigned room, she saw her best friend.

"Hey you!" Hope yelled. "Welcome back to the dungeon." With a slight, casual embrace, they started talking. "What's going on so far today?" As if it mattered that they had just discussed it yesterday on the front lawn.

"Well, Hope, I have to say I have soooooo many classes that are stupid. Like literally this —" she pointed to a piece of paper in her hand with a dot-matrix schedule — "knitting and home economics? I'm 13 and going to college....I don't want to have to be a grandma yet. I can smell the formaldehyde baths we're going to have to take...."

It already seemed like the year, barely 5 minutes old, was already destined for the doom of the doldrums. The late bell had not even rung, and her friend – or at least her good neighbor – was already in the red when it came to the attitude. For Hope, this was both the time to not only turn things around and do a favor for a friend, but to keep her own sovereignty. "Well, don't worry about it. We have class together, like, five times this quarter! You'll like it, I guarantee. We'll have fun, don't worry. Hey, we have Boss Ross the art teacher together!" It drew a smile from behind the glasses for Adriana, and helped her rise from the depths of the profundal zone of despair.

Without another word, the bell rang. "Hey, we'll be good together. I'll see you later, Hope. Like, 12:30, show up in gym! Let's cut class!" Hope smiled – *and then realized she had not found her locker yet.*

 Rushing towards the end of the hall where the note that had been left in the mailbox, and then placed in a side pocket of the bag by Carrie (keep in mind that a 13 year old girl may know what makeup she needs, but can't comprehend the intricacies of being prepared for the most important pedagogical steps of tweenhood pseudo-academia) said where her belongings should go, she began a sprint for adequacy.

There was a definitely rushed occurrence in the making, where clumsiness and nervousness got in the way, but then it only got more complicated in the worst way from there. Turning a corner, she slipped on water, and in her way was the monster herself.

A girl of almost 14, and mature in all ways except to the common courtesy, Dari Collins stood in Hope's way. A product of an upper-class family that was trying to assimilate to the life of a suburban drama princess, for she had not acquired the jewels and coat of arms requisite of dealing with things such as school buses instead of the subway and occasional BMW ride, recess on open lots rather than on fenced rooftops, and the fact that her parents now could drive 15 minutes to the country club rather than make it a weekend to head upstate, she hid her fear of social mediocrity by a certain type of prudent and forceful arrogance. She had 6 months to form her clique, and all she needed to do was sniff for the upscale department store perfume to track down those whom owed servitude to the Holy Grail of the puffed-up life. (Trust me, it's not that hard to discern it.)

The collision took all of a split second. In the scene of the dark halls, one could view conceivably that while Hope fell, the decline of Dari was the books flying above. It was war breaking out in heaven, and Michael and his angels fought with the dragon Dari, and suddenly, the angels were cast out as Hope hit the floor.

Dari left nothing for the young girl to waste. She literally went after the poor girl. Mouth wide open, she looked down at her merino wool sweater, light blue and with argyle in grey and white, and yelled "You bitch! This sweater is one hundred dollars! This punch is going to take a customized fritching tailor to get this out!"

Hope didn't know how to react. Avoid conflict at all costs, her father would usually say. Just go with the flow. "I'm so sorry. I need to get to class. Where's Mrs. Donaldson's room?" One of the problems with being so protected is that it offers those with little social practice to, eh, acquire the right etiquette. It was a hard-hitting reality, quite literally.

"You, had, better be kidding, you. Get out of here before I call my lawyer and turn your panties into pissrags." Dari literally granted her *the* free pass to class. It was singular because it would be the only one for her. After all, it was the first day; Dari had her seemingly inordinate but obviously obligatory schedule to maintain her status at the top of the totem pole.

As Hope ran off, Dari laughed in extreme anger, and pulled at her shirt, fanning out her tank underneath. That little beaver breath better not be in my grade.

She got into her room, her bookbag still quite full. Taking a deep breath, she sat down, and looked into the front of the room. *Thank God for late teachers*, she thought.

TWO MONTHS LATER

The first signs of the manifestation of fall were in the air. Slowly, the sun began to set earlier; the sheer tops and flip-flops lost ground in the popularity game to the letterman jackets and Chucks. Football was the name of the game, at least to the middle school gathering which would drop by the stadium to cheer on their older brethren. It was the calling of the young, the mating season for all the young biota, and it proceeded to give a sense of refreshment.

Not to be confused with the above, Hope Malott was still in the game. Eighth graders had to take a health class – the "wonder of wonders", as the teacher, a former gym instructor named Denise Ohmer. More representative of the masculinity of a bodybuilder than the psychological caress of what women would expect, Ohmer had short, butch hair with what appeared to be the beginnings of a mustache fit for diabetes commercials. And she had the attitude of "don't trust anyone". With a voice strained by years of Camels and hormonally compromised students, she had the whip of an angry dominatrix. More importantly and somewhat noticeably, she also was the one to go to the board and separate the sexes in class. She said "The boys don't need to know how to insert anything into there in as much as the girls how to grab and feel the gourds." It could only be pictured on how that conversation went for vote.

"Ladies, welcome to Sex Ed. Have you ever wondered about your body, and why it reacts so, well, special? You don't have a damn clue –" and out of her pocket, she whipped out an unwrapped, unused tampon, pulling it overhead, holding it like the Host on high – "and this thing here covers up for all your un-Godly mistakes." The class began to giggle, and rightfully so, as many young curious people had never expected such a dramatic introduction to personal cleanliness since they found out that 12 years indeed do need deodorant. Even if they do shower and groom like their Mommies and Daddies order every day.

In the front row, Adriana and Hope were quickly becoming the most conspicuous victims to the fallacy of intensive teaching. "Hey, maybe we can shove that in her piehole sometimes. The thing barks too," Hope whispered to Adriana, trying to hold back the mist in the eyes. They both began to feel the animal instinct that has befallen every girl who becometh a woman, and it was suddenly seizing their brains.

It was a first for them to feel this way. Being a teen female going through the first stages of being a woman is equivalent to being high on painkillers while feeling like you've been hit by two trains. Nothing knocks sense into you like a little bit of hormonal discharge. And it had to happen right in the presence of the master of health deviance.

Despite their best efforts, the angry schoolmarm spotted the conversation. "Hope Malott! Adriana Mendoza! You have anything to say regarding your health?" She began tapping her foot on the ground, the class falling as silent as the playgrounds outside in the morning. She growled, the folds in her face giving the look of an aged set of Victorian drapery.

Adriana felt the pain come on. Her shyness and retracted ego suddenly took over her mouth, bypassing the id. "Well, ma'am, we don't understand why hygiene has to be, well, such an adventure."

Never the one to hold back, her friend spoke. "Besides, we already have those. Every purse in this whole friggen school has one of those. You have the principal to thank, Mizz Ohmer. Our taxes at work, right?" For one of the first times, Hope was beginning to come out of her politically correct, super-polite ways, and indeed, she could feel the hormones come on.

"That's enough, Miss Malott. Either you take this device here – or you get out. You will understand it someday. I hope, dearie." The teacher pulled another wrapped tampon from her back pocket, putting it barrel-length to Hope's temple. Adriana looked at her best friend, being pressured, albeit in the most awkward way. "Just take it," she said with a dirty look and the roll of an eye.

"OK, Mizz Ohmer, I'll take it, with one condition." She paused, and with the raise of the teacher's eyebrow in the most vulcanized way, the student immediately spat out, perhaps in a moment of surprise and pure petulance "If this thing gets jammed in there, are you going to pull it out with those long whiskers on your upper lip that are hooking? I'm sure they'll carry bait, for all I care." Instantly, the whole class began laughing, and immediately thereafter, Hope was on her way to the principal's office. Or so she thought.

For a while, the girl who had been protected and honeysuckled into being an upper-class model for society by her parents, nurtured endlessly, and grown up well ahead of the precociousness of her bloodlines, suddenly was a rabble-rouser. Yet, she felt an overwhelming feeling of satisfaction and gratitude, a contentment that flowed through her body like cold antifreeze. She smiled as she walked down the hall. She held her head high, and said to herself *I'm sooo not going to the principal or counselor. I'm going to go down and sit and watch gym class.* But there was someone watching from around the corner – someone that would turn her fortunes and turn that girl into a lady. Dari slid a sly eye from around the corner.

All of a sudden, she felt a sudden pain in her stomach, like someone had taken a blow to her stomach. Her muscles tightened, her chest began to deflate like a balloon. She had never felt this way before, but she knew what it was - and she knew that despite the fact that she had gotten thrown out of Ohmer's class, it was true that she really did need that little cotton thingy.

Running to the ladies' room, she closed the stall, tried to apply it, in a mad panic. She couldn't think, couldn't go for anything, forgot being thrown out of class, or the fact that not only would her friend be considering her absence, but now the whole school administration would be wondering where Hope Malott was....and why she had acted so out of character.

Within seconds, the moment of truth had come. She fumbled it into the commode, it going in, in a split second, her innards had rejected the applicator. And she sat down, feeling like God was trying to bend her in half and give an appendectomy by severe pressure. She closed her eyes...

All of a sudden, the stall was lit in a bright glow. Hope could not see it – she pictured everything that had happened earlier, the voices intertwined in a jumbled mess. Somehow, the words didn't make sense, but within seconds, she felt anew – like there was no pain at all, that someone had lifted a giant burden off her shoulders. And she opened her eyes, and saw stars, like she had been punched square on the bridge of the nose. She took a moment to breathe, and found the pains of years had left her. And she suddenly realized her stall was actually glowing – all over the place! It literally had light, a bluish-green tint representative of the burning of the brightest methane. It looked like a giant star had nested in that ladies' room.

The door opened. She took a breath, and looked up....and there was Dari. Startling Hope, she said "Hi there."

Hope didn't know what to say, except she could only say one thing. "Look, I'm sorry about the first day..." she wanted off the hook. *This is not the time for conflict, dammit.*

I need quiet, she thought to herself in that little voice.

But Dari was there. "You know, you are pretty kooky sticking a glowstick in there. I've known of a lot of people sticking stuff. Fingers, johnsons, heck, a clothes hanger, heck, my aunt even stuck a cigar in there and called it a Clinton's Classic. But you, my friend, are one of a kind. Really...." She began to encircle the energy-drained girl. "I wonder when that little donger's going to stop glowing. You better flush it – " and without another word, Hope reached for it, figuring that she had seconds to bail before she got in trouble.

Throwing it at the intruder to her newest private catastrophe, Hope picked it up and splashed the preppy princess of purgatory power in the face, with glowing dots sprinkled about the girl, who began screaming with interspersed "Ewwwwww"s and the crimping of fingers.

But perhaps the strangest thing was as she began running, she realized that the dots on her fingers were still glowing. She stopped running, and began looking towards her fingers, as if she had discovered something was terribly wrong. On the surface, it was too much of an adrenaline rush for her to complete the thought in her mind. But then, it was something wrong in the end. And she knew that her priority was to make sure now that this happened, that she had to set it right.

ONE HOUR LATER

Time is a unique property, a unique dimension to analyze. Rationed arbitrarily, but yet all in the same the constant, it is ultimately the judge of everything of dimension, and it being the fourth essential to the sciences, it has its own imperialistic sovereignty.

For some, time flies past. It could have not done so for Hope, who sat in the back of her biology class. She was as confused and wondrous and perhaps a bit bitter of oneself of the events of what just happened. Slumped in her seat, she rubbed her eyes, and began to look outwards toward the crisp October sky.

The image of the glowing fluid, whatever it was, that had emanated from her innocence, stuck in her head like no other. She tried to reason exactly how this could happen; perhaps it was something she ate, or a trick of the lighting in the building.

Yup, it had to be that, she thought. *Food poisoning*. To most, it would have never been the monstrosity that lay before her. But yet to someone who was so sheltered from drama most of the time, she was in an alien world, one that could not seek respite from explanation. And it felt strange, to say the least.

A young man walked in the class, his tandem gait representing that he was not well, perhaps the effects of the environment. Smiling, he looked through his glasses and handed the instructor the paper, then immediately, as if in a militaristic manner, rotated one half turn and walked out. The teacher, an older gentleman with eighties-style double bridged glasses, looked through his bifocals, and said "Hope? The school nurse and vice principal need to see you. Immediately." The whole class turned around, suddenly falling silent from the usual whisper-and-note passing, and focused on the sight of what they saw to already be a downtrodden girl going to what they knew was the imminent doom of the house disciplinarian.

The walk was undeniably the longest of her life as she clomped down the hall with her boots clicking sharply beneath her. Even though she had to go about 300 feet, down a flight of stairs, and make a U-turn, she had plenty of time to think about her actions, however involuntary they were. For her, she had always prided herself on being a good student and a role model; it was instilled in her from birth that in order to make a difference, one must break from the mold. And now, her mold of hormones and a freak show had placed her in the bastard bin of the school.

Taking a deep breath, she grabbed for the door handle, looking down as she stepped closer. Turning it slowly, she made her words in her head. They never came.

The nurse looked up, and next to her was Dari, bandages twirled around her face like a papered tree. Her normally well-manicured hair stuck out in hay-like appendages randomly scattered about, lending an appearance to a palm bush after a severe hurricane. With no relent or tact, the postal prep got up, pushed the nurse out of the way, and said "You and your freakin' kiddie toys burned my face! You know that? You are going to have to have some nice lawyers...." She began to grasp Hope's neck, and reached for her hair. Already confused, Hope could do little but try to pry the angry girl's hands off of her neck. She was mixed between trying to get the hands or push the intently gripping body away. Little muscle tone was used, but it was reinforced with the anger of pity and the impasse of purely haughty attitude.

The principal stepped in between. "Ho, ho!!! You two stop this right now! Stop it! –" as he used all his might to separate the two.

"She burned my face! Underclass bitch, you don't know what you did –" the girl in the stained sweater yelled out loud. Her makeup was rubbed all over the sweater, obviously submitting to the fact that yes, the damned thing was filthy – but not as filthy as the skin beneath it and the heart that it covered.

[28]

"I don't know what I did! I didn't mean you any harm – you came after me...."

"You know darn well like what you did to me – this ain't the fourth of July on the beach...." It was beginning to show pure anger, and the argument descended from pleas of implied guilt to a pure contest of wills, with the antagonist becoming perhaps not so obvious.

The principal set them apart. "Girls, you can't keep doing this. Now, explain what happened – " he turned to Hope, and gave the look of trying to establish some sort of lawfulness in the room.

"Mr. Perry, I got thrown out of class earlier today because I think I was....eh, having some lady stuff go on – " she barely finished her words, almost out of breath.

The prep rebutted. "So she got thrown out of class and decided to go do this. You should be suspended – " to which the ever strict principal responded "Shut up, Daria."

It gave Hope a minute to catch her breath and establish a quantum of sanity. "It's not about that. I got sick in class, and something very weird happened to me. I tried to handle it, but I couldn't."

"Right, Hope. Nora, is Dari alright?" the principal turned to the nurse.

Just about as flabbergasted as a wrinkled *Viejo* nurse could be, Nora laughed. "Well, she's probably a little anxious from being sprayed, but overall, as long as no one notices the bandages, she's okay. I don't know what it is, sir, but it made for a lot of red face. "

With a pout and a look of stupor, the burned braggerette said "No one notice the bandages? I'm not going to a Halloween party! Homecoming's next week! I can't look like a zit face." She was angry indeed, but Perry was insistent that she leave.

As she walked out of the room, the principal turned to the young girl. "Now, miss Malott. We went to the lavatory a few minutes ago and couldn't find anything except a used tampon and, well, other stuff that our, eh, normally clean washrooms would see. Damn custodians and their union labor. $27 an hour...."

The nurse gave a chuckle and shook her head. Fool. Perry noticed, and realized he had been distracted. "Now, tell me if you had a glowstick or toy or something that you used to assault Miss Collins over there. We will find it, so you better come clean now, or else we're going to turn you into the magistrate, and you will be suspended.

"Do you understand?" With a nod from the student, he said "OK, now, tell me what happened.

And she began to elaborate about her motion for cleanliness, the oncoming, violent cramps she had, the barely making it to the bathroom. She mentioned how the bathroom glowed, the interruption of the girl she had run into earlier, and everything in between. For the principal, he had heard many stories about what the teachers called "disrespect" as a blanket statement. Even though the principal had moved up the ranks, including several in the military, he had never heard this type of story. It dumbfounded him, struck him as disturbing.

So instead of dealing with it by keeping Hope Malott in the office, he did the school administrator's thing – and sent her home. That car ride was strange – but in it, she would have her epiphany of a life that was one of a kind.

1:30 PM

The car ride home from being dismissed early from school is usually one of the most awkward rides one can have in a young life. It seldom is a friendly ride – usually, the kid may be outwardly angry, but in mind, is afraid of the consequence. Many a family feud started not because of a poor answer to a survey, but the mom trying to let the kid saunter in his room over the dad wishing to take more empirically corporal means. Either way, it could be best said that the conversation was minimal.

As soon as the door opened to the car, Carrie looked in her daughter's eyes. "You need to get in. I know what happened, and it's probably better we discuss on the way." Without a word, her little Hopie got in. Schoolteachers never cease to give all the bloody details, so to speak. And Carrie had rehearsed her speech on the way, as she had always practiced. Sure, she wanted to give it on the couch at home. When she was ready for it. Or even make it both of them ready for it. But like facing the death of a friend, it often never really fully manifests itself in the mind until it is too late. And then emotions can take over even the best of us.

As they pulled away from the school, the silence rang like the call of the coyote in the evening forest. "I didn't do anything, Mom. I was scared." She felt ready to cry.....she had taken great pride in practicing good intentions and citizenship. She felt that her lady parts had disappointed her; after all, she was innocent, and Principal Perry knew she was a good student, most likely the reason she was released instead of turned in to the authorities.

Carrie took a glance at Hope's sunken face, her emerald-laced eyes gazing out into the distance. It took a minute for her to swallow the lump in her throat. "Look, Hopie....what I am going to tell you....you cannot tell anyone. Not your friends, not your aunts and uncles. No one. You....you are a special daughter of mine. A very special one, in a way that no one else can say." She had tears in her eyes, and a pale, sincere, and regretful

[31]

look on her face. She looked straight ahead, gripping the steering wheel with equal parts vigor and indecision.

Hope was puzzled, somewhat skeptical. Even in her most conceited moments, she had not seen her mom like this. But she had been of the same blood, for which she knew her thoughts. "What's wrong?" She was trying to hold back her emotions.

She let the story roll off her tongue, in the darned best way she could.

APRIL 11, 1989

UTAH

The alarm sounded at the crack of dawn, a version of Stevie Ray Vaughan's rabid guitar playing. It was energetic blues, to say the least. It echoed through the apartment like the sound of a wailing wind through the forest; eclectically emotional, it felt like the nightclub atmosphere.

Alex Malott and his new wife Carrie were dozed out on the couch, layered on each other like a stack of deli turkey and curled around like the twist of a pretzel. They both ended up there because of a late night at the mine. Tru-Col Industries, a miner of various ores, such as aluminum, silver, copper, and iridium, mined in the Rockies for many years. They were each pulled there for different reasons; Alex by the fact that he was a mechanical engineer, six years into earning his PE, and Carrie by her necessity of finding a job that paid well and fit her needs, despite the fact she was literally a liberal arts college graduate with a couple of chemistry classes that she had taken in her free time – ones that through a scheduling conflict, made bureaucracy – and a few labs – attainable for ample work on the base. She was 24, Alex 27. They both had their young hearts, wild, perhaps not so much free for love, but free to the openness of life, the unquestionable ability to make one's own path, which befit their daily journeys out of town through the buttes and mesas of the lower Northwest.

"Hun, it's early today. Who's going to shovel all that snow, though? We gotta work!" Carrie laughed, looking into the still closed eyes of her dearest.

In response, he yawned, as if to acknowledge the futility of her pleas. He often did that, although it never really bothered her. Resilience was the key to her studies at school – she had often gone into the activism of the late eighties of saving the Earth and everything connected. It was quite an admission of guilt, perhaps. But she was in for it with him.

"Come on, it's like 6:30. Project's due today, project for compound 402."

They both tried to get up and out the door. As they walked down to the car, the sun shone bright. A newly fallen snow set an indiscernible fade into the low haze in the sky over the mountains. The route was plowed clear, and the roads were dry as a bone.

They were out to the plant on the side of town. Many of the cities represented the mining boom towns of yesteryear; small rows of houses stretching like leaves off of the main street trunk. It was very quaint, a sort of town that reminded one of simple lives of the Fifties. It did, in effect, make a big impression for them when they raised the then twinkle of their eye Hope. Driving through town made them think not of the isolation of moving from the big city, but how lucky they were to witness God's work in this town, the countryside, a landscape Currier and Ives paint of mountains of silver with powdery caps of white.

Even with this bucolic beauty of the environment, one could not have been more anticipatory for antithesis for their work at Tru-Col. As part of the testing team, they often skirted the borders of the legal, the sensible, and perhaps most sensitive of all, the environmentally sound. Their work was often skirted in secrecy, and any conversation with the public often went from topics of "Oh, that's cool, so you're a scientist?" to the inevitable "You guys are poisoning the environment." They had an older Chevy Nova for the particular reason that a new car (and they had them) would often be covered in paint, egg shells, the windows cracked and the headlights bashed in with baseball bats. They could also recall how the tires were slashed and a late season June snow left them marooned at work at 11 PM on a Tuesday night.

They went into work that fateful day at 7:30 AM. Before parting for the day, they would hold hands at the entrance, give a kiss, bump heads like many young couples would, and depart for the day. The guards in the plant, often older gentlemen who would wear suitcoats and a tie, would often smile, recalling their own youth and offering a genuine smile in a gesture of approval.

In many ways, everyone knew everyone at Tru-Col. It was not a very large plant by any means, and those who were employed there for long enough often would become celebrities in their own way. As they passed each checkpoint, the guards would wave hello, ask how they were, their kids were, and all the responsibilities of keeping "safety first". Before the final checkpoint to the lab, though, was a special gate. The guard would often be in simple personal protective equipment. Behind him was an airlock, guarded by a thick, safelike door. Entry was only by mutual swipe of a card, and one of the first of a litany of biometric devices, put up by the US government. The door would open with a hiss, and Alex had to hang up a special pink name tag outside on a hook, putting it back on upon leaving the room for any reason.

 The reasons were many; for one, it was an account of someone being in the room. If an unfortunate event occurred, such as an accident, explosion, or of the like, the body count would be simple – just check the tags on the wall. If they were there, the rescue and search crews knew who and how many employees to look for. Furthermore, there was security reasoning behind the matter in addition. Should some of the materials be lost or stolen, an account of who was in the room would be taken. Only then would there be a scan of all bodies in the room by the man outside the vault.

The door opened to the foresaid room. Inside, it was as clean as the dreams of an obsessive-compulsive's bathroom. Everyone worked indirectly in the area; separation from the studied chemistry was a must, with a few exceptions obviously for stuff that could be taken home. The company took great pride in never having an incident on their records of death.

"G'morning, Ed," Alex wished his co-worker as he walked in. With the same coming back, he began talking about his work today, particularly the compound 402.

Compound 402 was a combination of suspended radioactive components, mostly lanthanides with a potassium buffer. A lot of it was supposedly known, but the secrecy never really broke; they just never discussed it. The compounds themselves were extremely unstable; a single jolt the wrong way could send them into a fission reaction which was almost completely uncontrollable. Despite the fact that this was the truth, many of the workers would handle the smaller tanks of C402 on a daily basis, especially when they were in their casings, a lead "picnic basket" which weighed more than 100 pounds but felt lighter to the strong men. Within that was a vacuum chamber along with several vials of the compound on the rack. The daily struggle was to shuttle the vials themselves between the laboratories. Often times, they would have to be carried well out into the unprotected abyss of the outside offices. Out there, there were few vestiges of protection, should a spill occur.

Placing his gloves on, Alex began to prepare for his job that day: to place the vials in a chamber to test their volatility to a ceramic-iron polymer tank. Lead was both heavy and expensive to take places; furthermore, the lead baskets themselves were a health hazard, as they caused birth defects – and thus, diligent hand-washing to the point of chapping of the skin was often completed before break and leaving. By using the polymer, they hoped to develop a lighter-weight means of transporting C402, and it was hoped that by using this powerful compound, less radioactive compounds, such as plutonium, neptunium, cobalt, and the like could be moved more efficiently.

The process itself required a delicate hand. Despite management's pleas to keep the yellowish-green soft drink-colored compound out of the lab and in the hood, Alex insisted on using moon suits and the personal touch for his placement. He trusted the robotic arms and the tinted glass; what he did not trust was the fact that machines glitch, analog controls fail, and the inept and unintentional movement of a metallic claw could mean the compound's natural state of being would create resemblance of the property and vicinity to a meteorite strike from long ago.

Perhaps the big objective of the day was to allow for Alex to not be forgetful. One of the biggest hazards of any workplace is obviously fatigue. However, in many places, fatigue is connected with small things – perhaps falling down the stairs or mistyping a macro in Excel. A mistake here could mean the death of many, and a disaster zone that may never be able to be touched again, especially with the 4 billion year and one second half-life of the compounds in C402.

Counting the vials through a piece of Plexiglas and his visual shield, Alex was worn out. He didn't really want to be at work that day. But he needed to brush up for the boss.

25, 26, 27, 28, 29. Oh shit, I'm missing one, he thought to himself. The rack was missing one. With the standard rack of 35 being somewhat hard to notice that he was missing one, he went back to the sealed hood to slide a vial towards him, pull it out with the protected gloves, and put it in the case.

Just then, Carrie came in. "Hey babe –" and with that, the vial slipped, but with a nimble hand, Alex grabbed it before it completely left the glove. Alex gasped, and then smiled after he realized he had averted the disaster.

"Hey, you. Can't startle me like that, dear. Goddamn thing almost turned us into roast chicken and our building into Three Mile." Alex was serious, but Carrie put her left index finger in the "quiet" position, and ran it down his cheek. "How the hell did you get in here? Ed –" but no one was in there except he, his wife, and a case of highly explosive fluid in a black case.

Carrie was laughing. "You know, we never had that honeymoon we promised. You know, Acapulco – "she began to laugh, and pull on his lab coat. "And those guys over there —" she pointed towards the glass, to see the guard, Ed, and a couple of other women, all gathered around — "and we are going at the end of the week."

Alex wanted to say something, but he didn't. He grabbed the vial, wrapped it in his shielded glove where it would be protected and padded, and put the other glove next to it and walked to the gate. The airlock opened, and cheers rang out through the room. They all jeered "Hun-ee-moon! Hun-ee-moon!" as they walked out. The door slammed, and all was good, almost hitting Carrie in the rear. It seemed like good luck, but it was more than fortunate the door was there — for everyone's sake. And then, it was over.

Suddenly, the room filled with a flash of light. The slam of the door meant that the glove had slid off, hitting the ground. The still-open lead case created a military-style flashbang of the entire contents. They said afterwards that had Carrie and Alex been in front of the windows, they would have been killed. It was a dramatic sequence, but there were little stories to be told, and none should have been shared despite. A momentary lapse of judgment and a sure violation of workplace rules by the same government that celebrated his final celebration of his honeymoon now meant that the lives of many were changed.

PRESENT DAY

She had heard the entire story for the first time, and Hope still could not stomach the revelation, a secret that had burned inside her every action, but never voiced before. The fact that she had tampons that glowed meant a heck of a lot more than some would believe, but the truth hurt Hope like she had never felt before. Even when she sprained both ankles riding a bike, got cuts and bruises on fences - even fell off a jungle gym once, it did not overstate how this pain was worse than them all. It was not just physical pain, but it was an inner pain. For the first time, she felt like something different – something great was running through her blood. It stung like no jellyfish or bee or knife could ever do. It felt like she had to do something about it. But she didn't know what.

The mother walked up to the stoop of her house, and shut the door gently. "Hope, I never told you this story because I didn't want you to do anything you wouldn't want. You were not the age of reason yet – and I was told not to let anyone know."

"Know about what?" Hope was puzzled. She had already broken this covenant.

"Well, after what happened at our company, the doctors inspected us and gave us a physical. They wondered why we didn't pass away like the others. They took our blood, looked us all over, nary a scratch. But your immune system, and partially mine, was compromised on that day. And my reproductive organs took the brunt of the radiation – it was condensed in the eggs in my uterus. Your dad's privates, too."

"So why didn't I come out with three eyes, or five arms, like they show in the movies?"

"Well, they couldn't figure that out. All I know is that the C402 directly hit us on the skin. Your T-cells in your body are one-thousand times as powerful as that in your friends, Hopie. Your cells – and anything that your blood or bodily fluids run through, all have powers that are beyond

[39]

the human comprehension. You possess the only body that will likely ever have that capability. You are…." The mother began to water her eyes – "an unfortunate angel. A gift from God. And dammit, I'm not going to let you go for it.

Hope became instantly scared for herself, but also for her mother. No longer could she proclaim her innocence, or that she was just a normal girl trying to wade through the murky waters of middle and high school or the social life. Every step she took from here on out was a new step, a fording of a new river, the first of a thousand Confucian journeys, all wrapped around the concept. "But what am I supposed to do, Mom?" she asked.

The answer, plain and simple, was this. "You do nothing. You tell no one. Too many people know already what happened. If this breaks, we could be in big trouble. It was already too much for this to make it to the news of the building. God….God save our souls.

"You have great power, Hopie. You really do."

FIVE BLOCKS EAST

4:47 PM

Inner beauty often shows on the face of the bold, it was once said, but outer beauty seldom penetrates within. Somehow, there was a loss of beauty in the home of Daria Collins, the screaming of a girl gone too far into the self-absorption of ego, true to nothing but one's own will. Her clothes in tatters, she was taken home and essentially carried in by her father, as she was what many call a "hot mess." Bandages on her face and her apparel in disarray, her psychosis of double the drama and a pinch of sweet revenge by Hope the Omniscient, she was thrown on the couch. Something had gotten into her, but she couldn't figure it out. But it didn't help that a little bit of drama between classes didn't do the trick. She had indulged in drama, and was now taken over by the anger of the girl she barely knew but so much wanted to block out because she was an enemy.

"Daddy, I want to have a drink. Perhaps a little bit of rum," she said in a slurred voice. "My panties feel like a piss….rag. Oops." Her father had no part of it whatsoever. Called home from work to pick up his daughter, he had been through these struggles several times, and usually, the outcome was such that she would get a slap on the wrist, and he would get a strongly worded email in a week asking for a conference with the guidance counselor. It was a loop of inevitability that proceeded to energize well into the future.

"Daria, you know you've gotten into trouble so many times, love. You don't need any more of this so called mean girl shit any more. Come on, you aren't even in high school yet! Look at you, dressed like this. I'm sick of it." He began to go and fumble about the room, looking to complete his executive privileges and ford on with his life.

"Eh, I just hate that lil' bitch Hope Malott. She got all these special things, she likes being clumsy and nerdy and putting toys up places….but I'll get her one of these days." She turned on her side, and let her arm hang over the side of the leather furniture.

The dad would have no part of it. "You know, you get yourself into these circumstances and start wars and stuff. Look at you now. You don't get it, do you? Your face is probably gonna look like a corncob 'cos you got burned, and you're going to have to go out and go with Morris Bodart like that. Shame, isn't it?" He turned away.

These were shocking words to the spoiled surrogate. Her father would usually just solve all the problems by throwing money at her; the obvious servitude to the apoplectic was financially backed. And so, she expected to be rewarded for her tantrum. But her father showed a small candle of light in the darkness.

"You know what, Dad? I….don't…care! This girl ruins everyone else's lives, now YOU are ruining mine!" She got up and stumbled up the stairs to her bathroom. "I don't care, I don't need you….I don't need Hope, I don't need that little tramp Adriana…" she began to mount the stairs, and was failing miserably. Initially grasping the bannister, then the rail, then down on all fours, she grumbled incoherently. The bandages were blocking her vision, and she began to cry out loud. "I can't….shit….stand this anymore!" She buried her head in the rug of the oaken stair, and began to rip off her bandages. "Come and get me, tramps! You won't let me hide from you!" So she ripped off her bandages.

In a fit of anger, the downtrodden ditz had yanked her protective layers to bare her deep inside. But little did she know that where beauty in rhetoric lay, sometimes beauty in reality also took place.

Immediately, the effect indeed took place on her father. "Daria. You need to see this." She didn't realize it, but it was there. She collapsed on the stairs. And then, as her last view turned to a vanity mirror hung delicately on the wall, inner beauty began to show…and only then, was it evil.

"Oh, my God." She caressed her face.

[42]

THE NEXT DAY

8:45 AM

The 47th day of classes began like many in southeast PA; rainy, a bit chilly, winds out of the west. They tended to blow the direction of where the spirits of yesterday wanted to travel, and this was a bitter one to say the least. It chilled Hope in her light blue American Eagle Outfitters hoodie to get out and face what was promising to be a strange day. Hope didn't know about what her teachers would say about not being in class, whether or not she would have to make up any courses or homework, or where she would find the solace to admit the strange things happening. Most of all, she feared about the return of Daria. Like many things in school, word travels, especially among the popular people: jocks, preps, geeks, all the social groups. As many of the "others", the somewhat unaffiliated breeds discovered, these exclusive gatherings tended to have the biological equivalent of cross-breeding and cross-populating; whatever sphere of influence induced a problem, the others would eventually grab hold of and then likely exploit the morsels of deceit and contraband of words.

She got out of the car to see a much more subdued crowd. Few were gathered outside of the school. Instead, students were filing into classes, and little was said to each other. It felt strange, and then it just got worse.

As she walked up the stairs to the entrance, people began to stare at her, giving the effect of tunnel vision. As that feeling made those darkening hallways spin, the omnipresence of a violated social clause in the pedagogue had surface. She knew that word had leaked, for which reparation and penance consisted of the old fashioned standard of the silent treatment. All of the feelings that she was not supposed to worry about, at least in her mother's oversight, yes, they were all coming back in spades, all at once.

[43]

She got to her locker, putting her books down. Looking for her best friend for some consolation, Adriana was nowhere to be found. Her long brown hair, semitan skin, and large geek glasses were as easy to spot as an albino rabbit in a wine vintage. Hope became afraid, a fish of radiation out of the water of the cooling pipe. She took a look in the mirror at her eyes. Somewhere, she could see a shine in them. But it wasn't evident because there was just a sign of fatigue placed right on top of them, a tarp placed on the blue that she had seen so many times in that same reflection. It scared her to think that, but it was there. And fair game.

Just then, a tap on the shoulder came. Intense and alert with 1000 cubic centimeters of adrenaline flowing through every part of her body, much less the blood that got her this way, she screamed as loud as she could. She gazed into the mirror in suspicion. But the voice took over her senses. "Hey, you little weasel. Turn around." It was Dari.

Everything in Hope's body wanted to not look around. She was afraid to see what could have happened to her, especially with the concern that a girl who had prided herself so much on her appearance could look like. But then, a slight tinge of bravery ran up her lungs, and into her neck muscles. She turned around.

There was Dari.

She had no bandages, no burns.

And then skin that was as perfectly virgin as a movie star's complexion.

It gave Hope immediate relief, perhaps a little bit of respite from what surely was anticipating a mud fight, cat fight, or otherwise a deal of hair pulling best fit for a B-rate smut show.

"I don't have any makeup on, ditz." She looked serious. Grabbing Hope's bookbag, and forcing her to not turn around after she tried several times, she gave a serious look. "Whatever the hell was in that glowstick you shoved in your jewels, I want it. You killed all my acne." And then she smiled.

Pensive and waiting for what she thought was sarcasm to end, the shy girl gave a slight couple of nods, and began to smile herself. Dari's muscles relaxed, and let go of the young deviant. And for that moment, the explosives sat in the powder room, away from the matches of young hearts ready to ignite. It was all in the frightened look on the outcast's face, her blue eyes showing fear and a definitive sadness that gave the chiseled jaw a look that few had seen. And Dari was as ambiguous to it as she was her boyfriend's after-school rituals.

The day proceeded along reasonably well for the first few periods. However, the inevitable question that was on the shining innards of her mind, and the blood running through it also doing so, was how much was snuck out in a twist of fate and a moment of impeded judgment due to stress? Did Dari see the glowing tampon? Hope's mind began to race.

If she said it was a glowstick, maybe she thought it wasn't a tampon. But even if so, where do I say I got it from? A department store? A Jamaican witch? A rock star's cocaine closet? And if she finds it and feels it, what do I say, I got glowbugs and fireflies breeding inside me? And what happens if I can't shut up unless she kills me?

It was taxing, to say the least, on the girl. Certainly, this wasn't the way she planned to start the last year of middle school.

The bell to announce the end of third period had rang. She was headed to see Ohmer in health class. Certainly this would be a unique experience. She honestly didn't know what to expect – would she be given a lecture about her disrespectful ways from yesterday, the benefactor of the first true blossom of womanhood hormones? Certainly, a health teacher would comprehend the effects of premenstrual syndrome, much less the old codger of a principal. Or would she say something about what happened?

[45]

Nah. Hopie reasoned somewhat in attempting to convince herself anything but the truth. She didn't know.

She entered class very slowly, clutching her books tight to her chest. No one even noticed her entrance, until the old woman of the handful of beaver cushions began to speak. "Hello there, Miss Mal-Ottie. How are you feeling today?"

Pausing and waiting for a quick comment, Hope muttered in great uncertainty "OK. I want to sit down." With a nod from the teacher, she went to the back of the classroom, straight in the middle, waiting for the worst to happen. And it should have, and it did.

Hope's eyes began to pulse as they shook. She could feel that presence of her world spinning, the fact that all eyes were on her once again. Many times in a young person's life, that is just the anxiety of being peculiar to one's image. But yet it felt so strong – and somehow, with the burden of what she had done, it was too strong. Wordless, she sat in her seat, and covered her head. *I need to cool myself down*, *Hopie*, she muttered under hear breath. *For just a few moments*.

She turned to her left after putting her backpack down, two minutes in. Dari was sitting off her port aft side. Looking at her lovingly, Hope smiled. Let's talk, she saw Dari move her lips, and pointed out towards the hallway. "Miss Ohmer, I have to go to the lav. Gotta go service the gonads." She pulled Hope behind her, trying to keep up in her platform sneakers and flare jeans. The teacher had little to say to the two of them. She was too tired to deal with why two girls, of opposite candor, character, and concern, would book at the same time. And the coffee in the teacher's offices was just that damn scorched from the pot that had been reheated so many times. She had a lesson to teach, and she'd be damned if these 8th graders didn't know how a vas deferens worked.

The door slammed to the broom closet in the corner. "Don't worry, they don't bother checking these rooms 'cept at open and close. We may have an Arab and a Hispanic custodian, but neither are terrorists. At least on the district dime."

Without another word, Dari went on. "Look, you little screwball. You ruined my nice Express sweater from the mall. That thing was no dishrag, mind you. I should rip every single hair from your head for doing that. But I'm not going to."

Scared out of her mind, and not knowing what to expect next, she looked straight into the devil's eye. "Well, what do you want?" The same sharp tongue that had got her into this situation was about to do her in again.

The prep's blonde hair shined bright, and her demeanor firm. "I want you to help fix me for homecoming –" she pulled her sweater aside to reveal a huge blemish, a big red zit that was the size of a quarter, missed by the splashing the day before – "you can bust zits with your specialness, now bust this." She smiled, and stated boldly "Homecoming is next week, young lady. I have a date with Mo Bodart. I'm not wasting this. If you want to get off the sweater, I suggest you cure this. My bustline must be perfect. These boobs are my assets, and you're the banker, dweeb."

Hope laughed heavily at the sudden exposé. "Well, I don't have any glowsticks or the such. Nothing. That thing in the bathroom....it was a tampon. You'd have to bleed me." She laughed. "Now unless you want this to look like a 1950s Lon Chaney movie, I suggest you go down to the drug store and use the crèmes like everyone else. They're on sale this week. Dab twice, apply daily, results in three weeks or your money back. Now let me go." The firm but fearful girl of fair skin and fluorescent innards reached for the door handle, and then felt the grasp of the determined Dari.

For the first time, Dari's veneers showed, a pearl opaque white, like rice grains in the swamp. It was evident she had evil plans. "We have ways of doing that." She pulled out a nail clipper, and began rotating the tip of the file around. Scared and slightly skeptical, if at all, she saw the tip was sanded down to a point. Her eyes focused on the apex of the tip. The lights from above made an angelic gleam on the top, shining like lightning in her eyes. The gleaming blade was a monolith that she could feel cold in, even though she was not touching it. Somehow, Hope knew what was next.

Grabbing her arm, Dari smiled, and said "Just a small prick." She then reached back, and drove the nail file into the arm full bore. The sting was inevitable, and Hope let out a scream as the terrorist's nail file went into her flesh.

Immediately, blood began oozing out of her skin. When it hit the air, it began to glow like a magic fairy dust. Words could not describe what the two of them were seeing: to Hope, it seemed like a bright, blinding aura, like arriving into a Florida summer afternoon after hours in a movie theater. Perhaps it was the pain of her body instilling such adrenaline.

To Dari, it looked very much in contrast. Knocked off her pumps by the impact, she saw a clear, emerald-pearl fluid. In it was glitter and potential. It looked like the seminal call of the angels – and she stared at it intensely, as if there was nothing that could stop it from solving all of her problems. More specifically, if need be, only hers. "Holy shit," was all she could say.

For a few seconds, this was the impact. Then, as if it were suddenly on cue, the glow began to reduce. Hope's flesh had begun to heal, just like it did for Dari's pimples. Slowly, the blood hitting the floor began to slow, sizzling as it hit the tile. The light curled and winded, the cut slowly diminishing like the sun hiding behind the dark clouds of that same Pennsylvania afternoon.

Dari panicked. She knew she had only one chance. "No, NOOOOOO! This can't happen!" She began to approach Hope, going for the arm where the calling of a perfect face come the next few days beckoned.

Hope closed her eyes tightly, expecting impact. She could feel Dari begin to clutch at her arm, and then she felt her anger release. And yet it felt like nothing outwardly out of the ordinary. Just that the spinning wouldn't stop.

Moments passed, and a whole lineage of thoughts and feelings, a barrage of colors and pain, joy and defeat, went through. She opened her eyes very slowly, and saw Dari in the corner, slumped up against the sink. Her mascara had run all over her face, and her hair in a heap like a pile of hay blown by a windstorm. The sweater she had championed just a few minutes ago had dirt and seams in it that ran down and split, showing a halter top at the bottom. Her shoes, glittery ones she had bought from a really cheap clearance sale just a few days before, had flown clear across the room, and one laid in a sink, the other hanging from a light fixture. It had happened again, only this time, she had felt it a thousand times more. The impact was immaculate, and it was duly powerful.

Inside of her, Hope felt a great pain, one of disappointment and one of anger and uncertainty. She tried to put into words what she felt, but it really felt like nothing at all. In some ways, she just plain felt weary. Going to her feet, she began to get up. Her inner safety mechanism, one that had protected her up to this point, said Run, you twat, run. This girl is evil. But somehow, she didn't want to.

Dari began to hyperventilate. Looking like a drunk, she began to come to awakening. All of a sudden, she started laughing. "Oh, shit, you. You little brabusting bitch, you.....I....ain't going to forgive you for that. Hahaha-haaaa..." she began to shake her index finger like an old schoolmarm. Her face looked angry and downtrodden.

Immediately, the scope and weight of the situation began to take her on. The bathroom began to spin in her vision. She knew she had been forced to blow her cover to everyone. But what could she do? Certainly, those who cared enough about Dari – even though in all honesty, the skanky girl could only get teachers to write another of a million tardy-truant slips

[49]

on her, put in the back pocket of her letterman jacket – would be out to find her. And there was no way that she would be able to get past what appeared to be described only as a drunken stupor.

Hope began to pull on Dari's sweater. Dari's nearly disrobed and definitely disheveled body was as limp as a noodle. Her legs dragged behind her as Hope slung her over her shoulder. Hope had a robust body, and Dari was too damned concerned of image to put bulk on her frame. Yet this was not her calling – she never felt the power to handle someone else's body. Immediately, she began to think that the only way to get her out of the situation was to do something painfully obvious – make it look like Dari had done the jock thing and a high school thing, maybe even give a $5 store-look-like-she-was-drunk pose to her, possibly again. It didn't have to make sense at all.

Knowing that it probably could pass, given the obvious track record and suspect appearance, Hope prided herself that she may have gotten away with it.

Covering up for it, she took a small bottle of body spray and quickly and rather nervously sprayed it on her. *This will help cover up for the liquor smell that should have existed, but didn't*, Hope thought to herself. As she sprayed, she failed to notice one thing: Adriana was standing there.

The neighborly nincompoop watched as Hope dragged the body into the stall. She watched as Hope sprayed, slung two arms around the bowl of the commode, and placed the broad's head resting on the seat, hair in the bowl draped and half-soaked for added effect. Dari had still not stopped laughing, and her speech had degraded from simple English to pure babble, unintelligible to even Hope's ear. "There ya go," Hope said, and slammed the door shut. Content with her cover-up, Hope looked to see Adriana standing there, upon which she dropped her books. It was surely a catch, but this was a hook, line, and sinker.

"Hi, Adriana. Look, it's not how it looks…." Nothing could make her look any guiltier than seeing her take out the prom queen that had picked on her.

And it didn't work. "I can't believe you. What the…..faaaa…..what went on?" Her eyes began to fog up as much as the mirrors above the sinks. "You just couldn't get over the revenge on her. What did you do?"

Stunned, Hope began to lunge for Adriana's arms, an attempt to console her and act in a way to convince her that she was sincere and trying to protect her. Before she could get there, Adriana pulled back. "Keep your hands off of me!" the dark haired, precious young lady cried.

The situation was deteriorating, and then it hit rock bottom. A groan from the stall was followed by the tinkling representative of the shattering of glass. "What did I do?"

Before Hope could explain, her now-distant friend yelled "Did she poison you?" A groan, then a laugh followed.

Desperation followed for the superlative girl, who was trying to save her hide. "Adriana, please listen to me. She tried to hurt me – "as she displayed proudly and purposefully the wrists where the prep had sliced her open, but they were uncut and unbruised – "You need to listen to me. You cannot tell anyone what happened in this room. Never."

"I already get it, Hopie. I got it all. I thought you never changed. But you have," she stuttered. Turning away, she began to weep openly, and took off down the hall, untying her hair and giving the mane of brunette, freshly conditioned hair a flow in the breeze.

Hope dropped her bottle, and began to walk out in a form of catharsis equivalent to the knowing that all the words in the world could never cover the actions which were shown in that room. Never before had she felt this way; she felt the anger of Dari transported into her, the disposition of Adriana, the disappointment loosed from her conscience. It was a cornucopia of pain, but indeed, this was the way she should have felt.

The bell signaling the beginning of a new class period rang. Hope walked slowly to her class, not really engaging in any conversation at all with anyone. She had felt like sharing words was putting salt on the wounds of her outward character; surely, she had given too much of herself already for perhaps the decade.

But there surely had to be Mo. The athletic idol of the school, he was a surprisingly good student, especially with the school's stringent policy of academics over athletics. Still, it was always a mystery how he never really spent a lot of time answering questions in class without coming up with some wisecrack about a teacher's chain smoking or the fact the driving teacher looked like "a mushroom with a pile of pubic hair on the crown" for which he was promptly sent home. Amazingly, the dude skirted fate all the time. But he always backed it up with the fact the classes with the teachers that did see a bright spot in him would give A's. Some just plain said it was bipolar disorder. Most just thought it was a trophy fetish.

Mo Bodart walked into class, looking with a puzzled smile. It was pretty much the policy of the ugly girls to smile, look shy, and then right of breast, never making eye contact. It could have been an old southern mood of master and slave regards if it had to deserve nomenclature; it was more or less a common courtesy. The more slightly girls never really had to deal with it, because they were essentially always taken. Plus, the wrath of Dari would always be on their minds, and with Dari being the ringleader, it was important to give to Caesar what was Caesar's, and Dari what was Dari's.

Ascending the social ladder by will, Hope returned to feeling in her place by now. She saw the somewhat aloof look on the icon's face, one that seemed to emanate that he subconsciously knew something was going to go wrong. It was perhaps just a whim; after all, she was removed of all feeling not too soon before by what happened with Dari. But then again, it was like she had begun to feel for Mo – and it was different, because she had looked at the lean machine of a stud before, and never really had this feeling. Somehow, she had to try something she never did before. It felt like the only way to make this better; an immediate need to placate her anxiety by indulging in an addiction that was forming: the addiction of cheap love.

She got up from her seat, and began to walk towards the football player. He did not even notice her somewhat luring dance of movement towards her, instead conversing in the normally useless banter typical of the early teens. Only when she was immediately in his presence did he turn around.

In a way, Mo gave her the room, but not the floor. He was always used to the not-so-popular girls coming up to him. Usually, he would do the service of saying hello and feeding their sex drives enough to get them to smile, feel good, and then move on. It was a positive flirtation, but he was good at playing the game – and possum – at any time.

He smiled. "Hi there. Feeling good today, Hope?" he said, with a sly giggle. A pause followed, with Hope looking him dead in the eye. Without another word, she pulled near, reached for his cheeks, and kissed him.

It had been only five hours since Dari kissed him before class. But this kiss was different. It felt like they were in a different dimension, the each of them indulging in an act which gave a spiritually satisfying burst. They both were transported to another place, another time; they were no longer standing in the room.

For Mo, it was like all the things that he had done recently all came to him. The overlap of sounds in a jumble, from phones ringing to female voices to his mom yelling at him, the hut-hike of the football practices, it all came together. And then there was Dari, holding his hand. They were both in there, he wearing his outfit for football, and she was in there, wearing what he had a secret "like" for....wearing her cheerleader outfit. They both embraced, and all felt good. "Where were you all this time?" he asked her.

She smiled, and without an unpleasant word, smiled. "I was always right here, hunny." And soon, they were both sitting there, just two soon-to-be-grown-up schoolchildren just having fun. All the pain was out of their bodies, and it felt like there was a passionate connection between them, like Juliet prior to the poison of fairness. They drank water from the river Jordan, and it was baptizing them with fire. He began to wish this moment could last forever.

With a flash, the dream was over. His body was covered in sweat, but he didn't mind. The problems had left him, and his only complaint was the taste of a chicken salad, which came from the person who had so enamored him to the opportunity.

With a smile of contention on her face, and a smirk thereafter, Hope walked away. *That one was for you and your girlfriend, MoBo*, she thought. "You're welcome, dickhead", she said, walking away with pride. It was something she had to do. But yet now, in that kiss was something else: the fact that there were two witnesses to the surreal. And it would mean that in Hope's irresponsible actions, her inability to control her teenage wants, she was now spreading her seed, a seed that could only mean more issues.

In that moment, something about the repetition of an act was truly proof that it was scientifically possible to have something. Yet there was a silence about to be broken. And at the heart of it was Dari Collins.

TWO HOURS LATER

COLLINS RESIDENCE

It was inevitable that the same thing had to happen again to the girl who had done this so many times before. It was Dari who was once more a hot mess, but nevertheless was falling to pieces. The father, so much an almsgiver, had felt that this time, this mess, was just too much. He had been to teacher conferences, detention hearings, juvenile court, and now had Dari completely trashed.

He didn't think about anything except now that Dari had drawn the last straw from his patience. All he knew was that after Dari had been discovered drinking allegedly, the smell of alcohol somewhat absent, but nevertheless not unexpected, he was a very disappointed man.

Dialing the phone, he called someone who he knew could help his troubled daughter. It was the most resolute thing to do, but yes, it had to be done.

A man of clear accent answered. "Yes, Attrition Home?" he asked over the phone of the place. It was a home for clearly disgruntled and misdirected boys and girls to go to. Attrition was a place where it was halfway between juvenile detention and home. Nestled in a grove in the middle of grassy fields, it was a refuge of sanity in a place where anyone, young or old, could gain back the calm. Unlike a home, though, it was rigorously managed.

The man on the other side of the line listened to the description of what happened. He took careful notes of the proceedings, and became extremely interested in the story of how this Hope girl, you know, the one who had poured secret jelly into her body. It all came rattling off to him, but little did Mr. Collins realize that the questions the man was asking were more to do with the intruder to Dari's temple of the body than Dari. But like many in money, something doesn't register.

There was an evil plan, but no one knew it.

ONE DAY LATER

A knock on the door came all too strongly as Dari lay in bed, quite stunned from the effects of the C402. Her father had kept her home for some really odd reason; she could only be described as somewhat pathetically out of touch this time. Dari was never this kind of naïve, no matter how much it didn't make sense. But when she tried to go down the stairs with her high-heel boots tucked into her leggings while wearing a pajama top and gym shorts on top, and a sock draped over her right boot like a flag, its match tied as a ring around her hair as a scrunchie, never mind the makeup...it was time to keep her home.

The father answered the door. "Gentlemen, glad to have you here. I didn't think this day would come."

The men were very strict and showed little emotion. "Good morning, sir. Jeff Mellanby, Department of Health. We need to speak to your daughter." He began to walk forward, bypassing what was the gatekeeper of the house to get to the true story buried deep inside.

The second agent came in quietly. "What's your name, uh...." the rich patriarch laughed.

Quietly, the agent gave a glare, and stuck his upper lip, turning away. "Uh, okay, play that way." He was not even amused.

As the investigative visitors made their way into the house, the groans of the daughter were becoming even more evident. It sounded as if she began to sing a combination of Lorde and Bruce Springsteen; the lyrics jumbled even more by the cavernous bowels of the tudor house.

"As you can hear, gentlemen, I can't figure out why she has turned out this way. I think she had a little accident at school a couple of days ago..."

Mellanby turned around. "So you say that she had an encounter with a girl who had something glowing that she was putting on in the

[57]

bathroom?" He began to interrogate openly as he led the way towards the incoherent grumbling in the distance.

The elder Collins laughed. "I don't know. It was this girl, can't remember the name...you see, she's been like this and I can't understand her, but it's like she's in euphoria for some reason..."

"Was it a girl by the name of Malott?" he asked curiously.

The father was confused, but could lie through his teeth if need be. Years of cutting deals and leading the office gave him empowerment. "I think it was it, but I don't know, sir, I really don't," he began to speed up his mutter.

They made their way to the door of Dari's room. "Sir, I would knock first – " the father suggested openly as the unintelligible speech was ever louder.

As fearless as could be, nevertheless, Mellanby opened the door. When it opened, he briefly saw the whites of her eyes as a bottle of moisturizer flew six inches from his chiseled face. "Don't bother me, you business brawler! I had enough of you – and my Dad too! Hope, you're going to Hell and you know it! Glitter eater!" she screamed.

This could have not been less solace for her father, although it was fair game for commitment, which he did not omit from his proceedings. She was going to high school, the place where the drama could not have been stronger. She was new in these parts, but it scared him to think how hormones were starting to reform her in more ways than the 28th day and the fact that she couldn't fit into the same shirts that she used to. It was time. "I'm sorry for this, but that's why." He gave a weak smile.

The agent whispered something to Mellanby, to which he nodded. "Wait here," he told Collins.

The door closed, and the agent began to have his way. Grabbing Dari, he pulled on her blouse and sat her up in bed, much to the chagrin of the girl. "Dari, we're going to sit up and be a big girl now. You've been through a rough few days, right?" The impersonal physical altercation silenced the girl, as she was stunned. He knew about this process because he had seen it before.

Dari let out a scream at first, thinking in the manner of bloody rape. But then, she began to silence. The agent was a man of forty, but there was something about him that she found comforting. "You are a big dude, a badass one... hey, why are you touching me? I could have you arrested and – " she began to run her mouth.

Yet the agent would not have any of it. "Right now, your body is the property of the Commonwealth of Pennsylvania. Because you are on the verge of being sent to the hospital. So you're either going to listen to me and tell me about a girl named Malott or to the white room, you go." He sat down, and shook off his hands. She was covered in sweat, her makeup dissolved in the beads within.

The tough love was bitter and somewhat cold, but it worked. Dari gave a huge smile, one fraught with the feeling of conquest over the demons she had to fight. They were almost as cold as the agent before him. Even if they were just that, Mellanby knew that the facts Dari would spout would net him the information his supervisors had sought deeply for years.

She laughed. "You know that girl, Hope Malott. She is such a little twit. Walking around with her friends."

"What did she do to you, Daria?"

"Well, she went out and did this thing with a tampon tube one day. Stuck a freaking rod, 'bout this long, into her growler..." she began to gesture with the agent's hand, pulling at it like she was unaware, drunk, high, whatever to call it.

"So, how did you end up this way?"

Daria gave a giggle. "That little nerd blew me away and got me drunk. Whatever she had glowing in there, in her arms, it made me sick as, like, when I got drunk on my dad's oxycodone."

The agent was rushing through, but he had experience with interrogation. He literally had to be upfront to get his answers. And lo, he succeeded tremendously. "What color was this stuff that you saw? Whatever it was…"

She laughed. "Looked like she was sticking a fluorescent light. But it was green. Blue. Red-green, sometimes. Can I have a beer, by the way?" She giggled, not realizing that she was somewhat distracted.

The agent laughed. "I can give you beer if you let me ask one last question." Her face lit up, and her angst went away. He leaned in and said "Would you want to get rid of her?"

She gave her giggle, knowing her revenge was there for the taking. Even if it was a poorly subjected, slightly asinine character. "That little turd deserves whatever she gets."

The agent got up without another word, and walked out, not thanking her at all. He was deep in thought, but knew he got his answers. She asked for her beer, to which he looked at her and yelled "You don't even need that now, hun. Stick to your Starbucks lattes and Pom juice."

As he closed the door, not knowing what went on, the father relentlessly and curiously asked for his offspring's status. "So, how is she? Will she come back to normal? Do I have to send her to Attrition?" he asked innocently.

Not to be outdone by his mission, Mellanby covertly performed his best government action and provided some spin to divert him. "Your daughter is fine. No committal necessary. But I'd strap her down and hide all the platform boots she has for winter. Last time I checked, those things can carve holes into your walls, sir. Good evening."

And without another word, the men left. And without another word, the stage was set for the greatest suffering of all, albeit at the hands of an inadvertent slip of the tongue, done thrice to the hand of God.

III

The Cover-Up

THREE DAYS LATER – THE MALOTT RESIDENCE

10:12 PM

Being a caring, loving, and true father to her only child, Alex Malott could sense that his only daughter was in trouble. At least to the extent that he knew that she may have stepped off the beaten path and gone into the indivisible and infinite abyss of the unknowns of teenage life. She was going to be 14 shortly, and it was bothersome, especially to him, that no one could really predict what would happen. Even if she was a perfectly normal teenager with perfectly normal friends and normal hormones and all, she would still have the struggle of her life. But here she was, witness to her own unharnessed vitality. It made her wonder.

She cuddled in her bed, turned on the bedside lamp, and summoned her father over to her side. "Dad, have you ever felt like there were things in your life that you wish you could change? Like you never experienced them, and you could take 'em back?" She looked for guidance.

Alex was sincere. "We all go through things that we wish we could have never done. But it's the way you build character. That's the way you get experience in life. The good things in life make us strong, but the bad things we go through make us stronger. And sometimes, the most incredibly cruel things happen. But Hopie, they make us the strongest. We don't learn through good things always. Sometimes, we fear things."

"But I'm scared of myself. I mean, I did something at school that, well, I wish I had done differently." Hope started to cling to the comforter, feeling completely helpless to her own will, wherever it was.

Alex found resolve. "I heard about what happened at school a few days ago. I know you're scared about all of that. Look – " he grabbed her hand and held it as tight as he could – " when I had you, the doctors told us that you would have this defect. Where you may or may not live a normal life."

"But why didn't you let me know when I was little, Daddy?" Hope asked a big question. It was due, at least in her mind, for some solace.

With a look of sincerity, he did the thing he should have – looked her straight in the eye. "Because of two reasons. I didn't think it would help you to know that and re-iterate it to others. You possess a gift, Hopie. A very great gift. And people are going to judge you on that gift, no matter what you do. You have to use it the right way. When you experienced, well, your lady thing, it was a release. You were anxious."

But she was still curious. "But what was the second reason?" He looked up towards the sky, paused, and swallowed the lump in his throat. "Hopie, it was my call. I wanted you to find it out for yourself, so you could decide on the good – or bad – you would do with it. Because I don't have that power, sweetie. You will be a full grown woman in a few years. If I told you what to do with it, it would be severely irresponsible of me. I love you, and one of the things that a parent, a Daddy like me can do, is make sure when my flesh and blood mature, they mature in all aspects of life – physical, emotional, spiritual – they all receive their due. And I think God wants me to put that in your judgment."

Hope barely held back tears. Clutching his hand to her heart, she grabbed both hands and wrapped them around her dad's fist. "I love you too, Daddy." She kissed her palms.

Alex felt content with what he said. It was the truth, after all. "You must always keep in mind, though, that I will always be with you. Some may label you as a figment of science or a chance or a twist of fate. You are more than that." He patted her on the head for the final time of the night, and gave her a kiss. "Go get some rest. Tomorrow's Friday, after all. Ice cream day."

The light turned off, and the LED nightlight produced a glow of cool, relaxing blue. The door closed, echoing off the wooden floor and walls. A ray of moonlight shone on the dresser, where she kept her pair of wing earrings. It was the room that had the most light, facing out towards the front, where the sun could shine in the morning on the brightness in the Malott's life.

Walking down the hallway, Alex bumbled towards his bedroom. Long in length, the floor creaked and was dimly lit from the old vapor bulbs that he used. It fit well with the ivory-colored walls, lending an orange glow. He found himself deep in thought about his daughter, what she meant to him, and where she could go with her life. It gave him due pause to think that she was discovering herself twice at this age, both as a woman and as a person who controlled great abilities. It gave him a smile on his face.

Just then, his smile would go to frustration. With a loud bang, the downstairs door opened. Fearing a burglar, Alex took a peek over the loft into a mirror. He could see red lasers going through the freshly churned up dust. Immediately, he ran to the master bedroom.

"Hun? Be very quiet. We have unwelcome visitors." He ran to his drawer, pulled out the key, fumbled a bit in anxiety, and grabbed his handgun. "Stay in here, don't make any noise." Carrie grabbed her blanket and covered her body. Alex quickly began pushing bullets into his gun.

Carrie's voice pitched high "Should I call the police? I mean, they will be much better at shooting the bastards than you will. When is the last time you used that hunk of medal?"

Not fazed by it, and feeling purpose and suspecting a backstory, Alex cocked the gun hurriedly, knowing full well time was never on his side. "Don't even bother. It won't even help." He put the last bullet in the gun, and said "I'm going to get Hopie." Running down the hallway, he almost tripped over his bedroom slippers, piling through the door.

Carrie gave one last yell. "But honey – won't they kill you?" to which he replied "I know who they are. They aren't here for us or our goods. They are here to do what they felt like doing long ago."

Hope was already up. "What's happening, Daddy?" she asked innocently. "I'm scared."

Alex knew exactly what was going on. Given the news of the past few days, and the fact that chances are a leaky faucet seldom keeps itself to the drain, he realized that they were no burglars, especially ones wearing all black, talking out loud, and having laser sights.

The door banged open. Hope screamed out loud as high as she could. "Malott, you know what's up. C402 has infected your body. You weren't supposed to disclose any of this shit."

"Dad, he knows your name. How did – "

Alex interrupted. "Don't say anything, dear. These people are bad people. They are out to get you and make sure you don't exist."

The man behind the tactical glasses and mask was not showing any fear, like any government law enforcement would do. "Bad people, Alex? No, we're just the gatekeepers. You broke into our property, and now you're paying the price. Give us the girl. NOW. "

"No, you're not getting her. You'll have to kill me first. This shit is on me. RUN HOPE!" Carrying her teddy bear, she took off for the door, slipping through the hands of two of the uniformed men who had come to take her. She immediately began to run for her mother in the other room.

The man pointed the gun at Alex's head. "You know we'll have to do this the hard way. I have orders to eliminate you, if necessary. But I'm not going to." He dropped his gun and readied the safety.

Just then, the door to the bedroom slammed, a guard securing the hallway to make sure no one else would step in. In the moment, one of the men who saw the gun in Alex's hand, reacting on pure operational adrenaline, pulled the trigger in panic.

A scream from the other room arose. And just like that, Alex was dead. "What the hell was that? You stupid shit! Safety your weapon, officer! Get the girl now. I'm not dealing with a fail of the mission and an unnecessary casualty. Your ass is in trouble, Cox. Let's evacuate."

They ran to the other room. With the pointing of a gun at Carrie's head, Hope Malott was now the possessive right of the government. And there was nothing they could do about it. Taking Hope to the car, the men opened the door, tried to quell her screams as not to advertise to the neighborhood – or anyone else for that matter – about what already appeared to be a problematic mission.

From far away, a car on the street turned on its lights, and made a U-turn, squealing its tires in the process as it sped quickly away from the neighborhood.

Somewhere in that darkness, even with the neighborhood bedroom lights burning akin to the fire across the way, Carrie stood there, looking at her husband's body. She stayed motionless, pale as the moon.

But then it struck her. They loved each other so much to make third to their secret. And now three became one by the act of two.

10 HOURS LATER

FORT DIX MEDICAL CENTER

She woke up in a very comfortable bed, the daylight coming from a large window directly to her right rear. In a room all by herself, she recalled very little of the night before. She felt different clothes, her makeup smeared and her hair lay by her side, half-curled. The blankets seemed quite warm, perhaps a bit too warm. The room smelled of disinfectant. Soon, she thought, I'll get what went on.

The door opened. A woman, who Hope presumed was a nurse, walked up and grabbed her arm. "Hope, how are we doing today, dear?" She had a glass of water and a tray, with a syringe. "Rise and shine. We have a busy day today." She set the tray down on the table next to a lamp, and grabbed the syringe. "We need to do a blood draw on you. Right arm or left arm, babe?" She began to take the cap off.

Hope became scared, her face becoming even paler. "Who are you and why am I here?" she boldly and forcefully asked.

Apathetic as she was taught to be for a medical hospital, after all, emotions can get the best of you…she replied "You are here to see Dr. Copulus, dear. Take this tablet, it's time for your morning physical and your admission examination by the Doctor." Out came a pill, relatively large. It had the look and texture of a cookies and cream milkshake, with a pale milk ivory with specks of black dust in it. Hope didn't know what it was, and she looked at it funny. "Take it, dear. Makes it feel much better." She shoved the pill in her mouth, swallowed it with two big gulps of water. The nurse smiled and grabbed the half-empty glass out of her hand, turned around, and said "Dr. Copulus will be with you shortly." Without another word, or a sharing of thanks, she walked away.

Two minutes later, the obligatory knock on the door that every physician does for the purpose of assumingly not trapping a patient behind the door, and thus getting a copious settlement of malpractice sounded.

Hope swallowed the lump in her throat. It wasn't the pill, but it was similar. For sure, she needed to think and stomach what was happening. Dammit, she thought.

In walked a man in a suitcoat, tie, and glasses. He was obviously of Indian descent, although his name, displayed proudly from a tag hanging from his stethoscope, draped with a rubber pink elephant that creeped upon suspect pedagogy like no other, seemed to be very much Anglicized, at least to Hope. He smiled, and said "Good morning. My name is Doctor Bill A. Copulus. I'm the director of the Special Patients Ward here at Fort Dix. How are you doing?"

Looking eager to extract some information of her own, Hope relented. "I'm fine. I just took a horse pill after being kidnapped. I feel like someone hit me with a baseball bat, and – " she burped – "my stomach feels like shit right now. Yourself?"

The doctor laughed omnisciently. "I am doing just fine, thank you. I'm glad I've located you after all these years, eh…." He fumbled, and looked at the chart, scanning it over, "Mallory."

"That's Hope, sir. Why am I here, Dr. Copperless?" she asked, with a chuckle of relief. "Seems like you have been looking for just a short time. Are you one of those child predator dudes who get arrested on prime time TV?"

Not to be outdone, Copulus said "No, I am not at all. In fact, I am here to do what should have been done years ago. Your dad and I both concluded when you were born to keep an eye on you. It seems like you've found something you may not want."

Puzzled, Hope bit for the question. "Don't say anything about Daddy. He is dead and my mom is a damn widow because of you, Copperless. I am entitled to know what I want…." She was angry about the whole proceedings.

The doctor began to sit down next to her, holding the clipboard. "If you really wish for all your problems with your condition to go away, I suggest you lend an ear and please kindly listen, young lady." He quickly began to show some consternation on his face, apt to earn the trust of the girl. "I don't know if your dad told you this, but this is the true story. I was on the panel.

"Your dad was a scientist, a lab technician, at a gigantic plant out West. The people there all worked for private industry, not the government as you probably heard. They were testing out new compounds to prevent against radiation poisoning. After Three Mile Island, the act was relevant.

"We all looked around for guinea pigs. People who wanted to try our new compound, C402. Why, old Alex and Carrie….your mom and dad, Hope….they were so bloody broke that they would do anything. They got offered $1 million dollars to take the C402 compound, and they bit like a carp on the Delaware.

"We subjected them to radiation, although atypical radiation at that certainly. The C402 was taken intravenously, thinking its oral intake would pass through the bowels like a train does the switches on country roads at night. Why, damn, it worked excellent at blocking radiation. But it was like a sponge….our readers showed nothing on there, and we thought it was a success. We kept putting more and more and more of that sci-fi stuff in there, thinking we were so Goddamned amazing."

The nurse began to roll her eyes. "Pardon my curried tongue, young lady. Shall not swear again." Hope just giggled and rolled her eyes.

"But then we found out that our volunteers all began passing away after a few months…and a lot of them had brain tumors, kidney stones, leukemia. We wondered why your folks didn't get sick. We'd do anything, anything to not have someone subject to that. So we paid them. A lot of money. They had to do two things: never confess the problem and never tell what C402 was."

Hope was amazed. If this were true, at least in her decision making powers, it was an earth-shattering revelation. It was why she felt all the pains, why her parents were so awkwardly well to do with their suburban house and good jobs. Why they would do that, she could not figure out. She was still only 14 and could not interpret what was happening. "So now again, why am I here?"

A look only adequate to a politician after a sex crime followed, the frumpy look of the face ensued. "It was too much of a risk for you to start using those powers. You possess one of the greatest gifts of them all. Why, the thing is with those powers, you can command money, friends, fame. You'd be a damned millionaire and the healer. You'd give people Hope....in fact, that's quite likely why you were named that, young lady."

Dr. Copulus got up. "Look, it is not your fault that you are in this situation. I grew up during a time that folks like you, ambivalents and outcasts, were resigned to places like this: drab, squeaky clean, about as much personality as the patients in a psychiatric ward. You could be that way, but I gave you that pill to help you not do that." He grabbed Hope's hand, and shook it. "I am on your side, Hope. I understand your problems. I'll show you how I can help. If you would permit me, I have magical things I can do for you. Things you could never imagine. But you must permit trust in me."

Hope laughed nervously. "I guess I should trust you."

He got up. "Rightly so. I'm sending you to Attrition Home for Adolescents up the highway, a few minutes and a few miles. It will be a blessing, and all your problems will vanish – " he snapped his fingers - "like dust in the wind. But you must cooperate with me."

A few moments of silence ensued for Hope. The doctor's words were convincing – in fact, she had slowly begun to accept that perhaps her life was not so perfect after all. To many, it seemed like it was a scam, a lie, designed to explain a lot of things that really couldn't; the supernatural often solves its own conflict by extending its bullshit credit limit to even higher heights. It was almost like the government should have been a part of this. It was damned befitting.

"How do I know I'll be better?" she asked him. "I want to feel normal again." She got up, and began to walk towards the door, her flipflops clanging with a foamy clompclompclomp on the hard floor.

The now affirmed doctor turned to her, and said "There's someone I'd like you to meet. You'll look up to her." And so, they walked into the hallway, and off to destiny.

THE MALOTT RESIDENCE

ONE HOUR, 15 MINUTES LATER

The house had been turned over both in the materials and to the police overnight. Cars were stacked outside the residence in random array, and the coroner had a white blanket over Alex Malott's body as they pulled it down the stairs. All across the yard, and well into Lou Mendoza's, were small easels with numbers on them, showing evidence that something strange had happened. The neighbors were all looking around, especially at the tire tracks that had been made at the residence across the street, an older woman who had her son and daughter-in-law living on the first floor. People were wondering what happened; only one, Mendoza the elder, had heard anything, and ended up calling law enforcement.

In her nightgown stood Carrie, looking weary, alone, and bitter. Lou came over to console her, as she just looked around the yard, speechless, and completely disconnected. Reality sets in sometimes too hard, and for her, this reality struck so vivid that she literally had to disconnect. Somehow, she left herself for a few moments, and saw from a third person a synoptic view. That brand of disconnect left her feeling nothing in the end.

"I'm sorry all of this happened, Carrie. We know you guys are a good family, and you have been great neighbors for, what is it now, a decade?" asked the gentleman from next door, expunging what he thought was some necessary levity on the situation.

But there was none of that for Carrie. She could not believe it. "I lost my husband to some....some madman. My daughter could be any-where....maybe even nowhere except six feet under. My life is in ruins, Lou. Absolute ruins." She walked inside, trying to hide what was a burst of emotions, held back like the kink in a garden hose. Like the kink, she would let it trickle out for the world to see. But like the kink, if let out suddenly, the burst of water could take off a face. Her face.

She was used to that, especially in this world, where emotional discharges are championed only in the therapy of paid psychology, and even that, a treasured hour session every two weeks at $300 a shot. But she needed to vent it out, any way possible. But her feelings kept it bottled up.

Lou followed her in, knowing she needed him. "Look, Carrie, can I speak to you for a moment?" He shut the door behind him, and she looked at him with a somewhat critical set of eyes as they sat down in the living room. "I noticed that you have something which is bottled up right now. Perhaps there is something I can do…." He began to reach to embrace her, for which she pulled back.

"Lou, thank you. But this is a process of which it was somewhat my fault for not mentioning it to you. Hope was the reason for this. She did something – eh, you don't need to know 'bout it –"

As the words got out of her mouth, Lou seized the opportunity. "I know what it is. And I can believe it inasmuch as you can." He grabbed both arms, and pulled them to his sides. "You have something that I've wanted for years….a special daughter."

Carrie looked at him, as if he was being excessively ridiculous. "You are a fool. You have Adriana. I have Hope. You have your daughter. You have a nice house, and a clean lawn, and someone to tuck you in at night, watch TV, read books, cuddle. Tonight, I will go to sleep alone for the first time in two decades. And there is not a damn thing you or I can do about that. Capisce, paisan?" She was resilient, but before she could get up, another opportunity seized Lou.

"Look at this picture of Adriana's arm." He pulled out a Polaroid snapshot from when the girls were six. "You remember this? That first day, when Adriana fell, and Hope came to the rescue."

Carrie was skeptically befuddled. "Yes, but why did you take a picture of it? It looks like a bloody mess, and look here, there's a big piece of wood sticking out of it. Did you take it out?" she asked quite awkwardly, not exactly excited to witness more gore after she had seen such the night before, which was well bloody well enough.

Without another word, Lou had the haymaker of words and situation in his back pocket. "Adriana, come here." She walked over to the couch, and there, all by itself, was the large splinter of wood, about ½ inch across and about 3 inches long. "Show Mrs. Malott your arm."

Adriana pointed to her forearm. "It doesn't hurt, except when I exercise or do cheerleading." She said "But Hope picked me up, and Daddy told me not to take it out. Ever." The father smiled, and told her daughter to run off, asking her to water the flowers.

Lou looked back into Carrie's eyes. "Now, you know that would get infected. It would hurt. It would make the docs want to carve it out or cut her arm off. But the wound sealed before I could find anything." He grabbed Carrie, who was now becoming even more convincingly scared that the neighbors, on top of the rest of the kids at school and the such, were now in the loop. "You need me to help you with this. Let's stay in touch." Lou kissed her, to which she did not return the kiss.

Walking to the door, Lou said "I want to do the right thing for us." And Carrie did not utter a word, a sign of pure stupor.

IV

The Other

An old white police sedan trudged through what was left of the maple and oak forests on Interstate 95, thickened with afternoon traffic. The city part was incredibly concentrated: horns blowing, people yelling, the sound of trucks and people who didn't agree with cars having mufflers. It was slow, limited, and otherwise felt like the energy of summer had begun to finally run out. Depression and anxiety were sure to follow as the bleakness of winter awakened from its six month hibernation.

Hope Malott had felt pretty well up to this point of the day. Thanks to the efforts of the folks at the hospital, she had showered, hair trimmed and styled, and an outfit of a brown leather jacket, striped polo, skinny jeans, and riding boots made her look more attractive, or at least at comfort in her own skin. Consequently, she sat with her head held high in the backseat of the large Crown Victoria, looking out the window. She sat with her head on the rest, looking towards the shoulder at all the things the outside world had to offer: people shuffling their feet, birds flying in formation in the sky, a tinge of color on the trees interspersed in urban paradise.

The man in the front of the car, separated by a divider with a glass slide similar to a taxicab, looked in the rear view mirror. "You look absolutely tired, sweetie. Wish I had some candy to give you, but they won't let us give it out 'cos you might gag on it and commit suicide, and I would be in one hell of a pickle with that." His mouth was hidden from view, but his eyes in the mirror showed a rare glimpse of true compassion, one that had lacked presence in the few days before that.

Laughing it off from the backseat, she said "Well, I don't need any candy, anyways. I'd like a warm bed, some chicken soup, and perhaps a toilet that doesn't sound like a jet engine at night," she tuned.

The driver laughed. "Don't go now and pee on that backseat. Might look good, but this car already had a mass murderer vomit all over it and chances are two babies were delivered in it. Old cop car, lots of stories, but dammit, I don't need that, I just ate my lunch a half an hour ago," in a thick Northeast accent.

"Don't worry, I'm only 14. I won't pee on your seat. Or vomit, or poop, or anything." The driver thanked her.

A pause followed for just a few minutes. Hope sat back in the seat, looking at the dome light, and then out the window. She literally was lost in that big backseat. Confined to her seat, she felt trapped – but then again, was she on an adventure? Or was this a dream?

She pinched her eyes as tight as she could, and then opened them as wide as she could. It woke her up from many a set of rapid-eye, a paralysis sleep. But then, she was back there. It wasn't a dream.

The driver's eyes began to drift back to the road ahead of him, but then, he looked back. "You seem to be a little different from a lot of people I pick up and take to this place." He smiled and turned his head partway for just a second, looking towards her.

This was a due charm for the downtrodden girl. Not even her parents had praised her for being unique. Perhaps it was due to the fact that she grew up in the 1990s, where everyone was a winner, and received a trophy and told they were special. Alex and Carrie understood the only reward is through hard work, falling on your face, picking yourself back up, the way it was for many years. Some of the people who shared that same era of entitlement by age group, especially the girls at her suburban school, had parents who bit the mantra like a vampire would bite them for Halloween: nice cars, designer clothes, never having to do their homework alone. Sadly, it made her the lonely one in the school. She was a hard worker and never felt entitled, and it was her destiny to be that way. It became frustrating not having places to go or events posted online or in chats. Yet deep inside, that independence was vested in her for a reason: it was the right thing to finally grow up. Sadly, she knew at this moment, she would have to grow up more quickly than she had anticipated.

It felt so in her words, too.

"I've been on a journey, sir, that has taken me soooo many different places in the past few years. Some of which I want to go back, and a lot that I want to go back on." She smiled. "By the way, what's your name?"

He laughed. "Gary. Gary Patter." He paused. "Nice to meet your acquaintance." He reached his right hand over his shoulder, and Hope responded by taking his hand, a newly found mutual friendship just by chance. "You know, a lot of these folks remind me of when I was little. Crazy, outspoken, having problems. You know, people who don't want to associate with mainstream culture.

"I once had a Dad who was a pilot. Air Force pilot, 1st lieutenant. Very much an honor in my life, y'know. He would come and go from his job, stay late sometimes. But there he would be, even if it was the dead of night, who would tuck me into bed. Even if I was already asleep. I used to, heh, pretend I was asleep sometimes, and just as he closed the door, I would open my right eye and see him peek in one last time."

His passenger was listening acutely. "That sounds like my Dad, too. But he left us."

Gary continued his anecdote with added vigor and emphasis in his words. "It was all great, until one day, my Dad sat me on his lap on his recliner in our living room. I remember Carson was on, it was late. He looked at me, and said 'You know, someday, you have to be the man of the house. You have to mow the lawn, cook dinner for your wife and kids, even perhaps for your Mom. You gotta grow up and be a man. I'll help you there, and I will always be with you. But you are smart, and smart people not only go to school, but learn everything the world can teach us. '

"He smiled at me, and said 'But you can't hide your talents from anyone. You have to be bold, and set your own tempo.' He bounced me on his lap, even when I was 5, and we both began singing his favorite song from when he was in his youth – Rock and Roll Music.

"He left that morning and never returned. And that's all I remember of him." He turned and began looking back at the road. "I didn't need to tell you that, anyways."

Within seconds, the sound of a kiss went from the backseat, and a hand reached through the partition, placing the palm on the unshaven face of the storyteller. "Thank you for telling me that, Mister Gary."

A few minutes later, the two of them pulled into the driveway of the home. Unlike the industrialized, emotionless whitewash of the hospital, this was a very intricately positive place. The grass was carefully manicured, the last roses of the year still shining. A fountain provided a visual bifurcate of the drive, and bricks were complemented by Greek style columns.

"Well, sweetie, this is the end of the line." He reached around, unbuckled his seatbelt, and said "You take care now, y'hear? Don't let these folks put you through the loop." They both shook hands, and Hope said "You are a good man, Gary," for which he replied "Just remember that when they get the bill for the tip," and with a mutual wink of the eye, she got out.

A man in a black sweater vest and white shirt came out. "Hope Malott, I presume? Welcome to the Attrition Home for Adolescents. Come with me, and we will get you started on admission."

The day began to speed up for the downtrodden child. They went into the home, an elegant but somewhat sterile climate. The main atrium had a few people in suits and coats; Hope assumed them to be doctors or staff. Few looked like the stereotypical medical profile seen in all of the best B-list horror flicks. It appeared that occupation of the building proclaimed one had reverence and silence, a prayer to the gods for peace where many thought not to find it.

"Come in here, Hope." One of those doors in that atrium, the far right corner to the atrium with the winding staircase, opened before her. "We're interested with what you know and how we can help you." The door opened to a small room. On the shelves were stacks of books, interspersed with a potted plant, sculpture, or other comforting bric-a-brac.

They talked for about 10 minutes, essentially stating the same things that Copulus had mentioned, but the man began to indicate that it was time for Hope to begin to get assimilated to the building; he described the process as "a long period of healing for a deep cut that needs care and love." Hope thought of him as the ultimate of homosexuality; after all, there is no better judge of one's manhood than a promiscuous 14 year old.

Bringing what limited baggage there was, she was asked to go back into an annex to the building. The door opened to the third to last room. In it was someone who would be the catalyst for what she would expect in the next few years. "Hope, meet Duluth." Duluth Kane, a 17 year old girl, sat in the corner, staring out the window. She turned around slowly. Her eyes were a deep brown, her hair spiked up in highlights and buzzed in a brownish-blonde kind of pattern. Pink strands were interspersed within; Hope assumed this was the sign that this was not a police state, that someone could actually be unique in this place. She wore boots with buckles on them, and a tank top with leggings tucked into the riding boots.

In the best way she could, Hope decided to make the best of the opportunity to make a new friend. This isn't going to get better anytime soon probably, she figured. Guess I should just go and nip it in the ass. She approached Duluth. "Hi there. My name is Hope Malott."

She turned around, and gave a quick chuckle. "You're just another brick in the wall, Hope. Get used to it." She then started to look outside. "Nice to meet you, Hope Malott." Embittered, Duluth seemed to garner strength from the poorness and spite that echoed through the chambers of that mansion in spite of the colorfulness of her outfit in the sunshine that beamed brightly through the room. "You'll get used to it. Eventually staring out this window is all we have."

Stepping back for pause, Hope garnered every bit of strength not to flee. But the man in the sweater vest stepped back. "I'll let you two....eh, converse a little bit. Make some friendships, you two. This is your room. Dinner at six, 'k?" And with the door closing, the two of them were there to solve the problems they had for each other, and the world in general. They had to make things work out, or die trying. Or so it seemed.

Duluth turned around. "Did you take the coal pill?" She began to fumble about Hope's thin character, searching for the material that seemed to be of prime importance. "The pill, the one that looks like 10 year old asphalt. Did you pop it earlier? Stick out your tongue –" she reached for Hope's throat to gag her, but Hope stepped back, pushing the raving girl back.

"Yes, yes, YES! I did! What the heck is wrong with you, sis?" the newcomer questioned, sounding totally like ghetto trash. She had picked that up from the folks who lived in the western part of Philly and moved into the smaller rowhouses down the street. Sharing schools was like sharing beer with a pack of lepers: the risk was there, but you damn well couldn't believe what you'd come across in the meantime.

Duluth stated "Don't ever take that pill again. If you know what is good for you, you won't take it. Trust me, I found out about you. You have C402 in your system, right?" She looked somewhat empathetic to her friend. "Don't take the pills. Stick 'em to the roof of your mouth –" she handed her a package of gum – "and you will be fine."

Hope began to wonder why Dr. Copulus had stuck her there. It was not immediately illuminated, but somehow, she had her namesake. Before she could do anything, and seeing that Hope was worried and somewhat puzzled, Duluth reached for her hand. "Take this gum – and in my other hand – " of which she grabbed.

Duluth had put something on the half-chewed gum on her hand. It felt like she had either spit or bit her lip, but the gum stuck to her hand – and then, there was something else.

Within the blink of an eye, Hope felt the electricity of Duluth's words all flowing to her. A taserlike feeling of paralysis and hopelessness suddenly stung her body, and all her feelings were internalized; her senses had begun to fool her. She looked into Duluth's eyes, which began to glow behind her contact lenses in a hue of green, similar to that of the fireflies outside of the buildings. The difference was that while the insect glowed with a transient blink of an ecological eye, Duluth's eyes began to glow brighter as time went on. It mesmerized and told a million stories.

Hope could see the pain in her through the grasp of hands. But then Duluth's eyes began to fade, and the feeling in her hands began to come back. The stars came out of her eyes, and she realized that not a moment of time had passed; the clouds were still there, the room was in array, in contrast to what she had seen before. "That's why you don't take the pills, my friend." Duluth then pulled the gum out of Hope's hand, and tossed it over her shoulder.

Hope stood back. "So how did you know about my story? I mean, how did you find out about me?" She could not comprehend, but Duluth knew what she meant.

"Those pills are charcoal tablets with iodine in them. They are used for decontaminating blood from radiation. They take your powers away. Dr. Copulus prescribes them for the two of us — and just for the two of us."

Duluth got up from sitting on the window sill, and began to encircle her accomplice, educating her on the intricacies. "See, the two of us both have more in our blood than just two random girls from the hood." She grabbed Hope's arm, and pulled it out straight. "Look at your arm, and then mine. Those pills slowly make you more normal. Like taking your gift away."

"I don't understand though, DK, if I can call you that."

"Heh, I've been called worse. But I have been on those pills since I was 14. And now, they have taken most of my powers away. That's why I only lasted 12 seconds with you. And no, I'm not talking about sex. Don't get the wrong idea, young lady."

"But what about what Dr. Copulus said? About this being my father's fault?"

Duluth stuck her palms at her hips, encroaching on her friend, who was sitting in a chair the whole time, her hands shaking. "Bill told you that?

Seems like his story changes more often than he changes his underwear. Both are as full of shit as an invalid's diaper."

"Bill?"

"Doesn't matter. The guy has a mission to cover up for his mistakes. To finally put the death knell to a failed experiment. You know what it is?

"C402 was closer to your Mom's description. I felt it in you — I could tell it's what you felt. But here's the real story.

"It was a mistake for your dad to be handling that material — but it wasn't illegal or against lab rules. The fluid was radioactive the moment it got in that open beaker, but it didn't affect your dad. It literally did not make a difference, 'cos he was already immune to its effects. It was literally either a one in a million twist of fate, or the opposite....a serious design by someone — Copulus — who knew shit about it that we didn't." She grabbed a chair, and placed it sitting backwards, one foot from Hope. Sitting down with her front to the back of the seat, she placed her hands on the back of the chair, and stared at eye level directly into Hope's gaze. "I usually call it weird to have contact with dangerous materials without a whole damn suit of armor on. Copulus didn't care about it, because in the end, he knew his handling of the material would decide whether or not it would be successful — at least as its intended purpose."

Hope's face began to tear up. "So why did he tell me all that stuff? You know, about the injections, and such?" She inquired into the seemingly omniscient's face boldly.

"Your dad was one of the people who was being tested. He did need the money — but he also needed an escape as much as Copulus. But it got away from him.

"When he realized that it wasn't going to cure anything to make someone with super cells, and it leaked that your mom and dad were fornicating on the side, well, you know what? He took it to the next level.

[83]

And then....” She hesitated, and started to feel an immutable wave of emotions take over her. Her eyes began to tear up. “I was next in line. At least my parents were. The Kanes were the second wave. And I was already in the womb.”

Hope grabbed her, feeling some measure of sympathy. Her new friend could not hold it back any longer, as she began to sob openly. “Thank you.” She pulled her head off her shoulder, and sniffled back her last bit of tenderness. “I was a test for what was the moderating mechanism. The second wave. You were supposed to be the mistake, but the thing is I was born. And your parents probably thought it was pretty damn amazing when they found out. But then again, I had only token development. And to add it all, he just ended up making it worse in the end, too.

“He did a lot of things to me here, Hope. Lots and lots of things I was not happy about. Things I'd rather not rehash on. Memories that burn stronger than the blood that shines through those veins.

“Hope, you have the power to do great things. Don't let that motherscrewing douchebag take it away.” Hope nodded, to which Duluth said “thank you.”

Suddenly, a door slammed, and there was screaming out in the hall. The moment of sorrow and tenderness had turned into the moment of pure anarchy – at least to the newcomer's feelings. “What the heck was that?” Hope asked ambitiously.

Duluth rolled her eyes and looked in disgust. “Bob the oaf strikes again.” Hope ran to the door. “Might as well go see.” She creaked the door open, and Duluth came over to see the ruckus.

Outside were several men and a rather large boy, about 6'4” and perhaps 300 pounds. He was surrounded by women and a man, and he was shamelessly revealing everything God gave to him, both in words and physically. Hair covered every part of his body, but there was enough clarity of vision for Hope to realize that the man was indeed anatomically correct, although not very well endowed, to at least the naked eye, no pun intended.

"What do you call a video star who sells carpets? Bieber's berbers!" the boy yelled at the top of his lungs in a slurred speech. He ran through the hallway, up and down, occasionally in half and full circles. The people around him were yelling "Bobby, slow down!"

"Hey, calm down, and put some clothes on!"

And the occasional call to the radio "Central, call aid, inpatient out, inpatient out. Code 7-21."

For the first time, Duluth laughed, peering her head out the door. Hope was laughing the whole time. "That's Bob the Oaf, Hope. He feels a little bit like he has to do this every Friday afternoon. All thanks to TV ratings."

"Don't know why he would want to run around naked. Guy looks like he could sell me tires or a mound of half-melted ice cream. Ewww….." They both laughed, shutting the door for a moment, for which Duluth gave her a high-five.

Duluth chimed in, as she had done before. "He has moderate autism, but he does this occasionally to get attention. But he's a nice guy, too. He makes me picture frames for the past few Christmases out of craft sticks." It would mean a lot as time went on, but for the moment, Duluth and Hope were watching as the most entertaining form of cheap humor ran by, a Jello mold standing tall flying by in 113 different directions at one time.

The oaf ran past the hallway. "Oh, ladies! Go look at the running, flying Dutch dick wiggle!" he said, with the staff pursuing him at full speed. They laughed as the show and parade of medical waste of another type flew by the doorway. When the door shut, a loud thud followed.

Duluth gave an expected giggle, and explained the preceding arrangement as concisely as she could. "Ouch. Happens every time, Hope. Get used to it."

They both began laughing, covering their mouths like Japanese royalty. Indeed, they felt like princesses for the first time; they were part of the show rather than the stars. But for the first time, an inherent bonding began to take between the two, a compromise of hardship and the sharing of the common sins with equal penance. It almost seemed like they were forgiven, and all they needed was to hold each other.

Duluth sat down, and gave the last giggle. "Look, Hope. I sooooo much have to tell you something. This life sucks, but now that you're here, and we can pool thoughts, we need to start figuring out how to fix this bloody stool of a life. You seem like a pretty, eh, smart girl."

Hope calmed down, realizing that she had a truce in the works. "Yes, but how do you think this will work? We need time to think. And share our ideas, and feelings." She got up, and folded her arms.

Duluth was struck with an idea. I know how to solve things, she thought. "You know what I do to code my feelings – and keep my secrets also?" She lifted up her mattress. "When all else fails, pick up a guitar. Something a friend of mine taught me when I was, like, ready to puke from all the weird stuff that goes on. Why take it out on someone when six strings, frets, and a wooden box in the shape of a peanut smashed by an elephant can do it?"

"I've never really written a song before, DK. I'm more of the type where I pick up a CD at the store and rock out to it slowly." She watched Duluth bring out the guitar to the chairs in the center of the room. As she tuned the guitar, her friend sat back.

With a giggle of disapproval and sarcasm, Duluth said "Come on, it's not that hard. What the hell is wrong with you?" She plucked a C chord to tune up. "Just close your eyes and sing what comes to you." She began to

[86]

do chord after chord, humming in tune to what she played. "Here, you try it....I say this, you rhyme me. Best you can –" she played two chords. "There's a sunny side to it, the joy of life..."

Hope looked puzzled, but thought quickly. "But you're surely not clouding my day to be your wife."

Duluth chorded faster, her hands beginning to fly in obvious musical frustration. "Too many words, too many words." She stopped, and said "Do it not from here –" she pointed between the temples – "do it from down here – " she pointed underneath her right rib – "from the heart." She played another chord: "And your freedom lies where the flowers bloom...." And she looked to Hope.

"Waiting for my heaven to come oh so soon." With a nod in beat to the guitar by Duluth, they began singing – and songwriting. "And if my life someday isn't so well," Hope said, and Duluth replied "I'll surely take your Devil and send you to my Hell!" They both laughed.

For them, it was the building experience. It felt right, just in those few minutes they had been together. Surely, it had taken on a spectrum of both skepticism, but then, it was almost like the kaleidoscope of feelings began to take on a monochromatic agreement of just having to ford this stuff together, like they were sisters of the same clan. It was welcoming.

SATURDAY MORNING

10:10 AM

Demons arose from a long night of slumber, awaiting their next round of torturing those who seemed to enjoy their presence the least. It was a definite sign of the status of the girls that both seemed to have bad dreams.

Hope arose from slumber first, her head buried in a sofa in the corner of the room. Overall, Hope deduced the prevalence of a caste system of sanity in this home. Being that it was sort of a home for various castoffs, the décor ranged from a hotel-like experience in Duluth's room to almost a jail cell, with just a bed, sink, and commode, and a few books and CD's on a shelf (they had both sworn that they saw this in a lot of the rooms in the other side of the building). It seemed as if Dr. Copulus had put them both in the luxury suite; the room had plenty of space to move around, and was well-lit. This was contrasted with the lifeless, stoic glow of industrial fluorescent – and sorry, LED – lighting in some rooms. It lent to a sort of perfect system. She wondered why, down deep…

She looked around for her new friend Duluth. Turning towards the wall, she saw her slumped over a desk, hair combed down over her eyes. She had begun writing something, but all she could read was "You need to come here, Josh. There is no one….." and then the pen sat next to a blurb of ink at the end of the partially written E. It looked as if it had been hurriedly done; the markings tended to loop and twirl and the normal font of the millennial female did not seem to separate itself.

Hope embraced her friend's shoulders, and grasped them. "Wake up, Duluth. Wake up!" She got up slowly, and then went to look at the paper. "Whatcha writing about over here?" But before Hope could look, Duluth said "Oh, nothing. Just some poetry, I guess." She wrinkled up the paper and shot it basketball style into a can in the corner.

Not to be discouraged, Hope smiled and nudged her friend. "Did you have someone in mind for this?" It was an implicit hit on, well, it was obvious.

Knowing she was calling her bluff, Duluth stretched her arms and rubbed her eyes. "What, is this Nuremberg or Dr. Ruth? Go away. Fast." She had admitted guilt right then and there – and didn't even know it.

Duluth knew that the doctors would be around to give her the pills, along with a heavier dose for Hope. It was the first full day they would spend in the home, probably of many that they would, according to the estimates that they had made. They had to remain sane for the most part in the process of the experience at hand; as a result, they obliged to follow the recipe that ought to make sense at the time.

Putting her flip flops on, she strode into her shower. Turning on the knob, she stepped in as she disrobed. And then she shrieked for the first time that day – cool water. Turning the knobs off, she went outside, drying off what little of her lower body had gotten wet.

A puzzled roommate looked at her friend, sitting with her hair in a towel bun, even though it was not wet. "What happened? Did the boogeyman go and scare you?" She held a pantomime butcher knife, and gave her best horror movie impression.

"Nope. Cold water. I'm going to go down the hall. Friend of mine who is 16 has a nice shower. Newer one, I guess. This has happened before. Cheap twats, I guess."

"What about just yelling down and calling the custodian? They are trades, heh. Get paid $200 to fix that. If you're so spiteful, why not?" She giggled.

Duluth saw quick wit and upped her ante. "NOOOOO! Ever see that guy? 45 year old. He'll see my naked ass and start hitting on me. These breasts are for my man and that man is totally not a married, half bald, grayed out badass from Broomall. For-get it."

So she began to walk down the hall. Clomping down, she heard a banging on the wall near the center atrium. Curious to see what was the source of so much odd clatter, she approached slowly, as if a secret agent approaching a secret lair. She turned the corner, and what she saw was something where it should have been forgotten, and later there would be an attempt to make sure it was.

There, on the desk, was her doctor, laid spread eagle on top of what appeared to be one of the girls from another room. They were both talking in tongues that only meant one thing: bodily fluids were ready to be shared, and shared quickly.

The only thing that could be said was indeed. As the door cracked open, the young omnisciently omnipotent saw this. "You son of a bitch doctor." That was all that needed to be said. And so, she ran back to her room.

She got back, and Hope was sitting on the couch, her left leg on the cushion and right leg spread at a 45 degree angle to the floor. "How'd your shower go?"

And Duluth, shocked by the sight, stood in silence. "I don't think you need to know." She looked frightened. And Hope knew this was pretty much the way the Duluth was....a fearful girl, who didn't show outwardly her angst. Throwing her clothes on quickly, drops of water still coming out of her short hair, she nervously said "I don't need to know." Her shoes were on the wrong feet, and her socks sticking out of her boots. Her voice quivered in the way that she kind of knew there would be questions asked – and hell to pay, perhaps.

Just then a bang on the door, and a familiar accented voice came through. "Duluth Kane? Please come to the door. We need to talk."

It would have been foolish to think that actually opening the door would lead to anything good. But Hope made her fatal hero flaw and opened the door herself. She opened it, and laughed "Can I help you gentlemen – " but before she could even open it fully, the two men pushed her out of the way, blew the door open, and pushed Hope out of the way. "Duluth! Doctor Copulus needs to see you! Emergency!" And because Hope was fresh to the situation, due to the lack of time between event and personal explanation, Duluth was carried unhindered to the doctor's room, where presumably some evil, ungodly actions of fornication and undue predation and such had just finished.

Duluth screamed and the men picked up her body like a toy doll, her legs kicking as they carried her off. She began to writhe and scream, yelling futile profanity and otherwise trying to let them have mercy.

Immediately, Hope began to change her attitude about the home. It seemed as if innocence and help was not of the primary concern; rather, it appeared that she was in a place where the help could be overshadowed by the "help" of forced consent. The door slammed, and Duluth's screeching voice faded down the hall.

For some, this would have been a time for reflection or fear. To a 14-year-old who had just been introduced to the system, the prime mood was to inspect – and be curious, the scientist in her had already been primed in her own capability. Creaking the door open, she began to open the door and tiptoe down the hall. Luckily for her, the place had been just as deserted as it was before. She walked down, beginning to hurry her step. She saw Dr. Copulus' office on the left. Noises came from the room, ones that reminded her of movies that she couldn't remember the names of. But she felt pain coming from the room; it was perhaps Duluth's energy from her unfortunate elixir of C402, and it went all over the room. She came up to the room, with a glow coming from it, but she couldn't tell if it was just daylight or her blood that had been turned loose.

Curing her curiosity, she stuck her ear to the door, to which the door opened, luckily for her without a loud sound, just a couple of taps. Out of obvious and necessary curiosity, she peeked inside. What she saw, for all purposes, would define her stay – and path in life – here at the home.

There was Duluth, stretched across the table face down, just as much as the staff member she had seen before. The same two men who had taken her out of Hope's presence were holding her arms and legs down. The doctor, so compassionate before, had a wooden rod, and held it up, ready to pounce. They were both yelling at each other.

"You know you've been an atrocious asshole the entire time you've been here, Duluth. Now you give me reason to believe you've finally exceeded the limit."

"Chances are it's because you are, Bill. Now your asshole is finally getting pounded!"

"Yea, but it's finally time to straighten things out. You've ruined everything I wanted to do in this life, because you and your parents decided to send your sorry ass here. Should have went to college like they urged you – " and suddenly, the baton went down, and Duluth let out a primal scream. It exposed several blows, line marks of crimson that were all over her thighs. A single blow stretched across her face.

"You are a man of evil. A hopeless human being. And I'm not going to forget seeing your man thing in her mouth. She is absolutely beautiful. Your wife must be ecstatic about her property being wasted...."

"And what do you think I have that you don't? I have someone who loves me. You're going to spend the rest of your life – " a blow with the stick – " going about professing your disease –" another blow, this time with another scream – " not having a job because you scare the shit out of everybody – " another blow –" and you're going to die without a single thing except a really good story – " and then the doctor did what he shouldn't have, wound up, and said "you will lose face – " and threw the rod like a baseball player when he was walked on the fourth ball, and backslapped her in the face.

The doctor laughed as her body was exerting every single bit of remaining energy to break loose, and beginning to fail. "Take her out of here. 1

gram carbon iodate, and 5 milligrams Xanax with buffer. And give her a Vicodin injection, too. I don't want her bitching all night about how much her body hurts."

With a "yes, sir," they began to take her body away, the groaning still going on. It was a sure show of physical frustration, a type of signal that Copulus was the boss of the building. It just appeared to the shame of deriving such transgression of pain over something as little as a moment of impulsive joy.

Fearing the same for her, Hope immediately began shuffling down the hall, trying to avoid the sight of the men. She ducked into the men's room, which fortunately was empty. Keeping a peek out the door, she saw Duluth's body, looking as limp as a bunch of well-past al dente spaghetti. Her arms were still bound, and her legs dragged on the ground.

They threw her in the examination room. Shoving the pills in her mouth, the two men gagged her, forcing her to swallow by grabbing her throat and nose at the same time. She was too weak to put up any more fight. Her head cocked to the side, her eyes were rolled, unfocused through sunken eyelids into the back of her head. As Hope witnessed this, it made for an indelible inscription in her brain of the ramifications of her path. She immediately began to wonder whether it was worth continuing on and being so blessed to be able to resolve pain, but yet cursed by the lowest of Satan's demons to have to experience the pain over herself.

The heartless orderlies threw the straddled on the couch in the room that she and Hope shared, ignoring the fact that Hope was missing from the presence. They simply didn't care. The two men, their shirts torn by the struggle, and with marks from Duluth's boots, were filled with black streaks. A few marks of blood, probably both of the men and of the victim, were staining the light navy blue shirts. "She's a damn bundle of sticks, isn't she?"

"Yea, but she went down real easy. Not like that fat Downs we had in here. For an IQ of 40, she was like trying to tackle Joe Greene."

"Let's try and get her down here. Once that girl she's with gets in here, they'll do all that healing, and she will be OK." With a count to three, they put her down. Her body rolled, falling off the couch. "Who cares. It's lunch break time." They both walked out, continuing to converse.

About a half minute later, although feeling about half a day to the roommate because of the fear for her own well-being, Hope snuck in. The bruises on her body began to saturate with blood. They pulsed with a purplish, electronic-ink type of color changing. Duluth looked like hell, and had indeed been through it. Shaking her roommate's body, she said "Duluth? Duluth Kane, wake up. Please!" She turned her over. "Are you okay?" Shaking her newfound friend's body in the obvious attempt to renew her vitality, Hope bantered "I can't do this without you! What did you see that made him so mad?"

Duluth turned over, responding to her. Opening her eyes, before a single word was spoken, she spit out the pills. Then, in a very weak word, she said "Thank God I had a pack of bubble gum for my shower. I never go unprepared." She gave a weak smile. "Don't worry. Not the first time those eunuchs beat me up. I play helpless like a freaking possum - makes those dumbasses feel better."

For the first time that day, Hope smiled. "You little rat, you." She gave an embrace to Duluth, an impulse, and a pure one at that. Both of their eyes began to tear up. Even they had known each other for the scale of hours, a lifetime of pain and sharing of it started to stream between them in that moment. Hope gave a hug.

Looking at her eyes, the glow slowly started to come back. Hope's blue eyes began to show life, and as she had known, she began to try to help in more than consolation. "Duluth....how can I help?"

Duluth began to show her life back, too. "Just let me be. Let me sleep here for a second." She closed her eyes. "I'll be OK in a minute." And in a bit of quite requisite humor, she said "Oh, by the way, if I don't wake up, this outfit is a size 3, mid length. Boots size 8. Bra size....eh, you're better off not knowing. Don't try this outfit on unless you really like holding your breath in."

With an internalized sigh of relief, Hope let the words "Oh, you, what are we going to do with you?" She gave a push to the bruise on her arm, and suddenly, Duluth writhed in pain, but the wound began to disappear.

And so, Hope found out a lot more about herself through that moment. It was a mutual friendship finally; they both had connected in more ways than one through that hug. With her C402 in blood, Duluth rested for the night, and Hope kept watch as she sat there, and conversed. They had conversation, and it was strong. But it was best kept to the small talk, and they just had it clicking – and their lifeblood was back. At least for the moment.

SUNDAY MORNING

The friendly oaf was summoned to the office of Copulus. He was due for his semiannual evaluation, of which he was fully prepared. Usually, these tests were kind of typical of what you see of psychology in the movies, except they would ask situational questions and then watch and listen closely to your response. Oaf knew better than to give the same damned answers all the time, but he could seldom remember them from period to period. The staff knew this, and continued asking him the same questions as evidence he was not ready to reintegrate into society.

Oaf wished everyone hello and good day, then took his seat. Copulus was still fogged over from what he did the night before; certainly the witnessing, and later "necessary" discipline and "behavior control and audit" did a number on his concentration. "Good evening, Robert. Shall we begin?" With a lazy nod from his patient, they were ready to begin.

Just then, the door to his office opened. It was one of the lead nurses in the building. "Doctor, these are the documents sent to us by the Health Department's Legal Affairs. Please do read them…." He handed them to the doctor, who told her to come over to the side.

"What are all these, Jeffrey? I thought we were told to give the 302 committal papers." Copulus rubbed his eyes. "So we certainly cannot these girls in permanent care? We cannot bypass government proce-dure?"

The nurse frowned. "Nope. They are over 13, so they do not have to stay here if they don't want to. We can only make them stay if they have any medical condition that would make them a danger to society. And despite the fact you literally horsewhipped and beat Duluth Kane, we can't hold them here." He paused for a moment.

"Well, I mean, we can show the Board those scars and claim she did that as self-inflicted?" The nurse gave him a glance, as if to say Well… to which the doctor muttered "Very well."

Copulus was in trouble. Even though he was under government edict, he was not beyond the stage of the Board of Health. Already, he had been given probation for his commentary about a former female patient's dimensions that. Losing the battle of Duluth and Hope would be the last stake in his career. He was an older gentleman; his parents would never have allowed him to be dishonest or untrue to his practice. For the first time, though, he bowed his head. Taking the documents, he then came up with an idea.

"Hey Jeffrey?" he said in a midtone voice. "Is it possible that we can use that beating and say she was socially disobedient? And with violent tendencies?" Copulus said. "Between you and me, it's not a secret. But to everyone else...." And then Jeffrey turned to see Oaf, looking dead on, his eyes crossed and wandering the floor. His legs were shaking, and wrists uncurling and jerking all over, the telltale signs of his condition which had kept him under their care for many years manifested.

The nurse went and called the bluff. "What about Robert?" he asked. "We just said this all, and now he knows, too."

Copulus laughed. "Bob? Don't worry. He's not saying anything. He's as retarded as my dog. Ever see the way he shits his bed despite our calls to stop it? And the fact he's a moonlight streaker when the whistle blows and everyone goes home Fridays? No chance." He smiled, and signed the papers.

And for one blessing was another. Not only did they underestimate Oaf, but he heard everything. And his words would mean solid gold – and life for more than just two girls.

Oaf was released, his review sent to the Board of Health as it always had been. Usually, he would be glowing with joy as he came along, knowing in a simple minded manner that there was a chance that he would be released. Some people like freedom because they hate the regimen of being limited to property and/or quarters. Some hated the food or the lack of social opportunities. But for Oaf, it was different.

Oaf was placed in the care of the home after a childhood of despair and discomfort. Coming from parents of little money, he did not receive great care or proper education. Most of the kids would pick on him, knock him down, bookcheck him, and take his money. The kids' parents often would hire legal help or petition the guidance counselor to have his parents and their parents come in. Usually, the rich kids' parents would both show up with a note from a psychologist identifying their kids as model students with difficulties. Oaf's mom would show up with nothing but a purse and an old winter coat, her work uniform still on. It was a mistake to ever get him involved with mainstream school, but then again, there were a lot of mistakes – including Oaf himself, according to his dad.

But Oaf had not relented from making himself over. He deemed treasurable the simple things in life. Once he was able to get out, he wanted to get a job, collect some money, work hard, and pay back his Mom, whom he wanted to meet every weekend. Perhaps the reason why he ran through the halls on Friday was not because of simple medical illness, but perhaps a longing for a lost childhood, one that seemed to wreak anger and a state of disorganized flux.

The girls walked up the hallway. They saw Oaf over there, with a look of sadness and frustration on his face. Duluth, the senior member of the pair, said "What's going on, Bob?" She knew all the looks that the young man had from eating lunch with him seven days a week. "You look like you heard something."

"Perhaps I did," he said in a slow voice, weary from two hours of close verbal examination. "Did you see him last night?" He began to hunch over, as if he were out of breath.

In a bit of humor, Duluth said "Yes. A little too much, if you ask me." She showed the wounds from the beating she received. "These are that bastard's marks."

Seeking an opportunity, Oaf said "He told the nurse that....he was going to make up that you were a bipolar and were defiant. So you won't be released." He bowed his head in shame, even though in reality, he had done nothing wrong.

But it was little solace for Duluth and Hope. Duluth shook her head and yelled "THAT FOUR EYED SNAKE CHARMING BUDDHA RAPING JULAB BASTARD! I'll take him out myself – " and she began to run toward the office, when Hope grabbed her from behind in a matter of sanity. "Let me go, Let me go!" she let out in a scream with a few shrieks that could cut glass.

Hope realized that the situation was getting worse rather than better. The small frame of Duluth in her semi-army outfit was tackled to the ground. Hope yelled "So he's a liar, right? What are you going to do, dumbass, prove he's right by beating him up?" She looked with sincerity into her friend's eye. Something that had been taught to her in her early age was to never let the bullies lure you into a situation where you can get in more trouble – through discipline or by physical harm – than would the instigator.

Duluth kept yelling "That bastard's going to make me stay here! Stay here, all my life!" Her face began to turn as red as a beet, and her makeup began to run. Her tank top began to pop loose, exposing her halter underneath. She was a determined woman, indeed. But she had the terrible evil of false and somewhat unwise premise. That was a killer for her – and she knew that, but didn't want to admit it. Finally, Hope did what she had to, and smacked her dead in the face.

"Duluth! We need to think about this. Put it in a song. Let's stop panicking and start getting our stuff together. Perhaps you know something we don't. Let's nip him where it matters the most. " And so, they commenced a final act, one to show this man what two ladies who had so much bitterness in them from gifts so pristinely good could do.

And it would take some thought. Over a few really good hospital food sandwiches.

V

The Liberation

The most evil plans often had their roots in the best intentions, someone once said. Perhaps it was the teachings of Alex Malott, the impeccable father, one that had shaped the behavior and character of her daughter up to this point. Two years and some months older, her partner in crime did not have the path she did. For her, this was the breaking point of a terrific energy source. Her father, a loving and caring person, had tried to cover up what he had believed was the most terrible thing one could endow to his offspring: a birth defect not caused by luck, chance, or genetics, but because of his decision to go and involve himself in a matter to make a quick buck.

Chris Kane, now 47, was sitting at home 857 miles away. He was watching TV, but at that moment, he was thinking about a lot of things in life. When he had made the mistake of sending his daughter to see Dr. Copulus under the guise that "he would make it seem like nothing ever happened", he was content. But then Copulus pulled tricks of paperwork and the threat of incarceration to gain immediate control over the young science experiment. Prior to those years, he had tried everything: ballet, softball, dancing, acting, but then music took over her life. When she picked up that guitar, it seemed like everything bad that had ever happened to her went away. And it was consoling to the most point. But then it was supposed to all change. And now his little girl and her friend, two of one intention, sprung to it. Soon enough, the dwelling of his daughter became simply a function of pure apathy. It hurt to think of her, and he comforted himself by not thinking about it. And suddenly, it became separated from his paradigm, for which then it became invisible.

Hope commenced the ladies' plan and knocked on Oaf's door. Several times, she knocked quickly, trying not to be seen by the staff. She could hear him fumbling about the room, and screaming "Aye! Be right thereabouts. Stop acting like a Jehovah witness! I'm coming!" He ripped the door open. "Hope Malott. What can I do for you? Lookin' like Carole Bouquet from the movies."

A pause followed, as if Hope was like *Who the hell is that*? "Eh, okay, Oaf. You know how you heard that stuff from Dr. Copulus? You know, how they want us to be here forever, and like, all that stuff?" Oaf nodded, and she said "Well, you can help us in the best way possible."

She entered the room without asking him first, and shut the door behind him. Although this was a violation of his personal space, something she did not understand, the man was of common dignity and wisdom enough to see a determined girl with good intentions.

"Look, we all know about your habit on Friday mornings. If you want to help us, can you do us a favor and do it at night?" She looked him dead in the eye, and was as direct as could be.

Oaf laughed. "I do it when Ridin' Robert comes on. Daddy used to show us that." Hope smiled.

"Well, what I want you to do, Bob, is watch this tape after you eat dinner. It has an episode of that on here, the one from last week! Cole's Train Ride, right?" She handed him the tape.

Despite the fact that it was a meager offering, it was suitable enough for Oaf. "The best episode everrrr! What happens is when I'm going to see this, it makes sense now! Cole is like a cool, customer. Kind of like the lube when I rub it down here – " and lo and behold, he began reaching into his pants, hoping to grab something that was not exactly proper. Hope firmly grabbed his arm, as if to indicate you don't need to do that in front of me. Afraid to upset him and ruin his plans, she shook her head.

Hope was calm. "You do your thing tomorrow, 7 PM sharp. OK?" With a nod, the first piece of the puzzle was in place. She walked out confident, and knew she was in business. As Duluth walked by, she flipped the thumbs up slyly and covertly at waist level, to which Duluth winked and smiled.

Next, Duluth waited outside of Dr. Copulus' office. She needed some evidence, some material, to show what he had done. Copulus was out on his break; thus, Hope waited for the custodian to open the door to empty out the trash. Prior to being thrashed in there, the enterprising young adult had seen many things while she was in pain – usually the world moves slower when you have an adrenaline rush. She saw a stack of papers with the doctor's letterhead and cell phone number. Taking one of these would provide a place for her to dump any info on his actions to his wife, right at the house. She also had some plans to cover up for an escape route. But most importantly, she saw a tin foil wrapper, which she knew all too well that meant like an old Cutlass, they had swapped fluids when she caught them. The perfect way to implicate and extract revenge was the most perverted. Grabbing the papers, she pulled the rubber out of the garbage with a pair of gloves. She held onto the gloves, as she would need them later.

Walking back to the room, she showed Hope the rubber. Squirming, she told Hope "This is our key to a successful escape." Hope came back, and said "Ewww! Get that thing away from me! It smells like a horse's vagina! And it's filled with man bullion! Yuk!"

Duluth smiled. "And when you put it in the escape vehicle and park it in front of a house after you stole it from the PD…."

Hope smiled. "Yup. But how do we get the total setup to make someone believe it was truly evil? I mean, he could have done something really bad but we need something special. Like crime syndicate special." She waited, and then closed her eyes.

It was almost too perfect of a setup. But the cherry on top probably came from popping one surprise – a necessary one - of her own. She thought of revenge – but then, she got the perfect idea. "Here! Bleed me, Duluth!" who looked silly at her. "Bleed you?" "Yeah!" So she grabbed a pen out of her pocket, and stabbed Hope in the arm. Blood dripped like a fountain down, and Duluth stuck the condom underneath it. "Now, you have my DNA on a condom with Bill's mansperm on it. He'll be in jail for years!"

Amazed at what she had heard, the elder female laughed. "Sometimes, I think you are more than amazing. I love you. Barely know you, but I love you."

So, the second piece of the evil plan was put in place. Yet even with all of the plans to escape from the building, they needed a ride. It would be tough to get one out; after all, the gated community was quite a place to sneak out. She looked around to see what would be the best plan. Of the plans, she thought about what would be perfect; they were in a small town, and there were some trucks that went through town. Too gross, and perhaps they would not go into the town I wanted to go to. Plus what if they are perverts? She thought. Continuing to conjure up a bit of sense for the longest and perhaps most critical part of the story to make a clean escape, she looked out the window.

Then, she saw it. Coming up the driveway was a police car, a burgundy one. The local department was about half a mile down the road in the town. The cops would often pay a visit up to the home, as there were those sent by judges to the home in lieu of a detention center. Many times, they were required to transport them to and from their homes. Duluth knew that although they didn't have to deal with them (and for a fact, didn't want to; the kids were often hairless and were just about impossible to deal with because they would continuously hit on her in her presence). But if they could make it down to the station, perhaps they could snag a car. The plan was in place, and a healthy dose of ad-lib was necessary.

The next five hours were some of the longest that each had experienced. They figured that they had only one chance for the matter; surely, the tape would be discovered, and likely destroyed after this. No one wanted to deal with Oaf's streaking, and once he was known to have broken out, he would likely be sent to one of the solitary rooms in the center of the building. And the poor child would never want to do a favor for Duluth again, or probably Hope for that matter. They had to pray that night, and they did. Each of them said their own words of consultation with the Almighty, and somewhere out there, a star twinkled, as if He had given His divine approval for the matter.

It hit 3:27. Just about the time she would be getting out of school, the first time she had thoughts about the whole matter. Duluth curled up on the couch in the room, her feet curled in like she was bowlegged, in that cute little innocent way. Hope began to get this feeling in her veins like there was some sort of connection that had to be made, a feeling that she had not felt in a long time.

The silence was damning. Hope had to break it. "So, Duluth, I gotta ask you. Like, so you have a boyfriend…." She asked.

Duluth became defensive. "Yeah. So, is it like a bad thing? You seem a little unsure." The girl was nervous, and Hope just wanted to console her in her own way; a certain compassion that she felt both necessary and kind. She was just that kind of girl.

Hope laughed, and cupped her hands in curiosity, leaning forward. "You know, is it…." She twirled her fingers.

With a pause of drama, Duluth scowled. "You have no clue. You ever have one?" When Hope shook her head, Duluth almost preplanned it and said "You wouldn't understand, then." With a little pause, she relented. "He's a friend of mine, Hope. Used to be here when he was in rehab. Yes, at 14, he was in rehab." She paused again, and Hope uttered not. "Yes, he's good."

Hope smiled. "So you do have someone out there, Duluth." She got up, and sat down next to Duluth. "Seems like you don't have many friends, do you?" Hope felt the tension in the air beginning to release from her new friend. She had the toolkit to make sure that because they were in this together, that they would have to go forth and make these strides together.

Yet Duluth, in her automatically pensive way, felt as if the young girl was taking advantage to her. In carnal instinct, she took the defensive and got up, sitting where Hope was. "You sayin' I don't have any friends, Hope?" The sharpness in her voice suddenly became a little too much.

"Not really, but I don't know what, like, gives you this energy, Duluth."

A many instances, this would have solved the issue. But Hope's words stung her friend deeply. "I don't like talking about my social life. This was never supposed to be a permanent thing, staying here, Hope. Why the hell do you think I want out so bad?" In lieu of showing her tears, she slung back in the chair, stretching out like a Gumby doll, and placing her head back.

"Something hurts, doesn't it?" Hope said. "I can't feel your energy, but I'm a pretty smart chica, too." Getting up, she walked back over to where Duluth was, and sat on the arm. She literally could not let Duluth go. "Now I feel your energy. I can see your eyes, too. I might be going on a limb by saying this, but I have to say it."

For a moment, there was a tacit hesitation. In her way, Hope knew this was the one shot to get what she needed. Better yet, they both needed it. Duluth's eyes opened, and she initially turned her stare from the ceiling, and sensed Hope's energy in that very unique way, building up.

Her instinct began to take over once again. Yet now, it was focusing into the eyes of her only friend now. "You won't understand. But say it. I know you have to."

Hope looked at Duluth closely. The energy was there. "You were waiting for someone like me all this time." Three seconds passed, then four, then five. "Am I right? Please tell me."

Pent-up resistance began to compromise in the room, a certain type of stoicism that had made her go this far. Those boots, that short hair, the "Hawklick", a sort of cowlick that extended halfway back on her short haired head she would carry, Duluth's way of saying she was really like no nother - it all lent herself to the belief that even as a person of strong values, there was compromise. Confusion. A lack of personal identity in this damned strange world of hers. And she pinched her eyes shut and tried to forget the whole thing. She didn't know how to handle affection very well. There was little of it in the building, and she knew it.

All these days of hating the guys in her life because they were passive.

 All these doctors poking and prodding her.

The fact that she didn't know the life outside, where it was, how it formed.

 How she had to feel like it was a fish in a tank. *More than anything*.

And then, it was like somebody now was finally releasing that valve. The girl of remissive dreams nodded, and gave a small but honest smile. "Thank you. Well, let me help you then. Can you agree to that?" Hope's ability to cut through her was necessary. It was the way to success. Another nod came from Duluth, who could not utter a word. She was literally hooked and possessed by the presence of this girl, two years her junior.

Sensing the pressure, in a decision of careful, concise caretaking, Hope sat back down and allowed her friend to have room. "I don't have a whole lot of friends who are really good, either. We have kind of a clique, but I have one really good friend. She's my neighbor."

Duluth began to focus a little better, but she still had a sense of embodiment, a certain appliance and due affection there. Hope was entitled to her ear now. "I guess you two grew up together, right?" She didn't know the feeling, but there was a due obligation to ask. Deep inside, it was a feeling she wanted.

Hope smiled, and looked down shyly. "She's my best friend, Duluth. Even if she wasn't my neighbor, she would be my best friend. We did a lot of stuff together, made bracelets – " to which she showed it proudly, like a 10 karat diamond ring – " and we used to hang out in our room, play house, put on makeup, and such."

Duluth put her head down and looked at Hope. "I always wished someone would come in this room and do that. Would be kinda, like, special sometimes to have someone else in here." Her smile began to radiate throughout the room. "We had a girl in here once that was like that. But then I'd wake up and she'd be breathing heavily over my bed like she was having an asthma attack. Turns out I think she thought I was, like, butch or something."

Hope laughed. "What did they do to her? Oh my God." The girl talk slowly started to manifest in the room.

Loosening up, she rubbed her short hair. "I think they took her away and put her in a cell. Probably would have killed me, too. The way she held a hairbrush reminded me of a B-rate slasher porno or something." They both began to laugh a little bit as the sun began to shine in many rays through the room.

The bonding they had both prayed for was there. "I hope she wasn't the only friend you had here. That one was crazy." Hope laughed, but then, Duluth laughed, and then her face turned sour. She looked away.

Hope sensed a little bit of tension, knowing this may have struck a chord. "Lots of people come through here probably." She knew in the look on Duluth's face that a fragile part of her had been left out in the open, and now, it was slowly turning into the very reason that Duluth had so much sheltered herself in talking to anyone, even Hope. It was her only natural defense mechanism. "Too much travel and too much change."

Her friend was right. "Yea, there are some that really, like, make the difference, Hope. Too many times, shit like that happens 'round these parts." She gave a chuckle.

Hope gave it that she felt happy in getting this far. And it felt better, because they had both put themselves out there, for the first time.

Soon enough, it was 6:47. They were both in the room, staring out the window. Duluth was pacing back and forth, overthinking the matter. She had to hold back jumping for joy and being sad and unsure about the world out there, as she had spent most of her adolescent life in wards and pretty much her first precipice of legality in Attrition. Trying to not be detailed was her downfall.

A rumble came out in the hall. There was Oaf, running down the hallway, and as guaranteed, in the buff, his body in random motion like an amoeba in water. He was screaming "Yo, ho, ho! I'm a captain from down below! Shiver me timbers, until the break of winter, to sea, to sea, I go!" But amazingly, no one went to follow him. He began running down the hallway, and towards the room. "We're going for the gold tonight, ladies! Let's blow up Long John Silver's bounty!"

She slammed the door, cursing out loud as she caught her breath. The plan was failing – she had assumed the reaction of the staff would be immediate, but as it was off of schedule, it took time for the folks to realize it. Immediately panicking, she began to think about the dwindling time they had for an immediate effect. Her eyes began to glow in the hue that they had been accustomed to seeing. Sighting her guitar in the corner, and immediately ran to it, she sensed opportunity for music to bail her out of her problems one last time. Grabbing it, she stuck it out the door, and said to it "Sorry, Tacky, this is where you need to help me." Kissing the bridge, she said "Here, Oaf! Toy for you. Go smash this up!" Oaf took it, and ran towards the door.

Within seconds, the guitar was in pieces. And it also went as planned: Next to the door was the fire alarm. Every smash on the door had both a sad recall for her only escape from her life, but then, she anticipated the next escape, a much more fruitful one, to occur. *C'mon, Rosie. Get me the hell out of here*, she began to think. Every blow missed the alarm.

Then, the door opened. It was Copulus. "What the hell are you doing out here, Robert?" he yelled. The next blow sounded the fire alarm, which was a buzz and the burglar alarm together. Noise filled the room, and everyone began to come out of their rooms, down the stairs, and from all around to inspect.

It had worked...and not only that, it was helping all who were trapped there by the doctor and his evil staff. Duluth smiled, and said "Remember how I told you the music would save us?" she winked. They walked out to the custodial room. Hope wanted to leave the building immediately, feeling that an escape was more important and getting the hell out of there the biggest obstacle to overcome. But her new big sister knew that their outfits would give them away, especially if they were placed on the news.

Pulling the string, Duluth looked in the closet and turned on the light. "Here, put these on!" She went through the outfits, looking for the two smallest ones. "Put on this hat, too. We don't want to look like we just escaped from a mental home! They will be looking for people in our outfits and our hair color."

And so, they put on the outfits. Duluth threw a pair of boots at Hope. "Spare pair I had. Wore 'em twice. You'll look like you're ready to unclog a pipe with these on. Don't worry, I sprayed them with half a bottle of disinfectant." Hope laughed and scrambled to lace up the ankle boots.

"Where the hell did you get these boots, anyways?" Hope asked.

"We're allowed to get three packages a month. I had these shipped up six months ago. Grandmother still thinks I'm 15, but I have big feet. I am five-four, heh." Hope rolled her eyes, and put them on.

And so, they took off in the mob that floated out the door and through the building. They walked right out the front door, being sure to get out of the way of Copulus, who was as flustered as ever, and trying to avoid being trampled. He groaned as the people had freaked him out – his patients were now making him the victim. With rubber gloves in hand, the evidence in a small garbage bag, they walked out the front door, towards the town.

As soon as they cleared the fence, they saw a horde of cars, many of them marked police cars, heading towards the house. Many of the occupants were running around, some of which were trying to head for the main gate. Duluth directed Hope down towards a gully in the back. Here, a back road ran to the downtown area of the small town.

When they got to a fence, Duluth began to search around in a rush. "Here, come under here!" Things started to happen so fast, as Duluth pulled her new friend, her best friend, behind her like a modern day Sacagawea to the newfound friend. Both were exploring new territory, but for Duluth, this was the equivalent of a sensory overload; she had very rarely been out this far without someone reeling her in.

As they hustled down the road, boots clomping like lead weights, it felt like they were trying to carry the world on them. The not so subtle difference was noticeable to Hope. She was always used to flip-flops, clogs, and canvas shoes, and occasionally moccasins, all of which were light and airy. Duluth wore those too, but winter usually brought out the boots more than not – she idolized the rock idols from the classic era more than anything. Her calves tended to be much larger, although not really big at all.

They got to the police station, with Hope running out of breath. "I need a drink of water. Anywhere around here I can get one?" she half-laughed in a tired voice. "And how are we going to get in? Seems like this high fence means "no trespassing".

Not to be outdone, Duluth laughed it off. "Watch me. I'll surprise you." She went up to the fence with the lock, a keyed one with heavy duty fencing. Pulling out a hypodermic needle, she grimaced as she poked her finger and bled herself. The blood melted through the lock, disintegrating it. "Bet you didn't know you could do that, sweetie?" She gave a wink.

Hope was more direct. "OK, well, we're breaking into a police station. Can we get what we need and then the heck out of here? Isn't this, like, suicide for our plans? This isn't a video game." She had never been introduced to the idea of committing criminal acts. Alex and Carrie had committed themselves to raising a normal kid, and as thus, she had not been introduced to the more risqué aspects of living the life from the other side of the tracks. She stood there, and stared at the station, picturing herself in the station. It was a scary thought.

Duluth called her. "Come here. To this maroon one." They both ran over. She began looking under the car, reaching underneath every once in a while.

"What are we going to do, steal the exhaust off of this car?" a curious and sardonically serious Hope asked. "Shouldn't we just do like they do in the movies, and break the window in?" she laughed.

Ignoring her partially, and talking to herself, Duluth explained "If they see it broken in, they won't believe it. Plus we bleed, and our DNA will show we took the car. We have Bill's DNA...let's use it!" And then, suddenly, she said "Yes, here it is." The lights to the car blinked. "Get in! Hurry!" And so, Duluth got in the driver's seat and Hope rushed around to the passenger side as her accomplice started the car.

They both took a deep breath. "The PD here always keeps a spare car with the keys under the tire. We have a lot of emergencies in this area, with Attrition here, Fort Dix 30 minutes down, and the such. These country cops are just plain stupid sometimes, and they figure they can get away with hiding the keys if the gate's locked. Here – " she threw her accomplice a pair of fleece gloves – "take these off and keep them in your pocket. Your hands will sweat less in these, they breathe better than the latex gloves."

Duluth put the car in gear, keeping the headlights off. She talked to herself as the car pulled out with a couple of jerks. She had only taken some interest in driving; Attrition really didn't give the patients cars, but occasionally she would take some driver's ed courses in her excursions. Most of her knowledge of driving came from playing video games. Her reaction time was good, but even with the all-wheel drive Taurus sedan, she still was being careful. "Sorry, love. I just have to remember how to do this."

As they pulled out onto the main road, the headlights came on. "Let's get clear of the area. We have to do two more things before we can rest. First off, we dump this car. My boyfriend's house is right up the street from Copulus' house. 20 minute walk to there. His Dad's a rich guy, owns the building. He won't check occupancy." She laughed.

Hope was somewhat ambivalent. "Boyfriend?" she implied. "How did you keep this relationship, anyways? I thought you were isolated from the world. Or it was a joke. You were serious!" Somehow, things didn't seem to add up for her; this was supposedly a lone, sad soul. But she had her networks, and as anyone in the corporate capitalist world knew, it wasn't what you know but who you know. Or was it who you….something that rhymed with that.

[113]

Duluth laughed, speeding down the country road. She had not driven in a while, and forgot the idea of speed limits. Thankfully, the entire town was heading to Attrition, so they got away with it until Hope warned her "Slow down! We don't want to attract cops!" as Duluth underestimated the powerful pursuit-ready vehicle. But Hope was thinking about bigger things. "Dammit, Duluth, what did I do? Jesus, we are in sooooo much trouble when we get caught."

Duluth took her eyes off the road for a moment, and scolded Hope. "You are wrong. We are not going to get caught. For God's sake, don't say that!" She was right – they had to keep up a positive outlook. Sure, the effects of what happened were indescribable to the squeaky-clean girl, but they had done what they need to cover up what was now a significant set of tracks.

Hope feared for her life. "Where are we going to go to, a boyfriend's house? What if he is dating another chick? Will he just say 'I don't know you, bitch! Go away!' or something like that? Are we going to spend the night – the rest of our life in the car? Don't you think this dude might want an RSVP? You know boys..." She began to have a panic attack right there in the car. It took an equivocal of both words and actions to bring her down.

Without warning, Duluth slammed on the brakes right in the middle of the road. She put the emergency brake on, her body covered in a nervous panic of ashen skin, and looked Hope straight in the glowing eye. "Hope, we have gotten this far because of me. You helped me devise this plan. I came up with the intricacies of it. You have been trying to help. Put it aside now – we're in the middle of the brush, and you don't know if we are doing the right thing?" she cried.

Hope said "Yes, but you don't have the mutual permission any more. I don't know, I don't feel confident I'm doing the right thing!" she screamed. Banging her fist, she turned on the light bar in the back, and blue and red lights came on. Panicking and thinking they blew their cover, Duluth screamed.

"What the hell! Turn the lights off! We're in trouble!" She began hitting all the switches one by one, but all it did was turn on the computer, hit the lights in front, the strobes and wig-wags, and turn on the local country station and CB. The sensory overload had now become a jumble of lights, sirens, and every single thing that could add color to her life. It now was gibberish, and she cowered one more time, throwing her wishes to the Lord.

Citing that they had blown it, Hope yelled "I don't know how to! I'm not freakin' Dirty Harry. You wanted the damn pigmobile for a ride, you shut them off!" She threw the radio at the lights in the back, knocking them off. Pulling the wires out of the center console, the lights went off, the siren slowly autotuning down to a drone of a low wail. "There! Fixed."

A moment of pause led to them. Both turned away from each other. Duluth slammed her hands on the steering wheel. "Dammit!" she yelled, putting her head down in a private penance. Duluth looked down also, refusing to look her friend in the eye. It took them a few minutes to realize that this had become a little too real. They were stuck in the woods, neither of them had an idea of what to do at this point. With a sigh, they wanted to decry each other. But then, it happened.

For the first time, they looked at each other. It was their first argument, and fight, of their friendship. For a few seconds, they both were silent for that first time – two chatty young women with nothing to say. It was the time that they were able to finally analyze the caliber of their relationship. Before, it was a model of being two different people with a similar problem. But now, they were one person with the same problem but with different, and yet unique, approaches. They both laughed. And as they went on, they started laughing even harder. They had entertained themselves for the first time.

They pulled over at a house in the woods, one that was rather sizable, a ranch house with a two car garage. In the driveway was another sedan, just like the one they had seen. "Time to switch the plates." She looked inside and saw the lights out – the people who were there were unaware of the two visitors. "I scouted out this place when I was coming back from the grief clinic. Ford Taurus, just like ours. Police Interceptor." Quietly, they unscrewed the plate, and switched them. "Whacker patrol actually saved us this time. What kind of creeper actually buys old cop cars, anyways? Usually is something you don't want to be reminded of on a Saturday night." They both giggled.

Finally, to put the perfect the mastery of the illusion, they climbed back in the pilfered patrol car. Duluth took a break, and said "All right, so we did this all correct. The police will come looking for the car in the driveway, the guy thinks we're camped out there. Unless this car has GPS, which I don't think a cop would use, lest he would blow his cover, we're good. But one problem. This car still looks like a cop car. Like the light bar – " and they saw it sheared off in the backseat. "Hang on just a second." Duluth ran out the back, opened the back door, and threw it behind the clone car's wheels. "They'll think it's the car and all. Won't even look for us then." And they both let out a sigh of relief.

In some ways, this was the final piece of the puzzle for forging their relationship. Duluth admired Hope's ability for clear, concise, and proper thinking. She still had some of the goodness in her to be polite, but could see her breaking out of her shell and turning a girl into a full-fledged woman. Hope saw the big sister that she had always wanted, and Duluth knew it. Duluth, according to her thought, was a person who had plans and experienced the things she had always wanted to: being able to fend for oneself, and independent and resilient thought through an undying need to be productive and enterprising. Alex had told her many times that those were the friends worth keeping. And she felt it.

They pulled up to the alleyway near the Copulus' house. It was beginning to get late, and they feared about now being in the suburbs, and less than perfect individuals, hell-bent on robbing anyone who came across them being the norm. Slowly pulling in, Duluth set the car in park, shut off the lights, and told Hope to take the contents of the bag and throw them in the backseat through the divider. "That should be enough to get him in trouble." Putting the keys in her pocket, she gave a compensatory last look of approval at Hope. "Well, here we are. In the suburbs, out away from that screwed-up shithole of an asylum." Looking around, her eyes gleamed in the city lights. Her eyes began to change color, looking like lightning bugs. Hope noticed this, and looked at her. And Duluth noticed Hope's eyes were glowing, too. "You know, this was never supposed to be, Hope. I was supposed to be put down and moved far, far away, solitary life. Bill wanted to….that twerp, he wanted me to live on the military base all my life. Never see anyone but people who would understand my problems." She looked at Hope. And you made me bust that bubble when you came in."

Feeling the intimacy and eloquence of the moment, Hope felt like she had something to get off her shoulders. "You know, when I found out that I had this thing a couple of weeks ago, I was scared. I sat in the girls' room in middle school, having my first period. It was totally not like I anticipated it. But I prepared for it. Then, when I was there, and I found out I was pretty much getting rid of nuclear waste, I was scared.

"When Copulus sent them in to kill my mother, I was afraid. I didn't know what stage of my life was next. To be perfectly straight, when I checked in, I felt lonelier than ever. But then you were there. You have the same thing, but I really love the fact that you handle yourself, and your powers, with such power and grace. It's more beautiful than a flower."

They both looked each other in the eyes. Then, they did something they would have never anticipated – their lips locked, and tilted their heads right in that alleyway. For a few seconds, they were, well, just there, and just enjoying it. It perhaps was impulse, but for a moment, they felt as one.

In that kiss, they both felt each other's feelings. Being that they shared the same powers, the glow in the car began to show sparkles. Suddenly, sparks flew in more ways than one. A bolt of electricity shot from their hands, which were embraced. In that exchange, Hope suddenly felt the experience and angst that had built up, while Duluth felt childhood innocence in Hope. It was something that Attrition had taken away from her long ago. The car began to rock back and forth as their bodies began to pulse with energy. It was a beautiful act, and it was fortunate that no one was out walking for an early morning jog, mostly since if seen, there would be an unnecessary calling of the cops for a light infraction.

They slowly and quite unviolently separated. Duluth smiled. "I had to get that out of the way," she said, straightening out her shirt.

Hope felt strange, but she agreed. "Me too. Let's go to the house." And so, they dumped the car.

VI

The Reconciliation

Her last few days were a whirlwind of activity and a world of concern. She had seen her father killed, her body committed, her new friend of just a speck in time beaten, and a lot of other exposure to the real world. Now that she was out, and on her own, save for Duluth and her reacquired boyfriend, this was the time to start acting more adult. Her parents had taught her the values of independence; surely, the other person's dime was never suitable for one's own pride. But yet, she was only 14 at this point in time. Her world still revolved around beauty and outward appearance. She was holed up in an apartment with a girl she didn't know if she could trust, with a boy who seemed to come across as trustworthy, but several times would stay out late with Duluth. And only the heavens would know if Duluth was sharing information – or for that matter, her powers alike – to change the world.

They both got the first victory when they saw the car was gone. Hiding on public transportation, Hope saw a very pretty wife putting boxes out on the doorstep. She wanted to cheer it, but still, she feared the recourse of giving her identity away. She didn't know if law enforcement was looking for her, or anyone else for that matter; surely, the fact a police vehicle was stolen was a key crime in the city, one that would not fade away. But yet, after a few months' search, and the only evidence coming from a convicted criminal, Duluth and Hope were assumed to have passed away, and the search dropped because of it. Hope gave her name to the tearing up of papers that would take place, and she could feel it happening, if only a few miles away.

When Hope woke up that morning after, she saw Josh. A tall, skinny guy, he reminded her of the boys who would often go out and smoke. Slender as could be, he appeared to have a little bit of a visual instability; he smelled of cigarette smoke, and his smile kind of reflected a deep feeling that something was wrong. But he never triggered suspicion, and Duluth was happy. The biggest thing was that both understood that they had to keep to themselves; Josh pretended that Hope was just Duluth's roommate, and no one really bothered her.

After a few weeks, perhaps a couple of months, it really began to sink in for Hope that she was losing touch with reality. Like a modern day Apostle, fearing the Jews by shuttering herself in a room, the seasons began to pass and time slowed down. Duluth often would come home and throw her belongings on the couch; often times, it would be Josh's money that would pile up with a hoard of garbage to turn her on.

Yet there was this kind of resistance when she saw Josh. He always had a keen interest in Hope, even though for the most part, he knew that it would mean his anatomy to have any relationship with her. And she saw it in him, painted all over his face when he would come home and stare long enough to make eye contact, then look away when her blue eyes connected. Perhaps it was the shame of seeing Duluth in her.

The sadness in Hope's eyes began to take its toll. But she ate, she dressed, and she hung out, consuming news and digital cable.

For two years, she lived this way, under the radar, holing up at night, and going out by day to find food, clothing at the thrift store, and the like. They did odd jobs around the neighborhood for pocket money; Hope would often fix drapes, clean the tenants' rooms (many of whom didn't mind paying $20 to have an orderly apartment), and pump the drains. Duluth had work at her boyfriend's bike shop; she would learn her craft, upon which she would get under-the-table pay. For 25 months, this was the way they lived, and they were happy. Time flew by, the seasons blending into one another, the clock suddenly running thin. No one knew of the secrets they kept, not even the Dad, who was too busy to watch the news or view missing posters on the poles.

And then it happened. Hope woke up one month after her 16th birthday. She had slept on a cot on the floor, a barren room unsuitable for someone who had been so carefully sheltered for years. There was a lamp, a few plastic boxes for clothes, and a dresser, the ultimate vagabond life. But it was protection, and the heat was always on in the cold nights and the windows able to be opened by day.

She opened her eyes, and looked around. This morning seemed different; the sun was out, shining through the window. She had slept in a sweatsuit from the designer lingerie outlet, a teal blue velour outfit with the hoodie. Somehow, her right slipper had fallen off after she went to sleep, and her leg hung over the bed. Rising up, she heard the radio playing loudly in the other room. Slowly getting up and rising to, she bumbled to the living room.

It had appeared as if someone had left in a hurry; clothes were strewn about, the covers on the sofa pulled in a bundle, the TV remote thrown on the floor. Despite the haphazard life they had lived, and the fact that they were both in their teenage years, this was atypical for them. So she flipped off the radio, and slowly crept out on the porch from the third floor.

The church bells were ringing off the distance. It had appeared as if someone was about to get married, and indeed, there were. But Hope didn't mind; it was typical on weekends that there would be activity there. However, this felt different.

Questioning her inner monster, she picked up the newspaper off her neighbor's doorstep. Fumbling through the classifieds, she looked for the

[121]

church's name, and who was the new couple. She had a strange feeling, and it was confirmed: she did know who it was.

It had been quite a while since she saw her mother. She knew she was a strong woman, one of firm and ever-standing morals, of great character, and perhaps most importantly of great, intense passion. However, she also knew that in order to survive in this life, one must be able to direct both kinds of love to someone – love of offspring, for which they are flesh and blood, which no monster, dictator, or circumstance can take away, and the love of another of the opposite sex, for which no one can ever replace.

She also knew in tandem that her neighbor was an attractive person. After all, in the years both she and Adriana would play together, the two of them would often sit over on Lou's larger porch, in the glider discussing politics, how sweet the kids were, perhaps a little bit of sarcasm requisite for life in general. Alex didn't mind it all that much; he knew that there was no foul in having someone who could compete for your love in the presence of your love; after all, the greatest marriages subsist on that pretty little thing called trust. And Alex trusted Carrie more than any person ever could.

But now, times were changed. Alex was murdered, their only daughter was also dead supposedly, and she spent many days in that home, sitting in its bowels and cathedralistic cavernousness alone, and wondering what to do. Drawing near to her neighbor was of natural instinct for the widowed mother, and slowly, it developed into a long trust. She seemed to take great joy in watching Adriana grow up, and it was some solace for a life that had been lost to circumstance by the system. It was indeed the old widow's life; fading, remembering, and reflecting were now part of the fanfare. Except she was nowhere near as old as she somehow felt.

For a minute, she had to think deeply about what she and the recently abandoning Duluth had mentioned about relationships, and how they both had never experienced ones which were bona-fide true. Duluth was the senior member of the "team", who was probably out making love, or making trouble. It didn't matter. She thought about her mother as she stared off into the distance, trying to realize, to comprehend thoroughly what would make her want to cure her loneliness. It was hard even imagining herself being this alone; surely, Duluth had become sorority to her, but then again, even Duluth knew that she was steps away from being isolated again, and this quantum of having someone was just passing. Thus, she justified it.

Somehow, the feeling was intense, more than usual. Yet then again, it faded away. Those dreams and life were not peculiar to her mother. Even with all the time passed, the blood that ran through her veins ran through Hope's.

And so, it had to be done that things would need to be made right. The thought of her mother being in that house alone had become too strong, too taboo, a bitterness – it had to end finally. Putting on her jeans and a turtleneck sweater, she ran as fast as her feet could carry her towards the chapel yonder. It was of two priorities – the ability to grow up finally and break out of her shell, as she was becoming a young adult. But it was also of the priority to set things right. She could not continue to hide for the rest of her life, afraid of what people could and may do to her. She was trapped in her own body, one that made her seriously reconsider whether the lifetime of decontamination and assisted living was her destiny – and it sure didn't feel like it.

All it took was for the doors to bang wide open, with the white ribbon stretched down the aisle. No words were shared as Carrie and Hope made eye contact for the first time come two rotations 'round the Sun.

And life changed for the different beyond that point.

TWO WEEKS LATER

THE MALOTT RESIDENCE

In her old room, her old bed, Hope woke up at 3 PM that afternoon. She was still reacquiring her old way of life: doing chores, making her bed, going down to eat breakfast, and then packing for school. It was an honestly strange time as she arrived for 9th grade. As she had lived on the fringe for two years, her schooling had to be reaffirmed, and her subjects were lacking, as she had been strained for focus on those days back. Being a 5'8" girl and surrounded by somewhat underdeveloped girls around her, her first days back provided some uniquely esoteric exposition, to say the least. She was often times bullied, called names derogatory to one's intellectual qualities, and especially to her old classmates, now juniors, seen as a relic of failure. Everyone now knew Dari's story, and many did not believe her in the process. Since Dari and Adriana were the only ones adamant that the girl had secret powers, and Adriana confessed nothing under her Dad and new Mom's orders, that left no seconding to the school prep's argument. And Dari had been gone long enough for the pedagogue to abandon her ways, too; surely, the days after and the impending "reign of terror" left no girl without her red lips nor the willingness to spread false word, a seed that no one would ever sow on the stoniest ground.

School wore her down more than anything in the colder months of the Pennsylvania winter. Her appointments for social workers, speech therapy, emotional support, and trying to fire up a brain which had been wasted away for too long and dulled by the repetitive tasks of simple labor made it really hard to concentrate. The girls in her classes were like her when she saw Dari. Now, it was tougher. Dari had moved on to another school, went somewhere that she probably could have been fixed. In that way, Hope was happy.

Yet when Hope would hop on the bus with Adriana, the fact that she would be taking basic math and English, and Adriana was taking AP classes and making friends without the fraternization of Hope in permission kind of put her down. Sure, the girls in 9th grade were friendly – as friendly as a 14 year old teenage hormone-ridden pile of flesh could be. But Hope was more mature, and it was hard to make friends that way. She was the fool now.

The door opened slowly, and Hope slammed down her books, and kicked off her boots, which were covered in a thick layer of snow. Throwing her books down and hanging her coat off, she noticed the house seemed awful quiet. Her red and white beanie hat and snowflake scarf thrown on the couch, Hope pulled back her hair and replaced it in a bun.

At the kitchen table was her mom, rubbing her eyes at a pile of papers. Her face red, she was wiping back tears and clutching at a rosary, trying to fan through the papers. Hope was curious. "What's wrong?"

Carrie said it all in one sentence. "Your stepdad is coming home early today. He's been laid off."

THE NEXT MORNING

The last few hours had been quite the struggle for the recently reunited family. Many tears had been spread over the dinner table: some of uncertainty, some of panic, perhaps a mist of false hope that something good could come out of the matter. Needless to say, they had been thrown into a conundrum of feelings, for which upon they did what many well-to-do folks would: talk to someone.

The therapist was an older lady, mid-stature, lots of eye makeup but no cat eyes, and a perm, and definitely of the functional standard of clinical psychology. She took house orders, and Carrie and Lou felt like they were too ashamed to be seen in a "shrink" office, especially with a really "special" child in tow. Needless to say, she came to the house early in the afternoon.

She heard many stories that day, a lot of venting of anger and frustration, as the first 24 hours of panic began to subside. How they could summon such a degreed person on this short of notice was only left to the mind to decide and the heart to believe in. All those feelings flowed through those rooms in that old house like embers of a wildfire that consumed the dry wit of everyone living inside. But none were bigger than Hope's story.

Hope walked into that room, a den that had been set up in the corner of the house. The therapist took a seat facing the door, and immediately began to poke at her.

"So, you are a 16 year old girl, you've been hiding out with a friend you made at a halfway house for two years. You're in 9th grade, you have no job, no driver's license, no real connections. So how do we fix that?" the doctor asked.

Hope smiled profoundly and with great honor. The echoes of the old house wore her deep. "I don't know, but I have made it this far, Doc." She didn't want to blurt out her condition, for fear she would call for commitment. If only it wasn't for the fact that she already had called the bluff, she probably would have elicited necessary cracking of the shell to get that straight answer. But they couldn't fix her feelings for doing so. She would have to take that risk.

Crossing her legs and fixing her skirt, the doctor began to scribble down notes. "So you have to do something about it. You can't go on and be a 20-year-old senior in high school, plan on getting into college, getting married...."

Hope began to say what she thought. It was quite natural. "I don't plan on going to college. Ever see what happens to them? Loads of debt, can't even tie their shoes, and they get a shit degree and end up being a barista or such. I can do that with my 16-year-old brain."

With another few scribbles, the doc looked at her as if she was an uncircumcised visitor from the First World. "You have to do something with your life, though. Your stepdad is no longer a source of steady income – at least in the short term. You have to finish school. Strong, with honors and good grades. You and Adriana are both the age where you can add money to the bottom line in this house. Like, even if you work washing dishes...." The thick New York accent began to show its true colors when she was angry.

Resisting, the patient in the situation but hardly the subordinate of the discussion fired back. "Look, Doc. I don't wash dishes. I don't wait tables. I don't like the way my stepdad just launched in here and started putting my family through this needless, endless pile of bullshit. Witnessing what I did actually makes me feel like I'm like the outsider....and I have things I can do...."

The doctor laughed. "Well, you must do them. If you care about your father, you will make him proud, Hope. You must do that for your stepdad, also. Despite the fact that you may not always agree with him, you must be strong and make friends. Perhaps you should write notes to

[127]

him." Soon, Hope's thoughts began to resonate with hers, and the points were coming across strongly from the clinician.

Hope began to think of the next smart-ass thing to say. She wanted out of the situation. Thinking of all the decisions and trauma that had come up, the crooked psychologist had enabled her to vent all her inner struggles, as was by design. She knew it wasn't going to help to go and stomp her feet – surely, those who possess Ph.D.'s in mental health would be able to use the fits pitched by a teenager to advocate pharmaceutical disposition – so she gave it some thought.

Then, in a blink, a flash of light overcame her. Her eyes began to glow, and she told the person who had given her inspiration "I think I can talk to my stepdad about it." She called for him down the hall, for which he came. "Good move", the doctor insisted.

He came into the room, and looked into her eyes, which were still glowing. For the first time, stepdad and stepdaughter made eye contact. They had avoided each other for the longest time. Even if it was just two circles 'round the clock, surely they were not on the same page to the candid observer, for they placed money in a third party to get help. Hope craved that help, but she knew she would have to do something special.

Lou turned to the doctor. "Dr. Pauline, I have known Hope since I moved on this block 9 years ago. I have seen her grow up, become a young woman, and show her pride. She has done great things so far, but she must work at it." Turning towards Hope, he reached out an arm, and somewhat awkwardly gave his stepchild an embrace.

Hope began to be afraid. She had perhaps given too much away, but she felt like she had to do something to make Lou look responsible. "Well, I mean, I can work at it, but I have no real talent." She tried to feign a disappointed, helpless face, but she could only get out a smirk.

Pauline was not impressed with either one of them. "You are a smart lady, Miss Hope Malott. You can do anything you put your heart to. Not only do I want you to get job skills and begin earning a paycheck, I want you to begin a diary or journal of your feelings. You can do it in writing, in a private place, wherever. I will be back in one month to check it. We'll get everything you've ever wanted out of your system then."

Without another word, her stepdad nodded, and grabbed Hope with both arms. "Agreed. Plus, hey, look at the time! $400 an hour for this!" He began to want to complain about pennies and hoarding money, but then he said "But it was worth it, Doctor. Thank you kindly," after she began to lower her reading glasses and look with bloodshot eyes at the man.

And so, it was done. Hope did not know what to do, except think of ways she could please him enough to get both the doctor and the mother off her back.

The evening began to set, the twilight of mid-October lending a chill to the air. And it was scary to think what would be next.

In her room, Hope sat on her childhood bed, stretched out in a t-shirt and sweatpants. She knew that Lou was still a stranger to her, and somehow, the lack of blood between them gave some rough passages. He had different ideals, and seemed to have greed as his main premise behind a guise of work ethic and bootstraps. It was the ultimate sign of a liar and a con artist who was ready to pounce on the well-being of a family – and it would manifest itself readily, if only given time.

Lou opened the door. "Hope? I want to talk to you about Dr. Pauline. Just person to person," he calmly digressed, tapping the door behind him with a silent but firm click.

Hope became a skeptic no climate scientist would want sketching doubt in the models of his theses. She felt as if there was imposition to break her cover, the cover that had held so well for those two years she spent in hiding. It was covenant, and covenant felt like ark to her inner Moses.

"Well, I don't really want to talk about it, Lou. I feel like you stood me up in there, thinking I'd be able to go and be ambitious, sir…."

He butted in, defusing haphazardly the situation. "Well, I have something I need to tell you, so have a listening ear. Your mother and I are both trying to scrounge together pennies. I sold the house next door to move in here. It doesn't cover the mortgage or the utilities. We need every bit of help we can get here, Hopie."

Adamantly trying to not become too intimately connected with his moods, she replied "Well, I want to help. I don't hate you, but you are being a total Goddamned jackass about this too, Lou. What do you want me to do, exactly? Sell, like, the flowers out of my room? Make sandwiches for the upper crust in Fishtown?" She began to raise her voice with every word that came out of her mouth.

Then, it came out. Everything was revealed. "Hope, I want you to go and help this family by helping others. You made Adriana healthy when you girls were little. You can do a lot of great stuff with these – "he grabbed at her forearms, for which she pulled back and forcefully grunted, as if she was being controlled by an evil being.

She began to pull back from him, realizing she was being told to break a covenant that no one else had ever asked her to do. It was a violation of her raising to do this – and surely, she thought that the conversations and battles with Dari in middle school had begun to haunt her, all at once like a pack of evil spirits looking for a helpless body to consume their souls. And it hurt inside, a feeling of violation that made words feel like she was falling victim to raping of her gifts, a loss of innocence that was factor of someone who was supposed to love her. She had no time to think or consider.

Lou gave the best to seize the opportunity. "You only have to do it until we can get back on our feet. Just say that it's a mineral derivative, or a vitamin, or something. We make a few bucks off of it, keep food on the table. When it's over, and I get my job back, you can just say it was a side job. I promise nothing will ever be done without your approval." It was a hard deal, and Lou went into it with his head up high and his *huevos* down low.

Immediately, Hope felt the intense force of implied consent to a situation. She began to picture what Dr. Copulus said to her in those scant few days she had spent in the housing with Duluth. She pictured being able to help people, and the fact that she would be able to solve all her problems. She closed her eyes, thinking about her mom crying. How would her Dad feel, looking down from Heaven, and seeing this all occur. *Would he be happy*? She opened her eyes.

"Lou. You know I can't do that. I just went into hiding for two years. Two years!" She stepped up to her stepfather, towering under his iron jaw. "You mean to tell me that you want me to re-open this old, gangrened wound so you can make a whole few bucks with a circus act?" She wanted to hit him – and hit him so hard that it would take all her pain away. She stopped herself somehow from doing it. "I can't believe you! Who in their right mind would want to have that night – the night I feared for my fitching life – all over again!" She folded her arms and looked away, her face as red as a beet.

Something needed to tick with her. Hope looked to the side. There was Adriana, clasping at her dad's arm. Her clothes looked small on her, and it wasn't just a style statement. Her stepsister was indeed saddened, and she only wanted the best for her Dad. It was perhaps the most amorous thing she could do, and Hope just wondered if it was an honest attempt to deceive her into it. But she bit into it.

Hope sighed, fearing for her best friend, who looked very helpless and confused. The aura of Adriana crossed into Hope, and she felt the energy like a great wave of black, immersing her. She began to reason, knowing it was time to be a woman. Taking a risk she never would, the words rolled off her tongue. "I will do this for my Mom. I will do this for my Dad.

[131]

Someday, I may do it for you, Lou. You are family, and we are all in this together. But I am not going to save the world as much as I feel I should save you from yourself." And so it was, the first step in a direction that Frost would melt in.

VII

The Healing

SOLEBURY

And so it must have to be, the story of a girl who could only find herself in the company of others. They were in the car together, heading towards the suburbs, trying to set in stone the path they would take. It was a friend of Lou who was still in the luck of having work. The man was at the end of his rope, and felt ashamed to mention that he had what he believed to be a cancerous lump on his forehead. Under the alibi that he and Hope would just "pay a visit to say hello", they were invited to his house, a reasonably well-to-do one in an affluent suburb. Hope knew this, and wondered exactly as to what the procedure would be to break the news that Hope was no ordinary girl.

The car ride was one showered in the sound of silence. Lou felt ashamed to put Hope through all of this and potentially embarrass, if not lose, a friend. But the primal need for food on the table saved itself for all popular recourse. Hope knew this would be a rough one; her encounters so far with her inner gift had often been haphazard, spontaneous, and somewhat dangerous. Yet she had to help her step-parents and step-sister. And in the confused mind of a teenager lost in herself — and her feelings, mixed, perverted, and otherwise disintegrated, this was the process. And she could only pray that the process could lead to proper procedure – closure with the covenant between her two fathers.

They entered the house, a tall duplex that looked more like a rowhouse to the naked eye. "Hey, Mick. How ya doin'?" Lou asked. Hope stepped out of the car, hiding her hands in her gray hoodie. The man was a fairly young gentleman, average height and definitely not ill looking. Hope saw it as a sign that perhaps she was not being asked to do too much; her idea was to go in, start a conversation, direct it to the lump, cure the ill, petition for the greenbacks, and get the hell out – nothing more. They had been in the car, stuck in traffic on the highway for an hour, and they did not need any more distractions.

Mick welcomed them in. He poured a cup of coffee for each of them; Hope was the only one to not use cream or sugar. She mentioned that "it made the coffee last longer". It was partially true, after all, and she had a tremendous headache regardless, and didn't really have any remedy. Discussion started up, and for the most part, Mick was fairly happy, and the lump didn't seem to be all that nasty, seeming more like a bubbly brown mass, about a nickel coin in width. Hope took great solace in the fact that she had nothing to lose by helping this gentleman. To her, it was her only respite, a type of friendly relief that got her through the moments she knew would make her swallow that black coffee a little easier. Because it sure as hell wasn't her pride. Or so she was convinced.

Immediately, Lou began to fast talk his target. "How have you been in this house? Looks like you've kept it up well." He was dodging the obvious; trying to side track was enough of a feat. It made Hope quiver as she felt the coldness of the room, the bare walls with scarce a picture of black and white around. Being there was not one of her most pleasurable experiences, and she frowned upon it as she sat here.

Mick gathered his sweater. "Buncha commies been lookin' at this house ever since I took off of work. Some healthcare plan they have about this." He began to sip on his drink angrily, his teeth showing through the cup as the burgundy drink swizzled through.

"So, in other words, you want to keep this going? Like those assholes at work are gonna give a shit about you, eh, Mick?" Lou tried to draw humor from the deep and put it right out front. It was an act of almsgiving in a situation which felt as sour as the liquor he had seen on the table.

Immediately, the ill man began to laugh. "Don't even begin wit' me, Louie. I know I can handle it. Goddamned cancer won't beat this old chap." He grabbed a glass and began to pour what appeared to be a glass flask of hard liquor. As the cork popped, a waft of ethanol emanated through the room.

Sensing the opportunity, Lou grabbed a glass and began to anticipate a toast. "Well, Mick, here's to that. Let's toast." And so Mick poured a drink to his old friend, and they both giggled. He turned to Hope, and laughed. "Here, lil' rosie. Ain't too young to imbibe, ain't too proud to beg, eh?" He raised the glass, and his right eyebrow raised in salutation.

Hope began to glare, and couldn't believe what she was being told. Her bounds were beginning to be stretched enormously, and she wondered if the deal was ever going to be completed. Lou just looked at her like a millionaire in front of a pile of gold, just waiting to touch the riches. *Imbibe, drink, Hopie*, she saw in her stepdad's vision. *You have to do it for me.*

Reaching down in a moment of lapsed frontal lobe, she downed the shot. Many of the pains she had felt up to that point were discreetly harmful and obtuse, but the hard liquor stung worse than anything Duluth or Copulus could ever bring to her. Her eyes began to mist, enough to fog them over for just a few moments. Yet that drink, the aqua vitae of the Celts, was not long enough for her to ignore Lou beginning to grease the sale again.

And so, the drinks began to pile up. Lou and Mick were mediating each other, gathered around the dimly lit room, the console TV glaring behind

[135]

them in fine tune. Hope saw her stepdad beginning to slip away into the cusp of indecision. But Mick was just about the most affected; Hope thought fondly of the backwash syndrome, the essential part of copious drinking. She couldn't figure out where she learned it from, but yet it stuck. Too many mornings of those past two years, she had watched Duluth seemingly pour it, always with the quote "Lord, am I drunk!" as she and Josh would do it. And she'd sit there, just in awe. And that red-haired girl who would always party with them....then she disappeared. Oops.

A round of music had passed on the TV. Mick began to become tipsy, laughing out loud and increasingly becoming incoherent and unintelligible. Lou was apt to seize his opportunity, and moved the relationship along to conclusion.

The feeling of drink on Hope's thin body began to wear on her. She felt as if she had to get something out. Somehow, the bitter taste began to knock sense into her. She felt the urge of fear come into her. "Lou? Come with me. Now." She grabbed her somewhat illusionary stepdad.

With a giggle by Mick, Lou pointed to his daughter. She pulled desperately at his arm.

They went to a side hallway off to the side of the living room. Hope looked disgusted. "You never considered telling me, like, that you would do this. Don't 'cha think perhaps that this is a little bit too much? I mean, you're getting a guy with cancer drunk off his ass, Lou." She pouted and began to put her hand on her hip.

There was a quick pause, but Lou, even in his stupor, began to form his words. "I'm only doing it this once. Let it go, hun! We'll be in and out really quick. I get him drunk, you do your gadgetry and whatnot, he pays, we're out." He smiled and grabbed Hope by both shoulders, and gave a quick shake.

Becoming defensive, Hope cringed at the man who was supposed to be her leader. Lou's words, "gadgetry, magic show" stung harder than ever on her.

He, like, doesn't even have a full grasp of what I'm doing, she reasoned. Valiantly, she shook loose of his grasp. "Don't do this to me, Lou. This is stupid. Can't we just give the man some peace? I mean, maybe pay his doctor bills with the money you made from selling the house. I mean, come on."

The words bounced off of Lou like a waterproof membrane. "I got him drunk. You are here. Do this, or else. I promise I'll never repeat it. Ever again." He gave a wink and grasped her arm in a guardianship that felt all too much to Hope – by blood or by her gift – that it was a lie. She couldn't judge for it, though. Lou was too confused in his thoughts. And she needed an escape.

Sensing the end of the movement, the girl began to quiver. "OK, OK, I'll do it. Once." She walked in.

Lou piped up in temporal appropriateness. "So, Mick, I have a question for you. How's your recovery coming along?" He smiled, took a sip of the coffee, looking up towards him. It was one of the most awkward moments one could have; he couldn't outwardly say "cancer" or even "melanoma" without drawing harsh criticisms for reminding what kind of curse Mick was under. But then again, Lou made his living being blunt and to the point. It was befitting to have the case complete and the topic at hand made.

Mick smiled, and then sighed, as if to prepare himself for a bad statement. "Well, Lou, right now, they are trying to see if they can stop the growth. According to the doctors, they say no spread or metastasizing yet, although I'm going for an MRI next week." He looked disappointed.

Immediately, Hope began to fear what she would do. The ills she had fixed up to this point were minor – cuts to herself, breathing in and presumably sharing a gasp of air, which was filled with disease fighting T cells and immune cells. Never had she been put on the spot for this. Her mind began to race, thinking of a way to bail out. *What should I say to him about this*, she wondered. *What if I can't handle it?* She sighed out loud, too.

Immediately, Mick saw this, and understood it as perhaps implicit empathy. "What's botherin' you about it, young lady?" he asked. "Seems like you're in good health and all. Unlike me." He gave a discontent smile.

Hope looked for the right words to say. Her brain began to seek compromise, as if her words had to mean well. "I....I think that it's all relative, and all. I mean, you have to look on the bright side. You're happy, you have an awesome house and good friends....something not everyone has." She smiled.

Impressed, Mick began to open up like a storybook. "You know, money can't buy you that, sweetie. Money can't buy ya health, or friends, or a good life. Y'gotta realize that 'n all. I'd pay anything to go back and not be shitty to a lot of people in my life." He got up, and curled his hand, and said "Get up here." So Hope did, and he grabbed her hand. "You just remember this, Hope, my dear. Your dad is a good friend, and a good man. He would do anything for me, and I would do anything for him." He rubbed her hand.

Hope began to realize that this man either was flirting with her, or he was just a really kind-hearted, great person of superior character. As he held her hand, she suddenly felt the urge to do something about it. According to her morals, this man deserved her powers, and the full benefits. And Lou was just watching it, enjoying every last minute. "Hang on a second," she said. "Look me straight in the eye." She pinched her eyes shut, and stuck her hands on his forehead.

Dumbfounded, but nevertheless faithful, Mick got caught up in the moment. "What will you do, Hope, m'dear," he asked her. As she opened her eyes, the glow of her gift lit up the whole room. Her eyes first emanated greenish-blue beams of laserlike illumination, and her hands began to glow. She started to rub his forehead, her left thumb on the scar of the tumor on the skin. Mick stood still, paralyzed by what was happening in front of him. In that moment, she had felt so tense that she broke a sweat. And that sweat carried little parts of her. She didn't know what it was that was in it, but she placed her faith in performing the trick, whatever it was, and being content with it. She figured it was worth a shot.

The sparkles went through the air, falling like the dust of freshly falling snow behind a haloed Sun high in the sky. Lou had witnessed it for the first time, and it was addicting to him. Like no other point in time, he stood there, greedily counting his dollars as Hope worked the magic. She was completely on her own, and it was only a process that she needed to complete. And was she ever.

With a blink of an eye, the grains of sand floating through the air disintegrating, all of a sudden, it was over. The blue light faded to reds, then a purple. She reached for the cancer cells, and rubbed the forehead gently. The scab fell off, peeling with friction to the ground.

Stunned, Hope sat on the loveseat, collapsing and breathing heavily. But she had done her trick.

Mick smiled, and knew exactly what happened. "Thank you, Hope," he said. "You truly are a friend...because money can't buy that." And so it was, the first time she had realized her powers. He looked in the mirror, and saw his skin, which was glowing in a pale light. The marked signs of aging had disappeared in slight, but what was noticeable was that he felt refreshed and jovial; Hope had literally taken the angst of cancer out of her. The rest of his body was still under the ruse and consent of the disease, but streaks of light came from where she had grabbed. It made him give a weak smile, and he rubbed his face, the scabs, the dry skin, and the wrinkles. It was a moment where even he could not believe despite what the doctors had preached - that Hope had done this.

Mick was in a sudden euphoria. "What can I do to help? I've been fighting this….fighting it for years." Hope shook her head, but knew she would have hell to pay if she didn't take something.

Lou stepped in. "Can you buy us dinner for the week?" He laughed, and Mick obliged. Over a fried steak and potatoes dinner, the first deal for Hope had been completed. It would be the greatest form of modesty in her acts in the coming future.

The meal was sufficiently filling, as they sat around a dinner table that was too small. Mick kept a small lamp nearby, bills piling up like stacks of thin white confessions that he was indeed vulnerable. Hope just laughed as the Irishman would pour whisky on his meat, whisky on his soup, and starches, and a big shot of (surprise) tequila in his Coke – it was ridiculous.

Soon, it was time to make trails, and head on their way. Mick seemed a little drunk at the time, but his effervescent smile was satiation enough for the two of them. They both got in the car. Hope set her head back in the seat, trying to recoup her energy. She could feel her body fighting illness of some sort; her immune system had sent its best cells to her fingertips to complete the action on Mick, and she knew the recovery would take a while, but she didn't know how long. Slamming the door, she closed her eyes.

Not to be outdone, Lou jubilantly praised "You know, what you did was the right thing, Hope. You shouldn't hold that back – it's a gift." He kissed her on the cheek, an affirmation of a good dead.

But yet, Hope knew something was wrong. Sure, she had earned her money, although it was for one good minute. It did mean about a couple hundred bucks in food, but somehow, she felt empty inside, like one who fantasizes about their love, goes out and tries to fulfill it, but yet vicariously prospers under false pretense. It made her feel sad. "You know, we shouldn't charge for this. It's soooooo wrong, Lou. Really, it is." She refused to even turn her head, much less make eye contact with her stepdad.

Lou felt his guilt trip come in, too. He wanted to say what he thought, but his conscience put last veto on his words. "Well, think of it this way, Hopie. You did a service for someone, and you were paid. It's, like, doing business. You're earning a wage for a skill. And you should do that!" He grabbed her left forearm and shook it, as in an "attaboy" manner.

His stepkid had no part of it. Swallowing a lump in her throat, she said "Let me stomach it for a little bit. I need a rest, anyways." And so, they drove away, one mission completed.

As she rode home in the car, Hope stared outside at the city lights. The streetlights shone like little orbs of fire, the neon lights like a colorful streak of fire from long exposure film. Her eyes misted as she felt pain in herself. It was hopeful in the end; she felt like she had accomplished something, but it was an unfulfilling feeling, one that didn't satisfy her hunger for the meaning of it all.

And yet it had to change for the better. Soon enough, it would.

VERDE VEGGIE SUPERMARKET

It was shopping time for the family, and what little money they still had left was surely going to the food they would need. Lou put on one of his fleece vests over a dress shirt, while Hope kept moderate with a pair of jeans and a knit turtleneck sweater and moccasins. It was quite a prep show, but it was surely a veiled attempt at looking somewhat not broke and in trouble. The style was out, but it was quite a change from the underdressed bum look that Hope had made part of her character the past few years. It almost reminded her of the girls who would crowd in wearing ugly socks and yoga pants with their Sperrys just to kind of keep the guys off of them. But then again, she did it also in the realization that people would have to see her as beautiful, no matter what she projected.

They were picking out frozen goods last, like Carrie had recommended, so "they didn't spoil", as she would say in her thick accent. They really didn't need that much food, but they were four of the same pack, and despite the womanly approach of the majority, they still decided to pig out from home cooking rather than indulge in the famous cheesesteak of their hometown's namesake. That was for the folks from Jersey, Carrie would often explain during Hope's youth. And Lou was only the more of a scrooge (although he would sneak them in from work occasionally).

As they were pulling out the last bag of peas, a tap on the shoulder came from behind. "Hope? Is that you? Omagahhhh!!!" came a cute, squinted, tense voice. She recognized the voice as one of her friends.

The girl was dressed up for what appeared to be a date with a rap star. Hoodie strings hanging and baggy pants hanging, it was someone who she had gone to school with. "Kate Meroud. How are you doing?" she asked innocently. "Here, come here! Give me a hug!" She recognized her, and decided it was safe.

[142]

The story between Kate and Hope was extensive. Good friends for some time, they were classmates for almost every year between first and 7th grade. There were many times the two of them would sit on Kate's bed in her room, do their nails, watch some prime-time drama, and fantasize about teen stars. The time away had seemed to do some damage to her style; she had always been a child of very feminist culture and temper. Now, her hair was shorter, combed to the side, straight black, and a piercing hung from both her nose and lip. She took great pleasure in being trashed. Somewhat of a transformation, but yet not unexpected, there was a weak smile for Kate.

Hope was stunned, but nevertheless happy to see her. "How have you been, Kate? Can't believe you are still….well…." she scanned her friend's attire, trying not to feed impulse and call her something she would regret later, "a very good person and you have great fashion sense." She took a sigh.

Kate was unfazed, relieved to see her old friend. "Ah, don't worry about this." She tugged at the pockets on the knees of the cargo khakis. "This is a get-up to keep guys away. Look like a dyke, choose who you like." She gave a wink.

In a state of shock, her turtleneck-donning friend went for words. Playing with her shoe, she said "Well, I mean, I can't believe that you would still remember me! I mean, it's been like, a rough couple of years." She giggled. The awkwardness of the moment lent itself neither a measure of submission nor a sense of relief. Lou stood over the freezer a first down away, combing over the peas. Hope felt glad that he was too busy feeding his vegetable fetish from hunger to see what was going on.

"Well, Hope, I gotta admit, you do look rough. Hair all messed up, you got a sweater that looks like it's from 2002, and you're kind of messed up. But I still love ya, dear." She gave her a very tight hug which had a flair for not being so much one of friendship. In the exhalation, she took a deep breath, and inhaled, only to smell what amounted to a healthy waft of

Nautica Men's cologne. Grasping back, she patted Kate on the back, and wondered in the deepest and most sacred temple of her mind, *What is it about me that turns women on? Geesh, I must be like a man in this. Although what kind of man would wear this small of a sweater? And my boobs....*"

Immediately, Hope's dad made eye contact with Kate, which made her disengage the hug with some look of disgust. "That was sooooo good," Kate laughed. "Here, you have a profile? Take a picture so I can post it to my friends. Can't believe Hope Malott is here. You just started school back, too! Oh my God...."

And so, they began to take a picture. Smashing their heads together, they began fulfilling the prophecy of online social networking. All was well, and then, it was over.

Holding the camera up, Hope grimaced. "Hang on, Kate. Gotta sneeze." With a wave from her long lost friend, she turned around and began to raise her arm to obviously block what was going to come out. It all seemed to go in slow motion, those few seconds. As it came on, Hope prepared, as many would whom anticipated the cleansing of nasal passages through reflex. Forgetting to turn off the camera, Kate inadvertently left the high-definition lens pointed towards Hope.

The sneeze came out, and the droplets came out like a shower of glitter. Except instead of the natural light of the fluorescent industrial lighting typical of Pennsylvania supermarkets of age, this lit up the entire store. Like a small show of fireworks, the sparkles of cobalt emanated into the air like a tremendous celebration of independence. As the drops vaporized, a man carrying a handful of cans walked into the suspended droplets. When they hit his face, he squinted, but couldn't protect himself from the drops hitting him with vigor. It was like he flew into a sea of tracer fire in the battle between Kate and Hope, and unlike tracer fire, the shrapnel hit like bullets.

[144]

Lou saw the whole thing. His jaw dropped, and he took a sigh as the man with the cans, now blinded by the light, collapsed to the ground. The secret was no more, and it was about to be the Hiroshima of Hope's short venture in life. They had seen the explosion, and it was no longer the covenant on the mountain: untouchable, sacred, privy. It was now a public affair.

Kate froze. Her camera still rolling, she dropped her phone to the ground, it bouncing off the linoleum floor. "What….the….hell was that? You eating nail polish?" She was stunned, perhaps even more than the other persons who witnessed it. Already, some of the employees of the market were turned around, hearing the cans hit the ground and splatter. The floor beneath Hope's feet were interspersed with an elixir of beans, chicken soup, and what appeared to be a sea of shiny sparkles, effervescing and going through stages of pulsing. It was her first public showing of her bodily fluids, all interspersed with the effects of C402.

Without being able to handle it, Hope tried to eke out proper English to fulfill what was too great a need to satisfy her friend. "It was a sneeze. But I can explain. I….I have a cold, Kate. I'm sorry." It was pretty much the wrong words to say, insufficient and unacceptable for what happened.

She picked up her phone. "Now I know why you were out of school. You're a pica girl. You probably eat department store lipstick." Walking towards Lou, she laughed.

There was no mistaking of the consequences, and there was no way out of what she did. The damage began to add up in front of them. Videotape, even if it was in the form of a microchip, was the damning burden of proof that would do that damage. Even if she didn't know it was on tape, but the explanation of a girl who had disappeared from school suddenly for two years, only to reemerge, was something the gossip circuit was due and willing to handle. "Look, Katie. It's not what it seems. I just have a problem. Please, pleasepleasepleaseplease don't tell anyone. I have been out of school. I have an issue." Hope realized very little of the social impact; normally, her father would have taught her this, that tact always worked. Yet she was confused; these past years began to wear away at her father's rhetoric, like it had been forgotten over the course of a few years. And now, she lost that last vestige of her father's words, that the gift was special.

Unsatisfied, and in jest and total sarcasm, Kate laughed, and said "Don't like worry. I won't tell a soul. But you better go get the security cameras and eat the tape, too." And she began to quickly shuffle away.

Immediately, Hope began to tear up. She knew now that her special conditions were in the circuit of discussion. She looked at Lou, who gave an unsure look. Leaving the guy who had fallen to the floor, now seeing perfectly and not needing the glasses, Hope began to run to the restroom. And Lou broke gender and ran off, too.

The man on the floor looked at the ceiling, and said "I can see. Fresh, and perfecto. It's a miracle!" He got up, and threw his glasses on the floor. Picking up a dented can, and holding it to his slightly crossed eyes, he began to read the can out loud.

Beans, purified water, pork product, brown sugar, red 8, blue 4. Oh, my God, who was that?

And he was fitted with happiness. Immediately, a manager ran past Lou and Hope, and fearing a lawsuit, walked up to the man. "Sir, are you OK? Did you take a spill?" He reached to the man, who was on one knee after reading the cans.

The man smiled. "Yes, yes," he said with a nod. "But I'm alright. I think I'm good." He got off his knee and stood erect. "Perhaps God sends people my way. My crooked eyes needed that." He gave a laugh. Never had he expected having his wife sending him out for what she had forgotten would mean some random girl would play Jesus. Or at least one of those preachers you would see at 4 AM when he was up drinking. *Yea, those were just jokes*, he thought. *Better give to them this Sunday. No, perhaps to this supermarket. The worship of consumption.*

How seeing one clearly could cloud the mind. And how this would cloud the mind of that which had offered this opportunity to see.

In half a sigh of relief, and half a sigh of reluctant surprise, the manager nodded. "Sure. So you aren't going to need a lawyer, or a towel, or a new pair of shoes?" The manager in a tie and button down shirt and slacks began to shuffle the towel up and down the man anxiously. "Surely, you're going to want something for us. You have perishable goods all over you! I mean, you have a pile of beans in your crack, and if you go home, your wife will think you shit yourself...I mean, sorry, I shouldn't say that, perhaps you are incontinent or something....but I mean, no man should have to do that..." The manager, an older guy, feared the 88 million unemployed would be bearing down on him from below.

The man nodded with each statement. "Sure."

In a flash, the nervous manager calmed down. "I guess I should shut up now. Here –" he pulled out a half-used receipt, one he had picked up off the ground – "if you want a change of clothes or anything, call the store. We will buy you a fresh suit. With gas and charge card fees. And $30 for your time." The man nodded, and the manager scurried off, to his next cranky coupon customer.

LATER THAT NIGHT

COPULUS RESIDENCE

A lonely man, sovereign of his abode, began clomping down the stairs of his somewhat voluminous house. The woman of his dreams took the first taxi to the DelMarVa, as far away as she could get. The heater clicked on, offering some token warmth in an area which seemed to feel cold.

He tied his robe and sat down on his couch. The TV was blaring incoherently, the syndicated content offering cheap entertainment of shoddy illustration and even shoddier salesmanship. His glasses bridging his nose, he put up the recliner on the sofa.

A million things went through his mind, but none could justify what was about to happen. A knock on the door awoke the physician from his stupor; in a fit of somewhat unpredictability, he began to walk to the sound. Rubbing his eyes, he answered.

A man in a suit pulled a cigarette out of his mouth. "Dr. Copulus? Agent Mellanby. We need to talk to you." He flicked the stump onto the doctor's porch.

Sensing impending doom, he smiled. "Sorry, sirs, I'm tired. Potentially perhaps in the morning, we can talk," and with a smile, he began to shut the door.

The agent stuck his hand and pushed back. "Doctor, you don't want to do that." And immediately, the door sprung open, and Copulus was knocked down off his stance. He immediately was surrounded by large men, all wearing black tee-shirts and coats. They surrounded him, and said "Don't get up." His glasses had fallen beneath him, and his gray hair and dark skin had been contrasted with the whites of his eyes boldly shining in the twilight.

They went to the TV. "You watch this, you asshole shrink," Mellanby yelled. The report came in through the air, with the sound blaring through the echoing hallways like the banshee upon midnight.

MALOTT RESIDENCE

The fear of the unknown finally crept in after Hope had shuttered herself in her room. She felt as if she had finally broken free of her bondage to a secret kept too long. Her Dad would have told her to be a strong woman, and ford through struggles like she always did. And somewhere from Heaven, he was looking over her, and praising her in the like. But she felt afraid: afraid of what kids would do to her. Afraid of seeing the sparkles of her body become flares in the ice of the night, and whether or not she could keep the promise that she and Duluth had kept to never become specialties or omniscients just because they had a twinkle in their eyes that wasn't necessarily the one a woman could be proud of.

All of that had to be kicked to the side, though, as Hope turned on the television. The evening news turned on, repeating from a prior newscast. On it, the famous theme played, and the story came on after the close move was up.

"In Berks County, a man who was shopping reportedly was assaulted at a Verde Veggie Supermarket by a young girl earlier today, however with unintended consequences. The man, 48-year-old Terry O'David, was walking down the aisle when 16-year-old Hope Malott of West Philadelphia reportedly sneezed on him. O'David fell to the ground and then, found that the trauma that had occurred had suddenly repaired an astigmatism.

'Well, I was covered in beans, and pork, and corn, and uncooked carrots in chicken stew. When she sneezed, it was like she had fireflies, or something, stuck in her nose. It made the whole floor light up. It went in my eyes, and I blinked, and I hit my head. But I woke up, saw stars, and then, I could see without my glasses! It was a miracle!'

16 year old Kate Meroud, a former classmate of Malott's, witnessed the entire encounter as she had her phone going.

(Kate) 'You can see here that she has been out of the loop, wearing that old sweater from when my 27-year-old sister was in high school. But yea, it was scary, and that poor guy fell and almost, like, made a mess of his brains on the floor. No poor friend of mine would clean that up….and yea, Hope ran away, she was scared.'

Authorities are still looking for Malott at this time. According to Channel 6 News, Malott had recently escaped from a home for teens, but was released from charges after the physician on staff had forged documents.

If you know the location of Hope Malott, please call Philadelphia Police at (370) 555-5261. Live on Channel 6, Sherri Mewe."

She quickly turned off the television. In all the thoughts that went through her head, this was the one point she had feared would happen if she wasn't careful. And now, her preparation time was over. She expected it to be a school occurrence, and nothing more. Teenagers make gossip disposable and replaceable; it was only a matter of time before it passed. But, the catharsis began to set in; she felt damned to say anything. She just stared at the blank TV screen, clutching at the plush crab that she had won on the Ocean City Boardwalk at the squirt gun game some years ago on vacation. It finally stopped her brain from racing about two minutes later. She felt nothing but the chair she sat on, the light from the lamp on the bookcase that went to her loft, where she could hide for just a moment. She could only picture Duluth standing there, watching the news anchor, and feeling just as helpless as her. She could see her eyes glowing into the night. Her tears dripped like sundew onto the ground, melting away at the carpet. Her hair laid down in a comb, it felt like she could not take it anymore.

The word on the street was that Hope Malott passed away long ago. And for the most part, she took solace in that, the hiding alibi that gave her cover. With the report broadcast, however, her image came alive instantly. And that was the point in which she wished she was dead.

It was never the publicity that scared her as she sat in front of the glowing TV, contemplating absolutely nothing at this point. Rather, she felt obliged to have to come up with some cheapskate excuse as to why this happened. She began to paint different images within her lexicon of verbiage: the guy was a nut case, Kate a closet lesbian trying to enact revenge on an old love, the fact that the red turtleneck sweater she wore had some sort of laundry detergent with a surfactant that glowed in the darkness....the thoughts streamed through her head like a rushing river.

A knock came on the door. Not a word was said to answer it. Another round of knocks followed...this time, more noticeable and forceful. She didn't answer it, staring blankly at the screen, fireflies in the window.

The door clicked, the lock disengaged. It was Adriana, looking to speak to her sister and best friend. Opening the door, she saw a phased out girl, her legs crossed, staring at the screen. "Hey, sis. I just am coming in to ask you a question. You know, just something that's like, ticklin' my pickle." She came around front. Hope turned her head slowly.

The magic had gone from her eyes. "It's over, Adriana. Completely. I sneezed and blew away any hope for me to have a normal life." Her face pale, she looked towards to the window, most likely wanting divine intervention.

Taking a knee next to the chair, Adriana gave an embrace. She had been embittered from before, remembering what she had seen. But she had a different story, one that had been hiding away from her stepsister for a good amount of time. "Look, Hope, I know you think I'm upset with you. But I learned something." She stepped in front of Hope, grabbing both arms and looking Hope dead in the eye, taking a slightly lower profile and off to the right, as if she was looking up to her stepsister. Hope froze, her face pale.

"When Dari did that to you, I was afraid you had done something very criminal, and I couldn't believe that you were so, well, so evil. Two days later, Dari came back to school, and she had her friends in the clique around her. I was within earshot of them, and as she was pulling her sparkly black pumps – cheap department store ones, eight dollars apiece, they still had the sticker on them – she told me how she wanted to get you back. So she called her Dad, and Dad called the police. Or something Called some jerks because she was trashed. They were pricks to her and wrestled her around, made some advances, who knows. But she was laughing at you – and I felt bad. Bad for a friend.

"I went to her and felt the power to say something. And she brushed me aside, saying I was at fault because I didn't stop you from getting her totally in a hot mess. I told her she needed to stop taking those pills all the time. She didn't know I knew she was overdosing on bottles of Xanax every day. Made her drunk – not you. But she didn't know you weren't at fault. Just a reaction. Our Mom told us.

"They came knocking on your door because of her. Not me. But my Dad-" she began to look away – "my Dad married your Mom because you do have something special. But you shouldn't let those two jerks prohibit you from making a difference in this world, Hopie. You have to be the judge of whether or not you want to be a hero – or just be, like, the mayonnaise on a really good brisket sandwich. There for added effect."

Hope smiled. "So you are in this with me? You don't, like, think I'm a weirdo?" She gave a look of conceited regret, but yet, an overwhelmingly concise relief swept over her face.

Adriana gave a smile back, and said "We are in together. Remember this?" She smacked the back of Hope's hand twice, then the front twice, and Hope joined in in the secret handshake, in getting the fingertips together, and then said "Yea, man," in the most Rastafarian way. They gave a hug to each other, and it was made for good.

COPULUS RESIDENCE

"Please let this end, Mr. Mellanby," the doctor wept openly. "I should have never gotten involved with those two ladies in the first place," his thick accent cut through the night. "If I could catch her…" he cried.

The somewhat sternly obligating agent looked him dead in the eye, his brown eyes and jet black hair casting a shadowy stance. "It was your insolence and your irresponsible behavior that got you into this problem. Why the hell do you have to bone every single woman that ever comes through those halls?" He tucked his arms behind him and began to pace about the room, and directed anger, a tough cathartic front that had been called upon by his superiors.

Stung with knowledge, Copulus laughed. "Blame it on anything, the wife, the kid, the fact that she climbed all over me. Stupid zinc pill and oysters…" he shrugged.

Rigby pottymouthed back "You are just full of hormones, eh, Coppie? Those genitalia got brains of they own, don't they, sweetheart?" He walked up to him. "You just couldn't keep a handle on two miniscule girls, and now they got you on the hook, don't they?" He laughed.

The tides had turned for him. His unfaithfulness had gotten the best of him, and now he was paying the price. "But gentlemen, shouldn't you be focusing on trying to earn them back? I mean, look, the cat is out of the bag. Why not shoot the two girls?" Logic was there for the taking.

"Well, what do you think, ol' papa Bhat, we kill a miracle? We already killed the Dad, and it was all over the news." Mellanby grabbed the doctor's cheeks. "We tried that shit already. Nobody's going to believe us if we do it again." He grabbed the doctor, and said "You seem pretty numb to what's going on. Your balls are so sensitive that you need to feed them. So you want them fixed?"

[154]

Copulus said "Certainly I could definitely do for a little self-pleasure –" he giggled, but the agents never went to buy into it.

With a nod, a man in the back pushed Copulus down. Yanking his pants, the man pulled down the underwear, and grabbed a syringe. "You got caught with your jimmies in another woman, now you're going to pay. Consider this a gift – your final one – from your friends in the federal government of the United States of America and the Commonwealth of Pennsylvania." With that, the large man with the syringe shoved the needle into the place where no man should ever receive a sharp object. "You needed to lose the feeling down there. It's gotten you in a lot of trouble. Sayonara to ol' Winkie Monster." And with a groan, Copulus felt his privates go numb.

"Good," Mellaby replied. And then with three blows, he made sure the doctor would never let his sex life get the best of him.

"Let freedom ring."

12 HOURS LATER

The two sisters, not of the same blood, but of the same kindred and valiant spirit, both fell asleep in Hope's room, the bigger of the two. Adriana found herself highly defensive of her friend so true, and so much that she camped out on the couch by the window. The flickering light of the raised ceiling, an incandescent clear bulb which was obviously placed in by Abraham to light his shop to convince Abel to go to the Almighty for all good, was there.

Hope heard a banging outside, presumably one of the neighbors. Rubbing her eyes, she looked through the curtains. Seeing a pack of news trucks, with several of those foresaid neighbors all outside, arms folded in their robes, staring towards the house. Police had gathered around the periphery, but none of them looked anywhere nearly as intrusive as the tactically adept men who had killed Alex some time ago. Remembering that she had tuned in before, she turned on the television.

On the screen was Lou Mendoza, her stepdad. Microphones gathered in a pack, he was answering questions. He looked like a man committed, convicted, sure to get his message across. Like a salesman, he was providing his spiel, and talking like he was a policeman in the hunt for a serial sniper.

Hope saw the spectacle, and felt the shock of a lifetime run through her like fire in the dryness of the heated winter ventilation. "What the hell is he doing out there?" She ran up to the window, and looked down the slope of the roof. The only person she had of family in her life all the time was embarrassing himself publicly, and she, in her ultimate device, sprung into protectiveness. It literally was paining her from all sides to let him do this.

Wise to her dad's antics, Adriana went to resolve the situation. "Here, let me talk to him. He's my Dad, he'll listen to me!" She began to go for the door, barely able to walk down the hall in her pajamas and bare feet.

Adriana tried to solve it in the most simple way possible, helping out her sister the best she could. Hope saw the look in Lou's eyes, and saw it different. She knew that she got herself into this situation, and only she would be able to solve it. "This is my problem. Let me go down. They want me, Adriana. And only me." She put on her slippers and walked calmly and tactfully down the stairs.

She threw open the door, and raised her arms. Immediately, the crowd silenced, and the cameras were on her. It was like a police sting, guns of camera drawn and law enforcement of the mainstream media commanding her. "I'm here. I'm here, you guys. Like, what do you want? You have Hope Malott." She rubbed her eyes and immediately, the flash bulbs went off.

They began to work their way up. Lou found himself instantly swallowed into the flock of reporters and sight-seers, all anxious to analyze this new Hope Malott creature that they had now made public.

Immediately, the questions were asked that were appropriate. "Why did you flee after you hurt the man?"

"What did you eat this morning?"

"How did you make your nose glow? Was it the food?"

Hope began to answer the questions, stuttering in the limelight. But then, Lou stepped in between, wedging himself in the small gap between the bevy of microphones and Hope's tiny, thin body, and rubbed her black hair lovingly, gaining a grimace to the toddling teenager. "The services of Hope Malott are for private use only. But they will be provided for a small fee."

Instantly, Hope felt threatened and surprised at her dad's brazen attitude. She opened her mouth and frowned, gawking in disbelief. "Small fee?" she asked him, turning towards him in disbelief and pulling tightly at his arm.

Knowing shortly that her stepdaughter would slap her shortly, he said "Yes." He pushed Hope back, and looked directly into the cameras' eye. "$50,000 for a cure. No negotiations or price reductions. Effective immediately."

Hope ran inside, never so upset in her life. She wanted to hide, feeling betrayed beyond belief. Of course, this was something she wanted to do – help people. However, she did not expect it to be for such exploitation and pure greed. Indeed, she was witnessing a modern-day Scrooge take over her life. It was defying.

As she walked into the kitchen, her mom was stirring a pot of potatoes. Nervous as ever, she was facing away from her daughter at the sink, looking outside, and mumbling under her breath. Hope stood in the doorway, staring for a moment.

"Why I have to do this...every time.....I can't make an honest buck...an honest decision....an honest night in the bed....bad men.....God damn it!" She slammed the whisk down, the plastic shattering on the ground. The pressures of money and fame from both sides were slowly eating away at her mother. It wore on her usual free spirit like no other thing than she had ever seen. Alex usually would comfort her, and tell her it was OK. It helped her be proper and stoic, and she liked being that, especially on those days when she would be called to fancy parties. But this time, there was no stopping her. Her new husband did not give a damn about sensitive topics, or ethics, or putting thoughtfulness and peace into matters. Carrie had no choice. She needed the money more than the fame. But Hope knew the only way to go forth was to come clean – and she would.

Stepping outside, she went and returned the push on her dad. "Ladies and gentlemen, who can I help?"

Immediately, there was pressure on those who were listening in the crowd. Pressure in the folks who viewed that girl, that miracle, across the broadcast waves in the Delaware Valley. Somehow, the ideas of there actually being a person who could heal, someone who could take your pain away, were just too asinine and superfluous to the soul. It was not someone from Heaven that they sought; rather, it was someone who could make them forget. And so, there were doubters; and indeed, they were there. But then again, for every few people out there who were trying to not believe, someone out there was just desperate enough to relent to actually try this damn thing.

And as they went to bed that night, it was only a pair of desperate sunrises away.

TWO DAYS LATER

ROSENTHAL CARE HOME, HARRISBURG, PA

1:31 PM

The first of what she thought would be many obligations to use her powers in the way she had never thought would attend to was waiting inside the doors to a nursing home, about 125 miles west of the Malott residence. It was the first request they received; an older woman with dementia had a son and daughter-in-law who requested Hope's presence. Wiring the money to an escrow account in her stepdad's name, the car was started as soon as the funds deposited into the account. It was a long trip down the Turnpike to the capital city in PA; neither Hope nor Lou knew what the situation would bring.

Picking up an as-you-go smartphone from the cupholder of the car, as they were afraid a public number would result in what could be described as "security issues", they stepped out of the car. Presumably, the son and daughter were well-to-do; they had no objection to a quick depositing of the funds, taking less than 72 hours to round up five figures.

The sliding doors opened to the main hall. Lou put his arm around his stepdaughter, inviting her in. The smell of ammonia stung Hope like no other feeling experienced prior. Her mom had used it for years on the weekends while cleaning the kitchen, but something about the presence of so many ill people, those who were fading into the sunsets of their lives, the groans of the invalid, the plurality of vitality seemingly in slow motion as the brains and body parts showed mutual admiration of their imminent demise.

The nurse sat behind the counter. Hope looked around, perhaps in a bit of awe. Looking at them as being a pack of swindlers, the faces of the usually stoic personnel frowned, but nevertheless went through with the matter. "You Hope Malott?" Both gave a nod. "Room 1107. Rosemarie Benner." And so, the attendant went down the hall with them, inviting the two of them in the room. Taking a final jab at them, the nurse slapped Hope on the shoulder. "Don't kill the old lady. We have to have a paycheck in the morning, and already, the Health Department is on our ass." Hope gave a nod nervously.

The door opened. Gathered around the bed was a man, roughly about 40 years old, and a younger lady, about 30, presumably his wife. "Hope. You are here, dear. You have been prophesized by God to be here. Thank you." He stepped up and gave a hug to Hope, shedding tears almost immediately. In between sobs, he said "I hope you can help Mom. She is fading quickly."

For that moment, Hope did not know what to feel. It was awkward to be in this situation, especially because she felt nothing but regret for what she was about to do. She tried to shed tears, pinching her eyes ever tighter, and trying to feel it. Even with the embrace of the man, she felt absolutely nothing, no feeling or emotion through him. Perhaps it was acrimony that ran deep inside, almost like he felt absolutely nothing, a catharsis of disbelief.

And so she stepped up to the woman. She barely had her eyes open, her face pale, wrinkled with what was obvious: that years of torture and wear on her body had finally given in and showed. Her skin folded and creased heavily and hung off her facial structure as obvious signs that the lady had lost a lot of weight. It almost looked as if it was doing a disservice to let this lady live; surely, it would be best to take her out of this world, and place her in the hands of God, for which the ultimate judgment awaited.

But Hope knew she had to do it. Her stepdad needed it. And she needed to know. Taking a deep breath, she stuck her hand on the woman's eyes. The daughter began to cry out loud, "Please help her, Hope!" Opening her eyes, she began to rub her hands across the forehead of the woman.

Immediately, Hope felt the energy of the woman pass through her hand, unlike the numbness that had come across through the son. It shook her deeply, and felt like someone had given her a stomach full of silver, the chills going through. She pulled her hand back, and grabbed a needle off the table. Plucking her finger, the blood began to drip out, and she placed it in a cross on the lady's forehead, something that her Dad had symbolized as a gimmick to help sales (it literally meant nothing to the healing process...such a blasphemy it was, but sanctimony was not matrimony to the cause). The drops glowed more intense than ever, and ran down the forehead of the woman. The drops sizzled in the cool air, and off of it, for the first time, the darkness in the room showed a vapor of the blood evaporating.

For Hope, she literally had no guideline for what she was expected to do. She had never put any thought into how exactly her blood healed those around her - it just felt natural. She kept her hand on the woman's forehead, rubbing the blood with her forefinger and thumb in a circular motion. When nothing happened, she began to think that she had failed.

Looking around the room, the family and Lou, and also a few curious nurses, all stared at her, wondering what she would do next. Then, she placed a kiss on the woman's forehead. Slowly pulling back, the saliva and blood reacted, and her forehead began to develop a healthy color, as if years of age and rigor began to wear off. She didn't know if it had penetrated.

Taking a step back, she heard the patient's daughter beginning to sob. Lou began to openly look worried, and the stepdaughter began to show tears. "Please, God, let Hope help her," she cried. Immediately, Hope began to feel a certain kind of emptiness, and the sadness of a thousand sins. She looked into the mirror that was at bedside, and she saw the glow in her eyes begin to fade. She saw the same look in Duluth's eyes when she first encountered her, and it made her feel like she was out of her own domain.

I can't do this, Hope thought. *I don't have feelings for this woman.* She tried to feel the pity, the shame, the loss of someone. It didn't work as well as she thought it would. But then, her mind began to race, and she thought about her Dad, Duluth, and Adriana, all of whom had offered her hope and love.

She stepped up to the woman. Taking the needle between her forefinger and thumb, she drew an X on her wrist. The blood began to percolate quickly down her arm. There was a gasp in the room, seeing what otherwise appeared as the most graphic public display of self-mutilation. The blood had weaker glow to it, but still had a definite appearance of the compound that had altered it.

"Come on, Goddammit, Hope. Do this." She jerked her arm in a haymaker motion in front of the woman's head, as if she was the Pope commanding Holy Water over the woman. The blood began to soak into her mouth, and dripped in her nose.

Immediately, the woman, who had not been conscious for the entire time, opened her eyes. She looked at Hope, and then took a deep breath, for which Hope stepped back, rubbing her hand on the side of the woman's face. A group of gasps heralded the arrival of welcome pause and a feeling of contention.

Stepping back and admiring her work like Michaelangelo to his Pieta, whatever level of obviousness it was, she smiled. "Welcome back to the world, Mrs. Benner."

The lady opened her eyes, and saw the girl. "Hello, cutie. You have beautiful eyes....anyone ever tell you that?" She laughed, and her family began to openly weep, seeing that Rosemarie had come back to life.

Most relieved perhaps was Lou, who began to contemplate the possibilities of what Hope's seemingly white magic was creating. It was in some ways magical, but so much a responsibility. It was guilt that had taken over, but then again, he felt as if God had sent him to that house on that block with the Malotts.

Hope smiled. "My eyes are blue — they come from my father. My hair is long and black, and that comes from my grandmother." Stepping towards the woman, she clutched for her arm.

The lady gave a firm grasp of her hand. "You must have a beautiful family. You look elegant and have a very polite presence about you. It must be a tribute to your parents to be blessed with what you have. Don't let anyone ever take that away from you."

For that moment in time, Hope was frozen in time. She could feel the blood and muscles in her hands begin to absorb an exclusive energy. The verdantly glowing blood still dripping down her hands, it began to hit Rosemarie's arm in thick globules, for which Rosemarie began to feel as they absorbed into her skin, her cuticles and dry, worn hide slowly creating streaks of youth like a trail of tears — Hope's tears down her arm. Only they were tears of hope.

"Who did this to you, young lady? Such a shame for someone to do this to you." Her smile began to shut down, and an obvious sign of pain began to trickle through the elder's eyes.

"I did this. To help you, Mrs. Benner. It is my blood that made you better. I will heal in time, be assured. But you will be healed too." She began to grasp her hand, for which it seemed like the lady had more vigor, most likely because of the pain Hope felt in her arm.

In allusion, the lady said "That's a shame. But you did it for me, for which I am thankful. 'For the life of the flesh is in the blood…for it is the blood, the blood that makes atonement for the soul.' You are a saver of me. You didn't have to do it, little lady."

Hope grasped the hand. "No, Mrs. Benner, I didn't have to do it. I wanted to do it. I've been given a gift, something that my parents left for me. I have a gift of life that runs through my veins, runs through my blood." She smiled. "It's for all of us."

Rosemarie smiled. "Well, you have shared it with our family, young lady. You are a Hope for the world. Save your best for what you do for your best. And don't let this gift, this blessing, make you ill or make you want to give away the best you have." And those words stuck with her, as she pulled back and looked into the sunlight in the room.

THE NEXT MORNING

There was a definite type of vigor that arrived back at the Malott residence in the few hours after the action. Hope had spoken very little during the time that it took to get home that night; she was unsure if she was a bit dizzy from the blood loss, or experiencing the pressure cooker of what was expected of her, or if it was just the cold. Life went on for her, especially now that she was back at home, and suddenly, the expectations began to burden her once again.

Giving a very unfeminine yawn, she got out of bed, rubbing her eyes. In her flannel pajamas, she pulled at her t-shirt, hanging loose in all its plain whiteness. She always went to go grab Adriana on this weekend, as she always would. The cold weather outside had finally set in, and a somewhat tedious chill flowed through the house. The caloric of her pride began to flame out deeply, and it was burning her thoroughly.

Knocking on her stepsister's door, Hope needed to ask her something – it was always the thing of a young teenage girl, something on my mind that like hurts all the time and like that. They were always poking at each other, thinking that perhaps in a way that no one else would understand what each was going through. Hope clearly carried some of the most burdensome tasks as a localized celebrity; she knew to some extent that she had to be strong. But surely, the strength was not there for Adriana.

The door was locked to the room. Hope gave four taps and kicked the door with her slipper. This was to let her stepsister know that it was indeed her; she never did the knock when the parents were around.

After a few times through, and requests "Adi, it's Hope. Please, like, open up," and all of those matters, she looked down. Realizing that it could have been somewhat overwhelming to go through this repeatedly, the strong young woman walked away regretfully.

As she took down the first step to the first floor, she began to think for a little bit, pausing for what was definitely an eternity to her. She had never seen her sister this way, but somehow, it was becoming of her eventually. Despite her somewhat open gestures, Adriana was somewhat fearful of herself; her self-esteem began to fail considerably. She was afraid of hearing bullets whiz by her head, and knowing that the attention her best friend was getting probably established permanence, it was only expected she would do these things.

What really struck Hope hard was that Adriana seemed so normal at first, and was okay just a few days ago. What could have happened for her to change so much?

Lou was in the living room, sitting on Alex's very expensive couch. Laptop in front of him, he obviously was plotting his next attack – or simply put, the next "heal". This had become somewhat of a procedure around the parts, as he was playing Joe Jackson to the Ed Sullivans of the world, a sort of theatrical makeup that honestly became too much at the time.

Coming up from behind, he did not notice the somewhat disheveled stepchild giving an angry grin from behind. Barely awoken, Hope walked around front.

"Morning, Lou," Hope laughed. She knew something was up, much to the disgust of her promise with him. Quickly, he clicked out of whatever was open, trying to hide whatever was in that browser window.

"Hope, hello! How are you, sweetie?" he asked somewhat cautiously, lack of innocence implied by his distemper. "Did your cuts heal, hun?"

Hope was barely awake, and squinted as her blue eyes were hidden by her pupils not wanting to adjust to the brightness. "Yes, they did. Can't say though that it doesn't burn a little." She was being honest with him, a somewhat necessary cause considering she was not internal to her stepdad's seeming needs at the time.

But even in this, Lou was embarrassingly overburdened with his cavalier attitude. He smiled and said "But hey, we did this together! Look, we made enough money to pay off the car bill – " he handed her a check, signed Kaylee Benner, which kind of made her think: made Benner better. Bleh.

Hope felt a little hesitant to applaud her stepdad. She felt at a visceral level that she had done something good for someone, but it didn't feel fulfilling. Expecting to actually have some belief in her powers, she could smile for just a second. "Lou, I'm glad it worked for you and for Rosemarie." It was kind of the best thing that could come out of her mouth. Alex was watching over her diction, and somehow, stoically, she was able to halt herself from blurting out readily *You don't have any freaking clue what I'm doing right now, Lou.* It paid to be reserved and tactful in this case.

Getting up, Lou boasted "Aww, well, this is one of many. Smells like your Mom is cooking up a feast in the kitchen. Where's Adriana?" he began to let his smell sensory organs take over the fact that maybe something was wrong.

"I don't know, Lou. I went to knock on her door and she didn't answer. Probably just sleeping in, but I didn't bother." She went to the kitchen, attracted to the same pungency of burning bovine and porcine flesh that beckoned even the family pets.

And so, breakfast proceeded to go on. Adriana was missing out on a really great meal, one that they had not been able to afford for weeks. Lou was the most ecstatically positive of any at the table as the cold breeze began to waft through the old windows.

Carrie took the food off the cookware. She carefully spooned the food onto Hope's plate, serving her in a proper restaurant way. "Thanks, Mommy," she said in the voice that had been so enamoring for all of her life. Her mother gave a smile and told her she was kindly welcome.

Not to be outdone, Lou smiled. "Isn't that nice of your mother to do that. Great service! I could eat a horse right now, Carrie-" to which Carrie looked at him and slammed down the skillet, walking away as if to say *You eat out of this one. You think I'm some sort of mammy 'round these parts.*

Lou took the hint, said "Okay...." and began to scarf down the food. It was probably the first time there was some sort of disagreement between the two in front of Hope. Carrie had hidden it because she didn't want Hope to know that it was all for her. But somehow, she couldn't keep hiding it; it did bother her.

The silence in the room, save for the timing of clanging of the silverware on the plates setting the tempo of their hearts, felt as if it enveloped Hope. She took a few bites of her food, picking at it with some disen-chantment. And then it took her.

"I'm not welcome here, am I?" She looked at her stepdad, mother in the corner, and then went to see her sister upstairs.

For Hope, this was her welcome refuge: being able to speak to the person who would most be able to understand her. In some sense, the thought of Duluth had resonated through her: defend yourself and plan on people lying and cheating to get themselves any good out of life.

One turn at the poker table for all the marbles, Lou. *Bullshit*, Hope thought.

And then, it happened. As she got up to the top step, she heard groaning coming from Adriana's room. The doors and walls were thin, yet this sound resonated. No one else was around, and Hope knew it.

Immediately, Duluth and her survivalist side, the blood of life and C402 nevertheless, sprang into action. Living in the house had its benefits; she knew how to jimmy the lock to the room, as she had used the spare room so many times to pitch a tent and pretend that she and Alex would be "camping", even in the dead of winter. It was Adriana's room: simple, small, a place to hide that wouldn't cause sensory overload.

Nervously tugging at the door, a thousand words and thoughts flooded through the healer's head. Adriana was never one for drama, even with her somewhat reserved persona. When the door opened, she was stunned.

Adriana was draped on top of her bed, perpendicular to the grain. Her body stretched across, her head laid down over the near end, and feet towards the other. At her side, near her head, was a pool of blood, dripping down her arm. She had cut herself, and then attempted to do something, poison herself, whatever it was. She let out another groan.

The feelings in that room stung Hope tremendously. In there, she felt an immediate sense of pain that she had never experienced before. It was not the pain of illness, but the pain of desperation. She wanted to scream, but somehow, she couldn't mutter a single vocalization. Somehow, she knew that bringing Lou and Carrie into this was bad. She had to do this for herself.

"Adi, what did you do? Like, oh my gosh." Hope picked up her body, and threw it on the bed. She couldn't tell where the blood was coming from, but it kept coming from somewhere. As she pulled the body on the bed, the blood made contact with her skin. It seeped into a wound, perhaps a cuticle or a few apocrines, the sweat beginning to take her in.

Those few moments were powerfully substantiating. When the blood hit her, she saw Adriana and that moment when she left school. That day when she had to go alone to school without her best friend.

She heard Adriana crying, and then Dari standing there, smiling. She knew something that Hope didn't. Only one reason came to her mind, and it was obvious.

The smile on Dari's face, as she tugged at her sweater, trying to make her endowments robust to the extent that it was more attractive – it just felt wrong, for lack of better words.

Feeling this mood, and the fact that she saw her Dad suddenly being shot in front of her, and picturing Dari laughing, made her bite her lip.

Her muscles released. She was breathing heavily, but the blood dripped on her stepsister before she dropped Adriana. And she saw the blue and green in her eyes, the reflection going so strong through her cornea that it almost felt like she had been given the drug of her own endowments, except these endowments were not ignorable.

She fell back to the floor, and Adriana coughed twice. She spit out a razor blade onto the floor. As it fell, the room slowly began to spin for the both of them. Adriana had been cured of her pain by chance with Hope. But Hope had taken on a pain of her own.

In her mind, Hope could feel it ever stronger. Picturing this sister of hers, deciding to swallow a razor blade, that moment of truth, that this girl had felt so depressed that she would swallow sharp metal – it was over-whelming.

Adriana smiled for the first time in a while. "Hey, Hopie." She was high on whatever it was.

"Hey," Hope said. She couldn't say anything at all. The pain ran too deep, and it compromised her psyche to the point of verbal paralysis.

In there was a definite air of puzzlement, a sense of total disarray. Hope sat down on the chair on the side of the shadowy room.

Adriana laughed. "Am I more like you now, Hopie?" she said. "You cured me." She groaned out loud, thinking to herself that she was in the right.

Yet she was not right. In some sense, Hope became scared. And then incensed completely. "Why did you swallow those blades, Adi? Are you, like, crazy?"

The answer was rather vague. "I have lots of pain, lots of hurt, lots of things that stung in me. I....I didn't know what to do in that case. I wanted to do something, but I couldn't. Something to stop hurting.

"I saw you and your act, and I want to be able to get rid of my anger." She made reason to it, feeling the anger.

Yet this was not a concession nor permission for what she did. Hope knew what she did, and it meant the thing that she had feared: that she had set an unfortunate and dire standard, that people would come to her to help them with anything. And now, it was a visual and emotional manifestation. Hope responded by groaning and pounding her fists.

"God....damn it!" It was just as much anger at herself as it was to Adriana. "You can't be me! You have to be yourself! I'm not here to help people! I'm here to be me!"

Yet Adriana kept with her disillusion. "But you are my best friend! And I knew that if I could bleed, I could heal all my pain – " she laughed.

Not to be one with the humor of the moment, however delusional, Hope yelled – for the first time – at her sister and childhood *bestie*. "You are crazy, more than anything! This is a curse!" And she pulled the razor blade on the floor, and stuck it in her hands. As the glow in her eyes became ever stronger, she took the blade, with Adriana's blood in solution, and began to pick up the blade. She wanted to cut herself to spite her friend.

It was verity in the moment, and she felt deeply of her parents and principle by demonstration. But then she thought of her stepdad, and his reasoning. An eye for an eye makes the world go blind. Gandhi.

She threw the blade on the ground, barely sticking its sharp edge to her wrist. She knew this wouldn't work.

"Just don't tell anyone this happened, Hopie. Please." Her brown eyes suddenly resonated stronger than ever. And they didn't.

They both cleaned everything up together. It was that sisterly agreement that could only be described as something that only they would understand, a bond that was far more equivocal than equine, a chemical bond so strong that no quantum of energy could break it. And they said nothing. When they shared that effect, it transferred through them.

ONE MONTH LATER

I-476, EXIT 112

For many, the loneliness of winter in terms of life begins to set in around this time in November. Most of the trees have lost their leaves, the green hills of eastern PA begin to turn to a sad brown, and the last vessel of hope in the world comes with the holiday season beginning to set in. Surely, the gathering of families around the fireplace, sharing stories about the year in passing, seeing the smiles, how the kids have grown up, and so much of cheer...it was like the 1980s all over again. Before all the suffering, when the relatives were still alive, and the parties were in order rather than the exception – it was all a pipe dream.

There was no such premeditated joy for Hope in this realm of her life. Her stepdad was driving her to another appointment, another "60 second rescue", as had been advertised among the common media. Already, the hype began to rise. It was only a matter of time from the first confirmation of success until everyone began to want her services. She would hear stories about how people would sell life insurance policies, raid their 401(k)s, and in some cases, sell their homes, all to be granted the opportunity, the chance, the gift, to have that one minute where everything was free to happen.

Because of the impression she had left in those wallets, suddenly, she was able to acquire many material items. Her stepdad's old sedan had gone to an SUV, then a sports sedan to park alongside - with all-wheel-drive, of course. It cost nearly $70,000, but that had become pocket change to them, as the price that Lou was able to negotiate went up. She couldn't go anywhere without being recognized, and she would often pose for pictures. For the moment, she was treated as a queen, and she was happy for it.

Lou gazed deeply into the distance, the snow plowed freshly on the Northeast Extension part of the Turnpike. Like her feelings, the road was an afterthought to one of the greatest miracles of human invention – a quick way to travel from one sphere to another. It was there for the money now, and even though it had its glitz and generated money, it was just another waste of government effort to make someone's life easier.

"You know, this one's extra special, Hopie. We're going up to a hospital to help a girl. Parents are good friends of mine from a project I did in 1994. They paid good money to see you, dear." He rubbed her shoulder in good health.

Yet even with this show of perhaps tacit compassion, Hope looked outside towards the city lights flying by. Her consistent skill with sprinkling her blood and fluids had not done her out so far. She would go into the room, talk with the family and friends, and then commence. It required a little bit of showmanship; often times, much to the dismay of the Church, God bless, Lou would have clergy recite verses from the Gospel, especially towards the end of them and in particular affability to the Gospel of John, and those verses would echo in her head. To many of those same reverends and pastors, they would see her as being a gift from God, a true saint in the flesh, walking about those rooms.

"You know, Lou, I don't know if that will do that for me. I mean, we do this for money, and we are making money. Heck, we're having a garage built into the neighbor's yard. We have TV's, we have a nice Christmas tree sent from Ontario on the way. But how much more can we do before we call this shindig, eh, a victory?" With little feeling in her voice, she was trying to shy away.

Lou was taken aback. He had to continue the scheme; keeping Hope happy, her eyes aglow, and her blood pumping, was the deal. They had banked good coin for this so far, and the endless possibilities kept going. "We have to do this because you have the power to make people believe. Believe that miracles can happen. Believe that there is hope in the sun rising, the youth of the new day, Hopie. You have that power. Hashtag, a-course." Looking to be powerful in his words, going for big dictation was the trick. This was no longer to put a cup of soup on the table by now. It was to literally nail a Delmonico and gold potatoes with the Cristal on tap. Every week now.

And thus, if it did anything, it just made Hope irate. "Miracles can happen, Lou. You talk about believing….I believe deeply that only God, not me, has the power to make miracles happen. We just have to let Him decide about when the right time and place is." She looked at him, and with the silence, she slammed her head against the headrest.

"But you know, Hopie, perhaps this is the, like, making, the manifestation of a miracle. Wait until you see who you are helping tonight." He was beginning to fear that the mission had finally swung in Hope's reluctant favor, and he would be out of money.

They pulled off the turnpike and into the outer reaches of the same hospital she had been in nearly three years ago. Pulling in the lot, Hope began to feel the chills run down her back. A sense of fear grasped her like the cold of that November evening. The adrenaline began to shoot through her veins, and she looked herself in the vanity mirror. Turning down, she looked at the scars on her arms, which were now criss-crossed with lines from all the ritual bleedings that made it look like a Virginia ham.

To her, it struck a chord that these wounds would not heal as fast as they did initially. Her first heal in that bathroom 26 months ago was instantaneous; she literally was freaking out longer than it took for her body to right the ship. But now, she was going through this a few times a day. Lou had literally turned her gift into a huge commodity. And it shamed her to do it so many times; yet, in the end, she would just ignore it and pretend like it didn't really, like, bother her. Pauline was right about it: she needed a job, and unless it meant testing her healing powers on burger flipping grease burns, this was the modus operandi for the near future.

The doors opened, and immediately, a mass of people, reporters, nurses, and plenty of white coats all lined up. Lou had arranged security for her visit, and fearing the repeat of a governor's kidney operation, proceeded to have a queue roped off from the driveway to the door. It was like no other event she had seen, for she had become a celebrity in her own right. As the door opened to the front entrance, and the lot attendant got into the very expensive car, she covered her eyes. Let us through, let us through, let the girl through, the security told the people who watched. Arms began to go out of the crowd, and many of the people held diabetic syringes, vials, and a few babies for her to reach and heal. She indeed felt like a person of religious power, and believed she had the respect and blessing of God to go forth. It offered her resolve, but still fear. It was literally all in slow motion at this point in time.

She had remembered how she washed the feet of the sick at her church, how people of all ages and creeds were there to help. She spoke good words for seminars and for public speeches. But this was the primary task for the night.

The security was a surprise for Hope, who anticipated this would be a quick in and out job, one that didn't require much thought or fanfare. But it was different now.

The door opened slowly to the room in the children's wing of the hospital, not too far from where she had been lectured by the kooky Indian Dr. Copulus many moons ago. The smell of the hospital floor drew memories of when she was little, traumatic ones that gave her chills and blurred her blue as ice eyes. They burned with the want to tear up, fly away, and never have to deal with it again. "Here she is, Hope. Thank you for coming." The cameras closed behind her, and she was in the room with her Dad, his friend who had requested the visit, the mom, and what was presumably an aunt and grandmother, all looking lovingly at the new visitor.

The girl was different from the older woman she treated as her first case. She was bald, an obvious sign of the effects of chemotherapy. Her brown eyes pulsed with vibrant energy, her frail but overall well-looking body sat in the bed upright, portraying a significant amount of life left.

Hope began the conversation. "Hi there, little doll," she said to her lovingly with a supportive smile. "What's your name?"

The girl immediately smiled back from behind the cannula. "My name is Bianca, what's yours?" Her positive attitude only by a small child who seemingly had fought this for so long gave Hope a very contagious smile. "My name is Hope, hun."

Bianca looked in her eyes. "Mom and Dad told me you were here to get rid of the monster in my body. Is that true?" She asked in curiosity, her eyes beginning to become bigger and take over her head.

Not knowing what to do and overcome with emotion, the curer's face began to turn red. "Yes, I am here to take over the monster in your body. I have a thing in my body that helps fight monsters." It was simple, but it did the trick.

With a nod, the bedridden baby looked into her eyes. "You know, Daddy said when I was little that in order to fight monsters, all you needed to do was say 'Go away, monsters!' And shine a flashlight. A really big flashlight." It was incredibly right, and somehow, it was worthy for Hope to hear it, like the monsters had inadvertently turned on a new set of lights, one that had Hope's signature in it, in her eyes.

"Well, I want you, Bianca, to look in my eyes. They are very blue, but I want you to not stop looking at them. Pretend they are the flashlight now, 'k?" Hope knew she had to be as cool as a cucumber for the better of both of them. For the young one, it was over her head about this sickness; she understood it pedantically, like the way she knew the sun would always rise, because things would be alright.

[178]

This philosophy though could not have been more orthogonal to the older one, though. The way the few months, the rush of fame, this entire life of hers, a 16-year-old living as a modern day priest of the high church. But it was not the anointing of oil in the name of the Lord that they drew. This was part of her. And it was a part that was running out. In her way, Hope felt like staying cool allowed for a peaking of her sanity. The only refuge she had, as a result, was in the knowledge that she was doing good for someone. It was her opiate for her living, the stimulation and satisfaction of her days. And despite the toil on her face, she plugged on for all those months.

They began to hook up the machine that they would use to help cure the evil cancer that had taken over her body. It was simple: A needle would take a small amount of blood out of Hope's vein at a time. It would then be homogenized, cleaned and put to plasma and platelet, and then be deposited into Bianca's body. It was direct, but it was the best way to handle it. Plus, as a benefit, Lou had set it up to be the first demonstration of the machine, mostly designed to save on plastic for blood donation. It was Hollywood, for which Lou was Sam Goldwyn. And her eyes were as hypnotic as Astaire gliding across the ballroom floor. Or to just not let her know about the "pinch".

The nurse poked the girl's arm, for which she did not notice anything, mesmerized by the presence of the black haired, blue-eyed girl. She then took Hope's arm and felt for and placed the needle in her vein.

Hope distracted Bianca by keeping her speaking. "So, do you have any brothers or sisters, Bianca?" She asked very politely and conservatively.

The girl smiled. "I have an older brother, Michael, who is away at school. Dad says when he comes back in a couple of weeks, he's going to bring me back Birch Beer. Last time I tried it, it was good."

"Well, it is. How old are you? Thought you had to be twenty-one to drink beer," she asked in a feigning of naivete. "That stuff is bad, y'know."

The girl shook her head. "No, no, it ain't that. Tastes like root beer. But Mike thinks it smells like window cleaner." They both laughed, as the needles were placed in.

With a nod by the attendant physician, Hope began the procedure. "OK, Bianca, what I want you to do is close your eyes for a second. I want you to think about Michael. I want you to think about how much birch beer tastes good. I want you to think about playing outside with your best friend forever. I don't want you to open your eyes until I say you can, 'kay?" The machine began to buzz, and the thin tube began to show a glowing, radiant gel float by vacuum up the tube, into the machine. As it hit the pump, it began to turn into a ring of glowing fluid, buffered by a solid red inside that had sparkles in it. The doctor and resident both began writing on the chart about their observations. Her family began to smile.

For a moment, both closed their eyes. The girl began to speak. "I can see Laurie, and Tristan, and Taylor...they are all playing at recess. I can see them throwing the ball around....and oh, look, there's my little puppy Alice," she said in a train of thought.

"The sun is shining, there's a cloud that looks like an elephant." And Hope began to picture that in her head; and it did work miracles, as the imagery that the young girl described was as clear as the day she stated. She began to relax, and let the feeling overcome her.

Slowly, Hope opened her eyes. The girl began to look less frail. A small covering of fuzzy blonde hair began to appear on Bianca's head. The wounds that would not heal because of the chemotherapy began to glow, the blood finally circulating from Hope to Bianca's arteries. She began to smile. "Hope, I see you, all grown up, and there's a girl next to you, she has a skirt on, and looks like she is walking in the snow. Her hair is growing in, and her face looks like she has something to say, but can't say it. Her face is pale, Hope. Pale like the moon."

[180]

Immediately, she knew that something in her soul had come through that vein. She was immediately thinking of her friend Duluth….and now, in that blood, the thought had transferred over through that machine - and perhaps, in concentrate. "Yes, but what do you see, Bianca?"

Bianca, eyes still closed as by request, went and stated "She looks like she wants to talk to you, like her Dad is telling her to be quiet or she would be sent to her room without supper."

Hope's effervescent smile started to go away. She looked down at her arm, anticipating backflow. Sometimes, the machine would mix the blood and would give the ill person's blood in her system. But there was none.

She then could see what the small girl was seeing. It flashed for just a second. But it was enough to feel what was an intense pain.

Bianca began to say words that she could not have possibly thought of. And she vocalized them out loud.

We are more….

Than two random girls….

From 'the hood.

They were some of the first words that had been spoken from Duluth when she first met her. They were buried deep in her mind, but nevertheless formed the mantra of her healing mission. And now she shared them with Bianca, even at the subversive and subconscious level.

Immediately, a pulse of energy shot through Hope, and her arm jerked forward, knocking the catheter loose. The image of Duluth standing there, trying to grab and immerse herself in an embrace of the both of them stuck in their head.

Machines beeped, and everyone in the room began commenting. "Wait, Hope! We're not done yet!" But Hope began to feel an intense pain in her arm, one that by far overcame all the scars and feelings that she had felt.

Looking for her stepdad, she turned around the room, and headed towards the hall. "You are like a big sister to me, Hope! The one I never had! Don't leave! Help me!" She screamed out at the top of her lungs in a shriek.

Immediately, all of the energy that Hope had felt began to pulse through her blood. Perhaps it was being drained of resources or drained of protein, iron, or DNA, but she suddenly felt like someone was sending her to her stepfather. Blood running down her arm, staining her sweater top and running down in her moccasin shoes, she went towards the lounge.

Behind the door was Lou, and his friend. In there, the friend was holding a safe, one that was fireproof and sold at department stores. The man seemed very sad, and Lou was rubbing his hands together, inviting the man to shake his hand and hand over the contents of the safe. She glanced in, and saw Lou's back turned to her. The safe opened, and thick stacks of money, all orange in color and representing notes of significant value, were tied up.

The man looked sad, and had a frustrated and unfortunate look on his face. She could not hear what they were saying, but thanked God inside herself that she would not hear them. Immediately, all the feelings she had of being helpful faded. Like a drug addict on a hangover and withdrawal, the joy of her actions, all began to go back. She felt lonely, and betrayed. The opiate of her mind had finally gone to a hangover, and like a hangover, she felt pain.

The unmistakable, strongly burning pain of a thousand wrongdoings.

And then, the final conclusion of the matter in Hope's form of reality came in the look on the man's face. Bianca's father handed a bag over to Lou. And Lou screamed "THIS WASN'T IN THE DEAL!" The father was crying, and handed what appeared to be house keys, frustrated to the extent where he would do anything to help his daughter in her problems.

"Mr. Mendoza, I'll do anything for her. Even live on the street!"

It all added up to Hope now. She didn't have a father anymore. She had a greedy man who wouldn't do what this poor girl's father would: put the little one first. The manifestation of what Alex, the caring, loving man that had died for her a few years back had come to reality.

Running back to the room, she pushed open the door. Bianca was cured of her illness…but suddenly, Hope had one of her own. Quickly removing the catheter, and angrily pulling it out of her skin to a squirt of gel of blood, she said "Bianca, dear, I'm sorry. I….I can't do this, hun. You deserve better than this. You are cured." She placed a kiss on her forehead, and immediately, began to run down to the lounge, much to the dismay, but fortunately with a sigh of relief in the vacillation of appropriate time, of the family.

She opened the door. Looking at the safe, Lou said "Did you cure her, sweetie? We're rich, Hopie!" He fanned the money.

Doing what she thought she should, Hope slapped her stepdad, good relationship or not, dead in the face. "YOU BASTARD!" she yelled. "BLOODY, DIRTY, LYING, INCONGRUENT BASTARD!" She stormed out.

VIII

The Penance

An image of good lasts but just a moment, but the burning of bad inside can consume one's own being throughout. When someone tells the truth to you that you are the fool for believing them, should it also be true that being told the truth about a lie doesn't establish any creed, for the lie is inherent in the guarantee?

They had not spoken to each other for some time already, the stepdad and the daughter, two perfect strangers of ill content sentenced to their own lives and undoing. Both were angry at each other, mostly because of the lack of attention they had given to each of his or her wants. In terms of the scheme, this was a lethal combination.

Hope sat on the ledge of the window to her room, unable to speak. She had felt empty for the first time inside, a total shell of herself, like an eggshell without the yolk. The life inside of her began to wear away, and she didn't know what to think. She remembered how the doctor had told her to put vlogs on the Internet, and how they would work. Sure, they were a good way to spill her guts on what she thought. Most of them were fairly upbeat; she had many subscribers, and her videos would net thousands of views per day. Feeling obligated to be insightful, she would

[184]

often go to the library and find quotes from Buddha, the Dalai Lama, Mother Teresa, you name it, she used it. But inside, she felt bad.

She decided it was time to come clean on the matter, and to finally tell everyone what she thought. Opening her e-mail, "hopeforhealing" as her screenname, she saw endless requests. Many of them seemed to be hastily put together; mothers looking for children to be cured of diseases, developing countries where they asked for cures to leprosy and giardia, and often in poor English. It broke her heart every time to see what these people wanted her to do; many of them were poor and were willing to offer anything: land, animals, their entire life savings. The world had its eyes on Hope Malott, and she had to go and be responsible. But she couldn't.

"Here goes nothing." She turned on the webcam, this time for good. "Hi everyone, this is HopeForHealing.com, broadcasting live from the second floor. I know....I know a lot of times, I post stuff on here about how I find life in everyone, how I can help those who are helpless, how my touch can save you from the ultimate price in life. I am so glad I can help those in need. But I have a new message for you.

"Lately, there has been a push for me to charge more and more and more for the same service. My stepdad took 500 thousand dollars to help a girl with leukemia last night. I did my best to help her, and she is cured. However, I found that....well, her Dad and my stepdad, Lou, both had a business deal going on. I'm not a judge of emotions at all, and I can't tell whether or not someone is being serious or not.

"But the look on my stepdad's face was not one of the purveyance of a gift. It was not one of an angel looking to rescue an innocent child from the grasp of Hell. I didn't see that at all. I saw a man, taking the last penny from a desperate man who gave the ultimate price for his child, aside from his own life. And from the money he gave him, it damn well was his life.

"And then, I saw a man give up his shelter, his home, his castle. For his girl, his little baby girl. His daughter, the product of his raising and the proof of his love.

Hope sighed, and began to look outside to the sky. "You see, that kind of stuff doesn't happen for us heroes all the time. We are told that we can help a lot of people, and that we are gifts from God. All the time. They seek us, they realize we are in that room together, and then, for the moment, we have a covenant, a promise. But the promise is soon broken.

"I then had to go and try to reason why the manifestation of my gift is pain through desperation. Just don't get it anymore. It's, like, not worth it, world.

"And so, I would like to share this with you." She grabbed not a syringe, but a switchblade knife, illegal in the Commonwealth of Pennsylvania, but nevertheless acquired for effect (in New Jersey, of course). She immediately ran the blade lengthwise up her arm, making the entire room glow. "This, friends, is what I share with you. The vision of hope, of love, of caring. It's the best I can do without having my stepdad watch over me. I bleed myself for you, for the forgiveness and resolve of what ills you." She grimaced as her arm began to bleed profusely. "I am putting this blood in vials, in the darkest of my room here in my house. They shall glow for the common good, and it will be all that shall be seen." With a scream and a wince, she said *Haec quotiescumque feceritis, in mei memoriam facietis.* The knife fell to the floor.

She filled five vials, one for each member of her family, one for her, and one for her truly friend in blood, heart and soul, wherever she was. There were no more for them; she had to shoplift those vials from a drugstore in order to get them into her house, as she had no money, and had abandoned her job with Duluth's friend.

A knock on the door followed soon thereafter. "Hey, Hopie. It's Lou. Can you open up?" Fearing her life after the occurrence many years ago, she hid the vials in her walk-in-closet, and answered the door. "Hey, Hopie. Hey....I'm sorry about what happened today. I shouldn't have taken the money and the crib like that. It was awkward..." he gave an anxious giggle.

A tense moment followed, and it was something he had not expected. Hope dug none of the matter. "What do you think is funny of robbing a man of his last pennies? And his house, and dignity? Don't you, like, have a heart, sir?" she asked openly.

Lou began to show remorse outwardly, although it was not immediately apparent if it was just as much of feigning guilt as it was of typical. He began to mutter, "I trusted that man for a long time. He had a favor owed to me, Hope. He wrote to me, a letter, a freakin' handwritten letter, asking for my help. I thought maybe if you would not see the transaction, you would feel like it wasn't such a big deal. I mean, think about it this way, Hopie. If you were given all the money in the world to do one good thing for someone, and you knew you could seize it, and grasp it, and pull it out, like a weed in the sand – would you do it?"

Hope resolutely took none of it, and spoke back coherently "I would do it for free, because I always take it if that person is as good as he says he is, he would do the same for me." And she began to walk away. She did not trust her stepdad anymore, and didn't trust that he could handle the problems that conquered her path less traveled.

"Hope, listen. Before you go, I want you to do one more thing for me." She stopped in her path, and turned around, and took two steps back towards him. "For the last one, Mr. Timoni needs a cure. Rich man down the street has piles. He wants them cured. Guaranteed for $1 million dollars, covers what he would pay for surgery. Do this one, and I promise, I guarantee, you will never have to do another one again."

Hope seemed incensed. "The man has piles. He has a pain in his ass. I'm not sticking my finger in there, Lou. I'm not touching you, either, because

[187]

you're a pain in the ass also. You hear that?" She shoved him out of the way, and began working her way down the stairs.

She didn't have anyone to talk to at the moment. But that would all change in a moment. Coming up the walk, viewing her video, was someone who would change her destiny once again, forever.

She walked up the sidewalk, wearing a pair of ankle boots, a gray hoodie, and a tartan designed skirt and black tights. Her blonde hair was long and ran in thick bunches down her face. Nodding down in reverence to the headwind that blew down the street, her clothes were torn, her face red, and her resolve strong. It was Duluth, and she had come to rejoin her friend.

Knocking on the door, she felt ashamed after abandoning her friend that day. But she had to do something about it.

One of the tall security men answered the door. "I'm here to see Hope. My name is Duluth Amara Kane," the visitor proclaimed in deep breaths.

The security man had his orders. "Sorry, ma'am, but you have to go and register and make an appointment like everyone else. Please go to –" he began to ramble his speech, his obligatory tag line, but Duluth said nothing.

"Look, sir, I know what the website is. I've been there and all. With much appreciation, I'd like to see Hope. Quickly. Tell her it's a friend." She began to reach out and push the robust, muscular guard out of the way.

The guard began to grasp at her. "Miss, you can't come in here. Please go and set up an appointment!" the guard said as she was restrained, arms behind her back in law enforcement style. She screamed "Hope! Hope Malott!" as they carried her frail body, her long blond locks making her look like ghetto trash.

One of the men radioed up the stairs. "Hope and Louis, we have an intruder. Shelter in wherever possible, potential ill victim, not on appointment, do you copy?" the man went on the radio.

Lou went to the intercom. "10-4, Lamar. We're upstairs." He turned to Hope. "You see that? People freakin' rely on you! Why can't you do this? Buncha idiots who don't want to fork over the money. Ya gotta pay to play, I suppose," he giggled.

Hope looked out the window, always curious to see what people were doing. For some reason, she paid extra close attention that afternoon to the person in the hoodie. The overall appearance, the shaggy look, the pale face....and *yes,* that pale face was someone she recognized immediately. "I see that, Lou. I can do this." She ran past Lou, down the stairs, past the guards before they could get a word out, and Hope said "Let her go! Duluth! Duluth! Please let her go! I know her, I....know....her..." she uttered the last words as she broke the large guard's grasp over the girl. The guard put her down gently, and nodded in respect to her.

"Lamar, meet Duluth Kane," Hope said. "Friend of mine." The guard shook her hand, and apologized, to which the now-reinforced Duluth said in rubbing it off "No problem, Lamar. No worries, I spent three years putting up with various restraints. Chances are your ass would be on the Barbie if I had two more minutes. You never know..." she giggled.

Hope laughed. But then again, she knew that Duluth did not come all this way for a brief moment of levity. Grabbing her old friend, she said "What are you doing here?"

Duluth looked her straight in the eye. "Come with me. To a private place. I need your help." So they went to that place that Hope best felt would help, and found it in the master bathroom. Figuring the symbolism of how it always took longer in there than anyone else, she needed the time. As much as she could get.

[189]

The door closed behind them. Slowly taking off her hoodie, and dusting herself off from the confrontation, she put the lid down on the commode, and sat down. Hope sat on the counter and crossed her legs. "I'm coming to you, Hope, for a favor. I have a lot to explain, and I need to do it for you.

"You probably remember rooming with me and my boyfriend, right. Well, here's the story. I did leave that one day with him. He...he decided that it wasn't going to fly to have two girls in his apartment. Makes his Daddy think ménage a trois is going on, or some shit like that. Well, he took me out to lunch that morning. He told me he loved me, but he thought I was trying to gather up people to put on a show.

"He knew about my powers, Hope. And he worshipped them, intensely. So much that he would use my blood, my very own property, to do whatever he could. He did drugs, he smoked, he drank. And after a while, he began to be abusive.

"I come here for your help, and a warning. Please....look." She raised her top, a sheer one that looked like it had come from the summer. Lifting her tank top, she showed a scar, about a foot long, that ran up her abdomen. The scab was black, deep, and long. "This is what Josh did to me when he could not bleed me anymore. The charcoal was in everything I ate...cereal, pop, French fries, hamburgers...whatever he cooked, he put it in. He thought that if I didn't have powers, I was no good.

"And then he stabbed me one day. He was angry, said 'How could you do this to me, Dewey? I was so good to you....'" And she paused, holding back the tears. "I told him, 'Josh, I did nothing for you because I was special. I did it because I absolutely loved you." And that knife made me bleed my last drop of the life, the only life, I had. I survived because my body was able to heal with those last morsels of C402.

[190]

"So I am here for you. I want you to give me my life back. I have nobody, but please. Solve this problem of his damn scar." She held her hands out. "Please, for me. I saw your video, and I only have my friendship to give."

It took a few seconds of reservation for her to do it. But she felt like this was the only person that deserved forgiveness. After all, she had helped break out, unhinge an evil man who had done no good. Of course, she had told her stepdad that she was not interested. But she could find no better way to spit in the face of everyone who had ever wronged her than to give the life back to the one person who had helped her live. "OK, Duluth. I will do this for you."

Duluth gave a hug, and drew a heart with her finger over Hope's left breast. "Thank you, Hope Malott." She grabbed her arm, and pulled off what was left of the scab that Hope had done before. Sprinkling the blood, she pulled up the garments covering Duluth's scar, and began to close her eyes and used her opposing finger to smear the blood over the scar.

As this went on, Lou could hear and see what was going on inside the bathroom. He saw the light come through, and he knew that something was going on, that a healing was taking place, much to his chagrin. But he didn't know that it was a friend with the same condition, that same blessing, trying to reestablish herself. For Lou, it was betrayal.

Hope could feel Duluth's energy climb back. It began to take all her energy to put the glow back in Duluth's brown eyes. It took even more to make her seem normal again. The age on Duluth's face made her look 10 years older, perhaps either by the weathering of the cold and hard lifestyle, or the fact her lifestyle was devoid, and the disease which had kept her young was now killing her.

The window in the bathroom cracked, and a cold burst of air blew in the room, fanning the two girls' hair. It was like they were being as one, and as far as the people outside the room could tell, they were, for those few moments, one. It was taking all of her energy to maintain herself, and she became red in the face as she breathed forcefully, trying to let blood flow faster into Duluth. She deserved it in her heart, and the vigor she had given showed openly on the wall.

Hope opened her eyes, and then Duluth did. She lifted up her tank, and saw no scar at all. Hope looked into her friend's eyes, and smiled.

"Welcome back, Duluth." And she gave her a hug, a well-deserved one. Hope looked in the mirror at herself. The energy she had expended had made her turn pale, and now, Duluth had the glow in her eyes more than the donator of that energy did.

They both got up. Hope said in a whisper "I wish I could live this moment forever, what was it, 'Dewey'?" She was swallowed into the moment indeed.

Duluth smiled. "But the best thing for the both of us is that I must go now. Please...do help people if you can, Hope. I don't know if I will be able to do it, but I always wish I could have done more in this world. You have a mission, our mission, my love. Please don't let that stop you." She pulled out a pair of round, Lennonesque drugstore sunglasses, ones which still had the tag on them, leading to believe that she had shoplifted them. "Do what you can. Don't worry about the others." And she climbed up to the window, and jumped out without another word.

The words lived in Hope for that night. *Don't worry about the others. Do what you can. Don't stop yourself, Hope.*

12 HOURS LATER

The words "wake up, my dear," echoed through the room. Devoid of energy and feeling mostly apathetic to further healthy discourse, Hope awoke to her stepdad standing over her. "Wake up, Hopie. It's time for a little man-to-girl talk." She felt something tickling her nose, and so with rubbing her eyes, she saw he was holding a stopwatch, the fabric strap dangling millimeters from her nose.

She didn't want to awaken. "Come on, Lou. Please leave me alone – it's morning anyways. Speak words of wisdom, father Lou, and let me be." She tightly closed her eyes, but Lou would not let her awaken.

"If you don't get up right now, I'm going to take you and dunk your head in the commode, sweetie. Get up, rise and shine, hun." He was persistent, but nevertheless serious as ever.

Realizing negotiations were neither valid nor fruitful of one's verbal windbagging labor, Hope opened her eyes. "Whaddaya want? I feel like crap right now." And she did – sure, it was only evening, but the interaction she had with her best friend, wherever she was, had finally taken some of her permanent lifeforce with her. She stretched slowly, and began to see through blurry eyes that the room was in disarray, and there was Lou, holding a packet of neatly stapled paper, like a contract. And Hope, even in her modestly fogged mind, knew that it was probably a declaration of something rather official.

Lou began to speak with great vigor. "You know, I have to say about you, dear, that you really have become quite a rebel in those two years you spent being the vagabond of this family. You learned how to fend for yourself, to beg, steal, cheat your way into people's hearts. It's a sad life you've lived so far." He began to pace in front of her, thinking of going on the offensive.

Hope was puzzled. "I did what I had to in order to help a friend of mine. Her name is Duluth, and she is a very special friend." She didn't want to

[193]

go on the record and say that she also held the same powers. For one, it was uncertain whether or not Duluth had been completely sobered up and reinvigorated – her skin made her look much older than the 19-year-old petite she was. It was the cost of what she had done with Duluth in the bathroom the night prior – but no one knew about it at that point. Furthermore, it really was a knack for protecting her – who knew what Lou would do to find Duluth, and make a quick buck off of her, considering his enterprising at all costs.

The man stepped up. "It doesn't matter who you help. There are people out there who are willing to risk everything for a drop – a little, teensy-weensy drop of your blood. It means salvation. Life, Hope, life." He handed Hope the papers. "I got this paper from the man with the, condition, yes, last night. These are service papers, Hope. The man is suing us for jilting him. He paid good money, and his lawyer wasted no time after I called his room and told him you chickened out. He is not only going to get his money back, but he wants everything. Our house, our cars, our fridge. He's a very unhappy man, Hopie, tonight. Bitterly unhappy."

It seemed as if Hope didn't care all that much. She had had enough of this life, the one where she was expected to be everything to everyone. She began to vent her frustration. "Look, I know I can help people, sir," she rebutted. "But this entire thing of using me, using something God had granted to me as a gift, a certain ambivalence – this is too much, Lou. We need to go and start living life like we should.

"I know we're in money troubles, my dear. But we should earn it like everyone else does. I work flipping burgers. You fix roofs. Mom does odd jobs and housekeeping. Not this, Lou." She began to feel tears creep in her eyes, as she felt frustration. "And I have to ask this question, too, Lou. How can we lose the house? I mean, I don't lose all my money if I don't pick up your crap off the wood shop floor.

Duluth pouted. "And what the hell, too, with the house? You got your damn summer home from the last time, Lou. Why don't you tell this guy to stick it – and your begrudgingly large ego – up there so it will heal also? Maybe you two can live in that house together and see who can pillage the other first for their own humanity. I'll put my five dollars on you, Lou. Ante up." She wanted to slam the door in his face.

It meant a lot to her, but nothing to her stepdad. "Look, you don't have any job skills, Hopie. You ran away from the home, you hid for all the world's purposes under a bridge for months. What can I do to get you that job? For Christ's sake, you don't even have a school record, save this year!" His voice began to ramp up as he pressured his stepdaughter into making a contradiction of interests. "And you know what?" he said in pure guilt. "Angry people are in this world. A lot of them.

"They have miserable lives. Drink pure chemicals in their food and water. They do it every day because they feel better about it. Stuff their faces with crap. Period. And then they feel bad about it. Only they will step over our dead bodies to get their fix. Every time. You could change that. But when a guy is sitting at home wondering the next time he'll be able to shit in peace rather than pain –" he began to rant.

Resolute, she fired back at him in the crossfire. "You can't even speak your shit in peace, Lou. I did that out of pure necessity. I didn't do it because I wanted to pay bills. I did it because I was afraid. Very afraid, of people like you. People whose utter ambivalence to others shows so openly on their faces and in their attitudes. You don't care, do you? There's not even a look of caring on your face, Daddy. You have evil in your eyes." She called him Daddy for the first time, and didn't even notice. But it was subconsciously penetrating to her at this point.

Before there was another word, Lou's empty left hand struck Hope in the face. She let out a scream, and Lou yelled "You don't even get a clue about needs anymore, Hope Malott!" She began to run, but as she grasped for the door to the hallway that didn't seem to open, she was pulled in to him, turning her around. "Look, you can run to your Mommy right now and cry to her. She is downstairs filing ads for the furniture in this room online. There are tears in her eyes, and she sent me up here because she's too Goddamned embarrassed to look at you. Such a child, you Hope. What is wrong with you?"

The discussion was shifting gears, and she began to fear what was next. "MOM! MOM!" she screamed. "LET ME GO, LOU!" she said, her body beginning to flail as she tried to escape the grasp of what was now a very intrusive part of her life, living in her same domicile.

He began to clamp down on her. "Carrie is not going to help you on this. Either you calm down or we're going to go down to the police station. You'll spend the rest of your childhood floating between the detention centers and the psych ward. Do you want that? Huh, DO YOU?" he began to yell.

She began to realize the futility of her operations. This was a man who didn't want to budge. Hell-bent on making a quick buck, she calmed down. "What do you want me to do, Lou. What?" She emphasized the last word, and began to scream.

He let her go from being pushed against the wall. Taking a step back and straightening his collared shirt, he grabbed the paper. "I have a client who just had a baby two weeks ago. It is on life support because one of his valves is leaking profusely. The baby's hooked up to a machine, and the parents can only afford $25,000. You'll get your modesty and humility, I'll get enough money to get that pain in the ass – literally – to shut the hell up. Deal?"

There was some sense in the room finally. Shaking her stepfather's hand, they both reached an agreement. But then, there was something wrong.

The sound of crashing glass echoed through the room. Someone had thrown a glass jar in the window, lending a scare to the two of them.

Without regard for their security, they both peered out and saw many people gathered around, with signs.

Lou read the signs. "*God is watching you Hope. Cast not upon the man what ye owes to the Lord. Why can't you decide on your own salvation.*" The angry mob had seen enough. "Stay inside, Hopie. Let me handle those folks out there." He ran down the hall, to see Carrie running up the steps, tearing up.

"They have come for Hope. One of them banged on the door, saying that it was wrong for her to be asking for money." She ran into the arms of her husband.

"Screw them, hun. I'm going to get my shotgun and scare the shit out of them." Before he could go, Carrie yelled "No, dear. You have to go out there and try to calm them down. Chances are if you shoot first, they'll have every right to kill you, dammit, because they will have guns, too."

"Forget it," he yelled. But then she reminded him that this was the way her first husband passed away. "Don't do it, damn you," she yelled. He agreed, and he stepped out.

The mob went quiet as soon as he went out. Raising his hands, Lou smiled. "Folks, I am here to announce that we will no longer accept exorbitant amounts of money for Hope Malott's saving services. Effective immediately, we will only take what the person feels appropriate."

The heckling began. "How are you going to pay for your German meinkampf , you pompous ass!"

"Yea, but then are you going to pay people back if she can't get the moles off her dad's ass?"

"You're a cheap shit, and so is your daughter! Save people, don't take their lives for a fee!"

[197]

It was a high pressure situation, and nevertheless, a turning point in the story. But then again, Hope was going to experience one of the first chances to really return to normalcy – and that would come from the eyes of a child once again.

As she walked up the stairs, she took a look in the mirror at herself. And then she had to walk away.

IX

The Ultimatum

45 MINUTES LATER

FORT DIX MEDICAL CENTER, PEDIATRIC WARD

She could feel the pressure of the situation of the room as the winds of the positive pressure room began to blow out, blowing her dark black hair in the gust of wind as the door opened. In it was the beeping of meters, the dead and lifeless glowing of the instruments as a lone LED bar shone in the room. In it was gathered a bunch of family members, all with the sound of weeping as they were gathered around something, somewhere. She began to peer around the very dark room, wondering as to why so many people huddled around a campfire, and none looked very content. She began to wish perhaps that she hadn't taken this one on.

As she got closer, she could see what she thought was an incubator, and in it, a very small child, perhaps one that was born prematurely. The crowd parted as she stepped nearer. They all looked at her with a very loving eye, as if she was the tender of a gas station on a deserted country road in the middle of the night. Her glowing blue eyes, oceans of tempered glass that sparkled in the morsels of rays that emanated through the room, focused on this baby.

"Hope, please help her," one of the people said as she stepped nearer. "She doesn't have long." The incubator was sealed, but the baby inside showed signs of life, although with the cobwebs of equipment lending the fear of a matrix of problems, it stung the girl who was visiting to see this go on.

She looked into the bin, and saw the baby open her eyes. They were just as blue as hers, and the black hair, what little there was, seemed to flow back towards the fontanelle like the streams of hair that she had combed back on her own head for years. The face was pristine, a little angel looking for an act of God to save her.

Hope remembered everything her father said. She had done this many times before, but somehow, this felt like it had to go wrong. Seeing a version of her own birthing in this child, a sort of time travel in her mind and conscience – it was a terrible recollection of a lost childhood. She had literally grown up too fast, and it made her feel inside like vomiting. But she had to pass this blood on. It was only right in her mind. For in this, it was justification for all the things that were wrong with this world. She took a look into the lights, rubbed her hands through the waves in her hair, and said a prayer.

With a nod, the attending nurse began to depressurize the incubator, and a hiss followed through the room. This was it, and she felt suddenly that this was going to take every last bit of energy to complete.

Placing her thumbs on the baby's sternum, she licked her lips 6, perhaps 7 times, trying to get every last bit of the lifeforce on them. The air was dry, drier than she had planned, and she could feel the ambient flow of the air in the room dry them over and over again. She took to trying to circumvent it by thinking of dinner, a good fried chicken breast she had enjoyed some time ago. It was hard, but she felt like it was helping her.

She began to breathe, closing her eyes and holding the infant about six inches off the mat. Placing the baby on her face, she began to blow into the slowly fading baby's nostrils. She anticipated the room to begin glowing, the life going back into the baby and taken from her. She gave three breaths, then four, then six, then ten. Opening her eyes, she looked into the incubator, and could only see the child she was supposed to help slowly fade, its pale blue eyes beginning to fade into the darkness of that room.

Hope could feel the frustration begin to take over her. She wanted to prove her stepdad wrong, and it weighed on her like the force of gravity upon a neutron star. She could see herself doing this, like she had done with Dari, like Duluth, like the older lady. But somehow, she could not feel her energy, her eyes beginning to fade.

In a rush for immediate results, she backed the baby away and bit her own bottom lip as hard as she could, a haphazard and jury-rigging attempt to draw blood. It took some time, but she grabbed her nail on her thumb and slit it lengthwise, to which the blood began to come out. She saw it go down to the blanket, then on the floor, with a dark olive color that resembled the fertile soils of Mesopotamia, the cradle of life. But like the Crescent, this cradle with the baby would fall – and felt incredibly doomed to extinction and failure because the forces of life had gone dry.

The blood began to drip, falling on the floor. Hope panicked, and brought the baby closer to her mouth, allowing for the forest green gel to drip down the baby's throat. She breathed harder and harder, and began to curse out loud as to why she couldn't do this. The baby began to choke, and she realized that there was a point where this baby would asphyxiate in her arms.

The machines began to slowly beep slower and slower, soon beginning to flatline. Hope stumbled, feeling the effects of having both hyperventilation and low blood levels. She looked at the baby, its life beginning to end right there in her view. Her eyes blurred, she could see the family begin to caress the baby's hair, that same hair she could see herself in.

Lou began to approach the family, ready to cower and offer condolences. But the family literally would not turn and give him forum on the matter.

[201]

They were focused there on the child they were losing – and the failed attempt to perform a miracle.

The tones were steady, and it was over. Hope sat there, dejected in the corner. She knew that Duluth's interaction with her had drained her of every single bit of energy she had. She began to think about the time she had spent trying to hide this, how she had been suckered into doing this and taking advantage of people. She felt empty, a shell of herself. It may have been the meaning of what she had been warned about by her stepdad all along.

She cowered in the corner, looking at her body. Her outfit, once the pride of her status, was covered in blood and wrinkled. Her hair piled across her face, and her eyes glowed weakly as she gave the appearance of an angry witch, a dark angel. It gave such a deep contrast to the bright face she had always presented, happiness and sweetness. She looked tired for the first time. It was wrong, but it was the first time anyone had seen her hit by her mortal side.

The father walked over, his sorrow turning to anger. He had forced the god of greed before him. "Where is your father. I want my….my Goddamned money back," he yelled. But Hope did not look up, trying not to make eye contact. He pulled her arm up, rising her to her feet. "Where is he? He's a con artist, a liar."

Looking around, she saw that Lou had left the room. There was no one there to defend her, no one to tell this angry man who was down five figures of hard-earned money that it was all just a mistake, and that he would be repaid in full. "I don't know, sir, I don't."

The man was very incensed as to how Hope suddenly could not heal anyone immediately. Frustrated and overwhelmed by the stress, he could see his only opportunity come and fade like the comets through the sky. "I saw your ass on the news. You've been running this whole scheme so much…and yet you can't even do this for me now."

It was futile to argue. He began to wind up to hit the teen, but then, the mother, a bastien of fair attitudes, grabbed his arm, and said "Don't do it, hun. Let God decide on whether or not our baby deserved to go to Heaven." She pulled his arm back down to his waist. "But you still deserve your money back, though. Where is Lou, Hope?" she asked.

At that moment, she began to feel like fainting. The room began to spin, and soon, she could not hold it anymore, the words beginning to mush together like potatoes under the whisk. She knew nothing but to hold on at that point, and indeed, she did, until her head hit the floor.

It seemed like forever that she had been out of her universe, that little abode where she could be safe and sound, her beliefs fitting in the alternative to the rigors of her day. But then it was only a couple of hours. The doctors had come in and moved her to a wheelchair out in the lobby. She didn't have any identification on her, the medical staff refusing to believe in the black-magic witchcraft that Hope had presented. Although they had good reason to believe Hope needed help, they wanted to notify Lou, her stepdad, and he had bailed.

She opened her eyes, and looked around. The room was empty, and there was no one to help her. She could hear what she thought was her stepdad coming close. The wind gave a waft of his seemingly signature aftershave towards her nostrils. Still too tired to realize it, the unknown man, or perhaps Lou, grabbed the wheelchair, and began pushing it quickly away from the area. He was saying something, but she couldn't understand it. Her body was slumped over, resembling that of a heavy stroke victim. She was weak, and didn't know she was in danger. Her clothing was completely in shambles, and her face was pale and her mouth hung open, saliva covering her blouse and coat.

The man went to an empty room, throwing the lifeless body on the bed. Hope realized it was Lou, as he began to criticize her. "You know, all this shit about you and your gift is really pissing me off, Hopie. I hope you get my drift now." He pulled the chair away. "Your blood is the life of millions, saving us from ourselves. And making me filthy as shit rich. When you don't work, I don't work." He grabbed her, and she began to try to scream as loud as she could, but it seemed no one could hear her. They were somewhere, anywhere, but it didn't seem like anyone cared. The room was empty, and no one heard her screams as Lou had his way. Her body began to writhe on the bed as he walked towards the door, slamming it. "And you know what, if you don't do this for me, I have to do this for me. I can't have it like it is, you sure as hell aren't."

Hope did not know what to do, except to try and let out what she hoped for was a loud enough scream to be recognized. Still weak and disheveled, a medium peep was all she could muster. She felt the pain of Lou going through the room, his sweat dripping on her skin into the scars of the cuts she had made for months before. The pain was enough to make her diaphragm clinch like the sting of the first breath of cold December air that awaited her outside.

She tried everything to get out of the situation. Her body was paralyzed, not only by fear, but also by the true weakness that had seized her. Never before had she felt so bled of her inner self, and the energy within, that burned within her like a fire. It was extinguished with the holy water of Beezelebub, and it emanated within the room.

Lou was hellbent on getting revenge. He got close over her face, putting the examination spotlight directly over her head like an old-time interrogation of a criminal. The difference was that this time, the perpetrator was controlled the show – and it devastated her to be there. "And now, Hopie, this is the time I make all my money back. You have the blood – and now, this is the way we get it out." He pulled out the straps of the bed, which now was known to be capable of holding down less than mentally stable patients, tying her down in the equivalent of a straitjacket. She immediately gave in, her energy still rebounding.

He turned, and reached for a shiny object. She saw it at the very last moment – it was a scalpel, sharp as ever. Lou looked at it like a child, fascinated by its shine and gleam. The rays from the light over the head of Hope reflected off the scalpel and into the now glassy eyes of Lou, a sure sign of the anger and impasse of the man who had so dearly watched her be raised from next door, who had come to her mother's rescue after the tragedy that had happened thanks to another evil person not so long ago. Closing her eyes, she pictured herself being with Duluth, with Alex, with Carrie, and Adriana. Feeling the tears coming, but somehow choking them back, she pulled on the straps.

Lou smiled. "This is where the blood shed for our sins will establish the new covenant. This time, and every time." He pushed the scalpel to the left side of her neck, just by the glands. She winced as she felt the pain of the scalpel. There was no light in the room, nothing to stop and let her heal. Closing her eyes, she pictured herself in a place where she was happy. She remembered the words that Duluth had left her in closing: *Don't worry about the others. Do what you can. Don't stop yourself, Hope.*

And then she saw it for the first time: she began to think about Alex, and his right way of doing things. She saw that man, that father of hers, kicking the snot and the devil out of Lou, that bastard who had married his mom at gunpoint for her children's sake. And then she saw what she thought was Oaf, standing there over her, telling her in a loud, monotone "You can do this, Hopie! Yee-haa!" And she began to smile as Lou began to cut deeper and deeper.

Lou immediately began to panic. The room filled with light, a fountain of blood beginning to emanate from beneath her chin. She laughed and laughed, as she looked at Lou, whose face was developing shock. He began cutting and cutting until he could not push the scalpel in farther.

Hope smiled. "You bastard. You killed me, didn't you, Lou Mendoza? Well, here's to that." She chuckled, and saw her mother come into the room, her eyes showing clearly that she was worried. Seeing her strapped down to the bed, Carrie began to cry. "What are you doing to her, Lou?"

[205]

she asked. "Oh, my God, you sick man!" she proclaimed. She ran over to grab the scalpel out of his hand, but Lou did the final deed of evil, placing a zigzag cut of glowing angst across Hope's windpipe.

Hope continued to laugh, as she began to lose blood. Her wound glowed like a gilded necklace, and healed slowly. She only had minutes to live, but these were the best minutes she had. She saw her mother defend her against this evil man.

Most importantly, Hope Malott finally realized that indeed, her mother had done good in her life.

Carrie pushed Lou to the ground. "You don't deserve this, Lou. And neither does she." She pulled out a leg from an examination table. It was dark, rusted, and sharp on the end. "Here's to coming full circle, asshole." She then took the metal and drove the shard of the broken leg directly into Lou's forehead. She did it once, then twice, then three more times. Each time, the manifestation and anger of years of holding Alex's anger back, all those times when she had to hide her pride, all those times she had to go and explain about how Hope was a gift while trying to lasso her need for money and love, it all came out. And she had finally been able to release her of her sins.

She turned to Hope, who was strapped into the bed. By now, her entire body was covered in the blood she had shed so many times for the good of man and soul. And she was quickly losing the battle she had fought.

Carrie gave Hope a look. "Hopie, are you OK?" she asked in jest. "Got yourself a little boo-boo, hun?" She laughed, holding back what were definitely tears of regret and sorrow rather than happiness.

Seeing the light in her eyes in that dark room, Hope smiled. "I got a little one on my neck. I was playing, Mommy, with Adriana, and I fell on the fence. You know, that rusty one." She gave a chuckle.

Realizing that this was the end, because the wound had not begun to heal, and her blood was low, Carrie placed a kiss on Hope's forehead. "I found these vials, Hopie. I saw everything you said on your video, and you are right, hun. 'I bleed myself for you, for the forgiveness and resolve of what ills you.' So true for this moment, Hopie. So true."

Hope smiled for that one last moment, as her eyes began to glaze over. "You know, I have to say, this was an awesome time, Mommy. I remember the first time I found out about this entire thing with my blood, it was embarrassing. The first time I used it on someone, it was embarrassing. The first time I earned a dollar, it was embarrassing. But this time, the way it turned you from an average woman to a hero, the way it solved the problems....I feel...I feel like I've done what I needed, Mom. I've done a lot of things, made friends. You know, if you ever need someone like me, go and find her. She dropped in last night, Mom. She is here, on this planet, she's out there. She understands this far better than I do, Mommy. And nothing is better than her. 'Cept you, of course." Mustering her last breaths, the wounds from the scalpel began to make her throat whistle.

Carrie began to see the light at the end. The room started to fade, the light slowly shading from the light green and blue to a green, then beginning to turn yellow, like a coke oven. "I think you have done well enough. You're going to be 18, Hopie. You did your job. You saved so many, but yet, you suffered. That is not what God put you here for. You don't deserve this any less any less than anyone else."

Hope gave her last words. "You know....I should....should have never, ever went into horticulture when I was little. Too many damn old woods...old trees sticking into new growth." She knew exactly what had happened. She didn't know how, but the last feeling was that Carrie was there for her.

"Nah, Hopie. You would have found out next year that college sucks. Life sucks. You make your path. You'd probably end up like me." She put a kiss on her forehead, as Hope's eyes began to close. "You had 17 years. Almost 18. God looked over you, and He still believes in you.

For I know the plans I have for you, declares the Lord, plans for welfare and not for evil, to give you a future and a hope.

She pulled the scalpel out. "But I can't live like this anymore. That hope or any. One of us has to go. *Haec quotiescumque feceritis, in mei memoriam facietis.*" She pulled out the scalpel, and drove it into Hope's forehead, as the room exploded with light, the light of the world that Hope had hidden for so long. It was extravagant; it was enchanting; it was epic, and it was there for anyone to see, but only Carrie saw it in that room. It was all for herself. And the knife fell to the floor.

CHAPTER X: REMAINS AN X BECAUSE YOU HAVE TO PICTURE WHAT HAPPENS IN THE MEANTIME IN YOUR MIND AND HEART. BECAUSE THERE IS NO WORD THAT CAN EXPLAIN WHAT YOU TRULY BELIEVE.

A Drop of Cold Blood is dedicated to the lives of those who practice creative arts. Through the work of their hands, their thoughts and imagination, their voices, eyes, and wit, they create where others leave blank canvas. They make the common occurrence into art and the art into a lifestyle.

XI

The Prayer

The echoes of the organ flowed through the church like the blood of the Lamb poured for us all so that sins would be forgiven for us of the earthen state. It was a Thursday, albeit one that could only be described as solemn, but definitely not sacramental.

The small wooden casket made its way up the aisle. The pallbearers trotted forth, stepping in unison like soldiers marching to the beat of the gods. There were tears wept, and surely, the tears were of far less healing and much more the manifestation of pain and anger, perhaps sorrow. It was hard to believe for some that the ride was over; that so many dreams and possibilities, the sunlight glowing through the church windows painting the carpet like a golden kaleidoscope, now were turned to the sadness of a life's passing.

Somewhere in the darkness, Duluth Kane stepped into the church, removing her hoodie and sitting down. She was 19 and slowly ageing herself into oblivion. Despite her youth and being in the prime of her adolescence, her body was completely unrecognizable. Her hair, once her trademark from her days rocking to Eighties tunes at Attrition Home, was now combed over to the side and her buzz growing in and looked more blown than Blondie. In desperation and perhaps more of fear, she had lived a transient, shadowrunning lifestyle since Hope's passing; afraid that a single confession by the wrong person could send her to the same fate as her newfound, but yet late friend, she went into hiding. Her eyes, once the hook that drew boys to her like celebrity would to the cantor, were now bloodshot. She wore very little makeup, although she still had her twinkle.

In her mind, she formulated many reasons why she shouldn't have been there. But she had to have closure on what was certainly the only person who could understand her pain deeply enough, and yet find resolution. And somehow, the aura of the sarcophagus was producing much Hope. Somehow, she could feel that which had just passed, that newfound friend Hope, just sitting there with her, the blue eyes embracing her as she knelt in tune with the Mass.

Carrie Malott stepped to the pulpit. She looked down and began to fumble about her sheets, but yet she collected herself. This was a damned hard thing to do, and like most, she never could have prepared for this moment. "Ladies and gentlemen, we are all here today because we are remembering a great woman, one of many talents, an electric smile the ability to make someone's day just by being her."

Many heads bowed in sorrow. Duluth began to look at her body quite critically, in her own form of reflection. Somehow, when she stared into those arms, that skin, her emaciated legs, the chest in which she had seen the scars, she began to see her own demise down deep within.

"I watched Hope grow up in her house. Her Dad, for which they are both in Heaven looking down and praying for us, would often go and run around the house, pretending we were superheroes saving from the evil monster.

"She would watch TV on Saturday mornings, growing up, and sometimes we would cut old cloth and make a superhero cape for her. She was our princess, most of all. Alex, her father, he would get all whooped up. He would smile and tell her to go back to her safe house."

Chuckles began to go through the audience, weak, but somehow affirmatively present. It was very welcome levity.

[214]

"We would tie our hands together with duct tape, pretending we were captured. And she would save us.

"You now, we never thought that same person would take that simple superhero vision and make it such a bold and precocious reality. And it would help so many in all the ways a girl could. She had her website, her actions, and her ability to help those she barely knew. We did our best to raise her to use that as a springboard of neither for fame nor fortune, but for forgiveness." It stung some to hear those words, even those very close in the family. And somehow, there was infinity and back to the basics, from that which we were born, the soil to soil, and dust to dust.

"Forgiveness from the fact that we are bound to this Earth for yet a moment in time, a morsel of temporal goodness, a flash in the eye of the Universe.

"But what could we do in that time, oh, what we could do. Some see it as a struggle; others, a task we are indebted to for the time of our existence in the flesh. Hope saw it differently, my friends. Hope felt it to be a springboard to become a leader and a healer.

"And so, she took that, and lived her life thoroughly. And then again, she was so synchronized to what she had to do that she abused, and forgot, what she should do. And so, I give my salute to you, my daughter Hope Malott, in the words from which I read to you every night: "And so, I give you these words: He is not here; he has risen! Remember how he told you, while he was still with you in Galilee: 'The Son of Man must be delivered into the hands of sinful men, be crucified, and on the third day be raised again.'"

An earth shaking AMEN rattled the church as the seemingly forgotten mother stepped down, hiding the tears. It was the proper closure, and one that left some sense of resolve in the pain of many.

But through all the hugs and outward expression of sympathy, there was still one who was set apart from the others. One who felt the presence, perhaps of the dying blood in the casket some twenty paces away. And she knelt down to pray.

Pulling up her sleeves, she drew a glance from some onlookers. The scars began to draw attention, as the more well-dressed family mistook her for a lost drug addict, and somehow held back in solemn tact to not call the cops. They could sense purpose in her step, and it kept them at bay. Hope, in their minds, had gathered the destitute, the rich and the haughty, the proud and the strong, and took them in her arms. It was only right that despite the greed and strangeness, that it was no place for them to openly criticize what could have been a gift sent to them by her from Heaven.

They didn't understand how much of a gift this tattered girl of many levels was, the body sitting there. She closed her eyes and began to pray. Even though she was somewhat resonant to apostasy after a hard life had devoid her of any belief that God indeed was there in His highest intent to help her, she felt a breakthrough, a win in the eyes of a lost angel who had strayed down the path of lies, cheating, and ill courage. And so, it was due time to give thanks to that whom had protected her so far.

In her first prayer, she began to piece together words in the hope someone was listening. She closed her eyes, pinching them tightly in Baptist metaphor, thinking the evangelical route of mid-day television catechism made for the best selling point.

"God, God, it's Duluth. I....I know I haven't been exactly faithful. But I have no one in this world right now." She began to feel a warmth inside, like she was doing something good. In continuance, she became more vigorous.

"Can you please lend me guidance...tell me where to go and how to do these things. I would say I'm homeless, but I know I can pray to You; and I feel like my Dad is coming to see me. God, I hope he shows up, Lord. I just don't know what to do any more.

"Please, I beg you." The tears began to flow even more vigorously, and her hands began to clasp tightly as her body began to go limp. Her nutrition and the rigor of having to fend for oneself slowly began to eat away at her willpower.

As she opened her eyes, a tear fell on a tattoo on her wrist, just above a large scar. It was a Coptic cross, something that she had done under a dare, but now seemed to be a badge of courage and of honor where it once had been a sign of committing to the Devil.

As the tear hit, she saw something that had been avoiding her for so long. The bluish green glow of C402-infused liquid hit the cross and began to twinkle in the low lights of the church. It gave a rush of divine confidence and self-empowerment in that moment, something Duluth had searched for so long.

"Please, God, please. I beg you….in Your name, help me through this." She closed her eyes again.

The wafts of incense percolated through the air. She could feel the presence of something in the pew beside her. It had emptied out, the line to receive the Body and Blood removed from the presence. It most likely was a bit of that which had passed before her that presented itself in Spirit; but like the feeling of true love, it is only known best when the experience has presented itself prior.

She felt comforted, though, to know for perhaps a second that she was not alone. And she would need that in every single step she took in those boots, every single decision, the patience and serenity of having path where once there existed none.

TWO DAYS LATER

MALOTT RESIDENCE

The funeral Mass had long past the Malotts as they began the slow healing process for which the healer had been taken. The suits were packed away, the family and friends had returned to the normal life of celebrity correspondence and making money on what seemed to be the toughest economy that anyone had faced. It was the unfortunate consequence of dying: that there was support there for the family, but yet never sufficient consolation.

For the first time, Lou and Carrie opened the door to Hope's room. They had feared it for the longest time: the memories had shaken the room, and even opening the door to still smell the wafts of cheap department store fragrance that Hope preferred over name brand celebrity in the meaning of the simple life – it shook the two parents down to the bone and hurt like the stab of a stone-sharpened rod in the heart.

Lou could feel her in the room. Although something had given him a great deal pain, it was like a part of Hope was in him. He saw that mirror over in the corner, and could never recall why there was the omnipresence of a greater cause. But soon, it went back to sorrow.

They could feel all the memories come back at once, grabbing that door handle.

The wallpaper, a pink heart with green background, gave Lou a sharp memory on how they were able to pay for it after Hope helped heal a broken leg. He could still hear her voice echoing through the wood in the room….

No, Lou, this is the way we do it. I don't want this to look like a Lindsay Lohan painting.

That very way that the cosmetics were on the table, in front of the mirror. Carrie remembered how she had told Hope to do it that specific way so she wouldn't forget to put the foundation on before the rouge.

Don't worry, Mommy, I'll do it this way so we look good for Church.

She was only eight, and that voice echoed through the room, too. She had kept it that way in complete obedience. For all those years. And had left it there as a final covenant.

The way the bedsheets were tossed aside as they hurried out the door that day they went to the hospital. They were a complete mess by the standard of good housekeeping. But neither of the parents wanted to touch those sheets. They were left that way because that was the way Hope wanted them to be kept.

Both could see those last moments a few days ago: his yelling at her about the failed ability to help the main with the passage of stones from aft. Now they both felt like pains in that same part of one's anatomy, that somehow, they had forced it upon themselves; that she did not deserve to be put to her demise this way.

And the wardrobe, kept neatly, with the teddy bear sitting, legs crossed at the top shelf. It was that way because Hope knew her Mom would see that, somewhere, somehow. She knew it would make her day. Carrie picked it up, and began to pull it, the bear shooting a stare into the eye of the parent. As she grasped it, she gave it a hug so tight that it gave the feeling of Hope's last shades of love and kindness, her feelings taken to that bear also in a hug like she had done for so many nights during her stay on Earth.

As Carrie grasped it, a note popped out, a folded sheet that came from inside the bear's blue overalls. It had pink ink written on composition paper, in Hope's script and scribbling, looking as if it had been put together in a hurry.

Teddy bear, teddy bear
Wipe the tear from your button eye
Teddy bear, teddy bear
You don't need to know why

She grew up in a neighborhood of the house next door
And always yelled across the alley to my window for sure
We used to draw toy car maps on the kitchen floor
Our childhood days never were a bore

Teddy bear, teddy bear
Play high five with me in the backyard
Teddy bear, teddy bear
Why is life always to be so hard?

When you were eight on your birthday day
Your mom invited me for the night to stay
I gave you a small box that wasn't at bay
And it had a teddy bear in it, and you were on your way

Teddy bear, teddy bear
Tell me your best hug story
Teddy bear, teddy bear
About living in all the glory

Soon you turned into a teenage wonder queen
Better for anyone, the world has ever seen
I couldn't say in words what you mean
When I first saw your face, what you would mean

Teddy bear, teddy bear
Come to sleep in my arms at night
Teddy bear, teddy bear
Make everything in the world seem right

You had your friends after eighteen years
And suddenly they became your worst fear
Because the things they did to you were never mere
And now we cry for you are not here

Teddy bear, teddy bear
Now we will weep together
Teddy bear, teddy bear
Why do you cry for such bad weather?

When you passed on it was hard for me
To not see your blond hair and blue eyes to see
So your mom and dad wanted it well to be
They gave me your teddy bear so it could be free

Teddy bear, teddy bear
I can't love you like she would
Teddy bear, teddy bear
But if I tried, I really could.

HMDK2013

Those words could not have been more impactful. She didn't know what they meant, or who she was thinking of when she wrote those words. But in the final act, she tucked it right back into the bear's overalls, right where she found it.

Sensing the moment, Lou walked over to his wife. "You know, it didn't have to be this way, dear. I'm sorry it's been so hard." With an embrace, he sat down on the bed next to her.

There was no embrace to come back from her. "It was a strange life my daughter led. It was one that filled itself with so little energy and so little time. Time I will never, ever get back, Lou." It was hard to put that embrace into Lou. Carrie was indeed married to this man, and they were partners. But somehow, Carrie's interior love for Hope proclaimed that Lou's gentle purpose now overshadowed his deep need for personal gain. And so, she clasped away.

"But what are we going to do with all this stuff? This computer, these moccasin shoes, these stuffed animals? All reminders. Perhaps we should give them to Adi. She loved her stepsister very dearly."

But yet, Carrie picked up and clasped the bear ever closer. "They are relics. Golden calves, Lou. We shall not worship them henceforth." Carrie gave the hint through her words, but Lou was still digging desperately for the right words to say. They had been married for years, but still were thousands of miles apart when it came to each other.

"Perhaps Hope would have loved them to go to Attrition Home. They did so much good for her. Especially that girl she met –" but then Carrie began to hint at "no more."

"The place was cursed from the start," proclaimed Carrie. "Those folks killed my husband, Louis. What in the hell is wrong with you and your egotistical babble. You realize –" as she began to pound her fists on a nearby coffee table, making the picture frames rattle, "that you and your insistence of me shutting up has cost me so much, Louis. Too much. Too

Goddamned much." And she threw the bear across the room with a squeak on impact with the wall and ran down the hall, tears in her eyes.

"Honey...." But it was too late.

XII

The Tertiary

27 HOURS LATER

STEELTON, PA

A lonely man, worn thin by the cold nights of the Commonwealth, sat quietly in front of the fireplace, cuddled up in a blanket on his recliner. It was a fairly late evening, and the wind blew outside as the rain began to chill the air. Inside, the man's mastiff laid down on the rug, his cheeks flopping on the floor and looking as if he was ready to eat the rug whole.

As he snored, the wind outside would whistle through the bushes, lending an eerie feeling to the night. It was a dark one, indeed, and it could have almost lent creed to the mystery which would set in.

And it did. A gust of wind swept through the house as the window suddenly opened. The fire began to flicker as the ashes were blown about the room. The dog began to bark suddenly, waking the man from his slumber.

"Ah, shut up, ya rotten mutt!" the man screamed, half asleep. "These damn windows are so old they opened themselves all the time. Gotta call that plumber guy with the mustache I see all the time." As darkness crept over, the dog began to run towards the other room.

The man rubbed his eyes. "Aw, God, where did that dog go?" he asked in heavy Brooklyn accent. He threw the blanket off angrily and put on his slippers, thinking the dog had gone away.

As he turned the corner, he reached for the light. And then, he saw two glowing lights in the corner. Thinking of fireflies, he went to grab his newspaper. He was oblivious to what was truly going on. It was the first encounter of a predator. And it was the last thing he touched before the face of God. "What the...." It was all that could come from him.

THE NEXT MORNING

PAT'S PETROLEUM, LANSDALE, PA

An old truck, beat up and somewhat smoking up the neighborhood, pulled into the station. Pat's was one of the last stops before downtown Philadelphia on the highway, and the commander of the nicked truck was out of gas.

The lanky figure got out of the truck as it stalled next to the pump. It was a woman, in a trenchcoat and a hat. She could have passed for a man, but the long black hair coming out of the fedora gave her away. Putting on her black wraparound Gucci sunglasses, she obviously was in distress.

The attendant, an Arab gentleman who ran the convenience store, began to eyeball the character. Lots of folks would come in and out of this area, but she had a definite suspect appearance. Her clothes were worn and tattered, but somehow, she could afford specs worthy of the runway. He put one hand on his handgun, and continued to fuss about the lottery tickets. It perhaps was in his blood to be suspect about anything that didn't mean hot dogs and quick sales. She slammed the hood on the old beat up pickup. "Dammit." The truck was stolen from the night before, and she really struggled with trying to figure out exactly how carburetors flood when you push the pedal too hard. It was just fortunate enough the strange woman found a truck with an automatic.

Just then, a man stepped up to the side of the truck. "Hey, babe. You know, these trucks have the 350 in them."

The female was not amused. "Buzz off, bozo. Don't need no gearhead in here right now." She looked down and began to walk away, giving a nudge to the man.

Getting to the curb outside the door, she sat down and began to cry, her legs crossed in scissor on the curb and kicking her boots in her feet. She was tired, but systematic. She knew her mission was around there somewhere. Looking around, she saw a map, one that the manager of the store would put for travelers to find their way. (He was sick of dealing with people who were lost all the time, and felt it was better for them to help themselves. Candidly, he believed these Americans were stupid.)

Seeing the map displayed on the wall, she peered at it, and began to trace her way towards downtown Philadelphia. As she sat there, the tears began to run down her face. She knew where she had to go….it was deep inside her, like an irresistible glow that she could not hide.

The man, one much senior to the mysterious figure, and certainly of boomer age, rubbed his hands, sticking them in his pocket. To him, this was a young lady, not more than a girl, who needed help. He tried to hide his excitement by pulling his shirttail out of his pants, but somehow, things still "broke through".

He sat down next to her as she stared at the map. "Honey, babe, you a farm girl? Why you cryin'? Daddy throw ya outta the house? Daddy get drunk and beating ya?" He began to impose his will on her.

Again, the lanky woman relented. "Like I said, buzz off. Keep your stogie in your humidor. Walking around like that. *Lie to me, Pinocchio*. Loser."

Fleeing, she began to walk away and towards a slightly well-located pay phone, knowing that avoidance was solid gold – and she didn't like this situation at all. And so, the man began to grab her. "You know, you aren't from this part of town, are ya? You drive that old shitkicker and come in here lookin' like you just came from Pennsyltucky." He turned her around and looked her dead in the glasses. "You know, I have a place that you can clean up after exiting the mansion. It's called the Hotel Ronnie, and it's down the street. You leave that truck here, OK? I'll fix it in the morning."

"You don't get it, do you? I don't know who you are, dude, but look. I'm not going with you anywhere. I don't want to! And that's final!" She pushed him off and grabbed her trenchcoat even tighter, but he had a grasp on her.

Just then, the attendant had had enough. He mentioned in heavy British Arab accent "You two! You stayed here long enough! Off now! I call the police!" he yelled in broken English. They both could see the man with mace in one hand and something gray in the other.

Suddenly, the two were friends and confidants. The taste of hot lead began to run through their veins, sinking in simultaneously like a razor. "OK, alright, you got a winner. Down the street, that's it." He directed her to his truck, a noticeably newer one, to his source of life.

Arriving at the abode, they both began to smile at each other. He closed the door slowly. As she began to look around, he began to disrobe himself. She sensed it in him that he had some purpose. The living room presented itself as a well-to-do person's place of living. And then she spotted a picture on the desk, this man with a woman. She suspected it was not his daughter. And she felt a pain that would not go away. She knew what she had to do, to fix this ill person.

All it took was for her to enter to realize she had her way. Throwing those same Gucci sunglasses on his couch, she laughed.

"OK, hunny. You needed this one," he said. And the glow in her eyes and the "Yes, I did," was the last thing he saw. And then nothing.

The next morning, the man's wife came home from business. The door was left open, which was typical of her forgetful husband. He would often leave it open at night; she was ready to pound him, make love to him, and then forgive him. It was a relationship of typical middle-age dystopia.

"Ron, dear, where are you?" she asked curiously. "You left the door open again sweetie. Come on, wake up!" she playfully demanded as she went through the second floor apartment. The water was running in the bathroom, so she said "Ron, you in there?" The door was not locked.

[228]

Anticipating a moment of sheer intimacy, she pulled her bra strap loose and took off her coat.

"Ron?" She opened the door. In it was her husband. His head had been turned sideways, his neck broken. Mouth gasping for air some time ago, it dripped with a bluish, green slime that came out of his mouth like someone had blown up a glowstick in his throat. His pants were down around his ankles, his underwear still on. And his keys and wallet were gone.

It was only imaginable what Ron's wife did. And the whole neighborhood knew. The echoes of the scream were there. And it almost was loud enough to make it to the Malotts.

5:00 PM

30TH STREET STATION, PHILADELPHIA

She was down to her last $5, able to panhandle it off a businessman sitting outside a restaurant drumming away on two buckets to Hall and Oates. And now, she was ready to spend another night in the safety of the train station. Duluth had known that there were several folks down in the station; generally, the transit agency would not actively shoo them away, especially because budgets were tight and they were more afraid of guys with suitcases full of thorium. And so, she would tuck herself away in a back corner. She'd clean up in the bathroom and wipe her face off. But even with that, she began to find it hard to look herself in the eye. She knew the reason she was in this manner, tattered, broken, somewhat unkempt, would be seen in those eyes through the mirror. Her body knew that energy wasn't there anymore, and the eyes seldom would glow their emerald ruby, but she was obsessive-compulsive and wouldn't look, because it would make her think of how broken she really was.

The news came on with the famous theme. "Breaking news out of Lansdale today as a very vicious execution style murder takes place.

According to Pennsylvania State Police…" Duluth came out of the bathroom and looked up by chance.

"….this man, 47 year old Ronald Fitz, was murdered by an unidentified person this morning, apparently by poisoning. Fitz's wife had come home from a trip and found his body in the bathroom.

"Police found his neck broken and a strange unidentified substance with a neonlike glow coming out of it. Police have also indicated that a similar instance may have occurred twice in the past 48 hours as two other potentially related murders, one in Steelton and one just two blocks away

[230]

on Paulus Street, may be connected, as witnesses identified a female, about 5'7", with glowing eyes matching the Fitz description."

Duluth began to travel the distance in her mind. Experience had groomed her, but yet years of being constantly subjected to chemical intake and trying to put her music first had left her quite opaque of mind. But then, she saw the map, and then realized whoever it was had a plan to head towards town.

She looked up at the screens suspended on the pillars in the station. A man strode up to her side. "Funny thing these murderers are. What did they do, shove a glowstick in their piehole?" he said. "Don't turn out like them, young lady."

She turned, and looked him in the eye. When she blinked, her eyes flashed blue for just a moment. She knew it, but the man was just too intent on getting home after a long day's labor to notice. She saw him give a dirty look, but without a word, he shook his head and walked towards the platform.

Grabbing what was left of her belongings, she began to think deeply. And then, she remembered the glowstick. But this time, she felt like it was different. Hope was a bold and intriguingly curious person, but she could not have done this type of action. She was dead in that casket. She went to the funeral Mass. The open casket could not have been more gratifying. But then, it was over. That feeling just felt too foreign to her, yet it was apparent that deep inside, there was a drive that pulled them together.

Sneaking in the back door of the 46 bus, she knew she had one place to go. She had to save her legacy.

THE MALOTT RESIDENCE

"We can't keep them from knocking down our door, honey, about this," Carrie screamed at her second husband as the sounds of the masses penetrated through the walls. Everyone knew about Hope and her passing, but then again, this was not the gathering for healing, but one for hatred.

Adriana clung to her teddy bear, even at 16 a welcome respite for what was going on. Still reeling from her sister's passing, she feared the decisions she would make, if she did them at all. As she sat there on the bed, she saw the blades of scissors in the corner, with crusted blood on them from long ago. In her mind, as she hid behind those thick glasses, she felt like that blood of Hope was the one thing that held the two of them together. She caressed the wound every night from long ago, the plant long passed but splinter of which still alive, and she would nip at it, thinking somehow there were still parts of Hope in it. The ultimate sadness was in her every action and reaction, and she would never mention it to anyone. It was the beginning of healing for her from the cut that stung even more - that of losing her childhood friend.

"Well, what do we do, honey?" Lou yelled as he ran through the house, looking for something heavy to carry. The lynch mob atmosphere was beginning to antagonize the neighbors, and he was afraid that words would not hurt but sticks and stones were next.

Carrie felt angry. "You were the one who wanted to make this a public affair because your behind couldn't keep a job down at the Armory!" she screamed. She was trying to take all of her fears and put them in words. They stung enough as they left her lips; but yet, she was somehow relaying that feeling.

And then, Lou said the strongest and most bitter words he had ever spoken, a rash of viciousness he regretted as soon as he said it. "Well, you had to go out and play J. Robert Oppenheimer and now you have a dead girl to speak for it!"

But the mother of a passed girl never relented upon the hell and fury she hath. "You are a pig, Louis! You go out there before I grab the shotgun and turn you into a Ken doll! Damn it!" she screamed. She ran upstairs, expecting the fort of the home not to hold and the door to break down.

Lou came out, slamming his fist on his head. He knew he had gone too far, but didn't have the resolve in him to come back down from his seemingly haughty position. The funeral had just passed, and now, he was reliving the matter all over again. He held his fist high in the air, thinking God was punishing him for shedding the blood of a daughter that wasn't his for the mere benefit of a few dollars. He would look up at the ceiling, and try to see Him in the rafters, asking for forgiveness from this hell. In his deepest thoughts, he quoted Paul.

Likewise the Spirit also helpeth our infirmities: for we know not what we should pray for as we ought, but the Spirit itself maketh intercession for us with groanings which cannot be uttered.

It echoed through the room as he had decided to face the crowd. Once again, he took the deep breath and opened the door.

"You folks! Hey!" he screamed. "For Christ's sake, we just had a funeral! Why are you here?" The crowd all began yelling their insults, grasping at rocks and throwing them at him in lucid lapidation. He felt like he had committed adultery in front of the Pharisees, but that of the mind, where he had become so in love with the falsehood of using a gift for his own good.

"She's not really dead, you bastard!"

"Your daughter stopped curing and now she's out there killin' people!"

"Why don't you get her a job and reel your delinquent offspring back in!"

The words were in a mess, but each stung tremendously as they rolled off the tongues of the mob. He tried to say what he wanted, but there was no way to calm them down.

Immediately, the world for the family of the passed began to spin in a far different, more bittersweet way. The experience of the mobs was a common thing during Hope's lifetime and brief time in the spotlight, a sort of necessary evil for him. What waited outside, though, was not the mass of hopefuls, nor the desperation of the people for salvation through a little girl. Instead, they were out there, with the blood of Lou on their minds. And he couldn't swallow it, no matter what.

He slammed the door and took a breath. Hope, please help us. God....

A gunshot sounded in the distance, and everyone scattered. The window didn't break, but the three of them, all in the living room, ducked down, expecting any moment for the threshold to mount.

10:42 PM

As far away as Duluth Kane wanted to be from that mob, one could not have understood the sorrow and fear that her appearance would bring. She had hidden in the backstreets as she saw the mob gathered around the house she so much wanted to re-enter. The reaction of the public to this mystery woman made her fear her own life. Although it was probably faded so far that she would simply be the twinkle of an old man to his grandchildren, the night air and the faded moonlight meant you could see the glow in her eyes. She knew the general public nowadays was short-tempered and reacted with such reckless abandon that there would not be a word to explain, nor gesture to reason. The next moment she stepped into that mob would be her last. And she would not have the ability, damned as she was, to mend herself – or the broken fences she made.

And so, she let the setting of the Moon set the mood. The police had cleared the street, but garbage lay like it had blown in the wind from the docks. She stepped around it, her feet beginning to ache as her fishnets, torn and tattered, gave her the look of a punk, albeit unintended. She had to muster the strength to knock on that door one more time. As she walked up the stairs, she saw the behemoth of the house lay before her. The first time she stepped up there some time ago, the exterior lights gave it the look of warmth and a strong, fortlike experience. The guard at the front lent a sense of piousness and royalty, the virgin territory of life that she sought.

But months of war on the streets and dismay in the House of Hope had left the building in the state of shambles. The paint was there, but the house was dark and as cold as the night. There was no longer a guard, just bars on the windows, evident of the fear of the Jews of the public.

She swallowed one last gasp. She had no energy left in her, and this was it. She had not eaten that day, and her vigor began to carry to her blood sugar. It was that hunger, her hunger, of which gave her the push of attitude to get her up there. She could barely stand, but it made it for her.

She gave four knocks.

One, then two. A pause. Three. Then four.

She put her head on the door, and leaned against it, her arm across the screen. She didn't know what to say.

Lou opened the door. "Hi." She was startled to get such rapid response. "My name is Duluth. Duluth Kane. I was your daughter's friend. I need to know something – " she could barely get the words out before Lou, behind the screen began to relent.

After the fight and raucous discourse, he literally had no fuse, nor active empathy. "You just don't get 'Go away forever, you are meaningless to me', do you? I told you before after she died not to come here. At all." He began to close the wooden door in a near slam.

She gave her last bit of vigor, grabbing the screen door, and ripping it open, saving time to hold the door from Lou slamming it. He gave her forum. "You heard about the break-ins in this neighborhood?" She still could not look him in the eye. Perhaps it was weariness, or just the fact she had little respect for him at the moment.

"Yes, and God help you when you're in jail, young lady. You know I should call the cops right now." He held the door, and continued, expecting verbal crossfire to occur. He knew Duluth had lip to give.

The negotiating powers were in Lou's hands. She knew she had to take a different perspective. "They weren't me, sir. I'm scared about this, and I need your help. Do you think I'd come here, knowing you were the lifeblood, and kill you instead? Damn you."

Lou sensed the sharpness in her tone, but still held tacit. "How can I help you then? You want me to go and call your Daddy? Want me to go and hand you a bowl of soup?" He shook his head.

Her quick wit got back just in time. "Actually, I didn't think of that, sir. That would be pleasant in a moment. But it's a damn cold night. Let's come in and talk." It was a concise, blandly pointy hard bargain, but it was like candy for Lou's ego. And her lack of sweetness perhaps elicited the most savory response in the man.

He opened the door for her. Not knowing what to do after a hard day, hard week, heck, a hard year, for all purposes, he welcomed her to the manger. "Look, Duluth, I don't know if it's a good idea to have you in here. My wife is very upset, my Pook is up in her room crying her lungs out every night thinking about her sister, and you come in…and you, you're a reminder of everything I did wrong."

She thought about the natural quickfire back for a minute, the words and acetic soul that had kept her alive and opened the door. But she couldn't do it. "I get a feeling that there's something else that's in play, Mr. Malott."

"Mendoza."

"OK." She chuckled, and got a grin out of him as he sat back on the couch and closed his eyes, weary from having to explain to the police what happened. "I went to your daughter's funeral and prayed. For the first time. I feel like I have something more meaningful in life. I read this passage —" she unwrinkled a piece of paper that came from a hymnal in that very church — John six thirty five — "I am the bread of life; whoever comes to me shall not hunger, and whoever believes in me shall not thirst. " She wrinkled it back up somewhat hastily, and stuck it in her shirt nearest her heart.

Lou realized she had earned some points. He felt upset in his prejudice, that which was completely unnecessary. She had believed in inspiration, a total contrast to her somewhat agnostic discourse of the past. And so, the man gave alms for just a moment. "Well, thank you. I can't throw a fellow Christian out of the household. But you sure aren't going to find the life Jesus wished in this house. There's no life left here anymore. None of it. Hope is gone. In more ways than one."

Duluth grabbed Lou, who was rubbing his eyes. "I can offer you perspective. As a fellow life...uh, whatever you want to call it. I need time to clear my mind of this. I can't go back to Attrition Home. They'll kill me if I do. I don't have a boyfriend because guys are terrible. Two down there..."

Lou gave affirmation in a giggle. "...and nothing to spare. Amen, to that."

"I don't know who is doing this crap of burglarizing properties and killing people. They think it's me. But look at me! Do I look like that description? Do I seem like I'm here to kill? For God's sake, I can barely climb these stairs. I won't break a neck. Plus – " she ran her fingers through her hair, pulling at the short blond streaks, dry as a straw – " you think a wig would look sexy and stick to this? I don't match the description."

 Lou laughed. "Yea, you don't. At all." He snickered just a little bit at Duluth's somewhat weak but salient fashionista advice.

"I want to make sure we are all safe. We share a bond." She pulled up her sweatshirt, the one she had wore to rags all along. It was the last thing she grabbed before her boyfriend finally kicked her out. "Hope gave me this bracelet the night I came in here. I keep it on because it's all I have left of my power. It's loose now...I am hungry and tired. It's the power she had to heal people. I don't know if it's cutting off my circulation sometimes or what it is doing, but somehow the only thing I have left of her is here. And I don't want to lose that, sir." She was unusually polite, which stunned him.

[238]

But he would have none of it. He felt too sad. Reaching for the bracelet, he quietly relented. You shouldn't keep it, young lady. It's going to kill you like it did Hope, and it will me." In a fit of impulse, Lou reached for the bracelet, perhaps to grasp for that last vestige of sanity. It reminded him that Adriana had one too. And this was meaning his daughter, and also now Duluth....nah, they couldn't have shared that same bond, that same physical icon....and so, he had to break it. But then she pulled back. Duluth realized the chips began to fall in her favor.

"I'll get rid of it under one purpose. You let me stay here and call my Dad. I'll be like the wind in the night."

Once the person of some uncertainty, Lou felt resolve in the young lady presented before him. And he felt like Hope would have told him to let her stay. "You drive a hard bargain, young lady, Minneapolis, or whatever your name is. But by the will and name of my stepdaughter, Hope, you can stay here."

She gave a smile. It was the first time she had smiled in the longest time. The light of the lamp in the other room caught it, and it was warmer than anything Lou had seen. And it made another light in his heart as he saw for the first time the same glow he had seen in Hope. And it reinforced it. "For a little bit."

She laid down on the couch, and took her tattered clothes off. It would be welcome respite for the days ahead.

[239]

4:14 AM

A bright light came from outside the window. She didn't know what it was, but it was loud, like chainsaws that were too close. The house was nestled somewhat back from the street, but it sounded like it was closing in. Duluth awoke on the couch, her frail and thin body draped across the middle of it like a bearskin rug. She rubbed her eyes, and looked through the window. The sound quickly went away. She didn't know what it was, but now, her headache had become ever more potent. She needed a good dose of pain reliever. And she needed it now.

She got up and began to walk barefoot across the floor, trying in the dark to find the kitchen with only a small lamp, left in the dining room as a makeshift nightlight for the "young girl" by Carrie.

The ambiently buzzing sound began flowing through the air again, echoing throughout the house. Lights began to shine again. It was the kids in the street, she figured, riding their dirtbikes in the early morning.

Turning around to notice, she ran into the wall, hitting her head. "Dammit!" she whispered somewhat loudly. But the door in front of her opened, and she saw a light like no other. Except she knew what the light wasn't...and what it wasn't was just electricity in standing.

She quickly began to recourse through her memories. But then, she took a deep breath, realizing that this was a saving grace, discovered suddenly for the benefit of her, a gift from God. In the moment, she laughed. And then it became too much as she met the floor. The transaction was there, but then, suddenly, they cut the wire.

And in that moment, she was trying to hide what she had done, so much that she could never understand her procedure. The days of hiding and sneaking in to find what was inevitably a secret elixir, but yet so far absolved from the fact that she was searching for life, normal as it could be, took over her body.

[240]

Orion Prasda cracked open the window of the Malott residence. The house was somewhat dark, but yet there was an aura glowing from the Moon in the southward window. She knew something was there that she could not find. But yet, she knew this house was the spring of eternal life that only God could grant her, and her curiosity lent a great deal of strength coming from her heart and from her willpower to her already capricious muscle, nevertheless from the power she held.

The floor began to creak, frightening Orion as she perused the darkness. She could see a cabinet glowing in the distance, the door still open from the somewhat strange events of earlier. In her deepest interests, she knew exactly what was in the cupboard. And she would have to tread no more. She saw the girl on the floor, and knew this had to be the place from the small gobs of blood beaded on the floor, twinkling like resting fireflies in the garden.

A gun cocked in the background. "Don't move, young lady." She felt cold metal and the presence of a very angry and bitter father who knew all too well what she was doing.

XIII

The Reprieve

THE NEXT MORNING

FORT DIX MEDICAL CENTER

The planet had spun yet only a half rotation, but to the girl who had endured so much the past few hours, it was spinning for her heart in a tornado. Her locks of hair, grown and tattered, sat in a pile. Her makeup, already in overuse to cover up what was an emaciated body full of scars and weariness, had begun to cake on her sides. Her arms turned blue, she had little on her body to really cover up what was the decrepit avatar to what was once a proud teenager. She was almost 20, but age began to take its toll. Waking up, a tear came from her right eye, twinkling in the morning light and showing just one last view of what had given so much of her life. Saliva had come from the corner of her mouth, a tube placed to help her breathe. She was that close to losing it all; despite the power of that which bred in her like no other, there was very little life left to Duluth.

Lou had found her collapsed in the room after he had chased the intruder and called the cops. It was a bit hard to convince them that neither the owner nor the intruder had done so. So he did the right thing: handed her off to the medics and pretended he saw nothing. The story was a pain, but thanks to a little bit of Hope luck, he washed his hands of the situation. At least for now, he was rid of a side problem. Lou, the sad man he was, walked out with a pat on his own back.

The doctor came in and turned on the light. "Good morning, Duluth. It's very nice to see you." A man of decidedly opposite stance and impression to that which had forced medicine to make her so frail and meager, he was a broadly American male. Tall and handsome, he appeared to Duluth as a sunny angel brought by the prayers she had sent to Hope some days ago. "I want to talk to you about something. Something very, very important, my fair lady."

Even in the weakened state of her poor old soul, she felt the urge to acquire the hand of her Prince Charming. "Uh, hi there. Who are you?" she gave a laugh as she gasped her first large breath of the morning air, although somewhat unfortunately clouded with the smell of hospital disinfectant.

"Who am I....young lady, my name is Matt Bailey. I'm an experimental medicine physician here at our hospital. I specialize in adolescent and young adult cases. It's nice to meet you, Duluth."

It seemed to work to give energy to the lady of ethereal power as she lay in the bed. The color of her face began to return, as the cheeks of cold, fillet-like skin began to show color. "Why am I here?" she asked in a whisper.

Bailey laughed. "Well, as it turns out, it seems like you were a home invader to some extent. A Mr. Lou Mendoza brought you here in the back of his car. He says you were a friend of a Hope Malott – " he began to comb through his clipboard and nervously pulled at the frame of his glasses – "somebody who was here not so long ago, if I recall correctly." He pulled the sheets down.

Duluth began to rise and pulled her eyes from the ceiling towards the man in the white coat. "We were best friends. We had this thing together....well, it was a special thing –" she began to utter words, feeling the emotion, but yet an urgent emptiness take over.

"I don't think you are mistaken on this, Miss Kane. Unfortunately, the truth is that I also think that special thing is why you're here, and why I need to speak with you a little bit." He set the clipboard at the foot of the

[243]

bed, and pulled the sheet aside, showing her wrist. "I have worked with Dr. Copulus on this one –" and immediately, the tension in the room began to rise, springing from nothing into a great deal of pain from inside.

The room was silent but the attitude of the girl was screaming without the spoken word. She wanted out. Somehow, she began to wiggle in frustration. "Why is this….let me out of here." The doctor grabbed her and signaled for her to relax.

"You must stay here for now, Miss Kane." He realized that her body was too vulnerable for the outside world. "Dr. Copulus is no longer with us here. I'm actually working to make his somewhat, eh, radically esoteric practice of medicine disappear." He felt like vomiting because he could have ripped that clipboard in half.

She looked him in the eye, and said "Oh, okay. Haha, just checking." She rubbed her eyes and began taking her hand, running it through her hair. Gaining more energy, her eyes opened, shining brightly in the sun. They were two spheres of tiger's eye, with a black onyx center which had just the tinge of C402 blue in them.

The doctor continued. "Duluth, the reason why you are here is not because of your inability to find shelter, or food, or hygiene. When you were out, we did a variety of tests on you. Your blood sugar was low, your heart is working twice as hard as it should because you're dehydrated. However, we also discovered that the compound in your blood is low. Very low."

Duluth chuckled. "Copulus kept it low. Kept giving me iodine pills to suppress the C402. I tried to make him stop, but he wouldn't. Until I met Hope. Knew that bastard was up to something." She slammed her head on the pillow, raised up on the automatic bed, as if to give herself well-earned affirmation to years of struggle.

"Dr. Copulus did what he knew best. And he now is paying the price for his mishap. Duluth, you have a very serious condition. You have what is called myelodysplastic leukocyte syndrome. Your white blood cells are misshapen, perhaps a little too much. They look like little eggs on a skillet...not round but messy. In addition to this, the C402...the very thing that was given you so much healing power, is so low that it actually has corrupted your immune system.

Duluth looked at Bailey, completely mesmerized. She couldn't understand what he was saying, but somehow, it was penetrating. It was the load of seed that blew in the wind, only it was the poison of her own body attacking her. She began to mutter.

I don't want to die....

"The truth is, Duluth, is that your body is essentially being held together by what is left of the C402. I don't know how long you have in this condition, but we need to preserve whatever it is in that nasty chemical."

I don't want to die...I don't want to die...

"We're sorry that it had to be this way, Duluth, but we will take care of you. We promise. But I can't make any guarantees."

I don't....want...TO DIE!

Bailey stepped away for a second. He could feel Duluth's pain begin to enter his body in an aural manner. One of the main faults of the art of medicine is the fallacy of not being entangled into a single patient's backstory, their emotions, or their feelings beyond that of which is essential to one's practice. It is the toughest thing for a human to do to see the tears of someone and not want to weep for oneself. But it was there, and he cared for this young lady.

The nurse came in. "I'll be right there, Melanie." They walked out to the hallway. "I wish I could help her with this, but there's no way we can fix

[245]

this, dammit." The doctor had given in to his Hippocratic urge to never cut for stone, but yet he was never the specialist in this art.

The nurse began to rub her hands in her slightly tinged red hair. "I think it's gone too far with this. Can't give her chemo or radiation, correct? I mean…pardon if I'm the expert." She frowned a little bit, understandably pessimistic from too long of a shift.

The doctor looked down. "Not with her background. Could just make her sicker. And the sad thing is I don't know her next of kin, or if she has family…"

"Or insurance, sir," the nurse laughed, to which the frown of Apollo the healer came upon his face, as if to say *not funny*, to which the nurse said "Sorry. It's getting late my time."

There was a distinct blighted tone in the room, one that swamped like the thick fog of iodine gas which most certainly would have been of symbolic tone and placement for the awful acts of Dr. Copulus and the C402. Certainly there would be more to take.

But through all of this, the gut feeling of Dr. Bailey was that there most certainly was the one candle, the one that Duluth had lit years ago, that stood out in the darkness, and was a beacon from a mile away. He turned on the news, and saw what could have been said as the Lord Himself giving the poor souls on that floor a sacrament of forgiveness of sins.

Duluth smiled sarcastically. "If only that one shining star I saw before that damn board hit me in the head…." And it was the sign he needed that she knew.

Immediately, the doctor went to make a phone call.

ONE HOUR LATER

The doctor of many diamonds but perhaps of only one heart just left the police station. He was a bit bitter through his asinine thought process to proceed in this manner, but nevertheless felt quite resolute in his demeanor. He knew through years of relating to his spokesman Bill A. Copulus that he had business to do. It felt so wrong to allow for the survival of the last vestige of the C402 mistake rather than killing it, and destroying every single shred of evidence of what many years ago was considered to be the biggest under-the-table mistake the United States government had ever made, a series of three women who, through no fault of their own, were given the tremendous capability to undo what years of toil, environment, lost love, lost health, and the ever-present hourglass of life to which the sands of time dearly overflow, have done.

Deep in his heart, Dr. Bailey hoped there were only three. Supposedly, there were only two at first. That was supposed to be the way, just Orion and Duluth. But then, we found Hope. And now, she was gone. *Two, then three, now two.* It echoed through the chamber of his conscience like yelling fire in the Sistine Chapel. The burning question that would probably dictate his discourse was how he could have bailed out a burglar, and perhaps a murderer. It was worth it, perhaps. Surely, it had to be at least evident that he had to do something to Duluth, because she was in need of another's love.

The warden had wondered as to why this young physician had craved to turn free this criminal of another dimension. She had no identification, dressed like Columbo crossed with a severe case of Pat Benatar, acted erratically, and was being detained for potential murder (although they had not pushed it through yet.) Showing his Fed credential at the local "can" took a lot of gall and made his palms sweat, a calculated risk. He didn't know if she would go and kill him and head to the hospital, get all the drugs and whatnot she could, and then turn herself loose. But deep inside, when he saw her eyes, and the beads of them sent rigors down his spine that chilled him more than the cold prison air, it made for an extremely reactive situation. And thus, he knew it had to be that way.

"You know I need your help, young lady," Bailey spoke as he sped along the thruway. "I didn't pay for games." He didn't want to make eye contact with her, because he knew that he could not look into her eyes and see what was surely not a human – or at least in the spectrum of the common man.

She was silent. "I know what I need to do, sir. I'm doing this for a friend. And it sure as hell isn't you." She giggled in the most smartass way. "Let's get it overwith."

Bailey sighed. "Just the answer I wanted to hear from you. I know I can't win with you, but I'm not going to throw away two lives tonight." He rolled his eyes and grasped the steering wheel driving examiner style.

As they entered the hospital, people began to look at her. Orion's eyes glowed intensely. Her tall, lanky body gave her the look like a hoops star in the making. The blue eyes and long black hair was nestled in a bun at the back of her head. Wearing a Jack Daniels long sleeve shirt, dark gray slacks, and ankle boots, she looked more like biker bar eye candy than an innocent young teenager, one that so many had made mistaken for the befallen Hope.

As Bailey swiped to open doors, Orion looked around at everyone. She had become quite dizzy and overwhelmed by the seemingly not so stimulating to others atmosphere of a general hospital in a large city. She couldn't figure out why she had been sapped of so much power being there, but she understood that the fact that she was meeting someone who shared so much in common with her, but could never speak a word in parallel with Duluth, and that...that was the empowerment.

The door opened to the room. "Orion, meet Duluth Kane." What transpired next began to bring a perpetual light, a sort of easy, warm, aural sense of empowerment, and yet, such a relief. They were to watch.

[248]

Orion initially paused, and looked at Duluth's wasting body. She was speechless, and began to walk up to her, eyes open. "Duluth." Duluth was sound asleep, mostly because she had asked to be sedated by being somewhat mentally absurd to the staff.

Bailey took a step back and watched to make sure Orion wouldn't hurt the patient. What he saw was something that stole his heart away and made for an impact that years in the profession could not create. For 2 minutes, he watched it.

Orion grabbed Duluth's hand. She held it, grasped it, and rubbed the fingers. "Duluth." She sat down next to the bed, and kissed the hand as the scarred arm lay motionless on the elevated bed's rail. "Duluth....Kitty." She took the hand, and placed a kiss on it. The kiss glowed on the hand, for which she placed it back on the bed gently, and folded out the fingers as she placed the left hand on the heart. "Kitty. Duluth." She then walked around to the other side of the bed, and grabbed her other hand. She took the hand, and began to grasp it, and shook it. Unrolling the fingers, she slapped the hand in secret handshake mode, slapping the back, then the front. "Waka maka sing song, diddly diddly do..." She made the hand into a fist slowly. "Who in Attrition is in love with you?" She pounded the top of the fist. And then the bottom.

Bailey and a nurse sat there, and could not understand what was happening. They didn't need words to explain what it meant to see the two women together. But they didn't need words, as the actions spoke the tomes.

She sat down and began to rub Duluth's hair, which began to grow in. "You always kept that Hawklick, the half Mohawk, half cowlick, Kitty. Let me fix it for you." She spit on her hand, and rubbed it in. The spit glowed distinctly, lighting up the room. "They wouldn't let hair gel in, so this will do until July when your Dad comes in, Kitty." She took the hair and made it into the best damn Hawklick she could recall. It looked grand, and it was the best Duluth had looked in so long. "And always parted off to the

[249]

right side to go with the grain." She moved it off, setting the lick at a bit of a skewed angle.

The visitor then looked up. "Please, sir. Wake her up. She needs me." She grabbed the doctor's hand, and pulled him erect. "I want to help her."

Bailey took about three seconds to realize what he had seen. But in her grabbing of the doctor's hand, he began to feel the pain and angst that leapt through Orion's soul. And it felt like she had spread the acid of wintergreen on him, and it stung like a thousand wasps. "What do you want to share. You are taking me someplace."

And in passing, Orion said "You'll understand this when you come with me." She grabbed a syringe laying on the table. She stabbed herself with the syringe in the abdomen, and grasping the doctor's hand ever closer, she drew a small amount of whatever was near her navel, and pulled it out. The vial glowed so strongly that it made the room turn purple.

Puzzled, but somewhat suspicious, the doctor relented. "You know I can't do that, young lady." To which she smiled, and said "OK. Well, I'll do it." She pulled his arm, crunched his fist, and stabbed him with the syringe. She was not the weakest of women; on the contrary, the action she drew was a thousand times' the power Duluth exerted onto his appendages.

Immediately, the doctor felt what could only be described as the pain of the birth of a queen. He screamed, but no one could hear him. Paralyzed, his mouth opened, his breath taken away for that one moment, knocked forcefully from the winds of time. Flashes of light came over him. He could feel his arm slowly melting away. The loud sounds of clashing of metal and sharpening of a blade of diamond made him wonder if Orion had killed him and he was ready to visit his Creator.

And then he was silent. He opened his eyes, and was in the gardens of Attrition. He looked at his arm, and on the end of it was a little girl, with short black hair and blue eyes. It was Orion, although it was not the grown-up, but perhaps one of 6 or 7.

Through the beads of sweat, he looked down at the girl. She had pink overalls on, and a blue shirt with a small butterfly necklace on. "Why did you do this to me?" the doctor asked.

The little girl smiled. "I want you to come meet my friend." She began to run towards the house, pulling him with her. Somehow, he knew he had to come along. But why he did so, he didn't know. It was all a dream, so why did inhibition sting so terribly? He could see the house – Attrition.

They went in the house. It looked substantially different from what he had seen during his residency there a few years back. The inside looked like someone had repainted the entirety, and made it look strangely like a rich person's mansion. The white walls that echoed were of wood in this image. Lush couches and lounges lay in the lobby. The kids in the hall were all laughing, and there were no nurses or restrictive locks – it all looked as if there was no way this could have possibly been the home of mental cases and special needs, but rather a home where it seemed like children and their elders lived in community as equals of each other, a sort of island of contention. He looked at the Sun glowing through the windows on some daisies, blooming in the pot in smiling to the heavens.

The girl pulled her closer. "Come with me! I want to show you my friend!" And they ran down the hallway, past where the padded chamber was. It wasn't padded at all, but a small room with a window and a rocking chair. They could read to the kids there.

Past the places where so many tears of entrapment were shed. Past all of the places where doors were closed and the upset of mind and body were committed. And into that last room where there was one person to be seen.

The door opened. "Kitty! Duluth kitty, open up!" the little girl screamed. The door opened slowly. "Kitty! Look who I found! This man here is our friend. Introduce yourself, man here!"

[251]

The doctor kindly obliged. "My name is....my name is...." And with a look up from the girl's face, he said "Matt. Matt Bailey."

Duluth looked up. "Matt Bailey, you got it. Please enter. And wipe your feet! Y'know, this carpet ain't gonna clean itself." The image of Duluth was far different from the rebellious teenager he had seen in that room. Duluth's body was whole and virgin. She had a tank top on and a pair of butterfly jeans. Instead of piercings, tattoos, and boots, there was only the sunny look of a girl who hadn't experienced pain in the world. Instead of a dark cloud and even darker recourse, this girl...my, this girl didn't have anything but positive things to look forward to. She must have had friends. She must have had a Mom and Dad to take care of her. And Bailey smiled, because it was good. Her blonde hair had curls in it, and the bangs looked over her eyes. She had a small guitar in the room, and she ran over to pick it up.

"Opeeda, does this guy want to see me play on the guitar a bit? I know two songs." With a look to the elder, and a nod, she began to play. "My feet are feeling funny, and my hands are getting itchy. But I will tell you honey, what I say isn't Richie. Richie is my boyfriend and he is my kingdom coming. But when I see him, it sends the chicas running." She began to play chords.

The small girl in overalls began to smile. "Do you like her song? She made it up all by herself. Here –" she reached for a small tambourine. "You're an old enough guy. Please come play with us." And he obliged, as he had done for so long.

As he began to play the tambourine the best he could, he felt something that he had lacked for so long. It wasn't the typical feeling of happiness that one could get from a bottle of beer, or the winning of a game. For once, he had felt like he was doing something incredibly important: the ability to just destroy the things that had made his life so painful and so distracted. He felt young and ambitious. And he could tell that suddenly, this whole life didn't mean anything anymore. It was him being young.

And he looked in the mirror, and caught the sight of a man staring back at him, free of all the pain and suffering that had plagued him. It almost gave him a chill to think that it was him; and yes, that was a smile on his face. A genuine one. One that stood for more than hiding pain or pinching his lip to hide the words for someone who didn't need to know bad news. It felt pretty good.

"You play pretty good, Matt Bailey," the young Duluth smiled. "Better than anyone here. Did you ever think of starting a band? I bet you could definitely sell a few records." He nodded. The words just were suffocated out of his mouth, like someone reached in and took them away.

And then there was a knock on the door. To which it opened slowly, and there was the fear he had always felt. It was Bill Copulus, although a much younger one. The thick grey hairs from his dark Indian skin were not there, and his glasses were much larger. His normal suit and tie were replaced with a sweater. "Girls, it's time to go and take your injections. We're going to put them into your tummies this time." Immediately, he walked past the junior doctor as if he wasn't there, and grabbed behind the young girl's back, grasping to lead her off into the other room.

"Goodbye, Matt Bailey. Remember to start a band someday maybe," she said.

And so, he got up, and followed them out the door. He saw into the room where they were preparing what appeared to be two subcutaneous syringes. These syringes injected directly into muscle, and were typical of any medical operation. But these needles looked very strange, and then he realized that not only were these needles long, but he could see the chambers at the end begin to glow.

They had that tint – was it yellow, or green, or blue?

He had to say something, because he knew exactly what it was – C402. It had to be mixed in with the blood somehow. And it was definitely a plan to poison these girls. He wanted to scream, but he couldn't – the words just wouldn't erupt from his mouth. Medically, he knew that he had to support these girls, as he had taken an oath, his pure ownership of the MD, the meaning of years of preparation for situations like these.

Duluth was first. Copulus injected her with the liquid without much fanfare or resistance. Duluth smiled, as she had completed this so many times before that it seemed almost like nothing at all. Bailey knew he was doing something wrong. And then, he turned to Orion.

The injection went in. And she squirmed a bit, and said "Geez, this hurts more than I thought it would. Make it stop." And then, Copulus began to look away, as if he wanted to sneeze. Taking his hand up, he removed his hand from the needle and the injecting agent.

The sneeze came. And the reflex and jerk of his body knocked the needle longways, pushing it into Orion's stomach. She screamed as loud as she could. Bailey feared the worst. "Why does this hurt, Dr. C?" She began to cry, but the doctor could not recover. The C402 had been injected into the wrong place...and there was nothing to do.

"Oh, my dear God!" Copulus yelled. "Nurse, please! Grab sodium iodate. And a towel. Please, swiftly, do it!" Beads of sweat began to run down his suit as he removed the needle. Her blood began to squirt over the table, glowing brown with specks of green emanating like a fountain of light originating from her navel.

Duluth ran to the corner. "What's wrong with her? Is my friend OK?" She screamed out loud as the nurse held her back. "What's wrong with my friend?"

Bailey began to look upon the crying Duluth, and felt the urge to try to comfort her in the best way he could...an embrace, a hug, something. Copulus ran quickly from the room, and the nurses surrounded Orion as her body flailed in random directions, seemingly not understanding what sense of space or time went on. She was helpless to what happened. And she began to have more nurses try to control her, but somehow, this little girl's body, probably not even old enough to pick up a piece of lumber, needed several nurses to hold her down. They carted her body into another room.

Duluth sat down in the corner, tears coming from her eyes. She crossed her legs, and looked in disbelief. "What happened?" The nurses were paying no attention to her at all. She was isolated on an island for which her ferry was headed toward the horizon.

And then, the words came across like a rushing train heading west into the sunset.

She was the lucky one....

With a flash, the scene was over. Bailey took a minute to get a glaze of fog, of tears perhaps, out of his eyes.

They were back in the hospital room, with Orion looking deeply into the doctor's eyes, as they glowed, he began to glow. His arm, syringe still in it, had no hair or muscle in it. It appeared as if someone had made it completely anew. He looked into the eyes of the person who had put him through this, and he could see that she had purpose and resolve in them.

"That is why you must help her, Dr. Bailey." He gave a weak nod, and she pulled the syringe from his arm. He felt no pain whatsoever, perhaps from adrenaline, more from the fact that she had healed him of the pain in the meantime. "I'm glad you called me. This is my dream."

There were a few minutes in between the occurrence and what Bailey was suddenly obligated through physical covenant to complete. The feeling from just a few drops of Orion's blood still resonated through the physician's system. No one was in the room with him at the time, and he was quite unsure of what had happened. Certainly, he felt like there was some sort of mystical....mystical thing that he could not put into the word, or move the pen in the right way or quickly enough. His initial distraction was that he had been given a serotonin rush, that Orion had

[255]

given him drugs, or something that was so potent and at such high levels in the blood of that girl...but then, how could she have survived it? He didn't bother to ask. It was Divine and not for us to discover.

"You're going to help this girl, Duluth, aren't you, Orion?" he asked the tall girl. She looked into his eyes, and put a hand on his shoulder. "You didn't do this just for theater, right?"

She smiled, and her eyes began to twinkle. "I want to do this for a long lost friend. Don't be so freaking vain in your words. They speak nothing of your intellect. Please let me help her." And she pulled up her arm, which despite the drawing of whatever it was that ran through her veins, was completely flawless. "Pull as much as you need. The more, the merrier." And so, they walked over to a machine which drew the blood and purified it. Hope Malott used the machine several times during her healings, and it still was very functional, as the short period of time that she had shared her gift with the world had meant the machine was not even to its first maintenance point.

Nervously fudging about, Bailey's hands were cold and smooth to the touch like a lizard's skin. He could not get them to stop shaking, and suddenly, the task of threading catheter and a needle together was like trying to put a piece of yarn through a sewing needle. Perhaps while drunk to boot.

On the side, Orion began to think about what she was doing a little deeper. It was mysterious, but she knew she had to help herself as well as Duluth. But there were pains that she needed to share with everyone, and it could only be done by someone who could understand. To her, Duluth spoke a language that was the dialect of two. It was a secret club, an exclusive gathering, now with the exclusive credential of the ability to control the power of healing.

Before she knew it, the nurse began to fire up the machine. The nurse had witnessed everything before, but somehow, the dirty look that she wanted to give was held back. The whir of the blades of the machine began to draw blood from the elder female's arm. As it went down the tube, Orion began to mumble something under her breath. It sounded like she was praying to God, but it was just plain unintelligible. And Bailey began to close his eyes, and give a sigh.

On the receiver side of the tube, the fluorescent fluid began to go swiftly down from the machine. It hit Duluth's arm and began to flow into the muscle. There was a momentary pause. And nothing happened. The room was silent as the forest outside of night.

Suddenly, the electrocardiogram began to show a quickening pulse. Duluth's arm began to pulse and quiver, a tremor which began to flow into her shoulders and up her body. For a minute, there was an urge to investigate by the people in the room. She's killing this poor girl, Bailey began to think. Taking an involuntary look at the elder girl standing opposite, she saw a smile on her face, and a stare into the body on the bed. The glow in the tall girl's eyes shined as Bailey could see Orion's tears show a reflection of Duluth in the bed. It was as if she knew what she was doing, and it was all going to work. Bailey bit his tongue, felt like he had to let whatever it was happen. It took all of his good judgment – and perhaps a bit of willingness to risk his state license. But it was happening.

Duluth's heart began to race. She seemed to be in medicine shock, something that would probably have occurred as treatment and not as surprise.

Ten seconds passed. Twenty. Thirty. The blood began to become thicker and flowing faster. The panic button was there for Bailey, blinking ever so strongly into the morning air. He didn't know when to push it, but he had to believe. The nurse in the room began to swear out loud in the Holy Father's name. Some of it was probably in Spanish, but no one could tell. They could feel the power in the room, but it was all in the air.

And then, the body became limp. The muscles of the petite teenager began to slowly stop pulsing. Her heart began to rest. Duluth's body began to develop color. A collective deep breath was necessary to make things better for everyone in the room. As they looked at each other, they all emitted that effervescent sigh.

Bailey began to look straight ahead, as a ray of sunshine entered the room from the south window. There was no longer a glow to her skin. Yet in faith, he began to look closer. Orion gestured to the shade for it to be closed. And so it was then closed. She knew it was important to see what power was happening. And what they saw was a power of proportions that would shatter the stars.

Years of turmoil on Duluth's skin began to wear away instantly. Her face, once with the look of a 40 year old, began to slowly recede, lighten, and rest itself from stress. The scars on her body began to slowly pulse and glow blue, and then, began to pulse like a starry sky with sparks and flashes emanating through the sheets like fireflies in the night. "Look. Oh my gosh."

Getting up, the elder girl went up to bedside, just off the right shoulder of the patient. "Wake up, Kitty. It's morning in Hollywood." She began to shake her shoulder. Duluth looked as if she was 16 once again. Her hair fell out in a clump, but then it grew in long, mixed brown and blonde sheets, in waves of shiny, gorgeous mane, filling the bed. Her eyebrows grew in and stopped perfectly, giving structure to her face. The triangular cut of her chin began to come back, and the dryness of her skin began to replenish with fresh, new flesh.

Orion took Duluth's right hand, and squeezed it. She tapped the shoulder, and said cheerily in an almost childlike manner "Wake up. Wake up!" And slowly, Duluth began to open her eyes, which began to glow brightly. For once, the power that she had not seen in years because of the iodate pills began to replenish. The tube with the blood continued to flow, and Duluth grabbed back, and looked straight into the eyes. The bluish pools of light were like a private lake in the middle of the moonlit night in Kansas.

Duluth smiled. "I knew you'd come back to see me again. I thought they would have taken you by now." Her face began to turn red, not in the crimson of shame, but in the feeling that she had been long–lost.

"I wanted to see you again, Duluth. You needed me for this one. God, look at you, all grown up. You're beautiful. Worth more than gold to my eyes." She began to weep openly, and the tear drops sprinkled on the white sheets, buzzing like sparkling fireworks in July. As each one hit the sheet, it looked like shooting stars into the cosmos.

Duluth laughed, garnering all her energy. "You know, Opeeda, you drive a really hard bargain. Why the hell are you here? You should be hiding –" she began to wear out. Comprehending something this deep was too soon for what she had been through.

"I've been searching through the houses in the neighborhood. Got me in a bit of trouble with the LEO's in this city. But I also am glad that Dr. Bailey here has found you. You may have gotten sick just at the right time. It was your destiny, dammit, Duluth. Your destiny. I can't believe it's happening to me. Right now."

"Did it finally happen? I must have missed it. We got tied up with Hope and her ways. I tried to warn her –" as Duluth began to feel a burst of energy she had not felt in so long.

Smiling, the tall girl stood over the bed. "Not yet. But I have a feeling it's going to happen if we don't start taking action about it."

Bailey, inquisitive as can be, made the timeout signal with his hands. "Ladies, wait a minute. Warn her...about what?" he asked. "You two aren't going to be, like doing something bad. I don't want you committing a crime...another crime for you, Prasda. I don't know but this is –" another cut off speech, as she walked over and put her right index finger

[259]

to his mouth, as if to say shush in the most slutty, absolutely filthy dominatrix-style gesture humanly possible.

Removing the needle, and placing it on the table while the gel-like fluid still clinged in gobs inside, Orion went over to the window, and reached for the shade. It had a sharp cap on it, like the end of a garden stake. The brass shone brightly in the light, superceding what darkness seemingly was to take place. Stepping on the cap, she bent the rod and sheared off the tip, exposing a sharp, conelike ending that could kill.

"While I was separated from Duluth, I took tae kwon do lessons. One of the things they teach you how to do is use weapons efficiently and effectively." She broke the end of the pole, and handed the unsuspecting doctor the bar. "I want you to stab me with it. Go ahead, I won't look."

This was a complete shock to the doctor, who obliged seemingly one too many times. First, he had to trust bailing her out of jail. Then, he had to trust her in stabbing himself with her blood. But shedding more blood was just too much for the day, and he was still too much in shock to see what was quickly becoming an unwilling magic show for real life. Already, some of the staff of the hospital had come to see the ruckus of breaking objects and loud sounds to the normal tranquility of a trauma unit. Bailey just sat there and stared, dumbfounded, and probably just a wee bit ignorant to the outside effects.

He looked at the girl in bed, who sat in bed, closed her eyes as she rolled them, as if to say Well, I know what's going to happen next. Might as well just oblige and get it overwith.

Orion laughed. "You don't even have to stab me with it. Just hold it steady like this —" referencing in a joust-like manner. Closing her eyes, before he could react, the sharp end of the rod was suddenly lodged in her abdomen. She groaned, as if in a tremendous amount of pain. As she stepped back, Bailey let go of the rod in complete and dire shock. Taking two more steps back, she grabbed the rod.

Making sounds consistent with someone who was quite disturbed, or simply put, someone who had a large metal object lodged near one's kidneys, she began to pull at the rod. "Now, the trick is to get it out before the wound heals." She had the presence of mind to speak, but somehow, this foreign object didn't disturb her sense of humor, or her common sense.

She pulled at it, making groans, wiggling it, and slowly removing it from her muscle. Within seconds, a large amount of blue liquid came out, and began to sizzle like an egg on a Phoenix sidewalk in July.

And then, it was over. With one loud banshee scream, she pulled the rod completely out, as if she was pulling Excalibur from the stone. "As they said in high school, Duluth, *Whoso pulleth out this sword of this stone and anvil, is rightwise King born of all England.*" And in one large move, the rod came out, and fell to the floor, with the glow slowly fading, turning the room into a shaded refuge once again.

With her body completely healed, she walked up to the doctor, who was completely awestruck, and placed the rod, glowing tattered end and all proudly in his hand. "Here you are, Arthur. *Thou hast many times erred against thy Maker. Beware of everlasting pain.*" He could not utter another word for days. "You see, Copulus injected that C402 stuff into my fat cells instead of into my body like her over there. It's been stuck in there for about, eh, 16 years. And it is very much lipophilic. You know that means the fatter I get, the more is in there. I can't get rid of it, Dr. Matt Bailey. I might be going against your wishes, and I know I have a gift. But while Kitty...I mean Duluth, needs it to live, this stuff is going to make me live forever.

"I want your help to tell me what I can do about it, Doc." She patted him on the shoulder, as if it still wasn't registering. "After I grab myself a soda, of course." She smiled and walked out of the room.

Duluth laughed. "Whatever just happened, hope you got new trousers. Looks like somehow C402 has the side effect of either a priapism or incontinence. You're too young for that." She laughed. "Get me the hell out of this bed and open the window, Doc."

XIV

The Connection

FORT DIX MEDICAL CENTER WAITING ROOM

It was an obvious sign of the necessity of the times: they had finally reached the next of kin for Duluth Kane. And he was on his way into town to hopefully clear up what years of a mess of inconsideration and ignorance had left in its wake.

Christopher Branson Kane got off at the Greyhound station a few blocks away, trying to figure out his way to the hospital. The phone call he received was not a very polite one; it had awoken him in the wee hours after he had worked his shift at the office. He was the typical accountant: master's degree, CPA certification, loved driving his rather used luxury car. To him, life was a series of events, numbers, and then everything that clouded it in between. He had tried to forget the life he had before. Duluth, to him, was the reasoning behind his belief that condoms break, and 18 years of life can be shot to pieces because of it. Luckily for him, he had an excuse to go forth. As his only daughter was a baby by Copulus, and a seemingly "deformed" one at the least, he had a free pass to get rid of her by simply saying she was an experiment in progress. And yes, he did sit on the couch some night and hold the photo album from when she was 4 or 5...he couldn't remember. But he had no regrets. He made the mistake of being in the wrong place at the wrong time, and the money was worth it...to put that part of his life, that unfortunate circumstance in his past.

And for definite cause, in some ways, he would often think for moments about her. But it would fade into the night, as were many of his nights, consumed by the present.

Duluth stood in the doctor's office, her newfound friend out for a bite to eat. Her body had looked as well as it did in years; her makeup redone, an outfit of rather pristinely obnoxious clothing that was donated to the hospital was put on her. Her hair was in two small ponytails, a red shirt and somewhat baggy khakis were on her. She actually thought of a music video from when she was about 6 or so where there was a girl at the drive-in singing about candy. But what was it? She had no time to think. But it echoed through her.

Her thoughts were somewhat more complex. She really didn't have an understanding of her father too much; it was more or less a panoply of vague memories spaced over seconds of time, just little bits of knowledge. She could still feel them in her, but she didn't know if she would hear the voice, and they would all come back like a barrage of water during a tsunami. Or if it was like meeting a stranger. She paced about the room, her boots clomping in the linoleum lined room.

And there it was. The door opened, albeit slowly. Duluth sat in the chair in the corner, the scales and examination table lingering in the background. "Hi Duluth." It was two words in nearly 15 years. Time to get back.

She smiled. "Hi. I don't….know what to call you." She began to retract herself immediately as the man, this stranger, suddenly began to walk towards her. Beginning to feel a thick impulse of electricity through the air, she began to shiver.

Chris was there. "Do you remember you called me Dad at one point?" he muttered somewhat smarmily. "Dad. You know, father figure. *Papa. Tu padre.* Please." He sat down next to her.

Somehow, she tried to get eye contact with him. It was hard, because even in his presence, the scent of that cheap cologne, the unshaven face interspersed with red marks and a five-o-clock shadow of salt and pepper hair...she didn't feel trust in this man. But she also realized that it was someone who needed a limb, or a bone. Or something to trust in.

"I guess I can call you Dad. You are my father. Why? Why did you have to leave me this way?" She asked the most rhetorical of questions, something that really could have been more direct, but she really didn't want to say what she intended to say. It was just too damn strong for her.

Chris began to smile. "You know, I did this for you, dear. When you were little —" he began to go and grandstand and stump. It was probably his indoctrination as a businessman to wedge open the door and get in the face, agreeing disgracefully to nail it. However, one's business in real life with one's own blood need not have such imposing dialect. Especially when it came to opening old wounds.

Duluth began to speak over top of him, feeling the need to really lay it on. "When I was little, *blah blah blah*. You left me in the care of an angry doctor who tried to kill me so many times it was like someone just better go and stab me through my heart. All the time."

Chris began to do an about face. "I didn't try to do this because I hated you. I tried to do this for the best of both of us. You could have been sick. Doctor Copulus told me he would help. I knew he would help. You just didn't believe all these years that he could help. "

Duluth began to feel anger. "He didn't help one bit, Dad. He didn't have anything but stuff pills in my mouth and beat me until I couldn't take it anymore. Look at me, I'm emaciated. In a hospital. Dressed like a man. Homeless. Penniless. In need of a method, a means, a freaking definite path, of life."

"But why do you think I got on a bus for 35 hours, transferred 10 times, sat next to a nun, a biker, an Amish house raiser, and at least two men who were perfectly capable of ripping my testicles off and laughing the whole time, and at least one man who I don't know what the hell was wrong, but someone better let an asylum know....why do you think I came here?"

Duluth said it straight. "You probably wanted to get it off your chest that you suck as a man."

Chris had it about stated to him. "I think you're wrong, Duluth." He took a step back.

"Nah," she responded. "You came here to see me die." She ran out of the room, and slammed the door, running down the hallway towards where she believed where her true friend was.

The nurse quietly remarked "I'm sorry, sir, but I think it's better that you just leave Miss Kane alone. We understand that you are willing to pay for the hospitalization, and we will gladly do that for you. However, we think it would be good for you to follow our therapist's orders and not have further contact until we speak to her."

The father nodded. "Yes, understood, uh, Victoria." He laughed, and pulled out his credit card. He knew no better than to throw money at his problems. "Please take good care of her."

It was definitely not the experience Duluth wanted. Her frustrations took the best of her. As she drew stares from everyone, she turned into a public restroom and locked the door. Looking in the mirror, she saw her makeup, earlier done up in elegance and proper beauty, smeared all over the place. She began to throw water at her face, and moaned incoherently as she began to cry. She had lost it, and she knew it. But she didn't care in the least. Her father didn't speak for more than the time it took to cook a bowl of pasta in the microwave. But like pasta, it was warmth outside and around the edges. Yet deep inside, she could feel her Dad still being cold down deep, and it showed. The C402 that Orion had gave her that feeling back, that presence in the room. She couldn't turn him inside out for the life of her, and it was her worst nightmare.

She went to the corner and crouched down, her knees bent up in the air, sat against the wall. She felt helpless, but then again, she felt exactly the way she had thought she would: still alone in this world. She was in the same pose, her protective, sheltered pose, that had been there for her ever since the day she lost Orion for what felt like good. It was natural; but then again, it was entirely a figment of her being. Her protective side was once again there, and it scared her almost too deeply. She felt all those pains come back from long ago; memories of a small child in an even smaller childhood stung like hornets as she sat there in the darkened room.

Despite all of the eventful discourse, and somewhat legally skirting procedure had taken place, there was a great deal of relief that Orion had come into this situation. She had some sort of criminal past, but somehow, Bailey made it alright. They couldn't prove that she had done anything, so in a very little known Commonwealth Law known as the Gary provision, otherwise known as turning your back and pretending like nothing happened, Duluth was released to Orion. Take her home and care for her, they said. Sure, it was a bit difficult, but she had that characteristic sly smile, Duluth too weary. They hopped on an articulated bus and hid in the back. Chris Kane paid the tab.

And so, they had become somewhat a pair of friends that had a lot of catching up to do; the past few days were quite a rush, but nevertheless well spent. Orion had spoken to the hospital about her home in New York; it was presumed she had an apartment a few hours away, and her means of getting to the Delaware Valley meant she had a ride. But somehow, there was walking to do from there. And bumming rides from truck drivers, playing gigs with the house equipment, and letting the backs of trucks and the will of rural America guide her.

It was a lie that was practiced well enough to get her back with her friend for one more go after the layoff. Bailey called Mendoza, but there was no answer. He had turned his back on her. Or just plain didn't care. So he released her to the tall girl instead.

Sadly enough, the release was not without its "perks". Duluth had always been a bit virgin to the outside world's manifestations and actions. Orion, on the other hand, was functionally survivalist in every way. As they both sat in the very "fun" seat of the accordion in the bus, they began to plan what they would do. Going back to authority felt like complete suicide; Bailey was under the provision that through his "credential" that he was

[268]

freeing up two women who would hopefully bond together, work together, make a million dollars, and get the Goddamned monkey off his back and put the final posy in Bill Copulus' failed career.

And so, the perks began. The bus stopped in the small town, letting them off in front of a pharmacy. "Gotta do what we must, yet we mustn't," the elder laughed as she stuffed a handful of paper fiat in the farebox, much to the chagrin of the operator, who put it in the right way. *Buncha ignorant millennials*, he thought as he unwrinkled the currency.

As they stepped up the walkway to the pharmacy, a small one in the downtown area that reminded one of a modern Mayberry, Orion looked at Duluth. "One of the things that you have to learn when you are living a vagabond life is survival. Little money means little opportunity. You're a bit better dressed now, but God only knows when your next trip to the tailor is in order." She smiled, pulling the hoodie on Duluth and loosening it up. "Hide your boobs, they draw male attention." The elder zipped up the gray hoodie, and grabbed both arms of the little one.

"We're going to go in to this pharmacy. Little Jewish guy about *yay* tall owns it. He doesn't have a security staff and half the time, he's too busy ringing people up and filling old invalid's Coumadin pills 'round these parts to notice the shoppers.

"See those kids over there – " she pointed over to a group of kids, mostly hardened in view from less than fortunate circumstances. "They have a surprise here 'round this time of day.

"Smile and when these little kids run in, go directly to the aisle with the coolers and get what you need. You have about sixty seconds before he throws the lil' brats out, and notices and catches onto the heist. If he catches you, you have to fight and take off the hoodie." She turned, and laughed. "Oh, one more thing." He took a pair of wraparound designer, understandably male sunglasses and stuck them on Duluth. "You'll need these. 90% of law enforcement ID's come because of the eyes. Plus with that nice shot of C402 you have, the two of us with glowing eyes will be definitely given away. We have a gift...don't turn this into a liability."

Duluth slowly put on the specs. She was unsure about what was happening to her; she had seemingly gone from a nobody, flying under the radar, and living a somewhat weird but controlled life at Attrition to a street-dwelling free spirit, a petty thief in the interest of calories and satiation of one's primal callings and little more. Since she had been self-emancipated a few years, it was kind of a rush to create what was definitely a self-image problem. Her father had passed her off again, and the trauma of what he had said rang through her even more strongly than the pains of her reunion with Orion. Of course, she had to survive in whatever manner she could. Living the vicarious life through living off of subsistence had slowly eaten away at her willpower like a cancer that would not go away. And for someone who contained life to others, it was a pain that would not go away.

Suddenly, she found herself in the pharmacy. The owner, seemingly a bit older than expected, had two bottles in his hands, presumably for compounding. He turned his back for what was just a few seconds as the door opened. They both looked like two bombing suspects creeping in the store. However, this was just not the type of thing that stunned this owner. The mood was set.

Two kids hopped off their bikes, throwing them at the foot of the door in a heap of aluminum and rubber. Pulling a handful of currency and a couple of cigarettes out of their pocket, they stormed in the store. It was sinister, but it was a distraction. Just good enough, they thought.

Duluth began to run for the snack aisle, grabbing a few nutrition bars as the primal scourge of nutrition beckoned. She took them very gingerly initially and held them in her hand, not really causing a distraction. The pharmacist simply shook his head and looked away with a stubborn, what's wrong with these young people today look on his face. She had to continue to look at the pharmacist, who obviously kept glancing over his shoulder.

Her partner was not in the food aisle, but rather the medicine aisle. She was grabbing feverishly in the area of joint care. Assuming she probably was in a bit of pain after giving a lot of blood, Duluth was indifferent to it.

The kids made their move. The clerk at the front, an obvious youngster straight out of high school, began to laugh with the kids. The two boys threw the wad of cash on the counter, and pointed towards the cigarette dispensers. The act was in motion, one that perpetrated to the core; but then again, it was the norm around these inner city parts.

The owner began to look down the girls, and before he could do so, the kids reached for the cigarettes. And then he saw the kid reach into his pocket. In a natural defense, he began to scream "No tobacco for you kids! Go home!" He grabbed what looked to be an old broom handle and came out from behind the pharmacy counter.

 Orion screamed "Duluth! Now!" Taking two bottles of water, the granola bars, and a small first aid kit, they stuffed their shirts full of whatever they could as the pharmacist began to chase the kids. This was something that the elder had done so many times that it was almost like clockwork. They both began to laugh at the ease of it as they saw the glowing door to freedom almost too boldly.

Yet with all tall towers of unsteady preparation and lack of foundation, it all came down. As they ran for the entrance, one of the kids said "Old man, I'm sicka this bullshit! I need my smokes!" and pulled a knife on the two store workers. Immediately, the pharmacist froze, and it went from buying two packs of Winstons to a full-blown robbery. "Give me all the money, now! You're gonna learn, you old sack of shit!" The other kid pulled out a pair of brass knuckles, illegal to own in the Commonwealth but easily acquirable across the river.

Sensing the situation, and realizing that this wasn't expected, Orion panicked. This was not the usual grab and go that was typical of the time of week. These kids were turning it into the scene of a crime. Now, she realized that the security cameras would be looking at what happened. Normally, the elder owner would just write off his losses, knowing that it took too much trouble to prosecute someone for stealing a few candy bars and a bottle of cola. But the police would be watching this now as it was elevated – and it was going too far, too much for Orion's contentness.

"Kitty!" she screamed from the back of the store. "I don't know what to do!" Duluth suddenly realized she may have been all alone on this one. It was a foolish maneuver, and they both knew it. But they were both up to the tops of their boots on this one – and they were committed.

Immediately, one of the kids heard the two girls yelling, and said "Hey, who are those homeless dudes back there? Get your asses down back there." They began to run towards the girls. "We ain't leavin' no witnesses!" and they began to charge at Orion.

Duluth could only watch and pray for her friend. Once she was taken out, she only knew once again that she would be back to fending for herself. It all took three or four seconds, but the two young delinquents were unlike anything she had seen before. And she was scared as a direct result.

Immediately, Orion reacted in tribute and practice to her martial training. As the kid charged, she kicked him directly in the abdomen, making him wheeze. She took quick action while he was bent over, throwing him into a shelf, knocking countless bottles of cold and cough medicine floorward. She picked him up, grabbed the knife, and threw it to Duluth, who was standing by. "Here!" she yelled. "Take it!"

The kid began to look up. She responded by giving him a boot blow to the shoulder, causing a crackle, then a groan. "Ghetto trash."

Looking at the pharmacist, who didn't see any of the now-inflated chest structure that the girls had due to his adrenaline rush, and then to the other kid, she walked out.

The other kid laughed. "Dude, that bitch just beat the shit out of you!" he mercilessly lambasted his partner.

Not to be called that, she went back. "And this bitch has your knife and you on camera trying to rob this poor business owner. Shame on you. Your momma's gonna wonder why that condom broke while you were working out to Tupac." She signaled Duluth to come along, walking past the clerk and business owner.

Sensing the shockwaves, they immediately cleared the site of the store. Orion began to calm down, but Duluth was still hyperventilating. Neither of them had planned for this to happen, but there was an air of resolve around them. "What grub did you get in there, Kitty? Goddamn…"

"What the hell is going on! I just was part of a crime scene…and I committed a crime, and I could have been killed –" Duluth began to nervously ramble. Her eyes began to glow through the designer shades like moonlight through a shaded window. "What have I done?" She began to hyperventilate, and her skin began to turn just as white as it was during her hospital stay.

She received a hug from her friend, grabbing both arms and shaking her lightly. "You did good, Duluth. We got out of there in one piece with the stuff we needed. Mission accomplished, Kitty." She gave her a big, rich, loving hug, something the neither of them had experienced in a while. "It's going to be OK, hun, it's going to be OK." Duluth began to cry openly as the sirens began to gather from afar.

They both were scared out of each of their minds. Sensing the gravity of the situation, both gave a deep sigh of relief. Comforting themselves, it took a couple of minutes to realize that indeed, it was okay. They would have to pick a different little Jewish guy to shoplift henceforth, because

[273]

the guy could realize he was a little low on stock on the front two shelves, or the fact that some really tall high school basketball player wearing a zippered-out Temple University hoodie just beat the daylights out of two truant punks and would likely merit free antibiotics for life.

THREE HOURS LATER

QUAKER INN, EAST TOWN

The longest walk of the day took place after they were able to scarf down some of the cheap food they were lifting from the pharmacist. The riverside beckoned the elder lady for many of a reason, and she had her compass set for another thrill. Perhaps in the worst of unfortunate discourse, neither was seriously injured during the antics that had taken place during the time they had together. Nevertheless, there was some kind of polite discontent with the means of carrying on with this new lifestyle. Already, Duluth began to feel the adrenaline rush that was given with Orion's C402 donation. It was hard to know what it felt like when she was producing her own; certainly, it was not a proud moment of outward flair, but rather the quiet burning of a tableful of candles inside the Chapel of the Heart, giving light but not giving the grand show.

They stood in front of the hotel, which presented itself like Neuschwanstein in the September dusk. Duluth looked quite puzzled to Orion as they stood before the hotel in its supposed modernist grandeur of concrete and cheap Chinese shutters that served no purpose but to sell beds and sleep. "So, let me understand this. We have no money, no reservations, and we have two bagfuls of stuff. Chances are Mrs. Malott's going to be looking for us soon before she locks up the house. What are we doing in the middle of town looking at the only four-star suites in the area?" she asked.

"Play the game with me, Duluth. I know what we're doing." And with Duluth muttering I hope she does, dear Lord. I hope she does.

Going to the counter, they looked at the desk attendant, an Arabic man, who was fumbling about on the computer. "Can I help you ladies?" he said in a somewhat stern voice, realizing that there were two not-so-refined ladies tracking mud into the disinfected lobby, disturbing the sanitized equilibrium of what was clean tile and upholstery smelling of lemon.

"Hi, uh, Ahmad, right? We're here to see a Miss Erika Taylor. She is expecting us." Orion had the system down pat, and was beginning to sound like a seasoned salesperson of convincing others that she was real.

"Can I see ID?" he sternly jutted in. Duluth thought she was in trouble; even though she was known to the state, she didn't have the card on her. *Better off in case I ever get caught doing shit I wasn't supposed to*, she said. *Cops can't tell who I am.*

But before she could respond, her accomplice pulled out a card. "Here you go sir, and she's with me as a guest." The man looked hard at the ID.

And then he smiled. "Ah, yes. Mrs. Martinez. You're on the guest list. Rather unfortunately. Down the right hall, make a right, fourth door. And tell them to kindly turn down the music. It's getting late." With thanks to the man behind the counter, she was on her way. He gave a smirk in a very semi-facetious way, and Orion gave her smile. Duluth could see that one coming from a mile away.

"Money, money, Duluth."

"I can't believe it. How did you get that fake ID? Mrs. Martinez?" she asked. "How did you do that? How did you pass for a Mrs. Victoria Martinez?" she asked.

Victoria laughed. "I don't know, but you're going to have to ask her in person. I swiped this off the Internet. Turns out if you have people under, eh, a bit of threat of some serious disease at the DMV, you can get anything pushed through." She tossed the ID in the garbage as they turned the corner. "We share a lot in common, chica."

Still puzzled, Duluth wondered why they would be going to a party. "Have you ever been to a college party before? Turns out half the folks are so drunk that they set their keycards down to have a couple of Natties. And then they forget. You pick up the card and follow everyone else.

"This hotel always gets the Ivy Leaguers from UPenn here. Hop on a bus and travel down the freeway. The staff sticks them all together in one wing because all these rich folks don't like the noise made by them, and they leave too big of tips to turn 'em away. Especially during the offseason, when Captain James Negotiator comes and swipes the rooms 4-to-1.

"And you know what? I pass for a really sexy mom to these folks. Turns out you need a college degree to manage these damn brothels for the One Percent, but it means too that you're just plain retarded."

Duluth gave a half-smile, knowing that she really didn't have much to resent in that. And didn't utter a word, just came along.

As the door opened, she could hear the music playing somewhat loudly. These rooms were quite suite-like; there were dining rooms, a kitchenette, a couch, like a small condominium of sorts. She figured them to be leased out to the rich folks, and for them, this was no large issue, as they also knew that these students usually came from families with large endowments. So any broken tables would be covered up by the mommies and daddies.

She looked around at all of the guys in the room. Attrition had young males, but seldom ones that were this...this perfect to her. She saw guys all across the room, and suddenly, she was freed from her teenage angst. That boyfriend, that crazy, cutting, conquering bastard of a boyfriend...this was heaven. Living a life of isolation had given her a long trail of hormones. And she didn't know how to react to this many guys, except when Orion immediately looked over from across the room, holding a punch mixer in one hand and a Jello shot in the other. She lifted her arms in a toast as the guys said "Orion! Yaaay!" in already drunken stupor. The

[277]

boyfriend was nice, but intimacy doesn't take place in a crowded suite. At least before 2 am and in the main room.

But she had to take it slow. She sat down for a minute, and tried to think. She could feel the ability to love. But it was not a feeling she had been used to, like a great rise of possibilities. Her boyfriend was quite different than this; protective and restrictive, he often proceeded to defend her like a lion would the prized part of the carrion. But like the buzzard, she would often be cut and torn apart, again and again, by those around her. And in the end, he only wanted her for the abuse and to use her like a commodity. These guys were nothing like that. It was a blank canvas, a sure opportunity.

"Hey, you, young lady. You 21?" a random guy asked. "You seem lost."

"Haha, yeah, I guess," she answered. "I guess to...eh, both of them, I presume?" This guy was somewhat taken back by her shyness. It was somewhat of a dose of modesty that made her blush. She was over-whelmed.

The guy turned to her, and she turned towards him. It was a bigger guy, somewhat robust, thick glasses. Someone she did not dream of. The voice was luring, but the attitude was lax. He was hot enough for the Home, but she had to aim higher.

"You know, the playground is that way, if you need to go and find a place to cut yourself again. Leave it to the real ladies," he said, one foot and two puffs of unbrushed teeth-breath away from her.

She began to get up, but she was swamped. And her accomplice was nowhere to be found. She hadn't been in this situation, no matter what her personal training of years in social situations had allowed.

She began to cross the room, thinking that perhaps she could find respite in a lowly corner to regroup. She could not "just ease back and socialize", like the elder had suggested. There was always a feeling with her and her resilience that she would be okay with others, although her sheltered life had afforded her little opportunity to integrate herself into norms. She just knew what she did from the outcasts, and how to fend for oneself. And that was simply it.

The grasp of an arm broke her silence. "You're just out of your realm, aren't you? Here because you wanna get jiggy tonight, huh?" a noticeably Brooklynese accent broke through. A skinny guy, a noticeable goth guy, began to rub his privates and definitely intrude on her space. "And now, you are all mine, punk sista!" Beginning to do the grind, she put her hands up as she had him trapped against the wall. "You know, this is kinda the way I thought about it with a Temple girl! Like this and like that and like this and...." Then, he began to put his nose to hers, and she knew what was next.

Suddenly, she heard a groan. "Get off of her, you dickhead! Can't you get this outta your place? You know anyone here? Go home!" the noticeably more mature and gruff voice came to counter. She opened her eyes, and a man, a somewhat older looking millennial, came to the rescue. He had a polo shirt on, short buzzed hair, and defined biceps that were well-fit to his shirt. With belted jeans and snakeskin boots on, he smiled.

"Here, come with me. Let's get rid of these idiots. I have to talk with you." With a nod, she was swept off her boots and into the distance.

He took her in the bathroom, and he began to pat her down. "You OK out there? Don't trust these idiots at these parties. I just want to check to make sure you're doing well and all."

Duluth felt herself in the presence of a man, not a boy. And it left her speechless. "Uh, yea. But who are you?"

He smiled. "My name's Dylan. I'm a civil engineering major here. You?"

"Duluth." She could say no more. Josh was great, but this was pure. *How did a guy like this get into a party like here*, she wondered out loud.

"Well, hi there. What do you study?" He didn't hear her, most likely because he was a little out of his element, too.

She began to want to say "men, music, and morbidity", but she held back.

"I…I study, uh, medicine. I study healing medicine. And chemistry."

He fired back. "So you probably know about the angry professors in that department. Always have something to clean up." He began to rummage through the room, but then sat down on the ledge of the tub. "In a college full of idiots, you have to be careful."

She felt a certain measure of warmth inside of her, a genuinely heartfelt caloric like none before. The guys she had known never talked this straight up. Her feelings began to grasp her tightly as her old soul began to shine. "You know, most guys are pigs and suck. But you seem to have a little bit of a sense of yourself." She sat down next to him, feeling that closing in on him would give some sense of loyalty and friendship.

"It comes with the territory of being 'round these parts for too long. I'm not a brilliant person, and I'm 23. But I know too that I need to have a future in this world that doesn't consist of drinking my Fridays away and living at home, trying to explain to everyone why I'm different, but yet all the same. Work hard but be smart, Duluth."

"Yeah." She had the biggest grin on her face. She wrapped his arm around him. "How do guys like you stay single with all the women in this world? I mean…." She placed a kiss on his cheek. "You seem like such a sweet person to be hanging around these stupid parties!"

Dylan relented and looked down. "I have self confidence in myself. But I'm always fearful of relationships. One of the things I learned from people is that I can help everything within my sphere of influence. But it is hard to trust others when you know you are in control finally. I feel strange being attached to one person, like it's too unfair to everyone. I'd rather be everyone's friend..."

 She sat on his lap. "...and try not to piss anyone off because everyone's good inside..."

She wrapped her arm around him and kicked up her legs. "...and you know, you want to just carry this on..."

She looked him in the eye – "...and away we go, Duluth."

For the first time, she knew she had found the winner.

"Come with me, Dylan." She could not get the smile off her face. Perhaps it was Orion's energy inside of her. But yet, it was her energy as a strong woman, seeing a strong man in body, mind, and soul. They had both broken out of their shells, and it was like no other. Duluth didn't mind it as she glanced and saw Orion left behind – or did she? Her brown eyes focused on Dylan's face, and her blonde hair, the remainder of the essential gel somewhat nonexistent as the heat of the room had sweat her brow and left it in a somewhat combed mess, was blowing in the breath of her Prince Charming. Somehow, her adolescent identity crises and drama were blowing away into the Delaware. And it was good. The seventh day had come for her.

She wandered through the hotel lobby, pulling at doors as she pulled the poor, shy man behind her. She didn't care if it was someone else's room, if someone were having sex, or sleeping. A door had to be open. And for once, it would also be open to her heart.

Sure, Dylan gave his resistance. "Uh, Duluth, uh, should we be doing this?" Yet half her life was gone, her youth reinstated. If Bailey was there, he would have certainly seen that same image of Duluth from long ago; wild, free, innocent. And happy.

Room 472, at the end of the hall, had been propped open. But for these two, they were ready to love each other so much that the doors would be blown off in pure joy.

A FEW HOURS LATER

ROOM 472

For the first time in a long time, Duluth felt loved. She was 19, and sleeping in the queen bed of a King that lay downstairs. It wasn't hard to get in, and it was going to be even more amazing when Dylan Howley, her new love, woke up. He lay in her lap, both of them passed out from whatever it was that happened to them. They were both too drunk to remember it for certain, but she was sure it was amazing. But did he realize that in that kiss they had made, that she was glowing in more ways than just in the spirit? She hoped it was just him being drunk.

She woke up and turned slowly, squinting as her pupils constricted to adjust to the bright light. It was 3:32 AM. Hearing someone in the background, she went to investigate. Moving slowly as to not startle the passed out Dylan, she gathered her tank top and walked barefoot towards the bathroom. Every few seconds, a groan and then a bright flash of light would emanate through the dark room like a scary movie being viewed in the theater.

Somehow, they had found this room. Orion probably was tagging along, never leaving her new friend's side. As the rush of melatonin began to wear off, the sounds were quite erratic and disturbing.

There was her opposite, vomiting her guts out. Every time she would pulse, she would spit out a large amount of fluid. Duluth figured her to be completely drunk: not unexpected for a decidedly sorority-age girl. "Hey, Duluth. Sorry to be this way, but I have to get this out of my system. Too...much...alcohol." And with that, she pulsed again, choking out another bucketful of biscuit and brightness into the rather large commode. Orion gave a groan as if she was ready to pass a baby orally. It echoed through the room, and gave a definite sense of non-privacy to the two younger folk.

Duluth just passed it through her mind that she was probably dealing with a less than logical person. But it didn't bother her that much. Grabbing the bottle of vodka that she brought up from the party, albeit probably, she looked at the elder. "I think I better hide this from you," she giggled. "We need to get out of here before this dude gets up." She gestured, pointing to the other room, and turned on the nightlight. Under her breath, she said I think I had sex with him...and winking twice, she got a weak, yet politely supporting nod from her friend.

Getting up, Orion staggered to the door. "I need to pick up some ice down the hall. My head is killing me. Don't have the key obviously, so let me back in, hun," she muttered somewhat incoherently. When the door closed, Duluth rested, trying to be responsible and somewhat obsessive-compulsive, cleaning the quickly drying contents of her girlfriend's stomach. She was tired herself, and began to smell the booze.

It was all good, but then, something hit her. She took a sniff of the bottle, innocently wondering about how for a large woman, she got so drunk. Duluth had hung out enough at bars and clubs enough during her time as an independent; most of it was done sneaking in back entrances with the band, as many of the outer areas' businesses were seldom enforcing local liquor laws. She would go out and tempt guys with her guitar playing and songwriting skills, and before you knew it, she was kicking back and playing pop music from the radio at all sorts of places.

As she took a sniff, the bottle fell on the ground. Suddenly, the wafts of alcohol came through in all their volatility. Rushing not to blow the fact she was snooping on another's drinking habits, nevertheless also wasting a bottle of alcohol of which wasn't anyone's, and thus was a free gift, she picked the bottle up, cursing out loud.

She smelled the bottle. Instead of alcohol, it smelled like medicine. Really strong medicine, as if someone had put cream in it. Immediately, she wanted to see if she had mistakenly put something in the bottle. But then, she realized that there was no way she could have put it in there. Orion was drinking something else, and it was poisoning her.

For a moment, Duluth began to recall the somewhat disjunct memory of the Jewish man's pharmacy. It was a transient occurrence; she could recall somewhat that Orion had developed a keen interest in over-the-counter topical pharmaceuticals, but it didn't make complete sense at all.

Taking a small cup out of the bathroom dispenser, she soaked a tissue in the bourbon, and smeared it all over the cup. She had to know what was in there, and knew the perfect person to ask. And she was able to sneak out before the boy found out what happened to his booze, and probably a few months later, why he was itching. Leaving the door open with the stop cracked, she left to find the truth on the matter. And there was only one refuge for the solace.

She looked lovingly at her new friend, for one last time. She thought of having him tag along for the matter; surely, having her disappear would be the strangest matter. He would have questions, want to know about her more, her favorite color, song, flower, whatever. Heck, she hadn't even added him yet on social media, and here she was.

And yet, she looked down. Dylan didn't need to be brought into her world, Orion's world, any of their drama at this point. It was a sisterhood that the two females in that pilfered room had to still keep to themselves. Bringing a third person in reminded Duluth a lot of how Josh had led her to a demise of homelessness and survival. And she wasn't going to fall for the same gag, those men that suck, one more time.

So she ran, leaving them behind. She had to know why Orion had so much affinity for her itching to be someone else.

TWO HOURS LATER

MALOTT RESIDENCE

The remembered soul of long lost affection knocked on the door about six hours too late. Assuming that the folks of the house would be sleeping, and would have to probably sneak in the side window, she planned to pretend like she had cordoned herself in Hope's room for the past evening, unsure about how to explain her relative isolation. But the light was on in the house, and it was roughly 1 A.M., so it was cool.

The door opened. It was Adriana. "You know you can't be out this late all the time, Duluth. Mom's worried about you." Her brown hair was draped all over her pajamas, simply a halter tank and baggy sweatpants. A cold breeze blew in the door as the Moon began to cloud over.

"I'm here because I need your Mom's help. Pardon the look, but I got jumped coming out of the hospital." Duluth began to stick her hand to the door, expecting the resident girl to close it on her.

Adriana used her good health and judgment, and decided to accept the passcode. "Come in. Mom's sleeping on the couch." She unlocked the chain and opened the door. A long hallway was there, with stained wood that caused an echo as Duluth's bootsteps clicked on the floor. She was huddled in an afghan that looked more like a rag, and she cuddled herself into it as she slowly traversed the cavernous hallway to her judgment. She had taken it before she left the hospital; it was welcome for the chill outdoors, but yet such winds blew north in the house that the drape could never halt in their passage beneath.

And there Carrie was, her body draped across the large sectional couch in the living room. A single candle burned into the night like the fire in the hearts of a soldier. Her eyes opened slowly, and there Duluth was, towering over her like a god, with her green eyes cutting into the mother like no other.

[286]

"About damn time you're back. Next time you do this, you...you're going back to the shelter. No exception." Carrie gave a tired, sarcastically disgusted nod. She sniffed the air. "And God, have you been drinking? Ugh, you smell like Mr. Ames down the street. You're 19 and I'm not having two dead girls on my conscience."

Realizing that she was probably going to be going back to a really disappointed, and perhaps jubilantly angry Orion, Duluth rebutted. "I didn't drink. But I need your help. As a chemist. Or someone who has worked with this stuff before." She had a dead, cold stare into the eyes of her opposite, her sincerity intent on convincing her indefinitely to help.

"Isn't it a bit late to be doing work in the lab? Save it 'til morning to play Mr. Wizard. I gotta get up at 5 AM." She turned over in disgust, obviously trying to implicitly ignore the rampantly ruined chick.

"I just got back from being with Orion Prasda. She got me out of the hospital," she effectively quickfired back. "I want you to tell me what she's drinking."

Carrie's eyes opened so quickly that one could have believed she was being castrated with a bottle of whiskey and a machete. "What the hell were you doing with her? She's still alive? Goddammit, I thought we could have been rid of her long ago..." she muttered in continuously less scattered muffle to a full wake.

"She's alive. Bailed me out of the hospital a few hours ago. And I think she's, like, not up to any good." She pulled the sheet out of her pocket. "I need to know what's in here. I think it's itch cream and whiskey."

Carrie knew about her release, but was under the impression that Lou had picked her up, and dumped her out probably. He was under the assumption that Chris Kane showed up, they made up, and such. But it was late, and her temperance to reasoning left when she passed out for the night's slumber. She literally could not think.

[287]

They both went downstairs in the house. Carrie went slowly, her slippers clomping on the uncarpeted wooden stairs. Duluth came down behind her, with Adriana looking curiously from the climax of the stairs. The lights flickered on slowly, and downstairs was the most secret of the remainder of what had happened many years ago, a locked door to what was likely the most telling mechanism of the science behind the girls.

The room was a stark contrast to the rest of the house. White drywall and fluorescent light illuminated a very clean and organized room. Several tables were set up neatly across the floor, with beakers and Petri dishes lined up in rows. A small clock, showing the time in three dimensions, lit up the corner. It appeared it was left in a way for significant scientific study to be completed successfully yet succinctly. "I did this to try to figure out when Hope was little if she would ever be a normal kid. She was really afraid to come down here because she always feared I'd poke and prod her to death. Only got a couple of blood samples out of her, but it was never enough to really do a thorough study.

"Me and Alex both put a lot of money to make this a reality. But then after what happened a year ago, I haven't been back down here. Too many memories." She began to mist her eyes, her voice quivering into the room that made the walls echo in a certain way that kind of made it feel like the two of them were one in that basement, all alone for the world.

Duluth smiled, and placed a kiss on her hand, and touched Carrie's cheek. "Thank you. Hope used to do that all the time too." The girl gave a smile, which made the mom smile back. "But anyways, in that spirit, let's get this over with."

Through a lot of process, Duluth sat down in the corner, her arms folded. Her body ached from her travels that day. Even though she was energized and in good shape, the weariness from all the adventures began to suck the life out of her, even if only for the moment. The boots she wore were high and somewhat unsupportive, and her feet began to feel as if they were about to fall off. They were typical hospital loaners, mostly donated wear that was too bad to sell and too out of style to be popular. It was never about style, regardless, especially at the moment. She had a mission, a drive to complete. Tilting her head back, she tried to maintain a consistently caring and curious look to Carrie as she fumbled about the laboratory.

"So, there's everything in here, corn, ethanol, a little bit of cinnamon. But there's also something weird here...looks like some sort of cyclohexane, or something that smells like a cream. Was your friend taking antibiotics?" she asked.

"She had a tube of Maddox's Foot Cream near the bottle. I guess she put in the booze. Would it make it taste better?" Duluth asked curiously. "I can't imagine it being nice to smell like those shoes she wears."

Carrie fired back, her curiosity piqued. "What are the active ingredients?" She opened up a heavy book, and began to comb through. And then it struck her. "Main ingredient: Clioquinol. Good, God." She put her reading glasses on the table. "I can't believe she would do that to herself."

Duluth was puzzled. There was someone who was knowledgeable, frozen in time for a second. Something was definitely shocking Hope's mother. Not just caretaker or resident control for a homeless 19 year old girl. This was a woman who had the same things in her blood as her, someone who knew all the powers of chemistry, of substance, and of alchemy of things believable of evil. Duluth closed her eyes, hearing a sigh. She could picture a very inebriated and even more depressed young woman, knowing full well what she was doing. Crying as she poured the mix of alcohol and agent, knowing the effect and how it would destroy her, but doing it for no other choice.

"Duluth, you need to stay clear of this girl. This substance is a chelator of iron in the blood. It's very lipophilic; it likes fat cells. Did Orion say anything to you about it?"

Duluth replied "Only that...through feeling, she had an instance where the doctor was injecting her when I was, like, 6. The needle missed and she took it in the tummy."

Carrie's eyes began to look colder than the night outside, her face becoming pale. "So she's trying to harvest the C402 in her fat cells that is in there. This stuff...this can draw it out of the cells into her blood. She's using it to get it out of there and harvesting it, bit by bit."

"But why did she throw it up?" the little one asked.

In the best detectively Sherlockian way, Carrie said "Because I don't know if her body would be able to take that kind of chemical cocktail. She probably takes it with alcohol to mask the odor of it, because if she ate this cream raw, it probably would kill her. She's diluting it enough to get it in her bloodstream with the alcohol, and it gets to the fat through her blood, the chelator, this cream, goes and binds to the cells, and grabs the C402. She gets that burst, enough to do the trick in her bloodstream and spits out the rest. "

"How did she find out about it?" Duluth could picture it in her mind.

Carrie paused. "I don't know. She's very intelligent, Orion. I always thought back to when she was in that home, she always passed her tests. You might not remember it that much, but God, do I.

"Orion could do anything those folks at Attrition could throw at her. The problem is with that C402, she feared it. Deeply. But damn, she was a tyke. When she left that day, I don't know what happened, but essentially, she disappeared." Duluth nodded and gazed into the sage's eyes.

Carrie began to chuckle. "Orion...for her, she probably found out about it because she had to do it in order to survive. Literally. She's like Hope, but Hope was....well, I sheltered her and raised her the way I did for good reason, Duluth." Shaking her head, the mother of three walked over to the corner in retreat, deep in thought – and yet somewhat in a confued fright.

"Why, Mrs. Malott?" Duluth took two steps and began to wonder as she realized a personal connection was forming. "Why did you hide it from Hope?"

Carrie grabbed both shoulders of Duluth, pulling on the afghan draped across her small shoulders. "She was going to suffer the same fate as Orion. Copulus probably would have spilled the spiel eventually." The sense of fear became a spectrum of helplessness and a panic, and it was due for Carrie. Even if she was half-asleep, it was too real.

Duluth was shocked to her bones now, standing up and thinking about it. "He probably wasn't ready for it. Dammit." She now feared for her own safety, because there was someone who obviously had no contention with being who she was. Orion, in Duluth's mind, was the polar opposite of her. Duluth needed the energy to not age, and here it was, in an older woman who abused that privilege, not knowing of the supreme wealth she possessed. Hope would have seen it and thought of it as a gift. But to Hope's credit, she also saw the incredible demise it led to in the end. The two of them were in union of lifting the limits and telling those who saw the light to back off and go away. "What am I gonna do, Mrs. Malott?" she asked out loud. "She will find me again."

Carrie froze for a minute, and began to speak the words that stung like bees around a pear bush. She didn't think it would ever be possible to ask for this help, but it was the only choice. He would understand better than anyone about this. "I'm going to take you to the only person who would know. And I pray he will help you. God, damn it!" she screamed.

[291]

XV

The Fool

THE NEXT MORNING

THREE BLOCKS AWAY

There was a certain cold air of hypocrisy that cut through the even more chilly morning. What they were doing to someone who by act of defiance was taken both of manhood and of reputation was just despicable. The drive over was just about as sickening as a heavy dose of ipecac after a long night of eating and imbibing. Even though Duluth was in good shape, and cleaned up of all the dirt and grime and given some of Hope's best clothing to look presentable in mockery of the way she had left Attrition some years ago, it still was not enough to ask a man who was bitter for forgiveness.

They knocked on the door heavily. A distinct voice, with Eastern Asian accents intermingled with distinct Anglican rapport, said "I'm coming quickly. Hold, please." Taking a deep breath, they cupped their sweaty palms that were as white as the daisies on the lawn. Both wondered what he would say, or if he would help. It was a good explanation away from success, but one bad word from death.

The door opened. Both Carrie and Duluth had a necessary remorse on their face. The doctor had a look of disgust, and expressed himself in a direct, cold stare that cut through the night like blood of the Lamb. "Vanish, you two. Damn you from showing up here now. Such mockery." He began to close the door angrily, as he wanted to be rid of that generation of thought.

[292]

"Doctor Copulus, I know this is going to sound strange –" Duluth began to rebut as she stuck her hand on the door. She felt the situation begin to slip away, and like with Lou, she had to go again and put herself on the line one more time.

But the old doctor did not want to be emasculated again by verb this time. "I said go away. Vanish. You were done with me, so I am done with you." He began to reach behind the door, to which Carrie began to fear he had something more than just a fireplace stoke to attack the two women.

Duluth felt one last chance, and didn't want to burn it. "I know you think it's stupid for me to show up at your door. But would I be doing it if I didn't think going back to Attrition and risking that I'd have to deal through hell again and make you happy wasn't worse than what I was going to tell you? After the shit you put me through – see these scars – does it make any Goddamned sense to see your face?" She tilted her head, as if to say Does this make sense? And then, Duluth turned around and began to walk away, thinking this wouldn't work. Carrie looked down, and kicked a pebble for effect.

Copulus was bitter, but nevertheless feeling a quantum of rationale. "You have a decent point. Spit it out, now." He was going to give forum. Or else they were both dead.

Carrie motioned to open the door. Copulus began to express his rationale. "Mrs. Malott, I understand you would be here for moral support. Need I say that this girl probably hastened your daughter's passing, for which I send my deepest condolences. But what brings you here with her? I always believed that Duluth would have been a very poor influence, although I shall admit I administered equally poor medicine."

Carrie did not pay attention to a single word he said. Immediately, she said quickly, without making eye contact "It's Prasda, the other one. She's alive."

Copulus squinted his eyes and pinched his lips in the ultimate show of disgust. "Oh, dearest, her. Orion Prasda. I certainly hope she isn't in this city." He knew exactly what was in the terms of endearment possessed by the two ladies.

"She's here, and chances are she's looking for us. Turns out she may have been doing stuff that's made her a little bit...uh, eccentric," Duluth chimed in with resolve.

Copulus began to pace in his small, modest house. He knew what was happening. The memories began to flood in a rush of prolactin and a drain of serotonin, taking over his weakened elder body. "I knocked a dusty broom on the floor 60 seconds before she was in the room. And it's going to cost me my life. I don't know what she's here doing, but she is not like you, or Hope. She has it in her lipids."

The two women looked in silent belief for explanation. And he gave it.

"When I misinjected the C402, the chemical probably got in her fat cells. One of the things about it is that she has a storage reservoir of it...a large dosage right in there. We found out later that the reason why that chemical is so potent for us is that it can commonly cause beta radiation to the cells around it. Hope, your child, Mrs. Malott, had one big dose of it...your egg in your womb. Duluth, you had it in your bloodstream, although in a small dose. It metabolized in your system very quickly. But Orion Prasda..." He paused.

"Orion is going to have that in her body for the rest of her life. Unless she can flush all that subcutaneous fat out of her system, the dose I administered unfortunately means that it will forever loop in her immune system. Over and over again."

Carrie saw the look on the physician's face, and began to walk nearer, trying to console him. "She was also trying to flush it out of her system. Using cream clioqunol."

Copulus looked at the two, and pounded his fist. "I knew it. That bloody animal there, Norris." It caught his two visitors in stunned fashion.

He then gave a weak smile, understanding that it was fruitless to attack her now, many years in the future. "It's probably better off. Her ability to heal herself and her immune system is immeasurable. I bet she could probably cut her arm or leg off and reattach it as if nothing was wrong." With a look of *She already did it, dumbass*, by Duluth, they both continued.

Duluth never knew this moment would come across, but it was there. "Dr. Copulus, I've cost you a lot, but I need your help on this one. I'm really scared and I can't think of what she's going to do if she finds me. She could kill anybody. She could take all the bullets, and rip them out of her body. No cold will kill her. She's pretty much invincible." She stepped near to Copulus. "If it means going back and undoing what I did at Attrition, so be it. I was wrong." She reached to shake the downtrodden doctor's hand."

Copulus smiled. "You don't need to go back there, Duluth. You need to find your own place in this world. I was wrong, too. And I paid for it with losing my love, and, eh, my life. So there won't be little Bills running around. Nonetheless, a man is suggested to extend an olive branch every once in a while. I'll help you with this." She shook Duluth's hand, with a vigorous, professional, masculine effect.

Duluth took the hand, expecting the handcuffing she always feared in nightmares. But she felt the pain go in her, a pain that got to her heart, and gave a tinge of gray. But in a microsecond, she felt Copulus having opportunity of a different kind, one of resolve in his mind. And it made her give a smile and chuckle, making her brown eyes sparkle.

"Come with me." The two ladies went down the hallway to the kitchen. He opened a cabinet and he pulled out two vials, each filled with a purplish substance. "This, this is something I left in here after the accident with C402. I kept it in case you girls ever broke in, or any of my experimental study subjects did so. There's enough sodium iodate in here to permanently eliminate the C402 in your body. Please –" he handed the vials – "use very carefully. Next time you see her, find a way to get her to ingest this. Orally, intravenously, rectally, through the genitalia – but get it in her system."

Duluth took the vials. She stuck them in her coat pocket, the glass carefully wrapped up in the towel and gloves that Hope had mindfully left from last winter.

It was all making sense. But then, a knock came on the door. They all looked at each other, but in a flash, it was all over. They knew only one person could be there – and it wasn't a moment too soon that revenge was to take place.

She came in, breaking the door off the lock, the bar holding it clanging on the floor. "Duluth, how did I know you'd be here? And Bill Copulus, you piece of shit. You just couldn't keep your hands off her, could you. What a surprise, you bovine worshipping goat!" The attack was on.

At the first glance, Carrie saw Orion, and her memories began to erase. This little girl had grown up.

Thus, the mother chemist tried to explain to the girl she barely knew that reasoning was the way to go, and that it was better to discuss rather than dismantle. But interest based negotiations were ended when the tall girl threw her aside. Duluth began to run away, her shoes clomping on the floor. But she tripped, falling and barely hanging onto the glass vials that would save her if needed. She turned around to see Copulus on the floor.

Orion stuck her hands on the throat, beginning to gag the doctor. "You want me to break your goddamn neck? Open up!" The doctor's eyes opened extremely wide, his dark Indian skin beginning to turn purple.

Duluth, in a change of heart, felt sorry for the physician who, up until a few minutes ago, would be in this situation in the ultimate dream for the girl. "Please, Orion, don't do it. Stop it, STOP IT! PLEASE!" She cried weeping tears.

She lunged for Orion, but the extremely angered girl threw her aside. "Let me handle this, Kitty."

"Please, God, Orion, I barely know you!" the doctor gagged under his breath in extreme pressure and vigor. "Don't hurt me!" His body flailed excessively but helplessly as the tall and powerful girl knelt over his abdomen.

She pulled out pills. Even with the tears in her eyes, Duluth felt the adrenaline rush kick in, knowing full well they were the same pills that Copulus had nearly knocked her out with when he was caught cheating. They were sodium iodate. Even in the dimly lit room, the sense of them sent chills down her spine.

"You always had a fondness for these. Swallow them." In a maneuver attempted so many times at Attrition, she shoved the pills in, forced his mouth closed, and pinched his nose. In the extortion of asphyxiation, they would not open her mouth again until the patient swallowed. It was a cruel act banned later, but nevertheless rang strongly as a trauma on the conscience of Orion Prasda that she had to get back.

And then, she pulled out a dark brown bottle of peroxide. "An old trick. You never knew that the fire you started in us girls would come back to haunt you. Now you're going to feel that fire. As you taught us, *Nam omnes nos in ardentis ignis, qui datus est tibi erunt ignis*. Now you're going to eat your words *ad Latinum*, Bill." She shoved the bottle between the lips of the troubled man, who was only obliged to close them around the bottle by nature. It hit the pills, and suddenly, the last breath of Copulus was a scream which showed a man burning from the inside out. He spit fire out as the chemicals reacted in his windpipe, and the fire burned through him as the carnal cries of a man who was about to die after reconciling with those whom had pained him. It was coming full circle, and Orion didn't know it. But she looked in Duluth's eyes one more time, the bluish green showing in a flicker like a lizard. She kicked the burning flesh of Copulus body, snapping his neck. She disappeared into the smoke in the distance, leaving no trace except the embers of burning flesh.

The house was beginning to burn, the wallpaper burning fiercely as years of grease and spice smoked the walls. Carrie ran out the door, Duluth wailing deeply in the ultimate combination of fears of seeing what she did, and being scared to think. Her cries were as loud as ever, and the trauma was intense.

The next moment, she realized she was on the sidewalk, a firefighter consoling her. Breathing through an oxygen machine, her face was red, yet ashen. Carrie had been long gone, and so was the person who suddenly had become a very scary monolith in the face of Duluth. "You are OK, right?" the firefighter said. "I'm Dylan Howley, by the way. You remember me, right?" the man said.

She pinched her eyes shut, holding back the tears no more, and giving him a hug as she took some shots of pure caloric charm into her system. "I needed that."

Howley relented, somewhat scared. "This is a heck of a trip for a Temple girl out in these parts. What the hell were you doing here?" He knelt down across from Duluth's ash covered face, and gave a somewhat master-to-student look to her, something years of the Fire Academy had trained him in. He would not take an answer that didn't make sense.

For the first time, Duluth sat still. The girl of a thousand opinions, all worn on her sleeves like tattoos, now could not tell a lie. "I....I was out here with this woman....Carrie. She's....she's a friend." She shook her head as the man she had seen the night before looked on in disgust, also kneeling in his coat and hat, wordless also. "It's not good enough of an explanation, is it?" Years of being outward and lying had trained her not to panic in a situation like this. But now, she had to panic.

"I don't know how you get yourselves into these situations, Duluth, and I hope you don't anymore. You are too nice of a girl and too smart and attractive to do stupid stuff. Glad you're OK, by the way." Instead of criticizing her, and breaking her heart as she expected, he placed a kiss on her forehead, out of sight of the rest of the folks on the other side of the truck, all talking to reporters and holding off the press.

Deep in her heart, Duluth could not believe the heart and compassion Dylan had. Josh would have ripped her head off, caused drama, created a scene. As Dylan clomped slowly away, pulling at his coat and off towards the light, she stuck her head between her knees and began to say a prayer. It felt like it was the time to finally come clean with herself.

MALOTT RESIDENCE

She was in the room that was only fit for someone who deserved the power to see through the hurt in this world, and yet be a girl. It was only fitting, and the elders agreed with it.

Duluth Kane sat in the chair that Hope would always put her makeup on in. It was an old style vanity mirror, with the white opaque bulbs and a large wooden vanity outfit that had flair and charm but really little substance. The mirror was oval shaped, and was large enough to show a full complement of a body presented before it. But somehow, there was emptiness there.

She looked in the mirror at her face. Despite her rather youthful glow coming back, she could see tiredness and fatigue on her face. Her hair, once finely manicured and trimmed with pink sparkles and a buzz around the sides, looked frumpy and somewhat representative of a haystack.

She looked at her neck, the muscles in it no longer defined. It was supporting a head that was losing its substance, and the necklace, which read "Fly Higher", hung quite loosely, more than she had ever noticed before.

She gazed into her shoulders, and pulled aside the sheer tee she was wearing and looked at her skin. The tan she had always wanted wasn't there anymore.

And so, she began to rub her eyes. She began to look at all the cosmetics that had been left there by the girl who had set her free, but yet left her with so much on the table with no way to explain it. She rubbed the eyeliner on her face. Her hands shook, and she couldn't put it on delicately enough, smearing it all over her bagged eyelids. Vigorously, she put on the shadow. It made her look even worse. She tried everything to hide who she really was, but she couldn't do it. Her face began to turn

[300]

more and more redden, and her eyes, beginning to pink from lack of sleep, began to weep. I just want to be a Princess for once, Duluth thought.

A knock on the door cut through the silence. It was Adriana. "Hey, DK, I want in. I have to, uh, ask you something. Girl to girl talk." She was serious enough for Duluth to quickly swipe the begotten beautifiers to the side.

Duluth wiped her eyes, and went over to the door. As it opened, Adriana's eyes looked down. She could not make eye contact to the restless older girl. She hid behind a button down pink flannel, and her thick frame glasses. "You know, this room is, eh, kind of off limits for us in the Mendoza household." Duluth began to roll her eyes, and wanted to shut the door. In the nick of time, the little semitan girl said "But if anyone could fill it with love, it's you. Can I come in for a few secs?"

Duluth was stunned. "Oh, thank you, I guess." Adriana closed the door behind her, and began to go to the bed, sitting Indian style on it. Duluth slunk back in the director's canvas chair, and looked at Adriana.

Adriana was still somewhat stern, her raising and rearing getting the best of her tactful discourse. "And you know, I heard everything. You shouldn't really move Hopie's stuff around here either. Bad karma." She began to look away once again, expecting Duluth to become somewhat hostile.

Yet she didn't. "Uh, I won't. Thanks." She sat back in the chair, trying to relax for the moment. "So, what do you need?"

Adriana came over. "I came in for three purposes. One, I wanted to give you this –" she opened the door to the walk-in closet, and pulled out a guitar case, brand new, still having the tag from Pratt's Music, a store that Duluth had frequented over time on her "excursions". "1960's rockabilly guitar. I had it tuned a half-step down, just like Mr. Pratt said you did. He said you preferred to do it like Stevie Ray Vaughan. Saved up the past few months to get it for you. He gave me layaway...youngest credit line everrrr...."

For all the gestures that Duluth could receive, this was surely the best. Adriana had been somewhat resistant to open up to the stranger of certain substance but unknown character for the longest time. It must have been hard for Adriana to do this, because she was always the quiet one, reserved, afraid, and resistant to change. But it meant that the flower that had blossomed was now ready to reveal its beauty to the world. "I needed this, Adriana." Those were the only words that the receiver of this beautiful gift of musical charm could give.

She began to strum at the strings, the sound echoing through the room. "You forgot two more. Two, I want you to teach me to play 'Be The One'. You know, the song from the Cinderella show..." to which Duluth obliged.

They started to play together, sing together. It was very off-the-cuff, but it only took perhaps a dozen moments to realize that they did have a connection. They fed off of each other. As Duluth's fingers flew like angels' wings in plucking away at the strings, they felt goodness together. They had wondered about everything about each other, what really was the bond between her stepsister and this older girl who had been through so much. As they explained their explorations and lessons to each other, however, they discovered an aura of happiness. Duluth began to show her where to put her fingers, and they sung the chorus three times.

And somehow, there, peeking through the door, was Carrie. She just stood there, smiled, and after a few seconds, walked away, her hand on her heart. "Thank you, Hopie. Thank you, Alex." She blew a kiss towards the Heavens, folded her hands, and said a quiet psalm, just her and her Father.

Adriana then said something that she really wanted to. "You know, but that's not the reason why I came in here. You know, ever since Hope died, I've been missing something in my life." She gave a weak smile. "When I was little, I grew up all alone, and Hope was my neighbor. She was the first one I met when we moved in. She healed my cut. We played house, we played in the garden, we grew tomatoes. And then...then she became my half-sister.

"You know, my Dad tried so desperately with my Mom to have another girl. But Mom...she was absolutely not the person you'd want to hang around with. She thought it was more important to go out drinking with friends, to have a social life, to forget us two.

"She went out one night, saying she was going down to the mini-mart to pick up a loaf of bread and a gallon of milk. She promised she would bring home a pack of chocolate and a soda. Instead, she brought home a guy. I don't remember his name, but this guy was sweet. Hot. And dumb as could be.

"It was the first time I ever saw my Dad cry. She, like, sneaked him in the back door, like no one should notice. She was too drunk to realize too much of her drama had left him to the couch most nights.

"He wanted so bad for a hero, and my Mom was a hero for the longest time. But she isn't anymore. I can't even, like, talk to her on the phone without hearing my Dad and her yell at each other like a daytime soap opera.

"But anyways, when she left, I always wanted to have someone like a big sister in my life. It was impossible back then, but I think I found one." She pointed to Duluth, who was absolutely amazed. Putting her finger on her heart, she said "I know my big sister would have to have a big heart. And yours is special."

Duluth felt the pain inside of her suddenly radiate outwards in the brightest beams she could ever feel. Suddenly, the painful experience of the misguided and misaligned discourse that Chris Kane had spread in those token few moments some time ago didn't feel like such an imposition. Instead, she saw resolution – and someone she could finally trust. She reached out and gave Adriana a hug. "I'll be your big sister if you want." They nearly choked each other in simple unison, but it was a feeling of goodness.

And somehow, the powers that were in each other felt like they disappeared. Duluth felt a great deal of pain in Adriana, but she felt like it was flowing through her arms, into her abdomen, and up into her head. But this time, she closed her eyes and suddenly, after a few moments, she saw the hug she had first given Hope some time ago when they had bailed out of Attrition Home. Damn, it felt the same way.

They both let go. "You know, DK, I've felt a lot better about myself."

"In what ways?"

Adriana showed definite externalization and extroversion. "Well, the thing is up until right *fitching* now, I've had this bracelet on every night. It was my stepsister and me's sisterhood promise that we made, me and Hope. She made two of them, one for me, and one for her." She bit at it and took it off. "You can have this one. Hope took hers to Heaven. You're a lot closer to her than I am. You're still the sister that I never had."

Duluth began to become scared. "Don't say that about Hope. I knew her for just a couple of years. She is a damn good sister. I know because she saved me from myself. At least a few times." She took the bracelet and tried to relink the henna. "You know I can't do this to you. I mean…" she chuckled, "What can I do? I can't live forever, and this is proof." And then she pulled up her sleeve, and showed Adriana that she had one already. Although tattered, and slightly pulled at by Adriana's father, it still stuck.

But Adriana pushed aside the honest letdown, and began to look straight in the eye of Duluth, seeing the sincerity and reluctance in the blue coming from them. "You don't have to live forever to make a difference in this world, *chica*. You won't really truly die until your legacy goes out.

So you just make your legacy a little longer. Hopie isn't here, but I see life in you. You gave it to me a few seconds ago."

Duluth smiled. That was true. She said it in her mind. She knew it.

"You know what?" Adriana asked. "We're, like, in one with Hopie." She put it back on. "And one in the same, but not the same. It can mean two things, Duluth." She smiled. "Thank you."

Adriana went to her new big sister, and pulled her up on the bed. They both sat with their legs hanging over the side. "So, big sis, here's something we do in this house. Hopie and I used to do it. It's called 'Concentration 64.'

And so, they began to play it. Adriana explained to her how to play. Duluth knew it off by heart, but she felt like she needed to hear about it just one more time. It was the fact that it just seemed to make her happy to see that she was loved for the first time in a long time.

Concentration, is the game.
No repeats, or hesitation.
The category...
Names.

"Duluth," said Adriana. To which her opposite responded "Adriana". And then, Adriana began to say Hope's name, but then dropped her hands. Duluth felt pain in the room, but couldn't identify what it was.

"I can't do this. I'm sorry, but I can't think of Hope right now." She began to fold her arms, and walk away.

Duluth got up and gave her little sister a hug. She could see something else was burning deeper inside of her, one that gave a bigger pain. As she hugged her, suddenly her eyes began to glow in a way that she had never seen before. Her muscles began to contract rapidly. Adriana was not sad, but was having a panic attack. Duluth felt the sweat of Adriana's body begin to take over. In those beads, she could hear the voice of Hope, all too familiar, echoing through her head. Hope….Adriana….I always let her take my name and I would take hers.

Duluth began to feel dizzy. She had to let go. There were many things that she could feel, and years of having the seeming gift of C402 had meant feelings were everywhere, in every substance, every single item, the silverware in the house, the toys in the room, the car that they travelled in. Duluth began to give damnation to it all in her mind. It was becoming too much.

Adriana began to openly cry. "I'm sorry I did this to you, Duluth. I….I, kinda, like, just miss having her here. But you are now my big sister, DK. You can help me get through it. We're together." And then, the second hug took place. This time, they both felt each other deep inside. They couldn't let go.

And then, it hit Duluth. She had seen them before, but she looked at the glow of her arms wrapped around Adriana, and then saw the closet downstairs. "I think I know maybe there is a way we can make this last longer. I can be your big sister, like forever."

The door to the closet opened. It was the most taboo of everything she had known of. The four vials glowed in the deepness of the hole in the wall. It was the golden calf, unbeknownst to them at the moment, but then, the reverence took over.

Adriana turned away at the relic, in fulfillment of the Scripture. It was the last thing that was living about her sister, except in the bracelet she wore and the memories. A modern day act of Aaron, and despite the wars going on in her mind and her musical upbringing, the sound of singing was never to worship, but to seek atonement.

She didn't expect to find this, but somehow, she knew it was there. The presence of it was too powerful. "I don't want to see that. Don't want to know," she forced out in curing herself of the deep pain.

[306]

"Adi, this is something we have to do if you want me here. I'm weary and this is the final gift that we have in common." The glow came out of the side of the room, and they were opposites. Duluth could not take her eyes off of them, thinking of herself. But yet she could not do this without the person who knew that blood the best. "You know that she lives on in me already. Why not make this the way it should be? *What did I do to you, that leads you to stop me and not do this*?" she asked out loud.

It was futile discourse for the little sister. "What lives, lives in all of us. What is left out of us to die, shall pass, too." She had heard her Dad say that so many times in the time that had past. And somehow, Duluth knew it was an impenetrable defense given her reasoning.

She could only muster her best reasoning. "Well, I know this: I was told by someone before that I had just one life to live. One dream, one love, one opportunity. Why just make it like it's a joke?'" she said.

The words were Hope's. She had never told Adriana that she had shared those words with anyone else. "Don't....say....that, Duluth. You haven't lived this life like hers." The glow of the blood went off of Adriana's eyes like moonlight on the pond. She had left her glasses upstairs.

Duluth saw the reflection of the blood in Adriana's eyes, sincere and golden. It reminded her of her eyes before she had gone down the path of straying. She used to be able to see that every day, but then again, time and anger, passion, lust, and greed, had taken it away. She knew she had damned herself in this way.

"Well, we both have her in us. So why don't we both take it then?" Duluth reasoned in compromise.

Adriana saw this. "I don't need her. But you do. You understand this." She saw the glow in Duluth's eyes too. In her deepest wishes, she missed seeing that when they played together. When they were playing on the bed, she saw a little bit of it. It wasn't enough to back her up. But then again, it made it feel good again. "I don't want to lose you again, Hope."

"Then you must let me take what is mine."

XVI

The Ghost

THREE DAYS LATER

ST MARTIN OF TOURS, NEW HOPE, PA

It was only appropriate that in the true spirit of finding a new sisterhood that they went to discover a new Hope by going to the town not so far away that bore its name. Carrie had seen the way the two girls were beginning to bond, and she felt like it was needed for them to have a sort of social activity to bond. And so, the first excursion the two had together was a church carnival along the banks of the Delaware. A warm summer night, with the sky clearing, save for a few hazel clouds in the east, was in order. The place was well-lit with incandescent bulbs strung across the main spread. Popcorn and funnel cake caused hunger as its delectable smell wafted through the air. Bells and whistles and the occasional scream of a raffle winner emanated through the space.

"You know, Adriana, I've never, ever been to one of these. We didn't get out much at Attrition. Mostly it was just mall trips once or twice a month. Highly supervised. We couldn't run away and hide in the back of the skater stores 'til they closed." She looked around. "I always thought this was like fireflies off in the distance. Could never understand a word." She pointed to the target range. "But this...this is something I wanted to try."

Adriana, much more the veteran of the discourse, wanted to go and pretty much play stuff for stuffed toys. Or pictures of Cole Hamels and Rocky, one of her favorite movies. There were even raffles for Flyers jerseys, for which she wanted so dearly. But she was OK with it, at least for now. A little release probably was necessary, and in her own somewhat uniquely befuddling and complicated way, she was cool for it.

[309]

They stepped up to the range. A young kid with a visor and a "DUMB PEOPLE SUCK" shirt covered up partially by a blue vest laughed. "Can I help you ladies? Wanna shoot?" he laughed. "Two dollars. Don't hurt yourself now." He changed the twenty note for a handful of wrinkled, sweaty bills that were sure to be gone, thanks to feeling the power of God opening up the collection plate through the parish fair. And they felt like it was due.

Duluth grabbed the gun, a rather lousy BB gun with a crooked barrel. She studied it, lifting it and looking down the barrel. Looking at it, she closed her eyes for a second.

Drawing the attention of the teenage attendant, he said "You might want to shoot. Otherwise, you can't win these nice little moo-cows." He began to approach her, and grabbed near the barrel of the gun. "If you need my help, miss Benatar…"

"Take a hike, chump." She stuck her hand on his shoulder, and gave a moderate but firm push aside. "This girl can shoot." And so, she looked, to the stunned guy, who was high on hormones and low on appeal. And it was worth it. Ten BB's took out the star in a little over 3 seconds. Not a shot was missed.

Both Adriana and the boy, who was now trying to hide his "excitement", were stunned. "Geez, you chick. You come in here looking like you're going to rob a piercing salon, and you take out the target with this crooked eyed gun and still have half a magazine left. I guess I should hire you to guard my Mom's house at night." He smiled as Duluth allowed Adriana to point to what she wanted out of the array of prizes.

Duluth laughed, and looked him straight in the eye, her brown eyes flickering and scaring the boy. "Never underestimate a female with a gun." She slammed the magazine on the ground, and spit just for effect. "And you're this old and still moochin' off yo' mama. When you get more mature, you'll get chicks like me. Until then…" she pulled his shirt – and the rest of his body – close, and met him two inches from her face "you're going to have to deal with all the preps.

"Mo Bodart."

She walked away. Adriana was stunned. "How did you know it was him? And how did you learn to shoot like that?" She cuddled the small elephant dearly, as it was the first prize anyone had ever won her. She never was out for this type of fair before. Mostly, she feared the public setting, being too timid.

"I can answer that in one sentence. When you live at Attrition and have a boyfriend you'd rather be without, you can find out things that you want to know just by asking. Or else just being with the right people."

Adriana went back, her face kind of straight and unemotional. "That's two sentences. You said one." Expecting a fireback, she smiled.

Duluth laughed. "Oh, shut up, you." She gave a playful nudge as they both laughed, enjoying the moment together. After getting a blank stare from the nerdy chick, she said "Plus after you've been on the streets, you tend to learn from the trash. Walking through the downtown at 2 AM with those folks is a five letter word." In the sense, she didn't like talking about the past. It was no more. "Let's go and see what's going on at the stage. Looks like a band is playing. And look at that dude. Up to no good." The man was holding a set of knives, examining them quite carefully.

"Looks gruesome, a potential for supreme disaster, Duluth." She paused again in dramatic discontent, trying to fight off her timid outgrowth. "Let's watch it." And so, with a nod, they sat down.

They took their seats and began to view the show; or lack thereof. The show lacked the excitement of a circus act; the juggles were slow, the sideshow of a man talking through a bullhorn loudspeaker, perhaps the pastor, was dictate of those on heavy sedatives.

"Alright, so this guy's initially going to juggle batons. Sets him up by setting the bar low." Duluth still had her acetic wit within her, and it showed out loud. A couple of people began to look at her funny.

Adriana gave her a giggle, kind of continuing to bond. "You know, he was at another show a few years ago in high school. Only no knives. I think he had glass rods filled with Jello." They both gave a giggle, as to say how corny.

The sideshow was really depressing entertainment. Like every teenager, they had to distract themselves. It was just too damn monotonous – this was to be an exciting night out, and alas, this would not fail! So they did what most would – relieve the call of nature.

The bathroom was typical of divine indisposal: a small, old tile bathroom, with a couple of lights, tinted windows, and toilets that probably would have survived the fallout if the Soviets struck. They were that crapping old.

Adriana walked up first, waiting in what was a makeshift line. Duluth was paying little attention, save for the ever-boring show off in the distance. The hallway was dark, but somehow, she was attracted to what looked now like a set of rods that would light up in sequence.

Somehow, Adriana disappeared. Her partner in crime didn't know how they became separated, but she assumed that she simply was somehow distracted and left. Ah, Adi, you and your ADHD got you again. It didn't matter anyways; she had a duty to do. Just to get out of this funk, she had to go and clear her mind.

The door opened to the dimly lit room. She looked herself in the mirror, at her face. She did admit to herself that her youthful beauty, something every girl of fair mind and virgin soul would want, was there, although she could tell somehow that it didn't feel right. So, she washed her hands, sprinkling the water all over her face. Even though it removed some of the makeup she had "borrowed" from an old friend, it seemed like for the first time, in those moments tonight, she felt beautiful.

As she gave a smile and looked in the mirror, she saw the glow in her eyes for once, and didn't feel as if it was a bad thing. It felt like there was Hope in her. Duluth never felt that beauty, that poise, that inherent self-confidence.

And she would later find out why. The door opened, and an older lady limped in. Her hair pushed back, she grumbled to herself.

Duluth noticed this woman for some strange reason. She literally could feel a presence in there with this lady – she felt like she was going to attack her for some reason. Perhaps it was the scary thing that this woman was stumpy, ugly, and had a haircut that reminded her of what she saw in the mirror. But the woman had no poise - or anything Duluth thought she had herself.

She spoke to the young lady. "You usin' this sink? I gotta get this damn piece of parsley outta my teeth." The woman was physically imposing, and Duluth kind of felt her personal sphere shrunken to the cutaneous level.

Duluth stepped out of the way. "Uh, you OK?"

The lady was somewhat verbally subordinating, too. "Hun, I gotta tell ya. When you are old enough to have gingiva that have rotten down to the root, you'll get freakin' oaks stuck in there." She then began to pick at her teeth openly, grossing the young girl out.

Sights of such things were criminally asinine to the young woman standing next to her. This woman began to then pick at her upper lip, and the hairs. They were gross. She was completely ignoring the surprised, somewhat shocked look on the face of Duluth.

She had had enough. "You know....you know I've seen you pick at that for awhile. Soon enough if you pull hard enough....those will grow thick enough to actually get you it! Bitch!" Duluth had blurted it out. She knew something was wrong immediately, gasping at her mouth in disbelief. This person was a stranger, but yet there was a linkage.

"Excuse me, young lady?" the woman said. But by then, Duluth was gone.

As the night wore on, she began to look at the lights in a different manner. Even though it was early evening, she rubbed her eyes somewhat, and explained it to Adriana as "I just have a headache. You know, from the C402 and blood I took." Her opposite knew no better, as most of what Hope had done was kind of off-limits, at least in her mind. She didn't want to know about it, regardless. But as she sat there, Hope's blood began to impact her. How did she know about Mo Bodart? She could picture him in her mind, but couldn't remember where she met him or how. In her blood was the memory. And she could feel it in her. It was Hope's last pain as she ingested the last vial.

In a split second, this all was destined to come back. The man began to ambitiously toss the knives in the air, aweing the audience. Out of the corner of Duluth's eye, she could see a man with a cola. Somehow, he tripped.

In half speed view, it took a long time. The adrenaline rush could not have hit her in any worse time.

The cola flew in the air. And the knife, supposedly to go safely in the air over the stage, flew into the audience. And it hit a boy. A very small one.

Immediately, the boy screamed, the knife stuck in his arm. His mother began to yell in the Lord's name. Running for a bit, and then collapsing, blood began to spill on the pavement and the rented chairs. "Somebody call for help!" People gathered around, but no one would touch this boy, because no one knew how to help him. They were all afraid: afraid of lawsuits, afraid of hurting him further, afraid of getting gory innards on

[314]

their Sunday best. The outbreaks announced on the news lent themselves to even more caution.

It struck Duluth all of a sudden, a feeling she never had before. For years, she had tried to hide what some would call a gift, but others a curse. And now, she was honestly stuck between her will and doing what she could.

Immediately, she began to close her eyes and start to think about options. She needed them. The headache she had went from a dull boil near the back of her cerebrum to a full-fledged wailing of the pain sirens. She began to breathe heavily, worsening her oxygen deficit and furthering the pain. She could feel Adriana's hand grasping tightly at hers, the rings on her fingers that she had carried stinging like cold aluminum.

The boy needed help. No one was coming. She could see a medic off in the distance, and someone running to ask for necessary help. The boy's pain, and his blood-covered t-shirt, rang too many pains that she could not ignore. She knew it was Hope channeling her from wherever she was. That blood was poisoning her. But it made her do something she wouldn't. Despite her knowing that this was reopening an old wound by curing a new one, the impulse was too big. And it overtook her sanctity.

She stepped up, and forced the people aside. "Let me help him. Please." The crowd parted, and the boy silenced himself for a moment. She crouched down in a baseball catcher's position, going eye to eye with the boy. Not knowing how Hope handled it, she sighed. "Hi. Looks like that stupid guy over there was too stupid to pay attention to where he was throwing those crazy knives." This made the boy stop crying, and give a weak smile through the tears. "My name is Duluth. Like the city."

"My name is Colin. Colin Norris." He smiled. "Can you make this stop hurting?" he cried, extending a rather placid aura that surely felt like it was coming through the air in the seats.

"Alright. Well, what I want you to do is close your eyes for me. Just for a second. I have...to...pull...this...out..." which she did, and the boy screamed, the makeshift gallery gasped. "OK, ok, so that didn't work. Here – " she pulled off the black hoodie she had on. "I want you to hold this on here for a second." She stepped back and tried to think about how Hope would have handled this. Knowing that there was procedure, she went back to her adoptive sister. "How did Hope do this? I mean, how did she heal people? I've never done this...."

A man yelled. "The boy is bleeding, ya dumb stooge! Help her!" And so, she stepped back, and thought to herself.

C402, it's in my body, it's in the blood...it's in the blood!

She grabbed the knife, covered in the boy's blood, and immediately, she cut her pinky finger on her right hand. She squirmed as the bluish-green blood emanated from it, and suddenly, people were screaming for the two of them, although it was most likely that everyone was regretting allowing Duluth, a perfect stranger, to openly gore herself, creating the conundrum of two wrongs being right. It was worth a shot.

"OK, Colin hun, I want you to take my pinky and show me where it hurts." He pointed to the cut, now starting to ooze more than gush. She began to apply her pinky, and her blood began to mix with his.

Not knowing what to expect, Duluth was openly sweating, not only because of the heat of the atmosphere in thermal but of that of the air of pressure. She began to throw off her sheer top, exposing a sports halter she had thrown on at the last second. She had felt a species of nervousness like she never had experienced before. Praying for Hope's guidance from beyond the grave, and that of a higher power perhaps, she squeezed her finger like she was testing for blood sugar.

Her blood began to pop and sizzle, supposedly helping to cause clotting. For this cut, it wouldn't usually do it. But somehow, slowly, it did. The boy began to feel her blood, and less and less pain. It began to seal, and he gestured his contention and easing by beginning to move his fingers on the injured arm. It was Hope Malott, her legacy everlasting, coming to the rescue once again.

She took one last gasp, and turned back towards the arm. The scar had completely formed, and the boy smiled, as he looked at the knife. "Thank you, miss Duluth." And as the boy's mother smiled, she was overtaken by the drama. Rolling back her eyes, she hugged the boy and didn't say another word.

Duluth smiled as the boy walked off, the crowd absolutely lost in the moment, even more than the girls were. "Don't tell anyone about this! But you can go show the priest!" she yelled as the boy took one last glance and waved to her through the crowds down the hill, as her mom pulled at his newly healed arm, wondering about what type of miracles could happen at a church carnival.

She parted the crowds, but thanks to the benefit of technology, this would not be forgotten. She had begun another chapter in a story that was due to shake the world one more time.

TWO DAYS LATER

MALOTT RESIDENCE

The news on the television had never ceased to stun those who had seen it all before, although this time, it felt a lot worse because the stakes had changed. No longer was it true that Hope's healing processes were a controlled experiment. The world now began to question what was going on: why the break-ins were occurring, was this the girl who broke in, was Hope really dead and had plastic surgery, the ridiculousness of it all was quite a stir. And then there was Orion, somewhere out there, and not knowing what she could do, it was all beginning to turn into the late Bill Copulus' evil experiment, gone totally to the bastard of Unpredictability, somewhere in there.

And through it all, there was Duluth, cuddled in bed with a cold. She couldn't figure out where it had come from, although she had assumed that in her exploits in the many days passed, she had probably received it from someone – perhaps the two boys in the pharmacy, or the kid she helped, or the gun she had clung to like someone from Alabama – but she was wondering about it. She had her demons, and could not wait to speak.

Carrie brought some hot chicken soup up to the key-shaped bedroom in the old house. Hope's bed, with its pink comforter and lacy sheets, never felt so good for the petite Duluth Kane. She cuddled as she took her first "selfie" in bed, barely able to mask her illness from the eyeliner and messy blonde hair that was beginning to grow in.

Carrie set down the soup on the TV tray, and looked into Duluth's eyes. She had seen the same look in Hope's eyes several times when her stepdad was on his mission to bring the family out of bankruptcy. It looked like the sadness of a thousand puppies which just lost the bone for the day. Duluth was weak, and she knew something more than a cold was wrong. She rubbed her fingers through Duluth's hair, and began to look at her, as she was wordless and just afraid of it all.

Most notably absent was Lou, who had been seldom seen around the house with Duluth. He felt embarrassed at this moment to ask her in front of everyone else about her "heal"; surely, that which had been sold as a lure before had become damaged goods in the cold house, especially in the nights where Carrie often would spend time looking down the halls, expecting Hope to come out from the closet she had hid in so many times to say *It's OK, Mom*.

I just was hiding here with mah dolls 'til you cooked dinner.

When she had to pick up Duluth from that carnival, she knew little of what had happened. Duluth was smiling from ear to ear, and Adriana was cuddling with her nice little orange tiger. Both seemed like little children again, and it almost created a sort of maternal reflex emotion in Carrie, like she had been granted a second chance. Only these were not her children. Somehow, it took a damned long time to convince herself that they weren't hers. But it was a good thing; Hope would have wanted it that way.

The doctor came and made a house call as quickly as possible. Many thanks were extended to the Malotts for their contributions to wellness and research. It was one of Hope's last wishes to help people in any way possible in those moments, and one of the things that they had agreed on was that because of the circumstances regarding the exposure to C402, that Carrie and Louis could ask this doctor to help them in any way possible. It was the emergency that they had always mentioned, the release valve. And his name was Dr. Matt Bailey.

"Welcome back, doc," was the first set of words that came out of the mouth of the ill patient that had helped another weakened person just a few bats of an eye before. "I kind of missed your ass the past few days." She laughed, and then sneezed, covering the doctor with spit. "Sorry."

He just smiled, and said "It's okay. Chances are I've probably gotten this one already." He began to take samples, swabs, needles, skin samples, you name it, he had it in his kit.

"You know, there's something that's been bothering me about you two girls. If you don't mind me asking…." He chuckled a little bit, with the bedridden blonde obliging. "What is it that makes it so you guys don't glow in the dark at night? I mean, wouldn't that keep you up?" He was trying to add the timpani of levity to a boring orchestra of drabness, the rain pouring down on the window outside.

"I don't know, Dr. B. I just close my eyes and it doesn't bother me as much. I just, like, don't know better, I guess." She garnered a laugh from him as he click-closed his case. "You might have to give me a couple of days on that one."

Bailey was contrite, polite, and pleasant. "You got it, Duluth." He shook her hand, to which she didn't want to let go. That sweet gentleman, she thought. God, do I love him.

It would only take the balance of the week for that love to turn into confusion and angst. For which there would be no equivalent for reparation.

ONE DAY LATER

FORT DIX MEDICAL CENTER

The family of seemingly endless cures sat in the room for a little over an hour while they tried to find out what exactly was Duluth's illness that had been bugging her. She had been through many colds before, but they found it odd that they would be called in for more testing. Bailey had the best poker face when it came to medicine and breaking bad news; Duluth was well aware of it, but the other three housemates were just about as fresh as the morning dew on it.

She sat hunched over, a Care Bears blanket wrapped around her. Her face showed extreme redness, bags appearing under her eyes, giving creed to her fatigue and tiredness. She had been up for nearly three days as the cold, or perhaps flu, was taking all of her strength. Since Bailey had made the house call, he had been busy at work, and she went from the sniffles to a cough to nearly not being able to eat at all. The craving of sugar probably made her angriest of all, but yet she had trouble putting herself to eat anything because it made her already tender stomach even more uneasy.

As she sat there, she looked down at her arms. Once scarred, they looked reasonably fine to her, not really anything she hadn't seen. The dosage of sodium iodate she received was so long ago that she couldn't really explain this by taking away power. She was also sure this was no normal cold. After all, C402's effects gave her the immunosuppression system of a god; but there was no deity except to which to pray to exterior. She gazed curiously in the mirror at herself, peering across the lab table sitting in the corner of the office. Looking closely, and peering nearer, her eyes made her look very old and sick. Trying desperately to add verity to her not being 20 yet, she sat back.

Adriana, not to be put aside, sat in the corner with her stepmother. She felt like there had been an effect on Duluth that she caused, a guilt loop that was killing her. Not knowing the results, she prayed that it was just another case of a young woman, underweight and overambitious, getting hit with the zeitgeist bug of the month.

And then, the doctor came in. For anyone, this moment of truth, so anxiously awaited, leads to no dose of closure. Closing the door quietly, his eyes were misted. Bailey had never looked like this before...no doctor had ever done so, not even when Duluth nearly passed away not that long ago.

"Duluth, you're 19, right?" With her nod, he said "I....I have to ask you, because of government regulation if you would like these folks to hear our diagnosis for you. Because...they aren't your family or guardians, you don't have to let them know."

She felt strength come through her for once. It was amazing to her, and it was the blood of the healing that had taken her. "Well, they are my family now." She smiled. "Might as well get it out because they'll be figuring it out probably online in the next hour."

He smiled. "OK, fair game. I ran some tests on you, and I wanted to ask you if before a few days ago, if you did anything with injections, or needles." She explained to him about how she had taken in Hope's blood through the old vials, and how it had energized her and made her feel very young again. She explained to him then about the event at the church fair.

Then, the doctor asked a very intriguing question. "Was there blood on that knife from the little boy?" When she nodded a great nod of remorse, the doctor turned away. His answer was "OK." He gave a great sigh, and it pained Duluth to see the sigh. For the first time, she knew that something was seriously wrong.

"OK, Duluth, so here's the problem. We measured your platelet count, your white cell count, your bone marrow count, your leukocytes, everything. Your white cells, the ones to fight off infection, were extremely low. Your bone marrow showed little to no rebound.

When we looked at these details, we saw a raised level of C402 in your blood. And then, we saw something in your blood, under the microscope, that we've never seen. When you took in that boy's blood, it changed your body's ability to make white blood cells to the point where it cannot make anymore. Those cells have no ability to do anything but eat themselves as they form."

In a bit of puzzlement, and misunderstanding, Duluth shook her head and pinched her eyes. She had heard this before. "Dr. Bailey, eh, Matt. What does that all mean? Speak normal." She could remember those last few words that he had told her prior to Orion's *retrouvaille* from the darkness, but couldn't mince the words. She felt ill, and her mind was weary.

Bailey could do little to mince words as he tried to coat it softly but stay informative. "Duluth, your immune system is compromised. I don't know if we can fix it, but we can try, and pray. Normal therapy may or may not work, but I think the dose of Hope's blood was something your body wasn't used to."

For the moment, there was silence in the room. No one could believe what the physician of good standing had said. They all looked at each other, expecting the other to pick up where he had left off.

Deep inside, Duluth was confused. A low level of C402 in her blood nearly killed her. A high C402 content in her blood was going to kill her. It wasn't the same C402, but the blood itself was different. What was she to do? She tried to reason it out. But even her greatest senses and quick-draw thoughts wore heavy on her conscience.

But then, it really struck Duluth this time. She had feared death for the longest time, but now the words had given up on her somewhat adolescent typicality that you're going to live forever. She said to the doctor "How can this happen to me? I mean, I was OK a few days ago...." She shook her head, her face beginning to melt slowly away as her youth trickled down the legs of the chair.

"The fact is, Duluth, I don't know. The difference is last time, I think that it was fortunate because you had Orion by your side. I know you said before she isn't here, but there is a modest difference. Your body was weak, but it was surviving because you fought on your own. And now...I don't know, but it may have been that you had so many blood types in you that your body doesn't know what to do, hun." And with a pause, and a look of inquisition, he said "This time, there's no way she can help you. You can try to get her to give you her blood, but I don't know. If she is really that way, considering Hope was of good mind, body, and soul, I don't know if I would want the sanguines of alchemy of whatever she had in there in you. You may not be able to handle that energy, Duluth. It could inspire you, it could make you want to rip someone's head off – or your own."

This began to weigh deeply on the mind of the two landlords of the house, the hit of the words ringing a bell that tolled in all too familiar of a tone to be comfortable. Hope's passing was sudden because it was by fatigue and trying too hard. She died with peace and her mother knowing that it was the best for her. She had suffered for too long, in her mind. Too many people had taken advantage of her. But it was also a sharing of the good memories that gave her the strength to make positive of the passing.

By comparison, here was a woman she barely knew, but suffering all the same. The difference was that in effect, she had only seen caricature of the past few weeks in living in her house. But somehow, this was an extension of Hope – never mind that Hope's blood ran through her, and it felt like by taking her in, that she and her husband had been granted a second chance to make things right. Duluth was a forgotten child, one that didn't have the somewhat sheltered, semi-normal rearing that Hope had had. Duluth never had a day in her life that she didn't have to defend herself or find morsels and turn them into meals. She had been tortured too long, but this time, there was no resolution on Duluth's face. She had left it all in the prior years. And it hurt because she felt like she had failed.

"How long do I have to live, Dr. Bailey?" she asked.

"You must go and get Orion back. Perhaps she can help. She wasn't that crazy, Duluth. I can't let you die..." Carrie pleaded in folded hands. "I don't care about what she did or how she did it. I don't want another daughter passing away, Goddammit! Please, doctor, can I do something?"

The doctor began to wipe a tear from his eye. "Many times, I feared that when these girls grew up, that we would have to face these issues. Dr. Copulus and I both knew that we couldn't let the story go on forever without poor consequence. The truth is that when Dr. Copulus was murdered, a great deal of knowledge went with him. He was the only one who had the skills and intellect to actually have this stuff figured out, Carrie.

"I was just following along with him, trying to control the pain. Bill had his way of handling things, albeit with a stern face. But he also understood that no, he wasn't an angry doctor, or an evil man. He had a lot of pressure to pretend that miracles couldn't happen without someone knowing about it. What your husband did was sharing the miracle. And it cost Bill his ability to spread his seed. When Orion came out and showed what the curse was about one slip, and especially what one mismanaged bastardization of procedure did to a single innocent girl's being, it cost Bill his life.

"The truth is, Duluth, is you were condemned the moment you were born. It isn't your fault, sweetie. It really isn't." The words became too tense to say any more. He grabbed Duluth, and shared a hug with her, putting his Hippocratic hindrances behind him. "It's my fault. I should have let you go. Look at me. Damn this stethoscope. Damn this white jacket."

Immediately, Duluth began to feel the pain that Bailey had. She closed her eyes as the tears hit her skin. The pain she felt before in these cases was so minute, and it would pass. What she felt then and there was something that even the blood of Hope couldn't extend.

It wasn't the pain of a cut, or a tumor. This was years of hidden feelings, hidden hurt, things he could not release. It built his character and made him who he was. But it was all coming out in streams as they embraced. The room began to shake as the lights began to flicker. Duluth could see this man begging Copulus to stop putting the needle into Duluth and Orion. To stop playing chemist with people's lives.

Bailey grasped Duluth ever closer. The light began to emanate from every part of her body. "Duluth, wipe away these sins. Don't let go," he said in the strongest voice he could. Her body began to convulse, but she knew she couldn't let go.

She saw him grow up, and have the coat put on him. Class of 2008. "I swear to fulfill, to the best of my ability and judgment, this covenant..."

Don't let go....

She saw his first patient, a young boy who drank a bottle of chlorine. She saw him administer a bottle of ipecac and how the boy vomited all over his slacks, but then smiled and said how his tummy stopped burning.

Don't let go....

She saw the residency in the emergency room in Florida. How he tried to help everyone, and kept positivity, despite the long hours.

Don't let go....

And then, there was Orion, when she got out of the jail cell and shook the hand of the doctor, and placed a kiss on his cheek. "You are one of the best gentlemen in my life." As he signed the release for medical supervision, she sat there, coddling her hands.

Duluth began to say the words out loud that she had felt in him. The pain was so emotional that they both were in a sort of electrical contact, where the muscles of each of them could not let go of the opposite. They were in harmony.

They both began to cry out loud. It was dark in the room. The lights somehow were not on, but it was probably by layperson's means. They were just that bright.

And then, Duluth felt the greatest pain of all. The doctor's nails grasped into her skin, and blood began to ooze in earnest out of her left arm. "Please, Matt! Please, let go!" Carrie and Adriana pleaded.

But he was crying out loud and the muscles wouldn't relax. Finally, the little sister got up, felt a great deal of necessity and resolution, fought her insight and reservation, and grabbed the doctor, pulling him off. He was sweating profusely, and he collapsed to the floor, breathing as if he had run the hundred meters.

Carrie switched the lights on. There was Duluth, with burns on her body. She laid there, lifeless and most likely overwhelmed by the feelings and energy she had felt in those 90 seconds both she and her physician had embraced. Slumped over, she appeared unconscious, her head bowed and arms draped lifeless across the edge of the bed.

Adriana fell backwards, her body hitting the floor as Bailey stumbled, catching his breath on the table as he leaned against it.

These moments were never to happen. But they had to.

EIGHT HOURS LATER

It was a long night ahead for that family which had been through so much strain, so much frustration – and then again. They had sat very patiently but anxiously in the emergency room lobby, to which Duluth was transported to shortly after the doctor's visit. They had been in this lobby too not that long ago, counting down the last few moments of their pride and joy's life. The news blared through the empty lobby, and it was scary.

"This is Sherri Mewe reporting. Tonight, a scary sequence of events have wrapped up in a confession and confirmation of events that took place a week ago. In Solebury tonight, 21 year old Orion Prasda revealed that she, along with another two unidentified young females, were indirectly responsible for the potent first aid rendered at the Saint Martin At Tours parish carnival in New Hope. It is understood that Orion was the donator of a now-released secret government compound with the ability, once injected into the skin, to be able to heal any disease. Prasda took the podium tonight at Town Hall outside of Philadelphia.

'I am here today to tell you that thanks to the folks at Attrition home and the extensive medical research at Attrition Home in Solebury, that we have been able to come up with a cure for any disease, any illness, any time. This compound in this vial is able to stimulate the immune system when injected transdermally within 24 hours.'

"It is not understood if these events were connected to last year's surge of seemingly unexplainable healings completed by Philadelphia resident Hope Malott, who passed away earlier this year of an apparent suicide. However, Miss Prasda has indicated that the other unidentified females are actually living at the Malott residence as transients.

"Phone calls to Attrition and the Malott residence were not returned."

Lou Mendoza clenched his fists, and picked up the coffee mug he had been drinking from, throwing it on the table, and smashing it into a thousand sticky, hot pieces that spread over the stainguarded carpet. It

[328]

was obvious that she had gone behind the backs of the entire family after disappearing for a few days, and had made a spectacle of herself. She had been seeing Attrition as a place to avenge an old friend – and make right for what had been done wrong from so long ago.

"I'm going to kill that bitch!" was the only thing he could say. He stormed out of the room, and through the doors. Hospital security began to follow, but the elder man, seemingly the commander on duty, saw it, and put his hand across the breast of the younger guard, as if to say *Let it go. There's mental patients coming in soon. Don't wear yourself out.*

Carrie followed him out. "It's not going to help if we just get mad about this, honey –" but he was enraged beyond her control.

"We went through this all once, and now we're going to have people banging down our door again! I'm going to get my goddamned Ruger 45 and find this girl and put so many bullets through her that she won't see the light of day! Jesus Christ…."

Carrie yelled "It's not going to help to shed any more blood! Besides, she will eat those bullets and rip your head off in the process!"

"I know these C402 kids and they are not invincible, Care. They are just like any one of us. They have a heart and soul." He began to have the folks out in the parking lot turn towards the two, as they drew attention to themselves, an obvious domestic violence case that was all too frequent of inner city healthcare.

Carrie fired the final bullet. "Then why the hell are you treating them like they don't?" She slapped him and stormed back in. He wanted to say something, but he took the word of Lincoln and didn't remove all doubt.

He walked in, somewhat restrained. "What do you want me to do, honey? What can I do? These people are going to kill us…if she doesn't first!"

Carrie was the only one who knew the pain that they had all been through. She was blood to these three young women, and she knew exactly what they wanted. "We need to make Duluth the complete opposite of Hopie. We need to hide her. And make these last days of hers special. We did a damn good exploitation of a child already. It's time we give it up and do something right. For Hopie. Please, Lou. Please, I beg you for the love of God, don't put us through the moneymaking vaudeville acts. It's enough." She sat down and covered her head in shame. He had the common sense to walk away.

The nurse came out to the waiting room, with a smile on her face. "Mr. and Mrs. Malott? Duluth is back in the room. She said she wants to see you two." And it immediately felt as if the situation had diffused itself in some way, that she was responding on her own accord, her own words, that she was not a carcass. They could make it last another day. And every day was a gift from now on. And they were thankful.

The curtain opened. Duluth's body was burned, her hair nearly gone, singed off in clumps. They hadn't shaved it off, but somehow, when they entered, they could see that despite the tenderness of her emaciated body that was taken over by the supremely large emergency room bed, that she was in good shape. All they had to do was look into her eyes. In their ever-present glow, even in the dark brown of contrast to the others, they were her trademark revelation.

"Hi, folks. Care to have a chat?" she said with a smile, with surprising exuberance. "Mind that I might have to go to the Max Factor counter in a little bit." It was a shock that she had recovered so quickly, but they couldn't figure out how. She didn't have any bandages to her name, but it was okay. It was the truth that they loved her just the way she was. And after she threw them off in her stupor, they weren't going to even try. Bailey had stopped them, anyways. Let her be, he probably said. Girl's going to be her own beauty. Plus I got a secret. What a fool.

"Duluth, honey, what happened?" Lou asked out front. "What did you see when the doctor grasped you, hugged you?"

She laid back her head, rolled her eyes, and laughed in an almost eclectic stupor. "That experience was the best of my life, Lou, hun.

"For the first few seconds, it was pain. Pure pain and anger. Like someone was mad at me. I felt everything that doctor had experienced, a lifetime of guilt and pain. It was in his tears, and when he grasped me and cut my arm open —" she gestured to her intravenous tube-punctured arm - "he began to transfer his illness to me.

"But then, Adriana grabbed the doctor, and pulled at him. When she did that, all of a sudden, his fears went away. For, like, two or three seconds, I felt Dr. Matt Bailey send me to a better place. In his words, he said that he had faith in me. It was a feeling….like when I prayed at Hope's funeral, that someone would save me. Someone would help me.

"Adriana grasped at him, and she must have had something on her hands that went through Dr. Bailey. Don't know what it was, but it probably saved both of our lives. For a moment, the three of us were all together…just like I had wanted it to be. The reason why Dr. Bailey let go is because he knew that somehow, it was all complete then and there. Like it was in Luke….'Look at my hands and my feet. It is I myself! Touch me and see; a ghost does not have flesh and bones, as you see I have….' And there were the three of us together. We all had a party for those few seconds." She began to laugh and pound her head back and forth in the chair.

The nurse began to chuckle. "We gave her a bunch of painkillers a few hours ago. She needed them because she's all burned up. Don't know how much she is going to look from now on, or if she's going to live a normal life. But we'll try to get her a little bit better before she is discharged." Walking away, chart in hand, she gave an indifferent sigh, as she tried to pass off the occurrence.

[331]

But Lou had better things to say. "When he had said this, he showed them his hands and feet. Adriana!" She ran over. Pulling her hands palms up, she showed them her hands.

What they saw was incredible. Her hands were completely blue and green, like the eyes of Duluth. She had been hiding them in her pockets for some time, but there they were. "My hands, Daddy, they were bleeding when I touched Doctor Bailey. I was scared. I had poked myself, cut myself earlier when Duluth was in the hospital. I was scared, Daddy. I cut myself because I didn't want to be here without her.

Lou hugged her. "You may have hurt yourself. But you saved Dr. Bailey and Duluth's life through your blood. Your blood, your normal, human, unchanged, no radiation, no C402, your blood! You did it!" And without Duluth noticing because of the indifference of severe painkillers, the covenant was made, and it came full circle.

"She would have wanted it that way. Mom and Dad, I guess I did good for once." She smiled, and the three of them all hugged together for the first time.

ONE WEEK LATER

MALOTT RESIDENCE

The worst part about being burned is that it takes a while to heal and forever to become recognizable. However, if anyone, or anything, could beat the odds on that matter, it was Duluth Kane. She was on the best antivirals the hospital could provide, and it completed its due process in sure procedure. And thanks to the C402 and the blessing of Hope's blood, she had one last shot at life.

Looking in the mirror over those next few days, she saw the burn marks and the singed hair. It took a little while to get used to it, but the strangest thing was that she thought herself to be beautiful. And yes, she would see that glow in her face. Blushing sometimes did more than just warm her gestures; it helped her re-establish her identity. It was a gift that she had seldom had for herself, but it was damned peculiar that it would happen this time, this way. When she was 16, she was often regarded to be one of the little "butterflies" of Attrition Home, a positive but feisty little girl that really no one knew about. Hope helped her break out of that bubble a little later, mostly because of the way that Dr. Copulus had tried to shelve her and her "specialness". But what happened in tandem with her escape from the home and resulting emancipation was that she had to grow up. She didn't have the family to go to; her own father was too far away and too indifferent to actually try and link himself to her.

And so, she had to fend for herself and pretend like it was normal, this Kerouac life of hers. And it showed over time; her sunny adolescent face had begun to age tremendously. Months of lack of sleep and poor nutrition gave her bags under her eyes and a lanky frame with pale skin.

And then it came, a second chance. All of a sudden, she had life again, youth. It was something that many have searched for, sacrificing life and

[333]

limb to get the fountain of it, and be able to cancel the immeasurable and irreconcilable hell the Demon of Time places on all of us. It was somewhat true in Hope, but Hope too was aging and growing up. She had the power, but not the escape velocity. And it took her years too soon.

But yet, what was Orion? A freak of nature? A sign from God that it was OK? That there was life after death? And it meant we could live forever?

Duluth pondered those questions over and over again when she would in bed all those nights, applying the prescribed antibiotic cream to her face. She thought about what she could do with Orion, should she be in her presence again. To be a young woman, once the cutest of creatures with her unique hairstyles and pixie look with those skirts and tanks and military boots that went up to her knees...she had defined herself so well. And in all honesty, it went wrong just by having that relationship with Hope. She felt terrible for it. And sometimes, she looked in her eyes and saw the confession of Hope, and closing those same eyes for a second, felt her hands being placed around her body and just saying "It's OK, DK. I did this for a reason."

All this would go away as she returned into Hope's room. Because of the impact she had presented in the past few weeks, she had a warm bed to sleep in at night. She had a little sister, and a Mom and Dad who cared about her. She didn't have to worry about a warm dinner or whether the guard would allow her to sleep at the bus terminal at night. All things being said, the burns and temporary loss of beauty were worth it. And that's why she could smile when she would finally retire at night. She had lost her face when she gave that doctor her embrace. But now, she knew she could save face in the end. And it was about time.

In that week, her body began to change and the last push of her healing capabilities began to take shape. Her face became more recognizable, her hair growing without the Hawklick, but in a beautiful, long mane that was about shoulder length. It was scary when the bandages were removed every day because it meant the soreness would come back for just that

[334]

little bit. She had eyebrows and lips and a nose and could put on makeup. Her body wasn't moving swiftly in healing, and she knew it would take patience. But this was not little girl, preppy particular about her body Duluth. This was a woman who had long term plans on her mind. And the healing process was still fast, faster than she had ever seen before. Except Hope would have seen it clearly in her kindness and giving – and not Duluth's journeys.

She put on her pajamas, even though it was 2 PM, and sat on a beanbag in the corner. It was far less painful to her because it meant that the burns from Dr. Bailey's hug on her back wouldn't touch and she would grimace in pain. But she picked up that rockabilly guitar for the first time. She hadn't played in months, but it was like the ethereal riding of a bike. But she had to write about something. Her mind was still a garbled message. Anger and confusion took over, and it upset her greatly that the one thing that she had going for herself, the hope to be a musician of notable stature one day, was fading fast. Strumming a few chords, she lost herself in her music.

And then, the situation stung enough, even more than her burns. That consuming flame in her gave ambulance from the bed and put that guitar down. Turning on Hope's computer, she began to look for something on there, perhaps an internet site, to really give a sudden stimulation to whet her appetite. As she opened the browser, Hope's website opened.

She had never really looked at the site before, as it was too painful because there were only a few videos. She knew that Hope's site was more of a testament to her struggles and the inner conflict of what she went through. Duluth knew that if she watched it, she would be witnessing her own death in return. And no damnation of mankind is worse than forecasting accurately the terms of one's own demise. She closed the link.

A message popped up as she visited a video search site. "Do you still want to upload 'One Dream, One Life, One Opportunity'?" She immediately wanted to reject it, but somehow, she knew it was Hope's last say into our world, meager as all worlds.

It took ages to upload. She cursed at the computer, hoping that the poor customer service of the local cable company based downtown would not fail her this time. And when it completed, she watched the video.

There was Hope, sitting in a park somewhere, on a checkered blanket. It was debatable whether the weather looked warmer or Hope, who obviously did not have the rigors of her calling weighing on her.

"Good afternoon, everyone on HopeForHealing.com, this is Hope Malott. I've been vlogging a lot the past few weeks about how frustrating life is and the fact sometimes, it frankly sucks. But I want to do something I've wanted to do for a while. I have an OK singing voice, but I'd like to sing a song I wrote. I don't play anything, but I'm sure there's someone out there who can probably put the music to this. It's called 'One Dream, One Life, One Opportunity. Let me do this." She looked down.

Duluth began to watch.

If you had one chance to make this world better
What would you do tonight?
If you could make the sun shine brightly under stormy weather
What would you do tonight?
You know we all have weight put upon our shoulder
But what would you do tonight?
And the burden climbs higher as we all get older
But what would you do tonight?

We have one dream that we all live in
And one life that goes by ever fast and slow
But there's one opportunity to never let you go
We have pain in the air but love in our eyes
And in them we see

One Dream
One Life
One Opportunity.

Duluth paused the video. She grabbed her guitar and began to play along in somewhat decreasingly haphazard syncopation.

If you had to kiss one person to love them more
What would you say tonight?
If you gave your hand to make them soar
What would you say tonight?
You know there's life in love and friends
What would you say tonight?
And with each other it will never end
What would you say tonight?

The refrain went on again, and Duluth suddenly found herself together with Hope, there in that room, by means of magnetic disk. They were together for that moment.

She paused the video for a moment, and put Hope's favorite pair of pink headphones. Going into the computer's directories and software, she began to remix it. And then she hooked the guitar into the computer. Not realizing it, she began to feel like she was back to being open, being creative, an artist who could create great works on the canvas of the ear.

There's always time for us to put
What things can go away
And if I were with you tonight
Oh, the things I would say
We had so much fun when life was good
But we have to give it all we got
And then one dream one life
Opportunity came to an end
And we gave it our best shot....

[337]

She began to play faster and faster, her fingers began to fly once again. Even though they were red, they didn't hurt. Even though she had only picked up a guitar once in the past two years, she knew what she wanted. And she found herself recording chorus and making an MP3 of her recording.

It perhaps was the last gesture that Hope could offer in those last few moments of life. Duluth had her most tender, vulnerable, scared moment, and here was Hope, speaking from beyond the passing, helping her out just that one more time. And she was thankful.

When she finally shut down the computer that evening for dinner downstairs, she put it on her guitar-shaped studded flash drive, and put it around her neck. Hope gave her a gift, and it was her restless tendencies to make the world better that made Duluth the better.

Turning around, she felt a great deal of energy, a certain resolve that had set upon her. She failed to notice that she was beginning to take on more of being Hope than she had ever expected. She rubbed her eyes, ran her fingers through her hair, and felt good about herself. Closing her eyes as the temptation of food wafted through the dry air of the room, she smiled.

As she went down the stairs, she smiled and believed in herself. And her capabilities. Smelling the warm rolls and beef brisket, she turned the corner.

Lou turned around, expecting to see Duluth raring to eat. He responded by dropping the plate.

"Oh, my God." The au jus splattered, and the beef stuck to the floor like glue.

Not knowing what was wrong, Duluth became frightened by her adoptive stepparent's reaction. She walked over to the mirror, and took a glance.

Hope had given one last means to become one with her friend.

With a glance in the mirror, the shock rang through. There, looking back at her, was the eyes and face of Hope Malott. Her hair was now long and what had grown presumably since her rising was dark black. The only difference was that Duluth had her brown eyes, and not Hope's blue. But there, yes, it was Hope's face, placed on the head. She screamed the loudest scream she could do. It of course was proportioned to Duluth's head and holes, but it was a decidedly Malott face and not the Nordic one she had seen for her entire existence. It was not an exact match, but she could see the structure, her emotion, her cheeks and jawline molded in. She did not notice that her face was completely healed, with nary a scar in sight. This was Hope's way of living another day. It almost was slightly parasitical, but somehow, it was being her too closely without embracing Duluth herself.

Running back up to bed, she slammed the door shut and realized that perhaps, she had become too much like that which she was not. She was beautiful in her own way, but somehow, this was indeed a sign that things had come too far. She ran up to bed and put her face in the pillow, unable to look.

In a panic, Carrie called Dr. Bailey, his arms still in bandages. He had little memory of what exactly went on, but he understood in tandem that Duluth was probably in most need of all of his patients. So he put on a good suit jacket to hide the "battle scars", and hopped in his BMW and drove over.

Perhaps the biggest effect of all was not on Duluth, but on her new shared "sister". Adriana sat there, trying to look at Duluth's face. She was understandably curious as to what had happened to the beautiful Duluth Kane, but every time she tried to look over at Duluth, she could only keep her spectacled eyes on her for a few seconds before she had to look down. It was a resurrection, one that she could not understand in the least bit. And every time Duluth would see Adriana's reaction, she would go over and try to hug her "little sister". But she would cringe away. With each time this happened, even in a few minutes of passing, it hurt because there was no understanding.

Dr. Bailey did all he could to explain this one. The only words that could come out of his mouth were "I don't know." He tried almost to the point of exhausting his wit to give the words, but he couldn't say it. Given this, Duluth knew that it was Hope's blood and the burning of her face that did the trick. She knew it when he looked into her eyes and saw his greatest mistake. He wanted to hug her once more, but realized it was the common embrace that meant she would never have an identity other than that of someone else, an identity which she could never live up to, nor surpass.

The situation felt almost too awkward to put words to. So she didn't. But then, she realized that Hope was alive again...and now, with any single person knocking on the door, she would have to cover up for the entire family, because no one knew it was her.

A few moments later, they all agreed to give the freshly faced Duluth some time alone. Adriana looked from afar, peeking through the crack in the door. In it, she saw a woman who couldn't believe what her body was doing. Like an adolescent in identity crisis, she felt her new skin. Running her fingers through her hair, she picked up the scissors to cut it all off. And then put them down after snipping off a gob. She put makeup on, playing with her nose and her eyebrows. Adriana could see that person, and for a moment, Duluth was lost in herself, with her eyes glowing ever so blue. She had prayed for this life for all time, and she was given it. But now, she wanted it all to go away.

"Stupid....Hope....why can't you just die? Ugh!" she did, pulling at her hair. In that vanity, she felt like someone else was staring at her, an entirely different being, someone who wasn't her. Every time she wanted to speak, she swore that Hope was speaking back to her. But the sadness in Hope's face was too powerful to ignore. It was not one of her relics or icons of deep Eastern European doctrine; it was a golden calf that she now had to worship; her self-image.

Through it all, Adriana was conflicted on whether to help her or not. When she remembered Duluth, there was this "punk chick of strength" image that had always run through her head. It was uniquely Duluth, and when she would tell her friends at school about her, the image projected boldly and with great signature style, a sort of monolith of standing strong where no others could. Now, she covered her hair, tortured it. She wore Hope's clothing now. She put on Hope's makeup, and slept in Hope's bed.

For a moment, Adriana had to convince herself that she was not falling in love again with her stepsister. Watching through that small crevice made her scared in a way that no other moment had ever done. She wanted to say something, but the words couldn't come out. She didn't want to hurt her feelings, or further inflict trauma from what was already in active progression. It felt like she was witnessing the destruction of someone from within. Knowing from the Eriksson book she read in high school, there was an identity crisis. And sadly, the girl who had prided herself outwardly about being strong now showed her true hand of feebleness.

Duluth got to the point where she began to look away. Her new friend closed the door, to not disturb further what was already a definite disarray of massive proportions, scattered about the conscience like a confusion no one had ever felt before.

Duluth sat there in bed, just thinking. With literally nothing to say, she looked in the mirror. "Hi Hope! How are you? I'm fine. I wanted to meet you at the restaurant and ask you...." She pulled at her cheeks, pulled at the clothes which had belonged to Hope not that long ago. "I wanted to ask how...you did your hair! So beautiful and so black! You must dye it in 40 weight!" She tried to pull at the hair. That hair was the last vestige of her identity, something that had set her apart for so long. Now it was Hope's hair. "You win, Hope. The blood is all over me now. I had to be you. We promised we would be together. But look at this damn mirror of yours, Hopie. You win. Now let's go and make a million dollars!" She said not another word.

Realizing this was a bit futile to begin to hurt oneself to avenge the image that really was hurting herself, albeit for no reason at all, she sat on the bed. And for once, she knew she had to begin to think. Seeing Hope, who would have said to think, was almost too damn symbolic for it to pass up. She wanted to say it to counteract Hope, but yet she understood in tandem that she had to take Hope's place in this world – and to go forth from this room.

At dinner that night, Lou gazed into Duluth's face intently. His image of Hope with contacts and a little bit of chin surgery burned into his head. It took him all the strength in the world to not tell whatever it was that was curling Carrie's spaghetti around a spoon across from them at the table that he was sorry. But how could he say that he was sorry? He really wasn't for Duluth. The poor girl was living her penance, he would think for a few moments. She was the one who dropped in and took that last morsel of life that my baby had.

It was such a comforting mechanism for him to have that delusion in his head, an auric anarchy that really hid what truly was killing him: denial. And yet, he realized that the proceedings had done what was coming to him: a sign from God that Hope would not go away except by Duluth's blood and spirit. And so, he let Duluth and the icon in Hope live there. It was the only way he could survive.

10 HOURS LATER

Carrie began to pace quickly about the foyer of the house, trying to think about how to explain to everyone outside that she still was not hiding Hope, even with the revelation that indeed, Hope had passed some time ago. The people she knew would be certain that it was not the perfect doppelganger, but still, to the foolish masses of sheep, would not pass for perhaps a grown-up Hope Malott. In that period of time, she thought that she would be able to say it was just a stranger, and an even stranger coincidence, that the houseguest was indeed not her daughter. But crazy people would do crazy things, and when they saw the glow in her eyes, there would be hell to pay.

A knock came on the door. For the fifth time of the day, it was someone from the press, obviously out to investigate. The two tone hair and chiseled face of Duluth had not been released to the public, but it was going to have to be disclosed in the most discrete manner possible.

They shooed the reporter away, as always. Lou closed the door, and looked at Duluth. It was almost like he couldn't believe that this could happen – that Hope had indeed come back to haunt him, to preach to him about the ills that had taken place over the past few weeks. Only now, it was not the quiet compassion of a well-versed young woman who would rather avoid conflict, but one that hated him deeply, hated this life, this damned streak of unfortunate occurrences that had plagued them for nearly two decades. It was the unchangeable path that had finally hit Lou like the dagger that had been forced through him some time ago. He couldn't figure out who brought him back, or why he had been cursed to live it all over again.

Duluth had the inherent sadness in the situation, though. She had little to say since she had recorded that video, and she knew she couldn't say anything. She didn't want to be Hope. Hope wasn't her. Hope would have been brave in this scenario. Duluth was just scared. And so, she had to make it so she could have made Hope proud.

[343]

4:02 AM

The elders had retired for the night, obviously in turmoil as to what lay ahead of them in the ultimate healing process. There was an air of rejection, perhaps a sign of surprise that had emanated from those floors, those walls, and it echoed like the acoustics of Carnegie Hall in mid-movement.

Duluth could feel that strange lost, confused persona in her, and confirmed it as she looked at the face in the mirror several times. It was as if someone had given her a second chance at life, but yet, so much was abandoned from the first. She could have only wished for a healed face, a healed body, and it was there.

When she tried to put on her eye pencil, she couldn't help but stab herself several times, the awkwardness of the body taking over it all. Feeling around the bones, the lips were understandably smaller, the nose smaller, the cheeks chiseled but yet would often take that youthful glow that she never had.

In an instant, she began to think about getting away from this. For the past few months, she finally had a home, a family, a place to live. It echoed in her mind over and over again. But yet, she felt like there was something more to be done. Perhaps something that could tie up the ultimate loose end. The catalyst was Matt Bailey. He was the link to a success story in the end, the cornerstone for what would have to be a normal adulthood. And when he said he could not help, it became clear that she needed someone who would understand.

And so, she gathered up her warmest clothing, put on a pair of Wayfarers, placed on her newly christened head a slightly mauled military hat, and opened the second story window. She had to find Orion.

Wandering the streets, she tried to remember the exact way that she had come home. Surely, Orion had some sort of residence, or some sort of place to sleep at night. In her mind, she tried to channel the elder's way of thought: what she would likely seek, where she would eat, sleep, socialize, drink, anything that would come up. It wasn't extremely apparent to her at first that perhaps she would never find her in this big city, although it was also apparent that there was only one place where if someone with Orion's drive to right a wrong, she would have to be in one place.

XVII
The Betrayal

THREE HOURS LATER

ATTRITION HOME

The girl with the vagabond heart fell asleep to the gates of the home, cuddled up and leaning against the lamppost like the gangsters of the Roaring Twenties. When she awoke, a car was coming in, with somewhat phantom ethic; a large SUV, it had blacked out windows and an appearance lending to believe it was law enforcement carrying in the newest patient. Not noticing her there, she ran behind the vehicle as the gates closed behind it.

It sent a shiver down her spine to think she would be back here after so much wanting to get out. It was almost the suicidal instinct in her that had driven her to keep going through the cold and walking all those miles in those heavy boots. *Why did I wear these again*, she would ask herself. *Hope's Chucks were even better than this*. The sweat on her brow kept her going, though. And she couldn't dress like Hope, either. *No way.*

Watching the car doors open under the porch, she hunched behind a bush. Two men in constable's uniforms opened the doors. And there she was.

Orion got out, and opened the door to the building. She was there for a mission, and it wasn't by force. As the door closed to the home, Duluth could see the lights come on, unusual for an early morning.

She ran up to the building, and pulled on the door. Anxiously, she tried to remember how to jimmy the lock, as she had done quite experimentally over the years. She pulled and shook and turned the handle. The light came onto the porch, with the realization that Attrition had plenty of cameras, and if she did any more, she would be detected.

Ducking into the shadows, she realized that getting into the building was going to be tough. But then, in a search of the mind, she knew there would be one person who, by venture of his rabid foolishness, would probably let her in.

One, two, three, four, five windows down.... She pointed, counting the windows, jogging her memory. And then, she pointed to the one with the cross in the window. It was Bob the Oaf's room. If he was still there, he would be the entry she needed.

She climbed over the bushes, smiled, and brushed her long, brunette hair aside. This was the only chance she would get, because by morning, the grounds sweep would probably see her. Videotape from the cameras in the morning would blow her cover. But would anyone recognize her? On one hand, her return may have elicited a prodigal approach, perhaps lending her a home. Copulus' death had probably meant that someone of better character had been put in his place. But then again, she did not look the part from long ago. And Attrition was a state home, for which she knew trespassing was punished by jail time.

She saw him cuddled up, a book in his hand, his blanket half on, half off. He was still the same old guy, and he was going to help her one last time. Knocking on the window, she smiled, and cupped her hand to her brow, trying to look in.

It took several knocks on the glass to get his attention. She didn't want to give up that easily, but she had to maintain her posture. The light came on, and Oaf began to grumble.

"Who goes where no one else can go there? Who does it knock on these windows tonight?" And then, he came up to the window, and grabbed a broomstick. "Who is it that knocks?" he screamed, grabbing his belt.

Duluth put her finger to her mouth to politely shush the grandiose grump. Her memory of Attrition was that anyone who stirred the pot in the morning would quickly be investigated and promptly sedated, to which meant that she would probably be spotted.

She pushed her hands down and said "Bob, Bob, it's Duluth, Duluth Kane! I'm back! But be quiet! I need your help."

In reference to his acuity, he had a look of confusion on his face. "DK Duluth ran away with Hopie. So long ago. She had light hair. Short hair. A guitar. You are not her at all. Go now. Goodbye." He grabbed the window, and prepared to slam it.

Just then, Duluth stuck her hand under the window, and it stopped. She wanted to let out a scream, but just grimaced, clenched her teeth, and crossed her eyes.

Why do I have to keep getting doors slammed in my face so much? It's almost like I'm a Jehovah's witness, she thought.

Someday, I'm going to slam a damn door in your face. Whoever you are.

"You put this damn thing up Oaf, or you're not watching Ridin' Robert again. Do you remember we used to sing the theme song together?"

And so she began to sing the words. One by one, she used the power of the memory of her voice to stir the deepest parts of the modest intelligence of the boy. When she got to the third line, they both began to sing together. And then they even messed up the lyrics, like they both would do. She laughed as they both could never forget that second part of the bridge. They both laughed when they realized it was old friends.

"You don't have Duluth's face. You don't have her hair. But you have her beautiful voice. Somehow, methinks I am speaking to Duluth. Therefore, I must be speaking to Duluth."

She smiled. *Attaboy*, she thought. *But let me in first*. Before Oaf could make alternative judgment, she pushed the window past its safety, nearly knocking the entire pane off its housing. As she closed the window, she sighed, and said to herself "OK, now the hard part."

Turning around, there was Oaf, standing there, wearing nothing but a smile. "Remember Ridin' Robert?" Duluth gave an unfortunate biting of the lip, knowing that she had left some business unattended to. She tried not to look at his somewhat lumpy anatomy, and to the sadness of it all, it could have been put somewhat bluntly that he indeed missed her a lot. But she could not let him run about. Not now.

"Bob, um, we can do this later. Right now, I need your help with this." She looked around. "Why does this room smell like disinfectant? I mean, I've never been in here, but it sure as heck is clean."

Oaf walked over, nearly brushing into Duluth's arpeggio of clothing. "We have a new fine physician in the building. His name is Bob, too. Bob Norris. Dr. Bob." He smiled and sat Indian style on his bed, still in the buff. "He's been very nice, but he makes us keep these rooms super special clean." He was speaking louder and louder, his tone beginning to worry Duluth. So he tried to calm him down.

Somehow, the name rang in her head. Norris. Bob Norris. She passed it off as just being a coincidence.

"OK, so this Bob Norris guy, what does he do 'round these parts. Does he take good care of everyone? Is he nice to you?" She sat down in the corner, cupping her sweater to soothe sitting on a hard wooden floor.

Oaf smiled as she gestured to calm down. "Dr. Bob was brought here after Dr. Bill had his anatomy changed and was fired. There was a nurse that he was caught having marital relations with, and it made a lot of people really unhappy.

"So they went and found this new person, and he found this amazing girl. I think her name is…"

Duluth interrupted. "Orion Prasda? She's here?" She wanted to jump out of her clothes and say I hit the target. Thank God… But the senses came back and limited her.

Oaf smiled. "You are a smart girl, New Duluth. You are just like Old Duluth but with long black hair and rosy cheeks." She smiled and continued to get facts. "Orion has the same power Old Duluth had, but much more special. Like a million times what Hopie had, too."

Duluth nodded as she continued the last hour of interrogation. "So knowing that, Oaf…I mean, Bob, what does she do here? I mean, don't you think she wouldn't like it here, like Hope and me would?" She was keeping the questions simple, to keep the trickle of interest flowing in her old friend.

Oaf smiled and put his hand to heart, the other one beginning to gesture randomly. "Well, Orion is trying to help us heal a few people who are here. Really sick little bitty boys, maybe as old as you when you first came here."

"So she's really trying to share her wealth with others."

"Only she is going to have a really big meeting tomorrow. Why, Channel 6 and Channel 3 and Channel 10 are here tomorrow. She will have all the cameras, like a big Hollywood scene. She wants to try to make a statement on 'the biggest heal of all'." The last words came out like Oaf was revering them, giving them an almost immaculate status. It created a resonance in Duluth that meant she had to see this in person.

"OK, Oaf. I have to ask you a big, huge favor. Actually, two. No, wait a minute, three." She looked at him.

"Anything for a friend, New Duluth. Even three things." He gave his best smile, as he folded his arms and shook his hips, thrusting his anatomy about like a gelatin mold in the summer heat.

She paced about the room as she shut off the lamp and let the moonlight enter through the somewhat unsteady window as it whistled in the wind, half broken and somewhat incredibly flimsy. "I want to stay the night here. I'll take these little blankets and cuddle up under your bed. That's one."

"Two?"

"I'm going to go to that meeting as a press person. If I remember correctly, you still have your kiddie clothes. I'm going to suit up and look like someone from TV."

"OK. Three."

She laughed. "Three, I shouldn't have to say this, but put some clothes on. You're a very beautiful person, Bobby, but I think we need to let God keep His blessings on your body to Himself."

And so, they shook hands, and she spent the night there. She really didn't plan on the drag or the dragging, the snoop or the score, but it was covenant indeed.

THE NEXT MORNING

She woke up very early, the somewhat uncomfortable lodging accommodations, haphazard and temporary as they were, lending to a very slight sleep. But it was a worthy slumber nonetheless; weeks of keeping to the streets and stations meant she could probably sleep on a bed of rusty nails. But it was sufficient solution to her energy inside. Knowing full that she probably would be on the radar screen at the Malotts for sneaking out the window, it was on her mind that she would have to either explain her mission or somehow get up on the roof, up the tree, and back in before breakfast. She was known to be ill, so she could just say she was sleeping.

She grabbed Oaf's clothing, digging through a chest for some old, tired clothing that would pass for an honorable female of rank and file in the press. Grabbing a pair of slacks and a blue shirt, she could have passed for a military lieutenant. But it would not fly for anything but a trip to the picture show.

Digging deeper, she found what appeared to be a coat, a nice faux fur one. Geez, for parents dumping him here, he sure was probably stylish in the day, she thought. Although how could they afford it? Bob was broke back in the day. It would have to do for now.

Covertly, she glided out the door, Oaf nowhere to be found. They were already gathering in the foyer as the cameras began to gather in the back. She sat down, with the memories of the room ringing deeply through her mind. She wanted to close her eyes and forget it all, but the bright lights and the morning sun made the sounds that echoed through the chamber too powerful.

"Excuse me, young lady, but is this seat taken?" Duluth was startled by the voice. It was the same nurse who, a few years ago but not that long in her memory, force fed her pills quite against her will. She wanted to grab her gum and pretend it was all over.

"No. No, it isn't, ma'am. You may sit." And so the nurse nodded, and sat down, her *Viejo* past still echoing though Duluth's heart, causing it to pound strongly. She swallowed the lump in her throat as she tried to calm down.

The nurse, attuned to the vital signs of a person, looked at her funny. After a few seconds, she said "Mighty warm to be wearing that in here. You know, you might feel better if you just go back to the suitjacket. What rag you work for?" she asked.

Duluth could not stomach her fears. The only words she could think of were "South Philly News. Observer. Picayune." The simple smell of that woman's perfume, the connection to the pheromones of the past, simply was too strong to ignore.

The nurse laughed. "Never heard of that one. You're a young one by the way. Got a good voice too, like something that would catch an ear. They must be turning out journalists, rookies, all of them nowadays. Not like the days of old, I say." The nurse laughed as Duluth tried to hide the fact that there were memories in that voice, the only thing connecting her to a rather shady past.

She immediately began to look around. There were things that were changed, but she couldn't tell what. She would listen in – and everything would begin to make sense.

Her heart raced, as she anticipated the next few words. What she would hear would lend a share of her fire into the morning, but yet burn through her like a consuming flame.

The meeting began officially with some haphazard awkwardness, a typical discourse for such a place where the confused were sent to be fixed or scrapped – a choice. They were all gathered in the main room, with the shades of the morning sun coming through the skylight. Duluth noticed how warm it was in the room. Most of it was due to Attrition loving to have the spotlight on them. The lights shone bright, but they also produced physical heat, and it burned through everyone in the room.

Dr. Norris came up to the podium first. Orion sat in her boots, skirt, and suitjacket, much to the fashionable dismays of Duluth.

"Good morning folks, we are here today at Attrition Home to present to you the Orion Prasda Life Without Bounds Project. This project is something we have wanted to take on for years here at Attrition Home.

"Through the past 20 years, we have had a number of patients arrive at our House to cure many diseases. From multiple sclerosis to degenerative muscle diseases, to AIDS, cancer, and mental disabilities, we have been able to help many young people recover and then prosper through cutting edge research and care.

"I present to you today one of the premier examples of what the healing process can do. Seated next to me is a very special young woman, Orion Prasda. Orion was once a patient here at Attrition Home, and was under the care of the late Doctor William A. Copulus, who was a leader in research in regenerative cell processes and developing through chemistry an approach to preserving life whenever possible…"

These words began to cause the young Duluth to cringe at the words that were spoken by the physician. She knew that they spoke of C402, with Orion's presence on stage. But she also knew that Dr. Copulus was trying to get rid of the impact of C402 on the public, not promote it. She wondered as she glanced at Orion, her legs crossed as she smiled in the most fake forced type of electrical shock to one's face she had ever seen, whether there was something hiding behind this matter. In the deepest way, she absolutely refused to acknowledge a complete one-eighty degree turn on the subject. They just didn't get it that closely.

Yet in the crowd, she could not see Dr. Matt Bailey, who was supposed to be taking over. She knew that he would have been disgusted by the proceedings, and would have stopped her from doing so. But Bailey was also tremendously injured, burned in his mind and into his flesh it would travel. Such things were never destined for reality, but here she was, and here, he wasn't. For now.

"...and now, we are pleased to introduce to you the founder and director of Life Without Bounds, Ms. Orion Coppell Prasda." The applause piped up as she put her skirt aside and stepped to the podium.

The audience, especially the old friend in somewhat sudden masquerade, watched her every word closely as she spoke. "Good morning, and thank you very, very much, Dr. Norris. I so appreciate this," she stated in a quite ditzy and somewhat adolescent tone. "As someone who has been blessed with such an ability to heal others and stay young at heart and in body, I have taken up this project to share my gift with others."

Douchebag, Duluth thought. *Up yours, cabrón.*

"As you probably have already known, our town was blessed with people who could do this. The one girl who was blessed a year ago with the ability to heal others, Hope Malott, was taken from us too soon. However, we have developed and synthesized her healing power, developing this new substance, C402. This vial of red liquid contains enough of this awesome substance, injected into the bloodstream, to create an increase in white blood cell and platelet count. I have been blessed to be the first recipient of a dose of this miracle drug when I was younger, and as you can see, I have aged very slowly, to the point where

[355]

my body still has not outgrown adolescence. There are no scars, no trauma, no bags under my eyes." A round of applause followed.

Duluth got up from her seat, and walked towards the center aisle, folding her hands and staring Orion dead in the eye. She could see the nervousness in the elder's eyes, suggesting that she did have something to hide. Looking at her gestures made Duluth want to vomit. But she knew that it wouldn't do no good to pass more sputum.

She worked her way through the halls, recalling where her room was. She didn't know if it was still open, although she considered the fact that the memories may not have been something she would have absolutely preferred at this point. But then again, who else was in there?

One of the benefits of the big press conference was that the pharmacy was quite understaffed. A single nurse sat behind the counter, wrapped up in a book that reminded Duluth of her days as a teenager. Not so fortunate of days, either, she thought.

She opened the door slowly, trying not to startle the guarded woman. In her power, she silently prayed that the door would not creak as much as the old oak structure would allow. She could feel her footsteps making unwelcome noise; in that balance, she hushed her boots as best as she could.

Ducking behind the wall, she grabbed a bottle of mepivacaine and began to fill up a syringe. She still had the two vials that Copulus had given her as the last relics of a life gone bad. Not knowing what was in them, she placed a large towel around the vials and protected them from any physical damage. Knowing things would get rough in this building was a given; and yes, she knew that once you were taken down, the next place was a room where you could be fed, beaten, and ultimately stripped of all of your powers, rights, and thoughts. It stuck in the back of her mind like a deep burn.

"Come on, baby," she whispered as she drew the anesthetic out of the bottle. As she filled the needle, she could see the nurse begin to turn towards her. The pharmacy had two sets of stacks of medicine in which Duluth could hide in; the opaqueness of the walls was the key to the development of her plan.

Out of the corner of her eye, she could see the nurse begin to turn towards her position. Duluth ducked behind an endcap, pulling her coat nearer to her. And then, she knocked over a bottle of pills, sodium iodate. They had done it to her once again.

"What the..." the nurse whispered. The curious medic hushed towards Duluth's position, an obvious note to the sound. Her brain began to produce solutions immediately, but somehow, she knew that it was going to take a miracle.

Holding the syringe like a spy with the gun needle up, she ran to the back wall. As soon as the nurse turned the corner, she stabbed the nurse with the needle in the jugular. "I'm sorry, ma'am, but I have to do this," Duluth said in the most schizoid murderous fashion. "Where do you keep your C402?"

The nurse went to move, gasping. "I don't know, who are you?" she questioned confusingly as the young girl approached from behind her and whispered in her ear.

"My name is unimportant. What is important right now is that you don't make me inject this anesthetic in you and turn you into a useless pile of flesh. Mepivacaine, 2 percent. This shit will kill you like it almost did me. Move." She stuck the needle deeper into the nurse's flesh.

The nurse became quite scared, but then she began to recount her memories. A voice came into her head. "You know, I think you need to go back. Duluth, you must have come back for a reason. And God, you should be thankful Miss Prasda is going to help you." She put her hands up in a show of submission.

"Don't move anything, Chrissy. I knew it was you. You did your hair and your nails and lost weight...but somehow you and your trade school by night education never failed to get you deep in the shit you have to deal with in this place. Well, not anymore. Where's the C402?" Duluth asked again from behind.

Chrissy fired back. "And you must have taken the heaviest dose of it all. You look like the other two girls, you have it in your blood. Their blood. Why the hell do you think Orion and Hope look the same, and now you?" She smiled and began to give a somewhat cynical smile.

Her threat became somewhat nervous, as emotions began to stream from her, affecting her stability. "Well, you know, it doesn't matter to me because this is over with. I'm sick of you and Orion and all the people who made my life like it wasn't worth it in this Goddamned building." She thought for a minute, and began to feel her finger want to push the plunger so badly that it almost made it tremor. But she couldn't be the sacrifice of blood that would save hers, so she relented.

The nurse began to gasp. "Well, you push that thing in and do all this. What do you expect for us to do, Duluth Kane. We're only people taking orders. You have the gift, too, why don't you use it like Hope Malott did? You're only concerned with yourself. Your pain. Your unfortunate circumstance.

"At least with Hope, she went out at a much younger age than you and helped people. You, on the other hand, have had a beef with everyone you've met who couldn't get you money or a warm place to stay or get you laid. And every time you had a warm home and someone to give you a chance, you went and burned every single bridge you've come across.

"And look at you now, you can't even look me in the eye. You're wearing drag and you look like crap. You even had to dye your hair. So in that manner, Duluth, I'll show you where the C402 is if you pull this damn needle out of my neck." It was her schooling to deal with psychiatric

[358]

cases in the best means possible, and even the quick willed Duluth Kane had to defuse the situation.

Duluth pulled it out. "You don't know how it feels to hurt so much inside. So much and no one would listen." She began to sob, understanding that perhaps this nurse was right about her. But Duluth knew not only had Chrissy negotiated her release, that she, for once, was agreeing with someone on the staff. It established a severely lacking rapport that had plagued her in its lacking for years. A slight nod gave them the agreement.

They went down the hall to the broom closet. Opening the door, a safe lay on the ground, propped up on a concrete block of about the height of a small shelf. It was understandably to keep flood waters, should they occur, out of the safe. "I hate to say this, hun, but I don't know the code. Otherwise I would give it to you. We need to get rid of this stuff anyways."

Duluth raised her eyebrows and threw the syringe down. "Why get rid of it? I thought it was something you just said was a help?"

Chrissy sighed, and said calmly "This isn't the same C402 you've had, and Hope had. This stuff was Copulus' mix.

"After what happened in that room that day, and the accident that went on at the plant, Bill got curious as to what exactly gave the ability for the white blood cells to reproduce so strongly. As it turns out, it's not the effects of the radioactivity. It's the fact that there's a whole bunch of other stuff – minerals, biphenyls, stuff that was picked up in the lab and mixed in at the end that caused the effects.

"Duluth, pure C402, the stuff in this safe, is pretty much snake oil. Your body is aging so much because you're cutting yourself off of that exact sweet spot of all the crap that was in that desert factory."

She sat back, and began to kneel down, grabbing her head in disgust. And then, she wondered. "But how did Orion get all those powers? I mean, she literally could rip holes in herself..."

Chrissy sat back, and rubbed her eyes as she tipped her glasses. "What Orion has is the one reaction that we always feared about.

"When you get those ferrophilics in your fat cells, Duluth, they just stay there forever. Don't deteriorate at all. The problem is that Orion...her...when she took that vitamin injection during Copulus' weeklies, she began putting other stuff in her. God, when she was here, she would stab herself, play in the dirt, get cut, heal, you name it.

"As that stuff built up, the C402 wouldn't help her heal until it was in her permanently. For a long time. By God, Copulus wanted to stop her and try to control the damage. But it was always too late because at the end of the day, like any old person to a kid, he was just one big damn prick and annoyance."

Duluth smiled. She felt a lot better about the situation, especially now that she understood how things started to fit together. It was refreshing to hear the truth, especially because this nurse, who she barely knew, was giving her a straight answer for the first time. And it scared her to know that this may have been it.

"So, in other words, Chris, Copulus may have just been tapping the liquor by chance then the day I recall her leaving." She chuckled. "But how did he hide it so well?"

Chrissy sighed. "I don't know, Duluth. All I know is that it happened before I got here, and no one discussed it for years. I found out after he left that, well, he was pretty much the guy that everyone listened to because he was a stupid Gandhi-like character with an evil side.

"He kind of just wanted you to be the last one left. Orion got away and she was sent...sent somewhere, I don't know. When he found

Hope....when that rich dude called and Copulus paid him all that money...ridiculous."

The pharmacist gave her time to let it sink in for the downtrodden girl. It was necessary. "So what do we do, Chrissy?"Duluth asked. "What do we do with Orion."

Chrissy, realizing the situation was efficiently defused, opened the door and walked out. "Do what she probably wants to do. Give her life. I saw that bottle of weed killer she was drinking beforehand." With Duluth in the dark, she closed the door.

And so, she took that C402, and wrote "Life Mix Alpha" on it. She stuck it in her pocket, wrapped it up in some shop towels, and went back towards the floor.

Orion, swarmed with attention, saw the black-haired semiclone on the hunt. She stopped, seeing the glow in the eyes. "I would like an interview with you, Ms. Prasda," Duluth iterated, not to blow her cover. The voice was recognizable to only one. But it echoed to the masses.

The press, anxious to gather for the star of the show, was put off by the adolescent push. Orion gave her forum. "It's okay, folks. Little Miss Intuitive here wants to talk for the school journal. I can spare a moment."

They were side by side down the hall. "Look at you, Duluth. You did your hair, you did your brow, you even got a quick lift down at the spa! All to look like me for once! I'm proud of you, hun..." She began to embrace her, drawing the cringes of the staff who looked on. She never looked at us like that, they giggled. But she's going to save us from evil, so who cares?

Duluth was resolute and direct. "So, if C402 is the stuff you've been trying to get rid of for so long...oh, you didn't think I knew? Why were you drinking so heavily and puking your guts out like it was dinner night at Anorexics Anonymous?" she demanded.

Orion could sense the acrimony. "Look, you're 19 and you don't understand the road life. Everyone who's popular at our age does this stuff regularly. I played bars every night for the longest time. Travelled many times, many miles. That stuff is great for when you're getting laid by the best damn cowboys you can get. It works like magic. My innards glow and it looks like a *freakin' tunnel of love*. You can't deny it, sweetheart.

 "And you know what? Look at it this way: my health is good, unlike yours. Why, I know exactly why you came here, little girl."

She paused, and grabbed the little one, and looked her in a parental way. "You came here to show how I look good. Sexy in that. You couldn't dare look like your own. Gives me an affirmation that I am beautiful. And you need me more than anything in this life. Why, let me remember, Duluth: you were dead in five minutes before I showed up. If it wasn't for the warden not having to deal with the drunks that night, you'd be history like Hope Malott. Yea, you would.

"And now, you're the vicar of someone who's going to heal the world. Something you'll never do in your cavalier way of sleeping under bridges and panhandling for dimes."

Duluth smiled. "Well, I didn't need to have to prove it by putting on a show. I'll die once, and that is for sure. But you've been dead, Orion, ever since you thought it wasn't good enough to have a gift of life." She smiled and walked away, holding the vials in her pocket. "It was good to interview you," she yelled down the hall as the somewhat nascent philanthropist looked on in disgust.

Orion knew the intent of Duluth. The blood that ran through her veins and flooded her brain with the thoughts of confusion, and yet decision, echoed strong. She began to plan, hoping that it would not be too parallel.

Her thoughts began to turn from anger to resolve. Something had to be done about this woman's fakeness, her seeming will to absolutely piss on Duluth's ability to reason with her powers. Anger did its toll on the young woman for a few moments. And she had to clear things up for a moment, because she knew Orion was going to be much more acute to the situation. Simply going to call her out wouldn't work; she was the hero of the moment. So she took a look at the vials, and began to think deviousness. Think evil thoughts. Something that was so nasty that it had Copulus' name written all over it. She gave a smile, and immediately had her plan.

Taking the Copulus Life Mix Alpha vial out, she approached the bottle of whatever C402 was to be demonstrated. Dumping it in while taking a peek over her shoulder, she tapped the bottle in a show of theatrics. It just made her feel better. Whatever was in there had to be neutralized, and immediately. "Come on, baby," she whispered covertly, being sure not to draw attention to herself.

As soon as the first drops hit the greenish mixture, clouds began to form in the liquid in a deep purple, a sure contrast to the clear, almost fluorescent mixture. She cursed in the name of someone who didn't deserve it at this point, and so, she began to shake it, thinking it would dilute it.

And she shook, and shook, and shook. Every moment passing added nerves to her already unsure position. Should they come back for the demonstration, she would be flagged immediately. And this was the worst place to do it. A positive ID, plus tampering with medical procedure and poisoning, would at least land her in not so pleasant accommodations. A return to this house, she knew, was the least of her worries.

She gave it her all, and then heard footsteps down the hall. She took one look at the mixture – it began to translucently fade. Putting it down, she walked into the ladies' bathroom.

[363]

What it was, was. Closed case, and here we go, she thought. Her heart beating a thousand miles a minute, she wiped the sweat from her brow. It was way too close.

The jug went down the hallway. In her mind, she began to reason whether to make an escape for it, knowing that the results would be surprising, or to stay there. Certainly, it was known if no effect were to occur, then Orion might attempt to place the blame on Duluth. And they wouldn't find her again for a while, yet at its core of intent, it was a return to whence she came, being under the radar. That was not the life she wanted. It was enough of a damn procedure to get here, and she knew what she did had to be witnessed once and for all. It was a burden on her mind that she could not bear any more.

Loosening her coat, she went down the hallway to witness her fate. Orion stood at the podium, and didn't even notice Duluth in the background. "And now, ladies and gentlemen, I am pleased to demonstrate the power of C402. This is Daniel Allen, who suffers from cerebral palsy. Daniel is 14 years old, and cannot walk as a result of the terrible illness that has made it so he can't run with the kids, or climb jungle gyms, or play tag.

"For his entire life, he has wished for a miracle as he has lived in Attrition Home, being cared for by doctors, nurses, and medical professionals. But today, you will see something unbelievable. We are currently filling this vial with pure C402 mixed with my blood and platelets. This mixture will be injected under Daniel's skin in the fatty tissue in his abdomen."

There was no saving grace then. Duluth knew the moment of angst had taken the best of her as she swallowed the lump in her throat. Daniel was a good friend and a little brother to her during the time they were both in the home. Putting the mixture in his body would mean that he would never believe in medicine again. She had made the mistake of a lifetime, and now it meant she was likely denying a person she could help. Her insistence on killing the path of Orion could possibly mean killing one more person, one that did not deserve this judgment.

[364]

They began to inject the mixture into Daniel slowly. His legs in braces, he gave a small but strong smile, knowing full well he would walk off that stage being forgiven for his original sin.

Duluth wanted to yell "wait!" But she couldn't blow her lead. Something held her back.

The mixture flowed through the intravenous contraption and into his stomach. She looked lovingly at him, in the same way she had looked at Duluth. Slowly, his legs began to move. As time passed, the poor boy began to realize that he could do this; that it was the one piece of hope he had. And Duluth sighed, knowing that there was no way to stop Orion now.

In a covert way, Orion gave a brief glance for a brief moment to Duluth, who was leaning against the backwall. "Daniel, I want you to take off those braces. And I want you to walk over and throw them off the stage."

Daniel began to try out his legs that he almost never knew. They were atrophied, scarred, and worn, like the rest of his body, but certainly not his demeanor. As the fluid was pumped in, he could see muscle build in those legs as the potent elixir hit the bloodstream.

The emcee gave the nod. Slowly pushing himself up, he began to walk in the best way he could explain. It was frightening to see the mixture work, but Duluth knew that it was too much to take revenge on an enemy than to prohibit the forgiveness of a friend.

"Ladies and gentlemen, Daniel Allen, through my blood and through the use of C402, is now able to mobilize himself. His blood will continue to absorb the C402 and his body will heal." Gasps, and then a polite but emphatic applause followed.

Orion began to walk over to her seat. Duluth knew this was meaningless, but how could she stop it? It was all the bigger matter.

Daniel began to breathe a bit heavier, but it was expected. His muscles long needed exercise, and Orion put her hand on the back in false lovingness, and said "He'll need rehabilitation, but don't worry. He'll probably be in a dance marathon in college!" Everyone laughed for a little bit. And he nodded.

It then happened. Suddenly, he fell to his knees, and began to look as if he wanted to vomit. The room fell silent, and Duluth, in subconscious care, pushed herself to the front of the room. She took stewardship of everything that was about to happen. Her guilt now burned in her just as strong as the effects of the C402.

Daniel began to vomit. All of a sudden, the same thing that she had done many times before came out. It was a thick, purple, beetlike slime –the unmistakable signature of sodium iodate. Orion said "No, this isn't a joke! Get him some help!" The nurses began to run on stage as the boy convulsed, increasingly spitting the mixture onto the lemon fresh structure.

And then, she saw Duluth standing there in her alternative face, shrieking in surprise. She had a look that put thousands of years and millions of criminals' guilt in one. Orion and Duluth made eye contact for one, forever second of a moment. "You sick…. Folks! There….there is someone who doesn't deserve this! An escaped girl! Duluth Kane, right there! She hated the healing process, and she's escaped! Someone, please, catch her!"

And then, she realized she had to run. *Quickly.*

She grabbed the jug on the way, holding it under her desk. But no one noticed – they were intent, the cameras and press, and staff angered as ever – that the Prodigal Daughter had returned for her last shot at the legacy of evil.

MALOTT RESIDENCE

It was the event that everyone had not wanted to watch, and all for the reasons listed. It perhaps was curiosity that led the shiest and most apathetic of the members, Adriana, to turn on the TV, the public access channel. She saw this moment happen, and then, it was apparent that something had gone wrong.

She ran down the stairs, almost tripping over the carpet. "Mom, Dad! Duluth is at Attrition Home! I just saw her —" and pointed to the TV blaring in the corner.

Lou switched on the TV and saw Duluth running, the cringing kid on stage a sign of her act. He immediately looked away, and bowed his head. "We should have never trusted her, dear. What can we do? She is bitter and she went back there – why? Why would she go back? She was just too deep in her own world to realize that there's no place in the world for her." He switched off the TV. For him, this was the final closing of the door. The image of her guilt, her risking everything, the haunting of Hope again, still burned in his memory. And now, she was done. It was the end of the relationship, a very tenuous one that was fraught with disdain.

"Dad?" Adriana said to her father, walking in front of her. "Help her. She is my sister."

"Honey," her father responded," Hope is your sister. This Duluth character took her blood and spilled it for her own good. You are best to walk away and cling to that which you have remaining. A stain on the carpet.

Just then, Carrie walked into the room. She had been listening to the whole deal. Lou went and smiled to Carrie for moral support, but Carrie, in total disbelief to the husband, grabbed her car keys.

"I love her like a daughter, Lou. And if you don't want to help her and forgive your sins, I will." And off they went.

[367]

As she picked up her car keys, though, Carrie saw on the counter next to the clump of steel a bandage.

The bandage was something of importance. Someone needed to be in on the matter. Matt Bailey. Carrie huddled into the Benz that Hope's money had earned, and dialed up the one man who would be able to get her – and everyone else – exactly what was needed.

ATTRITION HOME

She slammed the door that had closed on her so many times before, all in the fear again. It was Dr. Bill Copulus' office. The last time she had been in there, she had seen the act of adultery on that desk. No one had been in there since, and the dust had accumulated. Putting a broom through the door, she locked it and prayed that the window would open.

Suddenly, the entirety of what had happened in the past three years became just a moment. She had fled this same building for the same reasons she was here. It was all a lie, and somehow, her need for revenge and angst towards the condition she was born with had caught her. And she was probably going to die for it now. For her, it was a roll of the dice. One that had best never been taken. Surely, now, the warmth of the Malott household seemed a lot greater now. She could see the disappointment in Carrie, and the anger of the nonbeliever in Lou. But perhaps the biggest sting was Adriana. She had done so much to try and convince her that they were sisters – and it was all a con. She had it all, only to give it away. And it stung worse than any pain that C402 could give. It wasn't the chemical doing this – it was her. She now had nowhere to hide, and she had lost her identity completely. A bitter shell with the reminder of both the peace of Hope and the melancholy of Orion remained.

She crouched under the desk as the door banged. In one last fit of anger, she banged on the desk underneath four times. She was getting it out before she was bound. Knowing her weaknesses, her sanity had finally compromised, and she was back there, in that room: little Duluth, her blonde hair and overalls, caving in and trapped in this home. Once again, she was back in full circle. She felt anger in herself, but this time, not a single ear was lent to hear her scream. And she screamed loudly, as she took it out on the desk.

One last hit, the strongest one came. A boot blow to the side, which hurt her deeply. Out came a glow which was nothing like she had seen before.

A suitcase revealed itself, hidden in the bowels of the desk, a secret passage. Copulus had one more surprise for them.

The door burst open, and she was there, next to the suitcase and jug. She had ten seconds before she could go. So, she guzzled as much as she could, figuring it was the Last Supper before her eventual demise that very good Friday. Sticking the other jug in the desk, she raised her hands as the flashlight hit her.

They brought her into the main room, holding her arms. Duluth knew one of the policies of the demerit system at Attrition was to face your accuser. So they held her limp body, pulling her up on stage in front of Orion. Placing the jug on the table next to the other one, they said "Duluth Kane, you have a lot of explaining to do."

Duluth smiled. "Yes, I do. That jug I have is the true C402. It works just as well. I don't know what is in that girl Orion's blood, but she has poisoned it herself. If you take a blood sample, she has a chelator in there. Drinks alcohol and poison. She wants to get rid of it. All of it, in one big swig. She's a drunk, a bum, and y'all know that, big time."

They let Duluth go. Like Matlock in the court, she pointed out that Orion had taken that bottle and used her blood. A nurse nodded in disbelief. What that nod did could have written a thousand books. He really wasn't sure, but it was certain that Duluth got away with a lie. "She told me to hook it up after she took the injection this morning," was all he said.

Orion gave a dramatic face that could only have been suited better on the girl that had brought Hope to her there in the first place. It was reliving the entire story, as if it had come full circle. "That's total bull, Duluth. You poisoned this yourself. Look at this – you couldn't even leave it here." The bottle was just as empty as the other one was, so they all assumed it was the same.

Duluth was resolute. "Want me to drink it myself? I'll do it, right now." She stuck out her arm, and reached for the bottle.

[370]

Just then, Daniel reached for it. "Let me do it. Duluth is a good friend of mine. Like a big sister. This Orion person is new here, and I don't know where she came from."

In that moment, Duluth began to smile, looking at Daniel. For once, she was unafraid, knowing full well that the joke was over. She knew that this was her fate, and that not everyone there had bitterness and a vague fog of distrust, lying, and false witness. "Take it, Daniel. You already know who I am. You've suffered enough."

"I can't go back to having a life of being a crippled retarded boy. As you'd say, 'lend me a G and one for the road, jack.' Before any nurse could react, he dumped the C402 on his legs. "This doesn't have any blood in it, does it?"

And then, the legs began to glow brightly. The sores began to bleed slightly, lending the blood. It crept in, and ran through his veins. This time, there was no way that she would have to fear the recourse. The boy had grown up, knowing that Duluth fled in good intent, and had come back in good intent. He stood up for the first time.

Orion stood there, stunned at the result. She had been duped, but could not explain it to the least. Instead, her snobbish mouth came out and took the mic from the crowd, as the press gathered in a lynch mob. "What are you going to do again, piss on my leg this time?"

Daniel smiled. "Nope. Feel great." And he took his right leg, and kicked her directly between the place where her mind was and her mouth should have been. She fell over.

Everyone gathered around Duluth, their faith beginning to grow in her ever stronger. "Now, folks, one more thing. Take a blood sample of this woman, too. I betcha she isn't such the philanthropic piety you thought she was." The nurses began to walk over to pick the former fallen hero up from her collapse of ego and of posture, to face her judge.

[371]

Orion knew she was toasted. No one would believe her story, and Duluth had testament and believability because they knew she was telling the truth this time. Why else would she come back? After what happened with Copulus, and knowing he was in his demise, she probably had to do this for good. Before they could get to her, she grabbed the table leg.

"You know what, Duluth, I don't care. Well, folks, it was worth it, but you have to remember that Dr. Copulus guy had taken all the life out of this woman. I've felt a pain. For years. Too long, too much, too late. This garbage, this C402, is buried in me. It's a part of me like a cancer that doesn't go away. For her, it's healing. But this stuff is going to lead me to suffer through it all.

"You can say this is good. It is. But look at your hero, Duluth." Orion's face began to sweat, turning red, tears running down her face for the first time. "But look at her face and her blood. You'll see me. Forever. Evil Orion Prasda. In her. I didn't want to live forever. But I will now." Like the time she had done it to Bailey and the weakened Duluth, she stuck the stake in her.

Duluth walked up to her. She knew this was the last lifeline she had. For once, it was her decision to end her life. She knew that Orion had life in her. This was killing her very deeply, and it was a shared pain. She saw the tears in Orion's eyes, the fear in her. It was the same fear Duluth had when she had been homeless a few days before. It was the fear when Copulus would shove those pills in her, the fear she saw in Hope's eyes. The bluish green glow was something they shared, and now, it was the parting message. It made Duluth's hands quiver.

"You put those hands on that damned stake, Duluth. Kitty. You will do this yourself. You and I will die. But I will die in no pain, and you'll be dying a thousand deaths knowing damn well you blew it in this moment" The words of the young had been turned back, and they were aflame in the air. Her hands quivered as she felt the rod begin to be swallowed by the immediate healing of Orion's body. Orion grabbed the IV, and stuck it in her arm. "I'll even help you. That stake there? I'll put this liquid on it, too. You believed in it, and it will kill me. This time, it won't be like your Dad, Lou. Yea, I put that through him.

The anger pent up in Duluth's eyes. Lou didn't deserve to live after Carrie went in. Hope's blood gave her that insight. She didn't know it then, but she would have to explain it to her new family. It explained how she knew everything about the family – she was there, in those last moments of Hope's life, and yes, she probably stared into that body when it lay limp. Her hands began to quiver, and it took all the energy in the world to not bite into her gums in the angst.

And then, she felt it.

And so sepulchred in such pomp dost lie, that kings for a tomb would wish to die. John Milton.

She drove the stake in with all the energy she had. And Orion screamed as the room lit up. It was the moment she had missed for so long, but it was the thing she had wanted to do. It was her decision to fade away, and it was hers alone.

20 MINUTES LATER

ROOM 15

She could hear the clock on the wall ticking in the background, and it was an analog reminder of the analog to the life she would now have to live. It was scary for her at first, because this was the one opportunity to escape the thing that had worn her down to her last wits, and her last bit of energy. In reflection, she kind of felt perhaps that she should have taken a little bit of blood. Perhaps enough to get her the recording contract she always wanted with a big LA record company. Or a few gigs at carnivals, at bars, at parties. She didn't know how long the face of her would begin to fade back into the face of Duluth, if ever at all.

But it was not Orion's face that she saw. She was still Duluth inside. And that was all that mattered.

They opened the door to her old room, still in the shape they had left it, albeit with a bunch of dust. "Crime scene, I guess," the nurse she was almost ready to kill said. "Might as well make it home, hun. You know what you got now."

They both sat down. Duluth looked into the nurse's eyes. "Need to go to confession, Kitty?"

Duluth laughed. "No, just probably to an exorcist." She paused for a minute, lending necessary humility. "You know, we can't keep these powers. We had three of us. Now two of us are dead now. And I'm the last one, sis."

The nurse laughed. "Hun, you have awhile. For once, why don't you live? You're 19, so you don't have to stay here. Obviously we can't 302 you in the matter. You just solved a crime and prevented a disaster, so we might have to make you at least, like, a staff physician."

Duluth looked down, and folded her hands in her lap. "No, Chrissy, I too shall pass." She gave her a hug. "But we can be friends in the meantime. Much nicer than stabbing each other with anesthetics and butch rape on furniture."

For a moment, they both laughed. It was needed. But then, the surprise of a lifetime – perhaps another one to be, came along. Carrie opened the door. And Matt Bailey was right behind.

"Hi ladies. Chrissy, Duluth." They both nodded in response, recognizing the faces as Carrie smiled. "Just so ya know, uh, we saw everything on TV. It was filmed. But you know, I can't go around this place without touching and exploring, because this place still reeks like an old dustmop. So I went in Copulus' office, and found this."

She flipped open the suitcase, an obvious side object that Duluth had completely forgotten about knocking loose. "I've been looking for this for years. Thought it was in that safe. But when I saw it, I knew I had to open it. And what I saw was amazing." Carrie had the mist in her eyes like no other. This was a special case indeed. "Consider this an early housewarming gift."

She opened the case. In it were levels and levels of vials, all labeled with Duluth's name and some with others of which years of fading of ink had made the script unreadable. But all of them were not glowing, but rather of the color of blood and plasma. They did not glow, but rather had the appearance of the blood of anyone, a mere mortal.

"You've lived in this house for so long, almost all of your life. Copulus was an ass, and you probably think your life was wasted, and this house damned you for it. But I will tell you all these years were wasted.

"Copulus kept all these vials on him to keep track of your progress, and all the other C402 studies. He hid these because they were proof that you were in fact normal. You didn't have C402 born in you, Duluth. And you can go back. All you do is take what's in here. It's your blood, Duluth. Your body will accept it."

She closed the case quietly, and placed it on the ground, treasuring its presence. The one man who had beat her, tortured her, and stripped her of her powers had saved one last surprise for her – and yes, he could her him laughing in the other room in his thick accent.

In that moment, Duluth was elated. "So when can we start getting this junk out of my body?" She obviously was pushed to apply herself and turn her life around for good.

Chrissy laughed from behind. "You're at Attrition, dummy. We seem to have plenty of needles and syringes here, right?" She winked. "I make for a hell of a ruckus, too. If you want, I'll get Bob to distract you."

"OK, you win, Chris," she laughed. "Just no misfires this time." And so, she began to comb through the vials.

But not before she handed the suitcase to Duluth.

"Be strong and courageous, for you must go with this into the land that you were given. Do not be forsaken. Do not be afraid, or discouraged."

She looked lovingly at them. "Life is back, I guess."

"Come home with us, Duluth, too. We could use a little help with laundry nights. Also, too, Lou tends to like his 80s music. You do any of that?" She nodded. "And dammit, this time, no more of that hairspray! Smells like someone opened up a salon."

"I think I could do that, Mom." It came out of her mouth so easily, so suddenly, and then so comfortably in the end. A slip of the tongue felt more like slipping into bed; of which she so completely desired at the moment.

Carrie turned around, and just smiled. She knew for once, Hope was back with her. They all walked into the sunlight and out to the world.

Bailey, with his bandaged arms, laughed, and said not a word. He didn't want a hug this time.

EPILOGUE

THREE MONTHS LATER

It felt like forever to finally break free of their slavery, the Pharaoh of time weighing heavily on the ability to convince themselves that the chain of healing, suffering, then again the confusion – it was all like a dream at this point.

On the last injection, they were at Dr. Bailey's office. He was definitely obsessively happy to help the remainder of the "special" girls he was so enamored to help. So much that when it was finally clear that the experiment had to end, that a conclusion was made, and now it was past theory and into scientific law, it was a deep relief.

He looked into Duluth's eyes. Initially, the bluish green glow was hypnotic when he first saw her. It was seeing into the girl's soul at first: the happiness, the pain, the suffering was all there. It explained everything that he needed to know about this field.

However, in the process of putting her blood back in her, he was able to kill the glow for this last time, it felt like it was giving new life. Her hair began to develop that Nordic blonde again, just like she had when she was little. The black began to fade as Hope's blood began to recycle out of her system, and Duluth suddenly became, well, Duluth again.

"You know, I was ready to begin bleaching this black hair, Mom," she said to her foster mother, laughing for the tenth time that day. She was very happy to have the burden lifted off of her shoulders finally; and relaxed a little bit more every day. "No offense to your genetics, but I like this blonde better. Goes better with the punk image."

Carrie could have been angry. She should have. "You know, that hair is a family trademark, dear. Hopie tried to do that too many times when she was 13. I kept telling her that she was beautiful – " and she laughed in memoriam – "but you know what, I guess that's the old way of doing things.

"Let's not do that again, right?" She winked at Duluth.

Adriana sat beside Duluth in the office. She took off her glasses, looked into Duluth's eyes, and smiled. It was, for the first time, that she had seen true happiness. They both felt an explicit comfort in being there for each other.

"You know, DK, I have to say to you….like, *chica a chica*, that you're going to be 21 in, like, a flash and a bottom of a bottle. Legal drinking age. Heck, you can play hands of blackjack in Carlisle. I gotta ask you…what are you going to do with your life now? I'm like, you can't heal anyone. You don't go to school that much. You're kind of isolated in a sense, have no job skills. How do you keep so cool?" She was still very much Adriana in a way; completely unable to enjoy the moment.

Duluth felt a little awkward, because she wanted to say something. But then, Adriana got up, and said "I don't even care how you do it. All I need to do is know it's possible, DK." And she gave her a hug.

Carrie enjoyed this moment. "So, you know what's really strange, you two?" They both turned around, still in each other's arms, looking like twins, embracing each other in the last vestiges of life. They needed that. "Here I am, in a house with four people from three different bloodlines. Pretty much everyone is not bloodline to my first marriage. How do I keep so cool?"

There was a sense of a little bit of urgency. Perhaps it was the stark contrast in the words, that she felt left out of that embrace. There were her children, although from different parents. She was a foster parent, to some extent. "I keep cool by knowing despite the fact that I've been through a lot of bad stuff in my life, that I can do it and still love everyone

[379]

in the process. Because love is God, and God is love. And you all are blessings."

Duluth said it best. "Get over here." And then there were three of them in embrace. It was a genuine moment, one that would have never been possible with Lou in the room. And even if he was, well, this was for them. Adriana didn't even bother to think where her Dad was, but he was probably still at home, grumbling about something.

Bailey came into the room, and saw the embrace. He gave his best "medicinal humor" out front. "Well, if you must be that way, girls, why not give this old man a hug, too? I need it." He clenched his clipboard tight and began to look with glassy eyes akin to a kitten in true need of love. "May I?"

Duluth looked at him, and gave him a nod of approval. That was all he needed. She grasped, and then thought Wait a minute....

As she held him, she realized that her powers weren't there anymore. It was the strangest feeling, to have that embrace and not share something more. So she closed her eyes, and then realized that the feeling she had was human – and genuine in emotion – and it didn't take C402 to do it. Bailey didn't see it or feel it physically, but the emotion he felt with her was simply amazing. And it was like it was with all his other patients.

In this moment, the doctor also knew what he had to say was even more perfect for them than the first true hug Duluth had ever experienced. Perhaps it would be, he hoped. "I actually took a while to get in touch with someone for you. Turns out you may have met a Dylan Howley before. He's actually a good friend of mine, ladies. We worked together on his grad school application."

Immediately, there was tension in the room. Duluth felt the urgency of the situation begin to eat away quickly at the positive attitude. She feared her reaction to a moment when she was absolutely confused, befuddled, and otherwise forced into a situation with her primal needs for adolescent hormones taking seizure of her.

Perhaps the biggest thing would be Carrie's reaction. "So you have a boyfriend, Duluth?" she asked, stepping back and thoroughly dissolving the huddle by folding her arms. "You never told us that, sweetie." She really didn't have anger or disgust in her plans, but she would have loved to hear the story – and be told.

Unknowing of what to do, as she had never been faced with the like of this situation before, she stuttered and gave her best nervous smile. "I just kind of picked him up in the process of being a girl. He was....smoking hot, per se. Remember, we hung out at Bill's house?" She kind of wanted to panic, but then again, why would she?

He stepped around the corner and smiled. "Hi, Mrs. Malott. Duluth, and you, miss...." He smiled and reached out his hand to each of them.

He looked at Adriana in pure friendship, but she had different plans. "Adriana Mendoza." She said her real name for the first time. They didn't know about that meeting with Hope, but she didn't feel like her soul was stolen. "Nice to meet you." She made eye contact for the first time also. Duluth and Carrie could see it in her eyes. She would have literally curtsied if she could.

Dylan had been estranged for a while. Duluth remembered that moment she snuck out while he was asleep. She could even more vividly recall him saving her from the fire. But now, she had to face him on his terms.

The poor girl was sad. "I'm sorry I'm a stranger, Dylan. I'm just....just not there with you. I had some issues...."

And then Dylan was playing it hard. He knew what had to be said. "You know, you have this kind of abject resilience in you, like the toughness of a round steak. You don't listen, you hang out with murderers, you rob stores, and beat homelessness by being taken in by a family who believes that you killed your daughter due to your selfishness." He began to rattle things off in quick succession. It felt as if she owed him something.

"I don't know, Dylan. Blame it on the fact I'll never be normal. Again." She looked down and puckered her lips. "I'm here at this doctor's office because I'm trying to take some stuff, some things that make me normal." She tried to smile, but she couldn't. It just wouldn't seem right.

Dylan looked her in the eye. "I don't like normal anyways. All the chicks who are normal never loved me. I don't know what the hell was wrong with you, but Bailey, this guy, brought me here because he wanted me to know that you weren't normal. And I'm ready to take it on in full stride."

Duluth smiled as her love gave a peck on the cheek. This was perfect. It had to be this way.

Not to be out of his appointment window, Bailey became the pillar of conciseness and prompt, direct discourse. "Now that you've met each other, something else has come up. As a physician, I want to tell people about things that may affect their lives. I've told you about healing, about platelets, chemistry, and the such. I have never, ever...." He chuckled out loudly, in true nervousness that he could not hide, " had to tell someone this." He held up the test results and pointed to hCG.

"Duluth, you...." He smiled. And her jaw dropped. So did everyone else's in the room. "You're going to have a baby." It was the best thing he could say. "Congratulations."

He just stepped back and let them enjoy the moment. Perhaps the biggest surprise was on the guy's face. He had some explaining to do to the mother he had just met. "I'm sorry, Mrs. Malott. Beer got the best of me that night." He gave a pat on the shoulder of Carrie, the best way he could ever explain to someone that it was pretty much a twist of fate.

Carrie didn't even look him in the eye. "So you did this out of wedlock. Out of school. To a girl with no job or skills. What the hell is wrong with you?" She primed herself to jump all over him.

Instantly, Dylan had to use his brains, his engineering marvels, his study skills, to gain some quantum of explanation. It was needed. "I....I actually didn't think something like this would happen." He began to walk over to Duluth, giving her a hug. "I'm sorry, sweetie."

Carrie could see the remorse in his eyes. It was the same remorse that she saw 18 years ago to the day when Hope was born. It perhaps was the intelligent man's way of dealing with crisis: facing it, admitting it, and going to do the damn best he could to make the most good. As she saw the embrace, she began to feel Alex there. It was a presence that broke through the doors of Heaven and laid there for all to see.

"I have to say, this is a surprise, children. A biggie." She grabbed Duluth. "But you know what, too?" She felt the newly discovered mother's muscles clinch tight, as if she was going into a set of rigor mortis. She was scared, and she could feel it. It wasn't C402 in her blood anymore. It was just reading her face. "I wanted so long to make this right. To make it so this damn cycle won't last anymore." She smiled. "I would love to have my daughter back. Let's make this real, DK." She then placed a kiss on her cheek.

It needed no more explanation. "Yep," the daughter laughed. "I will need a hand."

Bailey laughed. "If I told you folks perhaps I saw it was a boy...." They all kind of laughed in disbelief. "What would you say?" He giggled for a minute. And then he gave the ultimate guilty smile, as if to indicate I'm not bullshitting you on this one... "I'd say I have no experience, as all of the babies with C402 were females."

Carrie gave the last word. "But who says they are C402?" With a nod from Duluth, she shrugged her shoulders. And so did everyone else in the room. She felt the resolve, and agreed thoroughly to put it on the record. "We need a new start, anyways. *Omne novum indigent aliquo principio ad finem.* "

A NOTE FROM THE AUTHOR....

I wanted to take this opportunity to thank everyone who has contributed to the process of writing and inspiring this book, from start to finish, this has been a great process, and one that has taken a significant part of my life to complete, but makes me incredibly proud. There are too many to thank in this short note, however, I can tell you by name that there are several who are important.

Most important is my Mom and my stepdad John, who are firm believers that this is not just a hobby, but a true expression of one's abilities. To my best friends, Ashley, Alexa, Caitlin, Rene, Debbie, Shirley, Kristen, Marc, Jim, Ricky, Dale, Shelly, Doug, Emmilie, and Chuck (who is my primary reviewer and thinks this is awesome)....you believed in me when no one else did.

To all my family who have contributed their efforts in letting me know this is worth something to write.

To Megan, Kat, Amanda, and MP, whose efforts may never be paralleled because they will never know how much their artistry has pulled me through the tough times and writer's block.

To the Duquesne and Penn State Libraries, who have picked up this book for the general collection.

And finally, to my neighbor David. Lord knows how this book wouldn't have been done without a lifetime of beating my ear in about continuing to write, and how I ignored you. Until now.

THANKYOUTHANKYOUTHANKYOUTHANKYOU! Even if you are reading this now, it is important that you have been this far. I appreciate the fact that you have chosen this book for your leisure or inspiration. I don't write for my own testimony or my own thoughts. I write because I love to do so, and I want to make a difference. And I think I have.

With all of my love and thoughts,

Steve Zwolinski

Updates on "Hope For Healing" and "A Drop of Cold Blood"

Future Publications

Interesting Blogs

Movie and Theater Adaptations

Visit Steve Zwolinski on Twitter at:

@JingleBeau4

And book updates @TheSanguines

http://stevezwolinski.wordpress.com

Like us on Facebook: www.facebook.com/TheSanguines

For signed copies or licensing information for this text,

Email at steve.zwolinski@rocketmail.com

DUST WAS THE DAY

A Western Duo

DUST WAS THE DAY

BOOK ONE

CHAPTER ONE

THE FIRST CONFESSION

My Mom was a good Christian woman and attended one of the town's two Baptist churches most every Sunday. She sung in the choir, although, in truth, I have to say she couldn't sing a note or hold a tune, but the congregation was forbearing in that respect, as most folks generally liked her. She helped out like she did and was active in plenty of church charity work. Ma was a homely enough looking woman but was kindly with it and would never deny no one. Ever-suffering too, given the way me and my younger brother behaved. Our Pa was working on the big dam the President was building back in '31 and got killed there in an accident when we was young and I guess the two of us ran a little wild after that, leastways we was often in trouble and Ma was always there for us no matter what we done.

Anyway, before she passed, Ma asked me to write this down as I remembered it. I don't know why, maybe she thought it might answer some questions for me. And maybe it did, I ain't too sure on that score even now.

We lived on a small five-acre plot out in Benopé,

East Texas and I was home on embarkation leave and no more than nineteen years old at the time, when Ma called me into the kitchen one day to run an errand for her.

'See here,' she said. 'I made these two pies and I want you to take one over to the Brannigan place.'

'To old man Gabriel?' I asked. 'Is he still alive?'

'Yes indeed, advanced in his years and in some need of care and attention.'

I remembered old man Brannigan from when I was a kid. Seemed like he'd been around forever and he was an ornery cuss sure enough. He lived alone in this rundown shack with a tin roof he had built on the bottomland long before I was born. We'd be out cane pole fishing in the creek running through his property some days and he'd give us merry hell if he caught us, even set his dog on us one time as I recall. A grouchy old fellow who avoided folk and they mostly avoided him.

'You dress up smart now, in your uniform,' my Ma said.

'Aw, hell, Ma,' I complained. 'I don't want to go call on that miserable old man in my army outfit, it's sure to get mussed in the mud down there.'

'Do like I say, Jonah. He's one of God's children just like you and stop that cussing, I brought you up better than that.'

If she had been with me and some of the other gyrenes during Basic she'd have heard a lot worse than that and I sure heard enough later on that would turn her ears blue. Saw things too, things that no woman should see, nor no man if it come to that.

But she was a good old girl and I did as she said and took the pie along.

It was a fine day I remember, and there was some mist still laying in the bottoms it was that early. The sun was milky bright and shone through the cottonwood branches along the creek cutting some pretty shadows across the layers of haze as I crossed over the small plank bridge leading up to the Brannigan place.

He was sitting on a rough wooden bench in the sun whittling on a piece of wood outside the sorry shack he called his home when I walked up. He looked ancient, all wrinkly and with dark skin the color of an outhouse door. A tall fellow and lean as they come although he was bowed over some now with broad shoulders that told he must have been a big man in his day. It looked like he hadn't shaved in a while too, and had those wide sideburns like they used to wear in the old days, the ones that ran almost to the chin and his long untrimmed white hair that probably hadn't seen a brush since he'd been born and now trailed over his shoulders in two pigtails, plaited with rags like the Indians do it.

The dog noticed me first, some kind of rangy mongrel he had lying at his feet. It gave out with a low growl and he looked up from his whittling. The thing I noticed right off is that his expression never changed. You know how most folks will maybe give a start when you come up on them unexpected and they'll offer a smile and a howdy-do, well not old Gabriel, he just squinted into the bright sun and assessed you, his face staying solid as a rock.

He waited for me to come up on him, just sitting there, cool as you like, with this air of fearless confidence almost as if the self-assurance he owned was written on his skin and no sorry looking young soldier boy was about to bother him. Nor even a whole goddamned army if it came down to it.

One thing I did notice about him that was odd at the time was how his right hand left off the whittling. Almost as if it were a habitual thing that he did, he dropped the piece of wood and his hand lowered to his side. Then he fumbled there as if he had an itch or there was something lost in his pants pocket but I could see in actuality it was a way of hiding the instinctive movement of some memory from long ago. I never knew what it meant until later.

'Mister Brannigan,' I greeted.

'What you want, boy?'

It wasn't much of a greeting and he growled it in a low voice that the dog imitated, getting up on its hind legs and baring its teeth at me.

'Settle down, Boulder,' he said and the dog dropped down immediately but didn't let its eyes rove away from me or lower the hackles on its back. That was one protective guard dog with a rack of fine teeth and I watched it as carefully as it watched me.

'My Ma said to bring you this pie she made. It's an apple 'un.'

He frowned, 'She did?'

'Yes sir.'

'You're Mrs. Cord's boy, ain't you?'

'Yes sir, Jonah Cord.'

'Two of you, ain't there?'

'That'd be my little brother, Ahab.'

He smiled; at least I thought he did. There was a kind of tightening of his face and his lips, that looked as dry as summer cordwood, sort of stretched sideways and set his crinkles off like crazed paving.

'You ever read about the great white whale?'

'No sir, I never did,' I said wondering what the hell he was talking about.

'You read the Bible though, ain't you? Your Ma's a God fearing woman and she'll have seen to that.'

'Sure, I read it.'

'So you know about Jonah in the belly of the whale then?'

'I heard that one, I guess they named me after that fella.'

'And you never read no Herman Melville, never heard of Moby Dick?'

I shook my head, still holding onto that damned pie and wondering what he was rambling on about.

'See, this here white whale was as big as a house,' he explained. 'And a right devil back in those whaling days and this ship's captain called Ahab he had a bone to pick with that whale. It took his leg right off one time so he meant to get his own back and would move heaven and earth to do so. Your Ma and Pa must have had a sense of humor to name you two boys like that.'

He looked off somewhere distant over my shoulder and gave out with a rusty sounding chuckle.

'I like that,' he said, bringing his eyes back to

settle on my uniform. 'By the looks of you, young Jonah, appears you're about to be stuck in the belly of something right big real soon as well.'

'I'm off to fight, sir,' I said it with that fool pride we all suffered under then. All of us had it, me and most of my buddies from town that had enlisted. Little did we know we weren't about to go have no whale of a time, whatever that old man might say, no siree, not at all.

'That a fact?'

'Yes sir, we aim to do our duty.'

'Yeah,' he twisted his lip and gave out with a sad puff through his nostrils. 'I heard they got another damned war going on.'

'Aw, they say it'll be over soon enough once we get into it. Now, look here, will you take this pie?'

He rubbed a horny hand over his chin and I heard it rasp on the unshaven hairs there, 'I surely will and I'm obliged to your Ma for her kindness.'

'She'll be pleased to hear that,' I said, handing him the dish.

'What'll you be now, nineteen, twenty?'

'I'm just turned nineteen, Mister Brannigan.'

He nodded knowledgably, the dish sitting cupped on his lap and the dog for once taking its attention from me to sniff at that fine pie.

'That's about the same age I was when I set off to go fight.'

'That so? Was that back in the Great War?'

'*The Great War?* Hell, yes, I was in that one but no I meant the big one before that, the War Between the States.'

I looked at him in disbelief, 'You ain't talking about the Civil War, are you?'

'Sure am, boy. Year of 1861 when they put me in and I weren't nothing but a younger like you, damn fool that I was.'

'Mister Brannigan, if you was nineteen in '61,' I said, my mind racing with the mathematics of it. 'Why that makes you something like ninety-nine years old.'

'Well,' he said blandly. 'That or thereabouts, I ain't too sure of my exact moment of birth.'

'Hellfire!' I gasped and then quickly excused myself. 'Sorry, but that is unbelievable.'

His brow furrowed into a million crinkles, 'Well, how damn old did you think I was?'

'I don't know,' I fumbled, still bemused by the confession. 'Seventy or so, I guess.'

'No sir,' he said confidently. 'I was there, I done it. I fit with all sorts, Johnny Rebs and Indians, Mexicans and white men. I laid my share of grief on this world, that I surely have.'

'Sir, you are remarkably well preserved, if you don't mind me saying so.'

'Well, thankee, boy,' he chuckled again, a thin heh-heh kind of laugh. 'C'ain't run like I used to, nor get my leg over like I did, but give me a chance and I'll sure try.'

I shucked out a cigarette just for something to do whilst I considered his antiquity and I had it in my lips before I remembered to offer him one.

He shook his head, 'Thank you, no. Never could abide them machine made things. I done twist my own for many a year until I took to shot-gunning for the stage.'

'You rode shotgun on a stage line!'

'I did, that's when I took to chawing tobacco. See, you had to keep your two hands on the gun. Wouldn't do to fumble with no butt if some road agents came calling. 'Sides, you riding behind a six-team traveling fast and the wind's fair like to blow it away. My driver, an old buddy of mine called Teddy Bones, now he favored a pipe and would suck on that while he handled the reins. Kept it in his mouth with bowl turned down so the ash wouldn't blow in his eyes. I sure miss old Teddy. He passed, why, Lord! Must have been fifty or sixty years since. Bought his ticket down in San Bernardino, was just walking down the street, you know? Innocent as a bird, when a few local fellows had an altercation of some kind and began shooting it out in the street. Well, one of the strays hit poor Teddy and blew his lights out, just like that.'

'Lord Almighty,' I breathed. 'I never knew we had nobody like you as neighbor, I mean a real piece of history living here.'

'History,' he mused. 'Yeah, I sure could tell you some history. I seen a whole heap of things in my time.'

He had me hooked and I could tell it was some kind of offering he was making, a willingness to impart information. Maybe he knew his days were numbered and he just wanted to share some of his story before he went or maybe he just saw an eager young fellow on the edge of going overseas and willing to get his ear bent some by an old man with a tale to tell. Anyway, before I knew it I was sitting down beside him on the bench aching to hear more.

'So you was with the Union troops?' I prompted.

'Uhuh,' he agreed. 'For a spell anyway.'

'What did your folks think on that? Mine ain't too keen I can tell you.'

He shrugged, 'They didn't have much say on it as it happened. See, my Daddy was a hunting man and aimed to do some trapping when he first came out West to Oregon, he took to going off for week's maybe months sometimes catching up bear and beaver pelts. I can still picture him; I reckon we saw him so rare he kind of stuck in your mind as I can remember him today like he'd just walked out the door. Anyways, he was a big bearded handsome fellow who stood as tall as a barn door and maybe just as wide. He allus favored this buckskin shirt he had traded for with some of my Ma's people one time, claimed he liked the pretty beadwork on it. Now my Ma was a simple and uncomplaining critter, one of the Eastern Shoshone people and whatever life threw at her she took it all as it came. But that shirt, he called it his Spirit Shirt, and one of them Hawken rifles was what Daddy held most dear in life. I still don't know if he cared one jot for the rest of us, he was a pretty independent soul most of the time. One day he took off and we never seen him again, what happened we only heard as whispers. He was off with a team of four other trappers up in Green Valley country, it was said they was in argument and it didn't end well for my Pa. Anyways, it left me as the only one to bring food to the table so I filled his shoes and went off to do the hunting. Got to be a fair shot that way.'

He set down the pie dish beside him on the bench and growled a warning at the dog that had sat up and begun to take an unseemly interest in that sweet smelling pie.

'You had a big family?'

'Sure did, Daddy was most prolific. I think maybe that sometimes he only came back home when he did to lay down more seed. They was eighteen of us all told and it was me set to feed them all.'

'How old was you then?'

He pouted as he calculated, poking out that thin dry lower lip and jutting his grizzly chin, 'Maybe I had twelve years on me at that time so I had to do the hunting for us most times until he was lost to us for good, I ain't rightly sure of the exact time but when he passed that's when things really changed.'

'Gee! That's mighty young to be going out on your lonesome.'

'Sometimes I had me some help from the Indian people. I mean to say I was half in and half out of the tribe thanks to my Ma and they would show me a trick or two so I could catch things. I got real good at moving quiet, you know? It got so I could step through the wild woods, like that there mist lying in the hollow, light as air without moving a leaf or bending a stalk of grass and that got to serve me real well later on in life.'

'What was that like living with the Indians in the old days? I seen these moving picture stories and they certainly look wild enough in them.'

'They was just people like us, some good some bad, some wise some stupid. Lot of white folks think on them as dirty and savage and some of 'em were just like that it's true enough. But they was also some fine people too, wise folk and good, with big hearts that you couldn't fault. Hurt me bad to have to go killing some of them later on.'

That one shook me, 'You had to go killing your own relatives?'

'Nah!' he looked at me with momentary disgust and irritation. 'Don't be so literal, boy. No, I'm talking about the Indian Wars. When I was scouting for the military and had to do me some killing then, but I never did take to it so. Got under my skin every time I'd see one of them Cheyenne or Lakota warriors, even if they was old enemies of my own people, lying there dead in his Spirit Shirt, that got me to thinking of my Pa and saddened me some.'

'What's that like?' I asked him in a subdued tone. I was stupid and on the brink of life, about to head out to fight with an enemy I did not know and I guess that was the big question that bugged me and maybe why my Ma sent me over to see the old man in the first place.

'What's what like?' he asked.

'The killing part.'

He mused on that a moment, 'Depends on your reason, I guess. You protecting your own life then it comes real easy and you don't think no more about it. You doing it 'cos you has to do it out of duty then it ain't so simple. Lot of guilt can travel with that one.

I still got Mex faces that ride on my dreams from when I was a Ranger on the Border.'

'You were a Texas Ranger?'

'Yes indeed, rode with Company C under Captain Brooks.'

'And you was hunting down Mexicans bandits?'

'Sometimes, them buggers could be awful tiresome raiding across the Border, taking cattle and sometimes they would do a whole lot worse. Most of them though was just po' boys in need of a feed but some was real bad and we needed someone down there to do the policing as the goddamned army weren't up to much. I seen that General Pershing when he come after Pancho Villa, hot he was and mighty full of himself after already slaughtering plenty of our boys in the big one overseas, he comes down like some avenging angel. Son-of-a-bitch couldn't catch a cold and old Pancho had him chasing his tail for a twelve-month.'

'That troubles me some,' I murmured. 'The killing part.'

'Yeah it ain't pretty, you'd best prepare yourself for that. I reckon you'll see men's guts spread about and bloody wounds before you've done your time, young fella.'

It didn't mean much to me then, it was just a story the old man was telling. Interesting to hear but I hadn't seen any of what he spoke about back then. Later it was a whole different ball game.

'So how come you ended up in the army in the first place?' I asked.

'You really want to hear about that? It's a sorry

tale I hasten to say, ended up in one of the bloodiest most goddamned awful battles they had down in Virginia.'

'I'd like to know.'

'It may take a while.'

'I ain't got anything pressing.'

He took himself a deep breath, 'My Lord! It's back a long ways now. It really started, I guess, when we got word of my Pa's demise. Yeah, that was when it began... Back when I found out who murdered Pa.'

CHAPTER TWO

ALIVE AND KILLING

The Lipton Tavern up in Green River country was a trapper's hole-in-the-wall kind of grubby place that was just one room basically. There were some chairs and one or two tables on the beaten earth floor but mostly the men who came there chose to stand and jaw. For as long as they could stand, that is to say.

Lipton brewed his own brand of liquor and it was renowned throughout the county. It tasted like river dredge but it was the after effect that counted. Most seasoned customers knew to mix it with well water but the innocent new boy would sup it right down and as sure as a chicken comes from an egg within a minute or two of imbibing he'd be flat on his back on the floor without a memory of how he got there.

Mule Kicker - they called it and they sure were accurate there.

Old Lipton himself, was a cadaverous looking fellow, who would sit silent and stone faced behind his bar, which wasn't so much a bar as a shelf across one corner of the room. It was more like a kiosk really, just a closed in counter were he kept a few bottles of his demon drink and a collection of mugs and empty pickle jars for his customers to sup with.

He made a pretty penny in that place too. Menfolk would come from miles around just to prove they were man enough to handle the mind-bending liquor, so it was right popular. What with making so much cash, and although old man Lipton never invested in any furniture or fancy trappings, he did buy the best oil for his lamps, that pure kind they harvest from the whale's skull, the one that gives out the brightest light.

He had such a lantern hanging over the table right next to his bar and that's where the four of them sat.

Gabriel Brannigan saw them the minute he entered.

Mole Janus was facing him and so lit up by that lamp that he stood out like a rose bush in a Louisiana swamp. He had on one of those red Phoenician caps that the Frenchmen favored above the border in Canada and at the particular moment he was sitting back resting against the wall behind and fiddling with a strand of fringe on the breast of the buckskin shirt he wore.

Gabriel recognized that shirt right away, it was his daddy's Spirit Shirt and around Mole's neck he wore the beads and amulets and the little leather medicine sack of magic stuff a Shoshone shaman had given his Pa. That pissed off Gabriel right well and he bow-waved his way through the crowd heading for that table.

Maybe it was the surprise of seeing folks getting hustled so rudely apart or just that he was such a youngster amongst the mean crowd of hoary trappers that occupied the drinking house, whatever it was, Mole just frowned and pouted curiously as Gabriel neared.

But Gabriel did not hesitate he barreled straight in. They had taught him well, his mother's people. Even as a child amongst the Shoshone all the young boys were shown the way of the warpath and how to strike without hesitation. Gabriel lifted up the long Kentucky rifle he carried, hooked back the hammer and straight away, like the poet says, he blew a hole in Mole that took its toll and released his soul.

To Gabriel's right, sat a big buck called Lomas Chain (some said he was their real true leader) and Gabriel swung up right off and swiped him mightily across the jaw with the stock of his now empty long rifle. What few teeth Lomas had left in his head went sailing across the table and lay scattered in an unpalatable heap of brown and rotten bone amongst the drinking glasses. Lomas himself was stunned; he swung sideways and fell plumb into Redbone Clames, who was the youngest of the four. Now Lomas was a big fellow and heavy with it so he kind of locked Redbone in his seat as he flopped over him.

Next to the pale and bloody figure of Mole, who still sat bolt upright and pinned to the wall behind like a prize specimen in a collectors cabinet, sat Holly 'Lightways' Restitution. Holly was a sharp little red headed fellow and he was making a fast play for the Dragoon flintlock pistol he kept in his belt. But Gabriel was onto him. He carried this bayonet by his side, a long needle pointed triangular blade and as Holly had half drawn his weapon, Gabriel drove that blade straight through the man's gun hand and into his gut, nailing him as neat as a New Testament dissenter on the cross.

Without drawing breath, Gabriel swung around collecting the hatchet he carried stuck down the back of his pants. He came onto the recovering Redbone with a backhanded swipe that sent that steel blade straight into the trapper's throat and gave him a second chin. Redbone glugged a while with the axe head transfixed in his neck, he was trying to say something but whatever it was, was lost forever as he keeled over and fell heavily face down on the table. That completed the driving force of the steel blade and it did a good job of severing Redbone's topknot completely from the rest of his body. With a nasty sounding thud and a floppy roll, Redbone's decapitated head bounced across the table and landed in Holly's lap. But Holly wasn't complaining as he had already left the room, the planet as well as it happened.

That left Gabriel with the sole remaining Lomas Chain, who was shaking his numbed head and wondering what had hit him. Gabriel spotted the broad, bone-handled butcher knife Lomas wore in a scabbard at his side and Gabriel ripped it out and grabbed Lomas by the hair. Swinging him around in his chair, Gabriel stood facing the room and the knife close under the Mountain Man's bearded chin.

The rest of the place was in uproar by now. There was a lot of shouting and shoving from the back to get a better view whilst them in the front wanted to get back and out of range.

'You feller's better stand away,' Gabriel hollered. 'I got something to say.'

That stilled the noise somewhat as they were all curious to know what this was about.

'These here men killed my Pa,' Gabriel went on. 'And I aim to find out why.'

That was along with everybody else in there, so a deathly stillness fell over the room and even old man Lipton momentarily came out of his comatose state to take an interest.

Gabriel tugged on Lomas's head of hair and hissed in his ear, 'So speak up, you son-of-a-bitch, why'd you kill my Daddy?'

'We never did,' gulped Lomas, lisping badly as his dentures were now scattered over the table like burnt out popcorn and all he had in his mouth was his tongue. He could feel a trickle of blood coursing down his neck from the razor sharp edge of the blade at his throat and it encouraged him to answer promptly. 'Swear to God, he died in accident.'

'That ain't what I heard. I have it how that bragging bastard Mole Janus there been saying he done for Brannigan and I see he's wearing Daddy's favorite shirt and all his talismans. Now my Daddy would never have parted with that precious shirt or them magic things without him being killed in the process. So tell it, you murdering dog, before I cut off your wind permanent.'

'Well, it weren't me,' Lomas complied nervously. 'It was him,' he said, rolling his eyes over at Mole, but of course the corpse had little to say on the matter so no argument came from that direction.

'What happened?' pressed Gabriel.

That's when the world went black for Gabriel. There might have been some pain, he wasn't sure about that and all he did know was that there was no more for a spell. It only started to make sense when he woke up in the jailhouse with Sheriff Anders Doolittle looking down on him.

Doolittle was a tired and depressed man. He stood tall at over six feet and was of a rugged disposition but he had been trying for too long to control the misbehavings of the trappers and roustabouts in his small town. He felt his only surviving means of serving out his term of office was to remain indifferent to all conditions and whoever presented them. World weary and only wanting to leave and fulfill his lifelong ambition of opening a needlecraft shop, Doolittle went through the motions, praying for the day when his retirement arrived and he could indulge his love of cross stitching and embroidery to the full.

'Come on, boy,' he said gruffly as he nudged at Gabriel with his boot. 'Get with it, will you?'

Gabriel rubbed his sore head, he was dizzy and his swollen tongue felt like it was exploring a dry riverbed inside his mouth.

'What?' he choked. 'What the hell you hit me with?'

'Just get up. Come on, on your feet, I ain't lifting you, I got a bad back.'

Slowly, Gabriel eased his rubbery legs over the edge of the cot and looked blearily around. He saw he was in a bar filled cage with a stone built wall behind and the pervading scent of urine pretty much everywhere.

'How'd I get here?'

'They brung you in,' Doolittle answered with unsympathetic brusqueness. 'You got a date with the judge so move your ass will you, I ain't got all day.'

'You got a drink of water? And what's that stink in here, don't you ever clean this place out?'

Doolittle unceremoniously grabbed him by the collar of his shirt. The shirt was poorly made, it being a simple thing of poor homespun cloth, as his father had always insisted that his children be dressed as white men and never as Indians. So, Gabriel's Shoshone mother had been forced to attempt hand made numbers that never fitted too well and were wide in the leg and uneven on the shoulder. She was more used to sewing skins with bone needles and sinew and not the white man's fragile cloth with cotton thread. As a result, the collar parted company with the shirt and Doolittle was left holding a ribbon of material in his fist.

'Goddamn it, Sheriff!' complained Gabriel, shaking his head and wishing he hadn't. 'That there is my only shirt.'

'Should have got up when I told you,' growled Doolittle, throwing the rag aside.

Doolittle hustled him out of the cell and down a short corridor to an outer office. A solitary man was waiting, sitting behind the Sheriff's desk and looking as if he owned it. He was a bewhiskered and florid figure wearing a beaver skin stovepipe and smoking a cigar that stunk worse that the urine taint in the cell.

'This the reprobate?' he asked, brushing idly at the ribbons of ash marking the waistcoat that covered his ample belly. In fact he was so fat that the bottom buttons were left unfastened and his rumpled shirt and undershirt were visible bulging out.

'This is him, Judge,' Doolittle answered, pushing Gabriel forward to stand before the desk.

'You killed three men, boy,' said the Judge sternly, chewing on his stogie and eyeing Gabriel resentfully from under bushy eyebrows. 'And sorely wounded another costing him a mouthful of dentures.'

'If'n the Sheriff hadn't slugged me, it'd been all four of them was dead,' growled Gabriel, equally resentfully. 'How'd you get up behind me, Sheriff? I never seen you coming.'

'Weren't me, boy. It was old man Lipton, he don't like having his nightly income disturbed. That was three of his best paying customers you laid out.'

'Simple case,' the Judge interrupted decisively. 'Murder, plain as day, we ain't got any argument on that. I find you guilty, whoever you are and whatever your name is.'

'Now, hold on,' pleaded Gabriel. 'Those suckers killed my Pa...'

'Seeing as you're so young, I've a mind for leniency,' went on the Judge, going cross-eyed as he stared down his nose and estimated the impending collapse of his cigar ash. 'I give you two options, you can take thirty years of hard labor on the State farm or you can go serve out your time in the regular army. My brother-in-law, the respected and revered Colonel Benson T. Ashford is raising up a regiment of infantry to preserve the Union and has need of young blood to meet his tally requirements.'

'Don't I get a chance to...'

'That's it then, case closed and court dismissed,' said the Judge, slapping his hand down loudly on the desktop. 'Aw, hell!' he cursed as the sudden movement jolted the inch long tube of ash tumbling down to explode over his waistcoat. 'Take the prisoner out of here, Sheriff. See he gets down to the depot, the Colonel's a-waiting on his new recruits.'

'Do I get to see my Ma afore I go?' Gabriel pleaded.

'You're a breed, ain't you?' asked Doolittle. 'What the hell you want to go see a squaw woman for? That's what got this whole mess started in the first place.'

'How's that?'

'Your Pa, boy. Brannigan was a fool taking up with that Shoshone woman and then not wanting to share her around. T'ain't natural to get so fussy over Indian tail. Sometimes, I do wonder at folks manners, I surely do.'

'*Was* that it?' mused the Judge, with a mild show of interest. 'This whole sorry affair was over some no-account Indian woman, I just don't know what society is coming to these days, I really don't.'

'Right you are, Judge' snorted Doolittle in disgust. 'Anybody'd think they had a right to be here, the pesky savages. Ask me, Washington ought to bring in some legislation agen it.'

With that, the Sheriff grasped Gabriel by the arm and dragged him out into the street and headed off towards the train station.

CHAPTER THREE

DOING TIME

It was June and should have been glorious but along with the battle smoke, young Gabriel smelled rain in the air and he knew they would all be wet by nightfall. Not that he wasn't used to it by now, it had been a long road and three hard years since he had first donned this blue coat, kepi and sky blue pants.

Roanoke Island, New Bern, Whitehall, Goldsboro and Gum Swamp, all of them were milestone names to mark his route and decorate his personal battle banner.

Gabriel had seen them all in his time with Company H of the Massachusetts Infantry. The battles and skirmishes across three years that had rousted the youngster from his youthful ambitions and seated him in a bowl of violence and intermittent boredom that saw him reach his twenty-third year with a hardened heart and a few scars to boot.

He had lost many of his young friends along the way, leaving their dusty and blue coated remains strewn across green hills and flower-ripe meadows where by rights they should have been running free and sparking with pretty Sunday School gals. The only love that Gabriel saw during those dark days was to shed his virginity into a sullen whore whose only true appetite was for the Yankee coin she hustled from each attending soldier boy before he'd had time to unbutton his pants.

Now, Gabriel stood in cover at the edge of the wood and eyed the explosive puffs of airburst above his head and heard the distant rumble of cannonade as he waited for the soaring shells to descend and rip up more sods of lush Virginia soil and maybe tear the limbs from some unsuspecting Northern son in the process.

Right there in front of him stood seven long miles of the Cold Harbor fortifications and every inch manned by eager Confederates intent on defending the city of Richmond not far south of where the army stood. They called the rebel General Lee the 'King of Spades' with good reason, he liked to have his boys dug in safe behind walls of earth and in trenches deep enough to keep the Federal musket balls away.

But the Rebs were on the run. Everybody said so. There was no way it could last much longer, just break this line and then charge on unchecked into Richmond and finish it. That was also Gabriel's fervent wish as he scratched his gaunt chin and checked his Springfield rifle for the hundredth time. His nervy survey went on as his fingers toyed and rattled the twenty rounds in his ammunition box—not that he, as a veteran, relied on that sole supply, for safety's sake he had another forty bullets weighing down his tunic pockets.

His small coterie of surviving friends stood around him, Josh Parker, Boy Robinson and Leeward Soils. They were the only three that still stood and had marched the distance with him since they had met up at the railroad depot three years earlier. Idly, Gabriel watched as Josh and Leeward wrote their names on scraps of paper and pinned the tags on the back of each other and he wondered if they had a kind of death wish or some premonition that led them to make sure their bodies would be recognized and their folks duly notified.

Now they waited and even with all their experience behind them they still felt the hollowness inside and the cold taste of fear on their tongues as every soldier does before battle. It never wavered, that sensation, the tightness that gripped the gut as each canister shot burst, no matter if it was a foot or five hundred yards away down the line.

Gabriel sweated. He only half noticed the officers, all gold and glitter with gleaming sabers and shining harness as they wheeled their horses and sashayed up and down as if each was on a vital mission. His attention was fixed on the gray ripple that marked the ridgeline. That was where they had to go, across the open ground and up the slope into the belly of the beast. It was an animal that spoke with a fiery tongue and he knew it roared with a hail of blazing lead that would fall on them like God's angry word.

Flags were waving and bugles sounding, somewhere a regimental band was playing in a sorry attempt to rouse the blood and bring to light some fervor inside their collective fear.

A battery of twenty-four pounder howitzers let rip and their deafening roar still did little to instill optimism in the waiting troops. The air was full of the cannon's cordite stink and the mists of gun smoke drifted away across the waiting field of open ground.

The cry came down, repeated and echoed by officers and sergeants alike. 'Advance in line!'

Out they went, in a great wave of blue like a blossoming stain on the green grass as they left the cover of the woods. Some eager bunnies took off running and others kept a ragged line, stepping out and slow marching with their rifles held ready before them.

Gabriel and his buddies stuck together and shoulder-to-shoulder as they began the move towards the enemy positions.

It was a danged fool thing and Gabriel knew it, a charge on entrenched troops who held the higher ground, the whole escapade was doomed. Maybe every other mother's son here knows it too, was the thought that crossed his mind.

One foot in front of the other, that was all they could do. All the hollering, the urgent calls of the officers and hoarse shouts of the noncoms, weren't about to make one ounce of difference when it came down to it. It was all up to pure chance when the bullets started flying.

Gabriel heard it then.

A lone screaming order from the enemy that seemed isolated and weirdly alone in a brief lull amongst the heaving movement of the thousands of plodding troops around him.

The answering volley that came from the Rebs swathed through the advancing men, it cut them down like a scythe in summer wheat. The zip and crack of passing lead ball burnt the air and left a taste of cinders in the mouth as the men started falling around Gabriel. They dropped in their droves, some squealing in agony and others just falling where they stood as if their legs had suddenly been pulled from under them.

In front a sheet of rippling orange and red flame and a rolling burst of white smoke that spat out towards him from the ridgeline. The men kept falling and Gabriel stared around him in dismay as the troops were struck down, he tried to concentrate on movement onwards but tumbling bodies blocked his way. Stepping over the bloody remains and writhing wounded he struggled on, by some miracle he was unharmed and he marched with a mind numbed by the deafening sound of repeated volleys that beat at the advancing army.

'Gabe! Gabe!'

Dimly through the blood roar that filled his ears he heard the cry and turned to see that Josh and Boy were crouching over the fallen figure of Leeward.

Gabriel shook his head to clear it from the din and ran at an angle across the advance, battling his way through the men still on their feet and advancing blindly, until he reached his comrades.

'It's Leeward,' bawled Boy, his plump farm boy face crinkled in concern. 'He's hit bad.'

Leeward lay on his side with arms and legs extended as if he were still running, his waist and hip were a mess of blood and chewed flesh. The curve of shattered bone showed and appeared strangely blue in the afternoon light.

'We've got to get him back,' said Josh. 'Come on let's carry him.'

'Is he still alive?' asked Gabriel.

Boy, who was kneeling beside Leeward, leaned over and put his ear next to the fallen man's lips. He turned to look up at the others, 'I can't...'

His face vanished before their eyes, the cheek and jaw ripped away in a shuddering splatter as a bullet struck.

They were in a sudden intense hailstorm of zipping whining lead.

Both Gabriel and Josh dived to the ground and the earth around them erupted as if some strange invisible entity was tearing at the soil with hidden claws. The fusillade let up and moved away and both men raised their heads and looked at each other in wide-eyed terror.

'Great God Almighty!' breathed Josh, his lower lip flipping as if his teeth were chattering with cold.

Gabriel looked around him and only saw the humped backs of fallen men lying on the field around him, a great sea that stretched away in every direction. Gun smoke wafted down, sifting its way around them and dimming images of stumbling men half disappeared in the fog. Screams of agony and hollow prayers filled the air only to be beaten back by the blast of the continuing Confederate volleys.

'Hellfire!' whispered Gabriel, more to himself than to his companion. 'We have to get out of this.'

Both he and Josh hugged the ground, pulling themselves closer to the wall of dead that gave some protection from the relentless hail of bullets.

'*You men!* On your feet, get on!'

They looked up to see a bearded officer on horseback standing over them, his horse twisting in fear with white spume flying from the lips as the man dragged on the reins to keep the frightened animal in check. Amazingly he remained untouched, his face flushed with fervor and his eyes rolling wildly at them above his beard.

'No retreat,' the officer bellowed. 'On! On!'

He waved his saber and swept it threateningly over their heads. 'Get up you bastards!' he roared. 'I'll cut you down where you lay you don't move.'

Something about his twisted red face struck a chord in Gabriel's memory. He knew the man, he was sure of it. But never as an officer, it had been somewhere else.

The officer's mouth was open wide as he bellowed at them and as Gabriel looked into that dark pit he realized the man had no teeth. He wore false ones fashioned from wood, a not uncommon thing but still they gave the fellow a strangely ugly and ominous appearance.

'We have to get our friends back to the field hospital, sir,' begged Josh.

'Goddamn, you!' cried the rider, letting the saber hang from the cord at his wrist as he pulled out his service pistol and waved it threateningly. 'Get moving, you cowardly scum.'

Gabriel took it all in, in one frozen moment amidst a spinning world that had all the slow clarity of a dream. The whirl and crash of artillery and musket, the cries and pitiful calls for help and all the while the seemingly endless cascading snap of passing bullets. Above him the officer, a captain dressed in a double row of shining buttons and with fine gold embroidery patterning his sleeve, leveled the Army Colt at Josh and thumbed back the hammer. Obscurely, Gabriel noticed that his fine pair of pale white leather gloves were darkened in the palms by leather oil from the harness.

Lomas Chain!

The memory flooded back.

It was Lomas Chain, the man whose teeth he had knocked from his head back in the tavern.

Lomas, *a captain?*

'Curse you, for a yellow bellied coward!' Lomas accused Josh as he pulled the trigger.

'*No!*' bawled Gabriel, at last leaping to his feet and grabbing at the captain's waist.

Josh flew over backwards, his arms flying wide as a great smoking hole appeared in the chest of his tunic.

Gabriel hung on, trying to pull the sturdy figure of Lomas from the saddle, 'You murdering son-of-a-bitch,' he sobbed through gritted teeth, tears of exasperation starting from his eyes.

Lomas, struck down with his pistol beating at Gabriel's head and knocking the kepi from his head.

'Release me, soldier,' he snarled as he hammered downwards with the pistol repeatedly. 'There's Rebs out yonder waiting on us, so leave me be.'

One fateful smack connected with Gabriel's temple and he felt his fingers losing their grip as he slid away. Gabriel's legs went from under him and he fell to the ground. Through a dazed cloud he saw the figure on horseback spin around and waving the saber above his head charge off to disappear in the smoke. Tenderly, Gabriel explored his battered skull with his fingers and found blood on them.

Numb and only semi-conscious he looked over at the heaped bodies of his friends and his head dropped to his chest in sorrow. He sat there stunned, saddened and sick at heart, surrounded by his dead companions as unnoticed time passed by.

It was nine dazed hours later when he heard the retreat sounded and Gabriel joined the limping remnants of the army as they struggled back. Smoke hung heavy in the air and only limp banners and the scattered dead watched them leave. Seven thousand men fell that day and in sympathy nature wept and a summer storm struck up and evening rain fell from the dark clouds rolling overhead. The beaten and wounded survivors meandered down to find cover under the dripping leaves of the dark wood. It was a sad end to a disastrous day.

Gabriel shivered in the night, he was soaked through and hunched over as he rested against the bole of a tree, his hands clasped tightly about his knees. Around him shadowy figures moved in the lashing darkness and a continuous moan ran through the trees, whether it was the low wail of the wind or the depleted cries of the wounded, Gabriel could not tell. He felt hollowed out and only a meanness of spirit seemed to fill him. The whole of his despair was barely lightened by a curious consideration of the murderous figure of Lomas Chain and of how such a useless specimen could rise to the rank of captain in this godforsaken army.

One thing was plain to Gabriel; it was the only thing he had left to him now. He had killed and fought long enough for others. There was nothing left to hold him now and he would leave off this war. If it came to fighting from now on it would be for his own benefit and if Lomas Chain crossed his path ever again he had best watch to his defenses, for Gabriel burned with a promise of deep seated hatred and willingness for vengeance for what he had done to Josh. That killing and the death of his friends seemed to amalgamate into one hardened lump of resentment in his breast and maybe unfairly he blamed it all on Lomas Chain.

CHAPTER FOUR

ROAD RUNNER

His first hike lasted a week, flat out and with barely a pause for rest, after that he lost count of the days and weeks.

He wasn't himself, and yet he barely knew it. His head ached continually from Lomas's battering and he had not stopped long enough in his desertion even to wash himself clean of the blood that flaked on his face.

It had been three days since he had first felt able to eat. Water had come from brooks once his canteen had run dry and his old hunting skills paid off as he trapped rabbit and squirrel and ate them raw, uncaring what they tasted like.

He found he had brought little with him, only a few items carried in his gunnysack, almost empty, as he had not wanted to weigh himself down during the battle. There had been a crust of bread, a few biscuits and a cut of cheese but that had gone early on.

By habit, he stilled carried his Springfield and the load of shot in his pockets and he wished he had dumped the bullets and kept better provisions in his bag. But he had not been expecting this and he fled now, a little crazed, in random direction only aiming to stay away from resentful local southern supporters and any of his own military who would surely take him back for court martial and imprisonment or death.

Gabriel found himself talking to himself sometimes, then standing in a woodland clearing he would see Josh and Boy waving him on from the shadows under the trees opposite. At night, when he sunk to the ground in exhaustion, Leeward would come and sing him lullabies as if he were a small child.

These ghosts populated his scrambled brain and yet their presence strangely comforted him. He should be lying dead alongside them, he knew it and he wept guiltily sometimes in shame that he still lived.

The one thing that kept him going and burned bright behind the luminous light that flared in his eyes was the prospect of dealing out just reward to Lomas Chain. The bearded face with its array of wooden teeth loomed before him, like the goal of a distant mountain. It was the chimera of an end that allowed him to keep walking on relentlessly as his own beard lengthened and his forgotten tunic was torn and ripped about his unwashed body.

At night his gaunt frame shivered with the cold and when it rained he was soaked through and it was only the blazing madness burning in his soul that kept him warm.

He came on a lone cabin one time, an isolated place in a forest clearing with a few hogs and a moth-eaten looking mule standing in the yard out front. Like the scavenger he had become, Gabriel circled the place warily searching for the occupants. A rooster called and chickens pecked but nothing else moved and the house seemed hollow and empty, showing no sign of occupation.

In a scurrying rush, Gabriel made it to the wash line and tore down a few items of clothing. A pair of pants, a long shirt and some kind of scarf or bandana. He raided the hen house and gulped down the eggs he found there as he squatted in the straw, his eyes cautiously watching around like a hunted animal. In a work shed he found hanging an old farming hat, a wide brimmed floppy thing sweat stained about the seedy crown, the material moth holed and cracked at the brim.

He dressed himself in the stolen clothes and stole a hatchet and skinning knife from the shack.

Then came the creaking sound of a wagon approaching and he was quickly off, darting into the surrounding forest not knowing or caring who was coming just knowing he must flee.

One night, it might have been days or weeks after his theft at the cabin; he smelled the scent of frying bacon. His mouth watered at the inviting smell and he followed its perfume trail until he saw the glint of firelight through the trees. His discerning nostrils told him there was also steak or sausage in the pan and his imagination fantasized that it was eggs as well that filled that inviting skillet. Big, fat eggs frying alongside curling crisp bacon and a wedge of steak that hissed in its own fat, maybe some wild mushrooms as well.

It was a feast and his throat ran dry at the prospect of a proper cooked meal. It had been so long since he dared to even consider the notion of lighting a fire in fear of giving away his position that cold meals had been the order of the day.

He neared the campsite, coming as silently as only his Indian training had taught him.

There were three of them around the fire, two men and a woman.

The men were lounging on their saddle blankets whilst the woman did all the work and served them from the coffee pot and skillet she had over the fire. Slabs of bacon were sizzling and as Gabriel watched, the woman cracked open a couple of large eggs she pulled from a wicker basket.

It was too much for Gabriel.

'Hello the camp!' he called.

Like two snakes the men lithely unrolled themselves and speedily had rifles in their hands and gun belts close by. They were both on their feet and peering towards the sound of his voice.

'Who're you?' called the taller of the two. A man as thin as a beanpole with hair hanging to the shoulders but as he stood before the fire his face was in darkness and Gabriel could not define the features.

'Just passing by,' Gabriel replied. 'Name's Gabriel Brannigan and I don't mean no harm just hoping to beg a cup of coffee.'

'Stand where we can see you.'

Gabriel parted the bushes and rose to his feet, his

rifle held above his head.

The smaller man, a round-faced fellow with curling fair hair and a beard that ran around under his chin, gave a small chuckle, 'Well, come on in, stranger. You come peaceable and you'll get a welcome here.'

'Obliged,' said Gabriel stepping forward to join them.

'You on your own?' asked the thin one and as he was closer now Gabriel saw that one of his eyes was covered by a black patch, the ribbon running diagonally around his head and over his long hair that was dark as pitch.

'Yeah, there's just me,' said Gabriel.

The thin fellow watched the bushes behind Gabriel carefully for a long moment before he relaxed and lowered his rifle. As he did so, his partner also lowered his gun and held out his hand in greeting.

'Howdy, Mister Brannigan, we're the Stones boys, I'm Jake and this is my big brother Zebedee. Come on in now and set.'

Gabriel noticed that no mention was made of the girl who lowered her head discretely after giving him a swift look and then focused her attention on the cooking over the fire.

'You hungry, Mister Brannigan?' asked Jake. 'We got us plenty here if'n you care for some.'

'That's mighty neighborly of you, sir. I could sure do with some vittles and that there smells real good,' said Gabriel as they seated themselves before the fire.

'There, girl!' barked Jake abruptly. 'You heard the

man, set him a plate.'

The woman hunched over at his sharp call as if she half expected to receive a beating and hurriedly began to shovel food on a tin plate.

'Don't pay her no mind,' confided Jake. 'She's a mite simple and don't do nothing less you tell her.'

Zebedee sat aside solemnly and said nothing. He gazed into the fire's flames but Gabriel had the distinct impression that although he appeared careless, his attention was sharp as an animal and his senses alert to any anomaly.

'So, where you heading, Mister Brannigan, if I may ask?' said Jake as he passed across a full plate to Gabriel. 'Here y'are,' he added, handing over a fork.

Taking the implement, Gabriel nodded thanks and by the firelight he could see it was a fine piece of cutlery. Gold with a bone handle and obviously a delicate thing unlikely to be in the constant company of two dark men out in the woods.

'Thank 'e,' said Gabriel, deciding to make nothing of it as he dived into the plate of bacon sides and fat fried eggs.

'So, where you heading?' Jake repeated.

'South,' Gabriel mumbled vaguely, his mouth full of food. 'Lord, this is good.'

'Give the man some coffee,' Jake ordered the girl, who promptly began to fill a mug. She was more a grown woman than a young thing and Gabriel put her age at twenty or so. Yet her dirty face and unkempt long brown hair could not hide the prettiness of her looks and the capable way she carried herself.

'My word, you is one hungry soul,' said Jake as he

watched Gabriel demolish the plate. 'Been a while, huh?'

'It has,' agreed Gabriel, slurping a gulp of hot coffee. 'What about you boys?'

'Oh, we're just making do,' said Jake airily. 'Ain't that right, Zeb?'

His brother grunted incoherently and continued to stare into the fire.

'You been with the fighting?' asked Jake. There was a catch in his voice, a slightly cautious tone that he could no disguise.

'No, sir,' Gabriel lied with quick caution. 'I'm just making my way south, hoping for a new life.'

'So you never enlisted then?'

'Ain't my quarrel so I never answered the call. Best let folks fight their own battles is my way of thinking.'

'Yes, sir,' agreed Jake. 'Couldn't have put I better myself.'

His belly full, Gabriel settled back and used the tines of the fine fork to pick at wedges of bacon stuck in his teeth. He was guessing these two were renegades or maybe deserters who lived rough and probably preyed on outlying homesteads and isolated farms and that explained the surplus of food they had in these desperate times across the country.

'You like that?' laughed Jake, nodding at the fork.

'It's a right nice piece,' agreed Gabriel. 'Don't think I ever seen one better.'

'You keep it, fella. We got plenty more, ain't we, Zeb?'

'Why, I'm obliged to you.'

'Yes, sir. We do all right, don't we, Zeb?'

His brother nodded slowly then spoke in a low tone full of menace. 'I reckon you got us figured, ain't you, stranger?'

'That ain't none of my concern,' Gabriel answered carefully.

'Ain't too hard to work out is it?' Zeb went on. 'Not when my fool brother hands out gold utensils like they grows on trees.'

'I guess not,' Gabriel agreed.

'How you feel about that?'

Gabriel sighed, 'I ain't no better. These here ain't my duds, I stole 'em.'

Jake husked a laugh, 'I thought so, the minute I seen you. Youse just like us, making your way best you can, ain't you?'

'I had it with the army and lit out,' Gabriel confessed. 'Figured there's a better way.'

'So that Springfield ain't no stranger to you then?' observed Zeb.

'No, sir,' said Gabriel, toying with the gold fork and watching its glint in the firelight. 'I done my share with that particular item.'

'Me too,' agreed Zeb, idly stroking his patch with one finger. 'Lost me an eye and figured that was enough sacrifice for the cause.'

'Yeah,' sniggered Jake. 'We call ourselves auxiliaries now, kind of independent raiders if anyone asks.'

'And what flag is that under?'

'Whichever one appears on the skyline,' chortled Jake.

'Sounds like a fine plan.'

'Maybe you'd care to ride along with us for a while? We could do with another hand,' offered Zeb, his sharp eye roving over Gabriel speculatively.

'Don't mind if I do, I ain't got nothing else pressing right now.'

CHAPTER FIVE

HANGING WITH HANNAH

That was her name it turned out. Hannah. But he never did find out her last name.

She rode on the loaded pack mule whilst the brothers had a horse apiece. Gabriel walked on behind not yet having any other form of transport. He carried his rifle across his shoulder and kept watch on their rear whilst Zeb did the scouting ahead and Jake, who usually sang out with ribald songs and ditties, took the lead.

His opportunity came to talk with the woman when he asked for some water as they marched. Zeb was somewhere off scouting ahead and lost amongst the surrounding trees. Jake was content to continue his serenade with no audience but himself.

'I'm obliged to you, ma'am,' said Gabriel, taking the full canteen. The girl ducked her head, hiding her face behind a veil of hair. 'Have you been with them long?' he asked.

She gave a surreptitious and ambiguous jerk of the head that may have indicated either a long or short time.

'I'm Gabriel,' he prompted, hoping to get some response.

'Hannah,' she whispered, looking up briefly to see if Jake was watching.

'You wife to one of these men?'

She shook her head vehemently.

'They take you, did they?'

At that, she nodded agreement.

'Against your will?'

Again the nod.

'Hey there, Gabe,' called Jake, turning to see them both side by side. 'What you doing there?'

'Just getting me a drink of water.'

'Best leave that girl alone, Zeb don't like no one messing with his woman.'

Gabriel passed back the canteen and held up both hands in surrender, 'No offense intended.'

'If you're real good,' Jake chuckled. 'Maybe old Zeb will let you have a tumble but you'll have to wait your turn.'

Gabriel sniffed in distaste and backed off a few steps letting Hannah and the mule go on ahead. He had come across most types during his time in the army and he knew that the Stone brothers were of the lower order. Yet he himself now being a fringe participant also and with the low self esteem he suffered, the circumstance gave him the feeling that he was not one fit to judge others or how they behaved. The things he had seen and participated in during the war had left any sense of morality far behind and if it still lived in him Gabriel felt it was submerged below the years of death and destruction.

Since Lomas Chain, there had been a cold streak born in his character that he was only dimly aware of but he used the narrow stream of vindictiveness to sustain himself. And yet even despite this coldness he could not quite bring himself to see the girl without some sense of pity.

His thoughts were interrupted, as Zeb appeared holding up his hand to halt their column.

'Homestead ahead,' he told them. 'A lone place, there's smoke from the chimney so somebody's home. They got a couple of horses,' with this he gave Gabriel a knowing look. 'Be nice to save you walking, huh, Gabe?'

Gabriel nodded agreement.

'How many to home?' asked Jake.

Zeb shook his head, 'Don't know, couldn't see anyone. Can't be many though, it's only a small place.'

'Best we take a look,' suggested Gabriel.

The three men approached on foot and crouching down, viewed the property from the tree line on an overlooking hill.

It was small all right. A simple slope roofed building with an overhanging porch out front and a few sheds and an outhouse alongside. The pole corral out back held the two horses and a pair of saddles lay over the top pole.

'Look to me like military,' suggested Gabriel as he eyed the saddles.

'Uhuh,' grunted Zeb. 'Johnny Reb cavalry, I'd say. You got a problem with that, Gabe?'

Gabriel shook his head negatively.

A woman made her way out of the house as they

watched; she stepped off the porch step and crossed over to the outhouse swinging her gingham skirts and cotton apron in a carefree fashion as she went. By the look of her she was a fair-haired pretty creature in her mid-thirties and as she left the house a man smoking a pipe and dressed in the gray uniform of a lieutenant came out after her and leaned against the porch pole watching her go. He called out something and she turned and grinned at him.

The soldier knocked out his pipe on the heel of his boot and with a word towards the interior he went back inside the house.

'My guess is the soldier boys are visiting home on leave,' said Zeb.

'We got 'em penned, if they're all in the house,' added Jake.

'I reckon we get those horses and Gabe has one of 'em and the other we can sell off real easy.'

'Maybe they got some liquor in there too,' said Jake, licking his lips. 'I ain't had a wet for a while.'

'Okay, here's how I see it,' said Zeb. 'We come in from three directions. Jake and me'll take each side of the house, Gabe you can come in round back from the corral. Once that woman is inside we'll make our move. We all good on this?'

The other two nodded agreement.

'Right, let's do it. No mercy now, they want to make a show of it then we let them have it.'

With that they separated and began a careful approach down through the cover of the scrub growth on the hillside.

Gabriel dodged from building to building

amongst the shacks in the rear and edged his way alongside the corral. Both horses backed away neighing as he approached and he spoke softly to calm them. He froze and ducked down on one knee as the door of the outhouse opened and the woman came out, pausing only to straighten her skirts before, humming contentedly, she returned to the house. She had not given a glance in Gabriel's direction and once she was out of sight he crossed the bare earth yard to come up on the back of the house. The rear wall was windowless and only a closed doorway stood there. Gabriel gently worked the latch and it came up freely. He opened the door a crack and peered in.

He could hear voices and saw past the visible silhouettes of dark furniture the movement of the gingham dress flashing past.

Gabriel heard the heavy clump of boots coming fast on the porch and heard Zeb's harsh voice as he and Jake crashed inside.

'Don't nobody move!' Zeb hollered.

There was a gabble of voices and the scream of the woman as Gabriel pushed the back door wide and stepped in with his rifle held ready.

Chairs and a dining table blocked his way and Gabriel had to step around them to get a clear view.

The two cavalrymen had jumped to their feet sending their chairs flying whilst the woman, over to one side beside a range had been stoking the fire and was kneeling with both hands held to her face in horror.

'God's teeth!' bellowed one of the soldiers. 'What

y'all think you're doing?'

'Lift 'em high,' ordered Zeb.

The soldiers obliged but one of them held a pistol in his raised fist and fired off immediately at the two figures in the doorway. There was a loud cry of pain and the thunderous roar of gunfire as Zeb let loose with his rifle. The pistol-bearing soldier fell with a crash, firing off more shots as he went and his companion dived for his gun belt hanging from one of the fallen chair backs. The room was filled with smoke and the blazing flash of gunfire and Gabriel stepped into the cloud leveling his Springfield at the surviving cavalryman scrabbling on the floor.

'Don't do it!' Gabriel bellowed.

The woman screamed again at sight of the figure coming from the rear of the room.

The lieutenant whirled to see Gabriel and with a grim expression tugged out his service revolver and thumbed back the hammer. Gabriel shot him and watched as the man leaned up on one elbow for a moment, the round black hole in his forehead leaking a thin streak of red before his head wobbled on his shoulders and he fell back.

Zeb stomped over, working a new shell into his rifle. He stepped over the first man, who lay shivering, his booted feet kicking out at the legs of the fallen chairs. Zeb eased the chair aside and fired point blank into the soldier's chest stilling him instantly.

'*Ow! Ow!*' Jake called out loudly from the doorway. 'I'm hit, brother. The son-of-a-bitch shot me.'

'Goddamn!' snarled Zeb, turning to his brother.

Gabriel crossed over and knelt to check on the

fallen men and with one glance could see that both were clearly dead. He looked up to see how the wounded Jake fared and was turning to the woman when Jake called out again.

'Watch out, brother, she's got a gun!'

Zeb's rifle was still unloaded and he turned from tending his brother to stare with a bemused look at the woman and his good eye widened in horror at his certain fate as the weaving barrels pointed at him.

The sobbing woman had somehow got hold of a shotgun and was lifting the weapon in shaking hands when the wounded Jake fired his rifle from behind Zeb. His shot caught hold of the woman in the chest and ripped her across the room, sending her flying into a dresser stacked with dishes. There was the clatter and crash of broken crockery as the woman collided with the dresser and a final thin whine as she gave up the ghost, blood pumping from the wound between her breasts.

Gabriel climbed to his feet, automatically sliding a fresh shell under the Springfield's latch.

Jake had dropped to his knees and was clutching at the bloody wound in his side, 'Aw! Zeb. Aw! Zeb, I'm shot. Lord, I'm shot to death.'

'No,' said Zeb, lifting his brother to his feet. 'You ain't about to die. Come on now, we'll get you seen to. Gabe, come here and give me a hand.'

They helped Jake over to the long dining table and laid him down whilst Zeb tore away the shirt covering the bullet hole in his side.

'Get me some water, Gabe,' ordered Zeb. 'And find

some bandages, we got to stop this bleeding.'

'It hurts, brother,' whined Jake. 'I'm dying ain't I? God help me for a sinner, now I'm shot me all to hell.'

'Shut up, Jake,' snarled Zeb. 'Gabe, find him some liquor, that'll ease him some.'

The two Confederates had been drinking from a jug and Gabriel passed it over without a word. He stepped up to the stove and lifted a boiling pail of water and set that on the table next to the working Zeb.

'Go bring in the girl,' Zeb said over his shoulder. 'She'll do this better.'

On his way out of the door, Gabriel glanced down at the man he had killed and without a second's thought he collected the fallen soldier's gun belt and pistol and strapped it to his own waist.

Gabriel collected one of the horses in the corral and rode out to fetched Hannah who had been waiting patiently amongst the trees on the hillside with the mule and other horses.

'Did they kill anyone?' she asked tentatively as they rode back.

'Uhuh,' Gabriel allowed. 'Jake's been wounded though.'

He thought she grunted a quiet 'Good,' before she said, 'They allus kill them. They killed my folks before they took me.'

'That's too bad,' he murmured, feeling a twinge of guilt at his own participation.

'You a soldier?' she asked.

'I was,' he admitted. 'Fought with Union from '61.'

'So it ain't new to you,' whether it was a statement

or question he wasn't sure.

'Let's just say I killed plenty of Rebs before this one,' he said with a twist of justification.

She gave him a sidelong glance before observing carefully 'Don't make it right.'

Gabriel breathed a deep sigh and geed his horse on ahead. He clenched his jaw against the doleful reprimand and forced any ill feeling down under his mask of excuse. They had been the enemy and the death he had doled out had been righteous. But even so her softly spoken words still needled him.

Zeb was waiting for him on the porch, his face pale and drawn.

Gabriel pulled up and jerked his chin in query.

'He's gone,' said Zeb. 'Just like that, was calling for his Ma and saying how he'd bring the milk cow in and then he just went. Hot damn! Never thought I'd lose my little brother like that, it don't feel right somehow. I'll go find me a spade.'

With that Zeb turned away and walked off, his shoulders bent and head lowered.

By evening they had buried the dead and Hannah had cleaned up inside the house and managed to cook them a meal.

Zeb had remained silent all through the meal and now he began to drink. He had found the house store of corn liquor and hit it hard. Sitting sullenly at the table he began long blurred diatribes about Jake and himself.

'Ma won't ever forgive me,' he mumbled bitterly. 'Made me swear I'd care for him, she'll give me merry hell for this.'

Gabriel and Hannah ignored him and set about preparing some sleeping arrangements for them all.

'You listenin'?' called Zeb angrily. 'Ain't no call to forget. I lost me some kin here; we gotta hold a proper wake. You two set down and drink with me.'

Dutifully the two obeyed and set themselves down at the table whilst Zeb glugged down more of the strong liquor.

'Here's to brother Jake,' he called, swaying in his seat. 'Come on, raise a glass.'

'Zeb,' interrupted Gabriel. 'We're going to have to move fast come first light, best you lay off the booze.'

'Don't you tell me what to do,' snarled Zeb. 'Going to 'member Jake, best little old boy I ever had.'

It was dark now and Hannah had lighted a lamp and set it on the table between them. By its light the slurring figure of Zeb took on an evil appearance as he leered over the table menacingly towards Hannah.

'Reckon I'm gonna take you tonight, girl,' he said to Hannah. 'Goin' to need me some, take my mind off my loss, y'hear?'

Hannah lowered her head and said nothing.

'You see her, Gabe?' said Zeb, swinging on Gabriel and almost falling from his chair. 'Ain't a scrap of nothin', is she? Just a littl' slut for using, thass all.'

'Cut it out,' warned Gabriel, at last taking sides. 'That's no way to speak to her.'

'Wha' the f...'

He froze as they heard a call from outside the house.

'*Lieutenant!* It's time to leave. You ready?'

'Oh, Lord!' sighed Gabriel, sliding from his seat and making for the window. He edged around the curtain and saw a group of three travel worn Confederate soldiers on horseback outside, their restless movements barely visible in poor light coming from the lamp inside the house. Gabriel picked out the gray of their uniforms and the chevrons on the arm of one of the men.

'Soldiers!' he hissed. 'Three of them with a sergeant, must be the rest of the furlough men.'

'The hell you say,' snarled Zeb drunkenly. 'Bring 'em in, the more the merrier. Killed my boy brother and I aim to take me some more.'

He wove to his feet, letting his chair fall noisily behind him as he dragged out a pistol in one hand and lifted his rifle with the other.

'I'll cut 'em to ribbons, just like those damned officers of theirs. Lost me an eye but I'm still good for three pesky shavetail Reb sons-a-bitches.'

'These ain't shavetails,' warned Gabriel. 'They're Confederate cavalry and they look mighty well practiced I'd say.'

'*Hey, Lieutenant!*' called the voice outside, a touch impatiently. 'You coming? We got to make camp by sunup.'

'Come on ahead, you bastards!' roared Zeb, heading in a stumbling run for the door.

Gabriel dived around the table and taking Hannah by the wrist pulled her towards the rear door, 'Come on,' he whispered firmly. 'We're out of here, there's no stopping the drunk fool now.'

As Zeb sent the front door spinning back with a

loud bang, Gabriel opened the back door and pulled Hannah out after him.

The tattoo of firing from the front door hid their retreat and Gabriel gave a quick glance back to see the jerking figure of Zeb highlighted by flashing flares of gunfire. His silhouetted body spun and twitched as he was struck by a fusillade of gunfire from the alarmed troopers. Small pieces of flesh and jets of juice flew away from the body in the halo of light and Zeb appeared to be jerked by invisible strings before he stumbled back inside the house and fell to the floor.

Without waiting to see more Gabriel hurried Hannah over to the corral and whilst the shouts of the soldiers and heavy sounds of their boots came from inside they slipped two horses free and silently led them away into the shadows.

CHAPTER SIX

A KIND OF RESTITUTION

They married a year later.

It worked after a fashion and Gabriel began to settle down from his previous jaded lifestyle. He found his incipient anger slipping away and his new pose was augmented by the regularity of their changed life and the fact that he had to care for Hannah as well as himself, which ultimately urged him to find steady work.

He found it in the unlikely position of lawman.

The small sleepy town of Olive Tree Branch became their home. Well away from the war's end and the after effects of the final surrender and not suffering the political divisions found in many other towns meant that Olive Tree Branch held out a period of recovery for them both.

It was a simple place, the result of a failed silver mining discovery that ran dry, and no more than six hundred occupants remaining resident in town, the rest of the locals living scattered in outlying properties and farms. Twin rows of twenty houses faced each other across Main Street, with stores and a few offices occupying most of the lower floors. The early plan had been for an expansion that never came and the town stood frozen in time as a backwater bypassed by any main traffic.

Hannah was proving to be a quiet and taciturn creature that stood by Gabriel with a devoted show of silent loyalty and gratitude. For his part he found in her an oasis of peace after the stress and tribulations that he had experienced. To say it was a love match would be a stretch as they both came with baggage that they would rather forget. And although these earlier personal trials were suppressed and hidden away each was fulfilled by the relationship within the limits that their circumstances allowed.

Colly Tern was the nominal town leader of Olive Tree Branch and it was he that they had first met on the arrival. An elderly, outgoing fellow, often a dreamy character but of original settler stock and never one to forget how it had been for him in the early days, so he had treated the couple with respect and generous assistance. Colly had found them accommodation in an empty shack left by a recently deceased widow woman and introduced them to the townsfolk whom they found to be generally a hardworking and open-minded community.

Colly was sharp enough to see that beneath his rather harsh exterior, Gabriel held a potential that was worth prospering and it was by his efforts that he had been elected to town marshal.

It proved to be an easy task for Gabriel as there was little to challenge his position in the quiet township. An occasional fistfight, some arguments over outlying property boundaries and an errant daughter or two misbehaving were all that tested his capabilities. They had no jailhouse in the place and as there were never any serious offenders who needed imprisonment most offenders were put on trust and sent home with a sharp reminder to be-have. So Gabriel spent much of his day sitting idly in the small one-roomed office that was no bigger than a closet set aside for the law and whittling his way through acres of scrap wood. Come evening, he would amble his way home and find Hannah sol-emnly engaged with preparing his supper or wash-ing his clothes and he would gaze in amazement at her dutiful attention to his needs.

They did not speak much and she never criticized or nagged him and sometimes Gabriel wished she would bite back a tad just to bring some spike into their lives.

They made love frequently in their tiny bedroom and at first it had been an awkward and almost des-perate union but time had worn away the restric-tions and latterly they had enjoyed more freedom in their relations. It seemed to both that they were set to spend their lives in this contented and com-fortable state.

On the day it all changed, Gabriel woke as normal with the rising sun in his eyes. He stretched languid-ly, dressed and made his way out back of the shack to wash up. The early sun was warm on his back and he could smell the bacon and biscuits Hannah was cooking for his breakfast in her tiny kitchen. He came in behind her and stood for a moment watching her at work, still amazed that she could produce so much in such a tiny space.

He put his hands around her small waist and whispered a good morning into the hair at the nape of her neck.

She smiled briefly and tried to worm out of his grasp as she flipped the bacon in the pan. For sheer devilment, he tugged her about and kissed her warmly on the mouth. She bent to his demand as readily as any other time and with one hand holding a spatula and the other a hot pan cloth, she accepted his kisses and answered them as eagerly as they were offered.

When he released her, Hannah lowered her head and smiled shyly. She said nothing but jerked her chin in the direction of his seat at the table.

Gabriel shook his head at her compliant nature and returned her smile, 'You're a goddamned marvel, honey.'

'Go on,' she said. 'Go sit down before your coffee gets cold.'

Gabriel did as he was told and said, 'Colly wants me out at the Juniper place today, seems old man Juniper hasn't been seen for a week in town and they reckon I should go check on him.'

'Uhuh,' she nodded. 'Is that the one with the wooden leg?'

'That's him, lost it working on the railroad. Must have been one of the first to lay ties back east.'

'He's a sweet old fella so the ladies say.'

'Aha, you been gossiping again,' Gabriel eyed her with mock reprimand.

'No, no,' she said quickly, always taking him way too much to heart. 'I overheard them talking in the store, that's all.'

'That's okay, girl, I'm joshing you. You can go gossip all you care.'

She chewed her lip nervously, 'I ain't very good at it anyway.'

'Then it's about time you learned, that's a woman's thing or so I'm told.'

He laughed at her with his eyes and she admired the sparkle in them and felt a rush in her breast.

'Something I got to say, Gabriel,' she began haltingly as she held the skillet over his plate ready to offload his eggs and bacon.

'What's that?'

She looked at him nervously, and then in a rush, 'I believe I'm with child.'

For a long moment, Gabriel was silent as it sunk in.

'You're going to have a *baby*? Our baby?'

'Yes, I'm real sorry...'

'But, honey, that's great. Hellfire! A baby. Why, that's something else.'

Relief spread over her whole face, 'Then it's okay, you don't mind?'

'God Almighty! Why should I mind, Hannah? This is a wonder.'

He jumped up and swept the pan from her hand, dropping it on the table before he took her in his arms.

'Ain't that a thing,' he said softly, drawing her close and conscious of the press of her slender body against him. 'Who'd have thought it?'

'I was worried...' she began.

'No worries,' he said, tenderly brushing a strand of hair from her eyes. 'No way, it's wonderful news. I never thought I'd ever be a pappy, never in my whole life.'

'I'm so glad,' she said, resting her face against his chest. A slight frown crossed her brow, 'It'll be different, you know that don't you?'

'I guess so but not in any kind of bad way.'

'I hope not,' she murmured sincerely. 'You been so good to me, Gabriel, I wouldn't want to upset that.'

'I don't reckon you could if you tried,' he reassured her.

He kissed her softly on the lips and she pulled him tight, her fingers sinking deep into his shoulders in a grip of pleasure.

'I'm so happy,' she whispered. 'I never thought I could be so happy.'

'About time we had some of that don't you think?'

Solemnly she nodded agreement.

As Gabriel rode out to the Juniper place he pondered over the prospect of becoming a father. He thought back over his own daddy and for a moment the dark cloud of Lomas Chain and his cronies entered into his thinking but he brushed the thought aside and concentrated on the happier aspects of parenthood instead.

Mentally he listed the items he would need to find. A crib to make and he'd need to prime the midwife, then there were baby clothes, he decided he would have to have a word with Colly. Maybe the town ladies could get together some kind of sewing bee.

His head in a whirl of planning he hardly noticed the passing countryside. It was hot and flat country, covered by sagebrush, tumbleweed and clumps of cactus with only the occasional Judas tree standing dark against the baking sand and Gabriel rode through it without notice and almost in a trance state.

Gabriel was wakened from his thoughts as his pony descended a steep sided arroyo and for a moment he had to concentrate on where the animal stepped. He realized he was nearing the Juniper homestead and as he climbed the other side of the arroyo he saw the farm buildings laid out before him.

It seemed somewhat quiet; neither of Juniper's two dogs started out barking at his approach and Gabriel could see no livestock in the pens. He frowned as he felt the unnatural emptiness of the place. Something, he decided, was not right here and he wondered if the lonely old man had passed away or some accident had befallen him.

Gabriel called out as he dismounted outside the main house, on a slight rise behind stood the barn, its big doors swung wide and exposing the dark interior.

'Mister Juniper! You here, it's Sheriff Brannigan.'

But nothing moved and only silence responded.

Concerned now, Gabriel eased the pistol in his holster. He carried the Colt he had taken from the dead soldier and although it received little use he still maintained it with care.

He peered in the windows but saw nothing

untoward, then, knocking on the door, he found it swung open, as it was already unlatched. Stepping inside, Gabriel found only a dusty silence and a hollow sound as his boots stepped across the room.

'You here, Juniper?' he tried again.

A cold, half finished mug of coffee stood lonely vigil on the table in front of him. Drawing the pistol, Gabriel quickly made his way through the other rooms. The bed was unmade in the bedroom but no more than to be expected by a lone man. Washed socks were stretched on a drying string before the ashes in the fireplace. The whole place was deserted.

Gabriel made his way outside and with a sinking heart made his way over towards the uninviting entrance of the barn.

Looking around cautiously, Gabriel did not notice the object lying in the dust until his boot clipped the edge of it. He looked down to see he had disturbed a wooden rod. He knelt and lifted it to find he held the shaped wood of a peg leg. The one-legged old man's support.

At a run, Gabriel jogged up to the barn and fearing the worst he stepped into the sudden shadows inside.

He was there.

Circling slowly from the tight noose that stretched his neck to twice its length, the gaping face black and busy with flies. Juniper had taken a long time dying, Gabriel could see that. No quick neck break but a slow strangulation at the end of the coarse rope. His remaining boot had been kicked clear in his struggles and with sadness Gabriel looked at the pitiful sight of the old man's holed sock sagging from his foot.

'Goddamn you, old man,' he muttered. 'What the hell happened here?'

Gabriel cut down the body and then went outside to study the ground more thoroughly. There were plenty of hoof marks, especially around the stockyards. The old man's dogs were there, both of them shot dead. He looked for moccasin prints thinking it might have been Indians but all he found were heeled boot prints. So it was white men, he thought, and quite a few of them by the looks of it.

Something moved in Gabriel then. He had so long been sunken into the sense of safety and contentment that the advent of old dangers seared like a hot coal across his pleasant thoughts of earlier. It would mean a posse, he thought, but then he feared that most of the town's menfolk were ill equipped for such a task. They were simple folk and not sharp enough to take on a gang who thought nothing of stringing up a poor old one-legged man out of pure meanness.

How long, he wondered, how long ago had this happened? If it was the best part of the week since Juniper was missed then they would be long gone and all his livestock with them. Going by the prints and how little the wind and wild creatures had disturbed the tracks, Gabriel reckoned on three days at the most.

He would bury the old man, then take the trouble back to town and let Colly decide what best to do.

Colly shook his head from side to side and clucked his tongue sorrowfully.

'That's bad, Gabriel. That's mighty bad. How long, you say? Three days maybe. Hell, they'll be out of state by now.'

Gabriel looked across at the elderly fellow, his rumpled jacket dust marked, and with food stains on his worn waistcoat. Colly sported a handsome white mustache and side-whiskers, with the mustache over his lip stained with nicotine from the short cherry-wood pipe that was often stuck between his lips.

They were both wedged into the law office with barely enough room for one of them to sit whilst the other stood.

'Well, what do you want to do?' asked Gabriel. 'You want to raise a posse and try and track them down? Or you want me to head out and see what I can do alone?'

Colly sucked on his pipe as he considered, it was unlit and only gurgled emptily from the spit trapped in the stem.

'Sounds like there's too many for one man, Gabriel. Too many and too cruel by what you say.'

'They've had three days, so maybe made sixty miles minimum with the few head Juniper owned, depending on how fast and hard they travelled.'

'But who are these fellows, do you reckon?'

Gabriel shrugged, 'Renegades, bandits, hard cases left over from the war. Who knows? But bad people you can bet on it.'

'Heavens! I don't know what best to advise,' said

Colly, rubbing his grizzled chin.

'I don't reckon a posse from here will cut it. Maybe it'd be best I go take a look on my own.'

'You don't reckon they could still be around, do you?'

It was a thought that had not occurred to Gabriel, his past experience being so much of hit and run that the notion of sticking around the scene of any crime seemed unlikely.

He shrugged, 'Could be, I suppose, but I wouldn't count on it.'

'No, I suppose not,' agreed Colly.

They looked at the floor in silence, each pondering their own thoughts.

'By the way,' Gabriel said suddenly. 'We're having us a baby.'

'You are?' smiled Colly. 'But that's fine, Gabriel. Congratulations, my boy.'

'Thank you kindly.'

'Well,' beamed Colly. 'I should be handing around stogies on the basis.'

'I thought that was my prerogative.'

'Heavens, who cares? It's just damned good to hear, I shall offer my best wishes to Hannah first chance I get.'

'She'd appreciate that.'

Colly drew a breath, 'So, what do you want to do on this other business? I think its best you decide, I'd dare say you have more experience than me in such matters.'

'I'll take supplies and head out, their trail shouldn't be too hard to follow.'

'You aiming to bring them all back?'

Gabriel eyed him meaningfully without saying a word.

'I guess not,' supplied Colly, understanding his cool gaze.

'The way they strung up poor Juniper these are just mean-faced murderers, Colly. It wouldn't do to show them an ounce of mercy; they'll just spit it back in your face. No, I'll kill them where they stand I get the chance.'

Colly nodded his head in understanding, 'Well, you're the legal representative so you got the law on your side.'

'What I really need are ten good men as bad as those I'm going after.'

CHAPTER SEVEN

HOT LEAD AND HARD MEN

Black Jack Carnustie slid the spyglass shut but stayed where he was lying down on the ridge and staring at the town below.

'That the law?' asked the big man Dole Dougherty from behind him, the Irish brogue heavy in his low voice.

'That's the sorry son-of-a-bitch,' Carnustie agreed as he watched Gabriel leave the office and make his way towards a shack at the edge of town.

Carnustie collected his hat with the swept up brim and long white plume and eased himself back out of sight. He had taken the hat from a dead Confederate major. That and also the rest of the corpse's accouterments, sabre and pistol, fancy gloves and boots which he now wore with an affected show of dash. Not that he had killed the man, that had been the result of some enemy action. But it made no difference to Carnustie or any other of the seven men accompanying him, they all would have done it just as easily if the opportunity had arisen.

They were a band of fringe members of the past

conflict. Once they had ridden with guerrillas out of Missouri and professed allegiance to the South, then just as easily, switched sides and scouted for Union troops in the Richmond-Petersburg campaign. They were the vultures that gathered at the edges of any war, those keen to pick on the vulnerable bones of the defeated or any unfortunate non-combatant that their paths crossed.

Now the battles were over and peace declared they had drifted south to those states still sympathetic to the Rebel cause and that was why Carnustie had taken on the major's uniform.

But Carnustie's men had travelled far and were tired and needed a place to rest a while.

The old man strung up in the barn had burbled on about the town and its occupants and Carnustie had seen opportunity in the place. Small and out of the way, rarely visited except by a rare supply wagon and the occasional visitor. Guarded by some has-been wreck of a soldier all on his own. It had sounded like an ideal opportunity for a little rest and recreation.

'What you reckon?' Dougherty whispered, even though they were far enough away and well out of sight of the town.

He was a not-very-bright, and short, bow-legged beast of a figure sporting a heavy black beard and an open necked shirt that exposed the dense mat of hair that covered his body. An ape of a man, barrel chested with densely packed muscle that lay in slabs across his whole body and with arms that dangled down in simian fashion below his waist. Dougherty was Carnustie's long trusted associate and his second-in-command. And Carnustie prized him, not for his intellect, but because when roused, his normally placid and dim companion could unleash such violence that it surprised even Carnustie who was no fledging in the brutality stakes. Carnustie had at one time seen Dougherty go completely berserk and literally tear a man apart with his bare hands and from that moment he had kept the Irishman close.

'I think we should go explore,' Carnustie answered him blandly.

The rest of the gang waited patiently, they had little concern as to where they went or what they did and were happy for Carnustie to take the lead and tell them. The men smoked and squatted beside their horses waiting for the word. There had been only small pickings at the one-legged man's place and his questioning and subsequent hanging had provided them with little entertainment. The cattle they had stolen had been mean creatures and of little value and the one they had slaughtered and feasted on had provided little sustenance. They had discarded the rest of the animals as easily as they had taken them and now the prospect of women and drink in the town provided much more motivation.

'Okay, boys,' said Carnustie, slapping the dust from his hat against his leg as he approached them. 'We'll take the town. Maybe spend a few days there for a little amusement. What do you say?'

'You're the boss, Cap'n Jack,' said one tall figure, an unshaven man with sunken features and hollow eyes. 'Long as they got liquor and feed, I ain't concerned one way or the other.'

'Don't worry, Converse, we'll get you a belly full and a whole crate of whiskey as well.'

'They got women there?' asked a squat, frizzy haired young man with a cocky stance.

'Always the swinging dick, huh, Gilly Joe?' joked Carnustie.

'Ain't had me no diversion for a whole month now. It ain't good for my constitution,' grinned Gilly Joe flamboyantly. The young man bore an ugly scar that ran from under his left eye down to his jaw and he scratched it self consciously as he looked at the others, unsure if he was impressing them or not.

'Here's how it is,' said Carnustie, squatting down and outlining the township in the dust. 'We'll come in on all sides, just like we did back in Small Forks, you remember? We'll surprise the hell out of them and lock the place down before they know it.'

'What we got down there, Cap'n Jack?' asked Converse. 'Any resistance?'

'No more than farmers, shopkeepers and some lone star. Nothing to give us any problems, I reckon.'

'Who's the lawman?'

'Some stranger that drifted in, so the old man said. Back from the war probably and the only fool that's ever handled a gun, so they will have given him the job on that basis I reckon. He'll be a nobody.'

'When do we go?' asked Gilly Joe. 'I'm ready and willing.'

'Sure you are, you randy little goat,' sneered Converse. 'Just remember to keep hold your gun and not that thing in your pants.'

'Just 'cos you've forgotten what it's for,' snapped back Gilly Joe spitefully.

'Haw, haw!' mocked Converse. 'Listen to the baby jerk-off, will you?'

The rest of the men chuckled at the continuing confrontation between the two that had been an ongoing contest.

'That's enough,' said Carnustie, warning them off before things got out of hand. 'You can take it out on those town dummies down there.'

'Poor critters don't know what's coming,' chortled Gilly Joe, his eyes flashing with eagerness. 'We going to burn 'em out, Cap'n?'

'Not right off,' Carnustie answered. 'Let's see what we got here first. Right off we separate the men and women, anybody causes problems then cut them down.'

Dougherty sniffed and mumbled softly, 'What about the little ones?'

Carnustie knew Dougherty's strange protective proclivity towards vulnerable children, 'Ah, we'll not harm them, don't fear, Dole. They'll be your special responsibility.'

'No one touches them,' growled Dougherty. 'You hear me? You harm a hair on a sweet child's head and you'll wish you hadn't. By Jesus, Joseph and Mary, I swear it.'

'Don't worry,' Carnustie mollified him. 'Nobody will do harm in that respect, they all have it clear.'

'They'd better,' growled Dougherty.

'What you get so fussed over the kids for?' asked Gilly Joe, perhaps unwisely. 'They ain't but scraps of nothing an' more trouble than they're worth.'

Dougherty leered towards him menacingly, 'Just stay away.'

'All right, all right,' said Gilly Joe, backing away with open hands raised in a pretended show of fear. 'Don't get your underwear in a twist, I's just saying.'

'Best you understand,' rumbled Dougherty. 'Nobody touches the children.'

'Damn it to hell!' cursed one of the other men impatiently. 'Can we get on with this, I need my breakfast.'

Gabriel stood in the kitchen, a new 16-shot Henry repeating rifle crooked in his arm, a blanket under his elbow and the Colt strapped to his waist.

'I'm sorry about this,' he apologized to Hannah as she handed him a sack of supplies. 'It's come at a bad time I know given our good news but I got to do it.'

Hannah looked up at him warily from under lowered brows and nodded, 'You have to do your job.'

He could see the hurt behind her eyes and it troubled him.

'It'll only be for a few days, don't worry.'

'But there's so many of them.'

'Ach! They'll probably be long gone.'

She bit her lip, knowing full well that he would not give up and would track them down whatever.

'I might not even see them,' he added weakly.

Tentatively, she reached out and laid a hand on his arm, 'Just you take care, will you?'

'Be sure of it, honey. I'll be back before you even know it.'

'I...' she began, but a burst of gunfire and the thunder of hoofs outside in the street cut her off.

Gabriel spun around as loud whoops and strangled sounding Rebel howls came from the street followed by more gunfire.

'Goddamn it to hell!' he snapped. 'They're here!'

Shedding the sack of supplies and blanket, he worked a bullet into the chamber of the rifle and made for the door.

'Go hide, find yourself some cover,' he called over his shoulder as he swung the door back.

Stepping out onto the porch, Gabriel saw the billowing pillars of dust from whirling horses. He made out the racing men amidst the dust and heard the crash of exploded glass. Bullets whipped about, cracking and banging through the air.

'Come on out, suckers!' one of the riders bawled. 'Afore we come and get you.'

Gabriel lifted his rifle and took aim. He fired and lifted the offending man from the saddle, sending him spinning into the dust below his horse's hoofs. Quickly, Gabriel reloaded and ducking sideways, headed for the alley beside his shack.

'They got, Lou!' he heard one of the men call and Gabriel fired again into the billowing swirls of dust and then rapidly worked the lever on the Henry.

'It's that goddamned sheriff, go nail him.'

Horses spun in Gabriel's direction and he sped away down the alley and ran around back of his neighbor's house, one of the line of buildings that fronted Main Street and backed onto the open desert.

Gabriel stopped and stood where he was and

waited.

A horse rider, hollering wildly, burst from the alley, gun held high in his raised hand.

Gabriel crouched and fired twice from the hip, his bullet slamming into the rider and sending him over the side to crash into the wooden wall siding the alley. The man screamed in pain and begged for mercy in a high-pitched squealing voice as he lay squirming in a fallen heap at the base of the wall.

Gabriel did not hesitate but took off again heading along the back yards of the buildings, jumping the low fence divides and brushing through hanging washing. He tripped over a hutch and sprawled in the dust before, with a curse, he recovered and sprang to his feet to carry on running.

The sound of smashing glass and wrenched door frames, gunfire and loud curses followed him, the cacophony filled with the wails and calls of distress from the townspeople.

Gabriel loped along until he came to the alleyway beside his law office, a narrow overshadowed opening that led him back to Main Street. He knew he would need more of the ammunition kept in his desk in the office. Nobody had followed him after the first man and he came up on the alley entrance cautiously.

'Come on out, Lone Star!' he heard a voice call loudly. 'We got your menfolk here. You want to see them live, you better make a show.'

Gabriel shed his hat and peered around the edge of the alley. He had a clear view down Main Street and he could see the man. A figure dressed in Confederate uniform, striking a pose and dramatically holding a pistol pointed at the head of the kneeling figure of a shaking Colly Tern. Colly held his pipe clenched forgotten in his fists that were both held prayer-like before. Behind him, some of the mounted riders were driving members of the town into a huddled circle; a few had dismounted and were pushing men and women apart.

Six men, he counted, eight in all less the two he had put down. And that had been lucky, a thing they had obviously not expected, thinking surprise alone against the innocent town would win them the day. But it left Gabriel with a dilemma, he could surrender now but if he did the town stood no chance against these men. He could run and take his chance with some kind of guerrilla tactics but that might cost the life of his friend Colly. It was an unenviable decision and one he must take swiftly.

Gabriel clenched his jaw as his mind raced and then a cold objectivity descended over him and stilled his beating heart. He was Hannah's, and everybody else's only chance and he knew that there was no real alternative. He faded back away down the alley, the rifle gripped unnaturally tightly in his two hands.

Gabriel winced and lifted his head in silent agony as heard the solitary shot echoing after him.

'Told you!' called the Confederate. 'Come on now, we got plenty more here.'

But Gabriel was gone, heading into the open desert yonder, watching his trail and hiding his boot prints in the scrub and ground cover where possible.

He spent an hour scribing a wide circle across uneven ground and dusting his back trail where he could, and then he doubled back and struck off at angle heading for higher ground. At times he had seen a couple of riders searching for his tracks, weaving in and out of the sagebrush and around the clumps of cactus. Gabriel decided that they were an inept bunch and knew by their wanderings that he had covered his trail well; once again he was grateful for his upbringing amongst the Indians.

He found a safe place in a gully and sunk down to inventory. He had a few more shells for the Henry in his vest pockets and the Colt was fully loaded and there were bullets in his ammunition belt. He had no water and had left his hat lying forgotten in the alley. In his pocket was a small penknife but he had nothing else except the silver sheriff's star on his shirtfront. He unpinned the reflective surface and slipped it into his pocket.

He must find water, that was a priority; he would not last long in the heat if he did not. And then, perversely, he knew that without cover at night he would freeze in the desert chill. With a sigh, he set out, running at the crouch through the shoulder high brush and heading for the high ridge overlooking the town and then on to old man Juniper's place. There would be water there, maybe a canteen and food. Possibly even some weapons that the raiders had overlooked.

It took him two hours and at the end of it he realized he was sadly out of practice. Sweat dripped from his brow and his shirt was soaked through back and front; he had lived a comfortable life with Hannah for too long and was now paying the price. There had been a day when he was younger that he had been able to lope at a steady pace all day through the heat with his boyhood Shoshone friends and play a ball game of Shinny afterwards, now though, it was a different matter, he was dry as a pipe and his aching leg muscles missed a horse to ride.

Once again he stepped into the deserted house.

He found himself a canteen, filling it and quenching his thirst at the same time from the pump outside. Then he scavenged and took a wool blanket from the bedroom. After a quick trawl through the rest of the property he uncovered a heavy bladed Bowie knife and an elderly single-barreled shotgun that Gabriel decided to leave in favor of his Henry. He needed to travel light and freely so the less he carried the better. Tying the rolled blanket and looping it cross-wise over his back he tucked the knife into his belt and thought through his options.

They knew he was out there and he guessed they would be keeping watch for him, he also knew these kind of men would be unable to withstand the temptations that the town had to offer and despite themselves would not be able to resist. Nighttime would be best. He wished he had moccasins to wear and a bow to hand, as silence and the killing power of an arrow would have served him better in the upcoming fight, but he decided, unpleasant as it was, the close-in knife would have to do.

Hannah rose forefront in his mind and he had to

push the thoughts away as to have her welfare on the edge of his mind constantly would be a distraction and he knew he had to remain keen and focused.

The view down into town when he arrived at the overlook was not a pretty one. It was late and he had missed the first burst of murder and rapine activity and all that remained in the darkness of night was evidence of the aftermath. There was a strangely bruised solemnity about the place as if it hovered in a sluggish air of abused exhaustion.

A bonfire built of stacked household chairs and tables had been lit in the middle of Main Street and by it's light Gabriel could see there were bodies stretched out there. He was too far distant to tell who they were but he knew one of them was Colly Tern. A couple of young female victims were evident, one stripped quite naked, her pale body lying dead at a corner of the sidewalk as if she had been indiscriminately used and tossed there. The other, who looked like the storekeeper's daughter, although it was hard to tell as she had been leaned over and tied face down across a hitching rail. Her skirts were raised and tossed back over her head exposing her rear end and it was plain what had been done to her.

Near to her in a blanketed heap against the store wall sat propped a pale man stripped to the waist and covered by blood soaked bandages around his bare midriff. He appeared white-faced and slack jawed and Gabriel guessed he was the raider that he had wounded outside his shack and now looked as if he had finally given up the ghost.

Mostly the remaining members of the gang were lying around and listening to a piano being played. They had hauled Mrs. Mowbray's straight-backed instrument out of her parlor and dumped it in the street and she was being forced to play some gentle classical piece that really did not go too well with the surroundings. But that was all Mrs. Mowbray knew how to play so they had to settle for that. The thing was that the liquid sound of the tender music apparently had held some sway over the gang, as it seemed they were settled down with most of their rapacious energy already spent. A couple slumped drunkenly on the sidewalk with bottles and jugs in their hands and the few others wandered idly and picked through the items in the broken window of the store or gorged themselves on opened tins of supplies inside.

The guy in the Confederate outfit was leaning his elbow on the top of the piano and striking a soulful pose like some stereoscopic photograph of a lounge dandy back east. He had his chin cupped in one hand whilst the other kept a six-gun close by. There was a serenely poetic look about him as if he were enjoying the sound of the music, and Gabriel was happy as long as this kept his attention elsewhere for the time being.

Where the rest of the townsfolk were it was impossible to say as no one was in sight, and Gabriel guessed they were being held prisoner and locked up in one or two of the larger houses. He carefully noted the two guards patrolling the outer limits of the town. Two men that had probably not participated in the indulgences the rest of the gang had enjoyed. One had the solemn look of a black-clad Mormon or some kind of preacher about him and maybe avoided any such activity on the grounds of religious conviction, the other was an Indian and Gabriel reckoned the gang would not allow an Indian to mix it up with white men. The Indian was dressed in beaded buckskins and wore a big floppy hat with a bandana tied around, the loose ends hanging down the back over his long hair. To Gabriel he had the look of a Blackfoot about him and that made it easier for him as they were another old tribal enemy of the Shoshone.

The two guards circled slowly around in the same clockwise direction but at opposite points of the compass to each other. Gabriel timed their passage by counting out the seconds, and then when he was sure of the timing, he unfastened the blanket tied across his back and began to snake his way slowly down towards the town.

The preacher man passing by on his patrol neither heard or saw the covering of dust slide from the blanket as Gabriel rose from the dip he had hidden in. Yet even though it was only a soft silt of shifting sand, something instinctive must have alerted the man. He half turned but was too late, Gabriel was already on him. He swung the knife in a short arc but the half-turn had put him off his target for the aimed at windpipe and the blade sunk deep into the unresisting flesh at the side of preacher man's neck. Wide eyed the raider tried to jerk back and Gabriel pulled the knife out and tried to get to his throat and slit the windpipe before the man could call out. They both struggled, with the neck wound spurting artery blood in a violent jet over their fighting bodies.

Gabriel had his hand over the man's mouth and could feel the shine of his victim's teeth under his grappling fingers. Desperately the fellow kicked and shrugged, trying to shake Gabriel off. It was the kind of close combat that leaves each combatant only too well aware of his opponent. The smell of the blood, the struggle and sweat and stink of terror filled both men's nostrils.

Stabbing repeatedly, Gabriel plunged the knife in until he felt the man's knees give way. Soaked in the fellow's lifeblood, Gabriel could smell the terrible stink as the fellow voided himself in his death throes and fell face down.

Breathing heavily, Gabriel looked around but all he could hear was the tinkling piano still playing. He was shaking; the hand that clutched the dripping knife vibrating with the adrenalin coursing through his body and Gabriel slowly pulled himself upright struggling to throw off the sensation.

With a last look around he sloped off into the shadows of the surrounding desert and prepared to meet his next foe.

When the Blackfoot arrived, he started in surprise at the body of his fellow lookout. He dropped immediately to one knee, his rifle held ready as he searched the darkness.

He saw it instantly.

The twinkling sparkle like a star shining in the distance. It bobbed and jiggled and looked like the retreating attacker making off, some brass casings on his ammunition belt catching the light from the fire. Springing to his feet, the Indian raced off after the reflection hoping to catch up before it vanished from sight.

He did not make it as far as he had hoped as he swiftly ran full tilt into Gabriel's rifle. Rising up from cover and swinging the Henry rifle two-handed like a bat with all the force he could manage, Gabriel connected with the oncoming Indian. Gabriel heard the solid smack and felt the shock down the barrel as the stock hit the man full on the forehead and brought him up and off his feet. Tumbling down, Gabriel was over the stunned Indian in a second and delivered another stunning blow to the head half hidden by shadow.

The man flopped over with a soft groan and tried to worm away on his belly, crawling with both hands dragging him along. Gabriel drew the blade again and fell onto the man, using his weight to drive the knife in up to the hilt into the back below the ribcage. The fellow arched up and Gabriel heard his gurgling cry as he angled the buried blade upwards aiming for the heart.

It was over in a minute and Gabriel stepped away quickly from the shivering limbs.

He was stained with the two men's dark blood, it ran in streaks down his face and up over his elbows and onto his shirtfront that was also spattered and patterned with splashes. He looked a nightmare sight in the half-light with only his eyes glinting whitely in his darkly painted face. The killing mood was fully in him now; it was a primitive urge that superseded any display of simple humanity. Almost in a wild dream, Gabriel dived back angrily onto the fallen Indian and kneeling astride the body he clutched the head by the greasy hair and pulled it back. Then with the knife he carved a four-inch roundel of scalp free and dragged the hank of hair away. With the breath racing fast in his nostrils Gabriel tagged the scalp into his belt and climbed back onto his feet.

With one hand he reached up and snapped down the twinkling sheriff's star that hung from the tree branch. Then with one last look around, he made off into the shadows.

In a moment he was back.

With a grim smile, Gabriel worked the moccasin boots from the dead Indian's feet.

'*Eh-shun*,' he grunted in Shoshone. 'Thank you, brother.'

CHAPTER EIGHT

INTERLUDE

Here it was that old Mister Brannigan hauled off and said he was plumb tuckered out talking and still had some chores to do before dark and he'd leave off for now.

He had been nibbling at the corners of that pie-crust whilst he recounted his story and I guessed the old fellow was getting a taste for it and had excused himself as he really intended to go off and have a little feast of apple pie.

Whether or not he was just yanking my chain and it was all a tall tale or not, I could not figure out. If it was true, then it was a hell of a story and gave me a whole different perspective on my notions of the old-time west. This was no Tom Mix or Johnny Mack doing his gallant thing down at the moving picture house in town and nor was it the local guys in their spangled shirts, country music and pressed pants, no this was a whole different world.

I asked him once about how they did dress back then and he told me they more or less lived in the clothes they stood up in. Stiff with sweat and grease, coated in trail dust and out in all weathers, never seeing a wash tub from one year to the next except when it rained. In fact the only times they changed was when the damned things wore out and fell to pieces and they had to go buy new.

Geez, I observed, y'all must have stunk something terrible, how did that feel?

He explained in that dry old way of his, that most everybody else smelled the same so it made no difference whatsoever. He said that the one time he caught a whiff of a fine lady that was wearing some kind of rose water perfume and he near fainted with the shock of it.

Now that was the kind of extravagance that gave me cause for caution in his damned story. But he told me to come back on the morrow and maybe he'd tell me more. He also told me to bring along a quart bottle, didn't mind if it was whiskey or brandy, either would do, as he wasn't fussed. I guessed then and there that I was having to pay for my entertainment.

So I went off home and told my Mom how much he enjoyed her pie and how even his dog looked on it favorably.

Thing was it fascinated me, even if it was all hokum I just loved the story. Shoot-ups and a touch of romance, I guess it filled my young head with wonder and I was eager to hear more.

Next day, Ma was up early and by the time I had managed to get myself together I found she had baked not one but two pies, one regular size and a smaller one that she said was for the mutt. Hell! I couldn't believe it but that was Mom, generous to a fault even to a damned dog.

I picked up a bottle at the liquor store and took along a small box of cigars that brother Ahab had stashed away. He'd had them off his friend Emilio Solidade and they were those little slender Mexican ones, black as pitch and strong as old rope. We both tried them one time when Ma was out of the house and I tell you I nearly puked my guts they was that powerful. Anyway, I guessed the old fella was not above a good smoke to go with his liquor so I took them along.

He was there, sitting the same as before and braiding some kind of bridle from horsehair when I came up. He cocked an eye at me from under his hat brim as his nimble fingers continued working, then he let off his work and handed me the empty and cleaned pie dish without a word and I marveled that he had finished the whole thing in one evening. But his eyes sure brightened when I showed him the two extry that Ma had made for him.

The dog, Boulder was sitting beside him and watching me closely, with its head cocked to one side curious-like but at least it wasn't showing me its teeth this time. When I told Mister Brannigan the small one was for the dog, he chuckled some and thanked me. I set the bottle and cigars on the bench beside him and he licked his lips thoughtfully.

'That sure looks good,' he confessed, setting aside the braiding and fondling the bottle like it was a newborn baby. 'Doc says I ain't supposed to sup no more but shoot, in the time I got left who gives a hoot about all that.' He unpeeled himself a cigar, opened the bottle and drew a draught that left him lip smacking and gazing skywards.

'Bless me to my rock bottom boots!' he said. 'That is pure nectar, now light me up on this fine cigar and I reckon I'll be ready to bore you some more.'

CHAPTER NINE

SHOWDOWN AT OLIVE TREE BRANCH

Carnustie spat and cursed when Dougherty brought him the news about the dead lookouts.

'Goddamn it!' he bellowed. 'That's half our crew gone, who in the hell is this fellow?'

Mrs. Mowbray was continuing to play in the background, the dulcet tones of a Chopin nocturne carrying her away from the unpleasant scene surrounding her on Main Street.

'Will you shut the hell up?' roared Carnustie, his earlier mood of blissful audience swept away.

Unhearing him, Mrs. Mowbray's fingers swept along the keys, borne along on the trance of concentration that her playing allowed.

With a look of tiresome irritation, Carnustie raised his pistol and almost casually blew the top Mrs. Mowbray's head off.

'There's a time and place for everything,' he mumbled as the old lady flopped out of sight behind the piano.

'We'd best get off the street,' advised Dougherty.

'Indeed,' agreed Carnustie, looking around wildly.

Converse and Gilly Joe came ambling over, Converse was the worse for drink and mean in a rambling way whilst the sexually satiated Gilly Joe appeared jaded and rumpled.

'It's too damned bad,' he bitched. 'Just when we had it going fine, now some redneck's gotta go ruin it all.'

'Just let me have him for two minutes,' leered Converse dully.

Gilly Joe arched an eyebrow, 'You'd trip over your own feet you're so tipsy, you danged piss-head.'

Converse bared his teeth, 'You're asking for it, shit-for-brains.'

'Will you two give it a rest,' barked Carnustie. 'We've got other things to think on.'

'Never fear, we got us a town full of hostages,' remarked Gilly Joe slyly. 'And a few more gals amongst them.'

'So we have,' agreed Carnustie. 'But this is one clever lawman we have here, better than we thought. He must be to take down both the Indian and the preacher in stealth like he did.'

'Something you ain't thought of, Cap'n Jack,' slurred Converse. 'You suppose he's got kin here?'

'By heaven! You're right,' snapped Carnustie. 'Why didn't I think of that? Somebody here must be close to him.'

'Maybe not,' added Gilly Joe doubtfully. 'Remember he let you shoot them down cold in the street without a word of answer.'

'Depends, doesn't it?' butted in Converse, weaving slowly on his feet. 'Maybe we didn't have the right body.'

'Get them out here,' ordered Carnustie. 'All of them. We'll use them for cover and find out if any of them are his bosom pals.'

Gabriel was watching them from inside the angled shadow of the stone chimney on the roof of the blacksmith's shop.

He had scaled the building silently in his moccasins when he heard the uproar as the bodies of the guards were discovered. It had certainly lit a fire under the remaining members of the gang and with some sense of satisfaction Gabriel hunched down and waited for the opportunity to get another of them in his sights.

He had his planned run worked out, how he would take the shot and then slide down the sloping back of the roof onto a soft dune of raised ground behind. There was a water barrel alongside the next building but one and he intended to leap up from that onto the flat roof of the house and wait his moment from there for his next shot. One by one he would bring them down.

Gabriel raised the Henry and drew a bead on the figure in the Confederate plumed hat as he had him marked out as their leader. Without a leader, he reckoned, they would be in some disarray.

But before he could pull the trigger the four men suddenly broke apart and dispersed.

He swung the rifle following their rapid path and snap-aimed; his rifle shot cracked the silence of the night. He missed by inches and saw the white-feathered plume shatter into a cloud of particles. The four fled with Carnustie spitting loud curses over his damaged finery.

Answering firing came thick and fast but Gabriel was already carrying out his plan and as the blacksmith's chimney suffered a shattering hammering of flying bullets he was already riding the roof down onto the ground.

He dropped to the ground and continued with his planned route, leaping up onto the water barrel and from there silently onto the flat roof. He was pleased to see that his limbs were beginning to ease up and the activity bringing him back his old litheness. He crawled across the roof to peer over the edge and what he saw brought him up short.

The entire town's population had been brought out from their imprisonment and they were collected in a crowd with women sobbing and clutching their children whilst their menfolk held onto their families protectively. In the midst the raiders stood, covered by the massed crowd and leaving Gabriel without an open shot.

Gabriel searched the faces below, looking for Hannah but he could not see her amongst the milling mass of people. In fact, he noted, there were quite a few of the younger females missing and he wondered if they had been held somewhere else.

There seemed to be an argument going on between the Confederate leader and a burly bearded man and Gabriel heard voices raised in anger.

'I tol' you!' roared the bearded man. 'Nothing happens to the children.'

'But nothing will, Dole,' pleaded Carnustie.

'They're just here to give us cover.'

'It's dangerous, Cap'n Jack,' snarled Dougherty. 'They could be hurt. It can't happen, I'm taking them away from this.'

He turned away and began to attempt to coax children from their parents. Neither parents nor children took kindly to the ape-like man's attempts, no matter how well intended they were and soon arguments were breaking out.

Gabriel saw his opportunity and he called into the night, 'There's six hundred of you and only four of them!'

His cry brought stillness and then a steady mumble from the crowd.

'Don't even think it,' screamed Carnustie, waving his pistol about in warning.

The tall figure of Converse, still inebriated and tired of the noisy townspeople, pushed his way clear and stood staring into the darkness, 'Come on out, Lawman. Come on, get here and face me if you got the balls. I'll rip your heart out.'

Gabriel coldly leveled his rifle as the man came clear of the covering crowd. He eased the trigger under his finger.

'Don't be such a damned fool, Converse,' shouted a small scar-faced young raider from somewhere amidst the muttering townspeople.

'Shut up, Gilly Joe, I know what I'm doing, I'll get this sucker to come out and face us like a man,' slurred the drunken Converse into the night. 'You too chickenshit, you dumb lawman? You want to know what we done to your woman? You want to come down here and find out?'

Gabriel's heart sunk at the threat as he thought of Hannah and their expectant child, then his jaw tightened and he pulled the trigger of the Henry.

The boom and flash set off a backward sway in the crowd and Converse stood separate from them for a moment, tottering unsteadily on his feet. He looked down at his chest briefly in bemusement and dropped his gun. His fingers searched his shirtfront, ripping it open to look down for a long confused minute at the leaking hole in his chest. Then he fell, as if poleaxed, facedown into the dust of the street.

A collective wail went up from the crowd, as if the rifle shot had released them from all their inhibitions and they suddenly lost all fear and in an enraged moment they fell in a wave onto the remaining gang members. Gabriel watched the whirlpool of activity as, struggling amidst screaming vengeful townspeople, Carnustie and the others vanished under the heap of people. A gun was fired but that was the only sound heard apart from the grunting cries and screams. Something animal had been set free and a collective urge filled the normally restrained townspeople with a wild desire to rend and kill. Both men and women drove into the gang members, knocking them from their feet and then gathering over them and stomping down in a frenzied assault with fists and boots and whatever came to hand.

Only the bearded man survived the attack and he threw people aside as if they were lightweight sacks of grain as he rose up with a roar and carved out a clear space for himself amongst the encroaching crowd.

Gabriel dropped from the roof edge and loped across the street towards the big man.

He arrived to find the ape-like figure stopped in his tracks as he faced a small girl holding a rag doll. The child had been separated in the maelstrom of activity in the street and something like a smile twitched across Dougherty's face at sight of her. He forgot everything and holding out his arms he went down on one knee before the child. The strange anomaly that lurked in the breast of this grotesque creature, who was not far up the food chain above a feral beast, lightened his eye and gave him cause to forget all else.

'Come here, darlin',' he crooned. 'There's nothing to fear, I'll take good care of you.'

The little girl shrunk away and held her doll tightly.

'It's all right, it really is,' promised Dougherty, the smile in his black beard coming across more as a fearsome grimace to the child. 'There, there, baby child,' he said.

Her face crumpled and she began a high-pitched tearful whine of terror.

Coming at the run and fearing to hit the girl in error if he fired, Gabriel shed his rifle and leapt across the intervening space diving full force straight into Dougherty. He struck the big man where he knelt and was off-balance and the two of them tumbled, rolling into the dust.

Gabriel felt the mass of hard muscle under him as he connected and knew he stood little chance against such a monstrous and powerful man. It had to be finished quickly if it was to be finished at all. He rolled away, going for the knife in his belt. There were still too many of the struggling crowd heaving around to risk his pistol. Rising to a crouch and facing each other, the two circled each other warily, Dougherty confident in his strength and Gabriel wary with the knife held out before him.

A low growl started in Dougherty's throat and he bared his tombstone teeth, letting them show white and savage against his black beard. His long arms swung down, the fingers almost trailing on the ground.

Gabriel realized he was being stupid about such a creature, there was no way he could beat the man. Gabriel shrugged; he stood tall and tossed the knife on the ground before them. Dougherty grunted and frowned, looking down at the knife and then up again, wondering if his opponent was offering simple surrender. He stared questioningly at Gabriel through dim eyes, one eyebrow raised in query. They were no more than six feet apart and surrounded by a now silent crowd tense with expectation.

'Shame on you, you know you're upsetting the kids, don't you?' asked Gabriel, with a harsh tone of reprimand. 'Man like you should know better.'

'Me? What? No, never,' gasped a shocked Dougherty, glaring around guiltily. 'I wouldn't do that, I couldn't.'

'Well, you're sure upsetting me.'

In one smooth movement, Gabriel drew the Colt, thumbed back the hammer and shot Dougherty straight between the eyes.

The oafish character dropped instantly, still with a question marking his features.

A few of the younger and prettier women that had been kept separate had survived.

They were led out of the shed where they had been held, many of them bruised and partially clad in torn clothes, their faces streaked with tears. Rushing forward, relatives and friends enfolded them in sympathetic arms. The storekeeper and his wife were over covering the ravaged body of their daughter with a blanket, the mother sobbing in great heart wrenching sounds of anguish. Other townsfolk wandered around aimlessly, numbed and dizzily wondering what had happened and why this storm of violence had been wreaked upon them so suddenly. In the midst of their daze many wondered at their own burst of terrible revenge and with some sense of guilt they avoided looking at the crushed results lying on the street.

'It's not good, Sheriff,' said one townsman to Gabriel. 'They beat these girls bad trying to find out who you were. Then they did God knows what else to them in there. That little wretch there was the worst,' He indicated the flattened remains of the scar faced Gilly Joe lying in the street. The two trampled bodies of the raiders lay on Main Street amongst those others of their victims, they had been beaten into scraps of flesh and bone leaving nothing surviving that was recognizable amidst the slick pools of spreading blood. It was as if Carnustie and Gilly Joe had met up with a falling boulder and been squashed flat into the earth.

The man shook his head sorrowfully, 'Holy shit! Going to take a big shovel to scrape that lot up.'

'And Hannah?' asked Gabriel, already knowing the answer.

'Best you don't look, Sheriff. She's inside with a couple of the other girls who didn't make it.'

Gabriel sagged, feeling only blankness and sudden destitution and the man reached out and steadied him.

'We'll take care of it, Sheriff,' promised the man. 'You done enough for us, now we'll take care of this for you.'

Stunned by loss, Gabriel staggered away and the man watched him go wondering what had happened to this blood soaked man with a long scalp dangling from his belt. He certainly seemed no longer at all like the Gabriel Brannigan they had all come to know.

CHAPTER TEN

HIRED ON

Gabriel wandered back northwards.

He rode randomly having taken his leave of Olive Tree Branch without a word to anyone, just saddling up early one morning and heading out. He had paused only at the row of fresh graves on the hillside overlooking the town to lay his sheriff's star on Hannah's marker.

It occurred to him then that he had not seen his mother for some years and he had half a mind to go visit her and any of his siblings that had survived the war. But it was only a vague consideration and not one that he was determined to fulfill.

He was low of heart and the promising future so suddenly snatched from him had left him full of blankness and with little sense of purpose. It was as if an expected treat so surprisingly promised, like the sun shining on the prospect of a bright new day, had been torn from him. Wounded, not in body but in mind, he shook the dust of the town from his feet and with his leaving he hoped to forget all the memory of that gladness that would now never be realized.

In such a state he rode into the twelve-mile swing station of the Moulder Post & Package Stage Line at a place called Twin Bluffs, a small post run by a single lone man and not equipped to offer Gabriel more than a drink for his horse at the trough and maybe a cup of neighborly coffee.

The post manager was a hard-bitten soul called Jesse Stax. He was a thirty-eight year old loner, dressed in a grubby shirt and a three-day growth on his chin. He worked the station in a semi hermit-like existence never asking for or receiving any furlough and only seeing humanity as it passed by his door on the stage.

Their grunted conversation had not lasted more than a few words and that hadn't disturbed Gabriel, as he was not in any state for a feeble discourse on the weather or where he was headed. It had been no more than simple introductions exchanged and the offer to help himself from the coffee pot kept going on the stove.

Gabriel was standing in the doorway of the manager's shack, leaning against the frame with a battered mug of the strong black coffee in his hand when the midday stage pulled in.

'Get me them animals changed pronto, Jesse,' hollered the driver, a husky fellow with a fringed jacket and a worn crown hat with the brim pinned up in front. Angrily he rotated the corncob pipe in his mouth with one gloved hand and with the other he prodded the shotgun guard alongside him on the seat.

The guard was hunched over and moaning pitifully.

'Come on, Buck,' goaded the driver. 'What the hell's wrong? You been greeting and groaning the whole last stretch. Your bowels playing you up again?'

'I can't...' came the weak answer.

The door of the stage began to open as a curious passenger started to get out.

'Get your danged head back in there,' roared the irascible driver. 'We ain't stopping here; soon as we get them horses changed we'll be away. You get out here you get left behind, you hear me?'

Gingerly, the passenger, a thin pasty-faced man, pulled the door shut again.

The driver looked across at Gabriel, who was watching him and he jerked an aggressive chin in query, as if to say – what the hell you looking at?

Gabriel raised his mug of coffee in salute but said nothing.

They were both interrupted as the guard suddenly keeled over and fell out of his seat and dropped heavily to the ground.

'Damn me!' cried the driver, scrambling to climb down after the fallen man. 'What in God's name? Buck! Buck, you all right?'

Gabriel strolled over, mug in hand to where the driver knelt beside his companion.

'Well, Jehosophat! Will you look here?' said the driver, looking up at Gabriel, the corncob pipe still clenched firmly between gritted teeth. 'He's up and died on me.'

'Maybe it was something you said,' Gabriel answered without expression.

'I never said nothing...' The driver arched an eyebrow as he got the jibe. 'He's been bitching about some pain or other since Bedwater Springs.'

'Well, looks like you're short of a gun up top now.'

'Damn it,' grunted the driver, staring down at his dead guard and idly straightening the corpse's jacket lapels.

'Does this mean we travel without protection?' came a female wail from inside the stage.

The driver ignored the plaint and looked up as the post manager strolled over.

'Old Buck here has passed on me, Jesse. Can you take care of him? I got to keep my schedule.'

Jesse looked down dourly at the body and nodded sad acceptance.

The driver climbed to his feet and stared into Gabriel's face, 'You working here?' he asked.

'No, sir, just passing through.'

'You want a job?'

'Doing what?'

'Riding shotgun, what do you think?'

Gabriel thought about it a long moment.

'Well, yes or no?' asked the driver impatiently.

'Do I get paid?'

'Sure you do. Time we reach end of the line at Brummington, I'll see you set up at the office.'

'Then I'll do it,' agreed Gabriel.

The driver held out a gloved hand, 'Name's Teddy Bones and you are?'

'Gabriel Branningan,' he answered taking the

offered hand.

'Pleased to make your acquaintance, Gabe. Jesse, you find anything of a personal nature on old Buck and I'll be by to pick it up next time. He got any cash on him, although I doubt that, then remember it goes each way 'tween you and me.'

'That's pretty uncivilized,' came a mincing male complaint from inside the dark recesses of the stage. 'Stealing from the dead.'

'Damn you!' roared Teddy. 'It ain't stealing; me and Jesse are his legal inheritors. It's the custom out here; you die on the job you share out your worldly possessions with your nearest and dearest. And old Buck was a dear friend, almost as close as a brother, ain't that right, Gabe?' he asked, turning to Gabriel and fixing him with a glaring eye.

'If you say so.'

'There,' snapped Teddy. 'You have it so off my new travelling assistant and bodyguard, so you inside there, shut your trap and keep your nose out of stage line business.'

'You're ready to go, Teddy,' mumbled Jesse.

'Right you are,' said Teddy, clambering up over the wheel and into the driving seat. 'Come on, Gabe, we ain't got time for any more tomfoolery.'

Gabriel fetched his horse and tied it off at the luggage compartment at the rear then climbed up onto the driving seat alongside Teddy.

'You any good with that?' growled Teddy around his pipe and nodding at the shotgun in the seat well.

Gabriel shucked the weapon open and checked the load, 'I'll manage,' he said.

'Good enough. Hold on inside we're heading out. So long, Jesse,' with that he whipped up the team and the Concord jolted into action.

The stage line was one of the small set-ups that still operated outside any of the major railroad lines, it came down from Cold Fargo City and went all the way to Brummington running a regular for local mail and passengers.

Teddy told Gabriel all this as they jounced along, the Concord swaying on it's leather straps and bouncing over every rut and gopher hole in the trail as he drove the team on at a fast lick.

'It's owned by Mrs. Abigail Moulder and her daughter Evie,' explained Teddy around the pipe stuck forever in his mouth. 'Mrs. Moulder's a tough old gal but straight as a die, so don't mind her manner. Hell, she puts up with me, so she must be okay.'

Gabriel could hear gasping squeaks and moans of grievance from inside as the coach dipped and juddered, bouncing violently on the rough road. None of which seemed to bother Teddy who just roared at his team and urged them on even faster.

He cast an evil looking eye at Gabriel and grinned, 'Like peas in a pod,' he chuckled, obviously taking pleasure in his passenger's discomfort. 'I got Miss Evie's financey inside, him and a widder woman from up in Cold Fargo. He's a particular asshole and like to give me trouble the whole trip.'

'Remind me never to upset you I take a stage ride,' said Gabriel, clutching desperately onto the seat rail before he was thrown over the side.

'Yeah, it never does to do that,' growled Teddy,

slapping the reins and taking a corner so fast the coach came up on two wheels.

'The widder lost her hubby up there,' Teddy went on, hollering against the rolling sound of the coach and the pound of the horse team. 'Got hisself shot down, so they say. Some kind of venture man with attitude it appears, laid out when he had a run-in with this ugly son-of-a-bitch with wooden teeth. Now can you believe that? A set of wood dentures, hell, I thought they went out with bearskin hats.'

Gabriel who had been concentrating on hanging on for dear life suddenly took an interest in the driver's gossip.

'He have a name, this shooting fellow?'

Teddy looked over sharply as he recognized the tone in Gabriel's voice.

'I believe so. Feller called himself Colonel Lomas Chain, late of the regular army.'

'Goddamn!' sighed Gabriel. 'Bastard upped his rank.'

'You know this boy?'

'That I do,' said Gabriel grimly.

Teddy sucked on his pipe and mused a moment, 'That don't sound good.'

'It ain't,' Gabriel agreed but would say no more.

Teddy shook his head and decided it was none of his affair, 'Anyways, the snot-nose in there aims to marry Miss Evie. Some lawyer name of Tobias Grimes and you ask me, the pair deserve each other, old Mrs. Moulder done spoil that gal something terrible and you ain't going to like her none, I guarantee.'

CHAPTER ELEVEN

RIDING ON TOP

Teddy's assessment proved to be on the money and as they pulled into Brummington, Gabriel had his first encounter with Abigail and Evie Moulder.

The owner was striking a pose outside the stage office as Teddy pushed on the brake and pulled the Concord to a halt. She certainly gave off the air that Teddy had described, a stern, no-nonsense, sharp-featured older lady with white hair and arms folded across her flat chest and standing on two legs in tight riding pants spread wide in a masculine kind of manner. A six-shooter sat in a holster draped around her middle and she laid into Teddy the minute his team was still.

'Where you been, Teddy Bones? You're twenty-five minutes late. You know I like to keep a firm timetable here.'

'Sure thing, ma'am,' said Teddy, not in the least fazed by her abrasive approach. 'Old Buck went and died on me of natural courses over at Twin Forks, had to take on this feller here as shotgun.'

Abigail gave Gabriel a long searching look, 'Uhuh,'

she grunted. 'And what would your name be?'

'Gabriel Brannigan, ma'am.'

'Never heard of you and maybe that's good and maybe it ain't.'

The coach door swung open and the pale-faced male passenger stumbled out, his once neat suit rumpled and pomaded hair windswept 'Great heavens!' he sighed. 'What a journey.'

'That you Tobias?' snapped Abigail. 'What's the matter, you been sick?'

'*Sick?* It's a wonder I'm still alive, Mrs. Moulder. This driver of yours is a most inept and unruly character, rude and rough and he drives that vehicle as if the devil himself were on his heels.'

Abigail allowed herself a slight smile, 'Been laying it down, has he?'

The door to the office burst open and a tall; thin, ungainly creature with buckteeth and a horse face ran out. She was dressed in boldly clashing striped silks and wearing an extravagantly feathered bonnet and she let out with an ear-splitting shriek of greeting, '*Tobias!*

She brushed past Abigail and flew at the skinny guy, almost bowling him over, 'My dearest,' she oozed, falling into his arms. 'It's been so long.'

Teddy gave Gabriel a wry look, 'That's Evie Moulder,' he advised unnecessarily.

Gabriel climbed down from his seat and tipping his hat he reached into the interior of the coach, 'Ma'am,' he said, offering his hand to the lady in widow weeds sitting inside.

As Tobias Grimes and Evie Moulder fluttered

noisily at each other, making a great show of it for the entire busy street to see, Gabriel helped the widow down.

'You okay, ma'am?' Gabriel asked solicitously.

'My bag?' the woman mumbled.

'Sure thing,' said Gabriel going to the luggage boot. 'Which one?'

'Those leather ones are mine, the suitcase and the trunk,' butted in Tobias, reaching across the widow and pointing. 'See that they're delivered to the hotel, will you?'

Gabriel ignored him and he repeated to the widow, 'Which bag, lady?'

'Excuse me, my man,' snorted Tobias haughtily. 'You'll see my luggage is unharmed, won't you? Best leather brought in St. Louis at great expense.'

'The carpet bag,' the widow whispered.

Gabriel heaved the leather suitcase and trunk out and dropped them unceremoniously onto the dust as he levered out the poorer looking carpetbag.

'Hey there!' burst out Tobias, turning to Abigail. 'You see that, you see what he did with my bags? I must say, Abigail, not only have I suffered the torments of hell in this carriage of yours but now these rough fellows are abusing my goods.'

'Well, Tobias, if they're that precious to you,' said Abigail coolly. 'Best you carry them yourself.'

'You for the hotel, ma'am?' Gabriel asked the widow.

She inclined her head and Gabriel noted a flash of night-dark hair and a steady glance at him from under the veil that covered her face.

'If you'll allow, I'll see you over there,' Gabriel offered.

'I'm obliged,' she said softly in an eastern accent that was refined and of a class beyond the wild character of the Frontier.

Gabriel hoisted her bag and looked over at the large sign that read 'Gossamer's Hotel and Eating House'.

'This way, ma'am. Say, Teddy!' he called over his shoulder. 'Will you see to my horse? I'll be back shortly, we got some wages to discuss.'

'What am I?' spat Teddy in disgust. 'Your damned livery boy now? Remember *who* hired who here.'

His eye met Abigail Moulder's and Teddy saw the sparkle there, 'I like him,' she said quietly.

'Well, that's a real blessing,' grumbled Teddy, gnawing on his pipe. 'I thought maybe you was going to rip me a new one for Buck dying on my watch and me going off the reservation to hire some drifter.'

'Come on inside, you old reprobate. I think you need some refreshment.'

'Now you're beginning to sound like a civilized human being at last,' grunted Teddy, following her into the office.

Gabriel rang the bell in the hotel lobby and as they waited for the clerk to appear he studied the widow.

'Sorry to hear of your recent loss, ma'am.'

'Thank you,' she said, lifting the veil from her face and looking at him with a pair of deep blue eyes tinged with violet.

She was a beauty all right, Gabriel decided. A

gentle face, almost rectangular, with generous pink lips and a peachy complexion that glowed with a soft sheen under the fall of hair as dark in contrast as night is to day.

'I'm Gabriel Brannigan,' he said.

'Yes, I heard. And I'm Mrs. April Turner, pleased to meet you Mister Brannigan and thank you again for your assistance.'

'Your husband played the tables?'

She sighed, 'He did, much to my distress and his ignoble end.'

'It was an argument over some arrangement?'

'I believe so,' her attention fluttering away as she searched for the absent clerk.

'The other man involved, did your husband know him well?'

She studied him acutely at his continuing queries, 'Why the interest, Mister Brannigan?'

'I believe I might be acquainted with the fellow.'

'Is that so? Well, all I know is that he is a military gentleman, a Colonel Chain and a man of some ill repute. As you can appreciate, I have little to say of value in respect of the man and would rather avoid discussion of him.'

'Yes, ma'am, I understand. But if it is the same Lomas Chain that I knew, then I have equal feelings towards him.'

'Ugly creature,' she said in a momentary show of disgust. 'My husband and he had some kind of deal involving the red men's land, something to do with an ore discovery although not much was said about the matter in my hearing, so I know very little of the details.'

'Which Indians might that be, ma'am?'

'The fiery savages of the Sioux nation, I believe.'

'That so?' mused Gabriel as the clerk came out of a back room and interrupted his questions.

'Good day, lady and gentleman. Is it a double that's required?' he asked breezily.

'No, sir,' Gabriel answered. 'Room for the lady and separate one for me. I'm just hired on by the stagecoach so I'll be by with my possibles later.'

'Of course,' smarmed the clerk, eyeing April and thinking things he didn't ought to. 'And will madam be staying long?'

'I'm not sure just yet,' said April shyly.

'Well, I hope we can encourage you to stay with us here in Brummington; we are a growing town with business booming and much opportunity. Especially for ladies of quality and charm such as yourself.'

'We'll see,' whispered April.

'You allow me, Miss April,' said Gabriel. 'I'll see your bag to your room and then head back to the stage office.'

'Of course, thank you kindly.'

He handed her the key when they stood on the landing outside her room.

'I did not think to find a gentleman so considerate this far west, Mister Brannigan.'

'My pleasure, ma'am, and its Gabriel, if you've a mind.'

She offered a quick smile, 'Obliged indeed, Gabriel.'

'Ma'am, I'd be glad if you'd take supper with me

tonight?'

She cocked her head to one side, 'Perhaps not, Gabriel. I am so recently widowed it might be considered unseemly to be seen out dining unchaperoned with a stranger so soon.'

Gabriel offered her a tight smile, 'There's many that would barely notice, I'm sure.'

'Well, maybe at a later date.'

'Of course. Good day, ma'am.'

Later, in the warmth of evening, Gabriel sat at his hotel window, feet up on the nightstand and watched the town come slowly into its nightlife. The street below was full of the creak of passing wagons and the soft hoof beat of solitary riders. Not far off the saloon jangle of a tinny piano and the tobacco muted noise of laughter and conversation carried on the night air. The scent of cooking supper came up from the hotel kitchen and Gabriel wondered lazily if he should make his way down to the restaurant for a meal.

But Gabriel was comfortably enjoying the mellow and reassuring hustle of the town and instead he sat and took in the passersby on the street beneath his window. He saw Tobias Grimes and Evie, arm in arm, she with a tiny open parasol on her shoulder and strolling as if out on a parkway promenade instead of a dog-dropped cow town sidewalk. Both held their noses high with a show of inherent distaste for the rough odors of horse droppings and dust that invaded the evening air.

Gabriel smiled at their ostentatious display and was surprised when they both suddenly turned off and made their way into a dark alley to disappear from his view. He was leaning forward for a better view when he noted the shawl-clad figure of April Turner as she made her way out of the hotel and across the road. Her solitary figure hurried on purposefully and as Gabriel watched, she paused a minute, straightening her shoulders before entering the nearest saloon, a brightly lit place called The Broken Bucket. Full of curiosity, Gabriel was quickly on his feet and strapping on his pistol before he left his room to follow her.

The saloon was a busy place, the line of the bar along one side set with drinkers shoulder to shoulder along the whole length. Cigarette smoke lined the ceiling and the lamps glowed hazily in the fog. There was the noise of easy chatter and to one side lay tables and chairs occupied by sitting drinkers and a solitary card game in progress. A few buxom ladies in feathers supplied company and also served up drinks to the seated company.

Gabriel stood at the swing doors and surveyed the interior looking for April.

He saw her alone at a table towards the rear and no longer looking like a woman encased in grieving widowhood.

She had cast off her covering shawl and underneath wore an off-the-shoulder sky blue gown that did much to display her attributes. Her dark hair and the creamy skin of her shoulders shone in the waxy light of the lamps and a pair of drape earrings sparkled at her ears and gleamed silver against her dark shoulder-length hair. Her bosom had been elevated enough to render a swelling cleavage that was home to a small diamond necklace and her bare arms moved with dexterous ease as she nimbly ran out a pack of cards, spreading them wide before folding them down and executing a skillful riffling shuffle. It was all done with the aplomb of long practice.

Men gathered quickly at sight of the inviting female and before long a game was in progress with April dealing the hands. Gabriel ordered up a beer and stood at the tail end of the bar and watched April as she slowly and steadily built up a respectable pile of cash at her elbow. She flashed a genial smile often and kept up a line of patter that obviously allowed her fellow players to lose with no sign of discontent.

Gabriel shook his head at the complete change to the timid creature he had assisted from the coach.

It only started to turn rancorous when the owner came out from behind the busy bar to see the lone woman. He was a burly figure with garters on his sleeves and stiff white collar and cuffs to his striped shirt. He wore a diamond pinned tie and favored a broad mustache and slicked down center-parted head of hair that was so side-shorn that he appeared to be wearing a wig. A thick cigar jutted from his pugnacious lips and he frowned at April from under heavy eyebrows before swaggering over to her table.

'Excuse me, lady, but what d'you think you're doing?' he growled and April looked up to deliver him an engaging smile.

'Dear sir,' she said, her voice as mellifluous as an evening songbird. 'You must be the owner. Pray forgive my intrusion without permission, I just could not resist.'

'I don't know who you are, dearie, but we have an understanding here. I already have a dealer on the premises and I don't need no more.'

There was complaint from the rest of the table as most of the men were only too happy with April's company, in fact hopefuls were queuing up to take any vacant places.

'Firstly,' said April, a touch sharply. 'I am not your 'dearie', sir. I am late of Cold Fargo where I played at The Excelsior and The Grand Monarch, both establishments that I'm sure you will have heard of. I have held tables there for the past six months and were it not for the untimely demise of my late husband I should enjoy continuing the pleasant association I had with both owners. If you doubt my credentials I am sure they will oblige with references.'

The owner was too stunned for a moment to reply and his heavy brows wormed into indecision.

'I fully understand house rules,' April continued. 'And shall be sure to accommodate you with the normal percentage on closing down the table.'

'Well...' fumbled the owner, unsure of how to handle this quite elegant and forthright creature. Gabriel was also surprised by her confidence after experiencing the shy widow he had met earlier.

'I am Mrs. April Turner,' she said holding out a limp hand in a queenly manner. 'And you are...'

'You can't let this continue, Barnaby,' interrupted a sharp-featured dandyish character that had come up on the owner's elbow.

Barnaby shifted the cigar from one side of his

mouth to the other as he took in the gathered crowd of hopefuls and estimated their prospective pokes. 'I ain't so sure, Waxford,' he said.

'But we have an agreement,' complained Waxford, who was obviously the regular saloon dealer and not about to be dispossessed of his place.

'Yes but this here lady is drawing something of a following and if she comes as highly recommended as she says...'

'No matter,' barked the dealer angrily. 'You can't just forget our standing arrangement based on a pretty piece of ass that spouts goddamned fairy tales.'

Barnaby turned on him aggressively, 'This here is my place,' he growled. 'And I'll do as I please. You take your seat and shut up or get the hell out right now. In fact,' he said, turning back to the pleasantly smiling April. 'I reckon your employ is already terminated as it is.'

'God's teeth!' snapped the dealer. 'I won't allow it, you can't just throw me out like that, just because some hussy turns up showing her tits and turning your head.'

There was a collective rustle of complaint from the watchers at the crude comments and April momentarily arched an annoyed eyebrow.

'Now, now, boys,' she said. 'Let's not fall out, why don't we let Mister Waxford here continue at his table and whoever comes in with the best cash turnover across the evening continues to hold the post. Is that a fair hand?'

'No, no,' said Waxford, looking around at the

eager hopefuls gathered around April. 'That's no game, I ain't got the looks to compete with a pretty face.'

Barnaby was beginning to enjoy the competition and a half smile played around his cigar, 'He has a point on the looks score. What do you say, Miss April?'

'How about this then?' said April. 'Why don't we cut for it, high card wins the spot.'

'Sounds right enough to me,' said Barnaby. 'You both being of the gambling sort.'

'All right,' agreed Waxford nervously. 'But a new deck, not the one she's holding.'

'Of course,' agreed April. 'Bring it on.'

The sealed pack was brought over by one of the bar girls and another of the seated players broke the seal and made a swift shuffle.

'I hope you will take this in the spirit intended and will handle it fairly, Mister Waxford,' said April, eyeing him from under lowered lids. 'For you are about to lose your place here.'

'The hell you say,' spat Waxford. 'The day I lose to some high-toned fancy hooker is the day I turn up my toes.'

Gabriel moved forward through the crowd, irritated by the man's continuing foul and insulting language.

'I think you'd better curb your tongue and be respectful to the lady, mister, before someone curbs it for you,' he warned as he came up on the table.

Heads turned and April looked at Gabriel with a surprised smile.

'Good evening, Gabriel,' she said.

'Evening, ma'am.'

'Who's this?' blustered Waxford. 'This your pimp, is it?'

'I assure you not,' April said quickly. 'Mister Brannigan is a newly met friend and indeed more pleasant and well mannered than you, sir. Now will you cut the cards?'

Waxford drew a nine of clubs and there was a sigh of relief as April confidently pulled out a jack of diamonds.

'Damn your eyes!' cursed Waxford, turning away in angry disgust.

'Welcome to The Broken Bucket, Miss April,' said Barnaby, a greasy smile cracking his face.

'Why, thank you, sir,' April answered calmly and she was invaded by a flood of congratulations from those surrounding the table. Her blue eyes avoided them all and held onto Gabriel's over the gathered men.

'Will you join us, Gabriel?' she asked.

'Thank you no, ma'am,' Gabriel answered. 'I'm not much of a gambling man but I'd be pleased to walk you back when you're done here.'

'That would be most pleasant,' she agreed with a smile.

'I don't think so!' cried Waxford, pulling a derringer from the shoulder holster under his coat.

The crowd parted quickly with cries of alarm and men tumbled into each other in desperation to get out of the line of fire.

'I ain't playing second fiddle to no scabby bitch,

not on your life I ain't.'

Gabriel's Colt was in his hand faster than the blink of an eye, 'Put it away,' he ordered coldly. 'Before I put you down.'

Waxford spun on him, a sneer of anger marking his face, 'Damn you, you louse,' he screamed, poking his gun in Gabriel's face.

Gabriel's pistol cracked and a jet of flame and smoke leapt across the room. Waxford's hand flew apart in a bloody shatter of bone and tissue, his derringer flying up and away across the room in a spinning parabolic arc.

The gambler howled in pain and staggered back, clutching at the shredded remains hanging from his wrist.

'Somebody best go get the doc,' observed Barnaby in a bland tone. 'If you're going to bleed, Waxford, don't do it on my clean floor go hang your hand over a spittoon, will you?'

Without taking his eyes from the dealer, Gabriel spun his Colt in a fancy fashion on the trigger guard and allowed the smoking weapon to drop back in his holster.

'Anybody got complaint?' he asked.

'Only old Waxford, I think,' mused Barnaby, shifting his cigar and staring down his nose at the whimpering dealer. 'It's was a fair fight, no question of it. Waxford drew first.'

'Well I do believe I am done for the night,' said April, rising tiredly from her seat. 'If you gentlemen will excuse me, that is enough excitement for a new girl on her first night. Barnaby, if I may, I shall return on the morrow and these gentlemen can attempt to reclaim their losses is they so wish.'

She gave them all a brilliant smile that not one of them could deny and then turned to Gabriel and held out her hand.

'If you will, Mister Brannigan?'

'You sure had me fooled,' said Gabriel, as they left the saloon and stepped out into the street.

'I did, how so?' asked April, glad to be outside and breathing deeply of the night air.

'I took you for a fearful widow lady and certainly not a high flying card player.'

'It never does to show your full hand, Gabriel.'

'I can see that.'

They were strolling slowly, April with her arm draped casually through Gabriel's.

'You are indeed a forceful man,' she said. 'Thank you again for your help back there.'

'You're welcome. The man should not have spoken like that, he was an ignorant fool and I took umbrage at his foul mouth.'

'Indeed you did, he will never deal cards again but I'm sure you knew that when you shot him through the hand.'

'Just desserts, ma'am, he had it coming.'

'And so the cards are dealt,' she said in a sudden philosophical tone. 'And I always play them as they fall. We shall be lovers, Gabriel, if you so wish?'

Gabriel was startled by her brazenness but he did not allow himself to show it, 'Did you get into gambling through your late husband?' he asked, reminding her of her recent state.

'Ah, yes,' she sighed. 'My sadly deceased other half. But no, it was my mother showed me how to handle the gaming tables back east. My husband, I fear, was not much as men go and I was foolish to take his hand when offered but then, he had his moments.'

Gabriel was pensive as he silently considered her bold offer of a relationship. He had not considered another woman since Hannah and in the sullenness that he had felt after her death any desire for the act seemed to have eluded him.

'I should say,' he explained uncomfortably. 'I too was married before but she is dead now.'

'Mm,' she nodded understanding. 'You liked her, I can tell that. But have no fear, Gabriel, all will be well between us.'

'You're that confident,' Gabriel observed with some surprise.

'When you've been on the edge as often as I have, you learn to grasp the moment, Gabriel. It is all like a hand of cards and at some stage you must risk all. You assess the odds, count percentages and see what the other players hold in your mind's eyes and then boldly test them with coin until you show what you own yourself and allow fortune it's final say.'

'That's right poetic, I've never seen it like that I have to say. Not seen life in a turn of cards.'

'It's all a game, Gabriel, is it not?' she smiled with that coy smile of hers. 'I just hope you're not the joker in my pack.'

With that she spun him around and kissed him on the lips, her tongue playing inside his mouth. Gabriel held her close and felt the warm energy of her body pressed up against him. His hands enclosed her small waist, so tiny that his fingers almost met at her back and she panted a sighing breath before latching onto him again. Her kisses were fervent and full of desire and her hands explored his back tightening on his buttocks and drawing him in tight between her welcoming thighs. He was glad it was late and the street was deserted as she clung close in this fashion and stayed holding him with desperate urgency for a long time.

'Now,' she rasped, the breath coming fast in her nostrils. 'Now, you will take me. Be bold and strong, Gabriel, as it has been a long time since I have felt a real man inside me.'

CHAPTER TWELVE

MEETING UP

'Hot damn what have you been up to?' asked Teddy, taking in Gabriel's disheveled appearance and darkly ringed eyes.

'Had trouble sleeping,' mumbled Gabriel as he sluggishly heaved himself up into the driving seat of the Concord. It had been a long night and April's demands had certainly tested his resources to the full. She slept now in her room over in the hotel and when an aching Gabriel stumbled from her bed and struggled to find his boots, he studied the contented smile showing on her lips in the dawn light and knew that she was truly a bedfellow like no other he had ever known before.

'Well, we'll soon shake the doldrums out of you on this ride,' chuckled Teddy as he stuffed his corncob with dark tobacco.

'We going all the way?'

'Sure are,' said Teddy. All the way to Cold Fargo.'

'Well, go easy on me, will you, Teddy?' begged Gabriel.

'Don't know if I can,' Teddy answered, setting fire

to his pipe with a flaring Lucifer. 'We got company this ride.'

Gabriel raised questioning eyebrows, 'Who's that?'

'Couple of old friends. Evie and that Tobias fellow, seems she is intent on picking out a wedding dress and it has to be the danged best that Texas has to offer, so we has to go to Monsewer La Plank's establishment up in Cold Fargo.'

'Thought that fellow Tobias had enough of your driving his last ride.'

Teddy looked at him slyly over the smoldering pipe, 'He ain't seen nothing yet. Poor bastard's got foisted on the ride by Evie and Mrs. Moulder and not a word he can say about it.'

'Oh, God!' sighed Gabriel, fearing the effect of Teddy's venomous feeling's towards Evie's pompous beau and the result of the old hand's doubtless vengeful driving on his already jaded nerves.

Just then a bright and breezy Evie gushed out from the stage line office followed by a disconsolate Tobias and stern looking Abigail Moulder.

'Are we ready?' asked Evie in a high-pitched trill. 'Is everybody set. Oh, I am so excited. Come now, Tobias, do not look so down. It will be an adventure and I cannot wait to see the city.'

'Yes, dear,' mumbled Tobias, casting a wary glance up at Teddy on the driving seat who leered back at him through a cloud of pipe smoke.

Abigail brushed past the two travellers and heaved the canvas mail sack up to Gabriel, 'No fooling around this trip, Teddy,' she barked. 'You haul this rig up there and bring my girl back double quick, y'hear?'

'You got it, Mrs. Moulder,' Teddy promised.

'Please, please,' begged Tobias. 'I do trust we may travel with caution. Really, I am not fit for any rough transport, I am already all bruises and bumps.'

'Don't you worry none,' promised Teddy. 'Be like riding in a baby carriage. Kind of get you in mood for later on, Mister Tobias.'

Evie hee-hawed a shrill laugh at the oblique suggestion of such married bliss, 'Oh, do come on, Tobias. I am eager to be going.' She turned to her mother and offered her a peck on either cheek, 'Thank you so much, Mummy. We shall pick out a most wonderful gown at Monsieur La Planque's with the money, I'm sure of it, bless you for being so kind.'

'You just enjoy yourself, daughter. Come back safe.'

'Yes, yes,' fluttered Evie as Tobias helped her up into the coach interior. 'Goodbye, goodbye.'

'*Hey there!* Head out, you damned hacks,' bawled Teddy, slapping the reins down and setting the coach off with enough of a jerk so that Tobias barely had time to mount and in doing so, stumbled and fell inside with a shriek of despair.

'Oh, don't be so silly, beloved,' they heard Evie reprimand as she leaned out of the coach window and fluttered a handkerchief in farewell to her mother. "Bye, mama. Goodbye, dear mama!'

'But I am tumbled head over by that wretched man,' complained Tobias. 'Look at my sleeve; it is all dusty from the floor in here. Such filth! Why is the thing never swept out?'

Gabriel stole a look at the grinning Teddy and

said, 'Your damned horns are showing, you evil old man.'

'Never could abide a fol-de-rol asshole like that,' growled Teddy.

Gabriel was so beat that even Teddy's uneven attempts to hit every bump in the road could not keep him awake and the rocking stage soon put him into a doze. He rolled in his seat and dreamed over the pleasant taste of the past night, recalling every pleasurable moment of April's tender mercies.

They pulled into the Twin Forks station to find the dour Jesse Stax ready and waiting with a new team.

'How you doing, Jesse?' called Teddy as they drew in. 'You get old Buck planted alright?'

'I did,' answered Jesse, working with bridles and traces as he brought the new team in line.

'He leave us anything?'

'Nope, poor fellow didn't have no more than a two dollar pocket watch and the clothes he stood in. Even his danged boots had holes in them.'

'Too bad,' spat Teddy, twisting his corncob in his jaw. 'Buck never was the pecuniary type, fool drank it as soon as he got it.'

'Disgusting behavior!' they heard Tobias mutter from inside.

'Y'all comfortable in there?' asked Teddy, with a fake show of concern.

'We are, Mister Bones,' mumbled Evie shakily. 'Although I do feel a trifle unwell from all the swaying.'

'Like a ship on the sea, missie. That's what we

is,' supplied Teddy with a broad grin in Gabriel's direction. 'Just adrift on an ocean of sand.'

'Had a group pass through earlier,' advised Jesse as he worked reins through brass loops.

Teddy waited for more but it was not forthcoming. 'So?' he asked.

'Didn't like the look of them,' said Jesse.

'You think they is up to no good?' asked Gabriel.

'Maybe,' Jesse answered. 'Couldn't rightly say.'

'Well then what can you say?' barked Teddy. 'They look like they was going to a christening or a hanging, which is it?'

'Five of them,' said Jesse as if that answered the question.

'And...' pressed Teddy.

'Just,' Jesse shrugged. 'Had a feeling, is all.'

'What's this?' asked Tobias, leaning out of the coach window. 'Are we in some sort of danger?'

'Just you stick your head back inside,' growled Teddy. 'We'll let you know if your precious hide is at risk.'

'It is not myself I am concerned for,' complained an annoyed Tobias. 'My dear fiancé here is all I think of.'

'Nothing to fear there then,' whispered Teddy. 'One look at her and any road agent's about to surrender to the first hanging judge he meets.'

'That's it,' called Jesse, slapping the lead horse on the rump. 'You're set to go.'

'Right y'are,' called Teddy, whacking the reins and setting out. 'So long, Jesse.'

Gabriel watched the lone station keeper disappear behind them in the cloud of dust that marked their wake.

'Beats me how he holds to such a lonesome task,' he observed. 'Man must like his own company a whole lot for sure.'

'Lost his mother, wife and five kids to Indians,' said Teddy, snarling around his pipe as he worked the team into a trot. 'Ain't been right since.'

'Too bad,' mumbled Gabriel, lifting the shotgun and placing it across his lap.

'You think there's something in this team of riders?' asked Teddy.

'Couldn't say,' shrugged Gabriel. 'Best keep an eye out though.'

They were waiting for them at the foot of a red-rock mesa and crossed the road in front in a staggered line.

'How you want to play it?' asked Teddy grimly.

'Straight on through,' said Gabriel.

'Hell, yes,' agreed Teddy, leaning forward in his seat and bunching both handfuls of reins tight in his fists.

The five spread out across the road were wearing bandanas over their lower faces and calmly walked their horses out to block the way. One of the men carried a long-barreled sniper rifle propped on his thigh and there was no doubt that the group meant business.

There was no way to avoid them and they had chosen their ambush site well. On one side stood the rising crag of the rocky mesa and on the other a drop from the flat trail that no stage could handle without rolling over.

'Goddamn!' Teddy was muttering around his tightly clenched pipe as he spat out his tension on the team. 'Goddamn, goddamn! Haul on you sorry assed critters, come on let's move it.'

The stagecoach lurched forward with an extra turn of speed as Teddy encouraged the animals with his vituperative string of curses and a slap of reins. Inside, his passengers, thrown back at the sudden acceleration offered up cries of woe.

'What are you doing out there, you madman?' wailed Tobias.

'Best keep your heads down,' Gabriel called to him. 'We got company ahead.'

Tobias poked his nose out of the window and saw the waiting crew of patient bandits, 'Oh, no,' he moaned.

'What is it, Tobias? What is it?' asked Evie with a note of desperation in her voice.

'I fear we are about to engage with some unsavory sorts, my dear.'

'How many are there?'

'Five of the dastards.'

'Oh, dear God, what shall we do?'

'You must be strong, my love. It will be all right, I'm sure.'

'But what if they force themselves on me? All of them, taking me without mercy, I shall be ruined.'

'Not a chance in hell of that,' growled Teddy, hearing her strident sob of complaint, even over the rumble of the stage.

They were nearing now and Gabriel raised the

shotgun ready in both hands.

'Stop!' bawled the lead bandit. 'You hold up there or get your desserts.'

The outlaw horses were beginning to skitter nervously as it was apparent the stagecoach was not slowing down and coming head on at full speed.

'They ain't stopping,' cried the sniper, lowering his rifle to aim at Teddy.

'Go on!' urged Gabriel.

'What you think I'm doing, you danged fool,' grunted Teddy.

They swept in amongst the outlaws and Gabriel let go with both barrels at the man with the rifle. The load caught the fellow mid-section and blew him clear off his horse to fall in a cloud of dust as the rest of the bandits replied with a burst of fire. But their horses were rearing away and the shots only winged loudly past the two on the drive seat.

'*Yeehaw!*' yelled Teddy wild with relief and excitement as they burst through the ambush.

Gabriel rotated in his seat and drew out his Henry rifle from it scabbard stored on the roof behind.

The chase was on and Gabriel leveled his rifle across the bucking roof of the coach as the riders came on behind, driving their horses mercilessly.

'They ain't giving up,' grunted Gabriel.

'Neither am I,' replied Teddy, a glint in his eye as he kept the team going at full gallop.

The coach veered and zigzagged at the speed, it's tail end slewing on the track and a trail of dust billowing out from under the spinning wheels.

'Get on you miserable nags!' bellowed Teddy.

'Hell for leather, you pesky deadbeats.'

Gabriel heard the bang of following firearms and the zip of passing lead. A long splintered channel burst out of the woodwork of the roof alongside his elbow as a lucky bullet struck and he compressed his lips as he tried to bring his barrel to aim on the riders.

It was nigh impossible for either side to take accurate aim; both parties were jiggled and thrown about by their speeding passage over the uneven road. Gabriel shook his head in irritation but fired the rifle anyway, hoping to deter even if he could not hit anything.

Repeated, high-pitched screams came from inside the coach and Gabriel was undecided if they came from either Evie or Tobias.

A gopher hole or jutting rock turned one of the lead horses and it lunged sideways crashing into its partner on the paired team. Both animals sheered off and the following creatures pushed on straight ahead, losing pace as they miss-stepped.

'Whoa, there!' hollered Teddy, hauling on the reins as he tried to correct the line. 'Get back here.'

The front horse stumbled and started to go down dragging its partner with it, the team coming on behind lunged and jumped, crashing into the leaders and Teddy knew there was no stopping the immjnent disaster.

'We're going,' he bellowed.

Both he and Gabriel leapt free as the inevitable happened and with the sudden halt of forward movement the stage freewheeled on and pivoted over, turning in a slow sideways spin that churned up a bow-wave of dust. The coach crashed onto its side with driver and guard falling away and slamming into pillows of dust on either side before rolling on.

They were lucky, the pair of them, each side of the road was banked with soft dunes, and spitting dust but unhurt, Gabriel rose to his knees. Shaking his numbed head to clear it, he searched the road behind and saw the oncoming bandits looming towards them through the dust.

His rifle was gone, lost as he jumped. All he had was the Colt in his gun belt and he drew it now, stretching his arm out to take careful aim.

He fired twice and was pleased to see one of the men flip in the saddle and crouch forward over his horse's neck.

Teddy was helping a battered looking Evie who was trying to clamber from the overturned stage door and muttering plaintively, 'Help me, help me.'

As a shaky Tobias poked his head up from one of the windows and stared around dizzily, Gabriel knew it was no good to resist any longer, they were outnumbered by guns and he let his Colt slide back into its holster and stood with hands held high as the robbers rode up.

Their leader fretted on his sweating horse and rode it up and down before the surrendered Gabriel.

'What's the matter with you people?' he snarled irritably from behind his mask. 'Couldn't you see we was road agents? Don't you know you're supposed to stop at a hold-up? Now look what you done,' he gestured wildly at the wrecked coach. 'Damn fools.'

He was a figure dressed all in black, doubtless to appear more menacing, but in his state of annoyance all he appeared to be was a complaining felon bitching pointlessly.

'Well, you got us stopped, didn't you?' Gabriel answered coolly.

'*You!* You peckerwood,' roared the leader. 'You got one of my boys shot dead and another one winged, I ought to cut you down where you stand.'

'So what do you want with us anyway? We ain't carrying anything of value,' interrupted Teddy.

The leader drew a deep breath and looked them over, letting his eyes roam from Gabriel to the aggressive stance of Teddy and the willowy figure of Evie with her fancy hat askew and her dress torn and rumpled.

'Which one of you is Tobias Grimes?' asked the leader.

Gabriel and Teddy looked at each other curiously.

'What you want with him?' asked Teddy.

'I'm the one asking questions,' bellowed the outlaw. 'Just tell me, which of you is him?'

Gabriel stole a look over to the coach but there was no sign of Tobias, 'Well, it ain't me,' he said.

'Nor me,' added Teddy. 'And it sure ain't her,' he added, nodding towards Evie.

'Baines, go look in the coach,' the leader ordered one of his remaining men.

'Hey, boss,' said the one called Baines, tilting his head and leering at Evie. 'She's a sprightly enough looking little miss, ain't she? What you say, lady, you like a ride back with me?'

'Please,' begged Evie nervously. 'I beg of you, do not abuse me. I am a virgin about to be wed and cannot abide the thought of being deflowered here, like this out on the road.'

'Are you kidding me,' growled the outlaw leader. 'Heck! I'd rather take my pleasure with Baines there.'

Frowning over the questionable compliment, Baines ambled his horse over to the coach and peered inside and then he burst out with a bellowing laugh, 'He's here, boss. Looking a sight worse for wear an' all, ain't you, fella?.'

'Get him out of there.'

'Come on, Grimes,' the outlaw ordered, pointing his pistol in through the window. 'Haul ass out here.'

'I'm coming, I'm coming,' whimpered Tobias, appearing with both hands raised high.

'Get their guns, Houston,' the leader ordered his remaining rider. 'And then see to Ringo,' he added belatedly as his eye fell on the wounded rider sagging in the saddle.

'Damn you for that,' he spat, looking hard at Gabriel again.

'Hey,' said Gabriel. 'That's the name of the game, ain't it? You want to hold up a stage then you has to take the consequences.'

'That's right,' agreed Teddy, catching on quickly. 'You wouldn't be complaining if it was one of us that was shot up.'

'You have to take the knocks in your line of business,' Gabriel went on. 'Stands to rights, don't it? Kind of thing that comes with the benefits.'

'True,' said Teddy, turning to Gabriel as if they were in the midst of a private conversation. 'You know I never looked on it like that, but everything comes at a cost, don't it?'

'Sure does, that's a fact of life.'

'Will you two shut up,' shouted the leader. 'You sound like a burlesque double act.'

'Never did tell you about that, did I, Gabriel? Time I was appearing with 'Doctor Gobles Shine and Smile Show', it was over in...'

'SHUT UP!'

The exasperated leader turned to Tobias, who was shaking like a leaf in a strong wind, 'Where is it, Grimes?'

'Wh... What do you mean?'

'Come on, you little shit, don't be shy. That piece of paper, the government contract, I know you took it when my back was turned. You were seen, fella.'

'No, no I never did such a thing.'

'Yes you did, I shot down that sucker Turner and I know you hoisted it whilst I was doing it. Come on, give it up.'

'I... I...' stuttered Tobias guiltily.

'Please,' begged Evie desperately. 'Tobias if you have it, hand it over to the man, they intend to rape me here on the ground, every one of them one after the other.'

All the men looked at her and detected an almost hopeful twist to her voice.

'I don't think so, miss,' observed the leader gruffly, appearing slightly offended at the accusation.

'Oh, I don't mind,' chuckled Baines. 'Be glad to

help out.'

'See?' said Evie, with a quick sidelong glance at the outlaw and then at Tobias. 'This brute will manhandle me roughly and I will not be able to resist. I shall have to be sacrificed on the altar of his lust if you do not forebear.'

Tobias controlled his trembling and drew himself up majestically, 'I do not know who told you this fairy tale but I have not got this wretched piece of paper you refer to, I assure you. And be warned, do not dare touch my betrothed at fear of your life, sir.'

'You ain't about to get hitched to this daggy looking dog, are you?' asked the bemused outlaw. 'Grimes, I heard you was a lot smarter than that.' He looked from one to the other of them and with one finger tugged down the bandana covering his face. 'Or maybe it's something else, is that it? She a loaded female, eh? There must be some money involved here; you wouldn't go out of your way to line yourself up with... Hey, lady, you in for some money? Is that why old Grimes here is getting all romantic?'

'Certainly not,' snapped Evie. 'Tobias is a gentleman and his intentions are most honorable.'

'Yes, yes, it's true. It is a love match, Colonel. Love and nothing more.'

At sound of the title, Gabriel looked up sharply. He noticed the outlaw as he cracked a malevolent grin and saw the array of brown beneath his lips. Wooden teeth. It was Lomas Chain! Older now, with gray in his hair and beard but still with the same large frame and craziness in his eye.

Chain pointed a finger at Tobias, 'Baines,' he

barked. 'Tip this son-of-a-bitch upside down, shake out that paper from his pocket.'

'Say, boss,' interrupted the third rider. 'Ringo ain't too good, he needs some doctoring.'

'Yes, yes,' agreed Chain irritably. 'Once we've got what we came for. Get on to it, Baines.'

Baines dismounted and moved in, grabbing Tobias unceremoniously by the collar.

'Thought you'd get away with it, didn't you? Think I don't know that you and April were in it together, thought you'd take me for a ride, the pair of you. I take down her old man and we get the sole trading rights he's negotiated for every damned fort on Indian land. That was the plan, but April got greedy didn't she? Suckered you to go along with it, you being a lawyer and all. Now they've discovered gold in the Black Hills there'll be forts all over the whole damned state of Dakota and that contract is worth more than any goldmine.'

April! Gabriel started at the name. She can't be involved in this? For a minute he could not believe what he was hearing.

'Where is she, by the way?' Chain asked. 'Thought you two would be together all the way from now on.'

'Mrs. Turner is back in town,' said Tobias, looking at Evie cautiously. 'An old business acquaintance, dearest. No longer a condition to concern yourself with, I promise. It was merely an arrangement, I was to invoke the required legal actions, that is all.'

'You?' gasped Evie. 'You and that gambling widow? I saw her last night through the window of the alley, when we were outside the saloon, doing... Well, you know what.'

'Yes, my love, and wonderful it was too but she means nothing, it was no more than a business transaction.'

Chain yukked a long laugh, 'April Turner and you! That strikes a merry picture. But that's April Turner for you, why she'd ride bareback and play hunt the hot pepper with a horn-toed frog if it so suited. I never known such an ambitious woman get her legs in the air so often. Turned more heads up in Cold Fargo than a regular dance hall queen and then got herself bedded more times than the Whore of Babylon.'

'Oh, dear God!' spat Evie in disgust. '*You!* You have betrayed me, Tobias! I never would have believed it.'

Gabriel was silently suffering all these sudden declarations; his heart sinking at thought of April as such a conniving chancer and deviant. And to make matters worse, there was that piece of trash Chain, sitting smugly on his horse and spilling the whole sorry mess like garbage onto Gabriel's head.

The outlaw named Houston was making his way towards him and about to collect his Colt. Gabriel knew he would have to act now if he was to act at all.

CHAPTER THIRTEEN

COLD HARD FACTS

The arrow came out of nowhere.

The first Gabriel and the rest of the party knew about was when the bandit, Houston, tripped a few paces as if he were hot-stepping in a square dance and fell flat on his face the feathered shaft sticking out from between his shoulder blades.

There was a spatter of firing and both Chain and Baines spun around to look up at the mesa where a whole horde of Indians were showing their painted faces and whooping with expectation. Chain did not hesitate; he turned his horse and rode out fast. Baines looked around, not knowing what to do and Gabriel took the opportunity to dash across the open ground to the stagecoach.

'Get under cover!' he called to the others as he ran.

Baines finally took it into his head to follow Chain and he mounted up, one leg over the saddle as his horse bolted off.

Teddy had dragged Evie down under the fallen coach and Tobias was following in an awkward tumble of arms and legs. The three of them huddled under the floor of the canted vehicle, sheltering as best they could in the limited space.

Gabriel slid under to join them and pulled out his six-shooter as he did so.

'Holy Hell!' growled Teddy. 'Out of the fat and into the fire.'

'How many we got out there?' asked Gabriel.

'Fifteen, twenty, I ain't sure.'

Gabriel watched as Baines pounded out of sight followed by the catcalls and insulting cries of the Indians. As Gabriel watched a crowd of Indians raced out on horseback and charged in pursuit of the retreating figure. They all vanished from sight behind a veil of dust and Gabriel settled in to reload the missing bullets from his gun.

The occasional rifle shot and arrow ploughed into the woodwork but most of the initial firing had slowed down now.

'Are they giving up?' Tobias asked nervously. He was crouched down and bent over with arms wrapped tightly around his thin legs.

'Like hell,' said Teddy. 'They got all day for us. That's a war party out there and they like to play with their captives a little first.'

'We've got us a breather,' said Gabriel. 'They've taken off after Baines and Chain, so I guess they've left only a few here to keep us pinned down.'

Evie uttered a long quivering wail, 'Oh, dear Lord, to be taken by bandits and wild savages all on the same day.'

'Ain't nobody taken you yet, Miss Evie,' said Teddy, stating a fact and intending to encourage the woman who only allowed a plaintive hiccup in reply.

'They won't kill us, will they?' quivered Tobias. 'Surely not, it will go badly for them if they do. The military will see to that.'

'Maybe,' grunted Teddy. 'But it won't help us any by then, will it?'

Sounds of singing and loud war whoops came down to them from the mesa, where the Indians, sure of victory, were having a celebration before the fact.

'The horses, Teddy?' asked Gabriel. 'Did you see where the team went?'

'They'll be nearby, maybe over the other side of the coach between us and the Indians where we can't see them. They're all looped up with harness and won't wander off.'

'If we can get to them, maybe we stand a chance.'

'The mail bag,' Tobias said hurriedly. 'We must take the mailbag.'

'What's this, Grimes?' asked Teddy with an air of cynicism. 'You keen on playing mailman all of a sudden?'

'No, no, it's important.'

Gabriel was suspicious, 'What's so important? You got something special in there?'

'Of course I have,' supplied Tobias in an exasperated tone. 'You think I'd carry such an important document on me? No, I mailed it to myself at Cold Fargo.'

'So Chain wasn't exaggerating, you did take that contract.'

Tobias looked over at Evie guiltily with a hang-dog expression on his face; she stuck her nose in the air and turned away from him.

'I did it for us, sweetness,' he pleaded. 'For our future, we will be set for life if we take up the options offered.'

'And what part does April play in this?' asked Gabriel.

'It was her scheme from the start,' explained Tobias. 'She got the whole thing moving once her husband had won the contract, coerced Colonel Chain to pick a fight with her husband and then asked me to, er... take charge of the document.'

'He ain't no colonel,' growled Gabriel. 'But April double crossed him, is that it?'

Tobias shrugged admission.

'We ain't got time for this,' interrupted Teddy. 'We got to get out of here right now before them red men come down here and start investigating our hair styles.'

'Don't,' shuddered Evie.

'Hold fast,' said Gabriel. 'I'll go take a look.'

So saying, he wormed his way from under the tilting coach and crawled around to the side facing the mesa. Teddy was right; the horses were still there, one of them lying dead and acting as an anchor to the rest of the team who stood dumbly unmoving.

Gabriel was about to make his way back to the others when a commotion from the Indians caught his attention.

They were standing up in plain sight amongst the rocks and calling out joyfully and pointing.

Gabriel's gaze followed their pointing fingers

and saw the rest of the war party returning. In their midst sat the bound figure of Baines, tied fast with a tree branch holding his elbows back. Baines was hatless and looking the worse for wear as he bounced uncomfortably on the pony. Gabriel guessed he knew only too well what was awaiting him.

As the hullabaloo continued from the Indians, Gabriel made his way back to the others.

'What's all that racket about?' asked Teddy.

'They caught that Baines fella and it don't look good for him.'

'What will they do?' asked Evie in a trembling voice.

'You don't want to know,' grunted Teddy. 'How about the team?'

'They're there, one of them is down and all tangled in the harness rig but he's holding the rest in place. This could be our chance though; whilst they're occupied with Baines we might be able to make a break for it. Just have to be real slick about cutting those traces away.'

'And then outrunning them pesky redskins,' added Teddy gloomily.

'Just don't forget the mail sack,' reminded Tobias.

'You want it, you get it,' snapped Teddy. 'I'm more concerned with keeping my hair where it belongs.'

'Miss Evie,' said Gabriel. 'We're going to have to move fast, I'm afraid you'll need to lose your skirts.'

'*What!*' she said in shock. 'You mean disrobe and expose my limbs?'

'Afraid so.'

'Out of the question, it is most unseemly.'

'That corset thing too, I reckon. Miss Evie we have to move fast, I mean *real* fast.'

'Well, I just don't know,' she harrumphed. 'Everybody will see.'

'They'll also see the feathered lance sticking out your back you drag ass,' advised Teddy in ungallant fashion.

'Oh, it's *too* bad. You know I would do nothing of the sort unless it was a matter of life and death. Very well then.'

'Shall I assist?' asked Tobias obsequiously, as Evie began to unfasten her bodice.

'No you will not, you awful man.'

'Come on,' Gabriel jerked his chin at Teddy. 'Let's us go take a knife to all that leather hardware on the team.'

The two worked their way out on their bellies, both of them holding their knives in hand.

'Don't forget about us, will you?' came the timid request from Tobias.

Snaking over to the five remaining horses they could hear the Indians beginning to rev themselves up to something unpleasant for Baines who was already complaining loudly.

'That poor sucker's about to find out the real meaning of life,' whispered Teddy as they came up on the horses, who snickered restlessly as they heard him. 'Who are those Indians anyway?'

'Mixed band of Cheyenne and Sioux, I reckon. Now keep it down, we don't want to get the horses excited.'

Slowly they worked their way under the animals,

keeping the team between themselves and the war band. They were busily slicing through the leather harnesses and keeping a hold on each animal they freed when the screaming started.

The horses already nervous began to jitter and move around and Gabriel and Teddy struggled to hold the released animals steady.

'Poor devil,' mumbled Teddy, as another blood curdling scream echoed down from the mesa.

Then they heard the loud thud from behind that started the team scattering. Both men looked around to see Tobias struggling with the hefty mailbag in the well of the driver's seat.

'It's stuck,' he complained. 'I can't get it out.'

'You damn fool,' snarled Teddy. 'Get down from there.'

Gabriel hung on but the panicked horse he held was set to run and the powerful animal began dragging him through the dirt as it tried to make off.

A warning cry went out from one of the Indians above them and a volley of shots boomed out.

The released team bolted, swirling and raising a cloud of dust as they streamed away.

'Get back to the coach,' ordered Gabriel, letting go of his hold on the cut reins and allowing the animal to run off.

'I've got it!' cried Tobias in success, holding up to show them the mailbag.

With a surprised cry he suddenly shot off the coach as if he had been lassoed and pulled away by an invisible hand as he disappeared from view.

Scrabbling on all fours, Gabriel and Teddy

struggled to get back behind the cover of the coach as the ground around them was plucked at by flying bullets.

They rounded the corner of the coach to see Tobias lying on his back and spread-eagled on the ground whist a semi-naked Evie stared at him in awe.

'Is he alright?' she gasped.

'Afraid not,' said Teddy, taking out his pipe from his pocket and stuffing it in his mouth. 'He won't be getting no mail this trip. Guess his package already got delivered.'

There was blood on the shirtfront of the dead lawyer but he still clasped the heavy mail sack in both hands.

'Oh dear!' sighed Evie sorrowfully. 'Poor Tobias.'

They all heard it then, a distant sound but getting nearer.

'What the hell is that?' asked Teddy.

'Sounds like a band playing to me.'

'Naw,' spat Teddy. 'C'ain't be, not out here.'

By the time the column of cavalry arrived the Indians were long gone.

The Lieutenant Colonel's appetite for having his band play 'Garryowen' on the march had given them a very fair warning.

He rode in before his headquarters flag that fluttered red and blue with crossed sabers emblazoned and swept of his off hat in a rather dramatic fashion as he halted before the group standing in front of the ruined stagecoach. He was a tall man, almost six foot and looked a lean and fit figure, a handsome fellow sporting an extravagant mustache across his cheeks. Turning to one of his staff he ordered, 'See the lady is covered, will you? Madam, I fear you will catch a chill so undressed, if you will permit? A blanket perhaps?'

Evie, hands vaguely attempting to cover salient points on her underwear, dipped her head gratefully.

'I trust you gentlemen have not been up to anything unfortunate with the lady?'

'No, sir, Colonel,' stressed Teddy, casting a rueful eye at Evie. 'Not on your life.'

'We were hoping to make a break,' Gabriel explained. 'So Miss Evie needed to strip down for the run.'

'What happened here?'

'First off, we was took by road agents,' explained Gabriel. 'Then the war party come along and the bandits fled. One of them is still up there now though,' he jerked a thumb at the mesa. 'He got taken.'

The Colonel nodded to his Crow scout and the Indian rode off instantly to explore.

'Well, sir,' said the Colonel. 'We are out patrolling after a dispatches party of ours gone missing, then we came across this fellow travelling at some speed. What was his name, lieutenant? Yes, that's it, gent called himself Lomas Chain and he said a party was in trouble up ahead, so we came at speed.'

'Sure saved our hides,' said Teddy.

'And your party, are you all intact?'

'One of ours is down, Colonel,' said Gabriel. 'That reminds me, we have something that is of interest to the army.'

'Ah, yes, and what is that?'

Gabriel held up the mail sack, 'A contract, sir. Taken by the same Lomas Chain and in cahoots with our passenger, Tobias Grimes who you can see over there, slain by the Indians.'

'A contract, huh? Why so important?'

'It's a long tale, sir, but it involves the right to supply military establishments with necessaries, so I believe. Chain and Grimes were part of a plot to steal it and make an illicit fortune for themselves.' He decided to say nothing of April's part that he hoped to deal with himself later.

'And you? Who are you?'

'Name's Gabriel Brannigan, this here is Teddy Bones, coach driver and that's Miss Evie Moulder.'

'I see, well you make good report, Mister Brannigan. Perhaps you had better hand this document over to my lieutenant.'

Gabriel handed the sack up to the officer and just then the Crow scout came back and, siding up to the Colonel, he whispered in his ear.

'Terrible, terrible,' muttered the Colonel. 'These savages are quite unbearable. This fellow says they cut off their prisoner's nose and carried out other awful mutilations.'

'It's their way, Colonel,' explained Gabriel. 'You break his head open, cut his legs and arms and fill the body full of arrows it means the enemy can't do battle in the afterlife.'

'How absurd. Oh, I do apologize, madam. That you should hear such things, I hope we do not distress.'

'Quite all right,' muttered a muted Evie, obviously impressed by this dashing officer.

'Well, Mister Brannigan, you certainly seem to know your Indians.'

'Was brought up by the Shoshone, sir.'

'I see,' the Colonel's eyes sharpened. 'Well, I shall remember your name. It may be I shall call on you at a later date. I will certainly have need of able men with Indian experience in the near future.'

'Be glad to oblige, Colonel.'

'Excellent, so when you hear that Colonel George Armstrong Custer needs you I hope you will come running.'

'Oh,' fluttered Evie at the name. 'The hero of the late war, how wonderful.'

With a required show of embarrassment Custer bowed his head, 'You do me great honor, ma'am, but I am no more than a common soldier merely doing his duty.'

'Such a gentleman,' sighed Evie.

'I shall detail a party to carry you safely back to town,' said the Colonel. 'We must press on but you say this Chain fellow was part of the holdup team and also involved with this contract business. I suggest you carry tidings of him to the nearest law officer.'

'We'll do that,' agreed Teddy.

'So, a pleasure to meet you gentlemen and lady and glad we could be of assistance. Captain, order a detail to take care of this party, will you?'

His staff officer saluted and gave instructions to a sergeant riding behind.

'With that,' Custer said, tipping his hat again. 'We shall take our leave, good day to you all.'

'What a bold fellow,' said Evie, staring starry eyed and full of admiration as the Colonel ordered his troop on and rode away with flags flying and the band playing.

'Sure is,' agreed Teddy. 'Kind of fellow you'd follow into the jaws of hell itself.'

Gabriel scratched his chin thoughtfully; he was not so sure, he'd already seen too many officers who were all show and dash but not much common sense. But his thoughts had turned elsewhere; he was considering April Turner and just how he should handle the devious lady.

CHAPTER FOURTEEN

INTERVAL

Guess I kind of drew a sharp breath at that and dropped my jaw.

This old boy actually met George Armstrong Custer, the same Custer that met his end at the famous Little Big Horn Battle. It was something else and I wondered if the connection was leading on to that conclusion.

'You didn't get to be there, did you?' I asked.

'What? At the Big Horn engagement?'

'Yes.'

'No siree, missed out on that one, thank God. Wouldn't be here right now and telling you if'n I sat in on that particular disaster.'

'But you got to go scouting for him, didn't you? You said you was in the Indian Wars.'

'Sure I was,' he agreed. 'But don't you go jumping ahead. I still got some story ahead of all that.'

'Sorry,' I apologized. 'I didn't...'

We was interrupted by the far-off sound of motor klaxon horns and ringing alarm bells. Not that one never did hear such things but they was often a rare and far apart event in them days. Something one paid little heed to unless it was real close and at your own door.

But Brannigan looked up sharply at the racket. His eyes took on a misted appearance like the fast disappearing lowland fog over the creek. It was getting up to mid-morning and the sun's heat was breaking into the shadowy areas under the tree line and melting that whiteness away as if it were summer snow.

'What is that?' he asked, leaning forward in concentration.

'Sounds like the police and maybe ambulances,' I said, rather more eager for him to get on with his tale than worry about some distant emergency.

'That ain't right,' he murmured, his attention drifting away.

'What ain't?' I pressed.

He turned back to me and I could see this far-away look in his eyes as if he were focusing on something else.

'I feel a bad wind blowing,' he murmured.

With that I thought that maybe his ancient intestines was playing him up and could be I ought to move aside if he was about to crack a stinky one on me.

'You okay?' I asked.

'There's something out there, boy,' he said crossly, his eyes snapping wide open and alert again.

'What?' I asked, looking around but seeing nothing except dog trees, lowdown scrub and his grubby old cabin.

'I don't know,' he murmured, going back into that trance of his. 'But I feel it coming.'

'How's that?' I asked.

He drew a deep breath and surrendered to my insistence, 'You get to feel these things,' he said. 'You been around trouble long as I have and the wind can talk to you, tell you things ordinary folk can't hear.'

I guess I thought he was rambling, his tired brain surrendering to the fancies of old age.

'There ain't nothing out there, Mister Brannigan. It's all okay.'

'There's something out there, son, you mark my words. Trouble is, its coming this way.'

'No, sir,' I said. 'Those alarms is far off, they ain't near to hand. It'll be a fire or some accident, is all.'

'When there's moccasins in the woodpile, boy, best have a heavy stick to hand.'

I looked around searching the ground but couldn't see hair nor hide of any snakes or suchlike.

'Sure looks all right, to me. Maybe down by the creek but not up here.'

'Look here, you see Boulder?'

Sure enough, the dog was laid out flat yet pointing with its nose in direction of the wailing alarm sound. It was emitting a low continuous growl and the ruff on its neck was standing proud.

'Maybe its some critter out there?' I said searching the undergrowth. 'A possum, or coon.'

'No, it ain't that,' he was twisting his head from side to side as if trying to catch a scent or hear a sound. 'God Almighty!' he cursed. 'I sure lost my sensibilities. Don't get old boy, it's a regular pain alright.'

The alarm noise faded and disappeared way off into the distance and the bottomlands were filled again with only birdcall and the hush of the breeze in the leaves.

'Guess we're okay,' muttered Brannigan.

'What was all that about?' I asked.

Brannigan scratched his chin, 'No explaining it,' he admitted. 'Some call it sixth sense but I ain't sure what it is. Kind of comes over you when there's danger about, like a lightning rod up your back that sends signal to the brain. It's a telegraph wire of warning, that's all I can say.'

Sure sounded like a load of hooey to me and I reckoned it was just more of the old man's tall tale telling. But, I should have listened to him, maybe then I could have done something about what was coming down the line.

Still, all I was concerned with at that particular moment was finding out what happened to that vamp April Turner and whether he ever did get to grips with the villain, Lomas Chain.

CHAPTER FIFTEEN

DOG DAY

Gabriel found April running a game in The Broken Bucket when he got back. She looked about how you would guess, pretty as a picture and lighting the whole place up in a tight little red number that showed off her best attributes.

Gabriel never did learn to hold back so he strode right up to her where she sat dealing a hand.

'You been playing me for a fool, April.'

She looked up, a ready smile on her face that slowly altered as she saw he meant business.

'How so?' she asked.

'Your messenger boy, Tobias, is dead by Indians out on the trail but before he went he told us everything.'

She quirked her lip and continued to deal cards, 'Is that so? I'm sorry to hear it,' she spoke showing no outward display of how her mind was working. She was cool and calm and Gabriel realized that there was nothing much that could shake the woman as he noted her long fingers moved over the pack without any sign of the slightest tremble.

The three other players at the table were torn between concentrating on counting their cards and an avid curiosity into what this was all about.

Gabriel placed both hands on the table and leaned over, shunting two of the men aside, 'So why'd you do that?' he barked. 'Thought you'd get me to be your next protector since you lost out on Lomas Chain, was that it?'

'Oh,' she sighed, pouting slightly and placing the stacked deck face down on the green baize. 'I hear that Colonel Lomas isn't that far gone.'

'No, but the contract you had him kill your husband for, is. The army have it back now.'

She looked up at him then from under lowered lids, eyes cold as glass, 'You certainly are a fool, Gabriel Brannigan. It could have been you, you know? You and me. We could have done great things together.'

Gabriel straightened up, 'I ought to turn you in,' he rumbled.

'Do your worst, bucko,' she replied glibly, leaning back in her chair and staring Gabriel down. 'You'll find I had no hand in my husband's demise whatever the recently deceased Mister Grimes might have told you. He died from a gunshot but it was not by my hand and there is no evidence to suggest otherwise. Now, gentlemen, shall we continue? Sorry about this interruption, just another bad loser, it happens sometimes.'

'You dealt the wrong hand this time, April,' said Gabriel turning to leave. 'I reckon the Marshal will be calling on you real soon. It won't be me does the telling but the army will figure it out soon enough.'

April kept her head down, eyes on the table, 'So long, Gabriel,' was all she said. But it had a hollow ring to it and as Gabriel left the saloon and headed back to the stage office he wondered what she aimed to do now.

He arrived back at the office to find Evie fully dressed again and sitting sniffling into a tiny embroidered handkerchief whilst her mother cradled her and tried to offer sympathy. Teddy stood to the back of the room leaning against the ticket counter and reaming out his corncob with a pocketknife.

Abigail Moulder looked up as Gabriel came in. She was obviously at a loss, on the one hand her tough exterior told her that her daughter's loss was the best thing that could have happened to her and on the other she wept along with the girl in her distress at losing a husband.

'Looks like it was a hell of a day, Gabriel,' she said.

Gabriel nodded agreement.

'Lost me a coach and my baby here lost herself her man.'

Evie choked into another sobbing fit at that.

'There, there, sweet girl,' crooned Abigail. 'Don't you worry, there's plenty more fish in the stream.'

'No, Mama, he was the one for me. I can't envisage life without Tobias.'

'Come on Evie,' grunted Teddy. 'You heard him 'fess it. He was already playing fast and loose with you. You're better off without.'

But Evie was not about to be appeased and was making the most of the drama with another burst of waterworks.

Abigail, drew a deep breath and looked Gabriel in the eye, 'Well, I'm sorry, son, but it looks like you're out of a job until I can get me a new Concord. There won't be no mail coach running up to Cold Fargo until then. Teddy will have to ride the line letting the stations know along the way and maybe take what mail we get by pack mule but I'm a-feared I'll have to let you go for now.'

'I understand, Mrs. Moulder,' Gabriel answered. 'I see you got enough on your hands right now.'

'Sorry about that, Gabriel.'

'No matter, I reckon I'll be moving on anyway. That Colonel Custer said he needed scouts, maybe I'll take a hand at that.'

He crossed over and took Teddy's hand, 'Been nice riding with you, Teddy.'

'Same here, partner.'

Abigail placed a roll of bills in his hand, 'You've got this pay coming for your time, Gabriel,' she said. 'You go with luck, won't you?'

'Thank you, ma'am.'

Gabriel went back to his hotel room and began to pack his things. He was sad it hadn't worked out here and felt bad that April had turned out to be such a double dealer. When he was done he settled up with the hotel clerk and went off to collect his horse from the livery stable.

Three weeks later, Gabriel arrived at Fort Abraham Lincoln in North Dakota.

The place was obviously gearing up for war, built on an old Mandan village ground; it now sported nigh on eighty buildings and housed nine companies of troops. The United States and Seventh Cavalry flags flew proudly and men were busily stocking in hay and wood as Gabriel rode in. They had a post and telegraph office, bakery and guardhouse, a quartermaster's and laundry, seven officer's quarters and six cavalry stables. The whole place was mobile and full of activity with hardy non-coms bawling instructions and harassed troopers sweating and raising dust as they worked.

Gabriel asked direction from a passing water wagon and was given instruction where to find the Colonel and his party who were out picnicking in a grassy glade.

Custer was immediately identifiable as Gabriel walked up, he was at the center of attention holding forth on some wartime anecdote and waving his wide brimmed hat in emphasis. At his feet sat his devoted and pretty wife, Libbie and around them were posed attentive members of his staff.

'What ho!' cried Custer as Gabriel strolled up. 'What have we here? Mister Gabriel Brannigan if I am not much mistaken.'

'Good day, Colonel, ma'am,' said Gabriel, tipping his hat in the lady's direction and surprised he was remembered.

'You recall Mister Brannigan, don't you gentle-men?' asked Custer, and there were several nods of recognition. 'I do, quite well; he took hold of that unpleasant business involving road agents and Indians and saved his party. You did a grand job, sir,' Custer praised. 'The general was most gratified to receive back his contract. It appears your hand foiled a rather tidy plot there, could have cost the army a pretty penny, so I'm assured.'

'Yes, sir, glad to hear it.' Gabriel knew it had not been quite like that but was apprised it was best to let it slide.

'Well, what can we do for you, Brannigan?'

'Colonel, you made mention you'd be needing scouts and now the stage is gone I'm out of employment so I thought I'd ride up here and see if the offer's still open.'

'Indeed, well yes, there's no doubt we want men of your caliber. Pray go see my Officer of Scouts and tell him you have my blessing, he'll sort you out.'

'Thank you, sir.'

'I have an early patrol out in the morning, Brannigan and I'd like your attention on it. So be prepared for a quick start on the day. Abrupt for a new boy, I know, but best you get off at the deep end. What do you say to that?'

'Whatever you want, Colonel.'

'Good man.'

Gabriel respectfully tipped his hat again and turned to leave. 'Ma'am, gentlemen.'

'You ever catch up with that Chain fellow?' Custer called after him.

'Not yet, but I will.'

Custer guffawed a laugh, 'Good for you, give him merry hell when you do.'

Before he was out of earshot, Gabriel heard the Colonel returning to the tale he'd been telling at the exact point where he had left off.

Charlie Varnum was a twenty-seven year old second lieutenant full of pep and eager to cut a name for himself in the military. It was his job to oversee the scouts that accompanied troops on their various missions. He was accustomed to the Colonel going his own way and hiring men as he saw fit and the recent addition of Bloody Knife the half-Lakota scout who had recently left the service was a case in point. Bloody Knife had left the army a lance corporal with a few bonuses under his belt for services successfully rendered and Custer trusted him implicitly, so had asked him back in for his campaign against the Sioux.

With such ad hoc commissions by his commander, Varnum was not surprised when Gabriel approached him with word of the Colonel's request he be hired on.

Gabriel was given bunk space with Joel L'Homme Destrier another half-white scout who filled him in on the status of the scouting fraternity at the fort.

'Got yourself some Crow and Arikaree here,' he advised. 'The five Crow are the big wheels around these parts but I wouldn't give a plugged nickel for the bunch of them 'cept for Bloody Knife, he sure hates the Sioux, though Lord knows why.'

Joel Destrier was a po-faced fellow with a little chin beard and favoring a buffalo robe coat and low brimmed hat; he was the half-breed result of a dalliance between a French Canadian trapper and his Arikaree mother. Their similar origins threw the two men together, although each viewed the other with some suspicion until their capabilities were proven.

Instinctively, Gabriel felt uncomfortable about the man and although both were ordered out together the following day he kept his own council despite Joel's attempts to discover all he could about his new bunkmate.

'They's looking for a new wood supply along with keeping a presence in the country,' Joel told him as they sat together in the sutler's store and drank a glass of relatively good whiskey together. 'We got to find safe trail for the patrol. What you think on that?'

Gabriel supped a swallow and shrugged, 'Makes no odds to me. Reckon you know the country around here better than me, so you'd better take the lead.'

'Yeah, that's good, man. I'll lead them, you can fan wide and keep the flank covered. We'll have ten troopers and a wagon with us, damn thing'll be heard coming a mile away.'

'Better keep sharp then.'

'By God, you said it. The Sioux and Cheyenne are mighty pissed right now and they cut up rough whenever they can. Tell me, Gabe, what kind of work you do before this?'

'Nothing particular,' Gabriel said with a vague wave of his glass.

'*Nothing particular?* You must have done something to keep your kettle full.'

'Some of this and a little of that.'

Joel snorted a laugh, 'Okay, brother, I get it. That's your business and not mine, if that's how you want it.'

'That's how I want it.'

Joel sniffed and scratched dirty fingernails in his wispy beard, it was an unfortunate habit that pestered the skin rash he had developed and left his visible chin ravaged and raw.

'Is Custer commanding?' asked Gabriel.

'Naw, this is small time, be a bit beneath the big man, be one of his boy lieutenants I reckon.'

Gabriel recognized the inherent criticism; 'You don't think much of Custer then?'

Joel leaned across the table, hunching his shoulders so that his buffalo robe humped like one of the animals itself. He looked from side to side to see if they were overheard by any of the troops in the establishment before answering.

'He's got a mighty high opinion of hisself,' Joel confided. 'War hero an' all. An' I tell you this, that now that he's got hisself a pretty white wife he's forgotten about the Cheyenne squaw he took, an' I don't admire that too much.'

'He did?' Gabriel asked in surprise.

'Sure, girl by the name of Mo-nah-se-tah, daughter of Chief Little Rock. Seventeen years old and pretty as they come. Our Colonel here had her on the side and got a kid by her and you don't hear much about them now. Poor gal can't get wed no more with her own people since she had the kid out of wedlock.'

'Never knew that.'

'Well, then his brother had a turn at the girl and she got herself loaded with another half-breed brat.'

'Custer and his kin did all that?'

'Sure did, he only left off the maid 'cos he caught the clap up at West Point and it come back at him with a vengeance. Guess his lady wife ain't too keen on the whole setup what with one thing and another.'

'Shoot!' frowned Gabriel. 'Don't know if I want to know all this.'

'Show's a man's nature,' Joel expounded a touch pompously. 'You mark my words, that boy will make another signal mistake before he's done his military career. He's a reckless s.o.b. and it won't pay him well when he comes up against the Sioux nation.'

'Maybe you're right,' Gabriel answered non-committedly.

'Damn right I am, just hope I ain't riding his tail the day it happens. Fact is I'll make sure I ain't.'

CHAPTER SIXTEEN

RIDING POINT

As they rode out next morning, the patrol cut a fine figure with the paired column in smartly dressed ranks and holding position whilst leading the heavy flatbed wood wagon at the rear. Their officer was a young second lieutenant named Cyrus Lane, a fresh face and newly arrived. To keep him company, an experienced company sergeant rode alongside. Paddy Mulhoun had been provided to hold the inexperienced officer in check and advise against him doing anything too obviously foolhardy. Mulhoun had seen battle a-plenty since his arrival in the States from his mother Ireland and had risen to his rank and been broken down more times than the records allowed. He was a pugnacious little guy more fit for fisticuffs than leadership but this had been considered to be a domestic patrol and of little strategic interest so his attendance was thought fitting.

Gabriel did as planned and took himself away from the main column to scout the outlying country, as they pressed deeper into the forests. His route took him up high on the overlooking hills where he could see the company's progress below and also keep good lookout for any likely signs of ambush.

It was bright day and the sky was clear of cloud so that the sun was hot and shone down unheeded. After an hour of travel Gabriel took off his jacket and lashed it to the saddle at his back. Taking out a spyglass he stood the pony and quartered the horizon. Making out little amongst the dense clumps of trees they progressed through that were too young for the cutting, he moved position and noticed a thin trail of smoke rising from a clearing ahead.

Riding down he cut the trail of the patrol and reported his find to the lieutenant.

'Would this be a cabin or some homestead of sorts?' asked Lane.

'Not on you life, sir,' supplied Mulhoun. 'Not out here. There's little enough to keep a soul safe this far out from the fort.'

'Very well,' said Lane. 'Best you scouts go see what there is up there.'

Joel as lead scout looked over at Mulhoun for confirmation and the sergeant sniffed and rubbed his broken nose, 'Perhaps, sir,' he said. 'It might be better we send only one of them at this time.'

'You think so, sergeant? Very well, you fellow, Brannigan isn't it?' he nodded at Gabriel. 'You spotted this smoke, go ahead of the party and see what it is, will you?'

Gabriel touched a finger to the brim of his hat in casual salute and wheeled his pony around and rode off in the direction of the smoke. He was soon lost to sight of the patrol and moving alone through the forests of pine that enclosed him with a silence that was worryingly free of birdcall.

Gabriel slowed his pace and kept a sharp eye on the surrounding woodland. He sniffed the air but could only catch the charcoal taint of the fire burning ahead. Nothing moved and there was no breeze to tip the foliage around him. It felt unnaturally quiet and Gabriel felt the trickle of warning run up his spine. He lifted his Henry rifle from its scabbard and placed it across his lap as he walked the pony on. His nerve ends quivered and he noted a distinct sense of uneasiness as he pressed on into the gloom of the silent forest.

He was more than a thousand yards in advance of the patrol when he broke the cover of the clearing and saw the cause of the fire.

Ahead of him across the open ground and separated by fifty yards of long grass hung a figure stripped to the waist. Tied off from the sturdy overhanging branch of a tree, was a man hanging by his wrists. His features were blackened by soot and he writhed in agony at the heated coals that burned beneath his naked feet. The torture must have amused his tormentors as the unfortunate man wriggled and hopped in the air trying to escape the intense heat from below. The legs of his trousers were scorched and smoldering and his feet blackened and splitting where the baking skin had puffed and bubbled. A low continuous moan emitted from the dangling figure.

Gabriel dismounted quickly and searched for some sign of the man's attackers along the edges of the clearing. He could see no sign but they were near he knew it, they could not have left off their torture of the poor unfortunate long since. He was not yet dead and it was unlikely they would not have gone until that happened.

It was then he heard the sudden sound of shooting from behind. The concerted blast of Springfield rifles and the spatter of pistol fire tore the silence apart in a sudden cascade of violent noise.

The patrol was under attack and in a split second Gabriel realized the whole thing had been a ploy to bring them to them towards the clearing. Like fish in a stream to a baited hook they had ridden straight into an ambush. Screaming war cries and shouted orders came from his rear amidst the sounds of battle.

Gabriel was undecided, should he speedily return to the soldiers or rescue the torture victim? Just then the hanging man spotted him and uttered a loud cry, 'For pities sake!' he called. 'Cut me down from this.'

The call decided Gabriel and leading the horse by the reins he dashed straight across the open ground. Taking the man around the waist he swung him clear of the intense heat and with one hand slashed at the bindings with his knife. The man tumbled down with a groan and dragged himself on his elbows to rest his back against the tree trunk, where he lay propped and gasped his thanks.

'Thank God,' he wheezed. 'You come along just in time I was like to fry hanging up there.'

Gabriel peered at the blackened features; there was something in the voice that he recognized.

'*Chain!*' he burst out. 'Is that you, Lomas Chain?'

'Yeah, sure,' said the figure staring up at him. 'I know you?'

'Goddamn!' spat Gabriel. 'Of all the swine under the sun, it had to be you.'

'What?' struggled Chain. 'Who are you? What is this?'

'Damn you, man. You killed my pa, you dang near had me killed on the Cold Fargo stage and now I have to go save your sorry ass.'

Chain groaned again and tried to study his ruined feet, twisting his leg so he could see them better.

He sucked at his wooden teeth with a squeak of pain, 'Hell, I don't know about any of that and right now I don't care. You come with a party of soldier boys? 'Cos it sure sounds like they're catching a belly full right now.'

Gabriel realized he was right; the sounds of gunfire and warfare were reaching a shattering zenith in the distant woods.

'Listen, buster, whatever your gripes with me,' groaned Chain. 'We has to get out of here, those red devils will be back shortly to finish me off and you along with me we don't get going.'

Gabriel dithered, he was still in shock at the surprise of finding Chain here but he knew that what Chain was saying was true and yet his duty also lay in offering some assistance to the patrol.

'Come on, you ass,' burst out Chain. 'Get me up on that horse. I can't walk none but we has to move right now.'

'I ought to leave you where you are,' snarled Gabriel, as he dragged Chain to his feet. Chain howled with pain as he stood and Gabriel brusquely heaved him up by the seat of his pants and threw him across the saddle.

'Hurt does it?' Gabriel growled. 'Good, I hope it gets worse as we go.'

'Lord, have some pity, will you?' moaned Chain.

'Like you did for my pa and the folks on that stage. I know about your lowdown murdering deal with April Turner.'

'You know about April? How'd you know that?' asked Chain, for once forgetting his agony and looking at Gabriel in a new light.

'Never you mind, just hang on tight, we have ground to cover,' said Gabriel as he took up the horse's reins and started to lead off across the clearing at a jog.

'You ain't Brannigan's kid are you?' asked Chain with a sudden flash of insight. 'The one caught us all unawares in that tavern years ago. Cut down my three buddies with hardly a moment's pause. Yes, sir, I remember you. Damn! That was fine work for such a youngster but a hell of a long time back now.'

'I ain't forgotten you,' spat Gabriel. 'Not since you played at soldier and shot down my friend on the field at Cold Harbor.

'I did that too?' asked Chain in a bemused tone. 'How come I don't remember you with all that?'

'Because you're too dumb and stupid to know what you do.'

'Now wait a minute,' said Chain as they reached the cover of undergrowth on the opposite side. 'I saved your bacon at that stage holdup. It was me told that cavalry patrol where you was, I sent Custer himself to come rescue you. Hell, boy, you owe me your life and best not forget that.'

'I ain't forgetting nothing,' snarled Gabriel. 'Now shut your noise, we have a passel of trouble to get through here.'

Gun smoke was drifting through the trees towards them and the sound of shooting was gradually diminishing whilst the victory calls of the Indians were getting louder.

'They's nailed that patrol,' whispered Chain. 'Better we take another route.'

'I have to see,' was all Gabriel answered.

'Don't be a fool, boy. They're done for, we has to save ourselves.'

'Shut up!' snapped Gabriel. 'Or I'll leave you here and don't think I won't.'

'Damn me,' mused Chain. 'Brannigan's kid, your name's Gabriel, ain't it? Hell of a thing, who's have thought old Brannigan could raise such a hellfire runt.'

Gabriel ignored him and picked his way slowly and carefully towards the now dying sounds of the ambush. He sunk down amongst dense brush and parted bushes to see the remains of the fight spread over a track in front.

Blue-coated bodies lay at odd angles, some grouped together and others lying singularly dropped amongst the crushed and downtrodden brush. Buckskin clad Sioux warriors, in paint and feathers moved amongst the fallen soldiers, stripping bodies and joyfully carving up the remains with tomahawks and knives. To one side they held prisoner the survivors and Gabriel picked out the lieutenant and Sergeant Mulhoun with two other troopers hogtied and kept under the watch of three of the Indians.

Bowed low over the saddle, Chain followed his gaze, 'Those boys are goners,' he muttered. 'Won't be long before they join their buddies.'

'Maybe they'll string them up just like they did you,' Gabriel replied with spite.

'It ain't no way to go,' Chain observed with some feeling.

'That's why we has to save them.'

'Are you kidding?' hissed Chain. 'Look here, I can't move with my feet all boiled up and you are one against all of them.'

'Ride out,' ordered Gabriel firmly. 'Make as much noise as you can. Head for the fort. They'll come after you and I'll go get the others. See there, they're holding the horses close by,' he pointed at a lone young brave no more than twelve or thirteen years old who was keeping watch over the war party's ponies and the captured cavalry horse.

'You aim to take them all on yourself?' spat Chain. 'You gotta be crazy, boy. They'll rip you apart.'

'Not if you draw them off sounding like a rescue party. Holler orders and crash around in the forest.'

'Son, if I get going I ain't lingering none.'

'Give these fellers a chance,' pleaded Gabriel. 'Just like I gave you one. Damn it, Chain, I got enough grievance against you not to let you go at all, believe me. Just do like I say.'

Chain paused a long moment, 'You are one fool

of a life-saving sucker, that's for sure. Damn me if I ain't too. Okay, I'll do it.'

'Right, give me time to get in position, then let rip.'

Chain chuckled at Gabriel's intensity, 'Your pa sure named you right, Gabe, you is one guardian angel all right.'

Gabriel looked up at him, 'I ain't forgetting nothing,' he said coldly. 'I get out of this and I'll still come looking for you.'

Chain smiled broadly, his ugly wooden teeth a dark bar in the shadow as he backed the horse slowly away into the undergrowth.

'Look forward to it.'

Crouching low, Gabriel set off in a curving lope through the forest, cutting a circular arc to come up on the guarded prisoners. He moved elegantly, his moccasin boots making little noise as he ran on and came up on the youngest of the Indian guard.

The young man was a trainee buck, a youngster probably out on his first raid and his tasks were simply to cook for the older men and take care of the horses. Right now he was strutting, putting on an aggressive face for the captured soldiery and feeling that at last he had entered manhood as a warrior.

The two other guards were more attentive to the rest of the band who still ferreted noisily amongst the fallen, going through their uniform pockets and satchels and taking what they fancied from the bodies.

All heads looked up and rotated as the sound of a shouted order came to them through the woods.

'Company will advance!' Gabriel heard Chain

call out. 'Stand your line!'

This was followed by the crash and crackle of undergrowth, the thud of hoof beats and wild shouts of, 'Haloo!' and 'Give 'em hell!'

The startled Indians sprang into life, some of them making off on foot and others collecting their ponies before heading for the sounds of the oncoming army. In minutes the ambush track was clear and the young guard, now not so sure of himself, was looking around nervously. His two companions were torn between taking off for the fight or staying put and keeping watch on the prisoners. In the end the prospect of more scalps won the day and the two admonished the young man to hold his place whilst they ran off after the others of the war band.

Alone now, the young warrior leaned forward and innocently listening to the sounds of distant movement through the woods keeping his attention attuned to the deceptive struggle going on out of sight.

He never heard Gabriel rise up behind him from cover and only in the last split second did he hear him coming as Gabriel sprinted across the intervening stretch of ground.

Gabriel whacked the boy hard with the swinging butt of his Colt, bringing it down hard on the fellow's temple. The Indian's head spun aside, eyes rolling to white as he fell and Gabriel stepped over his fallen body and made his way across to the captives who all turned to him with thankful eyes.

'Hellfire!' rumbled Mulhoun. 'Wondered where you'd got to.'

'Come on, Brannigan,' urged the Lieutenant. 'Get us free, man.'

Kneeling to the task, Gabriel slashed with his knife and cut them free, 'Get yourselves armed, one of you go get the horses.'

One of the troopers did as he was told and brought up six of the cavalry horses whilst Mulhoun and the other trooper collected pistols and rifles from the heaped collection the Indians had made.

'What happened to Joel?' Gabriel asked the Lieutenant.

'The bastard turncoat is one of them,' spat Lane. 'He led us right into it.'

'You sure of that?' asked Gabriel doubtfully.

'Man, I saw him shoot down one of my men deliberately.'

'Never would have...'

'Look out!' bellowed Mulhoun.

Gabriel spun around to see the young bloodied guard leaping towards him, a tomahawk raised high.

Mulhoun fired the Springfield he was holding and the buck tumbled in mid-flight and rolled over shot through.

The rifle shot sounded loud and echoed through the forest.

'That's torn it,' said Gabriel. 'Get mounted, we has to ride!'

All them jumped to it and climbed into the saddle as the angry sounds of the rest of the band came through the trees. They realized they had been duped and were fast making their way back to the ambush site.

With a shout, Gabriel dug in his heels and set his horse off at the gallop heading straight towards the oncoming Indians. Behind and on either side the rest of the patrol followed behind, urging their animals on as fast as they could.

Before him amongst the undergrowth, Gabriel made out the brown shapes coming at the run, their flitting figures leaping and bounding angrily through the forest. The Indians ran in a ragged line roaring war cries, bursting through bushes and brushing past low hanging branches.

Gabriel fired to left and right as he was amongst them, each side travelling at a fast rate and colliding with each other in a collective crash of firing and loud shouts.

A raised lance, coming from a warrior rising up from cover at the last minute pinioned a trooper on the spear point, plucking the soldier savagely from his racing horse.

Off to his right and in front, Gabriel made out the dark shape of Joel in his buffalo robe coat and he angled his horse towards the traitor. Taking aim, Gabriel fired at the figure but the hammer fell on an empty chamber. In a last desperate attempt, Gabriel threw the pistol full force and was pleased to see it hit the scout full in the face and bring him up sharply. Gabriel rode on and charged over the screaming figure and Gabriel felt the thumping crunch under the horse as the steel shod hoofs met soft flesh and hard bone.

Two others of the party were leapt on as they passed and Gabriel saw only the tumble of blue uniforms covered by howling Indians vanish from sight as he broke through the last of the cordon.

Still lashing at his racing horse, Gabriel ran on and then looked over his shoulder as he heard thudding hoofs coming up behind and saw the bare headed figure of Mulhoun following his path. The two raced on together, spinning their sweating horses through the maze of trees and leaping fallen logs until they were clear of any sounds of pursuit.

'They got the Lieutenant,' panted Mulhoun.

'Okay,' said Gabriel, patting the neck of his horse. 'Go easy now, we ain't out of it yet.'

'How's that?' asked Mulhoun.

'Some of them took off on horseback after my rider, they'll still be ahead of us.'

'The bastards!' cursed Mulhoun. 'Who was that? I thought it was our own people coming.'

'No, a fellow they were torturing. I let him go and he made like it was another patrol out there.'

'Smart thinking and a bold move, Brannigan,' Mulhoun grinned. 'Brannigan, that's an Irish name, ain't it? Well, that would explain it.'

'You got anything but that rifle, sergeant?' Gabriel asked, realizing that except for his knife he was now totally unarmed.

'That's all it is,' answered Mulhoun. 'That and a handful of shells.'

'Well keep them close as that's all we have now.'

'Where to?'

'Back to the fort but we'll take a roundabout route and maybe avoid the rest of them Indians.'

'Lead on then.'

Gabriel took the high ridge route back, hoping to catch sight on any Sioux before they themselves were seen. He wondered obliquely how Chain had made out and whether the fellow had escaped at all. There was still too much hate in his heart for Chain to forgive him and in a strange way he wished that the outlaw had gotten away. He wanted the satisfaction of seeing to Chain's end for himself.

They rode on in single file, following a trail through scattered pine trees on the ridge and overlooking the rest of the forest below.

At last, Gabriel saw movement. He pulled Mulhoun to a halt and the pair sat their horses behind the cover of a clump of trees and Gabriel pointed out the train of five Indians below. They were moving slowly on obviously tired ponies. In their midst sat the half naked figure of Chain, slumped over and tied to his horse.

'Goddamn!' spat Mulhoun. 'That's a white man they got.'

'The fellow I told you about.'

Mulhoun shook his head sorrowfully, 'Brave fellow saved our bacon and now he's going to get the griddle again.'

'Give me your rifle,' ordered Gabriel.

Mulhoun looked at his questioningly, 'What you aiming to do?'

'There's not much we can do, except make his passing easier.'

'You're going to plug the poor fellow?' asked a shocked Mulhoun.

'Well, we can't take them all down can we? Our

horses are spent, we ain't got no ammo and but one gun between us. What else is there? We going to leave him to die hard? This way is the kindest.'

'Damn it, Brannigan! That's cruel.'

'Not as cruel as those Sioux will be when they see what we done back there to the rest of their party. They'll take it all out on that fellow there.'

'You shoot him,' Mulhoun complained angrily. 'And they'll come after us.'

'I don't think so, they're done and we're far enough away to clear out before they get up here. Now stop bitching and give me the gun.'

Shaking his head sorrowfully, Mulhoun handed across the rifle.

Gabriel slipped from his horse and made his way over to a straight pine tree amongst the grove and knelt down. He made sure there was a bullet in the chamber and steadied the barrel against the tree. Easing his neck muscles, Gabriel drew a bead on the figure of Chain. For a moment, the tip of the Springfield wavered as he considered what he was about to do. But Gabriel dragged a cold ring of merciless intent about his shoulders. He remembered all the sins the man below had committed against him. Of his father's murder and his soldier buddy on the battlefield, the rotten deceit of April Turner and the killing of her husband by Chain's hand. None of it he felt was outweighed by his rescue at the stage or this most recent attempt to assist him and save the patrol survivors.

He pulled the trigger.

CHAPTER SEVENTEEN

ANOTHER WORLD

That's when something happened that I'll carry with me to the grave.

Old man Brannigan was almost done in his story when a figure came running fast over the bridge. He was going at full pelt, kind of loose limbed and stumbling and you could tell he was in a panic.

It was my brother Ahab. He was bleeding down the side of the face and his eyes were wide with fear.

'You gotta come, Jonah,' he panted. 'It's Ma.'

'What happened? She all right?'

'No, she ain't,' he bent over, hands on his knees to catch his breath.

'Slow down, boy,' said Mr. Brannigan. His voice was steady and firm and the sound of his control eased you right off. 'You tell it so we can understand, okay?'

'There's this man,' gasped Ahab. 'He socked me one, see here?' he pointed to a gash on his forehead that was pumping blood. 'He broke in and he's got guns.'

'Name the weapons. Take it slow and easy, we

need to know,' said Brannigan, leaning forward attentively.

'What you mean...' I began, as riled as Ahab but Brannigan laid a hand on my arm to still me.

'Name the weapons,' he repeated.

'He got himself one of those guns with a round drum, you know like in the movies.'

'A Tommy gun?' asked Brannigan. 'Thompson sub-machine gun with a hundred round drum, haven't seen one of those oldsters in twenty years.'

'Yeah, that's it. Got it laid on the kitchen table in front of him. Gee! Jonah, he's threatening to shoot Ma.'

'Anything else?' pressed Brannigan irritably.

'One of them handguns...' Ahab waved his hand vaguely. 'A Colt, the automatic, like you showed me, Jonah. The one they give you in the army.'

'He got a name?'

'Says he's called Clyde 'Mad Dog' Cheetham, some kind of crazy all right. I reckon he's on the run, maybe a prisoner on the lamb or a bank robber, I don't know. Whatever he is, he's mean as a side-winder and been shot up too, he's got this bandage on his arm with a heap of blood on it.'

I took off then, running as fast as my legs would carry me. I heard Brannigan holler after me but I paid him no heed, I just wanted to get back home and see who this son-of-a-bitch was that was threatening Ma.

I arrived back home and burst into the house to find Ma bent over the stove and cooking up something there. This guy, this Clyde Cheetham was sitting at the table just like Ahab said he was and he looked at me without a blur of disturbance crossing his ugly mug.

'Howdy,' he says, cool as you like, though there was a glitter in his eye I didn't like. 'You the big boy here?'

I noted his finger curled around the trigger of the Thompson as he said that.

'What you aiming to do?' I panted, not even sure of what *I* was aiming to do.

'It's all right, Jonah,' says Ma, turning from her cooking. 'Everything's fine, Mister Cheetham here is just stopping by to enjoy breakfast with us. Now why don't you run along.'

She was worried, I could see it in her eyes and all she wanted was for me to be safe and out of there.

'I don't think so, Ma,' says this Cheetham, with a slow grin and no humor in his eyes. 'You just set a while, sonny.'

He lifts the Thompson and points it at the chair across the table from him.

'Your mammy's being real nice and cooking me up some eggs,' he said. 'I ain't ate in a while and I could do with a feed, ain't that right, Ma?'

'You on the run from the law?' I ask him.

Cheetham snorts a peculiar laugh, like to say, you stupid or something, 'What d'you think?'

'What you done?'

'We was in taking down that penny-ante bank you got here, Jesus! What a hole-in-the-wall joint that is.'

'Sir!' interrupted Ma sharply. 'We're Christians

here and I'd prefer you didn't take the Lord's name in vain in my house.'

'Sister,' sneers Cheetham. 'You'd best mind your own self and start worrying you get them eggs right. I can't abide runny, I gets runny and I's libel to lose control. You hear me?'

Seemed like he'd already lost control, his voice was on a thin thread as tight as a noose and the muscles on his face twitched and worked almost as if he could not master them.

'The bank?' I said to distract him.

'Oh, yeah,' he says, turning back to me and relishing his story. 'Well they even had a security dude in there, can you believe it? Even though there wasn't more than a few bucks in the place worth heisting. Young fellow sets off with his .38 and lands one in my arm, well he didn't last long...'

'Not poor young Mister Roanes?' gasps Ma. 'He has a wife and small child.'

'Whatever his fucking name is, he ain't wearing it now,' barks Cheetham. 'But what he did do is get the rest of them going. The teller and the manager starts to make a fight of it, hell! I didn't know they was all holding hideaways under the counter in there. What is it with you Texicans? Y'all got to carry hardware around with you? Cut down my buddy Simpson and then put Braxton over and that leaves me on my lonesome, so I made a mess of that place with the Thompson and got the hell out. Now we got cops and state troopers all over the county looking for me.'

'Well we won't stop you,' I said with a note of

desperation. 'Nobody here will hold you. Best you move on before they come looking.'

'Oh, I don't know,' he leers, his eyes jumping at me and all around the room like the law is in the woodwork. 'I kind of like it here and your Ma is real accommodating, it's kinda nice to meet regular civil folks once in a while.'

Ma laid a napkin and fork beside him and set a plate of scrambled eggs and some toast on the table, 'Please, eat and enjoy, Mister Cheetham.' She says to him as polite as if he's a regular friend or neighbor come visiting.

'Why, thank you, ma'am,' says Cheetham, lifting the fork in one hand and the Colt in the other. The Colt he keeps fixed on me whilst he eats with the other hand.

'Hunky Dory,' he praises after the first mouthful. 'Maybe I'll let you live, lady, you sure cook a mean egg, that's for sure.'

Ma and me both stay watching him wolf it down. Ma is standing beside me wiping her hands on a dishcloth, and me, I'm sitting there thinking on how I could maybe lift the table and turn him over long enough to get Ma out of there.

'You going to let my boy go now, Mister Cheetham?' says Ma, laying a hand on my shoulder. 'He's due back at his military camp and I reckon they'll be a mite upset with him if he's late.'

Cheetham glowers at me, 'You going off to do the government's bidding, are you?' he says. 'Going off to kill some poor jabbering idiots over there?' He nods in vague direction out the door. 'Fool's errand, boy. You don't get nowhere by doing other folks killing, best you do it for yourself if you're going to do it at all.'

'My boy's standing up,' Ma says proudly. 'He's taking his place for the rest of us against them cowards who ambushed our sailor boys at Pearl Harbor.'

'Pshaw!' spits Cheetham. 'Assholes should have been watching their backs in the first place.'

'Just like you did at the bank,' I snaps back at him. It was a fool thing to say, to irritate him at such a moment but I couldn't hold it back, thinking of all those good men lost to us doing their duty whilst a no-account wretch like him was stealing and killing his own kind.

'You got a point there,' he says and without more said he looses off a shot from the Colt. He didn't hit nothing but the lintel over the door but it was the noise and the suddenness that caught us out and both Ma and I jumped.

He starts off laughing at our trembling and says, 'They don't call me 'Mad Dog' for nothing, so best you remember that. Now, Ma, you got any coffee?'

That's when we get interrupted with a 'Hey there!' from the door.

It's Gabriel Brannigan with an empty pie dish in his hand. 'Howdy, Mrs. Cord, I just brung back your dish here. Mighty fine pie, I must say.'

Cheetham studies him coldly and levels the Thompson, 'How do, old fella, why don't you just step inside and join us?'

'Oh, I don't want to interrupt,' smiles Gabriel, as pleasant as can be. 'Just passing by.'

'You come on in,' snarls Cheetham.

'If you say so,' says Gabriel, still with that easy smile. 'You okay, Mrs. Cord? Seems like you're a mite concerned. This here fool ain't upsetting you is he?'

'Would you like to have some coffee, Mister Brannigan?' asks Ma.

'That's real neighborly of you, ma'am,' says Gabriel, as charming as you like. 'Hey, there, Jonah. You taking good care of your Ma?' He gives me a look then as if to say, that's what you'd better be doing about right now.

Cheetham frowns in irritation 'Who you calling a 'fool', old man?'

'Aw, come on, Clyde,' says Gabriel, stepping in over the threshold. 'I seen tinhorns like you all my life. Dim shits who ain't worth a plugged nickel unless they got a gun in their hand. You just stay sitting there and keep your fat mouth shut afore something flies in you can't handle.'

Oh, wow! I thought, now he's put the cat amongst the pigeons and I wonders what on earth Gabriel is playing at.

'Why, you punk-assed old fart,' growls Cheetham, tipping the table and beginning to rise to his feet, the Thompson and the automatic, one in each hand, with both of them leveled at Gabriel.

Then, way too fast for such an old man, Gabriel does his thing.

'Take care of your Ma, Jonah!' he shouts and at the same time underarms that tin dish, like a discus thrower in the Olympics, and he whirls it across the room straight at Cheetham's head. Instinctively, the gangster moves his head aside to avoid the spinning plate and that gives Gabriel time to haul out that Army Colt of his from the belt at his back.

I was busy going sideways and pushing Ma out of the way but had time to see Gabriel go into this crouch with his antique Colt held out in front like a dagger in the dark. He looks tight as a wire and all lean and mean, full of purpose and intent. No longer was he that fuzzy ancient bag of bones sitting on the bench whittling his days away and ruminating on past glories, it was a younger man I was looking at. That gun came out and his hand hooked over the hammer as he let fly so fast it was only a blur.

Bang! Bang! Bang!

Three shots, so close they seemed to be all of a one.

Cheetham staggered back, the Thompson going off skywards and stitching a ratcheting hole across the ceiling bringing down plaster and all sorts on us below. He was swaying there, kind of surprised and gaping at Gabriel, who calm as you like strode up to face him. Cheetham was bleeding from three holes in his front but still standing and trying to lift the automatic to put one in the old man.

'Goddamned fool, best you leave decent folks alone,' says Gabriel and cool as you like he lifts that Colt, sticks the barrel in Cheetham's face and puts one in his open mouth.

We all stand there a long moment in the sudden silence afterwards as the gun smoke wreathes out the door.

Then Ma surprises the hell out of me and says

calm as you like, 'Well, Mister Brannigan, I can't say I approve of your language but I must say you certainly seemed to have saved our day and for that I'm most obliged.'

Gabriel looks across at her, the Colt still hot in his hand and he replies with a shy look and a touch coyly, 'S'okay, Louella May, but I'm real sorry about all the mess.'

They both ignore the ghastly looking splash of blood and gobbets of brain on the wall and I'm sure he wasn't meaning that kind of mess but instead they concentrated on each other and a strange look passed between them. Something I still can't figure out. Ma kind of smiled in her eyes in a knowing way and Gabriel, for once in all my time with him, had a softer, kinder look about him. Nothing was said but something unspoken sure was and it beats the hell out of me what it was. I wonder now, thinking back on it, if at some other time and somehow in another place, the two of them knew each other. Never did find out, as when I asked Ma later she just clammed up and wouldn't discuss the subject, so I never got to know the truth of it but I got my suspicions, I surely have. It was the one and only time I heard Gabriel use my Ma's given name like that.

I never did get to see Mr. Brannigan no more than one more time and that was when Ahab drove me over in Senor Solidade's pickup. Ahab was taking me on to the station for my trip back to San Diego and Fort Pendleton as my leave-time was up, but first off, we dropped by so I could wish the old man goodbye.

'Sorry I never did get to hear the rest of your story, sir,' I said as he took my hand and gave it a good shake.

'Never fear on that,' he said. 'It don't amount to much anyway.'

'Aw, I don't know about that, I reckon it was real interesting.'

'Well, you watch your step out there amongst them slant-eyed guys, won't you?'

'I will.'

'No,' he warned sternly. 'You take care, I seen what they're like. I was over in the Philippines and they can be a crazy bunch them Moros, got these curly kriss swords and get themselves kill-crazy on narcotic drugs so they don't feel no pain.'

'*You were in the Philippines campaign as well?*' I gaped, hardly able to believe it.

'Sure, back in 1900 with the 4th Cav.'

'Hellfire, Mr. Brannigan, is there any conflict you ain't been a part of?'

He chuckled that heh-heh laugh of his, 'I guess not.'

'My,' I said. 'I'd sure like to hear about that one.'

'Well,' he hawed a moment. 'I guess I could set it all down, you know, kind of write it in letters.'

'Hey, that would be swell. Send it to me overseas; it'd sure help pass the time. Mostly we ain't got much to do, so I reckon I'll have ample time on my hands.'

He cocked his head on one side and looked thoughtful a moment, 'That might change, I'd say. But no mind, I'll see it gets done, don't you worry.'

'I'm obliged.'

'Well, so long, partner, just you come back in one piece, y'hear? And you...' He turned, frowning at sixteen-year-old Ahab, standing behind me. 'You're going to stay by your Ma, don't you go running off and joining up just 'cos your big brother done such a stupid thing. Your Ma don't need more than one boy in the army, we clear on that?'

'Yes sir,' Ahab answered dumbly.

And that was it. I was real eager to go and all afire with being a fighting man and maybe having in store as many adventures as the old man had. With a wave, Ahab shoved that truck into gear and we sped off down the road in a cloud of dust.

As I look back now though, I wish I'd made more of it, that last farewell. He was a regular gent, old Gabriel. A special kind of person, the sort that was the roots of America, and without him and others like him maybe our great nation wouldn't be where it is today.

EPILOGUE

LAST DAYS

They both left about the same time, Ma and Mister Brannigan.

Not in the way you might think though.

I was over there helping shut down a hell hole called Okinawa when it happened, up to my ankles in blood and body parts so mixed up you couldn't tell if they was the remains of the Japs or our own boys. It sure was a mess, I can tell you that as gospel. Earned me a hunk of shell splinter spliced with coral rock and a Purple Heart that rotated me back home with a leg that leaves me lopsided and limping to this day.

Ahab told me that pretty much most of the state turned up for Ma's funeral. The church choir came and sang and there was that many flowers that the whole cemetery looked like a flower shop. She was one popular lady and all her kindnesses came back to her in the way that folks were there and spoke out, each one having some story of how she had helped them out and given of herself so freely. It was the cancer that took her, so fast and quick that within a year it rampaged through her whole body and the doctors couldn't do a thing about it. She never said a single thing to my brother or me and it hurts me bad to think that she suffered that all on her own, but that was Ma, a regular saint of a woman and the mold was broke when she passed over.

Brannigan was good as his word and nigh on most every post overseas I'd get a pack of letters from him. They was all written in his scrawly hand, full of misspellings and scribed with a pencil that looked like it might have been made from one of his whittling sticks. Still, it was better than any book or magazine to read and it took my mind off all the mayhem. Heck of a tale and maybe I'll set all them letters out proper and in right order one day. Ahab's been real good letting me bunk with him and a guy at the Legion says he can help out with G.I. Bill and get me a course so I can get to do my letters right and Lord knows I got the time on my hands.

Old man Brannigan ended up in this old folks home, least I think he did.

They told me he left off his cabin one day, and just plain went wandering. Stole himself a horse, took the dog and that old Colt of his and just went. Riding down the highway like he was heading back to the open prairie and aiming at making hay while he still had some days left in him. The neighbors told the police how there was this hundred-year-old horse thief who'd lost his sensibilities and was wandering around and they put out a cross state all points bulletin looking for him. Found him in some juke joint down in Louisiana. The report said he was drunk as a skunk and spouting out about some old boy called Lomas Chain and how he was going to nail his hide to the wall.

Maybe old Brannigan did lose his marbles, a fellow that age, well you never can tell. Anyway, I'm told they waived any charges but the judge had him put in the old folks home for his own protection. His own protection! Had to laugh when I heard that one.

I was too beat up after my overseas venture to go check on him right off. I had a lot of issues to contend with right then so it wasn't until some time later I gave the place a call. They told me he was gone. Lit out one night, so it went. No one heard or knew a thing about it until next day when they found his bed made up neat and him not in it.

Where'd he go? Who the hell knows? I just hope he found his peace wherever it was. Me? Well, I'm still looking for mine.

There was one other thing that still leaves me wondering.

Ma left an addendum in her will, one that she had Mister Post the lawyer; add not long before she died. She said that if and when a certain Mister Gabriel Brannigan was to finally depart this planet, a wreath made up of local flowers, some Blue Bonnet and Zinnia, was to be placed on his grave, the cost of which was to be set aside from her savings. There was a note to be added; 'For Gabriel Brannigan, a loving friend and true guardian angel.'

Now, what the hell do I make of that?

DUST WAS THE DAY

BOOK TWO

CHAPTER ONE

REVISION

Well, here I am.

I got 'em all stacked beside me and a brand-new Royal Quiet de Luxe typewriting machine that Mister Parks down at the American Legion has kindly lent me. And there's quite a pile of them pages too.

Gabriel Brannigan, what a guy! He sent me all these letters telling me his story whilst I was overseas and I tell you, it's taken me nigh on a month to sort them all out and get them in order.

Okay, so a fair portion of them have got damp marks from the sea at Saipan and been bitten at by bugs on Tinian but they're a mixed bag anyway as old man Gabriel wrote them out on whatever came to hand. I got pages of the Phil Stagger Feed Calendar for 1942 with his writing all over the back, there's receipts and bills he used, even some handbills for the Benopé Rodeo. All of it written in pencil with that tight tiny hand of his that takes up every inch of white space on show.

And what a story.

You've got to remember my first outing with him.

He was nigh on a hundred-years-old back then but looked more like seventy and fitter than any at his age. A grouchy old buck on the outside but on the inside his heart was in the right place. He told me how his pappy was murdered by a mean piece of work called Lomas Chain and his partners and as a young man he went out and hunted them down. Then how he was sent off to fight in the Civil War and ran into Lomas again with the same bad result. After that he got to be a law officer but his new wife was killed by a band of renegades and he left off to go ride shotgun for a stage company. That led him into a liaison with a fine looking gambling lady called April Turner who turned out to be double-dealing on a setup with Lomas Chain, who just wouldn't seem to stay out of his life. But by then Gabriel was a scout with the Seventh Cavalry under Colonel George Armstrong Custer and getting involved in the Indian Wars. Finally he got Lomas in his sights and the last thing he told me was how he laid a bead on him and shot him down to save his old enemy's hide from being ravaged by a war party of Sioux warriors. Whether that was altruism on his part or just plain cold-blooded vengeance I couldn't say.

My Ma told me to set it all down, so I did, but that wasn't the half of the tale. She passed before I got back home from the army and could show her how it came out and I was right sorry about that as she was the finest woman I ever knowed and we miss her still. There was so many questions I needed to ask her about her relationship with Gabriel. And I would have asked him just that if he hadn't lit out and got himself busted up down in Louisiana in a juke joint called The Buckshee Drink and Dance Hall, him being all d-'n-d and raising Cain so bad that they put him in an old folk's home instead of jail. Well, he broke out of there and where he went after that I don't know. But I aim to find out.

If he's still kicking, he must be pushing a hundred-and-three years old by now. It's a long stretch but I guess if anyone could make it, he would.

My younger brother Ahab and his wife Cindy have been real sweet to me as I was pretty busted up when I got back from the Pacific, I near had my leg blowed off by a shell over there on Okinawa so couldn't get around too well. Yeah, that's right, my little brother got married whilst I was away and now he and Cindy have a little one coming, which will make them loving parents and me an uncle. I sure wish Ma could have stayed around to see that as she was a righteous and God-fearing woman and would have thanked the Lord for the blessings of having her two sons safe and a grandchild on the way.

Ahab's got himself set up right well and runs his own real estate office and makes himself a fair to middling income, so they're a real contented couple and I enjoy their company. They got this swell house, a Kelvinator refrigerator and a brand new Chevy Coupé and it's all a mite different than how it was for us before the war. Ma was on her own back then and brought us up on her lonesome but when she passed we sold the old place at Benopé and I had some severance pay coming and now I got a pension that gives me some leeway to play at being a writer.

Anyways, Ahab and Cindy let me stay with them and I have my own apartment over the garage that suits me just fine. I get around better now after all the rehab treatment at the Percy Jones Army Hospital, I still need a stick, but with the mobility I have, some time soon I aim to set out and find out what happened to Gabriel as best I can.

When I got back Stateside it appeared to me that the world had shifted and things had changed a whole lot in the country. We had dropped the bomb and were an atomic age but in Gabriel's time things didn't alter that much no matter whatever conflict was going on elsewhere. A man still carried an iron strapped to his hip and there was plenty that used them guns to make their way.

It seems that after he got free of the Indian Wars, Gabriel drifted back down south and took up for a spell as a Texas Ranger riding with Company C along the border. They was still tough old days back then and plenty of problems in that wild country. Mexican raiders crossed the border and Indian renegades still caused difficulties and it was down to the Rangers to keep the peace.

My name's Jonah Cord, I'm coming up on twenty-three years of age and whilst I try and find the old fella I intend to tap out Gabriel's story and bring it all up to date.

CHAPTER TWO

DOWN MEXICO WAY

Gabriel Brannigan nestled in a shadowed crevice on the northeast slope of Canyon del Infierno and kept his eye firmly fixed on the tin roofed cabin below. It was a rugged zigzagging canyon of blood-red rock with steep sides and a well hidden entranceway that opened into a narrow passage that eventually widened out into a flat sandy area that bounced the sunlight back into Gabriel's eyes with blazing ferocity. And it was real hot. The Chihuahua sun beat down with full intensity and Gabriel reckoned the temperature outside was reaching well over the high nineties. But he had chosen the ledge with that in mind and was crouched in a shady high overlook that gave him cover as well as protection from direct sunlight.

The canyon ran on a northwest to southeast axis and Gabriel's position on the northeast face meant he was safe until late afternoon when the sun's position came around enough to get in his eyes. But he was expecting company long before then. His partner and fellow Ranger, a young-blood called Prentice Jarrow, had drawn the short straw and occupied a sweaty site on the opposite wall.

True to say, Gabriel was somewhat concerned about the keen young man who demonstrated all the eagerness of his inexperience but then, as Gabriel philosophically considered, they all had to learn sometime.

He shifted position to ease his legs and set his Henry rifle on a rest between rocks to give him leeway for movement and stability when it came to making the shot.

Naranja Ned and his gang had hit the bank at Ramona just over the Texas border and Gabriel's captain at Ranger Headquarters had given the two Rangers orders to track the thieves down.

'If I was to hear of the complete and sudden disappearance of Naranja and his crew from the face of the earth,' Captain Brooks had said. 'I would not be at all surprised, in fact I'd be damned grateful. There would be a bottle of fine rum and two top class ladies from Madam Delphine's ready to hookup if that were the case. You with me on this, Gabe?'

It was basically an order to take no prisoners and one at that, to be carried out on foreign soil, if discovered the affair could be used to kick off an international incident by the Mexican authorities. But that was the way of it with the Rangers; they were not men to hesitate over such trivialities. It was a harsh country down on the border and they dealt in harsh realities, usually ones steeped in lead and blood.

Naranja Ned was an odd sort of character who at one time had decided to dye his hair bright orange, in the sorry belief it would put the fear of God into his victims. Where and how he had done it was a mystery, probably in some border town whorehouse by a dimwit gal who knew no better and had bleached his locks pure white with lye paste before applying the dye. The result had been, that although Naranja's hair was shaded a flaming orange, it had promptly started to fall out in clumps. Ruefully, Gabriel reckoned that the wanted outlaw would soon have to change his name to the more fitting, 'Bare Head Ned'.

The hirsutely challenged Ned ran with a crew of three others as equally unsavory as himself.

Jake 'Schlong' Otley was an ambiguous woman hater and abuser, a weasely little over-sexed fellow with a propensity for rape and female mistreatment, who was also said to own a flopper of momentous proportions that he used at every available opportunity whether his prey was willing or not.

The second member of the gang was a large bull of a black man known only as Blood Simple. A one-time slave reported to have broken out of enslavement before the war by taking the heads of his plantation owner's whole family, including the old mother, wife and two children by using the artless expedience of a long bladed machete that he carried still. It was said that the knucklebone necklace he wore about his neck was composed of the dissected elements of the unfortunate plantation owner's hands.

Castille Hidago, an erudite and darkly handsome Mexican was the third component. Once a land-owner of some note, his ranch and all he owned had been taken from him under dubious legal means by an official in the corrupt Diaz government and Castille had reverted to criminal acts to sustain himself. Fast with a gun and by far the brightest and keenest of the group he had sold his Catholic soul to the devil and no longer cared who fell victim to the gang's brutal activities across the border. His one true motivation was the downfall of the Porfiriato and all the servants of the president, Porfirio Diaz, who ruled Mexico in a cruel state of dictatorship.

They had hit the bank in the town of Ramona and it's small outlying military station and brought grief and vexation to the whole place with a rule of terror that had lasted two whole days. During which time mayhem and murder had operated on a major scale.

The sheriff's office, jailhouse and half of Main Street had been burned to the ground, the bank's coffers emptied and a debauch had followed that left ten dead and a variety of the female population in a state of expected pregnancy after Jake's rapine ministrations.

The few soldiers left guarding the small supply station had put up a lackluster resistance, and after some misunderstandings by the lieutenant in charge and four of the six troopers had been cut down, the survivors had departed in full retreat leaving the outlaws to their own devices.

All of which had led to Gabriel and Prentice following their trail until they crossed the Rio Grande and came to the Canyon del Infierno and the hideout in its depths.

Now he and Prentice waited for their return.

Given the odds against them, the plan was to nail the last member of the gang through the door and keep the rest pinned down inside until they either surrendered or made a break for it. Gabriel had enough water and supplies with him to sit it out and he had already made sure that every tin and sack of dry goods inside the cabin had been destroyed. The gang's water supply had been broached leaving anyone inside the cabin with nothing to sustain them under the blazing heat that the place was invested with at this time of year.

At the worst, Gabriel reckoned on three days, at the best they would try to run right away, and the Rangers would pick them off as they came out. There was no cover in the valley below, the gang trusting on the hidden entrance to keep them safe. The valley floor was a bare sandy hole that between the flanking fires of the two Rangers would become a killing ground if they tried to make a break for it.

The hollow sound of echoing hoof beats told them they would not have long to wait.

Gabriel leaned forward as the scattered riders of the gang rode into sight. They came fast as if glad to be back or maybe that was just the way that they travelled as a matter of course. At the rear, Blood Simple dragged a pack mule with a heavy load strapped to its panniers.

Gabriel hoped that the youthful Prentice was awake and not too tense to kick things off early.

The group dismounted, with the large black man given the task of taking their mounts to a corral amongst some stands of yucca growing out back of the cabin. The rest slouched inside, Jake jawing loudly to Naranja and Castille following solemnly on behind.

It would have to be Blood Simple who would be last in and Gabriel waited patiently for the Negro to make his appearance. He set up his Henry and took a mark on one of the porch supports at the entrance to the cabin.

Sounds of unrest came from inside and Gabriel realized that they had discovered the destruction of their supplies.

Blood Simple heard the uproar and came running, his lumbering figure a grim dark shadow against the glaring sand.

He was at the porch and stepping up as Gabriel sighted and his finger tightened on the trigger.

But then a rider came fast through the entrance of the canyon in a clatter of echoing sound and Blood Simple turned at sight of the speeding horseman.

Gabriel compressed his lips and halted long enough to take in the wide sombrero and grey uniform of a Rurale, one of the rough paramilitary Mexican force made up of convicts and outlaws that policed the outlying countryside. For a moment Gabriel hesitated, where there was one of them there might be more, and the presence of Texas Rangers discovered on Mexican soil could create a political problem. As long as they operated in secret everything would be fine but an obvious incursion could cause an international disaster and so he held off for a moment.

The Rurale swiftly dismounted and exchanged

hurried words with the Negro before the two went inside.

With their chance missed, Gabriel beat an irritated fist against the rock before him. But what, he wondered, were the Rurales doing conferring with Anglo bank robbers?

There was a burst of noise and Naranja and the Rurale came tumbling out of the cabin making their way across to the corral. Gabriel, impatient to get his man whatever the result, aimed again but the damned Rurale kept bobbing in front of his target and he could not get a clean shot.

The two made it to the corral and Naranja immediately hauled the pack mule across and began to unfasten the lashings on the panniers. He lifted a covering flap from the bulky load and allowed the Rurale to catch a glimpse of the pack's contents. It was too far for Gabriel to make out, but he thought he caught the glint of metal.

The two made their way back to the cabin and the Rurale nodded and shook his head in satisfaction before swinging up onto his pony in one motion and spinning it around to ride at top speed out of the canyon.

Naranja stood at the porch and watched him go. At last Gabriel saw his chance and he leveled the rifle. He let his breath out slowly and tightened his finger on the trigger; the strange looking head of sprouting red hair clear in his sights.

The porch post just above the clumped scalp exploded in a burst of splinters and the sound of a rifle shot echoed loudly.

Prentice! You damned fool, cursed Gabriel. The boy just could not wait and had let fly in his impatience. Worse still, he had missed.

Swinging low, Naranja ducked back into the doorway, already pulling the pistol from his holster. A volley of wild shots followed his disappearance, all of them coming from the cabin doorway and flying in every direction into the canyon.

The fusillade stopped as Gabriel heard Naranja bellow for a ceasefire.

In the silence following, Gabriel watched the billows of white gun smoke drift away and spread out in the hot breathless air.

'Who's out there?' Naranja called. 'What you want with us?'

Gabriel sighed in despair as he heard Prentice boldly reply, 'We're the Texas Rangers and we've come to take you in. Come out now with your hands raised.'

Now the young fool had given away his position and sure enough a volley from the cabin lifted dust and chips of stone around the young man's location.

'*We?* You said 'we',' called Naranja. 'Who else you got out there with you?'

At least this time Prentice kept his mouth shut and did not reply. Gabriel took the opportunity to consider the mule pack and he wondered what it might hold of interest to the Mexicans. Maybe, he thought, I should go down there and take a look whilst these outlaws are distracted by young Prentice.

'Come on, bucko,' called Naranja. 'You don't

mean to tell me you're on your lonesome, do you? I mean to say, one man against four, the odds ain't in your favor here.'

'Yeah, one little bitty Ranger against us big boys don't leave you with much hope of taking us down, now does it?' jeered 'Schlong' Jake as he joined in the attempt to rattle their attacker.

'We got us a whole company out here and we got you surrounded. Best you all surrender nice and easy,' Prentice replied but his voice held little conviction.

Gabriel took the opportunity of the exchange and as attention was fixed on the other side of the canyon he began to worm his way back down the rock wall.

'Sounds to me like we got us a boy Ranger here,' Jake called loudly.

'And a piss-poor shot as well,' said Naranja. 'Couldn't hit a standing figure at three hundred yards, what they got in the Rangers now? Babies still on the teat?'

'You assholes!' Prentice roared angrily and blazed off a few shots that panged off the tin roof.

'See that,' chuckled Jake. 'He hit the damned roof. Bit lower, fella, we're in here not up there.'

Gabriel dropped to the valley floor unseen and made his way cautiously between fallen boulders and through shadows from the overhanging rock towards the corral. He travelled lightly on moccasined feet, his education amongst the Shoshone as a youngster paying off as he slid silently through the wall of yucca and up to the pack mule.

'Let's see,' Naranja was musing loudly. 'They wouldn't send just one punk kid after us; he'd had to have a daddy figure to hold his hand. Now, who is it, boy? Who you got with you who's bright enough to hold his water and keep his mouth shut?'

'Never you mind,' came Prentice's worried reply. 'We got more than enough men out here to handle you. Will you surrender or take your chances?'

'*Take our chances?*' laughed Jake. 'With a shooter like you I'd take my chances any day. Come on down here and get me, sucker.'

Gabriel lifted the pack flap and saw the golden glint of barrels and a tied stack of oblong ammunition magazines. A Gatling gun! They were trading armaments with the Mexicans. Well, that explained the raid on the Ramona station; it was the military's weapons they were after and not the bank in particular.

CHAPTER THREE

NEW FRIENDS

The first Gabriel knew of it was when he heard the heavy thud of footprints.

He looked around in time to see Blood Simple bearing down on him with the searing edge of his machete raised and gleaming in the half-light of the shadowed corral.

The big Negro was grunting with effort and it was obvious he had found a back way out of the cabin with the intention of coming up to take out Prentice but had seen Gabriel instead.

The blade swished through the air and missed Gabriel's nose by inches as he backed off and collided with the mule. The animal hee-hawed and kicked out with its hind legs as it jittered away. Gabriel lost his footing as the support of the mule fell away and he went down and scrabbled to get away on elbows and heels with the big black man looming over him.

'I got you, white boy,' growled Blood Simple, his bloodshot eyes staring wide as he swung again with the machete.

Gabriel rolled sideways, the machete burying

itself in the dust where he had lain. The Henry rifle was out of reach, having dropped when Gabriel fell, and he kept rolling over as the lumbering Negro came after him.

Scooping up dust, Gabriel threw handfuls in Blood Simple's face covering him in a cloud of grit. Roaring with rage and half-blinded, Blood Simple kicked out as Gabriel began to climb to his feet and knocked the Ranger's legs from under him. Lying on his back, Gabriel was going for the Colt in his holster but its security thong tied down the hammer and there was no quick draw as Blood Simple was onto him too fast.

Desperately, Gabriel swung his moccasin boot up hard and raised a puff of dust from between the big man's thighs. There was an *'oof!'* of pain from Blood Simple who doubled over long enough to give Gabriel a chance to scramble to his feet.

Blood Simple's face was twisted in rage, his bloodshot eyes glaring at Gabriel with frightening intensity and at the crouch, with one hand on his aching crotch; he lifted the machete high over his head. Lurching forward the black man swung the blade in vicious flashes, zigzagging the broad blade before him as he drove Gabriel back towards the wall of Yucca plants behind.

Gritting his teeth, Gabriel flipped his Colt free and let Blood Simple have it.

Three shots in the chest and the big man was still coming, hollering loudly with blood staining his teeth, he roared in agony and anger still swinging the blade as he advanced.

In desperation, Gabriel raised his gun arm and blew a hole directly between Blood Simple's staring eyes. The huge black man stood stunned for a long moment as if only hit by a two-by-four beam instead of having his brains blown out by a .45 bullet. Then he dropped to his knees and tumbled forwards to fall face down into the dirt of the corral and lay still.

Breathing heavily, Gabriel dashed across to collect his rifle as he heard shouts and gunfire coming his way from the cabin.

He rolled over and collected the rifle coming up fast on one knee, looking around to see Naranja and Jake, both clambering through a hole broken in the planks of the rear wall. Gabriel cranked a bullet under the hammer and fired in their direction, his bullet kicking up a halo of dust from the wooden wall behind them.

Both men ducked instinctively and began a reply of firing that raised plumes of dust around Gabriel's feet and cracked against the surrounding rocks behind.

Gabriel stood his ground and worked the lever of the Henry loosing off a tattoo of shots that ripped the dusty air. Jake pirouetted in a whirling turn, the front of his shirt flying open and one arm spinning aside as his shoulder was shredded.

Naranja was racing sideways heading for the cover of the Yucca and Gabriel was quickly on his feet and paralleling his line of escape. The outlaw had his hands on a saddle pony and was keeping the animal between himself and Gabriel, his pistol leveled over the saddle. All Gabriel could see was the carrot clumps of hair sprouting in tufts from the otherwise pink skin of Naranja's skull. Both men fired at once.

Gabriel felt the slug hit him high in the left shoulder, the blow lifting him from his feet and sending him over onto his back.

Unharmed, Naranja was sniggering loudly in nervous excitement as he struggled to hold the pony still so he could mount.

From the lying position on his back, Gabriel lifted the rifle and aimed between his feet at Naranja's legs visible behind the pony's skittering limbs. Fighting the pain in his shoulder, he worked the lever and fired twice. And was gratified to see Naranja howl in pain as his legs were kicked away from under him and he fell heavily clutching at one shattered leg below the knee.

'Goddamn you, Ranger!' he bellowed. 'You damn well got me.'

Gabriel felt nausea rise in his throat at the burning sensation and needle-sharp sting as he struggled to lift the rifle again. Naranja was panting, his ugly face lifted to look directly at Gabriel when the Ranger fired and the scalp, full of scattered orange tufts, flew apart as neatly as if it were a breakfast egg being scooped out. Gray matter and ginger hair mixed freely in the bloody mist that erupted volcano-like from the top of Naranja's head and he bucked over and flopped down.

'*Prentice!*' Gabriel called as he climbed unsteadily to his feet but there was no answer from his companion. Trailing the rifle weakly in one hand, Gabriel made his way over to the writhing figure of Jake who lay on the ground in a spreading pool of blood. Gabriel stood over the wounded man and Jake looked back at him hazily.

'You shot me through, Ranger, have you done for me or not? I can't tell for sure,' he gasped.

Gabriel looked at the shoulder torn apart so badly the bone was exposed and at the ricocheting bullet wound that had shot sideways and transfixed the man's chest, ripping his shirtfront apart.

Gabriel toed the man's pistol out of reach, 'You're still breathing, ain't you?' he said.

'Hardly,' coughed Jake, spitting blood from between his teeth.

'Stay there,' said Gabriel. 'You got one more inside the cabin with you, ain't you?'

'Yeah, that sly faced Mex. But he's fast, Ranger, you'd better watch out.'

Gabriel moved over cautiously to the hole in the wall of the cabin and risked a glance inside. There was no movement in the shadowed interior, and nobody took a shot at him. It looked like Castille Hidago had gotten away clean. The gap in the wall faced the open doorway of the cabin and through the door Gabriel had a clear view of the patch of sand out front.

Lying, face down and spread out was a body he recognized at once as Prentice Jarrow.

'Oh, Christ, no,' breathed Gabriel.

He began to stumble around the corner of the cabin. He was barely able to walk now his shoulder wound hurt so bad and he dragged his rifle by the barrel as he wove past the figure of Jake still lying where he had left him.

'You going to just leave me here?' complained Jake. 'I been bad shot you know.'

'Sure, sure, I noticed. You stay there and don't you move.'

Jake coughed and spat a sidelong stream of bloody spit, 'Just like a Ranger. Got my arm near blowed off and he says don't move. Jesus! Where do they find you guys?'

Gabriel staggered dizzily over towards Prentice hoping to find some signs of life still left in the boy.

He was halfway there when he heard the voice behind him.

'He did well, your young fren"

Dizzily, Gabriel spun around; the movement lost him his balance and he fell to the ground. He looked up to see Castille Hidago sitting in shadow and propped up against the cabin wall beside the doorway with his legs spread wide before him. The Mexican was shucking out a cheroot and trying to light it with trembling and bloodied fingers.

'Don't try anything, Castille,' warned Gabriel unsteadily.

'No chance, senor,' said Castille, wryly lifting his jacket aside to expose a bloody wound in his side. 'The young one there, he has put a bullet in me before I could bring him down.'

'Guess you're my prisoner now,' said Gabriel.

Castille laughed softly, 'Much good it will do either of us. It appears you are hurt bad also.'

Both men sat facing each other, Gabriel feeling the hot sun beating down on him and Castille puffing contentedly on his cigar.

'I could sure go one of those right now,' confessed Gabriel.

'You come here, I have plenty,' offered the Mexican.

Gabriel obediently dragged himself across on all fours and slumped down beside Castille.

'Sure made a mess of this,' he said, gratefully accepting the offered cheroot.

'The young one,' said Castille, pointing with his cigar at Prentice. 'He was too ready, no? He could not wait.'

'Yeah,' sighed Gabriel in agreement. 'Kid should have held back, that was the plan.'

'Ah, well, it happens. Look, senor, what is your name?'

'Gabriel Brannigan.'

'A pleasure, senor Brannigan, but I have a suggestion, if you will permit? I know of a place where we can get help, it is not far. If you will allow this, we can make our way there and maybe get some treatment for our wounds.'

Gabriel thought it over for a minute as he enjoyed and savored his smoke, 'Why not,' he said finally. 'We stay here we're both buzzard meat.'

'What of the others?'

'Two of your buddies are already dead and one heading that way fast.'

Castille sighed, 'The world is a better place without, I think.'

'Well, *you* rode with them.'

Castille shrugged and then winced in pain at the movement, 'Needs must, amigo. When you are a renegade in your own country there is little in the way of options.'

'Can you make it to the horses?'

'Perhaps,' chuckled the Mexican. 'Perhaps we can help each other.'

CHAPTER FOUR

RESPITE

We got to take a short break here whilst I fill you in on where I was at.

I got me a vehicle off a used car lot, a Plymouth Chrysler, it had seen better days but I didn't have that much in the way of readies so it had to do. Packed my junk in the back and made my farewells to Ahab and Cindy, promising to be back before the baby arrived. Ahab wasn't too keen on me going, reckoning that my leg was still not good enough to make any long journey. But, if I was to tell you the truth of it, I reckon they was both a mite glad I was off. I mean to say, here they was, a young couple just starting out and with a kid on the way, who needed some beat up war vet hanging around with his bad dreams and moments of misery.

So, I lit out southeast on Route 90 heading for the Interstate and Louisiana.

When I got there the Buckshee Drink and Dance Hall wasn't as much fun a place as its name suggested, it was a beat-up joint on an unpaved road at back of a convenience store and retread station. A corrugated iron roofed wooden shack hosting a mainly colored clientele. The front was covered with tacky advertisement signs for everything from Jax to Wonder Bread, the rusty tin plates of the signage covering places where the planks had started to come apart. It was a high, step-up front and I struggled to make the climb, hopping along with my stick to help me up and groaning with the ache as I did so.

Now you has to realize this was Klan country with a bust-em-up body of rednecks calling themselves The Silver Dollar Group who were down for most of the killings and burnings of black folks in the vicinity and for a white man to enter a colored drinking establishment was not a welcome event at that time, so I walked in there with some trepidation I can tell you.

That kind of race shit has never bothered me too much. I just treat folks as I find them and I met plenty of fine black fellas during my time in the Marines. Each to his own, I say. They don't bother me and I don't trouble them. So I don't hold no grudge against them people and hope they can handle me the same.

It was a long hall inside with a dirty spit-stained floor and stale with the smell of old sweat and spilled beer. Posters proclaiming black performers I had never heard of papered the walls, with names like 'Slap-That-Plank' Doolittle and Rooster and the Raft Raisers. The dump had the overhang feel that on Saturday night it went wild in there but for the rest of the week it was quiet as the proverbial. It was pretty dark with only a few customers in residence, for which I thanked God. Though what heads there were in there turned to stare at me and you could cut the atmosphere of resentment with a paper knife. I walked in leaning heavily on my stick. I was kind of paining a little after my drive and with sitting for so long so I hobbled a bit which might have made me look kinda harmless, at least I hoped so.

'What you want?' boomed an edgy voice from behind the bar that consisted of a simple plank counter on trestles with shelves of soda and whatnot behind. The fellow behind the bar was a tall Negro man and as black as the shadows that surrounded him.

I stomped over to him, thinking to myself I had faced hordes of screaming banzai Japs in my time so why should I be a-feared of one man whatever his color or inclination. The couple of other somber looking clients were dressed in grubby farm-boy overalls and pull-down hats and sat on bar stools watching me closely like hungry bears at feeding time. At one end of the hall on a kind of raised stage made of beer crates, a skinny little guy was sliding out a blues riff on a beat-up guitar and he never let off playing the whole time I was in there.

'I'd like a Nehi,' I said.

'You know this place ain't for white folks, don' you?' said the bar tender solemnly.

'I know that,' I come back.

'Okay, mister,' said the barman. 'Yo' get your drink an' then yo' leave. I don' want no trouble here.'

'I don't want trouble either,' I said, propping the counter. 'Just that I'm kinda hot, is all.'

He popped the bottle of soda and placed it in front of me.

'Thank you, sir,' I said politely.

There was a heavy silence then, except for the guitar man picking out his haunting tune, a stomper that spoke heavily of sad souls and lost promises.

'Nice day,' I said to break the silence.

'If you say so,' was the gloomy reply.

'Say, I'm looking for a guy. Old white fella was in here some time back; he got himself busted by the police so I'm told. Name of Gabriel Brannigan.'

The barman pursed his lips, folded his arms across his chest and leaned his butt on the ice chest behind and shook his head from side to side, 'Don' know the man,' he said with a show of non-committal indifference.

'You has to remember the law coming in here,' I pressed. 'They took him off to some old folks home I believe. You know where that is?'

The negative shaking head again. These fellows just wanted me out of there.

A deathly silence followed and I sucked on the soda for a minute.

'Old guy,' I tried again. 'Real old, long sideburns and white hair tied in two pigtails, maybe dressed like a cowpoke.'

'What happen' to your laig?'

It was the blues musician suddenly calling out to me from the end of the room and I turned to face him.

'Stopped one overseas,' I admitted, as I didn't see no reason to be ashamed of it.

'You was in the army?'

'I was, 1st Marine Corp.'

'*Semper Fi*, brother. I was over there too, where was you at?'

'Any damned foxhole they sent me to on Saipan, Tinian and Okinawa.'

'Me, I was a little earlier, got mine at Guadacanal.'

I could see then there was a homemade crutch resting beside his chair and that he was favoring a leg the same as me, except one of the fatigue dressed legs was missing from the knee down. He rippled the strings a while, his long fingers sliding a bottle-neck neat and sharp over the frets without a glance downwards at where it was going.

'This old man,' he said. 'Why you interested?'

'He's a friend. Saved my ma's neck when she was in a spot of bother, he done me a lot of good as well.'

'Well, he was surely a hard and horny old character. Certainly tied on a load, old Joob there, the bartender, had to call in the police to pacify him. Joob don' want no trouble with the white folks, ain't that right, Joob?' The question was on the cynical edge as if the player didn't have a lot of respect for the barman.

The barkeep grunted and began polishing the bar with a rag a little self-consciously. 'You see that burned out old place up the road?' he asked.

I had noted the sooty ruin on my way down and nodded.

'That was Freddy Silvester's place, he used to repair shoes. Had a disagreement about some cowboy boots that cost him bad. They come held a shotgun on him whilst they burned his place down, then they pushed him back inside. He suffered third degree burns on that one.'

'I get it,' I said. 'I'm just looking for an old friend here, that's all.'

'He was hollering about a fellow named Lomas Chain,' said the bluesman, chunking down on a chord. 'Like it was the devil himself on his shoulder.'

'Lomas Chain is dead,' I said.

'Well, I reckon his ghost come haunt that old man then.'

'Where did they take him?'

'They said he wasn't right in the head and took him to the Arbuthnot Rest Home, though it ain't no good going there. He done break out of that place.'

'You know where he went after that?'

'No, sir. He just went.'

'Where is this place?'

'Down the road a spell,' he said missing a note to give direction with his bottlenecked finger.

'Thank you,' I said, dropping money for the soda on the bar. 'I'm obliged.'

I was at the door when the musician called after me, 'You're the second man to come asking,' he said.

I turned sharp at that, 'Another man asking after Gabriel? Who was he?'

The bluesman shook his head, 'Don' know 'bout that but he was a darned sight meaner looking than you.'

'How's that?'

'Big fella with a broke nose like it was flattened sometime, favored a snappy Fedora and nice gray suit though I reckon the bulge he carried under his arm weren't no Gideon Bible.'

'He a Kluxer?'

The blues player shook his head sorrowfully and shrugged before going back to his playing.

It was late and my mind was full of the mysterious stranger who was also on the hunt for Gabriel. It left me wondering why some gun carrying hard-hat could be after the old man. I had to think on it a while and I was hungry, so I found me a roadside diner and had a meal before asking direction to the nearest motel.

It was a hot night, sticky and thick with air like liquid oil, so I sat in the open doorway of my room looking through the screen door at the bugs playing around the light over the car park. I lit up a Lucky and pared down what the colored men had told me. Had Gabriel upset somebody else on his drunken spree, I wondered. It could hardly have been someone from his past, the irascible old man was so advanced in years that there was hardly a chance anyone was left alive from back then to bother him. Odd though, certainly odd and there was no doubt Gabriel had made plenty of enemies in his time.

CHAPTER FIVE

SUCCOR SUCKER

Gabriel passed out somewhere along the way, so he had no idea where he was when he came to.

All he knew was that he was in a clean and white adobe walled room with an open window that let in a fresh breeze. They were high up he guessed as the air was cool and free of the smoldering heat of the lowlands. There was the scent of the coolness of brittle rock and a sense of space out beyond the window.

All he could see through the window was blue sky and all he could hear was the sound of goat bells and the baaing of baby critters.

His shoulder ached like crazy but it was tightly bound in clean bandages and his body felt as if it had been scrubbed down clean as well. The bed he lay on was a simple thing and the blanket a plain Indian weave but it was comfortable enough.

He looked around for his clothes and pistol and saw them sitting on a chair at the foot of the bed.

He was struggling to sit up when the door opened and a young woman entered carrying a tray. She was not tall but full breasted despite her willowy frame, her features were that of a pleasant mestizo appearance and she had long black hair, night dark, like a cloak of shining silk, that ran down her back to her waist.

She smiled broadly at him, showing a row of even teeth that shone white against her bronzed skin and the darkness of her broad lips.

'Buenos dias,' she smiled. 'It is good you are awake, senor, but do not try to move so much. The wound, it is not yet healed.'

'Where am I?' asked Gabriel.

'This is the house of my father, Senor Alberto de Los Angeles, and I am Christina.'

'You doctored me?'

'Si, senor,' she said, setting down the tray on a small table beside the bed.

'Well, thank you, ma'am, I'm obliged.'

'It is nothing, senor.'

'Where's Castille Hidago? Did he bring me here?'

'He did, he is here, outside speaking with my father.'

'Maybe I should go see him,' Gabriel said attempting to get up.

'No, no,' frowned Christina angrily, pushing him back down. 'Will you destroy all my careful sewing? This will open up again, if you do so.'

Resentfully, Gabriel obeyed and slumped back down.

'Now, be patient, senor. I must see how the wound in your shoulder is doing.'

Her fingers were light and cool on Gabriel's

fevered shoulder and as she leaned to undo his bandages with her head bent in concentration, he surreptitiously examined her.

She was a beauty, there was no doubt of that and there was a honey scent to her skin that Gabriel breathed in. Her long hair trailed across him in whispers and distractedly she tucked it back over her ear with one hand as she worked. Her forgotten breath came heavy and regular close to his ear. Christina wore only a simple blouse with a deeply scooped neck that exposed the crests of her bosom and as he she leaned over him, he saw the weight of her unfettered breasts flow down and fill the cloth. It was with soft pressure that they lay pressing against his arm and as she wore nothing underneath and only a fraction of material kept them apart Gabriel drew a sharp intake of breath as, despite himself, a shiver of desire ran up his spine. She had no intention to create it but there was something inherently sexual in the sound and feel of her as she worked on him. Gabriel felt himself stiffening beneath the blanket and it was only the sudden sharpness of pain as she gently probed the wound that brought him back from his reverie.

'It is looking good, senor, there is no infection,' she said. 'It will take time but all will be well, I think.'

'Gabriel,' he said, the sound thick in his throat.

'Yes?' she looked at him in query, their eyes, only inches apart. His ice-water blue and hers deep brown and liquid like warm chocolate. There were hidden depths there he observed, obscure secret things that he could not determine and were denied to him like the meaning of graven images from antiquity carved in stone and he wondered at their undisclosed motivation.

'That's my name,' he managed.

'Si,' she flashed him her brilliant smile. 'Gabriel, I shall remember.'

She began to refasten the bandage, turning him to his side as she did so. There was something too intimate about the whole thing. Him half naked in the bed with her gentle brown fingers tracing his skin and although she appeared innocent of the effect she was having on him, Gabriel could not believe that he was alone in his response.

In this heady mix of pain and repressed lust he was rudely awoken as Castille Hidago entered the room. The Mexican looked pale and favored one side, leaning over with one hand fixed to the wound below his shirt.

'So,' he said. 'The warrior is awake and how does he fare, Christina?'

'Well,' she answered, concentrating on a final knot in the bandage. 'He is doing well.'

'How about you?' Gabriel asked the Mexican.

'Ah!' grinned Castille, spreading his hands wide but unable to disguise the wince of pain as he did so. 'I was lucky. There was much blood, but the bullet passed through, so Christina has tied me up like a turkey and I will heal with only a scar to mark the day.'

'As shall you both. There, senor Gabriel, I am finished.'

She gave a sigh of satisfaction and stood away

from the bed. As she did so, Castille draped his arm around her shoulders and pulled her close.

'She is a wonder, no, is she not, Texas Ranger? My little Christina,' he smiled at her affectionately. 'The best wife a man ever had.'

Christina looked back up at him and smiled in reply.

'You brought me here?' Gabriel asked, sullenly trying to hide his disappointment at discovering the two were a married couple.

'I did,' said Castille, looking down at him benevolently. 'You were barely conscious on the journey, but I managed to tie you to the saddle and bring you here to the mountains.'

'And where are we exactly?'

'In the mountains above Atahualpa. It is a secret place; we are safe here.'

'Safe from what?'

Castille shrugged, 'Why, the Rurales, of course.'

Gabriel nodded, struggling to sit and cradling his strapped arm as he did so, 'Yes, I remember the Rurale down in the canyon. You were trading guns with them.'

Castille smiled brightly, 'So it appeared but no, Naranja Ned may have thought so but no, senor.'

'Then what?'

'You are here, senor Gabriel, in a strong outpost of revolutionaries. We are all opponents of the president, Porfirio Diaz and seek to bring him and his vile dictatorship down.'

Gabriel noted that Castille's tone had changed; there was a note of bitter determination in his voice now.

'The plan was that we allow Naranja to make the deal with the authorities and that we should steal the guns before he was to deliver them. We, the revolutionaries, need weapons and we would have taken them before they could be given over.'

'You planned a double cross on Ned?' Gabriel asked with some surprise.

Castille shrugged, 'He was a means to an end, that is all. We could not go ourselves in force and show our hand, it needed to be Anglos that stole from Anglos.'

'And what of all the folks that got killed and their town burned down?' asked Gabriel with a touch of anger.

'This is a war, senor,' said Castille grimly. 'There are extenuating circumstances. I am sorry that this happened, and you should know I abhor the necessity but if you were to see what is happening down here across the border in Mexico, you would understand. We fight against a merciless regime that has all the military power and is unflinching in using it to bring the common people under its control.'

'So that justifies rape and murder in a Texas town?' growled Gabriel.

Castille pulled himself proudly erect, dropping his arm from Christina's shoulder, 'Thirty-four peasants from Rio Teocelo, a village near here, were taken from their homes yesterday, half of them hanged and the rest shot by firing squad. Last week in the village of Chahuapan, forty men were taken from the fields and forced to watch their womenfolk raped on the ground before them. Afterwards their execution was arbitrary and for no reason, they were all killed by machete. Did you know of this, Texas Ranger? No, this will not be reported in your newspapers, there is a policy of silence when it comes to Mexico.'

'It don't mean you have to take it out on Americans, it's your own affair.'

Castille shook his head, 'It is not that simple. You Americans have interests here that they do not want disturbed. There is much oil, copper and silver mined by American companies, there is the port of Veracruz with access for your ships to travel internationally. All of this the American government accepts from the hand of Diaz and they will say and do nothing to lose these benefits. And whilst this happens the land is taken by force from the starving campesinos, the rich ones in Mexico City want it all, so they take from the peasants to make themselves grand haciendas with rich lands.'

Gabriel shook his head, 'I don't know about any of that, I just know a crime was committed and it's my job to take you back for trial.'

Castille barked a dismissive laugh, 'You think so?'

'I do,' promised Gabriel with a determined glint. 'That and them guns you stole from the US army.'

'Yes, the guns,' said Castille, rubbing his chin thoughtfully. 'They will still be there in the canyon.'

'If your Rurales ain't got to them first.'

'No, they will not come until they receive the gold for payment from Mexico City. The messenger you saw will take verifying word back to his officer, then that must be told up the line of authorities and they will release the funds to pay. It will take a little while, things do not move so fast here in Mexico.'

'Then I got time,' said Gabriel, challenging Castille with his eyes.

The Mexican flashed a winning smile and turned to his wife, 'You see, my dear. This is the Anglos, they do not give up. Even here, this one who is lying wounded in his bed, he will not desist.'

'You should not think so badly of my husband, senor Gabriel,' said Christina, fixing a sad glance on her patient. 'His intentions are honorable, I assure you. We have all suffered at the hands of the regime, all of us here in the mountains.'

'Well, lady, whilst I'm obliged to you for your kindness, I still have my own duty to perform.'

Christina shook her head sadly, 'Perhaps you will change your mind, I certainly hope so.'

A few days later, Gabriel could stay in his bed no longer and was on his feet again and despite Christina's urging not to do so he left the room and went to explore the revolutionary stronghold. His shoulder troubled him, but his legs worked okay and lying around was not Gabriel's way.

Outside the sun was rising and he found the camp awakening. A collection of tents and crudely thrown-up huts sat on a broad rock plateau that was backed by a curving wall of rugged rocks and overlooked a wide vista that disappeared into a misty horizon. Women of the camp were starting breakfast fires and there was the early scent of cooking mixed with the rough smell of stables and wood smoke.

Gabriel breathed the air that was crystalline this high up and knew that if there was none of the dense early mist filling the surrounding valleys, he would be able to see for miles. Behind him amongst the rocks were the remains of buildings, now much crumbled with only walls and open window spaces left standing. The one remaining habitable building had been restored enough for it to house Gabriel in his recovery.

'It was an old monastery built by the Spanish fathers,' Christina explained, coming up behind him. 'The monks were an order that preferred isolation, so they lived up here like hermits but slowly they died out over the years. I think that maybe they were forgotten by the church leaders.'

'And these people here now are all revolutionaries?' he asked.

'Not all, some of them are campesinos who have been driven from their land and came here seeking shelter. They are simple people and are at a loss without their homes, it is very sad to see sometimes.'

'And the fighters?'

'Not everybody will take tyranny that easily, some of us must resist.'

'Like you and your husband?'

'Exactly.'

Children were beginning to come out and play amongst the huts, chasing chickens and calling to each other cheerfully. Their mothers scolded them as they flapped roundels of maize flour in their hands to make the morning tortillas they would cook inside the walls of heated field ovens.

It was a peaceful scene and Gabriel found it hard to believe that these people were so desperate that they would take on the military might of the establishment. Turning to Christina he voiced his opinion.

'It don't look like such a bad life,' he said with a smile.

The smile dropped from his face as he saw her drawn features and wide eyes staring straight out behind him.

Gabriel spun around to see a long line of khaki-clad men appearing out of the mist as they rose over the edge of the plateau. Everyone was armed with a rifle and at their head stood a tall figure, dressed as an officer and carrying a sabre held high above his head.

'*Rurales!* Christina breathed. 'We are betrayed.'

Something about the officer held Gabriel's attention, he was taller than the rest and wore a beard. His skin was paler than the bronzed Mexicans and when he opened his mouth to give an order, then Gabriel knew who he was. The dark lines of the wooden teeth replacing those Gabriel had knocked out years ago showed clearly against the gray of his beard.

'*Lomas Chain!* he gasped in shock.

The devil he had thought shot and killed in Dakota was here, alive and serving the regime. The man was back from the dead to haunt him all over again.

But there was no time to think about it.

The officer bellowed his order and dropped his sword and the advancing troops lowered their rifles and fired. The volley ripped through the peaceful camp in a blast of orange flame and gun smoke that billowed out amongst the campfires in a rolling cloud.

Women screamed in terror and Gabriel saw the hail of bullets rip aside tents and blow unsuspecting campesinos from their feet. Running children were mown down and fleeing women tumbled and fell as the remorseless troops advanced, firing as they came. Those amongst the revolutionaries that had weapons made a show of resistance, but the surprise was total and they wavered under the sudden punitive assault.

Gabriel grabbed Christina by the arm and hurried her back towards the ruins behind. Shot howled and whistled around them spitting fragments from the rock and ricocheting in screaming echoes.

Pushing Christina before him Gabriel tumbled back into his room and quickly grasped his gun belt.

He checked the load in his Colt and made for the door.

'Where are you going?' asked Christina.

'There's a man out there I must kill,' Gabriel answered grimly, his face set in a stony mask.

'You cannot, they will shoot you down for certain. We must go.'

'Not just yet awhile.'

Gabriel was at the door when Castille pushed his way in, a smoking gun in his hand.

'Good, you are here, Christina. Quickly, come with

me. You too, American, if you want to live that is.'

Gabriel stood a moment in indecision, and then Christina pulled at his sleeve and dragged him out of the room.

As they ran out Gabriel looked back to see the troops indulging in an orgy of vengeful violence against the beaten peasants. The Rurales had their bayonets out and were using them against the fallen; some of them even carried axes that they swung to hack at the wounded and unarmed men and women. Rifle butts rose and fell as skulls were cracked and blood spread in splashed pools on the plateau amongst the scattered campfires and flattened tents.

For an instant, Gabriel caught sight of the officer as he strode amongst the heaving bodies and through the fog of morning mist and gun smoke. He stood proudly, boldly striding forward through the struggling bodies slashing to left and right, his bloodied sabre held in a hand soaked red to the wrist.

Their eyes met and Chain's widened in surprise at recognition. Then he raised his fist and shook it in Gabriel's direction, his mouth opening wide in a roar of anger that could not be heard over the sounds of the massacre.

Gabriel turned and followed the others into the mist.

CHAPTER SIX

ESCAPE

The gray head that led them turned out to be Christina's father and he took the hurrying band down a hidden channel carved from the rising pillars of rock. They ran down the winding track to the clattering sounds of the mayhem behind that followed them in a chorus of echoing cries for mercy and the pitiless shouts of the victorious Rurales as they finished off survivors.

Senor Alberto found them a route to the camp's hidden stables in a cavern under a huge overhang and the four were swiftly mounted and quickly picking their dangerous way over a steep and almost vertical narrow path that curved down from the mountain stronghold.

It was the fog of morning mist that saved them from pursuit. The Rurales were unsure of the mountain pathways as narrow and winding as goat tracks and they balked at the prospect of such a severe descent whilst Senor Alberto was an old hand and knew the mountains well. Nimbly, he took them lower until they were onto the plain below and could urge their ponies on faster.

After an hour of fast riding they stopped to rest the horses and Castile and the old man engaged in a rapid conversation in hurried Spanish that Gabriel could not follow.

'What are they saying?' Gabriel asked Christina.

'My husband wishes my father to take me to safety whilst he collects the weapons left in the valley.'

'Is that right?' mused Gabriel thoughtfully. 'Well, maybe I should help him out there.'

She studied him shrewdly, 'Such a charitable offer, you think to take my husband captive, is that not so?'

Gabriel shook his head, 'I will do what I must.'

'Do not try this, gringo,' she said with a twist of anger.

'Christina, you're a hell of a gal and I wouldn't hurt you for the world but there ain't nothing going to stop me doing what I have to.'

'And this is after he has helped save you and we have dressed your wound and cared for you,' she said, the disgust plain on her face.

'Texas Ranger has to do what he has to,' Gabriel mumbled harshly. 'I gave oath on that.'

Christina eyed him haughtily, 'Some things are beyond duty, senor Brannigan.'

She turned away abruptly and went over to confer with the others. Gabriel stood alone and looked back the way they had come. His thoughts were on Lomas Chain and the improbability of him turning up in his life again. It seemed he was to be continually confronted by a man who should have died years ago by his hand. As he stood there looking over the arid desert land, he noticed that they were standing on a bed of flat rock and he swiftly knelt and, Indian fashion, placed his ear to the ground. Distantly, there was the rumble of hoof beats vibrating over the underground rock shelf. They were coming, he realized. Chain would not give up easily on his old enemy and now he was recognized, Gabriel knew Chain would not rest until one or the other of them met an untimely end.

Gabriel felt the Colt being quickly lifted from his holster and he spun around.

'Do you hear anything, senor?'

It was Castille standing over him, the pistol in one hand and with a questioning look on his handsome face.

Gabriel climbed to his feet, 'They're coming. It's me they want; their leader is an Anglo I've had run-in with before.'

Castille crooked an eyebrow, 'So? The Texas Ranger is hunted also, now perhaps you will understand how it is for us.'

'He ain't caught me yet,' answered Gabriel boldly.

'Then we separate, you will go with Christina and lead these men away from us.'

'While you go collect the weapons?'

'That would be a good plan, don't you think? I cannot ride far with this hole in my side and the canyon is not far from here, my father-in-law will help me. We can find out if the loaded mule is still there and stash the weapons somewhere safe.'

'They're coming fast, maybe thirty minutes behind. Do you want to risk Christina like that?'

'My wife knows this country well; she will find a safe place that the Rurales do not know.'

'You got a lot of faith in a woman.'

'Here there is no difference between men and women, we are all fighters against the dictator Diaz.'

'Mighty democratic of you.'

Castile smiled, holding Gabriel's gun in his hand and pointing it negligently, he shrugged, 'It makes no difference to me, gringo. You either do as I say or you wait here for your old friend with no horse and no pistol and I don't think the Rurales will be as generous with you as we have been. What do you say, amigo?'

'Don't look like I got a choice right now, but I'll come looking for you afterwards.'

Castille smiled confidently, 'If you must. Now go, the pair of you must leave a trail away from here and we will cover our own.'

Christina already mounted led over Gabriel's horse, 'Come, ungrateful one,' she said, eyeing him with resentment. 'Stay close and I will lead.'

'As you say, ma'am,' Gabriel answered swinging up into the saddle.

Castille laid his hand on Christina's where it rested on her saddle pommel, they said nothing, but a look of affection passed between them. She nodded once briefly before laying in her quirt and heading out at speed, not waiting to see if Gabriel was behind.

'Be seeing you,' Gabriel said in farewell as he followed.

They rode east into the rising sun and Gabriel saw that Christina was an able rider, sitting well in the high saddle and choosing their path wisely so as not to overtire the horses.

'Where are we headed?' he asked, drawing alongside her.

'To get help,' she answered abruptly.

'Look here, lady. I didn't mean no offence back there, it don't help to take on so.'

She cast him a rueful glance, 'You Americans are so pig-headed,' she said. 'We are on your doorstep here in Mexico and you choose to be indifferent to the cruelty that exists in this country.'

'Not me, ma'am. Maybe the politicos up in Washington but I see you're suffering, that weren't no battle back there that was plain bloody slaughter. Whatever you might think I don't hold with killing women and children like that.'

'It is our daily bread here, gringo.'

'I told you already, my name's Gabriel.'

'Well – Gabriel – behave like the angel you are named for and try to help us.'

'I ain't no angel, ma'am, that's a given, I fear.'

'Come,' she said. 'Less talk and more ride, we must get help for my husband and father before it is too late.'

Gabriel looked over his shoulder but could see no sign of the following Rurales and it troubled him, 'As you say.'

They pressed on and by mid-morning had come to an outlying walled ranchero that stood alone in the middle of an open plain with all the presence of a fortress about it. A run-down looking village of crude huts stood gathered around the outer walls and Gabriel could see that guards patrolled the high adobe walls.

'Do not be surprised by this place,' warned Christina as they approached. 'The huts are those of refugee Yaqui Indians who have come here for safety. Inside, I am afraid there are many bandits who have joined the cause. Now we must associate with these people as we need able fighters, but it is not a choice I would prefer. So, mind your tongue, Gabriel, these are dangerous men.'

'Who runs the setup here?' he asked her.

'A self-styled General, a half Indian called Celestio Lobo and an American who calls himself Shorthand. This one I do not like; I think he is dangerous.'

'How so?'

'Cold, you know? This one is not quite right in the head. He is one for blood and killing but for us he is a good fighter.'

'Nice company you keep,' frowned Gabriel.

'We are beggars, Gabriel, we cannot pick and choose.'

Within fifteen minutes they were both standing in front of General Lobo, who lounged behind a long table enjoying what appeared to be a small feast. Along the table sat a rough looking bunch, many of which were half-breed Indians and had a group of slatternly women perched on their knees. They all set aside their meal and studied the two arrivals with indifferent calculation.

Lobo was a man in his forties with small dark

eyes and a flamboyant piratical mustache and long black hair tied in a tail down his back. Silver rings covered his fingers and both ears wore small ear-rings. Down one cheek he bore the blue stain of a tattooed turtle that ran from eyebrow to chin. He sat at the center of the table in a high-backed chair and with both knee-high boots resting on the table as he gnawed on a chicken leg.

His eyes narrowed as he noted Christina and her companion and with a raised hand, he ordered the room to silence.

'Senora Hidago, a pleasure,' Lobo said by way of greeting.

'General,' Christina nodded. 'May I present, senor Gabriel Brannigan, who is riding with me.'

Lobo gave Gabriel the once over and sniffed, 'An American,' he observed. 'You have an American?'

'Temporary attachment,' Gabriel allowed.

'I too have an American,' Lobo said, a touch vain-ly. 'My good friend, Shorthand,' he waved in lordly fashion in the direction of a figure who rose slowly from the seat beside him.

Very tall and cane-stalk thin, the whip-sharp Shorthand, slowly moved behind Lobo's chair and studied Gabriel carefully. He wore a denim shirt and canvas pants and a curly brimmed Stetson set low on his head and in the shadows beneath the brim Gabriel noted the reflection of light in a pair of pale gray eyes devoid of color or feeling. It was all too apparent how he had earned his name; his left arm was missing a hand. The limb cut short at the wrist and the loss cupped in a blunt leather sheath fastened by thongs.

Gabriel did not need to see the pistol he carried cross-draw with the polished grip couched at wrist height, to know this man was a professional gunman.

'You will have things in common, no doubt?' smiled Lobo, exposing a pair of gold teeth, one replacing each incisor like glinting fangs on each side of his upper jaw.

'I doubt that,' murmured Shorthand, his accent Deep South.

'My General,' Christina interrupted. 'There is something I must tell you.'

'So speak,' said Lobo, tossing aside his chicken bone and wiping his greasy hands down the front of his embroidered vest.

'We have an arms cache in Canyon del Infierno, My husband and father are there now but there are a company of Rurales on the rampage. They have destroyed our camp in the mountains and killed many and now they come after us.'

Lobo languidly levered his boots from the table, spilling a jug of wine and tipping over a tin plate of bones as he did so.

'That is bad,' he observed.

'Someone has betrayed us,' Christina added. 'They came in force and knew exactly where we were.'

Lobo rubbed his chin thoughtfully, his stubby fingers twisting the tattoo on his cheek.

'You came straight here? That is not good, senora. Maybe they follow you and who is this traitor in your midst? Has he told the Rurales of this place.'

'That I cannot say,' Christina answered. 'But they were coming behind us at the canyon.'

Christina and Gabriel were standing on a tiled floor before the spread table, that had all the makings of some bizarre Last Supper, with the bandit General in the middle and all his acolytes stretched out on either side, their attentions firmly fixed on the two in front and all their food and women forgotten for the moment.

'And what would you have of me?' he asked. 'The guns would be a good thing, that is for sure.'

'Yes, will you send men to help my husband collect them? And maybe we can ambush these Rurales on the way. I would like to make them pay for what they have done.'

'How many of them are there?'

Christina turned to Gabriel for confirmation, 'I don't know, forty, fifty?'

'More like forty,' said Gabriel.

'What do you say, my children?' asked Lobo, turning to the men at the table. 'Shall we kill some Rurales?'

There was a roar of approval and wine cups were raised as eagerness mounted.

'You coming too?' Shorthand challenged Gabriel, his voice cutting low through the racket.

'Wouldn't miss it,' said Gabriel.

'You lose your leg iron?' said Shorthand, pointing at Gabriel's empty holster.

'The lady's husband is holding it for me.'

'Better we find you another if you ride with us.'

'Yes, yes,' Lobo agreed quickly. 'Give him a pistolo. Now, muchachos...' Lobo belched loudly and got to his feet. He was a tiny; round man and standing next to the beanpole thin Shorthand they made a comic looking pair together. 'Let us ride.'

There was noisy chaos as all the men rose and, laughing and shouting, clattered to collect their equipment. To Gabriel's eye there was no doubt that they were competent in one thing and that would be the killing, aside from that he had doubts about their motivation or any capacity for strategy.

'Twelve men against forty,' Gabriel whispered to Christina. 'You think this crew of misfits can cut it?'

'This is what they do,' assured Christina, though with a hint of loathing in her voice.

'Nice friends you have.'

'They are all murderers and villains,' she said bitterly.

'And not much of an army.'

'It is all the army we have.'

'Here,' said Shorthand, interrupting as he thrust an elderly looking Schofield pistol into Gabriel's hand. 'It ain't much but when one of these sorry assholes gets dropped you can pick up better,' he nodded in distain at the noisy gang of bandits.

'What's your story?' asked Gabriel. 'What're you doing here?'

Shorthand gave him a laconic smile, 'It puts bread on the table,' he said. 'How about you? How come you're in this shit hole?'

Gabriel shrugged and looked away from him forgoing any information as to his true purpose, 'They told me it was all gold and gals down here, thought

I'd take a look.'

Shorthand snorted a dismissive laugh, 'I don't think so, friend, you smell of lawman to me.'

'Well, I ain't looking for you, if that's what you're worried about.'

'Best thing too,' Shorthand answered confidently. 'I'd hate to have to bust your ass.'

Gabriel ignored the warning and broke open the tired looking Schofield and checked it was loaded on all cylinders, 'This thing fire at all?' he asked.

Shorthand shrugged, 'Guess you'll find out the hard way.'

CHAPTER SEVEN

TRAIN STOP

Lobo sent out scouts as they approached the canyon entrance and the two men came back riding fast.

Gabriel took one look at their faces and knew it was not good. He glanced across at Christina and saw that she too was worried.

'They are there?' asked Lobo.

'The old one, he is there,' answered the scout with a sad shake of the head.

Christina did not wait to hear more but lashed at her horse and sent it bounding ahead into the canyon.

'Wait!' cried Gabriel and when he saw that she was deaf to his call he quickly followed after.

Riding through the narrow opening at speed, Gabriel kept his eyes fixed on the heights above but it was only the echoing clatter of his horse's footfalls that came down to him. He broke the final bend and came fast into the dusty flat clearing before the shack and pulled the horse to a rearing halt.

Christina stood dismounted in front of the hut staring down at the riddled body of her father. The old man had been stood in front of a firing squad and cut down by rifle fire before being finally dispatched by a pistol shot to the head.

Gabriel quartered the area carefully as Christina sunk sobbing to her knees before the dead body of her father. The place had the hollow reek of emptiness and Gabriel was pretty sure that nobody else was in the vicinity. He found the dead pack mule behind the building, it had been dead some time, probably from lack of water and the carcass had already been picked over by buzzards and desert critters. The pannier packs loaded with the Gatling gun were gone. Gabriel studied the ground and found only a maze of hoof and boot prints, one overlaying the other in a massed confusion of sign.

He went back around the shack and found Christina, now on her feet and still staring sorrowfully down at her father's remains.

'Where is my husband?' she asked tearfully, looking up at him. 'Where is Castille?'

'He ain't here,' Gabriel answered softly.

Lobo and his gang entered the canyon, nervously spreading out and looking around cautiously.

'The Rurales have killed them?' he asked, riding up and staring down at the remains of Senor Alberto.

Gabriel nodded, 'Looks that way but they must have taken Hidago with them 'cos he ain't here.'

Lobo pouted and tugged at one of his earrings thoughtfully, 'Why would they do that?'

Gabriel shrugged, 'No idea.'

'They have the guns?'

'I reckon.'

'*Cabrones*!' spat Lobo.

'How long?' asked Shorthand, from where he sat his horse alongside the little bandit leader.

Gabriel pondered, 'Not long, the tracks are fresh and the old fellow's demise recent.'

'Then we will go after them,' growled Lobo. 'I want those guns.'

'First we shall bury my father,' snapped Christina, taking a belligerent stand and blocking his path. 'He must be treated with respect.'

Lobo chewed his lower lip a moment and looked from Christina to Gabriel, balancing out the prospect of such a delay.

'Very well,' he said. 'I shall send out scouts to see how far these dogs have gone. But hurry, they must not be allowed return to their headquarters.'

Whilst the scouts were sent out, Lobo hastily ordered four men to dig a grave for Christina's father and although they grumbled over the notion of physical labor, one hissed order from Shorthand had them jumping from their horses and finding spades for the task.

As they worked, Christina wept over her father's corpse, straightening his jacket and crossing his hands respectfully across his chest before laying a blanket over the body. Gabriel went over and helped her to her feet when she was done and she hung on his arm, diminished by her loss.

'He was a good man,' she muttered. 'A good father and loyal to the cause.'

'I'm real sorry for your loss, Christina,' commiserated Gabriel.

'But I do not understand,' she looked at him with tearful eyes. 'Where is Castille? What has happened to him?'

'They've searched the whole canyon,' said Gabriel. 'There's no sign of him here.'

Already doubts were forming in Gabriel's mind and he too wondered why Chain and the Rurales would want to take Hidago prisoner, if indeed he had.

When Senor Alberto had been laid in the ground, Lobo, still mounted, fretted impatiently as Christina made her final goodbyes and when she was done he wheeled his horse and ordered the band out of the canyon.

They had not ridden more than half an hour before one of the scouts was seen approaching fast.

'You have found them?' asked Lobo as the scout's sweating pony pulled up in a rearing slide.

'Si, jefe. They are by the railroad tracks ahead; Luis is keeping an eye on them. I think they are waiting for the train.'

'They are all there? All the Rurales?'

'Si, senor.'

'How's it laid out?' asked Shorthand.

'High hills to one side, the track runs on flat ground below and beyond is the desert where there is nothing.'

'Any buildings?'

'Si, it is a water stopping place. There is a tower and two sheds for railroad workers below, the Rurales are in the buildings and resting out of the sun.'

'Did you see the guns?' asked Lobo.

'No, senor, maybe they have them inside the hut.'

'The high ground,' barked Lobo. 'We must get to them from above. Lead us there.'

With that the entire troop wheeled off and with the scout taking the point, made off at a fast gallop.

Gabriel looked across at Christina as they rode, 'Are you alright with this?' he asked.

She nodded grimly, bending low over her pony's neck, 'We must help Castille.'

They walked the horses the last half mile in, so as not to give away their position with any dust cloud and Lobo had the band held back whilst he, Shorthand, Gabriel and Christina worked their way forward to lie at the cliff edge and peer down at the water stop below.

The scout, Luis, nodded a greeting to them as they lay down beside him, 'The fat pigs are taking their leisure, patron,' he muttered. 'But there is one there you should see.'

He pointed and they all focused their attention on a group gathered in the shade of one of the huts.

Gabriel felt himself tighten as he picked out the bearded figure of Lomas Chain, dressed in his officer's uniform with his peaked hat tipped back on his head and talking with a few of the Mexican officers. They all seemed relaxed and were smoking cigarettes and laughing together.

Christina suddenly grabbed at Gabriel's arm and gasped, '*Castille!*'

Sure enough, Hidago came out from inside one of the huts and stood alongside, seemingly as relaxed and at ease with the Rurales as if he belonged there.

'The dog has betrayed us,' growled Lobo. 'There

is your spy, senora.'

'No,' she blurted. 'I cannot believe it. He would never do that.'

But as she spoke, Chain slapped Hidago on the back and put his arm around his shoulders and hugged him affectionately.

'Sure looks like one of them,' observed Shorthand softly.

'I'm sorry, Christina,' said Gabriel, unhappily aware that his earlier suspicions had become a reality. It made sense to him that a man who would ride with such characters as Naranja Ned and take part in the murderous raid across the border had an alternative agenda. It was only the weapons he had wanted and those for his real bosses in the military.

'He has seen my father and our people murdered,' moaned Christina in disbelief. 'How could he do such a thing?'

'It is the money and power,' pronounced Lobo, with an air of high-minded righteousness. 'Some men will do anything for such things.'

Both Shorthand and Gabriel looked across at him quizzically, and then smiled at each other.

'What?' asked Lobo innocently as he caught their stare. 'What are you saying?'

'Just thought that was a tad rich coming from you,' observed Shorthand with his tongue firmly in his cheek.

Lobo pricked up pompously, 'Why you think this? I am a loyal servant of the cause, I am thinking of nothing but the good of the people.'

'Maybe an hour or so a week,' chuckled Shorthand.

'Enough!' snapped Lobo. 'We will go down there and wipe these wretches out for the good of Mexico.'

'Patron,' said the scout Luis, interrupting his leader with a nudge and pointing off to the horizon.

They all turned to see the faint smudge of smoke in the distance.

'The train is coming.'

'Then we must go now, there may be more troops on the train.'

'How we doing this?' asked Gabriel.

'From two sides,' said Lobo. 'We will divide the men and come at them like a pincer and crush them between us. It is the best way, we have done this many times before.'

Gabriel looked questioningly at Shorthand.

'He's right,' said the gunman. 'It works.'

Lobo was already scrabbling his way back away from the edge and heading towards the rest of the band. 'Come, hurry,' he said. 'We must strike before the train arrives.'

'Best you stay with the horses, Christina,' advised Gabriel.

'You think so?' she sneered, fixing him with fiery eyes. 'Whilst that traitor, my so-called husband is down there with his compatriots? No, senor, it is my intention to see I am divorced from such a man at the end of my pistol this day.'

Gabriel understood that it would be no use arguing with Christina, her determination was all too obvious in the grim set of her features.

It was with a great deal of noise and shooting that the attack began.

Both waves of riders swept in with clouds of dust and at their arrival the Rurales spread out and ran in panic. Some made for the open desert over the tracks and were cut down as they ran, whilst others huddled in the cover of the sheds and water tower and returned fire.

Gabriel kept close to Christina, he was sure that in her enraged rush to claim Hidago's head she would be placing herself in danger and he was determined that nothing should happen to her. Already he felt a protective urge towards the woman and even if his advances would not be well received, which he reckoned was highly likely seeing how recent events had impacted on her life, he could not deter himself from caring or taking her safety seriously.

He watched as she bounded forward blindly charging down amongst the Rurales. Gabriel followed on behind, the Schofield in his hand. Two of the Mexicans had her bridle in their hands and were trying to bring her down amidst the wild swirl of circling riders and Gabriel leveled the gun. He pulled the trigger, aiming at the lead Rurale and to his dismay the hammer collapsed as it struck and broke off from the aged pistol. Throwing the useless gun aside, Gabriel urged his pony forward. Kicking his feet free of the stirrups, he leapt from the saddle and crashed into the Mexicans. Both men flew sideways, and Christina's horse reared away. With the release she brought her own gun into play and shot one of the men down as he reached up to grab at her again.

Gabriel struggled to his feet in a blinding cloud

of dust that clogged his nostrils and dimmed his vision. He saw the dark shape of the other Rurale lurching towards him and struck out blindly. With a satisfying thump his fist connected with man's head and the Rurale staggered back, his cap flying from his head.

Gabriel drew the knife at his side and leapt after the man, now stumbling away in the dust cloud. Gabriel closed on him and swung the blade upwards in a searing arc, feeling it thud into the man's midsection below the sternum. Gritting his teeth, Gabriel swept the blade out as the Rurale dropped away from him. He turned about, searching for Christina in the maelstrom of bucking riders and gunfire.

He saw her heading for the shack that the officers had been standing outside earlier. Running, Gabriel chased after her. A swarthy-faced Rurale, teeth gritted in an open snarl, rose up before him, his rifle stock raised at shoulder height. As he lunged, Gabriel twisted aside and caught the blow on the shoulder that luckily was his unwounded one. He was turned about and almost lost his footing. Gabriel ducked down as the Rurale raised the rifle again, ready to club at him once more. He was open, looming above Gabriel who slashed at him with the knife, cutting through the man's shirtfront and raising a bloody weal on his chest.

Hesitating, the Rurale paused and Gabriel rushed in. He shoulder charged the man, swinging his blade up as he did so and driving the knife in under the jaw. Gabriel held the fellow pinioned before him, using him as cover as he sought out Christina again.

The prisoner gurgled and quivered helplessly, his head held on the buried point of the blade and his eyes rolling wildly as Gabriel spun him around.

Gabriel could not see Christina and then he noted her horse, it fretted nervously in front of the shed but she herself was nowhere to be seen.

Just then there was a ripping noise that chattered from the front of the shack and Gabriel felt the Rurale before him shudder under the impact of bullets from the Gatling gun. The man danced and juddered as the spray of shells ran over him and then passed by to race across the attacking band. Men flew from their horses and the animals screamed and tumbled as the bandits were cut down by the deadly swath of flying lead. The earth spat up chains of dust as the gun repeatedly sent a rain of bullets amongst the whirling horsemen, knocking down friend and foe alike.

Gabriel shed the sagging body of the Rurale and loped across to the shed, using his good side he shoulder-charged the closed door at the run and the tired wood gave way under his impact. The planks of the door parted, and Gabriel flew inside amongst the shattered timbers, sending clouds of splinters and dust into the gloomy interior. Gabriel rolled over and in a glance took in the two officers at the window manning the Gatling gun, one of them cranking its handle determinedly and raking the attackers outside in swinging curves from side to side whilst the other supplied magazines of ammunition.

In one corner, Christina was in the grip of a grinning Hidago, who held her by the wrists and seemed to be most amused by her struggles as she screamed wildly and attempted to claw at him.

One other figure stood in the shadows at the rear of the room and in the dim light Gabriel made out the wooden toothed leer and tall figure of Lomas Chain. Without hesitation, Gabriel launched himself towards the figure just as Chain fired his pistol.

The bullet caromed across the side of Gabriel's temple with a sharp crack before whipping past out of the open door and leaving him feeling as if he had been struck by a stone club. Spinning sideways, Gabriel tumbled away, his vision blurred, and limbs numbed.

Chain stood over him, his red-rimmed eyes glaring in the darkness.

'*You!*' he snarled loudly. 'It's you Gabriel Brannigan, you bastard.'

Gabriel was woozy, his only sensation that his body was not responding to his command to react.

Chain loomed nearer, the pistol held out before him.

'God! How I've waited for this moment,' he jeered.

Chain raised the pistol but just then another dark shape appeared in the doorway and at the same moment Shorthand's six-gun came through the broken window and fired rapidly, dropping both of the Rurale officers that manned the Gatling.

Chain spun up as the bandit leader, Lobo charged in through the doorway with a wild whoop, his gun blazing in all directions.

Lomas Chain did not hesitate but racked off three shots instantly, all the bullets making a bloody mess of Lobo's tattooed face. In the pace of the moment and as Lobo fell face down on the floor, Gabriel shook his head to clear it and reached out to grab at Chain. But the big man backed away from the weak attempt and lowered his gun to aim at Gabriel.

'Now, you son-of-a-bitch, payback for that slug you put in me.'

He pulled the trigger and all they both heard was the clack as the hammer struck a used cartridge. With a howl of anger, Chain threw the empty pistol at Gabriel and then turned to charge at the shed's rear wall. The thin sun-dried wood splintered, and Chain burst out through the opening.

'Later, Brannigan. I'll get you later,' Gabriel heard him call out as he disappeared from view.

Christina and Hidago were still struggling together, although now the smile had slipped from Hidago's handsome face and his features had taken on a more determined grimace.

'You stupid bitch,' he snarled as his hands closed around Christina's throat. 'Don't you see we could have been rich? I would have held high office in Mexico City and you would have had silk sheets to sleep on.'

'No,' Gabriel tried to say, as he clambered unsteadily to his feet, the room spinning wildly before him. His legs were still wobbling from the bullet's impact on his skull and although barely conscious he tried to make it over to the fighting pair.

Hidago struck out, swiping Christina a heavy blow across the side of the head and knocking her aside. Gabriel wove towards him and Hidago screwed his face into an angry snarl as he drew the gun at his side. No more the friendly smiling and handsome Mexican, now his features told a different story, one of anger and greed.

His pistol was out and pointed directly at Gabriel, whose stunned brain barely recognized the present danger, all he knew was to move forward and take the man down.

When Hidago fired, the fiery bloom of escaping gas shot from the barrel and lit a great flash before Gabriel's eyes. Temporarily blinded, he wondered why he was still standing. He was not wounded and yet with him standing directly in front, Hidago could not have missed from this range. Gabriel's legs began to give and he swayed sideways.

At that moment, two loud reports came from over Gabriel's shoulder. Christina screamed and Gabriel saw Hidago stagger as he twisted away, first one side and then the other, turning under the bullet's impacts. His eyes stared at someone behind Gabriel and his mouth worked silently in an ugly fashion before there was another loud retort and he plummeted over to crash into the wall of the shack before sliding down and lying still.

Gabriel turned and saw Shorthand behind him, a smoking gun still in his hand. His other, the handless arm hung limp and torn with a spreading stain of blood running down the sleeve.

'Thought y'all never get out the damned way,' he grumbled, before dropping to his knees.

'He got you?' Gabriel managed.

'Just a nick,' said Shorthand before he passed out completely and collapsed.

(JC Note: Gabriel's scattered writings from this time on take on a rather vague and sketchy collection of memories. Whether this was from a deep sense of guilt about his actions or whether they merely represent a unique period of uneventful and relative peace for him I cannot say. It appeared that he and Christina found a cart to transport the wounded Shorthand and the Gatling gun and before the train arrived with its possible troop load they made their way clear. Heading north and crossing the border they saw that the severely wounded Shorthand received prompt medical treatment at the Ranger HQ's well-equipped hospital, an act that fortunately saved the rest of his damaged left arm.

Gabriel quit the Rangers and set up house with Christina, and although they never married they lived together as man and wife in what appears to have been a contented relationship for some years and during which time Christina gave birth to three children, two girls and a boy.

Gabriel continued his partnership with Shorthand after his release from hospital and a close friendship ensued. With his savings Gabriel invested in a small ranch and for a few years the two tried to make a go of it as ranchers. It did not work, neither of them were equipped for such a life and before long Gabriel turned back to the law and became the sheriff of what was then a busy crossroads trading town called Grenadier Cross, still a busy place today but now abbreviated to Grenadier in modern times and not too far from my home town of Benopé. He took Shorthand with him as his deputy and the two served together for a number of years as successful law officers.

Gabriel had Christina bring her now widowed mother across the border and in time an uncle of hers and two of her cousins followed to come and manage the ranch. It proved to be a busy household with the three young children and all of Christina's Spanish speaking relatives and Gabriel felt increasingly marginalized. Over time tensions began to grow up between himself and Christina and after what had been an earlier pleasant relationship during the birth of their children bitter rows began to ensue.

Gabriel was a man who seemed better suited to being alone and the feel for individual liberty was strong in him. He took to excusing himself for any thin reason he could contrive and go riding off into the desert and roam for days with no genuine purpose other than to feel the freedom he found there away from civilized community and the social responsibilities that came with it.

It was not long before he discovered that Shorthand and Christina had struck up a more than friendly relationship. With his own notion of cutting the strings that tied and not wanting to deter Christina or his friend from what he felt was a better relationship for all concerned, Gabriel left the job as sheriff and, as was his way, one day took his silent leave and rode away without a backward glance.)

CHAPTER EIGHT

VISITING HOME

It struck me as I finished typing out the page that Gabriel Brannigan was truly one hell of a unique personality. If he was to be believed, that is.

Thing is, I still could not quite bring myself to credit that all he said was true. His life read like some twenty-five cent newsstand magazine story.

It had been fine when I had been a young buck and overseas ducking Jap bullets, a genuine entertainment in fact and I looked at all those mismatched papers with some kind of affection for the distraction they had given me back then. But as I came to see it now I wondered was it all real or just some old man's fanciful wanderings.

The thing that kept me going was the memory of him in my Ma's kitchen when the bank robber Mad Dog Cheetham had threatened our lives. That's when I saw something that could have been the Gabriel Brannigan I was reading about in his letters, a lean and mean man in his day and both quick and deadly when needed.

Somehow though, I still could not tie the two

images I had of him. This ancient fellow I knew, bowed and wrinkled with years and the tough and sharp gunman who's story was scrawled on the back of scraps of paper and calendar pages.

I determined to go visit the Arbuthnot Rest Home and find out.

It turned out that the founder, the Mister Arbuthnot in question had passed over some years previous and the establishment was now run by a protégé of his named Doctor Phreely Philpot. I gave them a jangle from the motel and fixed up an appointment with him for that p.m. the same day.

The Home turned out to be a rambling place built in dark brick in the vein of some old English manorial mansion set in rolling grounds. There weren't much grass to be seen but whoever built the joint obviously had that picture in his mind and would probably have preferred a golf course freeway to the dried out dust bowl it actually inhabited. Even the driveway was a heap of crushed gravel that allowed a tornado of dust to follow me as I rolled in.

Old folks were sitting about in bath chairs and kind of fluttering like flocks of pigeons. There wasn't much noise but then you wouldn't expect that from people on the doorstep to the next world. Most of them twitched a bit and maybe plucked at themselves in distraction, some of them tried to converse but I guess most were too deaf to hear what was being said anyway. There was a few nurses around, both male and female, hurrying about carrying trays of medicines and chamber pots and such.

Inside it had a distinctive smell. Not of death as

you'd expect in an old folks' home but something else. I guess these folks had seen a lot in their time. Two World Wars and in between the big influenza epidemic, bank closures, breadlines and the great Dust Bowl agricultural disaster across the Plains, enough human disaster to tire anybody. They were tired of life, these people, tired of the deceit and dishonesty they had suffered, tired of corruption and politics, of religious intolerance and taxes. And that's what it smelled of in that place. Exhaustion.

I was shown in by a huge guy dressed in a white coat, in fact all the staff seemed to identify themselves by wearing these kind of doctorial white lab coats. Anyway, this fellow was as solemn and as inviting as a stand-up refrigerator and about as big as one too. He was so big and wide on the shoulders that he had to duck his head and go sideways through doorways.

He tapped reverentially and let me in through the oak panel door with the title 'Dr. Phreely Philpot, Administrator'.

Doc Philpot was an owlish little fellow sitting behind a large desk piled with papers and lit by a set of narrow leaded windows behind him. He glimmered at me through these glasses that were so thick they magnified his eyes to the size of pool hall balls and his face wore a seemingly innocent looking expression of curiosity. There was the absent-minded professor about him, his white lab coat was rumpled and his gray hair unkempt and sticking out. Here was the kind of guy who would walk around with his shirttail hanging out his unbuttoned fly and not even notice.

He rummaged through the stack of papers on his desk a while and then said in a voice that creaked like an un-oiled door.

'And you are?'

'Jonah Cord, I made an appointment earlier.'

'Ah, yes,' he sighed, peering over the thick black frame of his glasses and studying me.

He noted my walking stick and promptly turned to the refrigerator who stood protectively guarding the door.

'Higgins, a chair for Mister Cord, if you please.'

The dummy obliged and then Philpot ushered him away with a dismissive wave.

'You are a veteran of the recent conflict, Mister Cord?'

I nodded agreement.

'Well done, sir,' he mumbled. 'Well done.'

I don't know quite what he meant by that but I guess it was some sort of praise for nearly getting my leg shot off, something I really had no hand in at all.

'Now, I must tell you, Mister Cord,' he went on. 'Our situation here at present is rather stretched and we have little room available. You see we take on 'clients', I prefer to call them that by the way, rather than patients, we are, after all, not a hospital here. Rather, we are a last way station on the great road of life...'

I let him ramble on in this rather affected tone for a while before I put him right.

'No, sir,' I said. 'It ain't a relative of mine I'm here to admit.'

'Not so?' he asked with a show of surprise that

rounded those eyeballs even bigger behind his glasses.

'Nope, I'm making an enquiry about one of your recent 'clients'.'

'Indeed, well enlighten me, Mister Cord.'

'Old gent called Gabriel Brannigan. He got himself in a spot of bother and was sent on here by the authorities.'

Philpot sat back in his chair and rocked there for a while, musing on that.

'And your interest, if I may ask?'

'He's a neighbor of mine and been good to my family. We kept in touch whilst I was serving and I'd kinda like to know what happened to him.'

'Well, unfortunately Mister Brannigan is no longer with us here.'

'Yeah, so I heard. Can you fill me on what happened?'

'I have to say in all truth that Brannigan was a most difficult client, Mister Cord. You will understand that given the nature of our facility we run a tight ship and I'm afraid that Mister Brannigan did not seem quite able to slot into our regime.'

I was getting the picture now and knowing old Gabe like I did, I guessed that he reckoned he had walked into seven kinds of hell with the strictures imposed on him by this snotty little creature.

'That so?' I said affably.

Philpot pressed his fingertips together and rocked some more in an officious mode, 'Indeed,' he said. 'He absconded in the end. I think it was that dog of his that upset him particularly.'

'His dog?'

'Yes, we do not allow pets here, you see? We do not have the capacity to handle the elderly as well as any livestock. But Brannigan insisted on keeping the animal nearby, he would feed it, you know? Steal food from the kitchen and keep the beast fed as it roamed wild in the grounds. Most unfortunate. I had to order Higgins to take a shotgun to it in the end. We can't allow that sort of thing here, you see.'

'*You shot his dog?*' I asked with some surprise as I had knowledge of just how much Gabriel valued the stray, he called Boulder.

'Sadly, yes. It was most upsetting and I'm afraid it drove poor Brannigan quite wild; we had to restrain him forcibly in the end. Some elderly, you see, can be quite dangerous when their faculties give way. The mind is not always able to handle the advancing years, as was the case with Brannigan. The sheriff's office had to bring him here after some discord in a local tavern, where he became the worse for drink and broke furniture and caused a great deal of distress.'

'I heard about that,' I said. 'The judge turned him over to you rather than the jailhouse.'

'Yes, that was the first time but I'm speaking here about his second bout of bad behavior.'

'He busted up the place twice!'

'Indeed,' Philpot pulled a sad expression. 'It seemed there was no holding him, quite surprising for a man of his years. Extraordinary, really.'

'He loved that dog, I know. I guess that's what got him fired up.'

I reckon there may have been a touch of critical accusation in my voice just then and you mix that with a twinge of distaste for this pedantic bottle-eyed creature and you get the picture.

'Oh, no,' he surprised me with. 'Not the dog at all, although I must admit there was some disturbance there. Poor Higgins suffered quite a nasty gash from a chair that Brannigan laid across his head over that. No, this was after he met Mrs. Muldoon.'

'Mrs. Muldoon?'

'Yes, one of our other clients. A charming lady of some years who has suffered a very unfortunate accident in the past. It's left her with some rather nasty scarring, she wears a veil now to conceal the unpleasantness.'

'And Gabriel knew her?'

'It appears so.'

'This lady, she here now?'

'Oh, yes, the dear woman occupies our lounge area and games room most days and occupies her time with playing solitaire. Was once a professional dealer, I believe, and she used to have quite a school going here at one time with some of the other geriatrics. Even the staff too on occasion, but we had to put a stop to that,' he offered a cough, or maybe it was a soft laugh. 'Couldn't have the place turning into a gambling den now, could we?'

'She's a card player then?'

'Of some skill, I must say.'

I was a tad suspicious of that right then, 'So after seeing this woman, Gabriel took his leave.'

'Not immediately no, but soon after. First, he

had to make his little demonstration at the tavern. A tantrum, you realize? Some old people will exhibit these urges occasionally, a kind of repressed desire to relive their past in some way. And, I fear that Mister Brannigan had doubtless engaged in moments of violence in his past that his fading brain needed to revisit.'

And then some I'll bet, I thought.

'You must understand, Mister Cord, we really cannot sustain this kind of stressful behavior here. It disturbs the other clients and causes all kinds of upset. I have to admit, I was quite relieved when Brannigan finally took his leave of us.'

'He just went,' I pressed. 'Just ran off?'

Philpot nodded, 'Yes, one day he was here, the next gone. I mean to say, it was quite unreal really, he had a gun, you know? When he first came here. A loaded pistol of some antiquity and he rode a horse and had that wretched dog with him. The man was quite delusionary and living in a past episode as if he were one of the cowboys that roved these lands in days gone by.'

'That would certainly be Gabriel Brannigan,' I allowed. 'I wonder Doctor, might I be able to meet with this Mrs. Muldoon?'

Philpot pouted as he thought it over, 'Well, I suppose that as you are one of our brave boys who suffered for our great nation and seem a reasonable man, I don't see why we cannot accommodate you. Mrs. Muldoon is still quite able and clear headed. Why not? I'll have Higgins show you over to the lounge. I'm sure she'll be there; she always is at this time of day. Probably the old lady will enjoy the company, she sees so few visitors.'

The refrigerator led me through the dark corridors of the place where the only sound was the squeak of our tread on the wooden floorboards.

'You had some trouble with Gabriel Brannigan, I take it?' I voiced, hoping to get some reaction from the giant.

'Sonofabitch!' he muttered.

'What's that?' I pressed.

'I ever see that sack of shit again an' I'll rip his head off,' he growled in a deep voice as hollow as the grave.

'You didn't get on with him then?'

'Busted me on the head,' he groaned. '*Me!*' And that he uttered that with such a shocked note of horror it demonstrated his total amazement that anyone could even dare considering such an affront.

He lumbered on a while down the gloomy corridor that looked like it went on forever and probably did.

'Old fella like that,' he continued in complaint. 'Made me look bad. Skinny old bastard busting my head over a damned mutt.'

'Guess he loved his dog.'

'I'd have shot him too given half the chance.'

'Tell me, Mister Higgins, where did you win your medical qualifications?'

He pulled up sharply then, turning and fixing me with a pair of piggy eyes.

'The Penitentiary,' he snarled with some kind of proud satisfaction.

I managed about as much innocence as I could and asked, 'What were you inside for?'

'I was no prisoner, numbnuts, I was a guard.'

'Oh, I see.'

'There,' he rumbled, pushing open a door. 'The old biddy's in here. Take a hint, asshole, don't play no cards with her she'll ream you out of every nickel you own.'

And he said that with enough venom to intimate that he had suffered at the old lady's hand.

The room was open plan and lit by a pair of open patio doors that showed the rolling drifts of the dusty freeway outside. There were tables scattered throughout, all but one of them empty. The lone occupant sat over by the patio doors, a figure dressed entirely in black with a dark lace veil covering her head and face. Thin arms moved slowly and methodically in spidery fashion as she laid out cards with neat precision on the table before her.

'Hey, Muldoon!' grunted Higgins. 'You got a war hero for a visitor.'

The covered head moved and looked me over.

'Very well, Higgins,' she said in a high toned, haughty and cultured voice. 'We'll take tea in here, if you will?'

'Not on your life,' snorted Higgins. 'You got fifteen minutes, buster. Then I come throw you out.'

'Too kind,' I answered deferentially.

Mrs. Muldoon continued to spread her cards in the game of solitaire without looking up as I stood before her table.

'An insufferable prick, I'm afraid,' she muttered

coarsely in a voice cool as ice.

'I'm sorry?'

'Higgins,' she said. 'I've known orangutans with more class than that simian creep. Will you take a seat, soldier boy? I can't abide cripples leaning over me whilst I play.'

I pulled up a chair and sat down, 'My name's Jonah Cord.'

'Indeed,' she said, flipping down a red nine on a black ten. 'Do you play, sir?'

'Afraid not.'

'That's too bad. Then I presume our time together here will be soon over.'

'I'd like to speak with you a moment, if I may, Mrs. Muldoon.'

'I do not know you and I cannot begin to imagine what we have to say to each other, therefore I should say this discussion is concluded.'

'It's about Gabriel Brannigan.'

Her head tilted slightly at that, and she froze rather like a bird taking note of a distant sound. I could not see any more than an outline under the veil, a flash of light from the open door rippled over seams of corrugated flesh but I made out nothing more than that.

'What about that ass?' she asked.

'You knew him I think?'

'To my sorrow.'

'I'm trying to trace his whereabouts.'

'And why on earth would you want to do that, young man?'

'He's a friend.'

'Gabriel Brannigan does not have friends,' she said in a tone slipping into bitterness.

'I believe you knew him well and after meeting you he left here in a hurry. I wonder if you know where he went?'

'And why should I tell you anything, sonny? Gabriel Brannigan does not mean a thing to me.'

'Mrs. Muldoon, or should I say, Mrs. April Turner, I really believe he does.'

That brought some attention out of her, she looked up sharply, 'Who the hell are you?' she snapped.

'Somebody that knows your story, does the name Lomas Chain ring a bell.'

'Another dumb loser,' she mumbled, turning her attention back to her cards.

'I know you had a deal with him that went sour and that you had an affectionate liaison with both of the men.'

'*Affectionate liaison!*' she barked. 'Is that what you call it? We fucked, that is all, buddy boy. Yes, I knew Gabriel and I must admit he was a well-hung stud in his day but he's just a bent old man now and of no interest to anybody.'

'Not so bent he couldn't sock out old Higgins there.'

She chuckled at that, a rusty sounding snigger, 'Yes, he did, didn't he? Fool shot his dog, never knew Gabriel to care about anything so much as that damned dog.'

'Will you tell me what happened, April? Where's he gone to?'

She spanned the cards in her hand slowly, rippling through them with a rapid shuffle.

'It was Muldoon did this, you know?' she said, tapping a bony forefinger on the veil covering her head. 'Acid. The bastard threw acid in my face. You wouldn't believe it now but I was a looker in my day, there wasn't a gaming table from Abilene to Galveston that did not know me. I was a queen of the gaming tables and played only with the best.'

'So, I heard.'

She sniffed and turned her head slightly to look out of the patio doors. By the light I could determine more of her ravaged skin that tugged down the right side of her face and ran ragged across her cheek. She had once been a handsome woman; I could see that. A slender frame that still bore itself proudly and wore the black clothes with a touch of elegance.

'They were good old days,' she sighed. 'My God! They were good. Money flowed and men were as busy as flies around honey when I walked in a room. I could have had any one of them I wanted, any time and anyhow. Dear God, it was fine, just fine and Lord, how I miss that time.'

'Chain shot down your husband, is that right?'

She nodded affirmation, 'It was a hell of a scam, but Gabriel messed it up. It would have been good with him and me if he had let it ride but he was all upright and righteous. Left me in a pretty pickle, he did.'

'He shot down Lomas Chain that time in Indian country, did you know that?'

'Shot him down, is that right?'

She turned slowly to look back at me. There was something in her eyes I could not quite credit, something challenging.

'So, I believe, then he ran into the man again later, playing as a Rurale officer.'

'He shoot him dead then too, I suppose?'

'I don't know for sure what occurred there, ma'am. I believe Chain made his escape.'

'You sure on that?'

'What do you mean?'

She chuckled then, a hoarse sound that developed into a bark of a laugh.

'He never got to kill him,' she admitted finally.

'What?' I asked curiously. 'You mean Lomas Chain got away? He survived and escaped Gabriel for certain.'

'That's right and not only that,' she chuckled, her eyes sparkling under the veil. 'It gave me a whole heap of pleasure to let Gabriel know that Lomas still lives.'

'So that's why he busted up the tavern.'

'Probably so, Gabriel never could abide Lomas. The two of them were enemies from birth it seems, it was as if they were crossed stars that were doomed to spend their lives fighting each other. I love it, it's a hell of a thing, isn't it?'

'My God! I never would have believed it. Chain's still alive, he had some years on Gabriel and must be in his dotage now and Gabriel still wants to reckon with him.'

'That's right.'

She was perking up at all this; the memory of the two old enemies enlivening her and her mask of crustiness fell away with the remembered years.

'I could have had you too, you know?' she said, suddenly coquettish and leaning forward and stroking her long fingers down my cheek. 'Pretty little war hero like you, you wouldn't have been able to resist and I would have played your pecker like a piccolo.'

It was a tad obscene somehow, this ruined crone in her nineties running her skeletal hands down my face and promising me a lot more than mere innuendo, I cringed away instinctively.

'Not now, huh?' she said, drawing back like a turtle into its shell. 'Not now, poor April is damaged goods. I killed him though, Mister fucking Muldoon, stuck him through with a butcher knife.' There was a touch of agitated wildness in her rising tone that verged on a kind of hysteria. 'He thought he could get away with it. I always went my own way, married or not, I took the bedroom as my own private territory; my sacred home but Muldoon never understood that. He thought because he put a ring on my finger he owned me. Well, he was wrong. The fool took it badly when he caught me humping his best buddy and took up with the acid trick. But I saw him out, waited my time and put that blade deep in his belly one night while he slept. Son of a bitch died squealing.'

'Jesus!' I breathed and have to admit that at that moment I felt a touch of dread at this fearsome old lady who owned such murderous intent.

'You want a hand of blackjack?' she asked suddenly.

I was still staring at her in some kind of shock.

'Come on, soldier boy. I don't get to play with anyone here anymore, I've cleaned them all out already.'

She shuffled and dealt quickly before I could

answer.

'What you got?' she asked, her voice brittle as glass.

'Where did you send him, April?' I asked.

'Beat my lay and I'll tell you.'

She was such a cunning hand with the cards I wonder to this day if she managed to shift me the two queens with the dexterous sleight of an old time card sharp.

'Twenty, huh? Well that beats my pair of nines,' she said with a snort, not even turning her own cards over.

'Tell me then.'

'Lomas came by to see me here one time,' she admitted. 'I think he wanted to start up again for old time's sake. He was a sly old dog, almost as sly as me. But then he saw my face and had a change of heart, he remembered how I was, you see? He thought we'd all stay the same forever, the fool. He was heading west, going on to Nevada, maybe Las Vegas. Had some deal planned out there, something that would make him powerful and rich, he said. Well, he wouldn't take me with him so I sent Gabriel on after him.' She nodded her head speculatively, the leafy rose patterns in the lace veil forming shadows like dark blotches over her damaged face. 'Let them sort it out between themselves once and for all, I thought.'

There was a hint of satisfaction in her voice, a gratified note of vengeance perhaps.

Hell hath no fury, and all that, I figured. And I could see how a once gorgeous woman like April Turner couldn't stand to be scorned not even now that her beauty had been ruined and her body withered with age.

'You'll be going too I guess,' she said. 'Now that you got what you came for? But there's more if you want it, you know? I ain't dead yet and can still turn a trick or two. What do you say on that?'

She leaned over hungrily and laid a hand on my chest in a predatory fashion with the fingers spread wide like claws.

I pushed back my chair and got up, 'Yes, ma'am. Best I'm gone, never could stand a cripple leaning over me either.'

Had to have the last word, I couldn't resist it but she only laughed. Long and loud as I left the room and her laughter had the sound of a younger woman in it, one that was raw with the strains of cigarette smoke and rotgut whiskey and reveled in the sound of squeaking bed springs.

Now wasn't that a thing?

It was back at the motel that I first saw him.

I'd been sitting in the doorway favoring my gammy leg and pondering on whether to make the trip out to Nevada or not. Should I just let it rest and forego any further chase across country after old Gabriel? Especially if the fool was chasing after April Turner's tale of Lomas Chain, I still couldn't quite believe that she had been telling the truth about that. More likely she had just wanted to piss off Gabriel and send him on a wild goose chase for the heck of it.

The man was stood leaning back on the hood of a parked car and smoking a cigarette. Big fellow dressed in a down-pulled Fedora so you couldn't see his face and a long wool overcoat with the collar turned up, neat but way too heavy for this climate. Like he had come from colder climes, New York or Chicago maybe. That gave me pause for thought.

Anyway, he stood there a long while and I watched him waiting to see if he'd look in my direction. But he never did, just finished his smoke, flicked the butt away and strolled off. Easy and casual with rolling shoulders like a boxer.

Maybe I was imagining things. He could just have been any kind of traveling man staying at the motel and taking the air. Was I getting jumpy? I wondered. Or was it that sixth sense that Gabriel had so often stressed about, it was certainly something that had stood me in good stead overseas. I knew how it worked. It came into play one day in this jungle clearing when I knew for certain that there was a minefield underfoot. Don't ask me how I knew it but it was like I could see it cold and clear in my mind's eyes, all plotted and laid out in traversing blast lines. I called out to the rest of the patrol, they thought I was crazy until one of them stepped out and lost both his legs. So here it was again. A certain sure instinct that told me that this fellow, whoever he was, was going to take some part in things as they played out.

Perversely, it answered my question for me; I was heading for Nevada. But Gabriel meanwhile, as it turned out, was heading for a mess of trouble in another time.

CHAPTER NINE

SIGNING UP FOR THE FIGHT

'Name?'

'Gabriel Brannigan.'

'Can you write?'

'Sure thing.'

'Then sign your name.'

Gabriel scratched his signature and the khaki clad regular army officer briefly perused the document, 'Right, you're now an enlisted member of the 1st United States Volunteer Cavalry, go report to the quartermaster sergeant and draw your equipment. Next!'

Gabriel left behind the long queue of hopeful volunteers in the bar of the Menger Hotel and went outside into the sunlit afternoon bustle of a busy San Antonio. There were plenty of other volunteers out there, joshing and chatting with each other and to Gabriel's gratified eye they all had the tanned and muscled look of hard riding outdoor types who appeared capable and eager to be about their business.

'You signed on, buster?' asked a regular army sergeant sporting a handsome mustache and a thick wad of forms.

'Yes sir,' Gabriel allowed.

'Right, give me your name.'

Gabriel told him and the sergeant duly noted it on a sheet and then said, 'Okay, here's what you get to collect over at the supply tent; one slouch hat, blue flannel shirt, trousers, leggings and boots. You want a bandana; you bring it yourself. You get a carbine and a .45 pistol on issue, some of you boys get to have a Bowie hunting knife as well, if the supply ain't run out.'

'Tell me, sergeant,' asked Gabriel. 'What kind of place is this Cuba?'

'Beats the hell out of me,' shrugged the sergeant. 'Just know they got Spaniards there and we aim to throw them out. Those local Cubans don't take too kindly to Spanish rule and its our duty to go help them get free.'

'So how do we find our way there?'

'Right now you'll be heading out to Port Tampa in Florida ready for embarkation. Now move along, fella, I got nigh on a hundred and twenty-five thousand of you fellows to deal with and I ain't got time for any more questions.'

Gabriel followed the drifting crowd towards the large supply tent and there he dutifully collected his gear from the overworked troopers inside.

'Hot damn!' said the young man behind him in the line. 'Look here; I got me a brand-new pair of boots. Lord! I ain't never had me no new pair of boots, I allus got me the hand-me-downs from my big brother.'

'Where you from, son?' asked Gabriel, curious to know where some of his new companions might hail from.

'Motem, Arizona, you know it?'

He was a tall fair-headed farm boy, a simple young man with shoulders that were obviously a sight bigger than his brain. He gazed at Gabriel with open blue eyes and a gullible expression.

'No, never heard of it,' said Gabriel

'I never been outside the State before,' the boy confessed. 'My name's Benjamin Bowrinkle, most folks call me Bo. How about you?'

'Gabriel Brannigan out of Texas.'

'Pleased to make your acquaintance, Gabriel. You mind if I try my new boots on right now?'

'Go to it, young fellow, enjoy 'em while you can.'

'I ain't too sure about this here gun though,' said Benjamin, laying down his gear and sitting in the dust to begin pulling off his shoes. 'What they call it? A Crap-something, foreign ain't it?'

Gabriel noted the boy had neither laces or socks and that there were holes in the soles of his scuffed shoes.

'It's a Krag-Jorgensen carbine,' he allowed.

'What kind of load does that carry?'

'30-40 army caliber.'

'Sheesh!' whistled Bo. 'All I ever shot before was my daddy's shotgun, this'll be an experience all right.'

'Guess so,' agreed Gabriel, amused by the fellow's naive innocence.

'You look a worldly kinda man, I reckon you seen

some times, is that right, Gabriel?'

'Some, I guess.'

'Yeah, a lot of these fellows look like you. I sure hope I ain't going to be the sore thumb around here.'

'Move along there!' bawled an aggressive looking sergeant, coming up and standing over Bo. 'What you doing sitting in the dirt, soldier?'

'Just trying on my new boots, sir. I ain't never had none before.'

'Don't call me 'sir',' roared the sergeant. 'I ain't no officer; you call me 'sergeant'. Now get on your feet, you're holding up the whole damned line.'

'Yes, sir, sergeant,' said Bo, hopping up with only one boot on. 'Sorry 'bout that.'

The long unmoving line of new men stretched back to the supply tent behind and on to another unknown tent in front.

'We ain't moving none, sergeant,' said Gabriel. 'He's got time.'

'Don't you argue with me,' snarled the sergeant, pushing his face close to Gabriel's. 'You better find out quick you ain't a civilian no more and what I say goes.'

'I got that, sergeant,' Gabriel said amenably. 'Just that we ain't going nowhere right now, so why not let the fellow get his boot on?'

The sergeant reared back, 'I can see we're going to have trouble with you. What's your name, old timer?'

'Brannigan, sergeant.'

'You done any army time before?'

'Yes, sir. Massachusetts Infantry during the war

and served with the Seventh Cav against the Indians, then the Texas Rangers for a while.'

'I see, so you know it all already, huh?'

'I didn't say that,' answered Gabriel easily.

'Say, that's sure is an impressive resumé, Gabriel,' cut in Bo with a show of appreciation.

'Shut up, you!' barked the sergeant, whirling on him. 'If you ain't being talked to you keep your attention front and center and mind your own affairs. We clear on this?'

'Yes, sir,' blinked Bo.

'I already told you, chucklehead, it's 'sergeant'.

'Sure thing, sergeant.'

'And you,' said the sergeant, turning to stare at Gabriel. 'I'll be watching you, soldier. Goddamn you fly-by-night volunteers, I had my way this would be a regular army show. Not no mob of circus riders and hillbilly deadbeats.'

He stalked off to be followed by a low derisive moan of complaint against his tirade from the other volunteers in the queue, the sound rising like a wave and following the sergeant as he marched off. The irate man glared at them and the wail died out.

'That there is Sergeant Onus Weather,' said the fellow in front of Gabriel, turning and giving him a broad grin. 'All fire and brimstone and he sure don't like you.'

'Onus Weather, huh? Well he sure comes on like a downpour,' allowed Gabriel.

'Howdy, I'm Mike Roundtree.'

'Sure thing, Mike, glad to know you.'

The two shook and Gabriel saw he was a wiry,

slender figure with a tanned face lined by the sun and wind. A fit looking man in his early fifties with somewhat hard boned, clean-cut features and a strong jaw and eyes that looked like they had seen some distance.

'Where you hail from?' asked Gabriel.

'Did my time as a grayback with the 1st Texas Cavalry during the war and then cowboying mostly, running cattle on the Double Zee spread out of Albuquerque, you?'

'Just drifting.'

It turned out that Mike Roundtree had been born to immigrant farmers in Missouri and his father had sadly died not long after his birth. His mother had raised him but when he reached the age of ten years she had also passed. Mike had been sent on to a distant relative but had fallen asleep on the train and not woken until he had reached Indian Territory in that part of the country that later became Oklahoma. On leaving the train a group of cowpokes had taken pity on the boy and he served as help to a Cherokee woman that cooked and cleaned for the ranch. He had grown up into his teens as a cowboy on the place until the War Between the States had given him reason to move on.

'Say, fellows,' piped up Bo, awkwardly hopping on one foot and clutching his unshod boot in his hand. 'What say we three stick together through this? I know I could sure do with some help from you old hands.'

'Suits me,' grinned Gabriel.

'You think they can stand us?' smiled Mike.

'We'll find out soon enough,' said Gabriel as the line shifted and they shuffled forward again towards the unknown tent in front.

And that was how the army turned out to be for the three new friends.

Mostly waiting around and not knowing what was happening next or where they were headed. There were drills of course, a great deal of drills and Gabriel saw that many of the volunteers were expert horsemen and that all displayed a keenness to be about their business and get to the fighting. Sadly though, the sultry climate of the Florida swamps accounted for a great deal of sickness and many in the force were laid low by Malaria and Yellow Fever before they even got a chance to make a start.

The waiting finally came to an end when they were ordered aboard a travel steamship named the Yucatan in the May of that year of 1898. With typical military mismanagement there was not enough space for the entire force of volunteer Rough Riders along with their mounts on the flotilla of fifty ships bound for Cuba and only two-thirds of their number set sail, the rest remaining in reserve in disease ridden Florida.

Arrival was indeed also a sorry affair. They travelled with a convoy of naval gunships and cruisers who made a show of it and paraded past the lush Cuban coastline of Cape Maisi and across from the aged fortifications at Santiago Bay where the battle ships bombarded the place as the troops were landed at the small nearby cove of Siboney. As they anchored offshore Navy steam launches set out and towed trains of boats packed tight with soldiery towards the coast.

Gabriel and the others stood at the rail and watched in dismay as their horses and cargo mules were sent over the side and expected to make the quarter mile swim ashore, the coastline it turned out was considered too treacherous for the ships to draw closer. Given the amount of horsemen amongst the volunteers there was a chorus of complaint as the wretched animals attempted to make the swim to shore with many of them drowning as they went.

'That ain't right,' growled Mike, watching the beasts struggle with the waves. 'They get water in their ears and they reckon they're gone and give up right there.'

'Damned stupid, you ask me,' agreed Gabriel.

'Look here,' added Bo, studying the floating bodies of drowned horses bobbing in the tide. 'What we going to ride on now?'

'Might be we'll be walking from now on,' observed Gabriel gloomily.

'I reckon you will,' snarled the irascible voice of the old trooper, Sergeant Weather from behind them. 'Like to see you wannabe fellows behaving like real regular troops on the march. Though given the look of that jungle out there, I reckon you'll be hacking your way through it rather than marching. You be doing that, you won't need none of them nags anyway.'

Sure enough, it turned out that Sergeant Weathers had spoken true and before long the volunteer cavalrymen were relegated to the ranks of foot soldiers.

They were to get their first taste of action at a place called Las Guasimas.

The uphill climb to the Spanish fortifications was through dense jungle on all sides and their first sight of the enemy came from Bo.

'Oh, my Lord!' he wailed, looking down at the decaying mess he had just stepped in. 'This here poor mortal's been shot dead a while. He smells riper than my daddy's pig pen.'

Gabriel looked at the pale festering corpse of the Spaniard lying in a dried puddle of blood and leaked juices; already the body was ballooning to twice its size and crawling with bugs.

'Ain't no more than a day dead,' he reckoned. 'Looks worse in this heat but it ain't that long.'

'Must have been them Cuban irregulars got him,' added Mike. 'They was up here a day earlier.'

'Well, I reckon this one's buddies will be waiting on us further up this danged hill,' said Gabriel.

It was hard going in the sweaty heat and they only had recourse to machetes to hack their way through the thickly tangled greenery that overshadowed them and cut off visibility to only a few feet ahead.

'Come on boys,' bristled their commander, the redoubtable and fiery general, 'Fighting Joe' Wheeler. 'I smell Dago up ahead.'

Wheeler had served as a Confederate officer during the Civil War and a certain yen for battle was revitalizing the warlike old warrior again.

The sound of shooting crashed through the jungle as the volunteers opened fire on the *fuerte* above them, one of the chain of Spanish blockhouses built around Santiago, all of them within sight of each other in protection against the local Cuban forces. Answering volleys came down in reply and whistled and cracked through the jungle.

'Where the hell are they?' complained Mike, peering through the leafy foliage as a swath of bullets slashed through the trees overhead. 'Can't see hair nor hide of where they're firing from.'

'They got them Mauser rifles,' explained Gabriel. 'The one's use smokeless powder, that's why you can't see 'em.'

The agitated Joe Wheeler lost patience and with a short-tempered roar he ordered a full-frontal assault on the defenses above. Such was his eagerness that he also lost sight of time and place and thought himself back in the earlier conflict.

'Let's go, boys!' he hollered with a loud halloo. 'We've got the damned Yankees on the run again.'

Lumbering upwards through the jungle, Gabriel looked across at Mike, 'This is a foolish charge,' he complained. 'God knows what they got up there.'

'They got the high ground that's for sure,' panted Mike.

Suddenly a huge bareheaded black man broke through the jungle before them and Mike raised his rifle threateningly.

'Hold on!' cried Gabriel, spotting the blue uniform and the horseshoe of rolled blanket slung around the Negro's torso. 'He's one of ours.'

The black man looked them over with rolling eyes, 'Which way?' he said. 'I done got lost.'

Gabriel pointed upwards, 'Always uphill,' he said.

'Thank you, sah,' said the black man, crashing off again and disappearing fast in amongst the curtain of giant palm leaves.

'What the hell was that?' asked a bemused Bo.

'He's with the 10th regulars, a Buffalo Soldier, one of the Negro troops,' explained Gabriel.

'Lord A'Mighty, we got colored fighting with us? I never knew that,' breathed Bo in awe. 'You sure know an awful lot of things, Gabriel.'

Gabriel snorted a laugh, 'It ain't any knowledge, Bo. It's just the years that do it.'

On all sides their comrades in the Rough Riders accompanied the three friends as they climbed sweating through the dripping jungle. Mostly they were fit young men looking for adventure that came from all walks of life. There were Ivy League graduates mixing with miners, and teachers, stockmen and clerks, all of them full of a youthful eagerness to get to grips with the enemy. In some ways, Gabriel felt a stranger amongst them. Few amongst his shave tail companions knew the true meaning of war and its results and he doubted that before nightfall not many of these brave young men would feel the same jingoistic fervor as they did now.

Grunting with effort and a touch of guile, Gabriel allowed the eager Bo to force a path ahead and he followed behind the big farm boy's flattened trail. Gabriel's blue flannel shirt was sticking to his back in the heat and sweat trickled down his ribs to run in a train until trapped by the canvas gun belt at his waist.

The jungle started to thin and Gabriel could see a

high cliff before them, its base surrounded by barbed wire. On the mound above sat the blockhouse with a low defensive wall raised over a trench in front. The building was a simple square structure, solidly built with a little lookout tower constructed on top of the four-sided and pointed roof.

'There it is!' said Bo in a loud whisper. 'We danged well got here.'

Figures were bobbing at the trench above and Gabriel pulled the bulky figure of Bo back out of sight.

'Just hold on there, hoss,' he said. 'They got us zeroed.'

As he spoke a fierce volley of firing came from the defenders in the trench and the large palm leaves around them flapped as bullets smacked through. It was as if a sudden squall had fallen and the jungle snapped and cracked under the fusillade. Twigs and foliage flew in a flurried cloud and splintered branches broke apart and rained down on the troops below.

'Holy shit!' snarled Mike. 'We got to get up *there*?'

'It's a dumb task all right,' Gabriel agreed. 'But that's what we got to do.'

'Well, I'm ready,' said Bo, staring boldly up at the hilltop redoubt.

'Don't you be *too* ready,' warned Gabriel.

'Hell, Gabe, they can't get me, there ain't a bullet made can drop old Bo. 'Sides, my daddy would never forgive me I don't bring him back a Spanish hairpiece. He made me promise, you know? You carry home one of them Spanish scalps to hang on my fireplace, that's what he tol' me.'

Gabriel could see the wild fever of excitement and nervous fear lighting up the youngster's eyes and he laid a restraining hand on his arm, 'Steady now, Bo,' he said calmly. 'There's plenty of others here willing to die for glory, just don't you be the first.'

'Hell! I'm going,' spat Bo, boldly wrenching his arm free and lunging forward.

'Aw, damn!' muttered Gabriel, bringing his rifle up. 'Cover him, Mike. Fool's about to get himself killed.'

The two men took up firing positions and laid down a hail of fire around the bounding figure of Bo as he ran at the crouch away from the jungle edge and towards the barbed wire defenses.

Gabriel picked his shots at any dark shape that appeared over the top of the trench. He was gratified to see his targets fall and figures pop up to drop away under his and Mike's accurate aim. Alongside him, Mike grinned as he worked his Krag-Jorgensen, 'Damn me, if this ain't like a goddamned turkey shoot.'

Others alongside were taking up the match and Gabriel heard the snap of an officer's Winchester and pop of a pistol amidst the sounds of carbine fire. Shouts of encouragement came from the volunteers as Bo closed with the low fence.

Then a Maxim machine gun began to rake the ground around Bo, the firing coming from an emplacement to one side of the *fuerte*. Bo stumbled, one leg spouting blood above the ankle, dragging himself upright he struggled with one of the support posts for the wire. He levered it backwards and forwards his heavy shoulders struggling to work the post free of the moist soil but it was deep set and would not come easily.

Gabriel worked himself around for better sight of the machine gun emplacement but to his dismay he saw that raised sandbags covered it and the gun team were hard to make out behind the cover of the sacks.

'We got to get that gun,' he called across to Mike.

Others of the volunteers were breaking cover now, encouraged by Bo's bold attempt they were also heading for the wire surround and attempting to break it down.

The machine gunner switched aim and pounded into the advancing troops and as Gabriel watched he saw one of the leading troopers take a direct hit, killing him as the machine gun bullets raked across his body and threw him down at the foot of the fence.

Gabriel saw his chance, 'Come on, Mike,' he called and set off at the run.

Thankfully, Gabriel heard Mike's heavy footfalls loyally coming behind him as the two pounded towards the fallen trooper, 'Grab an arm!' Gabriel called over his shoulder.

Bullets flapped around them, spitting up divots of dirt at their feet and hurling huge grassy chunks up high. The air was busy with the whizz and hum of bullets that sounded like an angry swarm of bees about their heads. Both men closed on the fallen body and still at the run, they each grabbed an armpit and hauled the figure forward with its feet dragging limply behind. Gabriel felt the dead man's cold underarm sweat tacky against his fingers but he gritted his teeth and hauled the dead weight up to the barbs of the fence, 'Over the top,' he called to Mike.

Together they heaved the corpse upwards and over the topmost strands of wire. The dead trooper lay fixed, his body-weight dragging the bands down in a sharp V-shape.

'Now, climb over,' said Gabriel, hastily grabbing the trooper's shirt at the back and pulling himself up. He swarmed over, clambering across the corpse, using it as a morbid and ghastly bridge. Bullets popped into the earth about his boots as Gabriel thudded down on the other side.

The machine gunner was trying to depress his gun but the sandbags, at once his protection now proved an inhibitor as he tried to bring down his aim more sharply onto the advancing Americans. The traversing field of fire had been set to aim at the jungle edge below the wire and no thought given to a possible break-through on the inner side. The Spaniards in the pit were jabbering at each other fearfully, some breaking away from the emplacement as they saw Gabriel and Mike nearing.

An officer rose up from the trench, waving his Mauser pistol threateningly and screaming at the retreating men to get back and man the machine gun. Gabriel shot him whilst on the run, hardly bringing his carbine above waist level as he dropped the officer. Mike fired into the remaining Spaniards in the emplacement as he did so and the two advanced steadily, stopping only briefly now and then to take accurate aim.

They both heard the wild war cries from behind as a troop of the volunteers broke through and charged after them coming over the side of the hill. The officer leading the charge was a wild-eyed Lieutenant Colonel with round gold-rimmed spectacles and a large set of teeth that showed white as he gritted his teeth like a mad thing and fired off his pistol in all directions.

'Look there,' said Gabriel. 'If that ain't that crazy s.o.b. Teddy Roosevelt come running up the hill.'

As Mike looked around, he noticed a bold Spanish sniper poke his head over the rim of the lookout tower and take aim at the officer with his Mauser rifle.

'Goddamn!' breathed Mike, bringing his carbine up fast.

He hauled off a shot just as the Spaniard fired, his bullet striking home and sending the sniper spinning. They both watched as Roosevelt staggered and for a moment dread ran through them as they thought him hit. But the redoubtable officer curiously lifted his foot and they saw that the Spaniard's bullet had merely clipped his boot and knocked the heel off. With a shake of the head, Roosevelt turned again to the business in hand and carried on towards the blockhouse, if at a slightly uneven run.

The Spaniards were retreating in panic, leaping and bounding down the hillside and making for the forest edge to the rear as fast as they could go.

With a jeering cheer most of the Rough Riders

congregated at the walls of the blockhouse and watched them go. But Gabriel was still burning with the heat of battle and he took position at the edge of the Maxim gun emplacement and began taking careful aim at the fleeing troops. Coldly, Gabriel potted at the runaways. He could hear one of them whooping in alarm as he ran, his loud cries pleading prayers to God and the Virgin Mary as he begged for his life. Mercilessly, Gabriel shot one after the other of the retreating men as they stumbled and ran.

'That's enough, Gabe,' said Mike, a little disturbed by his companion's blood lust. 'They're finished now.'

'Every one is one less to fight later,' said Gabriel grimly.

'They're done, Gabe,' pressed Mike, whose honorable nature would forgo shooting men in the back. 'Let it go.'

'Well, they shot enough of our boys,' Gabriel answered grimly, the breath coming fast in his nostrils.

At his words they both looked at each other as the sudden memory came rushing back to them.

'Bo!' gasped Mike.

'Come on, let's see if he's okay.'

Surrounded by crowds of backslapping congratulating troops, the two men pushed through and made their way back down the hillside. They found the spot where Bo had struggled with the fence post, but it was empty and there was no sign of their friend.

'Where'd he go?' asked Mike, looking around. 'He was hit in the leg he couldn't have gone far.'

Gabriel spotted the unit's respected and re-doubtable medic, Surgeon Church, as he treated a wounded man under a tree nearby.

'Maybe they took him back on a litter, we'll go ask.'

But when they approached the surgeon, he knew nothing of the soldier they described, 'Have to say I haven't seen him, boys,' said Church in his calm Washington accent. 'Plenty of others but not that one.'

'I seen him,' wheezed the wounded man, who had taken a bullet in the chest and was sitting up leaning back against the tree with a trickle of blood bubbling from his lips. 'I seen Bo.'

'Well, where is he, partner?' asked Gabriel.

'The Spaniards got him,' answered the man through gritted bloodstained teeth.

'What!' gasped Mike. 'They took him prisoner?'

'Yes,' nodded the wounded man. He was breathless from the wound that appeared to have clipped a lung but he managed to squeeze the words out. 'Bastards shot me whilst they done it too. There were a couple of them came running by. First off I thought they was Yanks, one was a tall bearded fellow with this funny looking mouth, like he had no teeth or something. He was a white man, sure enough, and dressed in Spanish whites but nowhere near as tanned as these local fellows. Well, they put one in me and then scooped up old Bo and ran off with him. He was limping bad, but they had him under the gun and off they went.'

Gabriel felt his heart sink as he heard the description of one of the Spaniards. The description fitted only too well the man he knew but it couldn't be, he thought. Not here, not now and not again.

Mike was shaking his arm desperately, 'You hear that, Gabe? They took him. Goddamn! We got to get poor Bo back.'

'Yes,' said Gabriel, looking off almost trance-like into the distance, his mind racing with the bizarre possibility that Lomas Chain had made an appearance in his life again. 'We sure have.'

'They'll be wanting to interrogate him,' added Surgeon Church. 'Want to know our disposition and numbers, that would be my guess.'

'Where would they go?' asked Mike.

Church shrugged, 'Daiquiri maybe, that's near our landing place, or possibly into Santiago itself. Forget it boys, they'll be long gone by now.'

CHAPTER TEN

RESCUE

Gabriel looked down the track leading away from the hilltop redoubt that the wounded man had indicated. It was a narrow and barely visible supply trail that led into the enclosing jungle below them.

'I'm going after him,' he said.

'Well, I'm with you, pard,' promised Mike.

'Come on then,' said Gabriel, loping off along the trail with a wave of farewell to the Doc and wounded man.

'Luck,' the trooper called after them.

They were circling below the incline of the hill and below the line of barbed wire heading for the opening in the forest when a harsh voice called after them.

'Hold on there, you men!'

Both stopped and turned to see Sergeant Onus Weather standing watching them, one foot higher than the other on the slope and a carbine balanced on his thigh.

'Where you think you're going?'

'They've taken Private Bowrinkle prisoner,

Sarge,' Mike replied. 'We aim to go get him back.'

'He's wounded, Sergeant,' Gabriel added. 'We ain't leaving him in their hands.'

Weather mused on it a moment, 'You know going off without orders puts you in an AWOL situation, don't you? Could be a Court Martial offence.'

'Don't matter none,' said Gabriel belligerently. 'Can't let our partner down and leave his fate to the Spaniards.'

For once the usually troublesome sergeant took on a suddenly more benevolent attitude, 'Appears to me you fellows did right well up there today. I reckon you will be more properly served in this venture if you have an accompanying noncom with you. Hell! I'm coming with you.'

'Well, come along then,' grinned Mike. 'We're losing time.'

'Bless me,' whispered Gabriel as the sergeant levered himself over the wire to join them. 'Who'd have thought old Weather could cut such a dash.'

'Maybe he's better than we thought,' replied Mike.

'Let's go,' growled Weather, breathing heavily with the exertion as he came over.

'Can you keep up?' asked Gabriel, noting the sergeant's sweating brow.

'Damn you, Brannigan,' spat Weather. 'I'll run your sorry ass into the ground any time, now lead on.'

With Gabriel in the lead they set off at a lope down the trail and were soon in amongst the heavy jungle again. The trail before them was clearly marked, the heavily trodden narrow path leading steadily downhill and cut clean from the surrounding undergrowth by machetes.

Behind them the sounds of victorious celebration on the hill faded quickly amongst the overhanging trees and vines and the three slowed their pace moving more cautiously as the quiet enveloped them.

Gabriel slid through the jungle with his senses attuned to any sudden anomaly, the tautness in him inherited from his earlier upbringing amongst his mother's people, the Shoshone. Suddenly, he held his hand up to halt the men behind and knelt on one knee listening hard.

'What is it?' whispered Weather.

'Shh!' hissed Gabriel as he strained to distinguish the sound he had noted amongst the birdcalls and other noise of indigenous creatures in the trees.

'They're ahead,' he said, sure he had heard the sound of heavy footfalls breaking undergrowth. 'They're slowed down by Bo, look here,' his fingers played amongst the dead leaves on the trail underfoot and came up stained red with fresh blood.

'Can we catch up?' asked Mike.

Without answering, Gabriel climbed to his feet and set off again at a faster rate.

Louder sounds came to them from ahead now and they were all suddenly pulled up by a steep shift in the jungle terrain. They could hear heavy wagons moving and the call of men coming through the wall of forest.

The three found themselves on the edge of an overgrown cliff face, the overhanging foliage draping thickly over the side with long twisted roots from the trees reaching down and vanishing

into the jungle below. Clearly seen was a camp in
a clearing, a line of barracks and outhouses built
beside a wide river mouth. There was what looked
like mining equipment and the nearby river held
rows of ocean-going craft drawn up on the beach.
Men in Spanish uniform moved about energetically
in the camp with mule teams bringing up howitzers
while sandbags were being stacked around gun em-
placements on the higher ground.

'They're getting ready for an attack,' observed
Weather.

'Yeah, must have heard the fight above and its got
them nervous,' agreed Mike.

'Look there,' said Gabriel, pointing.

They followed his finger and saw the limping figure of Bo being dragged into the camp by two men.
Bo was in a bad way, his torn trouser leg stained
deep red and the two captors beating at him with
their rifle butts and driving him on.

'Hot damn!' snarled Mike angrily.

'Watch where they put him,' ordered Weather.
'Though Lord knows how we'll get him out of that
hornets nest.'

'Must be best part of a hundred men down there,'
agreed Mike.

'Don't matter none,' said Gabriel grimly. 'We're
getting him out.'

His eyes were fixed on the taller of the two men
and a shiver ran through him at the recognition, he
knew that broad shouldered figure by its gait. It was
the same man whose teeth he had knocked out years
ago, the same one he had shot down to save from

Indians. The same man who had killed his father. It was Lomas Chain.

'What's wrong, Gabe?' asked Mike as he noted Gabriel's intense stance.

'The tall bearded one,' growled Gabriel. 'He's an outlaw and a renegade I know. A mean piece of work I have grievance against.'

Weather raised an eyebrow, 'What'd he do to you, Brannigan?'

'He killed my pa.'

'You don't say,' breathed Weather.

'It's a fact,' murmured Gabriel. 'I been chasing that son of a bitch across half the States in America, but the bastard always seems to evade me.'

'Well, he's close enough now,' warned Weather in a stern voice. 'But getting our boy back comes first, you can't let personal vengeance get in the way of this.'

'I know it,' agreed Gabriel. 'But if I get a chance, I'll put that sucker under.'

'So how do we go about this?' asked Mike, peering at the fortified camp below. 'They got an awful lot of guards on station.'

'They have, don't they?' agreed Gabriel, spotting yet another Maxim being dragged into position.

Weather shook his head as he too counted the guards below, 'That is way too many men for a site like this in the middle of the jungle.'

'And why the howitzers?' added Mike. 'There's no clear field of fire for them here.'

'You know what, fellows?' mused Gabriel. 'I reckon there's more going on here than meets the eye.'

Just then the rustle of undergrowth came from

along the ledge and all three quickly faded into cover as the sound of a body making its way through the forest came closer.

From within the cradle of a nest of overhanging palm leaves, Gabriel eased his carbine up as the sounds approached.

A panting figure pushed his way into the open.

He stood a moment wiping the beads of perspiration from his brow with a large spotted handkerchief. Red faced and dressed in jungle fatigues with a large portfolio bag strapped across his body the man noticed the campsite below and leaning over the drop, studied it curiously.

Mike rose up silently behind him, Bowie knife in hand. His hand clamped over the stranger's mouth and the knife's razor edge came up to rest against his throat.

The man gulped and stared wide eyed as the others climbed to their feet.

'Who the hell are you?' whispered Gabriel hoarsely.

Mike eased his hand away and the fellow began to gabble, 'Thank God, you're Americans, I...'

Gabriel hissed him to silence with a glance at the busy scene below them. The man nodded and continued in a quieter voice.

'Corbin Moon, Allied Press,' he explained. 'I was following the advance of you fellows up the hill and lost my way. Been struggling around in this blasted jungle for hours. What's going on here?'

'A damn news reporter,' snarled Weather in disgust. 'That's all we need.'

'Keep it down, Mister Moon,' warned Gabriel, thumbing the upward trail behind them. 'The Spanish fort's been taken back that way; maybe you should aim to head off up there. But for Christ's sake keep quiet, we thought a circus elephant had got loose in here.'

'Sorry,' apologized Moon, running fingers tentatively over his throat as Mike released him. 'That's a might sharp knife, young man,' he observed with a critical frown.

Mike arched an eyebrow and grinned, 'Lucky you was one of ours then, ain't it?'

Moon swallowed hard, 'I guess so.'

'Best you head out, sir,' urged Gabriel. 'We got business here.'

Moon bristled, 'As I have too, soldier. I'm here to report the war for the folks back home and it appears I have missed the main thrust so I'd appreciate it if you'd let me know what's happening on this front.'

Their hurried conversation was carried out in low whispers and Gabriel was losing patience with the delay, so he quickly explained their mission.

'Our buddy's been captured, and we aim to get him back but he's down there amongst that mess of Spaniards, so we're figuring on how to go about it exactly.'

Moon pouted and stared over the drop at the camp, 'Excellent!' he exclaimed. 'Just the sort of story I need. But how on earth can the three of you manage against that small army down there? Why? There must be nigh on a hundred men in that place.'

Weather rubbed his chin with a horny hand, 'You

got that right, a hundred men and a lot of artillery too. This ain't no place for a civilian, mister. Best you head off out of here.'

'Certainly not,' spat Moon. 'This is *news*, gentlemen, and that's what I'm here for.'

Gabriel looked away in annoyance; seeing that they were not about to rid themselves of the reporter he went back to studying the camp layout.

'Whatever they're all here for it must be mighty important, see how that big building has guards all around.'

'Some kind of headquarters perhaps,' added Mike.

'They took Bowrinkle in that same building,' said Weather. 'Saw 'em do it.'

'It has to be at night,' Gabriel suggested. 'That's the only way we can sneak in amongst them. See these roots hanging here? We can climb down and get into that place easy enough in the dark.'

Weather pulled out a pocket watch, 'A few hours to go yet.'

'You mean we have to wait?' asked Moon, slapping at a mosquito that was enjoying the hot skin on the back of his sunburned neck.

'I told you,' snapped Gabriel. 'Keep it quiet or I'll let Mike finish what he started.'

Moon gulped and nodded apology, 'You know, I did hear that the Spaniards were moving their gold reserve, maybe that's what we have here.'

The three soldiers looked at each other in a moment of stunned silence.

'*Gold reserve?*' asked Gabriel.

'Yes, you know? These fellows have been hauling gold and precious stones out of the Americas for centuries; the Spanish court was living off the proceeds for years. Well, it seems they had a hurricane off the coast here back in the 18th century, eleven treasure ships on their way back to Spain went down right here carrying a hoard of silver, gold, emeralds and all kinds of gems. The whole personal wealth of the viceroy of Peru was in amongst the ship's cargo. These fellows have been diving for it for years now, there was so much floating around they even found coins washed up on the beach. There was talk in the office back home before I joined the army group about how the powers that be in Spain know its all a lost cause over here in Cuba and want to get the last of their ill gotten gains out before they capitulate.'

'Well, they're putting up a right good show of it if this is capitulation,' grunted Weather.

'All just a temporary resistance. If that down there in that building is the recovered gold, then it'll be a real treasure trove and they'll be defending it with everything they've got.'

Gabriel breathed a sigh, 'That's a real help.'

'All we're interested in is Bo,' said Mike.

'Well, I don't know,' mused Weather thoughtfully. 'How much you reckon we're talking about here, Mister Moon?'

'Millions,' nodded Moon excitedly. 'We don't know exactly, but its all been taken off the local Indians over the years, maybe some of those golden Indian artifacts, precious stones and nuggets, old Spanish doubloons and all kinds of stuff. It's reckoned in today's money they had around eight and half million dollars of gold in the holds on those ships.'

'Well, a handful of that wouldn't go amiss now, would it, you fellows?' asked Weather with an overt air of innocence.

Gabriel noted the greedy glimmer in the sergeant's eye and shook his head, 'Bo is what we came to get and that's what I aim to do.'

'With you there, partner,' agreed Mike.

'A Bold Rescue by Daring Men of the Rough Riders!' exclaimed Moon, already writing the headline. 'I like it. It'll be a great story. If there's Spanish treasure as well, all to the good.'

'Yeah,' sneered Mike derisively. 'It's probably just a warehouse full of coffee beans down there and not a dime to be seen.'

'You think so?' frowned Weather, his disappointment obvious.

'We wait,' said Gabriel with a show of finality that brought the conversation to a sudden end.

But later as the sun set, it was the veteran Sergeant Weather who took final command.

As the light went beyond the jungle canopy he outlined the plan of attack.

'Mister Moon, you listening?'

Moon, who had been scribbling in one of his many notebooks, hurriedly put it aside.

'Yes, Sergeant.'

'You ever done any sailing, sir?'

'Why, yes indeed. Sculling on the Hudson in my youth whilst at...'

'Good,' Weather cut him off. 'Can you take on a little mission for us? It's important.'

'Of course,' beamed Moon eagerly, his teeth white in the darkness. 'I'm ready for anything.'

'I want you to take a circular course once we are down this climb,' he indicated the long growing roots of the trees that hung over the edge of the drop. 'There's enough light from the Spanish campfires to see your way. So make an arc around the outer limits, well away from their pickets and work yourself over to the river.'

'Got it,' replied Moon. 'You mean the boats moored there, right?'

'Exactly. Pick a good launch for us to make our way out of here once we've got our man. He's wounded so can't travel fast and we'll have to move it once we've picked him up. Do what you can to disable the other boats there, hole them or set fires if you can, just destroy any chance of us being followed. Think you can do that?'

'I'll do it,' said Moon firmly.

'Good man, it should be one of us by rights, you being a civilian and all. But we'll need all hands to get our man out.'

'No problem, Sergeant. This will make a great lead. Reporter Aids Rescue Attempt. I'll get a Pulitzer out of it.'

'Okay,' grunted Weather. 'Now listen up the rest of you.'

Gabriel and Mike shuffled closer as the sergeant issued his instructions.

'We stay in touch and move together, never lose

sight of the man next to you. Anybody has a problem, there's a sentry or somebody comes out of a tent suddenly, then we all stop until the danger's been cleared. Brannigan, you take the left. Roundtree the center and I'll be out on the right. Keep it quiet and move easy, okay?'

'Got it, Sarge,' Mike answered.

'Right, anybody gets separated then we meet up at the river. Save your strength, as my guess is that Bowrinkle won't be walking and we'll have to carry him and he's a big knothead, so get ready to do some work.'

A silent nodding of heads as they agreed.

'Then let's do this.'

They made their way to the cliff edge and each took a thick hardwood root in hand and swung out over the drop. Below was pitch black, the only light penetrating the canopy above a distant glow of the night sky populated with twinkling stars. Beyond the blackness below, scattered cook fires and the light from isolated hanging lanterns lighted the camp. Slowly the four men lowered themselves down the sturdy vine-like and knobby roots that were as thick in diameter as a fist and made good scaling ladders. In some places the smooth bark was coated with damp moss and it was the unfortunate Moon that first came across a patch and lost his grip, his fingers sliding over the slime as he dropped away.

The Rough Riders froze where they were, outlined against the cliff wall as Moon moaned softly in distress and disappeared from view raising a wild sounding rustle and crackling of undergrowth before hitting the ground with an audible thud.

All three held their breath and scanned the outer perimeter of the camp as they waited for some response from the guards.

Nothing. Only the sounds of the camp occupants going about their normal business came back to them.

'We're okay,' breathed Weather.

'Must have thought it was some animal out here,' Mike agreed.

Gabriel was already on the move, his carbine across his back as he dropped hand over hand into the jungle below.

Soon the other two joined him and they crouched together in the darkness.

'Moon?' hissed Weather. 'Where the hell are you?'

No sound came in answer and there was little obvious chance of finding him, as it was too dark to even see each other in the gloom.

'You think he's okay?' asked Mike.

'Poor sucker probably broke his damned neck,' growled Weather.

'Maybe he's already gone on to the river,' suggested Gabriel.

'Well, we ain't got time searching for him. Come on, let's get on with it,' rumbled Weather. 'Roundtree, take the point. We'll be close by.'

The three spread out and in a slow-moving line worked their way towards the camp perimeter making as little noise as possible. The muttering of men preparing their evening meal greeted them as they approached the shadowy outlines of the outlying huts. Somewhere a guitar was being played and a man singing softly.

The scream took them by surprise.

It was a long hollow wail breaking into a sobbing wrench of pitiful weeping. A dreadful sound, like the cry of some trapped and wounded animal calling into the night.

Mike stopped and looked over questioningly to the others, their faces barely visible in the shadows.

Weather shook his head in a signal to ignore the sound and with his finger he pointed ahead and Mike nodded and set out again.

They were in amongst the huts; the dark shadows black and obliquely angled around them. For moments Gabriel lost sight of the others as they moved steadily forward, slipping from cover to cover.

Voices came from some of the huts Gabriel passed, grunted conversation followed by the bawdy squeal of female laughter. There was the clatter of cooking pots and the rich smell of stewing meat in the air.

Gabriel worked his way around the pools of light cast by the fires and hanging lanterns as he loped through the shadows towards the large building at the center of the camp.

Another high-pitched warbling scream split the night and was answered by catcalls and cries of derision from the rest of the soldiers stationed in the camp.

Gabriel looked up sharply, the noise had come from the building ahead and he guessed that it was Bo who was doing all the howling. There was no doubt they were hurting him bad to get him to talk.

Grimly, Gabriel moved on more quickly and inadvertently stepped right on top of an unseen man sleeping on the ground covered by a blanket. The man complained loudly, and Gabriel swiftly struck down with his carbine's stock, ending the cries of irritation in a soft groan. He looked across at the others who had both halted and were waiting for him to give an all clear. Gabriel waved them on and then stepped over the unconscious man, holding his rifle ready at the port arms.

They reached the cleared land surrounding the large warehouse structure and sunk down as a couple of leisurely guards strolled by chatting and smoking cigarettes.

Weather signaled with his hands and both Gabriel and Mike slung their carbines and drew their Bowie knives from their belt sheaths. The two set off after the guards, paralleling the men's patrol through the huts. At last the guards reached an area of darkness and, quickly loping across the intervening space, Gabriel and Mike came up silently behind the two men. Both Rough Riders struck at the same time.

A hooked arm around the unsuspecting face and a knee placed hard in the back as the bodies were bent over. Sparks flew in the darkness as the cigarettes were knocked aside and the flash of the blades scribed a slash of brightness as both men had their throats cut. Booted feet scrabbled and dust was raised in the death throes. Blood, dark in the dim light, shot out in a geyser and the two guards tumbled down with Gabriel and Mike on top of them pressing the faces into the dirt to cut off any further sound.

So close to his victim, Gabriel smelled the body stink of chilies and onion in his final meal as the guard exhaled his last breath. The two Rough Riders dragged the bodies up into the shadows close to the warehouse wall; the only sign of their violent end a blood trail in the dust. Breathing heavily, they both looked back for Sergeant Weather and saw him with rifle raised, preparing to kick his way through a side door.

At that moment there was the boom of an explosion and a pillar of flame shot into the air from the direction of the river.

'Looks like Moon made it after all,' observed Mike.

Weather kicked out and crashed the door open. He stepped inside, firing his carbine as a roar of alarm came from the camp. Another bloom of light lit up the night followed by the bark of explosion and the crackle of fire.

'Geez!' said Gabriel. 'He's sure making a show of it.'

'Better than Fourth of July,' agreed Mike. 'Looks like that boy's found himself some dynamite.'

'Come on, best get after Weather.'

They ran towards the open door and the sound of gunfire coming from inside.

Men came bounding haphazardly from the direction of the camp as Gabriel reached the doorway and both he and Mike spun around firing from the hip at the advancing Spaniards. Most were half-dressed and unarmed and dashed about in confusion shouting out frenetic calls of, 'Attack! Attack!'

The racketing sound of a Maxim machine gun firing off followed by volleys of rifle fire split the night as another explosion roared.

Gabriel and Mike cut the running figures down, spinning the racing men into the orange dust haze cast by the firelight billowing from the boats harbored at the river. Reloading quickly, the two pressed into the warehouse doorway.

They both gasped in amazement at the sight that met their eyes.

Stacked on shadowy pallets from floor to ceiling and glittering in the mellow light cast from oil lamps hanging from the walls were layers and layers of gold bars. The vast interior was filled with piled ingots that had been melted down from the native gold raped from across the continent and from the treasure dragged up from the sea and it all made a wall of immeasurable value. Unsealed crates stood open, their insides filled with the shine of emeralds and rubies, of diamond studded hoops and glowing pearl and bead necklaces, the precious stones demonstrating a fantastic excess of luxurious wealth. Golden masks and headdresses in vibrant feathers stood hanging from stands and long feathered cloaks in a multitude of colors trailed over the floor. Ugly and grotesque statues carved from stone stood ominous and threatening in the shadows. Everywhere were signs of hurried attempts to pack the treasures ready for transport, timber, hammer and nails, rope and netting lay in heaps.

Gabriel pulled his eyes away from the treasure trove to see the figure of Weather sprawled in the shadow of one of the large crates. He and Mike dashed over to the Sergeant and saw he was badly wounded, struggling for breath his body palpitating with the sucking wound in the chest.

'Stay down,' rasped Weather. 'They're in there. Three of them and they got Bowrinkle.'

His head sagged with the effort and Gabriel crawled over him to peer around the edge of the crate.

A long table beside a smoldering brazier stood in a cleared area on the beaten earth floor. On the table lay stretched the stripped body of Bo, his limbs spread wide and fastened by rope. His pale skin shone pallidly in the dim light and was bruised and marked with savage stripes of red but his feet were the worst, the soles barely recognizable as more than stumps, blackened and with all the appearance of over-grilled hamburger.

Behind him, hiding behind the tortured man for cover, Gabriel saw the three men, all of them armed and looking in his direction. A rifle barked, the sound loud in the hollow space and a splintered crack split the crate above Gabriel's head. He ducked back swiftly as another shot roared and kicked up dust.

Mike was tying a looped sleeve cut from the Sergeant's shirt around his chest in an attempt to stem the blood flow. He looked up as Gabriel knelt to study Weather's wan features. Gabriel shook his head as he saw the coming death written there and Mike cursed silently.

'I know it,' said Weather, noting their expression through slit eyes. 'Set me up, I'll keep them busy whilst you two flank them.'

'You won't make it,' objected Mike.

'Don't damn well argue, just do it,' growled Weather. 'That's an order.'

'But...' protested Mike but Gabriel was already helping the Sergeant and dragging him near to the corner of the crate. Gabriel knew it was their only chance to take the defenders by surprise and he shoved the carbine into Weathers' waiting hands.

The Sergeant gave him a grateful wink, 'Thanks, Brannigan. You'll make a right good soldier one day.' Blood trickled from his lips and he snorted bubbles of red from his nostrils, 'Now get to it,' his breath rattled in his throat. 'Go save our man.'

Gabriel looked up sharply and indicated direction to Mike; he would take one side, his partner the other. Both slipped away as Weather unsteadily began to loose off shot after wild shot in vague direction of the defenders.

'Wait! Hold your fire!' came a call from across the warehouse.

Gabriel stopped dead and crouched down as he recognized the voice, it was Lomas Chain.

'This is damned stupid,' called Chain. 'We can end this peaceable right now.'

'Who the hell are you?' Weather answered weakly.

'A fellow American, that's who. I'm telling you we can make a deal here.'

Gabriel listened with gritted teeth as he heard his hated enemy propounding a share of the vast treasure surrounding them. With a deep breath of disgust Gabriel put aside his distaste and began again to work his way around the stacks of gold to find a clear overlook on the three men.

'You think you can make a deal with me,' snorted Weather. 'I'm just about done in, mister. Much as I would like to, I don't reckon I could carry away a nickel piece you put that bullet in me so good.'

'Sorry about that,' Chain replied unconvincingly. 'What about your buddies there? They got a say in this?'

'Why don't you ask them?'

'All right, I will. Hey there! The rest of you men, you want to live in luxury the rest of your lives?'

Neither Gabriel nor Mike answered, they were too busy worming the way between the heavy wooden pallets.

'Come on!' Chain jibbed. 'As much as you can carry, let's do a deal?'

'All we deal in, friend,' came Mike's cold voice from the other side of the warehouse. 'Comes in a brass casing.'

And he sent some of it slamming in Chain's direction. There was a cry of pain as one of the Spaniard's took Mike's bullet and flopped over.

'This is stupid!' roared Chain in desperation. 'We can all walk away rich men.'

Gabriel lifted himself above the side of the crate he sheltered behind and had a clear shot at the other Spaniard, crouching alongside Chain. Leveling his carbine he called out, 'You're going to get all you deserve, Chain!'

With that he fired and the Spaniard, a man with rolled sleeves and Bo's blood on his hands, dropped silently sideways covering Chain as he fell.

'*No!*' screamed Chain, recognizing the voice as he fumbled to throw the dead Spaniard off him. 'Not you, not Gabriel Brannigan.'

'I'm here,' said Gabriel. 'And I'm here for *you.*'

'Not so fast,' warned Chain, his voice deceptively calm with a warning sharpness to it. 'If you want to see your friend stay alive, that is.'

Gabriel peeked over the crate's edge and saw that Chain was on his feet and that he held a sharp-edged machete blade hovering over Bo's neck.

Bo was only semi-conscious, his head and eyes rolling sluggishly as he made half-hearted attempts to free his tied wrists.

Both Mike and Gabriel got to their feet, their rifles covering Chain, 'You're a dead man either way,' warned Gabriel, moving cautiously forward. 'You let that blade slip and I'll nail you within a heartbeat.'

'I know it,' said Chain, grinning broadly so that his wooden set of teeth made a dark bar behind his lips. 'How have you been, Gabe? Ain't seen you since Mexico. You make out with that fine piece of Mex tail you had down there, did you?'

'Shut your mouth, Chain, I don't like looking at those mucky wood teeth you got.'

'Well *you* put them there, you asshole,' Chain snarled. 'So, live with it.'

Gabriel noticed that he held the sharp blade so that if either Rough Rider risked a shot at him it would drop from his fingers and sever Bo's throat. They were at an impasse.

'That's our buddy you got there,' growled Mike

bitterly. 'What you done to him?'

Chain shrugged, 'Just interrogation, I'm afraid our Spanish friends can be a little crude in their technique. He was a tough old boy, your chum here, couldn't get a danged word out of him. Except for the occasional scream though, of course,' teased Chain spitefully.

'You bastard!' roared Mike.

'Hold it, Mike,' warned Gabriel. 'He's just trying to rile you.'

Both Rough Riders were close now, standing at a forty-five degree angle and covering Chain.

'How you doing, Bo?' Mike asked the figure stretched on the tabletop. 'We've come to get you out of this.'

Bo mumbled something incoherent in reply, his eyes rolling in his beaten face.

'Don't suppose it's any use surrendering?' asked Chain blithely.

'Lay aside that machete and we'll see,' offered Gabriel.

'Oh, no,' chuckled Chain in disbelief. 'We've met before, remember?'

The walls of the warehouse bowed as if struck by a high wind as another loud explosion came from the riverbank and they all ducked their heads instinctively as dust silted down from the roof.

'Sounds like you got the whole US army out there,' observed Chain with a bitter twist of his lip.

'Just your neighborly newspaper man,' quipped Mike. 'And you know how they like to overplay a story.'

'The hell with this,' growled Gabriel, lifting his rifle to aim at Chain's head.

'*No!*' cried Mike.

Hardly had the word left his lips when with a wrenching scream a support timber collapsed and the outer wall began to fall inwards. Timbers split with splintering cracks and the whole weakened building began to shift, leaning over threateningly.

'It's going!' bawled Mike, throwing himself forward to cover Bo's body as a rain of broken roof fell in around them.

Through the falling wood Gabriel saw Chain duck away, he managed one shot before the clatter of collapsing planks knocked the carbine from his hands. Another roaring explosion came from outside and it was as if a whirlwind had suddenly struck. All around him, Gabriel saw the building coming apart piece by piece as the walls folded in on themselves. Luckily the timbers were cheap sundried and rough-cut planks, quickly constructed and lightweight. As they fell, Gabriel felt himself swamped and knocked to the ground by a great rainfall of the planking.

The last thing he remembered as he was buried under the downfall was the sight of Chain's disappearing back haloed by the wall of flame visible along the riverbank.

CHAPTER ELEVEN
THE OLD FOE

I stared down the black hole of the Colt .45 automatic.

I knew it was an automatic as I'd already carried one plenty of time in the Pacific.

The back of my head was sore as hell where the fellow had slugged me as I came in the door of my darkened room. He stood over me now, the same man I had noticed at the earlier motel. He still wore the pulled down fedora keeping his face in shadow and had on the same woolen overcoat that was way too hot for the climate.

I dropped my walking stick as he hit me and it was lying between me and him right now. Seeing it, I tried to formulate a plan and drag my fuzzy brain into action.

'Who the hell are you?' I asked, my hand creeping towards the tail end of the stick. I reckoned if I could get the hook end around his ankle somewhere between his neatly creased turn-ups and nicely polished Florsheim shoes I could hoop him over and pull him down. He was a big fellow all right, looming over me and staring down hard but at the right moment if I could get him off balance...

'You following me?' he grunted. 'Why you on my tail?'

'I ain't following you, mister and that's no call to slug me like that.'

I was lying on the dirty carpet of my seedy motel room, in an out of the way nondescript place somewhere on the road to Nevada. I'd driven all day and just gotten in not more than thirty minutes before. And after a puny burger in the motel's flyblown diner that served passing truckers and mostly lone travelers on this deserted part of the highway, it had been a short walk to my room where this big ape had been waiting for me.

'Then how come I see you every place I go?' he asked.

My hand was on the ferrule at the stick end, all I had to do was wait for the moment then I'd hook it like a shepherd with a sheep and lift him off his feet.

With a tired sigh, he looked down and casually rotated his foot. The guy must have been wearing size thirteen's 'cos they were certainly large. He pressed down on the stick under his shoe, crushing my fingers as he did so.

'No you don't,' he tutted.

I gave up on the walking stick idea, this boy was not all brawn, there was a brain beating in there somewhere.

'You mind pointing that thing elsewhere?' I asked, nodding at the automatic.

'Depends, asshole. You going to spill it? Who set you onto me?'

'Listen, mister, I don't know who you are. I got my own business to attend to in Las Vegas and it's nothing to do with you.'

'What's your name?' he asked.

'Jonah Cord.'

'Never heard of you. You with the Miami Mob?'

'*Miami Mob!* What, you think I'm some kind of hoodlum?' I was kinda pissed just then, being sore headed and all, so I ignored the pistol and pulled myself upright whether he liked it or not. 'You mind if I get up now?'

He backed away a few steps still keeping me under the gun, 'Okay.'

'I need the stick,' I said.

'Right, just don't try anything clever.'

'Now,' I said, heaving myself to my feet. 'You want to tell me what this is all about?'

'I ain't telling you shit, fella. See who's holding this gun? I am, so *you* start talking before I get a mite miffed.'

His voice was gruff and sounded city born but aside from the rough accent I had to agree that he had me at a certain disadvantage.

'I'm looking for someone,' I said. 'An old fellow called Gabriel Brannigan enroute to Las Vegas.'

'Uhuh,' he grunted. 'And why you doing that?'

'He done me some favors in the past, I just wanted to see how he was faring.'

'Must have been one hell of a favor.'

'No, not so you'd notice. Saved me and my Ma from a shooting one time and kept me up to date whilst I was serving, that's all.'

'Uhuh,' he grunted again. 'Gabriel Brannigan? Seems like I heard that name somewhere.'

'He's just an old man, must be over a hundred years old now. Hell of a guy in his day though, now I just want to see him all right, that's all.'

'And that's why you're on this road?'

'That's it.'

I could see the fellow was relaxing some as he began to believe me. I mean to say it was an unbelievable enough story to disarm anybody.

'You some kind of hood, is that what this is about?' I asked. 'Some sort of gang war thing?'

The man chuckled and snapped open some ID from his billfold, 'Not on your life, pal. I'm with the Treasury Department in DC and looking into an old case. I thought for a while that maybe you was with the opposition.'

He had obviously decided I was on the level as he had slipped the automatic out of sight under his coat as easily as he had poked it in my face.

'A Treasury agent, that right, is it?' I asked with a note of cynicism. 'They got a lot of you bust-'em-up kind of fellows in Treasury now?' I was rubbing my sore head at the time as I asked that.

'Yeah, well, sorry about that, you being a cripple and all,' he made the right sounding noises but there wasn't much real apology in his tone.

'So, I can go about my business now, is that right?' I asked.

'Yeah, I guess,' he paused a moment. 'This Brannigan fellow, why's he heading up to Nevada?'

'He's looking for a fellow, an old adversary of his.

He hates this guy right well and claims he murdered his pa back in the old days and he's been looking for some come-back for years. I reckon I'm heading after him to save the old boy getting himself into any more trouble on that score.'

'He likely to do that,' chuckled the Treasury agent. 'Get himself into trouble? Really? I mean to say, you're talking about some antiquarian old coot who probably can't even get up the stairs easy.'

'Don't you believe it,' I said. 'When it comes to Gabriel Brannigan and Lomas Chain, then there's hell to pay whatever their age.'

The agent froze on the spot.

'*Who'd* you say?' he asked in a suddenly quiet and strained voice.

'Gabriel Brannigan.'

'No, the other one.'

'Lomas Chain.'

'Yeah, that's what I thought you said.'

'Why? What's it mean to you?'

He stood there a long moment, his large outline a dark silhouette in front of the flickering roadhouse sign outside the window.

'Best we sit down, and you turn the light on,' he said.

I did as he asked and turned to find him already seated on the edge of the bed. Slowly he unfastened his overcoat and leaned forward to rest his elbows on the knees of his razor-sharp creased trousers.

'You got anything worth drinking?' he asked.

'Sure,' I said, getting a half-finished bottle from my case. 'What's this about? You want a glass with that?'

He unscrewed the cap without answering and took a long swallow.

I watched him carefully, his battered features thoughtfully furrowed as he slugged back another mouthful. He walked like a boxer and looked like one too with a punchy, beaten-up face beneath a swollen forehead, popped-up cheeks and a busted nose. But there was a mellow look about his eyes, they were slate in color and shone with a dull shade of hope buried somewhere deep inside.

'My name's Bob Warner and as I said I'm a government agent, have been ever since I got back from Archangel two years back,' he began slowly. 'Seems like you and I have something to discuss.'

I pondered on what he might have been doing in the Soviet Union but let it pass and took the one and only chair in the room and sat across from him, taking back the bottle as he passed it across.

'You're talking about Lomas Chain?' I asked, noting that everything had changed in his demeanor at mention of the name.

'You got it,' he answered.

I sipped from the bottle but was far more interested in what he had to say.

'Lomas Chain is dead,' Warner went on. 'He died back on the fifteenth February 1932.'

That got me freezing that whiskey bottle halfway to my mouth, 'You sure on that?' I asked, not really believing it.

'Lomas made his mark before he went,' Warner continued without bothering to answer. 'Got himself quite a syndicate out on the West Coast, but he came out of nowhere. Guy was a millionaire and we don't know how he got his fortune, just know that he had a bucket full when he made his presence known. The word was he made it out of trading in Ecuador but there's no real evidence of that. Where and how, we don't know for sure but everybody guesses it was something illegal whatever the source.'

I scratched my head on that, thinking about Gabriel's story of his time on Cuba and all the gold he had seen there, 'So why are you fellows interested?'

'It ain't him no more, no, it's his son, Benjamin Lamtoc Chain.'

'*Lomas had a son?*'

'He did. We don't know the wife's name but probably some native girl he met in South America as Ben is somewhat of a darker shade than his pa.'

'And this Benjamin Chain inherited his father's cash.'

Warner shook his head negatively, 'No, it wasn't so straightforward. See, as you'd expect there were a lot of people interested in Lomas' empire once he passed. They didn't want the boy to inherit and they came on real strong in an attempt to push him to one side. But Ben wasn't having it, no sir, not him. Mostly these were all men who had held directorships in Lomas' various businesses; he had a whole heap of going concerns when he went. Air transport, haulage and shipping, that kind of thing. It was all kind of shady and some of these people were not, how can I say it? Not of the most noble sort, if you get my drift.'

I nodded understanding; most of the folks involved in large-scale transport back in the thirties had a big hand in illegal booze under Prohibition and that meant gangsters.

'So, Ben was hard put to claim his father's money, which believe me was now worth a king's ransom. I mean he had three houses and when I say houses I mean like palaces. They were all in different states in the US and then there were five more that we know of overseas. He owned a thousand-acre ranch, then some luxury retreat in Florida, a hotel in Cancun and a whole apartment block off Central Park in New York. Had a custom-built Rolls Royce and a personal airplane line and his very own ocean-going yacht. Last estimate by the accountants in Treasury was that he held something like five billion in readies and Lord knows what else tucked away in offshore accounts. We are talking very serious moolah here.'

'Still can't get over the idea that he's dead and gone,' I said. 'Is that a positive?'

'I've seen the certificate, liver complaint. He's dead alright, even his tomb over in Woodlawn is built like some damned palace, it's carved out of Italian and Portuguese marble and stands about as tall as the Empire State. Seems he went kind of doohlilly before he passed and favored the notions of ancient Egypt, thinking he was going to live on in the afterlife like one of them old time Pharaoh's or something. This whole tomb is built like a regular house with all the particular things inside that he liked and wanted to take with him, they say that there's even an alabaster bath tub with gold taps and running water in there.'

'Old Gabriel sure will be disappointed.'

Warner held out his hand for the bottle and I passed it over. There wasn't much more than three fingers left and he raised questioning eyes, 'You mind?'

'Finish it,' I said, feeling generous.

'But Ben was raised tough and he came back hard,' said Warner; licking his lips after slurping down the shot as if it were a Dixi-Cola. 'He bought himself a crew of hard boys and planned it all very well, every one of those suckers on his father's board took the big ride on the same day and at the same hour. It was a regular St. Valentine's Day massacre and not one of those bosses survived.'

'So, Lomas' son is now the big cheese, is that it?'

Warner nodded agreement, 'Your friend Gabriel might be walking into a world of pain he starts making waves in Las Vegas.'

'And, if I may ask, what's your part in all this?'

'Treasury wants a handle on Ben. He's not been forgotten by the old men in the mob and now he's climbed the corporate ladder and recycled his pa's fortune, we reckon he's doubled it with what he inherited and the extra he made during the war with his Black Market concerns. The mob are hungry for what he's got and most of them had friends that Ben disposed of back in the day, they want revenge and a slice of his pie, it could be one hell of a war that's brewing.'

I shook my head, 'And Gabriel's walking into the middle of it.'

'Looks that way, that's why I thought a head's up might help you get your friend out of the line of fire.'

'I'm obliged, I'll sure do my best.'

'There's another reason I'm telling you all this.'

'Uhuh, and what's that?'

'I need to go in there looking harmless and I reckon holidaying with an old crippled war buddy might make a good cover.'

'You mean you want a ride?'

'That's about it.'

'Well, can we cut out the 'crippled' angle, do you think? And, man, you have to lose that coat. You look like you just left the Polar Circle dressed like that.'

Warner shrugged, 'I feel the cold something terrible, that's all.'

'What, cold! Here? Friend, it's hot and sultry in here and nigh on eighty degrees outside, how can you feel cold?'

'You ever been on the Soviet run?' he asked me solemnly.

I shook my head.

'Listen, thirty days adrift in the Barents Sea in mid-winter and you'll never feel warm again, believe me, I know. I was serving on the US merchant ship Daniel Morgan when she went down as part of a Russian convoy in '44. Krauts had us cold, and that ain't a pun, but we fought real hard I can tell you, brought down two Junkers bombers before we had to quit. But the old girl was hit sore and we had to abandon ship and take to the boats. Would you believe a U-Boat captain gave us directions to land before he sunk her with one in the side?'

I guess I took it as gospel then, that as a Merchant Navy seaman, Bob Warner had served his country just as well as any in the regular forces.

CHAPTER TWELVE

THE LETTER

The letter, if that's what it was, was stuck to the back of one of Gabriel's missives. I don't think he had meant it to be there but somehow it had been included. It was a torn piece taken from a tinned peach label and written in his undeniable small hand on the back of the label that had travelled far and been inadvertently attached to his main letter by the remnants of sticky peach juice he had in all probability been supping on at the time. Folded many times and maybe kept in his wallet for a long while as all the folds were well worn. The paper was old and the writing bolder than his more recent letters to me, as if a younger hand had inscribed it.

Since discovering the note, I had pondered over it many times, not at first at all sure of its significance. It was a meandering script; a poor attempt at love poetry of sorts and that in itself was remarkable. That such a hoary old devil like Gabriel Brannigan could even bring himself to create such a thing, for I was sure it was his, seemed nothing short of miraculous.

There was no name or addressee, only one small

indication as to whom it was intended but the content held obvious deep feeling and meaning to the writer. Where it had been written and when, I had no idea, it may have been on some windy plain by a lone campfire in the dark of night or on one of his many campaigns when he had tired of all the strife and bloodshed and needed to hear a softer voice.

'The prairie wind still calls your name,' he had written. *'A sad refrain that sounds the same. Long and lonesome and kept apart, it's call rests hollow in my heart.'*

Hell! This didn't sound like Gabriel at all, and it was nowhere else that I had found any sign of tenderness in his rough soul but for this person whoever she was, that he had doubtless held great affection.

'When we played our game of love, I should have known it weren't enough. My eyes were young and too blind to see, the very best was here for me. I brought you flowers inside my hat and laid them down where you were at. We danced one time at your birthday ball, just as our summer came into fall. And I rode off full foolishly instead of dreaming how it might be.

That one and only time we kissed, the one and only girl I miss.

My heart was cruel and didn't know,

That maybe I could hurt you so.

And all the lost years in between, since that day you were seventeen.

None hold back the love I send, my one and only sweet LMM.'

That was it, the only clue, the initials of the love

of his life. Who was the 'LMM', I wondered, the amour of his youth who had touched the old man so much he had carried the memory of it in his pocket all through his adventurous life.

The thing that stuck in my mind was that look that had passed between them on the day when Mad Dog Cheetham had threatened us both and when he had spoken her name that only time, 'Louella May', my own dear late mother. Could it be? That somewhere in their youth the two had maybe had a fling together. I couldn't bring myself to think it so. She, an upright churchgoing lady, kind of heart and a goodly soul. Could she have ever found any friendship in a liaison with such a rough and way-ward fellow? It seemed an unlikely impossibility.

But then I reasoned it would have been many years since. When, as he says, they were both young and she no more than a teenager, perhaps they both had been different people back then. Who's to say that such a dashing buck could not have appealed to a simple and innocent girl on the verge of womanhood?

I scanned all the letters reminding myself of the women he had known, of the ones he had married or struck up a relationship with but none of them had names that matched the initials. What cinched it was my mother's maiden name. Mummers, Louella May Mummers that had been her birth name.

All of it got me wondering if maybe the old man had been letting me know the truth of it in his roundabout way. Had he allowed that note to slip in under the pretext of error and his real intention been to tell me that if things had been different that I, Jonah Cord, might have been his own son.

It was a mind-blowing concept; I have to tell you. And it got me to wondering if this whole thing had not been deviously stage-managed by the two of them before I set off to join the army. My father had been lost to us and could Ma have seen it as the one way to prepare me for the difficulties she knew in her worldly way that I would have to face.

Gabriel was a seasoned fighter, a man practiced in the art of war. Who better as a guide for her eldest boy as he set out to fight? Why else would Ma stipulate that a wreath of flowers be set on the old man's grave when he passed? 'A loving friend', she had asked to be written on the attached memory.

Damn them both! Who'd have known, as I carried that home-made apple pie down to the old fellow's shack, that they were both playing me like the innocent I was back then. Taking my careful education in hand with silent forethought and consideration, surely the rightful actions more proper for true parents to have for any child, even if I was not a product of their union.

Gabriel had loved my Ma but missed the opportunity with his own bold recklessness but then never forgiven himself for the error of that youthful mistake. How sad, I thought. I had loved my own Pa for the little time I had known him; there was no denying that. But now, Gabriel had a strong call on my affections and in all of it I found an even deeper love for my caring Ma, surely a woman and mother beyond all others.

CHAPTER THIRTEEN

ON THE ROAD

Bob Warner and I were on the road early.

We split the wheel and as we drove I asked him about his time at sea whilst he spelled me after the first few hours of driving.

'How was it on those convoys? I heard they were pretty rough.'

'You could say that. The Brits had it the worst though, they was at it a whole lot longer. What with Uncle Joe Stalin and Roosevelt both pushing for more supplies to aid the Ruskies it was a hell of a time. Seas like you wouldn't believe and so cold sometimes the sea would freeze thick on the superstructure, so heavy it threatened to roll us over. We had to hack it off with axes. But that old PQ17 convoy was the king killer all right. They thought the Krauts had that big gunship the Tirpitz out after us and dispersed the entire convoy, man, we was all alone and they picked us off like fish in a barrel. Twenty-five out of thirty-six of our ships went down.'

'Crazy times, huh?'

'How about you? Where did you earn that walking stick?'

'Saipan first then Tinian in the Marianas and after that Okinawa. After Saipan we thought it would be a walk in the park at Tinian. No decent landing sites so the Japs couldn't nail us on the beaches. Most of the island was farmed, so not a lot of jungle just sugar cane. We had more men, more hardware than them, we owned the sky and the sea and the Japs were on the way out but they sure didn't give up easy.'

'That old Banzai spirit, I guess?'

'More like Kamikaze, they just never considered surrender although they was beat, would rather swallow a grenade than give it up.'

'Hard to beat.'

'When a body's willing to die fighting like that there's hardly nothing you can do but kill and keep on killing. Those suckers went down in their droves. Hell, I've seen Seabees having to put them underground with a dozer they was so many bodies lying around.'

'And what happened to you?'

'That was later on Okinawa. The worst artillery and mortar fire I ever seen. Shell fire knocked me out and took my leg away.'

'And now?'

'I can walk some and I ain't dead, I guess I'm grateful for that.'

'Seems kinda weird you taking off after this old fella after all that, wouldn't you rather take it easy now?'

I mused on that a moment, 'I guess it don't leave you, you know? Oh, I can't ever lay to rest all the bad stuff I've seen and the buddies I lost but there's something else that lives on. Like a music note struck, you know? It kind of quivers in your mind and lingers. I still got the mood in me, I got to move, to do something.'

'I hear you, buddy. I really do.'

Took us four hours to hit Austin and we cut off US90 and headed northwest along Route 66. We aimed to clip through parts of New Mexico and Arizona before making Nevada. I reckoned it would take us something like twenty to thirty hours all told.

I was getting to like Bob right well, he was a quiet, steady kind of guy and he knew enough not to chatter all the while but just drive sometimes. With his big hands on the wheel I noticed the scars on his knuckles and guessed he might have been a street fighter or bar brawler at some part of his life. You didn't get cuts like that with gloves on and in a regular boxing ring.

It was somewhere out in north Arizona, early in the day as the sun was coming up and painting the skyline pink, when Bob suddenly plunked one of his size thirteen's on the brake and pulled us up real sharp.

'*What?*' I shouted, startled out of the doze I was enjoying.

We were passing through some small roadside town. A nothing kind of place, the main street holding not much beyond a bar, a pharmacy, garage and diner, all of it dead quiet with nobody about except for a few parked cars.

Bob was staring out the screen and I followed his glance.

He was looking at a white painted chapel, one of those single-story cement block built places with nothing much to say for itself except for the cross on top. Some one had scrawled on the wall in foot high letters; '*Gabriel Brannigan is the devil, the Lord knows his name and he is doomed for all eternity.*'

'What the hell?' I gasped.

'Seems like your man has made his mark here,' snorted Bob.

I frowned in consternation, 'Now what can that be about do you think?'

'Beats me, but maybe we should find out.'

He nodded his head in the direction of the diner and I saw a young woman unlocking the street door and going on inside. The lights inside flickered on and it was apparent she was opening up the place.

'What say we get us a coffee?' suggested Bob.

'You think it's *my* Gabriel Brannigan?' I asked as we got out the car.

'Seems likely the way you describe him,' he chuckled. 'You know? I'm kinda looking forward to meeting this fella.'

They had one of those bell things over the door and it tinkled some as we entered. The girl was behind the counter, tying on an apron and looked up as we came in.

'Morning, gents,' she said, giving us the once over. 'We're just opening up. I'll have coffee ready real soon. You want breakfast?'

She was a pretty little thing even with no makeup on and still half asleep with that dreamy look as if she'd just climbed out of her bed. Thin with pale features and frizzled hair that might have been blond at one time, but darker roots were beginning to show through. Self-consciously she dabbed at that mop of hair as she fussed over the coffee maker.

'You boys are out early,' she said, not looking at us.

'Yes, ma'am,' Bob answered. 'We've been driving a while and could do with a bite to eat about now.'

'Sure thing,' she said. 'Just give me a minute, how'd you like your eggs?'

'Over easy,' said Bob as we both took a stool at the counter.

'This your place?' I asked by way of conversation.

'No, it's my pa's. I usually work up the road at the store but he's a mite under the weather at the moment so I'm filling in.'

'You're an early starter yourself.'

'Seems that way,' she answered vaguely. 'Where you fellows headed?'

'Vegas. We're taking a break and thought we'd go lose some money at the casino.'

She snuffled a laugh, her head bent over the makings, 'You'll certainly do that up there.'

'Say,' said Bob in a casual manner. 'We saw that sign written on the church back there, what's that all about?'

She half turned to look at us, leaving the eggs hissing on the plate. 'The 'Gabriel Brannigan' one, you mean?'

Bob nodded.

'Well, it's a story all right,' she half smiled, lifting the corner on one side of her mouth.

'What happened?' I asked, trying to make it sound as if I was unconcerned.

She poured our coffees and brought them over, setting down the mugs carefully on the counter before us. Close up I could see she was maybe late twenties but with a worn and washed-out look that made her pale face appear older than it was. It was that small town look that spoke of knowing only the same folks all her life and the prospect of living her whole life in this dull backwater with nothing but marriage to a local guy and a parcel of kids to look forward to.

'He was just an old gent that came through here a few weeks back,' she said.

Her eyes were a bright blue and they kind of faded a bit as she recalled.

'There was a spot of trouble with Reverend Gaines,' she admitted, chewing at her lower lip thoughtfully.

'What'd he do?' I asked.

But she turned away without answering and returned to the eggs.

'An old guy and a minister who thinks he's the devil incarnate,' pressed Bob, with a laugh. 'Now you got me wondering, missy. What's the story here?'

'Ach!' she said, fiddling with strips of bacon. 'You don't want to hear it.'

'No, go on,' urged Bob. 'We got nothing better to do and a good tale over breakfast will make our drive all the easier.' He had a pleasant way with him and I could see his jocular manner was winning her over.

'Tell the truth,' she sighed. 'I ain't a 'miss', I'm a married woman and that's where it started. Mrs. Jane Burdough is my proper name.'

There was something in her that wanted to confide, you could see it plain. Maybe she had few folks to talk it through with or maybe the fact that we were passing strangers she'd probably never see again made it all the easier.

'Sorry, Miz Jane,' apologized Bob. 'Just that you look too young and pretty to be a married lady.'

She arched an eyebrow at him but smiled all the same, 'Get along, you wouldn't be joshing a woman now, would you?'

'No, siree,' said Bob fervently. 'I wouldn't do that. So how did being married get you involved with this old boy and the minister?'

She shoveled the eggs and bacon onto plates and popped some bread from a toaster and brought them over.

'Well, you see,' she said leaning on the counter and speaking in a hushed voice even though we were all alone in the diner. 'Reverend Gaines is a kind of old time preacher, he holds forth in a strong way if you get my meaning. Well me and Carson, that's my other half, we were having a tiff, as it were. He had got himself drunk again and I got to smelling perfume on him. He don't really mean no harm by it but, you know, he likes a taste now and again and when he's under the influence, well, he tends to misbehave a mite.'

Bob shook his head, 'Now that ain't right,' he said, forking a strip of bacon.

'I know, I know,' she said, shaking her head in agreement. 'I keep saying it, but things around here... Well, you know how it is.'

Bob nodded understanding as he filled his cheek with the bacon, 'Small town, not much going on. Yeah, I've seen it.'

'There you go,' she said, taking a deep breath. 'We live with what we got.'

'Mighty fine eggs,' Bob praised.

'Thank you. I try, Lord, I do try,' she wasn't talking about the eggs though. 'Well this old boy came in off the road one day, must have been lunch time and the place was full so I came along to help pa with the serving. Carson was sitting in the back, looking down in the dumps and hung-over and I wasn't speaking to him, so the atmosphere was a touch sensitive, if you get my meaning?'

I could picture it all as she told it, the place packed with farm boys. The young ones joking around and the old timers huddled in their usual places, smoking and gossiping. Joints like this always had their ghetto areas and nobody sat in anybody else's place on a regular basis.

Her pa would have been sweating as he cooked up a storm at the grill and the sallow looking Carson Burdough would have been glowering in the corner as his missus walked straight past him and angrily tied on her apron without giving him the time of day.

Maybe the hunched figure of old Gabriel wouldn't

have called for any attention as he creaked his way in and took a place at the counter. He was just some old deadbeat hustling along the road and ducking in for a quick feed before he went on his way. There was enough of the cowboy about him not to cause concern amongst the locals and therefore he'd go virtually unnoticed.

'I have word,' boomed out Reverend Gaines, making a full-on Biblical entrance by slamming the door and looming in. 'That there is licentious and sinful activity taking place in the roadhouse down the way.'

That would have caused a stir and the place would have gone quiet.

'Yes, indeed,' the Reverend continued. 'I have report that men with families and goodly wives are taking themselves into that sinful place and forgetting their vows.' Here he would have cast a gloomy and accusing look in Carson's direction.

A big man in stature, the Reverend would have been standing apart from the others, alone in the crowd, a position he believed befitted his station. A bumptious and burly figure full of self-importance and raised up in his own consideration by those in the community who admired his particular style of religious fervor. For he would have swung out his words in tent-preacher fashion and projected fire and brimstone like it was borne in his fingertips.

'Get me a coffee, Jane,' snarled Carson, embarrassed by the attention and taking it out on his wife.

Jane sniffed and ignored him.

About then, one of the young bucks would have stirred the pot a little, 'What are you saying, Reverend?' he would have asked innocently.

'Sin, boy! That is what I speak of. There are those here that do fornicate with wanton creatures and abdicate their responsibility under the influence of excessive inebriation.'

'Who you talking about?' the boy would have pressed, giving a sidelong grin at his buddies. 'Wouldn't be old Carson over there, would it?'

'You sit down and mind your manners,' Jane would have snapped. Loyalty rising over her irritation and not wanting her husband to be put on the spot any more than he was already.

'And you!' snarled Reverend Gaines, swinging on her and pointing an accusing finger. 'Allowing your promised partner to indulge in such fruitless and vile pastimes. You, should be ashamed.'

'*Me!*' gasped Jane, blushing to the dark roots of her dyed hair. 'What the hell have I got to do with it?'

'What? You would curse before a man of God?' burst out the offended preacher, slandered by her cuss word.

Here he would have puffed up his chest and crossed over to stand at the counter and leer accusingly over at Jane.

'Your task is to provide physical satisfaction to your husband and not send him off to find it elsewhere in low dives where the divine act is darkened by the shallow exchange of cash money.'

Shocked, Jane would have been stunned to silence by the insulting reprimand.

Just then, Gabriel sitting at the counter would have felt the big man's pressure close to his elbow and the big man's belly nudging his fork hand away from his plate.

'Say, fella,' he would have said. 'You want to leave off a spell, I'm trying to eat here.'

'Be quiet,' said Gaines. 'I am about God's work.'

'Sounds more like you're interfering in what ain't your concern to me.'

Gaines would have stared disdainfully down his nose at Gabriel, 'And just *who* are you to question the Lord's messenger?'

'I'm Gabriel Brannigan and I tend to mind my own affairs until they dig their way into my lunch.'

'Well, sir. I don't know you nor do I care to, pray stay out of this.'

By now Jane's pa would have been taking a hand and he would have waved a skillet in the Reverend's direction, 'That's enough now. Let's have some peace and quiet in here, I'd be obliged if you'd take a seat, Reverend Gaines and save your preachifying for a Sunday in the proper place.'

Gaines would have raised his hands skywards and taken a pulpit stance, 'Oh, Lord, forgive these iniquities. I am your humble servant and am ill served in this place of sinners. This wayward husband and his sordid concubine have steeped themselves in the pleasures of the flesh; they have drunk at Satan's well and imbibed the unhealthy cup of his disease. Cast them from Your recognition let them wallow in the mire of hell's swamp and...'

'Say, Preacher,' interrupted Gabriel. 'You want

to draw breath a moment? Seems these young people don't want your opinion on their private matters, that right you youngsters?' Gabriel would have asked turning to the two recipients of the Preacher's disfavor.

'He should damned well stay out of it,' snapped Jane. 'T'ain't none of his concern and that's a fact.'

At that a fuming Gaines would have reached across the counter and taken Jane by the hair and pulled her half over the counter. 'Demon witch!' he would have bawled. 'I will not have you hold me in contempt.'

And that's when Gabriel would have taken a more active hand.

My guess is that he would have used the fork.

Straight down it would have gone, making a deep impression in the back of the Reverend's hand and digging in there some. At this Gaines would have howled loudly and stared in disbelief at the physical attack on his person.

'You...' He would have blubbered. 'You, sir, are doomed to find the law at your door for this.'

'Is that right?' asked Gabriel and I could almost see the evil little grin splitting his creased lips.

He was old and his fist was more bone that flesh now but that bunched item could still crack a nice smack when it wanted to. And that's what he did, why he punched old Reverend Gaines a mighty blow that split his lip and broke his nose and send the big man tumbling back into the lunch tables behind.

But Gabriel had learned a long time ago that one made sure a man was down for good before he left off and as Gaines came back upright, well then he met another healthy whack that caromed off his jaw and left Gabriel shaking his sore fingers and sucking his knuckles.

'Goddamn!' cursed Gabriel. 'Been a long time since I handed out one of those. Guess I'm out of practice.'

Then they would have tumbled onto him, those other fellows in the diner. Once the Reverend was down, the locals would have felt a righteous need to play at protector and grab hold of the ancient stranger before he did more damage.

'Leave him go,' ordered Jane, brandishing a ladle. 'He's right, it weren't none of the Reverend's concern.'

'You heard,' her husband agreed, taking his wife's side and pulling Gabriel free. 'Let the man alone.'

'I'll see you in a prison cell for this,' mumbled Gaines, holding his bloody nose with a fork-pricked hand and trying to speak around a bleeding lip.

'Take a lesson,' advised Gabriel, shaking a bruised fist in the preacher's face. 'Them that judges others allus gets judged themselves by a mightier hand than they own.'

Well, that's how I saw it all happening and it was pretty close to what Jane Burdough was telling us. It seems that when Gabriel hit the road again he went with Carson and Jane's blessing and assurance that there would be no trouble with the law. As it turned out, Carson was kin to the local sheriff and would counter anything the Reverend came up with, leaving him with only the last resort of venting his spite in the lurid graffiti on his chapel wall.

So, continuing on like we never knew the man, we made our thanks to Jane, paid the bill and left the diner to carry on our way.

'Quite a fella,' Bob observed as he got behind the wheel again.

'They broke the mold,' said I.

CHAPTER FOURTEEN

VEGAS

The Spaniards called it Las Vegas, meaning The Meadows.

Well, it may have been lush grass and wetlands back in the 1820's but now it was all a part of the Greater Mojave Desert that spread out like a super heated stain across the land and sucked the very moisture from the air. Hot, dry and dusty with a dose of sunshine and infernal heat for practically every day of the year. With lax gambling and divorce laws it soon became a haven for the inveterate gambler and gangster. The air force base and testing ground nearby had provided a source of fun hungry young service personnel with ready spending power and that all helped the money flow. It was a honey pot for the predators where substantial fortunes could be made and not necessarily just by gambling.

We came off the highway and drove onto The Strip through the daytime glitter of the town, it was one of the first places to discover neon lighting back in the day so the town was awash with lurid signage lighting up the desert for miles around at night.

Right now though it was just brash images and reflected silver that sparkled in the bright sunlight.

One of the first Anglos to discover the place was a fellow called Fremont and we made it down the street named after him, heading for the El Cortez Hotel and Casino. They said that the town held more than thirty-five thousand residents and it seemed that most of them were out on the street right then. It was a bustling place, busy with cars and men in uniform, there were some real pretty girls walking about too and that was enough to get us rubber-necking like a pair of yokels.

We signed in and got us a room and were about to follow the bellhop up to our suite when Bob inadvertently jostled a handsome looking fellow in a fancy suit. The guy looked like he could have been a Hollywood movie star he was that pretty.

'Mind where you're going, you big lunk,' said the fellow, looking down his nose and brushing his sleeve as if to ward off infection. His eyes were poker black and belied the neat outer appearance with something that told you he was a mean one underneath.

'Excuse me?' said Bob, nice as can be.

'Just watch the suit, buster. These threads cost money.'

'And swell they are too,' agreed Bob, cool as a cucumber. 'You look real sweet in them.'

'You taking the rise out of me?' snarled the guy.

He was backed by a couple of heavy looking characters who did that thing, you know the one, they let their hands slide inside their jacket fronts like boys that really ain't reaching for their wallets.

Bob was not fazed though, 'Take the rise? How could I do that?' he said, towering over the no more than average height guy. 'You being such a big fellow, and all.'

The guy nodded and studied Bob, like he was making a mark on him in his little black book, 'I'll remember you,' he promised quietly with a cool air of menace.

'Be sure you do, then you won't bump me again, will you?'

One of the punks made a move but the guy called him off with a shake of the head. He looked around once quickly at the crowded foyer to see if anyone was watching and then he tipped his hat at Bob.

'Be seeing you,' he promised and moved off flanked by his two bullyboys.

With a snort of disgust, Bob jerked his chin at the bellhop, 'Who was that ass?' he asked.

'That's Mister Siegel, sir; he owns a slice of the hotel. You must know him, they call him 'Bugsy' Siegel on the street but never to his face.'

'Can't say I've heard of the fool,' observed Bob with a show of disinterest.

'Oh, Mister Siegel's a big wheel around here. Mighty important. Have to say I don't think you made yourself a friend there.'

'That supposed to bring on my palpitations?'

'He's a gentleman fronting for very big business interests back east,' whispered the bellboy, with a silent look of awe.

Bob drew a long breath, 'Like I care. I seen too many of them, son, and none amount to much when it comes down to it. Rip that suit off and you got a skinny guy with a dick the size of a wiener, it's all show, believe me.'

The bellhop shrugged and indicated the lift doors, 'Yes sir, whatever you say, this way if you please.'

I played my own part when we reached our room. I took the bellboy aside as if to tip him whilst Bob went on ahead into the room.

I held up a bunch of dollar bills, 'You know a guy called Gabriel Brannigan?'

The kid looked at me and then at the money, 'Maybe. Old fellow, I mean real old?'

I peeled off five, 'That's him, where do I find him?'

The boy shrugged, 'He moves about a bit, you could try The Plainsman, he hangs out there I believe.'

'The Plainsman, that a hotel?'

'Sure, hotel and casino like everything else around here.'

'Okay, thanks,' and I gave him another five.

They had it tricked out like an old time Western saloon.

The wooden Indian outside let it all down a bit, it was crudely painted in glowing colors and held about as much resemblance to a proud warrior chief as a lead toy. Inside they had stuck to historical relevance with a long bar, and I mean long, and everywhere had a sort of brown look to the décor as if was all part of an old sepia tinted print. They had Roulette and dice tables going along the opposite side of the big room with groups of customers dressed in

Stetsons and plain shirts and vests. The only thing missing was the gun belts and spurs, these fellows looked like cowboys all right but more like your regular ranch hands up here on an outing.

There were low hanging electric chandelier lights giving out a feeble glow that flickered now and then and behind the bar a darkly carved mahogany monster dresser with a huge mirror that reflected the ornate tin-finish till sitting in pride of place. They even had a brass foot rail and spittoons.

The crowd of drinkers inside was a dowdy looking set of guys that lined the bar and they all appeared slightly uncomfortable as if the size of the place diminished them and they'd rather be back home in their local ma and pa drinking hole.

I spotted him right off.

He was down the far end of the bar counter, leaning up with one boot on the rail and looking like he had been born there. He wore a wide brimmed black hat, a suit jacket and there was dust marking the knees of his trousers.

'That him?' asked Bob.

Without a word I moved down the bar towards him and he reacted like the very first time I had ever met him. Exactly the same, with that cool appraisal and no outward show of surprise or greeting.

'Gabriel Brannigan,' I said, standing off and giving him the glad eye.

'I see you're back from the wars, bucko,' he answered, with a nod at my walking cane. 'Buy some lead over there, did you?'

'How you been, old timer?'

'Fair to middling,' he said, allowing a faint smile to tilt his lips.

He had laid off the Indian style pigtails he used to wear and his hair was cut short, which made his face appear more gaunt than I remembered and caused his ears to stick out some under his hat brim. Other than that, he still had the same seamed and bronzed face I knew from earlier times even if he was a mite thinner.

'This here's a friend, Bob Warner,' I introduced.

'Howdy,' said Gabriel, sticking out his hand and giving Bob a shrewd eye full. 'You boys want a beer? I'm just about to get a refill.'

He tipped his head at the Negro tender serving behind the bar and held up three fingers.

'So, what brings you to Sin City?' he asked.

'You do,' I answered.

'*Me?* Hell, boy, what you want with me?'

'First off I got to thank you for all the communication you sent me, they was all mighty interesting.'

'Aw!' he waved it off. 'Weren't nothing but an old man's ramblings, that's all. Surprised you even read them.'

'Thing is I know why you're here.'

'Uhuh,' he grunted without elaboration.

'Lomas Chain.'

Gabriel rotated his head to fix me with a stern eye, 'Well, you know by now that's an old affair I still has to settle.'

'Thing is Mister Brannigan,' interrupted Bob. 'We know that Lomas Chain's no longer with us.'

Gabriel grinned, 'You think not?'

'I do, he's dead and buried.'

Gabriel shook his head slowly from side to side.

'It's a fact, sir. I've seen the certificate.'

'Piece of paper don't make a man dead, son. What are you? Some kind of lawman?'

'Treasury agent,' Bob admitted.

'Thought it was something like that.'

The beers had arrived and Gabriel lifted his, 'Here's to you,' he said.

'Health,' I said, toasting him.

I lowered my gaze as he set his glass down and wiped away foam with a finger.

'You heard about Ma?' I asked.

He pulled a face then as if a sudden pain had struck him in the side, 'I did, Jonah. I did and I'm real sorry about that.'

'She thought highly of you, you know?'

He dropped his eyes and said nothing for a moment, 'Saddest day of my miserable long life when I heard of her passing. She was the finest lady I ever knew.'

'I know that,' I said with feeling and he raised his eyes just enough to study me from under his hat brim.

'Then you know how it was? No disrespect intended, Jonah.'

'None taken. Ma wouldn't have allowed it.'

He nodded slowly in agreement.

'So, Mister Treasury Agent what is you want here?' he asked.

'We're looking into Lomas' son, Benjamin Lamtoc. It looks like he has a presence here.'

'You got that right,' agreed Gabriel. 'Son of a gun near runs the place.'

'But his daddy's dead,' I said, pushing my beer glass aside. 'Why're you hanging around here, Gabriel?'

'I been watching things Indian style,' he said, peering off distantly down the bar. 'Keeping my ear to the ground.'

'So, why?' I persisted. 'There's no good reason, you can't raise him from the dead.'

Gabriel smiled, 'Maybe not but I did hear some stuff about your own pa though.'

That one took me by surprise, 'My pa?'

'Yeah, you know he was lost to you when they was putting up the dam near here.'

'That's right, I was a kid when my pa was killed in an accident out here on the Boulder Dam, or Hoover Dam as they're calling it now,' I explained all this for Bob's benefit.

'So they say,' Gabriel continued. 'Although maybe it wasn't no accident.'

That gave me a frown, 'What have you heard?' I asked.

'Well, you know all the boys that worked on that dam back then used to travel the thirty miles down here for their rest and relaxation?'

I nodded agreement.

'Well, I met one old boy who was busy on the dam in those days and he says it weren't no accident.'

'How so?'

'This fella says your pa was one of the leading lights in trying to organize the workers. Well, it appears he upset a few of the big dogs amongst the six construction companies. Remember, those were hard times back then in the Thirties, most folks that made it here were only too glad of the work. So anybody stirring it up amongst the workers wasn't too welcome. Neither by the hired or the bosses.'

'You saying he was a union man one of those IWW guys?'

'I am. Appears there is some question about his accident and that maybe he was sanctioned off by the powers that be. My informant reckons that a contract was put out on him.'

'Who did that?' I snarled. 'Tell me who.'

'Yeah,' sparked Gabriel sharply, his eyes gleaming eagerly as he stabbed his finger into my chest with some satisfaction. 'Now you know what its like, don't you? You lose your pa to nefarious villains and you can see where I've been coming from all these years.'

'But I told you,' interrupted Bob again. 'Lomas Chain is dead, all that's left is his son.'

'He ain't dead,' spat Gabriel. He's alive and kicking, I know it.'

I was getting confused just about then, what with Gabriel's hints about my father's death and his own crazy insistence over Lomas, whilst Bob wanted desperately to get back to Benjamin Chain.

Gabriel sniffed and broke the mood, 'Let's go eat,' he said.

We settled on a steak joint called 'Mo Green's Hot Dog and Dinner Room' just up the way and one that Gabriel recommended as serving the only real steak he'd had since getting here. They were big all right those steaks, like about half a cow. So big the damned things near filled the plate and left little room for the potatoes and gravy.

'Good eats,' agreed Bob as he tucked in. There was no doubt Bob had a big appetite, well, he was a big fellow and he certainly was putting away that giant steak in record time.

'That ain't the only reason I come in here,' said Gabriel, waving his fork.

I noted that he wasn't really eating, more like picking at his food and I put it down to his advanced years and the tendency for the elderly not to need so much time at the trough. But I was wrong, he was using that fork to indicate a party across the far side of the dining hall.

Bob looked up from his fast emptying plate and followed Gabriel's direction across the crowded dining room.

'I see him,' he growled.

'You got it now?' asked Gabriel.

The party in question was behind me so I couldn't see them right off but I could make them out reflected in the long mirror on the wall across from me.

A large man was the center of attention at a table of equally big guys who sat together in a sectioned off banquette and were deep in conversation. He was neatly dressed but not extravagantly, in a simple gray three piece that brought out the tanned darkness of his skin. A square, no-neck block of a muscular body with raven black hair cut real short and sitting like a cap on his head with a severe straight fringe over seriously dark and slanted eyes. The Indian face was solid, as if carved from wood and it held little expression as he listened to his companion's intense conversation. Although he sat with the rest of them, he was somehow set apart from the rest and gave off an almost lordly impression of regal distance.

'Who's that?' I asked.

'*That* is Benjamin Lamtoc Chain,' filled in Bob.

'I've been tailing him for days,' said Gabriel. 'Watching his every damned move.'

'And what have you found out?' I asked.

'He loved his Daddy it appears.'

'How's that?'

'Well he's a regular up at Woodlawn. That's the cemetery here and where Lomas is supposed to be planted under this giant monolith of a tomb he had built. Dumb sucker never had no style, you should see the place.'

I nodded, 'So I heard from Bob, sounds kind of outrageous.'

'Yeah, well once a week, Ben there goes visit the place with a bouquet of flowers that he sticks on the grave. He clears out the old blossoms all respect-ful-like and replaces them with fresh cut, regular as clockwork. I ain't figured it yet but there some devious reason behind that, I can smell it.'

Just then another man approached the group and Bob started in his seat, 'See that?' he said. 'That's the same Siegel fellow that fronted me in the hotel.'

Sure enough, Siegel was smiling and patting backs and shaking hands all around.

Gabriel grinned, 'You already met Bugsy Siegel? You know who he is?'

'Some kind of businessman,' pouted Bob.

'No sir, that's the number one Black Hand outlaw around here. He represents the Mob back east and got hisself a franchise to run some gaming palace they're planning, a joint called The Flamingo.'

'Looks like he's real good buddies with brother Chain there,' I added.

Gabriel nodded and gritted his teeth, 'They're sure up to something.'

'And it looks like a something I should know about,' observed Bob.

'Maybe,' agreed Gabriel.

But I have to admit I was more interested in other things and whilst Gabriel was focused on the unlikely notion that Lomas still existed and Bob was into the prospect of his son and heir being at the heart of criminal activities, I was keen to hear more of what Gabriel had discovered about my father's death.

'Gabriel?' I said, bringing his attention away from the other side of the room. 'Any chance we can meet up with this old dam worker you mentioned?'

Gabriel pouted his lower lip, 'I reckon, he'll be back there at The Plainsman by now. We'll get along once we've finished up in here.'

Siegel was turning to leave when he spotted Bob sitting in his overcoat and rising head and shoulders above the rest of the clientele. He stopped a moment and gave Bob a slight smile before raising finger and thumb in pistol fashion and pointing it in our direction. Then, with a charming beam of a smile that had about as much amusement written in it as a rattlesnake's bite, he was out the door.

That brought Benjamin's attention around to us and his glittering eyes fixed on our table as he assessed the three of us. It seemed he narrowed out the aged figure of Gabriel and focused on him long enough for the rest of his pals to all give us a long hard look as well.

'Shoot!' said Gabriel. 'You boys draw fire like a turkey in the canebrakes. Let's get out of here.'

We hustled on down to The Plainsman for an after dinner shot and a chance to run into the old timer that Gabriel had befriended.

It turned out the old boy was called Cephus Long and was a quiet little gent that stood just a little over five feet tall. He was small and wiry and looked like he had seen enough of life and worked hard at it for a long time. He was one of those old timers who took the 'Hillbilly Train' and left Virginia to find work in the coalmines when it was plentiful. After that payload died out he was left high and dry without a penny to his name or a home to return to, so when word came out they were hiring at the dam he came along with all the other hopefuls eager to earn a living.

'They was an awful lot of us,' he confided, his worn hands cradling the beer Gabriel had bought him. 'They came from all over, maybe ten or twenty thousand with their families. Set up these squatter camps out near the workings as the companies only raised up living quarters in Boulder City for them that was hired and that was no more than three thousand of us. McKeeverville and Ragtown they called them and they was mighty poor places to be in, people making homes out of canvas and sticks. It was real hot that first year of '31 and damned unbearable out there,' he recalled. 'Sixteen folks died of the heat it was that bad.'

'But you knew my pa?' I pressed him. 'James Cord.'

'Sure, I knew Jimmy. Right fine fellow he was too, always keen to help folks.'

'So, how'd he die? We heard it was an accident, they told my Ma he died of pneumonia from carbon monoxide poisoning working in the diversion tunnels but Gabriel says it was something else.'

Cephus sucked his teeth and looked around the bar as if worried that someone might overhear.

'He was an activist,' he said. 'You know, back then the Six Companies ran everything, you wanted work then you did as they told you. They didn't give two hoots, there was more than enough hungry men out there on the breadline so they could hire and fire how they wanted. But Jimmy saw how damned cruel it was and he took up with them IWW union boys, you know, the ones they called the 'Wobblies'. They wanted to get the workers together and strike for a decent wage and such.'

'It didn't work out so well,' Gabriel interjected. 'The companies had the sheriff's office on their payroll and they soon saw the strike was put down.'

'Even so, Jimmy kept encouraging the men to hold off their labor and as you can imagine that didn't go down too well with the bosses.' He paused there, staring into his half empty glass for a while.

'What?' I pressed. 'What happened?'

'I seen him that last night,' Cephus confessed. 'Lord, we shouldn't have left him alone. He was stood over a cook fire and just left off a meeting with us all. I looked back and saw him; he was standing kind of tall and watching us all leave. There was a confidence about your pa, Jonah. He was a bold man, a straight fellow, if you get my drift?'

I had barely known the man, me being so young and him being away so often finding work and I tried to imagine him from Cephus's words. I knew my Ma loved him dear and always said he was a person of honor who wouldn't suffer fools gladly nor let the weak suffer, so that fitted in with what Cephus was telling me.

'He never died of no pneumonia,' Cephus went on. 'He died falling off one of them intake towers. Least that was how it looked but they was seen up there by some of our boys. You want the truth, it was a gang of them hooligans that threw him down.'

'Who?' I asked. 'Who did that?'

'There was only one body that did that kind of work for the Companies back then.'

'You want to guess?' cut in Gabriel.

'You're not going to tell me it was Lomas Chain?' I said.

'He was the one to expedite,' said Cephus. 'Everybody knew it. Chain had a whole gang of enforcers who handled troublemakers for the Companies by any means. They beat them bad or just plain killed them and the law and the Company's big shots covered it up.'

'Goddamn!' I spat, feeling a wave of hot anger run through me.

I hadn't felt that fire since the hell of Okinawa and it rippled through me like a bad memory, lighting up all the old feelings of hate again. Now I too had good reason to see that Chain and all his leftovers were brought down.

I looked up to see Gabriel watching me with a kind of half smile playing on his craggy lips. He knew what I was thinking, he knew that I got it, that we were one in our intentions.

'You ready now, son?' he asked. There may have been something paternal in the way he said it or maybe it was just that shared desire for payback; I ain't sure which it was. But it didn't matter much either way to me just then; I was too full of bitterness and loss at that particular moment. I thought of my Ma and all her years of struggle after Pa died, of all the lousy jobs she'd held to bring my brother and me up without a decent paycheck coming in. And I thought of the war too, of walking amongst the dead and dying, down amongst the rotten mud, blood and maggots whilst these bastards back home had been riding the gravy train.

I nodded slowly, 'You bet, let's get 'em.'

That was when something happened, I'll never forget.

The old fella Cephus suddenly gasped, 'Oh damn it! I'm really screwed now.'

He was looking over my shoulder at someone at the bar and I turned to see a guy the size of a Sherman tank watching us from along the counter.

This fellow had a bland expression on a decorated face that had certainly been in the wars sometime, he had a long scar on his chin and fistfight lumps that gave him a somewhat bloated appearance.

'What's that?' I asked. 'You know him?'

'Sure,' breathed Cephus nervously. 'He's one of Ben Chain's hit men, Todd Rooster, one mean sonofabitch and now he's seen me with you fellows I'm a goner.'

Gabriel only leaned across to Bob and asked quietly, 'You want to?'

Bob didn't answer he just got to his feet and went on over to the bar. Why Gabriel said that to him, I'm not sure. Maybe he just wanted to see what Bob was made of.

Anyway, it went down like this.

Bob fronted the fellow and some words were exchanged that I could not hear but next thing I know is that this Rooster is taking a swing at Bob. Bob didn't do much, he just kind of tilted his head to one side as the fist sailed by and missed him but maybe just brushed his shoulder. I was watching Bob's back under his overcoat and he kind of bunched up his muscles and brought one up, it was a jab but it came all the way from his feet that were both firmly planted. Man! I've seen plenty of bar fights in my time. I'm a Marine and Marine's will fight anything, friend or foe, They've done battle with Germans and Japs, I've seen them brawl with most every nation under the sun and when that's done they'll even fight with themselves. But right then I was given an education on how you really do it.

Bob socked that boy so hard he sent the guy sailing back against the bar. But Rooster was a big old buck and he promptly shook it off and went for that thing on the inside of his jacket. Bob delivered him a knee in the nuts, he must have missed some and caught him in the thigh but it still crooked Rooster over and as he bent down Bob rolled one up from mid-section that smacked around that barroom like the sound of a bullwhip cracking.

Rooster sailed back upright and Bob reached into his jacket and pulled out the .38 pistol Rooster had nestling there in a shoulder holster. With a look of distain, Bob tossed the gun onto the bar and swung another one that shook Rooster like he was made of jelly and that one dropped him. Down he went, stumbling on the slippery brass foot rail and ending up on his behind looking up at Bob with a faint gape of disbelief.

Bob leaned down to grab him by the lapels but the gangster had caught hold of one of those heavy spittoons and he swept it up, tobacco spit and cigar butts flying out in an ugly brown stream as he whammed it against the side of Bob's head.

That one shook Bob and he blinked some but Rooster wasn't done, he was up in a crouch right quick for such a big guy and he slammed the heavy base of that now dented spittoon into Bob's face. Bob's head went back and Rooster was on him, one, two, he hooked in a couple of heavy punches and a big one that sent Bob staggering away across the room. Bob tumbled over his own feet and fell onto a Roulette table that was behind him. The table gave way under the impact with a loud crack and sent betting money, green felt and local gamblers flying in all directions. The table folded up under Bob's weight in a v-section and he reached out to regain his feet to find that the Roulette wheel had shot out of its mounting and was under his hand. Without hesitation he swung that hefty thing is a looping discus throw that sent it flying across the room.

It reminded me of the same ploy employed by Gabriel when he had confronted Mad Dog Cheetham in my Ma's place and I glanced across at him. He grinned back at me and nodded knowing full well what I was recalling.

Well, that chunk of hardware caught Rooster hard in the gut and he not only gasped but also broke wind amazingly loudly at the same time, which raised a few eyebrows in that bar, I can tell you. The poor guy never had a chance after that, Bob shot across the room with that damned overcoat of his flying out behind him like a cloak as he set to. Now it was that I saw how Bob had earned those scars on his knuckles. He was in his element as he started in with blows you only dream about, hard knocks that sunk home with a vengeance and a satisfying sock of sound. One after the other they drove Rooster back against the bar so hard that I thought he might have broke his spine. But no, he still stood and was spitting blood in a red cloud as Bob laid into him remorselessly.

Bob was on fire and his face grim as a reaper as he worked out against Rooster's suffering body, every blow sending shivering quivers through the gangster's whole frame. Finally, Rooster reached out dumbly for the bar edge to support himself but his dazed hand slid along and he slipped over to tumble down. He fell, his head resting on the foot rail and his feet splayed out on either side of Bob, who raised one of those big Florsheim shoes of his and lowered it onto Rooster's throat. It was plain to see Bob had lost it temporarily and gone into a cold killing mood and you could reckon his next move was to heave down and snap Rooster's neck against the bar.

Gabriel was up on his feet real quick.

'Enough!' he barked. 'That's enough, Bob. He's done.'

Bob turned to look at Gabriel with glazed eyes that seemed far away and in another place.

'Hear me?' snapped Gabriel. 'It's over.'

Bob shook himself and recovered with a shuddering shake of his big shoulders. But something in him still sought blood and despite Gabriel's controlling influence he shifted his foot to rest it on Rooster's extended right hand that lay spread out alongside. There was a crackling crunch as Bob lowered his whole weight onto the fingers and Rooster howled in pain, as every bone in his gun hand was broken. With that, Bob reached down and jerked Rooster to his feet by his jacket lapels as easily as if he was hoisting a dinner plate, which was no mean feat as Rooster must have weighed nigh on three hundred pounds.

Bob pulled him close and looked hard into Rooster's one good eye, the other one was so swollen and puffed up he could hardly see out of it, and said in a low voice full of intensity, 'You tell your boss I'm coming for him. You got that? I'm coming for him.'

CHAPTER FIFTEEN

GRAVEYARD SHIFT

Next day, Gabriel and I set out to tail Ben Chain on his weekly visit to his father's grave. Bob had to take an early red-eye flight out to Washington to make report to his chief who had been hassling him for an update. He planned to be back by nightfall or tomorrow at the latest.

We set out and began following behind Chain's fancy Lincoln at a safe distance in an ignominious beat up blue Chevy hire car that Gabriel had been driving.

Woodlawn is big and flat, the various gravestones standing like dimples on the forty-acre plot. It was set aside about the time of the First Great War but now some of the markers still held memorial flags marking out those brought back from overseas from the last one. The flags were the only bright colors in the sun baked place but they hung in desultory fashion in the breathless air and looked a little out of place in the sad location.

The cemetery was edged by trees and it was amongst them, far back at the end of a purpose-built driveway that the Gothic monstrosity that Lomas Chain had ordered built as his final resting place stood. Chain's limousine drove right down that roadway and stopped before this bizarre temple to his outlaw father. It was big all right and looked to be about a hundred and seventy feet tall with two layers of steps in white marble that rose up to a sort of canopied bower at the top. Some kind of roll top bed affair carved in pink marble rested under a stone canopy with four pillars that supported a decorated roof rising up in a point to a gleaming metal spire above.

On a flat area above the first flight of steps was a church-type kneeling place before a large stone trumpet shaped vase. The vase, we could see from where we stood hidden in the shadows of a low shade tree, was full of dried out flower stems. Nothing could last long in the blasting heat out here and the exposed flowers were no more than husks and no comparison to the great mass of verdant blooms that Ben Chain carried in his arms as he mounted the steps. Reverently, Ben Chain knelt down and plucked out the dead flowers, he tidied the area and placed the lush bouquet in the vase before clasping his hands before him and bowing his head in prayer.

It must have been a quarter of an hour before he finished and climbed to his feet again, after a long look up at the spire above, he turned and made his way back down to wait in the cool of his Lincoln whilst one of his bodyguards went up to collect the dead flowers and clear them away.

'He do that every time?' I asked Gabriel as the

limo pulled away.

'Every time,' Gabriel answered watching the Lincoln leave the cemetery. 'Same ritual always.'

'Must have loved his pa all right, to spend so much time on his knees like that.'

'Seems that way but I can't figure it, who on God's green earth could ever love an asshole like Lomas Chain?'

'You notice anything in particular?' I asked.

'Like what? I must have seen this same thing happen exactly like this for six times at least. It's always at the same time and follows the same routine; he does this little procedure every week and then goes off to a clubhouse restaurant for lunch. Never varies.'

I looked out across the simmering heat rising in soft waves from the ground, 'No water,' I observed.

Gabriel looked at me questioningly.

'He never put no water for the flowers in that vase.'

Gabriel shrugged, 'So? Maybe he don't give a damn about the flowers. He can afford to buy a whole garden full if he so fancied, why should he worry about that bunch?'

'It don't figure,' I mused. 'He must know they'll be dead by nightfall, so why bother?'

Gabriel rubbed his unshaven jaw thoughtfully, his fingers rasping on the white bristle, 'You think there's some kind of message being left here?' he asked.

'I think we should go look.'

We crossed the deserted graveyard stepping between the headstones and made our way up the wide span of white steps. Despite the heat the marble was cool and the carved kneeler and vase were shining and crisp in the sunlight. I looked down at the magnificent display of flowers already wilting in the intense heat. Now why would he do that, I wondered? I guessed there was only one way to find out so I knelt down and lifted the bunch out of the vase. I saw in the bottom a grill that covered a dark hole.

'You see this?' I asked.

'I do,' Gabriel agreed. 'Some kind of drainage, you think?'

'For what, there ain't no water and why would you have drainage like that in the bottom of a flower vase anyway?'

'Well what then?'

I leaned over as I had seen Ben Chain do as if in prayer and said 'Hello!' The word echoed back to me hollowly from somewhere deep inside, the sound amplified by the trumpet shape of the vase.

'There's a tunnel down there,' I said.

Gabriel looked bemused, 'Why would they have that here?'

'Don't you get it?' I asked. 'He's talking to someone; he comes here to hold a conversation with somebody in there. Dear God! There's more than a dead body in this thing.'

'*Lomas Chain!*' growled Gabriel. 'The bastard still lives, I knew it. I could feel it in my bones.'

'Ben must come here every week to make report and receive instructions, that's what this whole thing is about.'

'But why the hell would Lomas bury himself alive like this?'

'That I don't know but I'll bet he's in there. This place is supposed to be built like a regular hotel underground and for some reason Lomas must have decided to hide out but still run his empire through his son from down there.'

Gabriel roughly brushed me aside and leaned over the trumpet mouth of the vase, 'I know you're in there, you sonofabitch!' he bellowed angrily, the words vibrating down the hole in receding echoes. 'I'll get you yet, I swear it, if my name ain't Gabriel Brannigan.'

'Hold up,' I said pulling him away. 'Don't you give him any ideas he don't have already.'

'Son of a gun!' spat Gabriel in disgust. 'That swine is still living, feeding off his rotten crimes from a hole in the ground. Goddamn, I'll roast his hide before I'm done.'

I looked up at the spire and bower above, 'There must be a way in somehow,' I said. 'He would have to receive supplies in there.'

Gabriel was already making his way up the second flight of steps, 'If its there I'll find it,' he panted.

'And then what?' I asked, hopping along with my cane and stiff leg behind him.

'I'll blast his ass to hell.'

'You don't know what's down there, even if we do find a way in.'

'There must be plans somewhere,' grunted Gabriel. 'I'll find them and figure it out.'

'Something this heavy must have support arches underground,' I observed. 'The foundations could run across a couple of acres down there.'

He was wheezing bad once we reached the summit and I was worried his old bones and heart would give out on him. But Gabriel had the bit between his teeth and he eagerly scoured the weird canopy and its bed-like sculpture inside. We both spent a half hour searching but could not find even the slightest crack to indicate any opening.

Cursing vociferously, Gabriel finally admitted defeat and we headed back to the hotel.

He was in a bad mood and fuming silently as we crossed the hotel foyer and took the lift back up to our rooms. I could see his mind was racing and knew he was planning something devastating. For a guy of his age you had to be impressed by his sharpness and acuteness of brainpower. Nothing except his physical attributes seemed to be diminished by the years. And although he appeared decrepit in many respects the bold heart that beat in his breast was still as strong and resourceful as the young buck who had first ridden the prairies when the country was young.

He slammed open the door to my room and strode inside.

'We need to see the city records,' he snarled. 'Find out how that sucker built that place; I'll get to him if it's the last...'

He stopped in mid sentence and I followed his horrified stare as we made out the figure laid out in an easy chair.

The wasn't much left recognizable of the bloody figure slumped there. They had worked hard on the body, beating the face to a pulped mass of meat and finally finishing the job with a bullet through one eye.

'Goddamn!' breathed Gabriel as he recognized the small figure. 'Cephus Long, he said they would get to him.'

'It don't take much to guess this is a warning,' I said grimly.

'More than that,' added Gabriel. 'I'll have it as a declaration of war.'

'We're going to need us some hardware if that's the case.'

'Damned right,' Gabriel nodded. He drew a deep breath, 'Feels like old times,' he said almost wistfully.

'What about the law?'

'These guys own the law, there's no help there, we has to go this one alone.'

'Can we hustle up weapons, you think?'

'Guns ain't a problem but I got to do one thing before that.'

'What? What you aiming to do?'

'Got to attend me a funeral,' he said.

'We're getting Cephus buried you mean?'

'Hardly,' he answered with an enigmatic air.

CHAPTER SIXTEEN

TOP-UP

Gabriel held me off until nightfall with his plan.

He went out on his own in the afternoon, just to arrange some things, he told me, and when I pushed for an answer he warned me to back off and he'd let me know when it was time.

The time arrived at ten thirty that night.

Bob had returned, a little beat up after his speedy journey to Washington and back and he did not receive the news of Cephus's death too kindly. He did not say much about his trip to Treasury headquarters, but I got the impression they had urged for some kind of early return and that Bob was under a deal of pressure.

Gabriel returned and called me over with a crooked finger but would say no more. We left Bob who told us he had decided on an early night he was that tired, and it was Gabriel who got behind the wheel of the Chevy as we headed out into the night. It appeared to me that Bob had caught some intimation that Gabriel was up to no good and decided to look the other way in case it would jeopardize his position as a Government agent. On this one it seemed to me he had decided to take a back seat and leave us to it.

'Where we going?' I asked, already knowing it was a futile question.

'You'll see.'

And that was about what I had expected him to say.

He drove around a while until we pulled into a Texaco filling station.

'You need gas?' I asked.

'Now listen close,' he said, turning to face me. 'Get this thing filled up. Then head out to the cemetery, I'll meet you there. Drive down that roadway to Chain's tomb and park off the road somewhere out of the way and wait for me.'

'What you aiming to do?'

He just grinned and gave me an impish wink, 'You'll see.'

Before I could say more, he was gone, slipping out the car door and disappearing into the night. The station attendant was at my window and I was distracted long enough to miss out on which direction he took once he was free of the filling station lights.

Wondering what the hell was going on I did as he told me and got the car filled and then drove out to Woodlawn.

It was kind of spooky in there, the whole place being lit only by moonlight that thankfully, was on the rise otherwise I wouldn't have seen a damn thing. Everything shone with a misty white glow and the silent gravestones were no more than black shadows spreading across the dry ground. I followed the pale driveway down until before me, Lomas' mausoleum rose up dark against the skyline. There was something menacing about the place in the darkness and I searched its shadowy surface to see if some chink of light would bear witness to our belief that Lomas was inside and living but none showed and everything was as quiet as the proverbial, which was quite fitting seeing as where I was.

I hauled the Chevy off the road and made for the deeper shadows under one of the shade trees then pulled up, switched off the motor and waited.

Not a sound reached me and there was only the Chevy's cooling motor ticking quietly as I waited. I spotted movement as something slipped between the gravestones and my heart missed a beat. But it was just a coyote on a midnight run as it sloped past, stopping only to give me a cautious look from baleful yellow eyes before it went its way.

I heard the distant roar of a truck and looked over my shoulder to see headlight beams split the darkness of the cemetery and come fast down the driveway.

A clunky looking gas tanker with the Texaco star emblazoned on the side sped past my hiding place at top speed. Without stopping, the hefty half-ton vehicle went straight up to the Chain tomb and using its six-by-six wheelbase forged on up the first flight of white marble steps. There was a screeching as the undercarriage ground against stone and jagged lines of oily dirt and broken marble followed the truck's forced passage. And that's when I knew for certain that Gabriel had arrived.

I watched in amazement as he pulled up and braked the truck balancing it at an angle on the sloping steps and climbed out of the cab, and then Gabriel busily set about unlatching the hose from the truck's side panel. Calmly he dragged the hose over to the trumpet vase and buried one end in amongst the now dear departed bunch of Ben Lomas' flowers. Gabriel gave a cheeky wave to where I sat in the Chevy and then spun a wheel and started to release the truck's seven hundred and fifty gallons of gasoline straight from the loaded tank into the underground tunnel.

Oh boy! I knew then what he was about now and continued to watch in awe as he bled the tanker dry. Gabriel allowed a dribble from the hose to run down the steps as he hopped down them with a kind of devilish delight. A match flared and he was running in that crabbed fashion of his that was barely above a staggering jog as his ancient limbs struggled to move fast.

The ribbon of flame sped up the steps swiftly and there was a soft *whoomph* as it disappeared into the bowl of the vase.

Gabriel burst into the car.

'Get the hell moving!' he panted. 'It's going to be like Vesuvius any minute now.'

'You dumb bastard,' I bawled as I cranked the car into action. 'What the hell have you done?'

'When you got a rat in the house there's only one way to deal with him,' he grinned.

I rammed the gear in place and spun that Chevy out of there fast, raising a cloud of dust from the spinning wheels as I went.

As I sped away down the driveway heading for the exit I glanced in the mirror and saw the reflected results of Gabriel's gross act of arson.

There was a kind of underground rumbling first; so deep I could feel its vibrations coming up through the car wheels. It was the sort of thing you might expect before a volcano lets loose and it reminded me of the sound of distant artillery fire. Then fire spewed up in a tall bright geyser of light that shot out of the trumpet mouth of the vase. After that the dry ground started to split open in ragged cracked lines and broiling flames rose out of the earth following the path of the underground tunnel as the fire below rampaged its way towards the center of the mausoleum.

We were almost out of the cemetery when a firestorm broke through and billowed up under the roof of the stone canopy. The curling pillar of oily flame rolled up into the sky spreading a bloom of light and black smoke over the whole graveyard.

'Yeehaw!' hollered Gabriel happily, his white hair ruffling in the slipstream as he hung out the car window watching the blaze behind us. 'Will you look at that. Goddamn you, Lomas! Go burn in hell.'

We hit the road as with a roar the intense heat and flame cracked apart stone and caused an explosive eruption that shot chunks of marble and splintered pieces of the building high in the tortured air.

Leastways, I thought, there ain't nothing but dead people in there to be disturbed by all the destruction. I spun the wheel over and fishtailing, we headed off back in the direction of town, leaving the great rising sheet of flame to diminish away behind us.

'You sure are a crazy person, Gabriel,' I complained, crushing the accelerator to the floor and trying to urge even more speed out of the pounding engine as the sound of fire bells approached from in front.

'Maybe,' agreed Gabriel, slumping back in his seat with a contented smile. 'But I sure feel a whole lot danged better to know that Lomas Chain is underground permanent. I can rest easy now and my poor old pa can too.'

'Wish I could say the same,' I muttered, thinking of my own father and his untimely demise.

'Well,' said Gabriel, staring ahead through the screen. 'We ain't quite finished here yet awhile, are we?'

'What do you mean by that?' I asked.

'Cephus Long, that's what I mean. That fella didn't need that kind of treatment and I reckon Lomas raised his son just about the same as himself, dark and mean. So we has to do something about Benjamin now.'

I sighed, 'Oh no, Gabriel. Not more of this, are we about to take on the whole damned gangster underworld of Las Vegas?'

'What's the matter with you?' frowned Gabriel. 'You was mighty keen a while back. What's changed your mind? You was a soldier, weren't you? Well its time to go to war again.'

He was right, of course. There comes a time when and if a thing ain't right and nobody does anything about it, then the wrong just festers and grows. Benjamin Chain was like that, sick from a black disease that he had inherited from his father. If such a man could beat up and kill an old fellow for just talking to us then he was capable of a whole lot worse. It just takes a good man to sleep a while for evil to foster, I heard that somewhere and had to admit it was a damned good homily to live by. I don't know if Ma would have agreed but I like to think she would have.

We got back to find that Bob had been real busy.

He hadn't slept at all and in reality had been out raising a whole arsenal of hardware for us. On the bed in the room and all laid out neat and tidy was an array of weapons. A Winchester shotgun, an M1 Carbine, a Thompson sub-machine gun and a Colt automatic, all with magazines of ammunition lying alongside. There was even a small crate of pineapple grenades in there.

'Where'd this come from?' I asked, staring down at the weapons.

'A Treasury agent's little bonus,' he answered enigmatically.

'Hey!' said Gabriel in appreciation, as he leaned over and picked up the shotgun. 'You got some lead in your pencil after all, lawman.'

'What brought this on?' I asked, giving Bob a curious sidelong glance.

'They're pushing me real hard in Washington. Say they want facts and figures to bring down Chain,' growled Bob. 'Tell you true, I'm sick of all their pestering. It's okay when you're sipping cocktails in Delmonico's and dishing out orders from behind a desk but its different down here on the ground. I come back and see Cephus sitting in that chair all bloody and beat up and I ain't about to go hunting for no account sheets just so Head Office can nail this fellow on some tax evasion hassle that takes years to bring to trial. I aim to go straight to the source.'

'Kind of talk I like to hear,' said Gabriel as he worked the action on the Winchester. 'Never did care too much to fool around with proper protocol anyways.'

It suddenly seemed to me as if I was in the company of a couple of damn fool avenging angels and I was a mite blown away by it. But I came to realize all of a sudden that I wasn't no different, I still had claim on Benjamin and all his dirty little shenanigans. Maybe he hadn't been directly responsible for my Pa's death but he certainly had been for Cephus's and by proxy that added up to the same thing in my mind. Besides, I wasn't about to let these two guys walk into a hellhole without backing them up; Marines don't do that kind of thing.

'How's this going down?' I asked as I picked up the Thompson.

'We need to clean house,' said Bob. 'Get rid of the whole nest of them. They're breaking ground on Siegel's casino building site tomorrow. Seems like Bugsy has arranged a little celebration for his backers, Chain and the rest of his boys are going to be there.'

'Where's this at?' asked Gabriel.

'A clubhouse called The Lonesome Dove, single story place, one of those flash joints with big windows, palm trees and a whole lot of car parking space outside. It's owned by one of Siegel's Mob boys and they're closing up shop especially for the celebration. So we'll have a clear field, there won't be anybody in there other than bad guys.'

'Time?' I asked.

'Midday, that's when the whole thing kicks off.'

'You sure of all this?' said Gabriel.

Bob eyed him, 'I got friends where it counts,' was all he would say.

'So, I see,' grinned Gabriel, gleefully picking up a handful of shotgun shells and stuffing them into his pocket.

'Best get some rest then,' I added. 'Sounds like a busy day tomorrow.'

CHAPTER SEVENTEEN

DUST UP

We parked the Chevy at one end of the car park and in the shade of an overhang.

The rest of the lot was empty except for a lineup of shiny motors out front that would have done proud to any topnotch car sales forecourt. Chain's Lincoln was in pride of place in the center so we knew he was in there as we exited the car.

Bob opened up the back and we took out our weapons, grabbing a pocketful of grenades each as we did so.

'When we get to the place, split up,' said Bob, slinging the carbine on its strap across his shoulder. 'One on each side and I'll go in the front and read them their rights.'

'You sure you want to do it that way?' I asked.

'Got to do it proper or it ain't lawful,' sniggered Gabriel cynically. 'Ain't that right, Bob?'

'That's the way of it,' agreed Bob po-faced.

We shouldered our arms and stepped out from the shade into the sunlight, walking across the empty expanse of car park side by side towards the gleaming windows reflecting the bright midday sun like shining mirrors.

It must have looked crazy to anybody watching. Like some High Noon shootout from the old days, with Gabriel carrying his shotgun at port arms and Bob with the carbine slung and the Colt held down by his side, then me limping with my stick and carrying the Thompson.

'You step inside and I'll distract them a mite,' whispered Gabriel, drawing the pin from a pineapple grenade with his teeth but keeping the safety lever down.

It was a long walk and seemed to me to go on forever, the hot sun beating down on us and rising off the asphalt in waves under our feet. Our shadows were short with the sun so high and made our isolation seem even lonelier as we strode steadily towards the building.

We parted company out front of the row of parked cars lined up before the picture windows. Behind the glass I could see the dim outlines of the men inside, we hadn't been noticed yet and that much was obvious as nobody was looking our way. I swallowed hard as I realized there must be nigh on thirty or so hard men inside that place, all of them villains and most probably armed to the teeth. I went off to the right and Gabriel to the left as Bob strode up bold as brass to the big glass-paneled double doors.

A sleepy figure smoking a cigarette stepped lazily out from the front foyer and was about to question Bob, who promptly slugged him with his Colt and dropped the guy before he could ask anything.

Strangely, the fellow slipped away with the cigarette still stuck in his mouth and he lay there sleeping like a babe with the butt smoldering between his lips.

Bob stepped over the smoking figure and swung the entrance doors wide and I heard him call out, 'Federal agent! Don't anybody move.'

'Fire in the hole!' Gabriel echoed his call, releasing the grenade catch and rolling it away under the parked cars.

With that I set off at a fast hop around the corner of the clubhouse looking for a side entrance.

With a rolling blast the grenade went off five seconds later and lifted the Lincoln high off its wheels, it shunted sideways and canted over onto a fine-looking Packard parked next door. Glass shattered as iron fragments spattered the clubhouse front and blew out one of the scenic windows, followed by a minor explosion as a fuel tank went up in a ball of fire.

I found the door I wanted next to some kind of utility yard and kicked my way inside. A short corridor leading to some toilets fronted me and through a swing door porthole at the end of the corridor I could see the mayhem that Bob had started inside the main room of the clubhouse.

Guys were leaping up from their smartly laid out dinner tables and loosing off handguns wildly in Bob's direction. A lot of shouting was going on as cool as ice, Bob walked forward, picking his shots and dropping fellows to the left and right of him as he advanced.

I pushed back the swing door and let fly at a

bunch of guys standing over by some kind of buffet bar. Now the Thompson can do some damage when its used right and I had plenty of experience of that, so I traversed a pattern along the bar from right to left, holding the bucking gun tight in a firm grip and letting it do its job. It cut down that row of nicely dressed hoods and sent them flying in a chewing splatter of flying blood and ribbons of expensive material.

The air was full of flying lead now and some of the clubhouse inhabitants were regaining their wits and had taken cover behind overturned tables and behind some square support columns that ran along the center of the large room. All was the roaring sound of gunfire, of smashed plates and glassware riddled by the recurring rattle of my Thompson. The surprised gangsters tumbled and fell, hollering and screaming as they were mown down.

With a boom, Gabriel made his entrance from the other side. The blast of the shotgun overriding the rest of the sounds of the gunfire and I looked across to see him offloading shot after shot as he worked the pump. Stepping up, Gabriel let one guy in front of him have it full on and I saw a bloody hole the size of a grapefruit open up in the back of the fellow's suit jacket as he was sent up in the air and sailing off his feet by the blast.

I caught a flash of white out of the corner of my eye and spun around to see a waiter in a pale jacket approaching on hands and knees. He looked up at me wide eyed with panic and held up empty hands to show he was an unarmed non-combatant. I waved him on with the Thompson, indicating he should get out by the door behind me and he scurried past.

Turning back, both Bob and Gabriel had run over and were pinned down behind one of the central columns. The cement block allowed them some shelter as a group stationed behind a bar area let fly and chipped great holes from the sides of the column, the bullets whining and cracking in ricochet.

Bob's arm was torn and bleeding and a gash marked his cheek. Each time he tried to duck around the corner of the column to return fire a tattoo of shots sent chips and cement dust flying. I couldn't quite see Gabriel behind him but both men were in a fix as they were trapped under the rain of firing.

It was the hefty figure of Ben Chain that rose up and loosed off with a hand gun as he urged his men on to keep up the fusillade. I had him in my sights and was bringing around the Thompson to let him have a burst when something hard hit me on the side of the head.

Next thing I knew I was staring at the floor and somebody was trying to drag the Thompson out of my hands. I struggled half heartedly as my head was still ringing from the blow. I made out my attacker as the waiter I had let make a run for it. He was leaning over me and grimacing with effort as he tried to pull the gun out of my hands.

With one hand he kept whacking me with the sap he held and had laid me out initially. The lead loaded leather hurt like hell each time he delivered a blow and I could feel my senses slipping. I let go the Thompson suddenly and he fell back, a smug grin of satisfaction on his face. But I swooped up my cane and two-handed delivered him a blow along the side of the head like a baseball batter at the plate.

That shook him some as the handle of the cane rattled off his skull, so I gave him another one. Following on as he scrabbled backwards towards the back door trying to shield himself from my continuing blows with the stick. I slammed into him from left and right, whipping his head with all the energy I could muster. He took a few hits and shaking his head lifted up the Thompson to aim it at me.

He was standing in front of the porthole window in the door when the front of his face was punched in by a bullet that went straight on through his head and shattered the circular halo of glass behind. The waiter tumbled back over without a sound, swinging the door open and lying half in and half out of the room. I heard the *ching* of an empty clip ejecting and turned to see Bob lifting up the carbine to shove in another load.

There was no time for thanks as I swooped up the Thompson again and swung around already firing as I came. Plates and glasses shattered on tables and silver cutlery leapt up as I curved the chain of bullets rotating across the set dining tables towards Chain and his gang crouched behind the bar. Bottles on the nicely mirrored shelving behind them exploded, sending shards of glass and spilling a deluge of liquor over those hiding under the bar counter.

That's when both Bob and Gabriel tossed a couple of grenades into the mix and I ducked down behind the cover of a table. There was a double boom of sound as the grenades went off, one taking the front of the counter and ripping it apart, the other grenade falling behind to one end and sending a couple of fellows spinning into the air.

The place was filling up with smoke from the gunfire and explosions and the stench of cordite was strong in the air. Charred furniture began to smolder as the blast from the grenades burnt black holes in the overturned tables and chairs.

Some figures were standing in the haze of smoke with their hands raised in surrender but Gabriel was having none of it and he continued to haul on the pump action and drop whatever came under his Winchester. It took Bob's steady hand on his arm to call him to a ceasefire.

Ragged bodies lay everywhere, draped over overturned tables and sprawled inelegantly on the floor in puddles of blood. It had been no better than bloody slaughter but we had laid out the best of the Mob members in Chain's gang, there was no doubt of that. I glanced over at my companions and saw that Bob held the carbine in one hand his other arm a soaking mess of dripping blood, Gabriel limped out from behind the pillar favoring one leg that had taken a bullet high up in the thigh.

I was the lucky one, all I'd had was a few cracks on the head and it was only then that I touched the raw spot with my fingers and felt the trickle that ran down the side of my face.

'You okay, boy?' Gabriel called, as he limped out with the shotgun couched on his hip.

'Better than you,' I said.

'T'ain't no more than a crease,' he answered, pressing down on the wound with one hand.

'We get Chain?' I asked.

'Go take a look,' said Bob.

I hiked over to the ruined bar and looked down at the heap of tangled bodies lying behind, all of them piled up on top of each other. The fragged remains had been torn apart by the grenade explosion and it was mostly a mangled heap of charred and bleeding flesh that I looked down on. Even so, the easily recognizable tanned Indian face was nowhere to be seen amongst them.

'He ain't here,' I said.

'Goddamn!' cursed Gabriel. 'Where'd the sucker go?'

I saw the opening set in the floor, a small doorway that led to the bar cellar below. The hinges and handle were smudged with streaks of red.

'They got a cellar here,' I called. 'He must have made it away through that. There's blood though, I reckon he stopped one.'

All three of us weren't fit enough to take up any kind of chase and all we could do was hold the remaining survivors under the gun as the sound of approaching police sirens came to us through the broken windows.

'Now the explaining starts,' sighed Bob, wearily leaning back against the pock marked cement pillar beside him.

EPILOGUE

LAST WORD

It had been a long-haul following Gabriel Brannigan across country and this is the record of how it ended.

Well, almost that is.

Bob saw us safely out of Vegas by making up a whole heap of baloney and lying through his teeth to his bosses in Washington by telling them such a pile of BS that they just had to let us go without any charges being brought. They knew enough though to see that the whole affair hadn't really been totally above board and legal and Bob suffered for it. They sent him off in all kinds of low-grade positions to no-name postings that nobody else wanted and when they offered him a desk bound position in a stationery office he had finally had enough and quit the Department. Last I heard he was making his living as a P.I. somewhere up in Oregon.

Me? Well I made my way back to my brother Ahab's and his wife Cindy's home in time to celebrate with them the birth of my nephew. A fine little boy they named James in favor of our father. So I'm back again in my apartment over the garage and typing out these last few lines to close this record. The nice thing about it all was that I met a fine and pretty young woman at the birthday celebrations, Miss Jenny Levane, a war widow and local school-teacher who lightens my days now. She's a wonder to me and who knows, maybe that's going to go somewhere, I kinda hope so.

And Benjamin Lamtoc Chain? Nobody knows. Did he survive? That I can't tell as no sign has been seen or heard of him since. If he did get away and recover he's certainly kept his head down and all the authorities reckon he lost whatever position he held with the Mob when Siegel was assassinated later on. With his father, Lomas gone, who it turned out was the real brains behind it all, and who, as it happened, had been diagnosed with a pretty disgusting skin disease (probably a bad case of leprosy he picked up in South America) that he had wanted to keep from public view, there was no one left to fund or advise Benjamin. They say that when the fire department finally put out the blaze at Lomas's tomb they found the overheated surface soil had caved in on his underground hideout and the whole place underneath, every tunnel and room in the vast complex was laced with a coating of melted gold. So all the treasure Chain had heisted from Cuba had found its way there and he'd kept it nearby only to have it go up in smoke along with himself in the end. All this we found out from one of Chain's surviving gang members who had turned State's evidence and spilled everything in lieu of a long prison sentence.

Gabriel? Well that's the sad part.

That bullet he took in the leg didn't fare too well for him. He was way too old to be cavorting about like that anyway and some kind of septicemia set in. Last time I saw him was in his hospital bed, he tried to make light of it by saying we were a matching pair now, both of us being a couple of hopalongs. But he looked a ghost of his former self and I could see he was wasting away in that damned bed. The medics said they might save him if they took the leg off but we both knew such an operation would surely kill him. He would have none of it and as was his manner and the style in which he had lived his whole life, he somehow made it out of the hospital unaided and went off to die in his own way and in his own time. I guess he's out there somewhere, in a place where he'd rather be. In my imagination he will have made it out to the desert and is lying on some lonesome hilltop and like the souls of his Shoshone forefathers will be watching the stars pass overhead and listening to the wind as he recalls all the many adventures he had in his long life. God rest him, he was fine fellow and I count him as a true friend.

If he has a last resting place then there's no telling where it is, so instead of carrying out my mother's wish to place a bouquet of flowers on his grave, I take them along to hers and set them down there beside her. Maybe she would like that, I sure hope so.

A LOOK AT: COFFIN JACK: A WESTERN DUO

ONE-EYED COFFIN JACK IS A DEADLY MAN.

Coffin Jack is a dark souled assassin that does not possess much; he lives alone with only feral cats for company in his isolated shack in the mountains and barely ventures down to civilization except when he gets the call.

Joined by his now partner, Lowell Devereux – a naive reporter who was unceremoniously thrown into the path of Coffin Jack while seeking uplifting stories to inspire the readers back east – the two are out prove all that they are capable of. Their wild journey takes them across country to confront a series of deadly challenges and plunge into an esoteric nightmare that transforms the pair. From there they are taken on a trail through the darker side of the Old West where factions differ and it is a new enemy they must face…

A tongue-in-cheek Western with all the blood and thrills of a regular rough ride, or as Coffin Jack might say, "Ya gotta own a pinch of salt for this one."

Coffin Jack: A Western Duo includes – Death-dealer and Gravedigger.

AVAILABLE NOW

ABOUT THE AUTHOR

Tony Masero grew up in a deprived and grey postwar London where the only relief from bomb craters and food rationing were colorful Western books and movies. The pictures on the screen displayed wide sunlit spaces, glorious forests, breathtaking mountain ranges and most importantly adventure and a great sense of freedom. His love of that early thrill has subsequently inspired many of his own books. Living far from the Wild West and any kind of armed culture he made up for it by practicing longbow archery in the forests of southern England.

At the age of three Tony Masero's father, a renowned woodcarver, placed a pencil in his hand, an act that resulted in a later career as a Designer and then Illustrator. Working in the international advertising and publishing world Tony Masero produced a great deal of art for book covers and through the research involved in their creation is where his interest in writing began.

Research is important in his own books and many of his tales are based around some historical incident or characters that truly existed. From there the imagination takes flight and for a person with a visual frame of mind his books are often imbued with a natural pictorial quality and full of human characteristics that are true to us whatever our origins.